TEAGAN

Deck the Headlines

A Small Town Enemies to Lovers Holiday Romantic Comedy

First published by Lightning Strike Press 2022

Copyright © 2022 by Teagan Hart

All rights reserved. No part of this publication may be reproduced, stored or transmitted in any form or by any means, electronic, mechanical, photocopying, recording, scanning, or otherwise without written permission from the publisher. It is illegal to copy this book, post it to a website, or distribute it by any other means without permission.

This novel is entirely a work of fiction. The names, characters and incidents portrayed in it are the work of the author's imagination. Any resemblance to actual persons, living or dead, events or localities is entirely coincidental.

Teagan Hart asserts the moral right to be identified as the author of this work.

Teagan Hart has no responsibility for the persistence or accuracy of URLs for external or third-party Internet Websites referred to in this publication and does not guarantee that any content on such Websites is, or will remain, accurate or appropriate.

Designations used by companies to distinguish their products are often claimed as trademarks. All brand names and product names used in this book and on its cover are trade names, service marks, trademarks and registered trademarks of their respective owners. The publishers and the book are not associated with any product or vendor mentioned in this book. None of the companies referenced within the book have endorsed the book.

Cover by GetCovers

First edition

This book was professionally typeset on Reedsy.
Find out more at reedsy.com

For Jimbo, Glenn, and "Lucy and Ethel" ... you two know who you are.

To Lucia, my first Beta and one of the best humans I know.

To Lucy Score and her incredibly supportive and loving BRAs

And to all my fantastically wonderful ARC readers!

"Hope never abandons you, you abandon it."

– George Weinberg

Contents

1	ELLA	1
2	ELLA	13
3	ELLA	19
4	ELLA	26
5	ELLA	40
6	ELLA	54
7	ELLA	65
8	CAL	74
9	ELLA	84
10	CAL	92
11	ELLA	107
12	ELLA	124
13	ELLA	131
14	CAL	139
15	ELLA	150
16	CAL	157
17	ELLA	168
18	CAL	175
19	ELLA	182
20	CAL	196
21	ELLA	213
22	CAL	221
23	ELLA	235
24	CAL	251
25	ELLA	260
26	ELLA	272

27	CAL	283
28	ELLA	297
29	CAL	319
30	ELLA	336
31	CAL	351
32	ELLA	368
33	CAL	379
34	ELLA	396
35	ELLA	411
36	CAL	420
37	ELLA	430
38	ELLA	436
39	CAL	443
40	ELLA	450
41	CAL	458
42	ELLA	466
43	ELLA	476
44	CAL	484
45	ELLA	491
46	ELLA	496
47	ELLA	505
48	Epilogue	514
49	Sleigh Ride Or Die Preview	517
About the Author		537
Also by Teagan Hart		538

1

ELLA

This was purgatory and Ella had to pee. The corporate majesty of the *Seattle Tribune's* hallway, jam-packed with other hopeful applicants, and her own crushing fear, weren't enough to distract her. It was a crappy entry-level junior copy editor job, but there were still at least thirty other people, dressed in their "interviewing finest" waiting to have their names called. And more kept arriving. The hallway was so full now if she left to try to go find the bathroom, some jerk was going to take her spot.

Someone knocked into her from behind and she staggered forward. She threw out a hand to brace herself on the wall and narrowly avoided a domino effect situation with the man in front of her. Sadly, this was not unusual for Ella. She'd been given long legs, a narrow stance, and a high center of gravity, but never really got around to reading the instruction manual that came with them.

"Oh sorry!" A deep, feminine voice said behind her. She turned to look back at a tall woman who was digging through a black portfolio.

"Oh, no worries," Ella said. "Honestly, this is the calmest rave I've ever been a part of. I'm starting to think I might be in the wrong place. I mean no one has those light-up pacifiers and not a stitch of neon mesh as far as the eye can see."

The woman chuckled but didn't look up, still digging through the stack of pages in her binder. A piece of paper slipped out of her fingers and fell to the floor. Ella bent down to pick it up for her. It was the woman's resume. Her eyes fell on the top heading under the woman's name: Relevant Work Experience. Six years at the *Chicago Sun* as a junior copy editor. Two more at *Washington Square News*, the student paper for NYU.

"Thanks," the woman said, holding her hand out to take the paper from Ella. She gave Ella a quick smile. "I've got so many resumes for so many different job interviews. Are you here for the junior copy editor job too?"

Ella couldn't speak. This woman had eight years of experience. *Real* experience. That was what she was up against. And this woman wasn't even the oldest person in the hallway.

Crap.

Ella had been a reporter for *The Monarch*, the Duwamish College's paper, but it was a small school and therefore a small paper. Nothing to write home about, as it were.

"There's a few of us going for it, huh?" The woman continued, either not noticing or being too polite to acknowledge Ella's speechlessness. The woman checked her watch. "What time is your interview slot?"

"Uh," Ella choked out, trying to find her voice. "Eleven."

The woman nodded. "You must be next." She smiled at Ella. "Good luck."

Ella tried to scrape together some semblance of a smile and nodded at her. The woman went back to organizing her portfolio and Ella leaned back against the wall, looking down at her own pathetically short resume, clutched in her hand. She'd graduated from college over the summer and taken a month off to binge Netflix and congratulate herself. She'd just always assumed she'd immediately get a job as soon as she started looking for one. But here she was, at the end of November, on the first job interview in her field. And she was surrounded by older, more experienced people for the same entry-level job. How was she supposed to compete with the people who *had* the experience when she couldn't get a job to *get* the experience?

Her phone rang, making Ella jump. She snatched it out of her bag and was about to shut it off, but hesitated when she saw it was her mom. If she didn't answer, her mom would probably call every one of her friends and then the police. Her mom was convinced that each day was a new battle for Ella to not get stabbed, raped, or kidnapped in Seattle. Better to just answer, tell her she was fine, and that she'd call her back later. She sighed and slid her finger across the screen to answer.

"El! I have some news for you!"

"Hi Mom," Ella said, dropping her voice to just above a whisper. "Can this wait? I'm about to…"

"Pippa has started working for the *Hope Hornblower*! I didn't know that until I stopped in to renew our subscription at the house and Pippa was the one that helped me. Did you know?"

Ella squeezed her eyes shut. "Yes, Mom." She hoped her mom could hear her desire to wrap this conversation up and get off the phone. "Pip called me the day she got the job."

"Speaking of jobs," her mom continued, missing, or ignoring the tone of her daughter's voice, "Clarence Ford is retiring."

The door to the interview room opened and a blonde woman in what had to be a thousand-dollar suit emerged. She smiled at the rest of the applicants and headed down the hallway toward the elevator, picking her way around the rest of the crowd.

"Mom," Ella said, jealously watching the woman go by, probably on her way to the restroom and then the rest of her life outside this crowded hallway, "I'm at an interview and I could be next. I need to…"

"Don't you remember Clarence? He's the editor for the *Hornblower*," her mom continued. "Well, *was* the editor."

"Sure," Ella said. "Of course, I remember him. That's great that he's retiring, Mom. I…"

"No, it's not great! Well, maybe it is," her mom said. "He just quit. He called Myrna on Sunday. He just told her he was done. He wasn't going to go back to the office. I saw Myrna at Bumble's this morning and she looked like hell. She said she didn't know what she was going to do without Clarence. He's not sick, as far as anyone can tell. He's just…sick of the newspaper business…or something."

"Guess we'll never know. Anyway, Mom, I love you, but I have to go."

"Why?"

Ella sighed and crossed one leg over the other, trying to stop squirming. "I told you, Mom, I have interviews today."

"Oh! That's right. Sorry, El. Where are they at?"

Ella turned to face the wall, hoping the sheet rock would help muffle her voice. "Right now, I'm at the one for the *Seattle Tribune*, and then I've got one at the *Northwest Signal*."

"The *Tribune* is a newspaper, but what's the *Signal*?" she asked, sounding like her mouth was suddenly full. "And have you been eating?"

Ella sighed. "Yes, Mom. I've been eating. And the *Signal* is an online news blog," Ella said, turning back around just in time to make awkward eye contact with the woman waiting next to her.

She heard her mom swallow whatever she'd been chewing and then sigh. "Is that a *real* job?"

Ella closed her eyes. "Yes, Mom. It's a real job. With a real paycheck and everything."

"Are you sure journalism is where you want to spend your time, Ella? It's just..."

"Just what, Mom?"

"It...it just doesn't make for a very happy home life..."

"Mom, Grandpa was covering the war. If I'm *lucky* the most I'll be covering is flower beard contests and silent discos. It'll be years before I'll get to cover anything that important." Ella could almost hear the thoughts moving through her mom's head. Ella's grandpa had missed most of her mother's childhood. As a result, her grandparents had fought daily until his death, five years earlier.

"I just . . . El, I don't want you to end up like Grandpa. I don't want you and Les to fight every day and miss out on your kids," she said softly.

"Ok, Mom, I love you. But Les and I are just dating, and there are no kids in the picture. And I really need to get off the phone before they call my name. I'll call you later." She hung up and checked the time on her phone.

Her interview was at eleven and it was now five 'til. She just had to get through this interview and then make it to a bathroom, any bathroom (seriously, she'd take a potted plant at this point). Two steps to success. She could do this.

The door to the interview room opened again. A very tired looking woman with a silver bun emerged. Her hair was pulled back so tightly that it stretched the skin on her face until she looked like Vincent D'Onofrio's character in *Men in Black*. She looked around at the hopefuls and cleared her throat. The hallway grew quiet, and she checked the clipboard in her hand.

"I'm sorry for the delay. But we're moving through all the names on our list as quickly as we can. Thank you for your patience."

She was lying. She was not thankful for their patience. She was taunting them.

"We're now ready for those of you that had interview slots between nine and nine-thirty. First, we have Alex Cartman?" A short man with thinning hair, straightened his tie and crossed the hall, smiling at the woman. The woman didn't smile. She held the door open for him with the energy level of a tired pet owner whose cat couldn't decide if it wanted to be in or out.

Ella was having a hard time keeping the pitch of her voice below panicked screeching when she turned around to look at the woman beside her. "They're running *two hours* behind?"

The woman shrugged without looking up from the paper she was reading. "It happens. It's an entry-level job. If there was something else that came up, they probably just got a late start on the interviews."

"But...but..." Ella said, pulling up the email on her phone. "It said I was interviewing at *eleven*."

"So?" The woman's voice was slightly annoyed now.

"And then I'd be done by eleven-*thirty*, and I'd have enough time to get across town for my twelve-fifteen interview."

The woman grimaced at Ella and sucked in air through her teeth. "Yeah, that's probably not going to happen."

It was a one-two punch to Ella's gut. First, because she'd been so naive, thinking that she wouldn't have much competition for the job. And second, because she had so little experience with these kinds of interviews that she thought she might actually be able to cram two interviews into an hour and fifteen minutes. Should she leave? Should she wait it out? She was frozen to the spot in indecision, although her bladder was definitely voting for her to go. But, leaving felt like giving up. She decided to wait it out. She stared at her phone, watching the minutes tick by as she thought about dry deserts and the scratchy sound of sandpaper on wood, and being trapped in a hot car without air conditioning or windows that rolled down. Anything to make her forget about the ticking time bomb that was her full bladder. Not to mention the closing window on travel time to her second interview. It was forty minutes later when the severe bun woman returned and cleared her throat. "Ok, Ashley Dayton?"

A redhead with black-framed glasses bounced from her seat and practically skipped through the door the woman held open for her. It was almost 11:45. The drill-sergeant part of Ella's brain, which El referred to as Helga, snapped her riding crop against the palm of her hand. Helga was the part that made her study, do the dishes, and get her ass off the couch before it entered into a symbiotic relationship with the microfiber. Helga was based on Maid Marian's chaperon in *Robin Hood: Men in Tights*. And any time El *did* make a stupid decision, she had the satisfaction of blaming Helga for not having her head in the game.

Now, Helga was telling her that she had less than thirty minutes to get across town to her second interview. Sure, it was a smaller news outlet. The pay was less and the commute from home would be longer, but the silver lining was the fact that she probably wouldn't have as much competition *and* she could go find a bathroom. With those happy thoughts in mind, Ella squared her shoulders and moved back down the hallway, away from the interview room. She moved with purpose, and she expected the other hopefuls in the hallway to call to her and ask where she was going. When they did, she would turn slowly to look back over her shoulder and say, *"I've got another interview to be at."*

Of course, she didn't get the opportunity to do such a dramatic look-back. Because no one, not even the woman she'd exchanged words with, called to her. At the end of the hallway, she finally turned back to look behind her. No one seemed to have even noticed that she'd left. The hallway looked exactly the same as it had when she'd arrived. As if she'd never been there. El wasn't sure why, but that kind of made her sad.

She swore she heard angels singing when she finally found a bathroom. Yeah, some of those other applicants had more experience than she did, but she had bladder relief and they didn't. She reveled in her triumph in the tastefully antiseptic bathroom and then sauntered back to the elevator. She only paused for a second to look back down the crowded hallway. Then Helga took over and she punched the down arrow before she could reconsider what she was doing. When the doors opened, Helga marched her into the elevator with a plan. By the time the elevator had reached the ground floor, she'd arranged for an Uber pick-up.

As she breezed past the *Tribune's* receptionist, who was almost vibrating in her seat behind her monitor and a stack of Starbucks cups, Ella took a deep breath. On to bigger and better things, she told herself. The snarky part of El's brain that Ella called Sarcastic El, told her this was bull, but Helga punched Sarcastic El in the boobs and told her to shut up and get in the blue sedan that had just pulled up.

The *Northwest Signal* offices were in a strip mall at the south end of Georgetown. Definitely not economical to make the commute by Uber every day. Helga was scouting for bus stops while Ella tipped and thanked her driver and climbed out onto the sidewalk. Her phone said 12:10. She hustled inside and stared at the empty desk in the *Signal*'s front office.

"H-hello?" Ella called out. There was only one other door in the small room. And it was behind the main desk. She wondered if she should open it and call down the hallway, but Helga told her to sit down and shut up. She decided to give this one the Helga. She'd already walked out on one interview today. She didn't need to immediately torpedo her shot at the other one. Thoughts of the crowded hallway she'd just left were making her sweat. Her subconscious was kind enough to conjure a new crippling fear. What if there were thirty other people already waiting in an interior hallway to interview for the job, while she was sitting out in the *Signal's* lobby like an idiot, waiting for someone to come get her? Helga told her to stop being paranoid.

She sat for exactly three minutes before she got to her feet to see if she could hear anyone on the other side of the door if she got closer to the front desk. For all she knew, the whole office could have gone out for pizza, or quit today. And then she'd just be sitting here, waiting, until the *Signal* was evicted from the premises. She inched her way around the edge of the front desk. She was listening with every fiber of the natural eavesdropper in her that had now been trained for four years to always try to get a story, even when, to the average person, there didn't appear to be one.

Silence.

She took another step toward the door, leaning forward, straining to listen. A hacking throat-clear on the other side of the door almost made her jump out of her skin.

The throat-clear was followed by a man's voice. "Yeah, Jem, I heard you the first time. I know it's not headlines. It's 'third page, below the fold' at best, but you didn't see what she was wearing. I'd have proposed on the spot if my wife hadn't been there." This was followed by a guffawing laugh and then the doorknob rattled. Before Ella could get clear, the door swung out, hitting her in the face with so much force that it had to have been kicked open.

"Son-of-a...," she hissed through gritted teeth.

"What the..." the man's voice again. He peered around the door to see Ella holding a hand to her nose. "What? Were you just standing behind the door like a personal injury lawyer, waiting for a payday?"

"What? No. I'm Ella Danforth. I have an interview at 12:15."

He looked Ella up and down and she immediately felt a wave of dislike for him, coupled with a desire to kick the door closed on *his* face. Over the years, she'd learned that there was a category of men that were obsessed with women that are built like giraffes from the waist down.

"Huh," the man said. "For what position?"

Yeah. This guy should have been banned from *saying* the word, "position".

"The job I'm interviewing for is Online Research Assistant," Ella said, trying to suppress her gag reflex long enough to hand over the remote to Helga in her brain. Let this asshole take on the "brick-shithouse-of-a-woman" personality that cut off a *Mindhunter* episode twenty minutes in to force Ella to study for finals. Helga seemed to be doing a pretty good job of making the guy think twice until his gaze dropped to Ella's black leather boots that stopped just below her knees. They were plain and matched her black skirt and suit jacket, but the way the guy was looking at them, Ella suddenly felt like she was wearing lingerie on her shins and her boobs and ass must have traveled south to join them. Helga wanted to snap her fingers at him and tell him, *"Eyes up here,"* but Ella took over. She cleared her throat and shuffled her feet. Finally, Mr. Boot-Fetish looked up at Ella and gave himself a visible shake as he settled back into what Ella was guessing was his baseline expression.

"Yeah, almost forgot. Well, it's just me here today, so let's get this thing going."

Super. Exactly what Ella had always hoped a potential employer would say to her regarding her interview. He turned and headed back down the hallway, not even bothering to hold the door open for her. Ella caught the doorknob just before it closed. She hesitated for a moment before following him. She glanced back at the strip mall parking lot behind her, out through the entryway doors. It wasn't too late. She could still leave. Have an Uber pick her up and then go get some frozen yogurt. Her head was aching from being smacked by the door, and being eye-doinked by Boot-Fetish Barry wasn't doing anything for her mood either. *Afterward,* Helga reassured her. *Just get this stupid job, and then to celebrate, we'll go get froyo.*

With that reassurance from Helga, Ella took a deep breath and forced herself through the door and into the hallway. It was narrow, and what looked like dentist exam rooms turned into offices stood on either side. They had no doors and were crammed full of what had to be garage-sale-specials or university surplus furniture. The man stopped at the last door and motioned Ella to precede him inside. She bit back the disgust she felt as she was forced to brush against him to squeeze through the narrow office doorway. His office had to have been a supply closet before the *Signal* moved in. It smelled like cigarette smoke and beef jerky. The desk had a pile of papers, a pile of McDonald's food bags, a pile of magazines, and a laptop. There was a gold nameplate with a badly-sized piece of printer paper jammed into it. The name Ernie Bleu was printed on it.

"Ernie?" Ella asked.

The man nodded. "But everyone here calls me 'Bleu'. I'm the Editor-in-Chief. Well, and the lead reporter. We've had to make a lot of cuts lately. The economy and everything."

A red light was blinking inside her head. Either this interview was going to be pointless because they couldn't afford her position anyway or (and her skin crawled just thinking about it) if she was hired she had a feeling she was going to be frequently asked to "perform duties outside of her job description". *Well, we're already here,* Helga told her. *Might as well see it through.*

She handed her resume to Ernie and he leaned back in his chair, put his feet up on the desk, and glanced down the first page.

"Duwamish College, huh? I didn't even know that place *had* a journalism program."

Ella felt her smile tighten. "Yep. I'm living proof."

He snorted and swiped at his nose with the back of one hand before returning it to the resume. He shrugged, set down the papers, and picked up his phone. "Well, tell me about yourself."

"I graduated this summer," Ella began. "I was a..." Ernie had started texting someone. She could tell because Ernie had evidently not figured out how to turn off the key sounds on his phone. The beeps were distracting, and Ella paused until Ernie looked up at her.

"Go on. I can multitask. It's kind of a skill you pick up working in the newspaper business."

Ella suspected "multitasking" could encompass any number of activities in Ernie's life. She gave herself a shake and tried again. "I was a reporter for *The Monarch*, Duwamish's student paper for three years. I covered the City Hall and Student Council beats, and..." Ernie laughed. Not at Ella. It was apparently in response to the dinging text message he'd just gotten in reply to his fumbled key stroking.

Helga had the market cornered on calm and patience, but Sarcastic El held all the cards when it came to verbal whiplash.

"Let me tell you," Ella said, "those City Hall pajama parties can be wild when you have to report on them. And trying to get them to keep their clothes on long enough to confirm statements and photo captions when all they want to do is streak and flagpole sit on top of the Space Needle is a full-time gig."

Ernie was back to punching buttons on his screen with fumbling thumbs. His poor wife. Probably lots of Xanax. Ernie was obviously not listening to Ella, so she decided to up the ante.

"And then the Mayor decided last Christmas that she wanted to slide bare-ass naked and backward down the railing outside of City Hall, while covered in whipped cream, and carrying two-lit sparklers. It took everyone in the room and her kids on the phone to convince her that if she did that, vital parts of her anatomy would get stuck to the railing like that kid's tongue in *A Christmas Story*." Ella paused, waiting for Ernie's reaction.

He burped. "That's great, Maggie. Go on."

Maggie? Where had he gotten *Maggie* from? He still had Ella's resume on his lap, which was making her a little nauseous, considering how intensely he was gazing at the new text message he'd just received. She didn't want to think about the fact that she'd touched anything that was now sitting on this man's lap.

"Anyway, after I downed the whole jar of green olives at the Christmas party last year," Ella continued, "they crowned me their queen of the moon, and now on every full moon they all must make sacrifices to me of blood and Twinkies."

Ernie was texting again, and he didn't look up when he finally weighed in. "Well, that's some good experience to start with. Like I said, we're having to make some budgetary cuts. We'll take a hard look at your resume and skills, and we'll give you a call next week about our decision." Not really wanting to think about who "we" might be if she was sitting across from the Editor-In-Chief, Ella quickly got to her feet.

"Thanks, Little Boy Blue," Ella muttered. "Have fun blowing your horn."

"You too," he muttered without breaking his texting non-rhythm. "Have a good one."

"I know *you* will," Ella said, heading back down the hall.

2

ELLA

Happy, Helga? El asked inside her head as she headed back down the hallway and into the reception area. Helga didn't respond. Not being one to relish the idea of rubbing someone's nose in their dashed hopes, El decided to move on from Helga's defeat and get herself an Uber and some froyo. The cold air outside the front doors of the cramped *Signal* office felt good on her skin.

According to her app, her Uber driver, Jatan, was on their way to pick her up, and her first stop was going to be at Seafrost, for a Pacific-sized froyo; kiwi, with a layer of cheesecake on top. She sighed and looked at her phone. Jatan was still five minutes away. This, unfortunately, left her mind open to five minutes of entertaining itself and the first thing that popped into her head was the phone call with her mother that morning.

She loved her mother, but anytime a conversation with her drifted towards talking about her hometown, Ella had this irrational fear that she would be put in some kind of trance and dragged back there. There wasn't anything wrong with Hope Island, per se... well, that wasn't exactly true. But the point was, nothing scared Ella more than the possibility of being stuck there and having her nose rubbed in every embarrassing thing she'd ever done, for the rest of her life.

It was why she'd studied journalism. It was a job that would take her far away from Hope, to somewhere she could cover something *actually* happening. Something bigger than Hope's summer bathtub races or the Baby Jesus Bazaar. She blew out a sigh. Of course, today hadn't done much to bolster her hopes of making her journalistic dreams come true. The first interview, or non-interview, had been terrifying and depressing. The interview she'd just walked out of made her feel like, after froyo, she'd need a shower. And some comfort.

Automatically, her thumb found Les's last text on her phone. She'd texted him, "Love you, babe", two days before when he'd been in class. Les was a philosophy student and still had a year to go before he graduated. He was studying hard, Ella had to admit. They were lucky that their friend Wendi was also in the program and could keep Les on task because as a rule, Les's mind tended to wander. That was probably ok for a philosophy student. Kind of like if an astrophysics student had a habit of staring at the stars.

Normally, she wouldn't have bothered him, but after such a shitty day, there was an ache in Ella's stomach. She'd only seen him at bedtime in their apartment for the past two days. And she missed him. The phone was ringing before she put it to her ear. It rang three times and went to voicemail. Ella stifled a sigh of disappointment just in time for the beep.

"Hey Les, it's me," she started. "I just had two interviews, back to back. The first one, well, it was a lot like the first *Tremors* movie, you know, high production value, but still nauseating. And the last one was like the fourth *Tremors* movie; mostly just nauseating." She paused to look down at the toes of her boots as they scuffed on the pavement. "So, yeah, like the *Tremors* franchise as a whole, my day is going down the crapper and fast. So, I'm about to go to Seafrost for a Kiwi-Cheesecake Pity Party. Can I pick one up for you? I...miss you." Ella paused. She hated sounding so codependent. That wasn't her. It never had been. But she guessed that some degree of codependency was just part of being in a big-kid relationship. Les was her first "serious" boyfriend that included cohabitation and the "I love you" exchange. She had to admit though, the exchange rate on "I love yous" tended to diminish over time. The frequency of anything in their relationship beyond regular roommate behavior had fallen to an all-time low over the last few months. Ella blamed herself.

Without class to go to every day, it had been hard to keep motivation up to do much of anything. But now, she was back in the game. Even if she'd whiffed on the two interviews today. There would be *other* interviews. And, she had to admit, the day didn't seem nearly as bad when she thought of Les's blue eyes and dirty-blond, shaggy hair as he gave her that crooked smile and tweaked her nose. The ending voicemail beep sounded in her ear, bringing Ella out of her thoughts. She hung up just as a tan Volvo pulled to the curb in front of her. She waved at the man behind the wheel before she climbed into the backseat.

"To Seafrost, my good man!" Ella said. It was redundant since Jatan already knew that was where they were headed. But Ella was so happy to be out of Ernie's office and on her way to froyo and possibly some stress-relief with Les, that she couldn't help sounding aloud her froyo battle cry. "Can I get you a froyo, Jatan? They have thirty-two flavors."

"Why thirty-two?" Jatan asked. "I've always wondered about that."

Ella shrugged. "Maybe they wanted to outdo Baskin Robbins with their thirty-one."

"So why not just come up with three more flavors and make it thirty-five or forty even?" Jatan asked.

"Maybe they didn't want to be showy about outdoing them," Ella said. Jatan grinned. "So, what about it?" she asked. "Feel like some tasty frozen yogurt? My treat."

"It is November," Jatan said. "It's too cold for frozen anything."

"So, we'll chase it with some Starbucks hot chocolate," Ella said.

Jatan chuckled and looked at Ella in his rear view mirror. "Thank you, but I'll pass."

"Ok," Ella said. "But you're missing out. Because I have found it."

Jatan glanced back at her again. "Found what?"

"The meaning of life," Ella said with a shrug. "The answer. It's not forty-two or a Monty Python sketch, though they've both been instrumental in bringing me to this point. The meaning of life, my friend, is a kiwi-cheesecake frozen yogurt from Seafrost. Size Pacific."

"The Pacific? Isn't that the one you get in a bucket?"

"Yep," Ella said.

"I thought they only made that size for parties and catering events."

Ella nodded. "So I've been told, every time I order one. But does that stop me? No."

"They actually give you a Pacific-sized frozen yogurt?" Jatan asked, his eyes widening in surprise.

Ella sighed. "No. They give me a lecture about forty-eight hours notice and then serve me an Atlantic-sized serving. But I think I'm wearing them down."

"Everyone has to have something worth fighting for," Jatan chuckled.

"Damn skippy," Ella said. She felt her phone vibrate in her pocket and dug it out. It was a text notification. She opened it and Les's picture popped up next to a text bubble under her "Love you, Babe" from two days earlier. *"I'm studying at Wendi's. Be home late."*

Ella tried to ignore the deflating feeling happening in her chest.

"Here we are," Jatan said as he pulled to the curb outside of Seafrost. Ella pushed her disappointment aside to make room for the pure ecstasy of frozen yogurt.

"Do you mind waiting for me?" Ella asked. "I'm springing for Starbucks if you'll drive me there next." Jatan nodded and six minutes later, Ella was back in the car, digging into the three pounds of froyo on her lap as Jatan wove through traffic towards the nearest Starbucks with a drive-thru.

"So, do you mind me asking what happened today that made you decide to eat your body weight in frozen milk water?" Jatan asked as he signaled and changed lanes.

"Two fhitty innerviews," Ella said, her mouth full of cold deliciousness. She swallowed. "And my boyfriend is studying and won't be home until late."

Jatan nodded. "I understand now."

Ella grinned at him. "Jatan, I think this could be the start of a beautiful friendship."

"And there's nothing like a Venti Americano to solidify our bond," Jatan added as he pulled into the line for the drive-thru.

While they waited for their turn, Ella stared at her phone. She'd wanted to call Les again, but if he was studying with Wendi, he wouldn't answer. He'd tried to explain his reasoning for this and the deep philosophical ramifications, but Ella had gotten lost in the name-dropping of the different philosophers and finally just nodded before going back to reading news articles on her phone. Still, there was a nagging feeling in her chest. She needed to see him. Even for a minute, just to hug him and know she still had something good in her life, even if it wasn't her dream job. It was weak and petty, but if she could just have that, she knew she could hand control back over to Helga and spend the rest of the night filling out another thirty job applications for anywhere that was hiring. As long as she had one stable thing in her life, she could face the rest of it being a shitshow and not finding her dream job for a while.

They ordered and as soon as Ella had put her wallet away, she gave Jatan Wendi's address. Jatan turned them toward the Capitol Hill district. It was convenient that Wendi's apartment was a short fifteen-minute walk from her and Les's. Wendi and her boyfriend Charlie were their closest friends and it made date nights so much easier. Wendi always had their double-dates planned, so it took the pressure off of Ella in coming up with something fun to do.

Jatan pulled into the parking lot for Wendi's building and Ella was ready to get out as soon as he came to a stop. She'd been spending the trip psyching herself up. Les was going to be surprised. She didn't usually do anything dramatic or romantic like just dropping by his study sessions to kiss him because that always sounded like it might be embarrassing for her. And more than *anything*, Ella hated being embarrassed. But today, she needed Les, embarrassment be damned.

She'd tipped Jatan ahead of time and with a rushed thank you, she held her froyo with both hands, led with her hip to get her shoulder bag out of the backseat, and nudged the car door closed before she could second-guess what she was doing. She took a huge bite of froyo as she got to the stairs and fought back the brain freeze that told her maybe Jatan was right.

It might be too cold to be cannon-balling frozen milk water. Oh well. She licked her spoon as she reached the top stair and headed down the hallway to 231B. She stuck the plastic spoon in her mouth so she could knock and then stuck it back in the ice cream so she wouldn't look like a four-year-old when Wendi opened the door.

At first, Ella didn't hear anything coming from inside the apartment. Then, there was a scuffling sound and a voice she recognized as Les's coming closer to the door.

"Don't move, babe. I'm sure it's just pizza."

Then, the apartment door swung inward and Ella was staring at her boyfriend. He was naked, except for a pair of boxers she didn't recognize, that he had put on backward.

3

ELLA

Ella and Les stared at each other for a full minute without speaking. It was hard to tell who was more shocked.

"So...," Ella finally said, pulling the spoon out of her half-eaten froyo. She licked it before pointing at Les's boxers. "Those are new." She felt Sarcastic El breaking free of Helga's hold on her. That was odd because usually in a situation like this, Sarcastic El would be holding Helga back as she powered up a head full of fire and righteous indignation. Number two on the list of things that Ella hated the most, right behind being embarrassed, was being lied to.

"Ella," Les breathed. "What the hell are you doing here?"

"Les? What is it?" Wendi's voice asked. Her hands snaked around his chest from behind and her cloud of red curls preceded her face as she peered around Les's arm. Her skin paled when she spotted Ella.

"Ella!"

"Sup, Wendi," Ella said.

The three of them stood very still, staring at each other and trying to get a handle on the moment. Ella was taking a mental inventory. Helga and Sarcastic El were both mouthing soundlessly like fish out of water, but for the moment, neither seemed to be able to muster anything as a follow-up.

Les Kugan, her boyfriend of the last year and a half, was cheating on her. It wasn't the first time she'd been cheated on. But she'd hoped

Les was different. She'd given up her apartment to move in with him. She'd...trusted him. That hurt the most. Ok. Hurt, that was a step in the right direction. *Uh, Helga,* Ella thought, *anytime you want to let rip with the righteous indignation, let's hear it.* But Helga was still. There was a new guest at the party inside her head. She was pale and emotionless.

"Ella..." Wendi was actually the first to speak, dragging Ella out of her head for a moment. "I'm sorry...it just...happened."

"Sure," Ella said, her voice cold and flat. "I mean, it's really the only thing you two could do. You can only study for so long, right?" The deadpan tone of her voice surprised even Ella. The hurt was quickly shifting into something else. She wasn't just disappointed in Les for cheating and Wendi for aiding and abetting in the cheating. She *was* angry. Pissed, in fact. But, she couldn't work herself up to yelling. It was odd. Inside her head, Helga and Sarcastic El were both just taking a step back, observing this new Numb Ella.

"Ella," Les said. "It's just that..."

She ignored him and looked down at her froyo. She scooped up a spoonful and stuck it in her mouth. "Sho," she said, pausing to savor the flavor which wasn't as intoxicating as it had been a few moments earlier. She swallowed and glanced back at Les and Wendi who weren't touching now. "How long has this been going on?"

"El," Les tried again. "This is why. This is exactly why this happened. You're-"

Ella raised her eyebrows and glanced at Les. "Oh really? Dazzle me. I can't wait to hear exactly how this happened and why it's my fault."

Les sighed. "I never know what you're thinking. What you're feeling. You don't let me in. You're so obsessed with *not* being the one to go out on a limb..."

Ella snorted. "Les, come on. It's hard to 'let you in' and 'go out on a limb' for you, as you put it when you're in Wendi's bed every day."

"El..." Les tried again.

She looked down at her froyo and she felt a mental box close on the scene in front of her. Helga finally found her opening, and with more enthusiasm than she usually showed, she started desperately pulling Ella's attention toward something that wouldn't make her eyes burn. Of course, it only half-worked as a new, smaller tragedy usurped the one framed in the apartment doorway. "Damn it," she muttered, "I left my hot chocolate in the Uber." She glanced back up at Wendi and Les, still standing there staring at her. Wendi had on a bra and panty set that Ella had given her as a Secret Santa gift the year before. And unless Les was "one of the many" he was wearing a pair of boxers that belonged to Wendi's boyfriend, Charlie.

Ella snorted to herself. Neither one of them was worth another second of her time. And number three on Ella's list of things she hated the most was having someone waste her time. *Well done, Les,* Numb Ella thought with another snort of laughter, *today you hit the trifecta.*

"What's so funny?" Les asked, narrowing his eyes.

Ella shook her head and turned away from them to head back down the hall. "Nothing. Have a nice life. Both of you." She was almost to the stairs when she heard the door to Wendi's apartment close. A second later, the door to the stairs in front of her opened and she was nose to nose with Charlie.

"Hey, Ella!" Charlie said. Ella's heart ached for Charlie when she saw he was carrying roses.

"Nice flowers," Ella managed to say.

"Oh, it's our two-year anniversary today," Charlie said with a smile. "I'm gonna surprise Wendi."

Ella took a deep breath. "You might be the one getting the surprise."

"What do you mean?" Charlie asked.

She couldn't let him just walk blindly into what was waiting for him at the end of the hall. "You want some froyo?" Ella asked, holding the bowl out to him.

"What? Uh, no ...thank you," Charlie said quickly, a grin starting to spread across his face. "Is...is Wendi cooking something for dinner?"

"Yeah, Kugan-werst," Ella muttered.

"What?" Charlie was confused again.

Ella balanced her froyo in one hand and put her free hand on Charlie's shoulder. "There's no easy way to say this. My boyfriend, well, I guess my ex now, is doinking your girlfriend in her apartment right now." Ella glanced down at the flowers in his hand. "Apparently on your anniversary." She sighed. "Sorry, Charlie." Charlie's lips were moving, but no sound was coming out. "Did you keep your own apartment?" Ella asked. After a moment, Charlie nodded. Ella smiled at him. "Good. You'll be ok."

She could feel her resolve starting to shatter as realization began to set in. *She hadn't* kept her apartment. The apartment she was currently living in and paying half the rent on was in Les's name. Ella could feel the hot knot starting to form in her throat as she gave Charlie's arm one more squeeze and headed for the stairs. By the time she reached the bottom of the staircase, she couldn't hold the tears back anymore. Damn him. And damn Wendi. And damn her for trusting them. She made it outside before she slumped down to sit on the curb. Her shoulder bag skidded across the pavement next to her as she shifted, settling the half-melted remains of her froyo on her lap. She felt sick. All the time and energy and care she'd wasted. And on top of that, she'd just embarrassed herself, and been lied to. That was what hurt the most. Les had known her history of being cheated on, and he'd done it anyway. And she'd wasted her time caring about him. Ditto that for her so-called friend Wendi.

A car was pulling to the curb in front of her, slowing down until the front bumper was just feet away from her legs. She looked up to see Jatan behind the wheel. She glanced down at her phone. Had she scheduled an Uber on her way downstairs without realizing it?

She scrambled to her feet just as Jatan rolled down his window and leaned across the passenger seat to smile at her.

"You forgot your hot chocolate in the back." Jatan pulled a fresh hot chocolate from his cup holder and held it out to her. "It was cold when I found it, so I got you a new one."

Ella burst into fresh tears at Jatan's kindness. "Jatan, you are one hell of an Uber driver."

"You look like this was a rough stop for you," Jatan nodded at the building behind Ella.

"Yeah, you could say that," she chuckled, before swiping at her nose with a tissue from her pocket.

"Climb in," Jatan said. Ella tossed the remainder of her froyo into a trash can and slid into the backseat.

She gave him the address to Les's apartment and Jatan took her there, off the meter. Ella pulled a fifty out of her wallet and handed it to him. He opened his mouth to argue, but she just smiled at him. "For the hot chocolate and excellent door-to-door service."

He gave her a half-smile. "You going to be ok?"

Ella shrugged. "Are any of us?"

"Good point," Jatan said. Ella watched him drive off and then turned back to study the apartment building she'd been calling home for the last year. She'd never been overly fond of it. It was new and shiny and modern. It wasn't homey, like her old apartment.

Ella could feel the tears starting to well up behind her eyes again and it was pissing her off. It was at that moment that Helga decided to take over, but she didn't shove Numb Ella aside. They were sharing the helm, both trying to get their asses to fit in the captain's chair. But, Helga was the first one to give her orders. *Get upstairs. Pack. Leave.* Three-step program for putting distance between her and Les.

The apartment felt cold to Ella now. She stopped in the doorway to survey the living room. When Ella had moved in, she'd gotten rid of most of her Craigslist and garage sale furniture because Les's father had furnished his apartment with designer stuff. Ella had missed the overstuffed chintz couch and scarred writing desk that was just the right height, but she'd convinced herself that being with Les made it all worth it.

Ella closed her eyes and mentally asked Helga and Sarcastic El which one had been responsible for that spectacular line of reasoning. She sighed when they both pointed at each other. *Don't reminisce.* Ella thought to herself. *Pack your stuff and get out.* Ella forced herself into the bedroom and avoided looking at the bed as much as she could. Still, she couldn't help wondering if Wendi, her supposed friend, had ever been in it with Les. She stuffed her clothing in her rolling suitcase and dumped everything that belonged to her from the bathroom into a backpack. She paused in the kitchen, thinking of her dishes in the cabinet.

"Nope," she said aloud to the empty apartment. They were all his. Anything that had touched his lips, especially after learning where else they'd been, he could keep.

She bumped her suitcase down the stairs and with each echoing thud, the realization of her day set in. Two terrible interviews (or almost interviews), followed by catching her boyfriend sleeping with her best friend in the city. And now she was homeless.

Ella was several blocks away from the apartment complex before she realized what she was doing. It didn't make logical sense, but she decided to just let her feet keep carrying her forward. They seemed to know where they were going. She didn't think it would help, but with two feet, her brain was outnumbered. A half-hour later, she was standing in front of the old red brick building where she used to live. She paused on the sidewalk to look up at what was once her living room window. Her comfy chair that she'd sat in to watch the sunrise had been replaced by a Christmas tree. As she watched, two small children carried ornaments over to hang on its branches. A woman appeared behind them, a baby on her hip, as she smiled at the progress. A new kind of hurt was erupting inside of her. It was almost December. Almost Christmas. She'd already told her mom that she and Les would be hosting Christmas dinner. And now, all of that, all the possibilities, any kind of future down that road was gone.

What was she going to do now? No more relationship, no home, no job. . . Panic was starting to creep in. It was too cold for her to just sit on the street corner for the night or in the park. She had some other friends in the city, but they all had roommates or lived in closets disguised as apartments. She couldn't ask them for help. Besides, how embarrassing would that be? She shivered at the thought of having to tell them that she'd just caught Les cheating on her. They'd feel sorry for her, but somewhere in the back of their minds, they'd assume it was because she hadn't done something right.

No. She didn't want to tell anyone in Seattle about what had happened.

Not when she was so pathetic and holding the short end of the stick. Something was fighting its way to the surface in Ella's mind. Something her mom had said during her phone call. She closed her eyes and groaned when she remembered what it was.

It was definitely not a Plan B or even a Plan Z. It was almost the worst scenario she could think of. It was embarrassing and it was a regression so it definitely counted as a waste of her time, making it a twofer out of Ella's top three. But it was also the only idea she had at the moment that would solve one, possibly two, of her immediate problems.

She pulled out her phone and dialed her mom's number. "Hi, Mom. Did you say they're hiring at the *Hope Hornblower*?"

4

ELLA

Ella decided not to take an Uber in hopes that Helga and Sarcastic El would figure out an alternative plan before she reached the Light Rail station and the shuttle to the ferry. Every possibility she could come up with presented itself to her and then quickly imploded as logic was applied. Going home was something she vowed she'd never do. Just because it would solve an immediate problem *didn't* mean it was a good idea. Coming home was a double-edged sword.

And yet, here she was on her way to catch the shuttle that she hadn't ridden for four years. She could feel a quilt of self-pity, depression and realization settling over her. But, she didn't have any other options at the moment. So, she just kept slogging along the sidewalk, wearing her shoulder bag and backpack and dragging her rolling suitcase behind her like a tourist.

Numb Ella was silently prodding her feet forward, while in her head, Sarcastic El started heckling every idea Helga could come up with as to how to keep Ella in Seattle. While her other two personalities bickered, Numb Ella said silent goodbyes to all of her Seattle haunts. Her apartment building. The bagel shop where she'd worked while going to school. The accounting firm that she'd worked at as a bookkeeper during her last year until she'd graduated and quit to find her "dream job".

She had to walk back past Wendi's building to get to the Light Rail station, but she picked up speed and looked straight ahead, definitely not wanting to accidentally bump into Wendi, Les, or even Charlie.

Helga and Sarcastic El had still not been able to pull any marvelous alternative plans out of their collective mental asses by the time she reached the Light Rail station. So, when the shuttle to the Anacortes Ferry Terminal came, she took a deep breath and forced herself to get on it. When the shuttle jerked forward, pulling them into traffic, Ella was forced to accept the fact that she was leaving Seattle. She stared out the window as the familiar sights of the town she'd called home for the past four years, rolled by.

What a difference a day made. When she'd woken up that morning, moving back to Hope was definitely the most unexpected and least desirable outcome for the day. Yet, here she was. She rested the side of her face against the cold window and stared at the gray sky. The ever-present rain began to fall and though it normally felt comforting to Ella, today it felt like a harbinger of doom.

It was really happening. She was going back. Back to the place where every single person over the age of thirty knew and remembered every embarrassing thing she'd done in the eighteen years she'd lived there. To say it was a depressing thought was an understatement. And it was almost December. The absolute worst time of the year to be going back. Why couldn't Les have kept it in his pants until the spring?

The line for the ferry that made stops at Selton, Raven, and Hope Island was predictably long. The Selton, Raven, and Hope ferry should have been the runt of the ferry litter. The combined populations of all three islands consisted of less than ten thousand people with Selton definitely having the lion's share. The ferry did make a final stop at Orcas Island, the largest of the San Juan islands, before coming back to port, but that wasn't why the line was so long. It was tourists. During the tourist season, Selton, Raven, and Hope Islands were stuffed to the gills. And the Christmas season was the worst. That thought made Ella want to find a nice hard surface to bang her head against. But she didn't want to lose her place in line since delaying her boarding wouldn't change the inevitable. Her mom already knew she was coming. There was no time left for her to run off and join an anti-technology commune. Her mom would have the Coast Guard, several news channels, and every able-bodied member of Hope Island out looking for her if she pulled something like that.

The line began to move forward and Ella resigned herself to her fate. She rolled her suitcase up the ramp and once aboard, she broke off from the rest of the crowd that was surging forward to occupy the bow railing. It was always crowded with tourists wanting to stand like Rose on the bow of the *Titanic* and feel the cold sea breeze and splash of the waves on their faces. She knew better. They were more likely to get dive-bombed by asshole seagulls who could hear a bag of Funyons being ripped open, three miles away.

Instead of heading towards the bow, Ella lugged her suitcase to the upper deck and found a bench at the stern railing. She wanted to look at the mainland for as long as she could.

As she stared at the trees and seemingly endless stretch of land in front of her, she was hit with the same feeling she'd had that morning. When she'd looked back down that hallway at the *Tribune*, full of junior copy editor-hopefuls who'd immediately filled the place where she'd stood, it was as if she'd never been there.

Was that all life was? Just people staring back at where they'd been and wondering if anyone would remember they were once there too? The shoreline and the people milling around on it seemed to have a mutual disregard for each other. The people spared little notice or thought for every rock and tree they passed. And the trees themselves were probably not making mental scrapbooks of every upright ape that wandered by. Numb Ella was apparently at the helm for the moment, deciding to lay some depressing philosophy on Ella. She did her best to ignore the skid toward the dark side that Numb Ella was trying to steer her into, as she breathed in the familiar smell of the sea air.

She wondered vaguely how the second round of Les and Wendi's "ugly-bumping explanation" had gone for Charlie. Would Les and Wendi start dating now? Would Les convince Wendi to give up her apartment and move in with him? If so, he was single-handedly creating more rental options for people in Seattle by convincing gullible women to give up their places. Ella gave herself a shake.

Too dark, Numb Ella.

In an attempt to distract herself, she gazed around at her surroundings and saw a news kiosk on wheels being pushed around the deck in her direction.

She bought a Twix bar, and after a momentary internal battle, a copy of the *Hope Hornblower*. Might as well embrace the inevitable. It was not a lengthy periodical. After all, how much news was a daily paper supposed to scrounge up when the entire town was five square miles with a population of just over three thousand?

The front-page headline announced the immediate retirement of Clarence Ford, the editor of the *Hornblower*. There was no picture. Not surprising. From what she could remember of Clarence, he never took pictures. When she was in high school, working at the *Hornblower* part-time, he'd always been the one to take the pictures at staff gatherings. Myrna had a theory that Clarence was self-conscious about the big scar on his cheek. The rumor was that he'd gotten it in a car accident when he was a teenager. It was as good a theory for Clarence being camera shy as anyone else's explanation.

Instead of a photo of Clarence, there was a large picture accompanying the story below that featured Esther Jacobs basically muscling her husband out of the frame as she held up wooden lobster-shaped novelty nutcrackers. *Ah yes*, Ella thought, *you know it's almost the holidays when the bizarre novelty nutcrackers start coming out of hibernation.*

Ella leaned back on the bench to read the very short piece on Clarence. After a few minutes, she'd moved on to the surprisingly playful piece about Esther's lobster crackers, when the sounds of a heated discussion drawing closer broke her concentration.

"If I'd known this ferry didn't go to Waldron, I wouldn't have gotten on it," a man's voice snapped. Ella glanced at the port that was now growing smaller as the ferry cruised past Burrows Bay down the Rosario Strait. The frustrated man looked about her age. He had tan skin, dark curly hair, and several days' worth of scruff on his face. He was tall and lanky, in an attractive way, and he stood like someone that wasn't used to being angry and frustrated.

The deckhand he was arguing with looked bored and when he spoke to the man, his tone was condescending.

"Sir, you can change ferries at our Orcas Island stop and take the ferry directly from there to Waldron." Without waiting for the man to reply, the deckhand took advantage of the man's momentary silence and strolled away.

The man watched him go before heaving a frustrated sigh and hiking his day pack higher up on his back. He glanced down at the ticket in his hand and then as if he felt Ella's not-so-subtle staring, he turned to look at her.

She almost choked on the piece of Twix she was trying to swallow when his gaze met hers. She managed to get it to go down just as he crossed the deck and flopped down onto the bench beside her.

"No offense if you're one of these island commuters or whatever," the man muttered, "but your ferry system sucks."

Ella nodded, not wanting to speak until she was fairly sure she wouldn't spew crumbs all over him. "No argument here," Ella said. "I've always assumed it was a conspiracy to deter island visitors."

The man nodded and gave Ella a lop-sided grin. He had dark brown eyes that lit up his face which, going by the laugh lines around his mouth, was now settling back into his usual expression. "A brilliant plan," he added. "Confuse them away." He sighed and leaned his head back against the seat.

Ella recognized the posture of defeat. Without pausing to think about what she was doing, she held out the remaining Twix bar to him. "Twix?"

He hesitated and she glanced over at him. He looked from the Twix bar to her face and grinned again. "You sure? I mean, I know it's Twix's ad campaign and everything to share, but I've never actually met anyone that offered to share their Twix with me."

Ella shrugged, feeling the slightest jolt in her stomach when he flashed that smile at her again. It was accompanied by her struggling to remember the last time Les had smiled at her. That had to be why she'd felt the sudden flutter in her chest. Maybe she'd forgotten what a smile looked like.

"Well, I like to subvert expectations when I can," she said. "Plus, you look hangry. And that deckhand is all bones and grizzle."

"I appreciate your thoughtfulness in preventing bloodshed," he said. "And . . . for preventing me from choking on a . . . deckhand bone."

Ella shrugged. "I do what I can."

She felt the long-forgotten, but still familiar, jerk of anxiety that always came as a medical side effect when she introduced herself to an attractive man. "Ella Danforth," she said.

Introducing herself to guys had never been her strong suit. Les had been a classmate in her Chemistry class during her first semester at Duwamish. Before that, she couldn't recall the last time she'd been single and introduced herself to a guy. All the guys she had dated in high school were the same ones she'd grown up with. She hadn't had to introduce herself. They'd all known each other since their mud-eating, pants-wetting, streaking-toddler days. But now, here she was, just hours after breaking up with her first serious boyfriend out of high school and she couldn't seem to remember how to casually talk to someone of the opposite sex. What if he thought she was nuts and didn't shake her hand? What if he just got up and moved? Oh well, at least she had a newspaper to bury herself behind until she could get to the rail and jump.

"I'm going to hope that that's your name and not some obscure island greeting that will mean I am thrown overboard if I answer it incorrectly," he said, reaching out to take Ella's hand. "Tony," the man said. "Tony Sanetti."

"Nice to meet you," Ella said. Tony took the remaining Twix bar and Ella was thankful for the excuse to break eye contact with him and wad up the wrapper. "So, I'm going to go out on a limb and assume you're not from around here," she said.

Tony took a bite of the Twix and waited until he'd stopped chewing to answer her. "Nope. Chicago."

Ella raised an eyebrow at him. "I've got some bad news for you, Tony. If you're planning to keep heading west until you get back home, it's going to be a long trip." Helga and Sarcastic El, who'd been watching with mouths hanging open up to this point did a double facepalm. *Strong move, whipping out the dad jokes, Ella.*

To her surprise, Tony chuckled. "You don't say." He looked out at the waves rolling by in the ferry's wake. "No, I'm visiting my aunt and uncle. They live on Waldron Island."

"They must be pretty hardcore islanders then," Ella said, looking around the deck for a trash can. She paused and glanced back at Tony. "Have you ever been to Waldron before?" Tony shook his head slowly. "Well, the population of the whole island is something like seventy-eight people."

Tony closed his eyes in defeat and chuckled as he leaned his head back against the wall behind their bench. "They forgot to mention that little detail when they invited me out for the holidays."

"Old island trick," Ella said, finally stuffing the Twix wrapper in her coat pocket.

Tony opened an eye and turned his head to look at Ella. "There's no chance that you're also headed to Waldron, is there?"

Ella smiled, mentally telling Helga and Sarcastic El to shut up. He was just being nice. "Sorry, Tony. You're on your own."

He sat up again and rested his elbows on his knees before turning his full attention on her. "Where are you headed then? Raven Island?"

"No one lives on Raven Island. It's just a place for photographers to take really awful senior pictures of pimply girls and for, um, you know... bird-ologists... to go study migratory patterns, or seagull droppings, or something."

Tony blinked at Ella. "Ok, there's a lot to unpack in that description. First, I'm going to guess that you had *your* senior pictures taken on Raven Island?"

"Oh no, my secret's out," Ella muttered.

"And second," Tony continued, "Bird-ologists?"

Ella mock-glared at him. "It's been a long day. You know who I'm talking about."

"Ornithologists?" Tony asked.

"Them too," Ella said with a grin. God help her, she was actually starting to like this guy. Not in a serious way . . . just as a welcome relief to focus her attention on and avoid thinking about Les, Wendi, Ernie Bleu, the *Tribune*, or what lay ahead for her.

"So, where are you really headed?" Tony asked. And there was reality. Back, like a tiny dog that wouldn't stop barking until you paid attention to it and even then, it was only a fifty-fifty guarantee.

Ella sighed. "Hope Island."

Tony grinned. "So you're a tourist, like me?"

"Sadly, no," Ella said. "I grew up there. And now . . . I'm moving back. For a little bit." She stared back at the mainland. "For the smallest 'little bit' that I can manage."

"Oh!" Tony said quickly. A note of excitement in his voice drew Ella's attention back to him. He was grinning ear-to-ear now. "Wait, my aunt told me about that place. Doesn't Hope have all these great holiday traditions?"

Ella sighed again. "It depends on how you measure 'greatness', I guess."

"She said there are all these bazaars, parades, and competitions. All that great stuff."

"That's an interesting measuring stick you're using there," Ella muttered. She hadn't allowed herself to dwell on all the Hope Island crap until Tony had started listing it off, forcing her hand.

"What? You don't like it?" Tony asked.

Ella shook her head. "I'm used to it. I grew up there. For eighteen years, participation in all the various *insane* traditions of the island was mandatory."

"But wasn't it fun?" Tony asked.

"Is Disneyland fun for the guy who wears a three-hundred-pound, black fur mouse costume every day in July, Tony? No. It was just a part of living there. If you're from Chicago, you have to hear about pizza and the Cubs all the time, right?" Tony nodded and she continued. "If you're from New York, it's the Mets and the cockroaches." She sighed. "If you're from Hope, it's the ice turkey bowling competition, the town-wide After Harvest Food Fight, the Island Yodeling Championship, etc." Ella sat back and reflexively smoothed the newspaper on her lap while a mental parade of every embarrassing task she'd had to do at a Hope Island event danced through her head.

"Is that the Hope Island paper?" Tony asked, pointing at her lap.

"Oh," Ella said, now wishing she'd rammed the damn thing in her bag. "Yeah."

"May I?" Tony asked. Ella shrugged and handed it to him. He studied the headline and grinned. "Why is it called the *'Hornblower'*? That's not a common name for a paper, is it?" Ella groaned involuntarily. "What?" Tony asked. "What is it?"

She shook her head. No escaping it now. She cleared her throat and sat up, rotating to put one knee on the bench and her arm along the back so she could face Tony. "Ok, fair warning, just remember that you asked for the following ridiculousness."

"I'm hooked," Tony said. "Reel me in."

Ella rolled her eyes, but when she saw Tony's expression hadn't changed from earnest interest, she pressed on. "So, Hope Island was originally settled by Swiss immigrants, back in the late 1800s. They'd come out on the Oregon Trail and then just kept going. Overachievers, in my opinion. Anyway, they originally named the island 'Hoffnung'."

"It just rolls off the tongue," Tony said.

"Exactly," Ella said. "Well, anyway, it means 'hope'. Later, as more English settlers moved out here, the name was just changed to 'Hope'. I think World War II may have had some influence on changing German names to English equivalents. Other places in town were changed to English names, etc."

"Ok," Tony said. "So that's the island's name. Why is the paper called the *Hornblower*? You're a story tease."

Ella snorted and shook her head. Ok. Tony was starting to make the day seem not as shitty. "Right," she continued, "the infamous Hope Horn. So, these Swiss immigrants brought their musical instruments with them, of course. One of them being the lovely, docile-toned Alphorn."

"Wait, you mean those big horns they use in, like, the Ricola ads?"

"That's the one," Ella said.

"Oh, I can hardly wait to hear where this is going," Tony said, inching forward on his seat.

"Well, don't get too excited. Anyway, there's one lighthouse on Hope Island, on the west coast. And the legend goes that one night, the kerosene ran out unexpectedly. So Hans Kruegelmier, the lighthouse-keeper, sent his wife, Anna, into the settlement to go house to house asking for more. In the meantime, Hans was worried that the ships offshore would run into the island because the lighthouse's beacon had gone out."

"A valid worry of any lighthouse keeper in an age without GPS," Tony said, nodding.

"Yeah, well, the only 'ships' that were off the coast at the time were two drunk fishermen in a rowboat, named Kurt and Johann. So, there wasn't a lot at stake, to begin with."

"You're making this up," Tony said.

Ella shook her head. "Sadly, no. Kurt and Johann have a children's playground named after them in town."

Tony started to laugh.

Ella raised an eyebrow at him. "Want me to finish or is your ridiculosity meter already off the charts?"

"N-no, I think it can handle a little more," Tony snorted.

"Well, ole Hans was so worried that he ran back to his house and got his Alphorn and stood on the cliffs next to the lighthouse, blowing the thing until his throat was raw, trying to warn the 'ships' that they were approaching the island."

"And?" Tony asked when Ella fell silent. "What happened?"

She frowned. "What do you mean, 'what happened?' Kurt and Johann started yelling at Hans to shut the hell up because he was scaring their fish away. They chucked liquor bottles at him. But of course, in their inebriated state, they didn't have a great concept of how much force it would take to throw the bottle that far inland, let alone up the cliffs to where he was standing. So, Kurt and Johann were probably the first polluters of the Rosario Strait and probably *shouldn't* have a kids' playground named after them. And after the uneventful night of them *not* crashing into the shore, the town founders felt they should commemorate this night where nothing happened, by building a gazebo in the center of town and displaying Hans's Alphorn forever." Ella leaned toward Tony, lowering her voice conspiratorially. "Personally, I think it was just some wise planning and a nifty way to separate Hans from his Alphorn. Legend has it that he wasn't very good at it."

"Is the horn still there? I mean, a hundred and fifty years of salt air and rain must have . . ." Tony started.

Ella shook her head. "No, it was replaced every few years until in the 1980s, the town council had the brilliant idea of replacing it with a bronze replica that people could actually blow on."

"Oh no," Tony muttered.

"Oh yes," Ella said. "Apparently, it was supposed to help the 'young people connect to their roots,' but imagine having something that is less sanitary than an old-school public water fountain, that when blown into, can be heard all over town. And it's ceased to sound like a musical instrument by any stretch of the imagination. In the summertime, because our tourism bureau is staffed with a bunch of masochists that hate the rest of us, they advertise to all the tourists that they can come 'blow our horn'. Which, come on, phrasing, people. So, imagine you're putting your contacts in, or defusing a bomb, or just put your kid down for a nap, and then the silence of a quiet afternoon is shattered by a noise that I can only describe as a whale farting into a kazoo, attached to the largest megaphone ever conceived."

"Wow . . ." Tony breathed. "That's . . . that's a sound."

"Yeah," Ella said, dropping her gaze down to look at the paper in Tony's lap. She felt heat rising in her cheeks, remembering being in the rose garden, half-naked, and under Brad Hartwell on Prom night when someone blew the damn thing and almost gave her a heart attack. Brad had screamed like a little girl and taken off, muttering about getting caught by his dad. Leaving her to make the "walk of shame" home with nothing more to show for it than bits of rosebush in her hair, scraped elbows, and no real "shame" to be walking off beside the fact that she'd been about to give up her virginity to a guy that had squealed and run off when someone had blown Hans's horn.

"So, to immortalize this thing that plagues your town, they named the newspaper after it?" Tony asked, glancing back down at his lap.

"Pretty much," Ella said. "It's a weird place, Tony."

"It sounds like it. But Christmas won't be so bad, right? I mean, if anyone tries to blow the horn in this weather, their lips will stick right to it."

Ella sighed and shook her head. "You'd think that would slow them down, but no. You'd be surprised how many people are willing to risk ripping the skin off their lips to 'blow our horn'. Especially during parades, bazaars, competitions, etc." She said, nodding as she repeated Tony's list of activities.

"Still," Tony said. "It's pretty cool that your town comes up with so many creative things to do."

"Hmmm, creative, insane, potato, pah-tah-to," Ella said, weighing the words in her hands. "I actually have a theory about that. I think that because we're so far away from the surrounding islands and the mainland, the crazy has nowhere to go. So, it just swirls around the island, getting more and more saturated every year. Each year the holidays and celebrations climb one more stair towards bedlam. Frankly, I'm kind of amazed that our island hasn't burned down yet."

Ella winced internally when she realized she'd been saying "our" about Hope. She wasn't even back on land and she was already slipping back into being an Islander. Hope Island was like the iceberg that sank the Titanic, but instead of there being more ice under the water, there were tentacles. And they may stretch and let their captives play around on the mainland, but sooner or later, they were going to suck them back. It wasn't possible to "Abandon *all* of Hope".

"Wow," Tony said, shaking his head and pulling Ella away from her thoughts. "I have to see this place while I'm here." He pulled out a full-sized map of the U.S. and spread it on his knee. He leaned forward, squinting at the islands off the coast of Washington. "Which one is it?"

"South of Lopez," Ella said. "It's the one shaped like a heart."

"A heart?" Tony asked. "I don't see one shaped like a heart."

"Oh, not the cute kind," Ella corrected quickly. "It's shaped like a human heart." Tony picked up the map and held it closer to his face to squint at the tiny shapes. Ella grinned at him and shook her head. She got to her feet and grabbed a folded map from the information display, bolted to the railing.

"Here," she said, handing it to him. "It's the ferry map. As much as I loved the Monty Python-esque sketch you were reenacting with that map, this one won't cause you to go blind or give your retinas a paper cut if you sneeze while squinting."

"You're too kind," Tony said, grinning up at her. The announcement that the ferry was pulling into Hope Harbor came over the loudspeaker. Tony got to his feet. "Well, Ella Danforth, it's been a pleasure." He reached out and Ella shook his hand. Their fingers lingered for just a second longer than the average handshake. Her heart was pounding in her chest so loudly she was afraid that Tony had heard it. But, she felt a small measure of relief when she studied him and saw the color creeping up his neck and into his cheeks under his stubble.

"Good luck on Waldron," Ella said, inwardly cringing at the pathetic farewell.

"Thanks," Tony said. "And hey, maybe I'll come back by and 'blow your horn', uh, as the saying goes." Now he looked even more uncomfortable.

In the spirit of throwing gasoline on the fire to put it out, Ella added, "I'd like that." She closed her eyes, gave herself a shake, and tried again. "I mean, I'd like it if you stopped by, you know if you got bored and didn't mind a different flavor of boredom."

"Oh, I definitely want to try all the flavors," Tony said.

"Great," Ella said.

"Uh, good," Tony added.

The ferry was at a standstill now and Ella quickly threw the strap of her shoulder bag over her head, swung her backpack back over her shoulders, and grabbed the handle on her suitcase, doing her best to hide her face from Tony. It felt like it was on fire. She didn't want to examine anything she'd just said to him too closely at the moment, let alone unpack what it meant that she was flirting with another guy only hours after breaking up with Les.

But, could it be called flirting if the phrase "whale farting into a kazoo" was involved? No. She was talking, not flirting. Tony wasn't an Islander and his trip out to the islands was temporary. Maybe she was jealous, or just hoping her trip would be temporary too. She gave him an awkward wave and hurried down the stairs, smashing her foot with her suitcase before turning to fall in line with the disembarking tourists that were heading down the ramp. She was one of four passengers that disembarked, so she couldn't even hide in the crowd. Once she was on solid land again, she turned to glance back at the ferry and saw Tony standing on the upper deck waving at her.

"Blow it hard for me!" He yelled. Ella snorted and Tony quickly followed with, "The horn, I mean!"

She just gave him a thumbs up and turned away, still blushing, unable to fight down the light happy feeling that was swelling in her chest. She hadn't embarrassed herself, at least so much that she could never show her face on the ferry again. And there was something else. Pride? No, confidence? Maybe. She'd managed to talk to a guy and he was actually *interested* in coming to Hope and visiting her while she was home. And that was even after the disclosures about how insane her town was, *and* the fact that she'd had to move back home. He hadn't treated her like she was a loser. Maybe she was going to be ok. She held onto that happy feeling as she turned back to face the footpath leading into town.

She felt the happy feeling starting to dissipate in her chest when she came eye to eye with the town's welcome sign. "Welcome to Hope Island, City of Hope, Population: 3,456. We HOPE you'll come blow our horn!"

Ella groaned as the flood of tourists walked past her, cameras out, pointing, and talking to each other. Yep. She was home.

5

ELLA

It was a steep climb uphill to get to the town center. Ella picked up speed, bumping her suitcase over the cobblestone streets and attempting to blend in with the rest of the tourists. Her plan was working at first. She'd found a husky man and a curvy woman to hide behind. They were moving at a good clip and they were almost up the hill when they decided to stop for a photo op, temporarily exposing Ella. And that was when Fate decided to tag in.

"Ella? Is that little Ella Danforth?"

Ella glared down at the ground. Why was it that the earth never opened and swallowed a person up when they wanted it to? The voice belonged to old Mrs. Thompson, Ella's fourth-grade teacher. Since the earth wasn't cooperating, Ella had only one option left to her.

"Hi, Mrs. Thompson," Ella said. "How are you doing?"

"Oh, I'm doing just splendidly, dear! And who wouldn't be? It's almost the most wonderful time of the year! There's so much to do! Did you come back for the festivities?" Mrs. Thompson blinked up at Ella, her eyes magnified behind her inch-thick glasses, making her look like an owl, clutching a bunch of mistletoe in her claws.

"Uh, not exactly," Ella said, not really wanting to give Mrs. Thompson any details to feed to the inevitable rumor mill. Mrs. Thompson had her next question at the ready, but the booming sound of a vibratory, wet whale fart blasted across the square, drowning her out.

"What!?" Ella yelled as the horn blasted again. Waiting for someone to *stop* blowing the horn in Hope was like people in Seattle waiting to go outside until it stopped raining. It never stopped, so might as well carry on.

"Are you pregnant?!" Mrs. Thompson yelled, just as the horn blast was cut short, most likely by the parent of whatever demonic child had decided to make it to first base with Hans's horn.

"Uh, no," Ella said, very aware of the overwhelming calm after the fart.

"Oh, really?" Mrs. Thompson squinted behind her glasses as she surveyed Ella's stomach. Now Ella was feeling even more self-conscious. She glanced down at herself.

"Oh, that's just a froyo baby," Ella said.

At the look of confusion on Mrs. Thompson's face, Ella quickly added, "Too much ice cream."

Mrs. Thompson didn't look convinced. "Dearie, it's almost December. No one's eating ice cream at this time of year. You can tell me if somebody got you in the family way."

Ella glanced down at the cobblestones. *Earth? Hell? Anyone down below? A little help here? Just make a hole, I'll jump in it,* she thought.

Unable to summon any help from down below, she instead summoned the closest thing to a smile she could muster and shook her head at Mrs. Thompson. "I'm not pregnant."

"Are you sure?" Mrs. Thompson asked again.

"Yeah, pretty sure," Ella said.

"You know sometimes a woman's body knows before she does." Mrs. Thompson was a bulldog with a squeaky toy and Ella could almost feel the eyes of passersby on her as the old woman went on and on about how her sister was two months along before she knew.

"I haven't had sex in three months," Ella finally blurted out, hoping it would end the discussion. Now she heard the sounds of footsteps pausing around her. She didn't care anymore. She just wanted this conversation with Mrs. Thompson to end. She knew Mrs. Thompson wouldn't be embarrassed by her admission. After all, the mistletoe Mrs. Thompson was clutching was "Young Stud Bait", as the old woman called it. Mrs. Thompson was famous in Hope for cornering young men and asking them to help an old lady put a piece of mistletoe up in every doorway in the downtown area of Hope. She'd look for fresh victims every year because only the oblivious ones never put two and two together and realized that she asked them to do it so she'd get a chance to check them out while they hung it up for her. After a second of silence between them, Mrs. Thompson finally just shook her head.

"That's too bad. You might want to work on that. Maybe you're not doing something right."

"That must be it," Ella said, deadpan.

Mrs. Thompson smiled and nodded, evidently missing the sarcasm in Ella's voice. "I could help you, you know. I've read a lot of..." Mrs. Thompson began.

"Eudora, she's back to interview for Clarence's job," a second voice called from the other side of the narrow street. Ella didn't even have to look to know it was Mr. Welks. Ella turned to wave at him. He looked as grumpy as ever, his black leather eye patch looking out of place with his flannel shirt and floral-print gardening gloves. The door to his greenhouse stood open, leaning a bit (like its owner) to one side. The aluminum frame was resting against his house, rubbing the paint off the siding when the winds from the sea jostled it. It was a common sight in Hope. People bending but not breaking to the nature around them. Hope was stubborn. Not unlike Mr. Welks.

Ella hadn't heard him moving around in his yard and now she wondered how long he'd just stood there listening before he decided to step in and offer the correct rumor material to Mrs. Thompson.

"Hi, Mr. Welks," Ella called to him. He gave her a dismissive wave and turned his frown back on Mrs. Thompson. Clearly, Ella was just a prop in this argument he was about to have with his neighbor. The pair were infamous bickerers and a constant headache for the town's overly-cheerful tourism bureau because every tourist coming into town via the footpath had to pass between their houses. To Ella, it felt like karma for the tourism bureau since the damn horn gave everyone *else* headaches.

"Eudora it was on the phone tree. Didn't you listen to it? Or were you too busy finding that ugly thistle to hang up all over town?" Mr. Welks barked, making a few of the tourists that were milling around pause and look over.

"This ugly thistle, as you call it, Fred Welks, has been responsible for the human race continuing all these years! Do you have any idea how many babies have been conceived because of this!?" Mrs. Thompson's nostrils flared as she pushed past Ella and marched over to stand in front of Fred's white picket fence. Her depth perception wasn't the best and as she shook the mistletoe in his face, there was a very real possibility that she might shove it up his nose.

"If that's what you think happens under the mistletoe," Mr. Welks bellowed, swatting it away, "then it's been longer for you than this one," he jerked a crooked thumb at Ella, "and you're in no place to give anyone advice!"

"It'll mean more to them if they work this one out on their own," Ella muttered to the nearest gawking tourists.

She was momentarily relieved as she took the opportunity to flee the interrogation and move down the street. Of course, because she'd lost her original tourist cover, Ella was acutely aware of how exposed she was as the path widened and turned into an actual street. There was a road that wound up to the town from the ferry for people bringing cars to the island, but she'd taken the footpath because it was shorter. Of course, the downside of the path was the fact that it took her right through the center of town. She blew out a sigh and quickly surveyed the path in front of her. She was a block from the town center and the gazebo. Her mom's house was another two blocks beyond that. Ok. Three blocks and one Town Square. That's all she had to do. When she'd been a cross-country runner in high school, the distance would have been nothing. Granted, she wasn't wearing the right shoes, she was still in her interview outfit, she was weighted down with about three pounds of frozen yogurt and half a Twix bar in her stomach, and she was hefting a suitcase, backpack, and her shoulder bag. But, maybe if she just kept her head down and hustled . . .

"Ella! Ella Danforth?! Is that really you?" Mr. Elton's voice boomed off to her right. The sense of dread in her gut ratcheted up another notch. Mr. John Elton (yes, his actual name) had been on Broadway as a singer, dancer, and actor and when he spoke, it always sounded like he was saying the few lines preceding a big song and dance number. Normally, Ella didn't mind it and just accepted that it was part of his personality. But at the moment, as she desperately tried to slink through town without getting the third degree, she wished he'd been a mime on Broadway. She turned her head and gave him a look that was more of a grimace than a smile. The broad-chested, movie-star handsome man was standing outside his studio, Mr. Elton's Academy, having a smoke. Through the open barn-style door, Ella could see about a dozen kids laughing and running around trailing long green and red ribbons behind them as they leaped around to the sounds of "Jingle Bell Rock".

"What are you doing back, girl?" Mr. Elton asked, his rich voice prompting Ella to cross to him, hoping he'd lower it if she was closer. He tapped the ash from his cigarette into a flowerpot that sat on the ground and raised an eyebrow at her. "I didn't think I'd ever see you back in town."

Ella sighed. "You mean you haven't listened to your 'phone tree' yet?"

Mr. Elton shook his head. "No, Lawrence usually checks the messages, but he's been working overtime getting probate work done on the mainland and I can't remember the answering machine pass code." Lawrence Elton was John's husband and the only lawyer in Hope that Ella knew of. "So, spill! What are you doing back in town?" Mr. Elton pressed.

She sighed. "I'm here to interview for a job at the *Hornblower*."

"Oh! Clarence's job?" Mr. Elton's eyebrows raised in surprise. "I thought you'd be working a big job at a Seattle paper by now."

"Well, sometimes life's funny," Ella said, feeling the sting in her chest. She'd thought the same, until today.

Mr. Elton opened his mouth as if he was going to ask her something more and Ella braced herself for the question. But, a scream, followed by crying erupted from the studio behind him and Mr. Elton quickly dropped his cigarette into the pot and hurried back inside. "Sally! Why is your finger up Juniper's nose?" she heard him say to the crying girls, hands on hips in the doorway.

Ella glanced up at the sky, put a finger to her lips, and then raised it up. "Thanks for that, Universe," she muttered.

She decided to just smile, wave, and keep moving past all the people that called to her as she hustled by Bumble's Market, Reverend George Anderson who was fussing with the nativity scene in front of Hope Church, Honey-Do Hardware, and The Spark Theatre. She'd managed to skirt the gazebo. Whoever had been blowing the horn during her interrogation session with Mrs. Thompson was gone, and the tourists that had disembarked with her either hadn't found the gazebo yet or had decided against taking the town up on their offer to "blow our horn". She was willing to hope that since they'd already heard what the horn sounded like, they'd decided to give it a pass. Or maybe their kids were just lying in wait until their parents were too tired to discourage them from donating additional lip skin to the damn thing. Either way, Ella was thankful. Blowing the horn automatically drew attention to the gazebo and as she passed by it, she gave the Universe another silent high-five for sparing her.

But the Universe was either feeling sassy or Ella's karma account had just been overdrawn. A quickly assembled crush of people was suddenly around her, moving fast and carrying her along with them, knocking her off course from her original trajectory. She was alarmed, until she spotted Esther Jacobs standing outside her knick-knack shop, Seaside Treasures, holding a wicker basket full of snow globes with a paper sign taped to the edge reading "50% Off Hope Island Snow Globes". The crowd was surging toward her, no doubt drawn by the banner above the shop's door, reading "Christmas Shopping Sale".

Ella started to sweat. Shit. If Esther spotted her, she'd be lucky to make it to her mom's house by New Year's Eve. Esther was a marathon talker. A triathlon talker, occasionally, when she was wrapping gifts in the shop, barking orders at her husband, and holding a one-sided conversation with a hapless victim. And it had never been definitively proven, but Bruce

Ellington had sworn on a stack of motorcycle magazines that he'd once witnessed a tourist's ears start to bleed after Esther had been talking to him for an hour and a half. The poor man had run from the shop, across the square, and right down the footpath to the ferry, never to be seen again. Or so the legend went.

Ella surveyed the crowd around her. Poor saps. They had no idea that one of them was about to be sacrificed to the goddess of gab as tribute. Someone brushed against her arm and a tall, broad-shouldered, thin man started gently jostling his way toward the front of the crowd. He was waving at Esther, trying to get her attention. If it had been the Hunger Games, and the guy had known what he was volunteering for, Ella would have let him do it. But as a tourist, there was no way he'd know what he was signing up for. She couldn't just let him roll in meat tenderizer and walk into the lion's cage.

She gave an inward sigh and moved to intercept him. "You don't want to do that," she said when she made it to his side.

He turned to look at her, confused. He had blue-green eyes and up close, Ella had to admit, he was pretty good-looking. If he'd been five inches shorter and five inches narrower in the chest, he would have been model quality. Instead, he looked like the human equivalent of butter scraped over a little too much bread.

"What?" he asked. His voice was a low rumble and Ella paused, caught off guard. She hadn't expected it to be that deep.

"Uh, Esther," Ella said, nodding toward the woman in question, who was now handing snow globes to the tourists in front of her. They were looking at the domes of glass and already shifting their weight uneasily from foot to foot while Esther started to tell them her life story. "You don't want to talk to her on a sale day if you can help it."

"I don't?" the man asked, narrowing his eyes.

Ella nodded. "She's a talker. So, unless you don't have any plans for the next week or so, it's better to ask her husband, Stanley, if you have questions. He's usually inside."

The guy turned away from her and started waving his hand, trying to get

Esther's attention again.

"Ok," Ella sighed. "Good talk. Enjoy. And FYI, bleeding from the ears isn't normal. So, when you're done here, Bumble's Market probably has something that will make it stop. Or, if she manages to suck out your will to live, the bay is that way." Ella thumbed over her shoulder, back toward the footpath.

The man's glare was icy and his tone was sarcastic as he said, "Yeah, well, thanks for your concern. I'll keep that in mind. Feel free to go 'help' someone else now." Ella had had it. If this jackass had a death wish to stand in front of Esther until his face melted off like the Nazis in *Raiders of the Lost Ark*, so be it. And screw him. Sarcastic El was giving her a standing ovation, but Helga just raised an eyebrow at her. Ella sighed. She wasn't really mad at this guy in particular. She was mad because she was back in Hope, with no definitive plan for how to leave again. And she was mad due to remembering that some of the many, many tourists who came to Hope were a-holes and that dealing with them would be a daily occurrence for her now. "And while you're at the market," she muttered, loud enough for the man to hear, unable to stop herself, "you might ask them for something to knock that stick out of your ass." Sarcastic El gave her a chef's kiss.

"Excuse me?" the man asked, turning again to look at her, disbelief, anger, and . . . something else on his face. Bemusement? No, it couldn't be. His nostrils were flared in anger. "Where do you get off telling me, a stranger, who I should and shouldn't talk to?"

Ella shook her head and turned her attention back to her suitcase. "Just trying to be helpful. Silly me. You're clearly suicidal, so don't let me stand in your way." She turned and started pushing her way out of the remaining row of tourists standing at the back of the crowd. She heard him mumble something behind her that didn't sound especially flattering, but at that moment, she didn't care. She'd attempted to do her good deed for the day. Hopefully, that was enough for the universe to give her at least an " 'atta girl".

She wheeled her suitcase around the last tourist and was within sight of the residential area. *Oh, thank god. Almost there!*

"Where are you going in such a hurry, young lady?" The raspy voice was one that Ella could pick out in any crowd. It belonged to Mandie Cane, or at least that was the name she went by. Everyone in town just called her Miss Mandie.

Knowing it would be much worse for her if she pretended she hadn't heard Miss Mandie, Ella took a deep breath and turned to wave at her. She was standing in front of the De-Floured Erotic Bakery, Hope's *only* bakery. Miss Mandie had been a porn star in a previous life and then used her earnings to put herself through culinary school before moving to Hope on a whim and opening an erotic bakery. It took both Hope and Mandie some time to adjust to each other, but now she grudgingly made loaves of plain bread and cinnamon rolls in exchange for being able to make every bachelor and bachelorette cake on the island. And the citizens of Hope had gotten used to seeing her famous "Double D-elicious" cupcakes with fondant nipples and nipple rings, sitting on the shelf next to their old-fashioned donuts and bear claws, which Miss Mandie had renamed, "cougar claws".

"Sorry, Miss Mandie," Ella said. "Just heading to Mom's house." Miss Mandie was the one person she didn't want to piss off during her stay in Hope, however long that might be. Her stomach lurched at the thought. Miss Mandie was the keeper of all things sweet and delicious and if Ella was going to make it, she was going to need sugar. Lots of it.

"Oh, that's right," Miss Mandie said, struggling to get a plastic light-up candy cane wedged into the ground on its plastic spike. "You're gonna take Clarence's job, aren't you?" Miss Mandie started swearing under her breath as she fought with the decoration.

Ella hesitated for a moment but remembering Miss Mandie's famous temper and the crowd it always drew, she quickly left her suitcase and went to assist with the candy cane . . . erection. With the two of them steadying and shoving, the candy cane was finally stable enough to stand on its own.

"Well, I'm interviewing for the job," Ella said, taking a step back to survey their work. The candy cane was still a little crooked.

"Oh, it's fine," Miss Mandie said, giving it a dismissive gesture. She met Ella's gaze with a grim smile and then let her eyes roam around the town square behind her. "This town."

Ella nodded. "Maybe it's because I've been gone so long, but I'd forgotten the kind of sale stampede Seaside Treasures could whip up."

Miss Mandie shook her head. "Yeah, Esther's got the tourists trained. Big sale on the last day of every month now. And she carries all the inventory for a bunch of the island artists around out here. Her monthly *Exclusive Sale* she's been calling it. It's like catnip for these day-trippers." Miss Mandie sighed as she and Ella took in the crowd. "I don't envy you. Having to try to cover and make sense of the coming holiday-themed shitstorm."

"I know," Ella groaned, turning to look at her. "But hey, maybe I'll get lucky and they won't hire me."

Mandie met Ella's gaze and chuckled. "Not likely, Cranberry Sauce."

The shock of a memory hit Ella at the mention of her old nickname and she felt her blood run cold in her veins. A cold sweat prickled at the back of her neck as the feeling of old and painful shame swooped through her stomach. Miss Maddie winked at her.

"You think I forgot? That Town Thanksgiving dinner lives on in infamy. Not a year goes by that someone doesn't tell that story."

"Oh," Ella said, her voice sounding faint and foreign in her ears, "that's so... nice." The story that went with the nickname was her single most embarrassing memory in Hope and one that had haunted her like a poltergeist from the time she was eleven until she graduated and moved away. It had been four years since she'd been called Cranberry Sauce, but less than an hour back on the Island and it had risen again to dog her steps. As much as she tried to press it down, she couldn't shake the vivid memory of tap dancing in that tin can cranberry sauce costume at the dinner.

The memory was burned into her brain with such awful detail that she could still smell the spray paint from the costume, mixed with her own panicked sweat. Of course, her karma had never been great, even as a kid. Her mom told her it was because she raised too much hell. Maybe she was right, but either way, her karma account had called the loan that Thanksgiving Day. While being forced to tap dance, dressed as a can of cranberry sauce, she'd tripped over Andy Belmont's brown "gravy" cape and fallen into Hope folk history. She'd crashed off the stage and onto the buffet table which promptly collapsed under the weight of the dinner, her eleven-year-old body, and the heavy costume. The chant of "Whoa there, Hoss! Hold up, Cranberry Sauce!" had been equal parts dumb and catchy. So, of course, it had become the thing legends were made of.

And it had been the mainline source of nightmares for Ella, that rose up every time she'd been singled out in class to go to the board or do any form of public speaking in front of any group larger than two people. It had actually been a big part of what had drawn her to journalism. She liked to be behind the story, behind the camera rather than in front. That was something she and Clarence had in common. A depressing thought hit her. What if she ended up like Clarence? Stuck in Hope for thirty or forty years until she became so fed up with the town and the newspaper that she just quit. Ella shivered. No, she had to make *sure* she didn't get sucked into staying any longer than she had to.

"What are you worried about?"

Miss Mandie's voice brought her back to the moment and she blinked at the older woman. "What?"

Miss Mandie turned away from Ella to plug the candy cane into the orange extension cord snaking out from the side of her building. "You're a shoo-in for Clarence's job, girl," she said around the cigarette pinched in her lips. "You grew up in this madhouse. You know what's coming. And you've personally participated in all of it. The best generals have spent time in the trenches."

Ella snorted. "General Patton say that?"

Miss Mandie straightened up and smoothed out her rhinestone-studded holiday sweater. "No, an old director of mine. She'd been a porn star in the 70s before climbing into the director's chair."

"Well," Ella said. "Thanks for the vote of confidence . . . I think."

Miss Maddie nodded. "You might want to get down the road to your Mom's house before Esther spots you."

"Crap," Ella muttered, glancing around her. "Thanks, Miss Mandie." From where she stood, Ella could see Esther, still on the front porch outside

Seaside, and as she watched, the old woman's laser beam eyes locked onto her like the eye of Sauron.

"Run," Miss Mandie muttered. "Just wave and take off."

Ella took her advice and was another block down before she heard someone calling her name. Ella picked up her speed.

"El! Slow the hell down! Where's the fire?"

She almost collapsed in relief. It wasn't Esther. "Pip! Sorry," Ella turned to see her old friend. "I thought you were Esther."

Fear flashed across Pippa's face as she quickly looked around. "Don't say her name. It's like Beetlejuice. You'll summon her." Pippa Donovan was two years younger than Ella, but they'd been close friends for most of their lives. She pushed her cloud of bright red hair out of her eyes and grinned.

"So? How does it feel?"

"How does what feel?" Ella asked.

"To be back," Pippa said. "Back in your old hometown! I mean, you haven't come back to Hope for what, four years?"

"Yeah," Ella said. "Just, uh, busy with school and work and all that."

Pippa crossed her arms. "Yeah, right, about that. You wanna share as to what prompted the sudden move home?"

Ella felt a stab of pain in her chest as her brain rewound through the day's events. But, Numb Ella came to her rescue, pushing the events out to arm's length. "Two bad interviews. Caught Les cheating on me with a friend and decided I didn't want to keep breathing the same air as him."

Pippa scowled and shook her head. "Les is a syphilitic dildo. I swear if some men didn't have penises, they'd have no personality at all. Too bad it's always the shit kind of personality in those cases."

"Preach it, sister," Ella muttered.

"But you just graduated, right?" She asked. "That's exciting. And now you're moving back here to interview for Clarence's job." She paused. "Right?"

Ella sighed. "Frankly, I'm surprised the town hasn't erected a billboard stating all of this. Maybe I should take the plunge myself. A nice banner would get the word out." Pippa raised an eyebrow, and Ella sighed. "Apparently, the rumor mill has been running at full force. Not that surprising, considering the fact that my mom almost hung up on me in her excitement to spread the word that I was coming back. I mean, I know my mom can move quickly, but it hasn't even been six hours and everyone except Mrs. Thompson seems to know why I'm back in town."

"Did she think you were pregnant?" Pippa asked.

Ella nodded. "How did you know?"

She rolled her eyes. "Because that's always Mrs. Thompson's first guess. I went to Bellingham to go Christmas shopping last year, and when I got back, on the same day, I might add, Mrs. Thompson stopped me and asked if *I* was pregnant."

Ella grinned. "Well, I suddenly feel a hell of a lot less special."

Pippa nodded. "You're welcome. But I didn't track you down just to confirm what I had already heard."

"No?" Ella asked. "What's up?"

"Myrna sent me to find you after Jack Sellers stopped by the newspaper office to tell us he saw you talking to Mr. Elton."

"Myrna sent you?" Ella asked. Myrna Ernhart was the owner of the *Hope Hornblower* and also the only adult Ella knew that insisted everyone, children on up, call her Myrna, not Ms. Ernhart.

Pippa nodded. "And she's freaking out. I probably don't need to tell you this, but Clarence quitting so suddenly did nothing good for anyone's blood pressure at the paper."

"I'll bet," Ella said. "What with it being almost prime tourism season for the holidays . . ."

Pippa squeezed her eyes shut. "Don't remind me." She opened them and focused her dark green eyes on Ella. "The point is, your mom called the paper to tell Myrna you were interested in interviewing and I half expected Myrna to erect a small altar to you and start burning incense until you got here."

"Really?" Ella asked.

The redhead looked at Ella like she'd just sprouted a duckbill. "Uh, yeah.

Who else knows the tinsel-tangled car crash that's about to hit the town and is *still* interested in covering it?"

Ella blew out a sigh. "Well, 'interested' is a strong word, and I am a glutton for self-flagellation."

"Oh good," Pippa said, "then you'll be right at home." She took the handle of Ella's suitcase and started wheeling it back toward the center of town.

"Pip, where are you going? My mom's house is this way," Ella said, pointing up the street.

Pippa shook her head. "Myrna says she wants to see you *now*."

"But it's almost six," Ella called after her, hustling to keep up with Pippa's power walking.

"Doesn't matter," Pippa said. "If you don't come now, I think Myrna will end up holding an all-night candle vigil until you show up and say you'll take the job."

Ella's one-hundredth heavy sigh of the day was drowned out by the sound of her suitcase wheels rattling over the uneven cobblestones. The buildings of downtown Hope were two-story, classical architecture brownstones for the most part. The *Hope Hornblower* was the only break in the tradition. It sat like a squat, gray, single-story bulldog on one side of the circular downtown ring of businesses that faced the gazebo.

As they approached it, Ella could hear more greetings from town members around her and her feelings of dread and suffocation seemed to be rising with every step.

"Oh," Pippa paused just before they got to the front doors and turned to look back at Ella. "Um, I guess I should warn you . . ."

"What?" Ella asked. "Warn me about what?"

"You aren't the *only* person interested in the job."

Ella wasn't sure why, but Pippa's statement didn't feel nearly as ominous as the wicked grin she gave her before turning back, tugging the front door open, and standing to the side, motioning for Ella to be the first to enter.

6

ELLA

Walking into the *Hornblower* felt like walking into a perfectly preserved memory. When Ella had worked at the *Hornblower*, she'd done filing, cut the clips for community scrap booking projects, made copies, and essentially whatever Miss Bee, Clarence's old secretary, had needed. Miss Bee had died the year after Ella had left for college and now with Clarence gone, Myrna was really the only relic of that era left. Ella hadn't made it more than three feet inside the front door when a squeal off to her right made her jump.

"El! It wasn't just a bullshit rumor!"

Ella turned in time to get knocked back by a very enthusiastic Maddie. Maddie Burke had been Ella's best friend through their formative years. She and Maddie had met in preschool and stuck like Velcro to each other until they'd graduated from high school. They'd picked up Pippa as their third musketeer in late elementary school, but Maddie had been Ella's first best friend.

"Maddie!? What the hell are you doing here? I thought you were in Boston for college?" Ella gasped through the tight bear hug Maddie had her in. Maddie squeezed even tighter and Ella thought she now understood how the mice on the nature shows felt when a boa constrictor got a hold of them.

"Same as you," Maddie said, finally loosening the hug. "Couldn't break the death grip the town had on me. I graduated in May and came back here when I heard the paper needed a photographer." Ella pulled back to give Maddie a "get real" look. Maddie blew out a sigh. "I never could bluff you out." Maddie shook her head. "I just . . . missed it here."

If Maddie had been anyone *besides* Maddie, Ella would have asked her if she had recently suffered any head trauma. But, Maddie had always been in love with the island. Like a love struck woman that only sees the good in her partner, and not the crazy; like the fact that said partner names their oranges before they eat them, or creates a patriarchy for their kingdom of potted plants. It was almost . . . endearing.

Maddie's expression turned to curiosity. "I do have to say, as much as I absolutely love that you're coming back, I was surprised when I heard." She paused and studied Ella's face. "Did something happen or . . . not happen?"

Ella heaved an inner sigh, preparing herself to retell the explanation she'd given Pippa, but was promptly cut off by the redhead.

"The jobs up there suck, and Les, her ex-boyfriend, and ex-roommate has been dipping his stick with a friend."

Maddie's happy expression turned dark faster than a derecho forming on the coast.

"Syphilitic dildo," she muttered. Pippa nodded in agreement.

Seeing her two old friends seething with the anger that she hadn't been able to muster, made Ella feel a little lighter. Yeah, it sucked to move home, but knowing that Maddie and Pippa were here with her, was the best thing to happen to Ella all day. Well, at the very least they were tied with the pleasant exchange she'd had with Tony on the ferry. Maddie still had Ella by the hand. She'd just dragged her over to the old photographer's desk beyond the reception area when Ella heard the sound of the front door jangling behind her.

"Oh, here we go," Maddie breathed, glancing behind Ella before dropping her gaze to study her fingernails. This was a classic Maddie-tell that Ella hadn't seen her use since high school when she'd had a crush on the high school quarterback and studied her fingernails every time he'd pass by them in the hall.

"Mads, you're doing the Finn Lonnigan crush thing," Ella said, frowning. "What's up?"

Pippa stifled a giggle behind a copy of the paper she'd quickly snatched off of Maddie's desk and peered over the top of it at whoever had just come in behind Ella. Confused, Ella turned to see what had them acting like they were back in school.

A man had come in through the front door. Ella felt the color drain from her face. Of course. The way her day was going, it was inevitable. Why wouldn't the man that was now standing in the reception area, be the man she'd tried to save from Esther? For the moment, he didn't seem to have noticed her and she had a chance to really look at him. He had his head down, the sleeves of his white dress shirt rolled to his elbows. He wore a leather messenger bag like Ella's and he held a pencil between his lips as he compared something on the screen of his phone in one hand to something on a notepad in his other. His dark brown hair was tousled from the wind and partially falling across his face. She quickly turned her back to him and snatched a layout mock-up off of Maddie's desk to hide behind. Maddie caught her eye, silently asking her what was up. Ella did her best to tell Maddie with her eyes to not draw any attention to her. Maddie seemed to understand, but unfortunately, Pippa missed the memo.

"Hi Cal, how was your first time covering a Seaside Sale?" Pippa asked. "Or, better known around here as an Esther-pocalypse?"

Ella peeked out from behind the layout mock-up enough to see the man, still looking from his notes to his phone. Finally, he slid his phone behind his notepad and took the pencil from his mouth to scratch something on the page. "Not my first, if you count the lobster nutcracker blowout sale, but this one was definitely more violent. I'm just glad I made it out alive. Between the tourists storming the shop like it was the beaches of Normandy, a really pushy blonde, and Esther Jacobs's long-winded storytelling giving me college lecture flashbacks, I'm thinking of asking Myrna for combat pay." The man glanced up, his gaze landing on Maddie. "I've got some pictures to send you . . ." His gaze shifted to Ella.

"Oh, Cal, this is Ella Danforth," Pippa said, pulling the mock-up out of Ella's hands and leaving her face to face with the man. For the briefest moment, they locked eyes.

The man looked surprised and then scowled. "We've met."

Without saying another word, he went back to his notes and breezed past them before disappearing around the corner that led to the hallway with the break room.

Ella felt heat rising at the back of her neck. So he hadn't been a tourist and he had actually needed to talk to Esther. So what? It was an honest mistake on her part. No need for Prince Humperdinck to get his panties in a twist over it. Still, Ella was shaken. She'd been back on the island for one hour and she'd already pissed off someone she was going to probably have to work with.

"You've already met?!" Pippa asked, turning to face Ella.

Ella sighed. "Yeah. I thought he was a tourist. He was trying to flag Esther down and I tried to talk him out of it."

Maddie shrugged. "Honest mistake. Anyone else would have been grateful for the heads up."

Ella gave Maddie a soft smile. "Oh, how I have missed you, Mads." Maddie grinned and tugged on one of the loose pieces of hair hanging around Ella's face.

"And that's why he's mad?" Pippa asked.

Ella shrugged. "Unless he's a magnet for pushy blondes, I'm guessing that was my starring role in his adventure." She paused and listened for the sound of his footsteps coming back down the hall behind them. It was quiet, so she asked, "Who is he, anyway?"

Maddie snorted.

"Cal Dickson," Pippa said, the evil grin spreading across her face again, "your competition."

Ella raised an eyebrow. "He actually *wants* the clown-hammer-induced headache that is the job of Editor-in-Chief at this sideshow?"

Maddie shrugged. "Apparently. He's new. He's been working as the main reporter for the paper for the last five months."

Ella shrugged. "Well, fine. Myrna should hire him and I'll take his old job as a reporter."

"Besides putting scratch and sniff stickers at the bottom of the city pool, that has to be about the worst idea ever spoken aloud." Ella turned to see Myrna coming out of the editor's office at the far end of the newsroom. She smiled when she saw Ella and there was a lot of relief in her smile.

A warning light began to go off inside of Ella's head. She had an idea of what the job would entail, but Myrna was looking at her the way a stranded sailor clinging to a piece of driftwood would look at an approaching Coast Guard ship. Nevertheless, she hugged Myrna when she approached. "Good to see you, Myrna."

The older woman shook her head. "I'd say the same to you, but it would be such a gross understatement that I'd just end up embarrassing myself."

Ella raised an eyebrow. "That bad, huh?"

Myrna's expression turned to weary annoyance. "You have no idea. Time for a chat?"

Ella nodded. "Since my mom already lit the bat signal, I assume you know why I'm here."

"Yes," Myrna said. "And I can't tell you how relieved I was when she called."

"That makes one of us," Ella muttered.

Myrna steered Ella into Clarence's office, which looked like it had been decorated in the paperwork equivalent of rock strata. There were piles of paper . . . everywhere. The bottom layers sitting on the floor, shelves, and desktop, had started to yellow with age. Ella half wondered if some of the paperwork she'd turned in to him five or six years earlier was somewhere in those piles. They'd been smaller during her time here, but even then, Clarence didn't like to file things. Miss Bee had even threatened to quit multiple times if he didn't let her file them. He'd eventually relent and give her a single stack of papers, but the rest he'd hoard. The meager amount that he would grudgingly let her file away wouldn't even put a dent in what was, even then, a three-shot combination of health, fire, and tripping hazard. Miss Bee had started closing Clarence's office door at night in case mice were burrowing through the papers.

"Nice to see Clarence kept up the tradition," Ella said, glancing around at the stacks.

"Yes, well, Clarence had his own . . . idiosyncrasies," Myrna muttered, carefully stepping around a precariously leaning stack of paperwork on the floor and moving a second stack so she could sit down in his brown leather desk chair. Ella looked around and realized that what she thought were just piles of old newspapers and paste-up layouts, were in fact, concealing a second chair. "Ella, before you commence excavation on that chair, do you mind shutting the door?"

She nodded and moved back across the office. As she started to close the door, she heard footsteps and Cal Dickson came into view. He was sipping from the dark blue ceramic mug with stars painted on it that had always been Ella's when she'd worked at the paper. He lowered it from his lips and glared at her. She returned his glare, with interest. The bastard was drinking out of *her* mug, after all. She closed the office door, probably harder than she absolutely needed to. The top pages on the nearest stack of papers fluttered. The whole stack shifted and for one heart-stopping moment, Ella held her breath hoping it wasn't about to topple over and cause a domino effect with the five stacks sitting next to it. The moment passed and she turned back to see Myrna's gaze locked on the same stack of papers.

"Well, that was close."

"Yeah, sorry about that," Ella said, glancing out the interior office window. She had a perfect view of Cal sitting down in profile behind a laptop on the otherwise empty desk right outside the office door. He'd started typing, but as she watched, he paused and raised the mug to his lips again.

"Cal," Myrna said, nodding when Ella turned back to look at her.

"What?" Ella asked.

"Cal Dickson. I'm sure Maddie and Pippa filled you in on him?"

Ella shrugged. "Just that for some odd reason he was actually interested in Clarence's job."

Myrna chuckled and nodded. Ella started moving piles of papers off the chair in front of Clarence's desk. When she finally sat down across from Myrna, she noticed the older woman had a large date planner open in front of her. Even upside down, Ella could read the December heading. She groaned when she saw the *Hope Hornblower* logo at the bottom of the page and the cramped black pen handwriting squeezed into every square, marking off the thirty-one days in the month.

"Is that . . ." Ella started, but trailed off, dreading the answer.

Myrna nodded. "Clarence's assignment book for December. Seems there are even more this year than usual." Ella groaned. Myrna lifted her head to study the young woman. Then she smiled softly before removing her glasses and wearily rubbing her eyes. "Ella, you were in my Brownie troop for three years, and then my scouts troop for another four. I never saw you back away from a challenge . . ."

"Well," Ella said. "There was the ropes course. And . . . arts and crafts when we were gluing feathers and rocks to those picture frames."

Myrna rolled her eyes. "You never backed away from a challenge when you thought it was something important enough to do."

Ella thought for a moment and finally shrugged. "I guess so."

Myrna sighed and looked around the office. "Well, my dear, this is going to be a challenge." She brought her gaze back to look at Ella. "And I know you may not see how important it is at the moment, but this isn't just some little throw-away newspaper. As you know, tourism is the money-maker in Hope." Ella nodded and Myrna continued, putting a boney finger on the datebook in front of her. "And this paper, its success in bringing *in* that tourism, can be the difference between success and failure for every shop and business in town." She paused. "Well, almost every shop and business. I don't think Frank's Taxidermy or Scelero Plumbing would fold, but if all their customers were forced to move because *their* businesses failed . . . well, you get the picture."

Ella nodded, a little stung that Myrna would think that she didn't know the paper was important to the town. "Myrna, I know."

Myrna gave her a quick nod. "Good. I thought so, but it's been four years since I've seen you and I wanted to make sure you remembered. Ok," her tone was lighter now. "The only thing left to do is the paperwork."

"Wait," Ella said. "That was the interview?"

Myrna smiled. "Do you want me to grill you about your extracurriculars, and ask you why you think you're the best person for the job, just to make you feel more at ease?"

Ella shrugged and glanced over her shoulder. "What about . . . uh . . ?" She looked back at Myrna and nodded toward the window.

"Cal," Myrna said, nodding.

"Right," Ella said. "Is he serious about being interested in Clarence's job too?"

Myrna sighed. "He is. But, Ella, I can't throw him in the pit when he doesn't even know what's down there."

"But you don't mind throwing me in?" she asked.

Myrna chuckled. "Cal's been in town for six months. He's been working here as a reporter for five."

And then, the last piece fell into place in Ella's mind. "Oh," she said. "He's never been through 'The Hellidays'. That's why you don't want him in the job."

Myrna nodded again. "Exactly. How could I ask an outsider to coordinate and cover the ridiculous quantity of events that this crazy town puts on every December? I couldn't. He'd crack. We'd find him in a bathtub full of gin with a straw and a wind-up toy boat."

Ella nodded. "Yeah. I could see that." And the vision wasn't entirely unpleasant if she was being one hundred percent honest.

"You, on the other hand," Myrna continued, meeting Ella's gaze, "have been training for this your whole life. I personally have seen you participate in just about every insane event this town could dream up."

"Usually under protest," Ella said.

"Still," Myrna added. "You've been through the war. You know where the tripwires are, where the stories are, the big crowd-pleasers, and I know that if Cal is overwhelmed, you'll jump on a grenade and cover the Santa Beard contest or the Baby Jesus Bazaar or the Parade of Trees."

Ella sighed. Myrna didn't want to hire her because of her skills or her education. She wanted to hire Ella because she was an Islander who'd lived through and survived everything this town had dished out for eighteen years. There was possibly also a contending factor, Ella noted, that Myrna knew how stubborn she was when it came to finishing something, probably hoping she wouldn't quit like Clarence. Ella's stubbornness was entirely the Helga part of her brain, while Ella's sustained survival of the town's insanity was due to a healthy dose of the Sarcastic El part of her brain. *That was why Ella was getting the job.*

"Do you think Cal will quit when he finds out you're giving the job to me?" Ella asked Myrna, resisting the urge to turn around and look at him again. Ella couldn't understand why, but she *wanted* to look at him. She wanted to savor the cold glare of annoyance on his face. Seeing that annoyance would make taking the job easier. After all, by doing this, she was saving the cranky jerk's sanity. He should be grateful. At the very least, he should give her back her mug. Ella forced herself to return her attention back to Myrna.

Myrna shrugged. "I don't think we have to worry about that. Cal moved here from New York. He's a very good writer. And he's dedicated. He works nights, and weekends, and picks up every story. Clarence used to split the stories that needed covering between himself and the one reporter we've always had on staff. But after Maggie got pregnant with her third back in April, and decided to quit, Clarence had to cover all the stories himself. Until Cal came along in June. December will be his sixth month here and he's covered just about every story since he came on board. I think the last piece Clarence wrote up was about the trophy fishing team he was a part of on Waldron and that was sometime in October."

Ella shrugged. "Well if Cal's that good, maybe he would be able to handle . . ."

Myrna was shaking her head before Ella could even finish. "No, you're not getting out of this, my dear. You know that summers on the island are cakewalks compared to the, how did you so eloquently put it, oh yeah, 'The Hellidays'. He's used to one main story, three to four column-length articles, padded with Maddie's photos, and two to three pages of ads and classifieds. He has never seen anything like the tomes that are the Hope Island Holiday Editions." Ella opened her mouth to protest, but Myrna held up a hand. She fixed Ella with one of her no-nonsense glares that made her feel like she was thirteen again and had just gotten caught being too rowdy in her tent at a scout camp out. "I'll make you a deal, Ella. I know coming back to Hope probably wasn't a part of your post-graduation grand plan, but if you'll stick it out through the holidays and keep the paper going, cover all the insanity, keep everyone afloat and the tourists coming, I will give you as many reference letters, phone calls, in-person character witness statements, and blood oaths as you want, to get you into your next job. But I'm desperate. Please."

Ella felt herself nodding. Seeing Myrna beg was freaking her out.

A look of relief washed over Myrna's face, followed by a wide smile. "Excellent. Thank you so much, Ella. And think of it this way, you can use this season to train Cal on the ropes so he can take over when you're ready to move on."

That thought lifted Ella's spirits. *When she was ready to move on.* Maybe as early as January. She could go anywhere, do anything. Maybe become a foreign correspondent stringer, or go back to Seattle with a little more experience under her belt. Granted, a few months wouldn't be a lot, time-wise, but if she took thirty-one editions of the *Hope Hornblower* with her and detailed everything it had taken to get them out . . .

Ok, that wasn't *as* happy of a thought. First things first, Helga was back in charge and breaking down the road ahead of Ella into manageable steps, as she always did. "You mentioned paperwork?" Ella asked. Myrna nodded and pulled a green folder out from under Clarence's assignment book. Getting a second look at the assignment book, almost entirely black with ink, made Ella's stomach start to churn.

"Oh, here," Myrna finally said, as if reading her mind. She picked up the assignment book and held it out to Ella with a grin. "Might as well start familiarizing yourself with it, Editor."

Ella tried to force a smile as she took the book from Myrna. She set it in her lap and stared down at it. Like the smell of peppermint TUMS and black coffee that seemed to ooze out of the office itself, the familiar scrawl on the page in front of her was so strong a reminder of Clarence that she almost expected to hear him cough and clear his throat beside her. She had so many memories of the man. Watching him on the phone with his feet on the desk, a steno pad balanced on his thigh as he wrote in that almost hieroglyphic short-hand style that was entirely his own. Luckily, in the assignment book, he'd at least used letters that were members of the English alphabet.

"Myrna," Ella asked as she rubbed her thumb over the divots in the paper from the force of Clarence's pen.

"Mmm-hmm," Myrna said, shuffling papers in the folder in front of her.

Ella looked up at her. "What happened to Clarence?"

Myrna paused and met Ella's gaze. There was worry, but mostly sadness in her expression. "He just . . . got overwhelmed."

"Overwhelmed?" Ella asked, frowning. It could be chaotic, Ella knew, but the *Hornblower* wasn't *The New York Times*.

"Tired, I think," Myrna said. She shrugged. "He'd been working here ever since he moved to Hope, back in 1980." She smiled sadly and shook her head. "He was the first person I hired after I bought the paper."

Ella looked back down at the assignment book in her lap. "One too many Helliday seasons, you think?"

"I mean, I'm not even hands-on and the stress of the season on the paper still feels like it sucks away a year of my life every time it comes around," Myrna said.

Ella nodded. "Fair enough." She thought about everything that had happened in her year, culminating in the events of the day. She pushed away another sharp pain in her chest. "I wouldn't mind having this year sucked away."

7

ELLA

The paperwork was pretty standard and reminiscent of the same application Ella had filled out to work at the paper when she was in high school.

"What? No 'forfeiture of soul' clause?" Ella asked when she'd signed the last page.

Myrna grinned. "You're about to take on the Hellidays in Hope. Do you feel like you need that part in writing?"

Ella sighed. "Probably not."

"Well, shall we make it official?" Myrna asked.

"Is there a goat sacrifice involved? Because I'm really not wearing the right shoes for that," Ella said, following Myrna out the office door.

The older woman glanced back at Ella over the top of her half-frame glasses. "What you, Maddie, and Pippa do after I leave is entirely up to you."

Ella shrugged. "Well, in that case, we'll probably just go out for beers."

Myna grinned. "I think I might join you if that's the plan. Monday nights are 'saber-tooths drink for free' at Fast Eddy's."

Ella squeezed her eyes shut. "Myrna, I love you, but please don't ever call yourself a saber-tooth again."

"Why?" Myrna asked. "It just means a woman in her sixties."

Ella shook her head, keeping her gaze on the floor.

"Doesn't it?" Myrna asked as Ella passed her and moved into the newsroom.

Pippa and Maddie were playing with the photo layout for paste-up and the only other person in the office was Cal.

"Everyone," Myrna called to the mostly empty room. "Well, everyone that's here, anyway. We'll have to catch the others up on the big news tomorrow, but for the rest of you, Ella Danforth is going to join us as the Editor in Chief for the *Hope Hornblower*! I know that most of you already know Ella and you know that with her experience, she'll do a fantastic job of steering the paper through the end of the year and into the next one."

It was a speech that didn't evoke a lot of enthusiasm beyond Pippa's initial squeal of joy at the announcement and Maddie's fevered clapping. Cal had gotten to his feet and was leaning against the edge of one of the vacant desks nearby, but still separate from the rest of them.

"We should celebrate tonight!" Pippa shouted.

"Yes! Jared, the bartender over at The Alphorn created this drink called Christmas Kryptonite. It's like a Long Island Iced Tea from the North Pole with a shit ton of peppermint schnapps in it," Maddie added.

Ella cut her eyes to Myrna. "I don't know, I heard good things about happy hour at Fast Eddy's."

At the sounds of interest from Pippa and Maddie, Myrna moved past Ella to tell them all about it. Ella's eyes fell on Cal. He was smirking at her, arms crossed and one eyebrow raised. He was *still* holding her mug, almost as if he was taunting her with it. No matter how much Helga tried to reassure her that there was no way that Cal knew that the mug had been hers long before he'd stepped foot in Hope, Ella didn't care. Today was not the day for Cal Dickson. Her bullshit meter had hit critical mass before she had even climbed off the ferry. She opened her mouth to share this fact with Cal. She hadn't completely worked out what she was going to say, but she had a feeling "give me back my mug before I bash in that smug grin with it" would be somewhere in the mix.

Cal's expression had shifted when she opened her mouth. The smirk had faded to annoyance and before she could say anything, he turned away from her and headed back to his desk. After a moment, she heard the sound of him typing again. Fine. If he wanted to sulk, he could. She'd get through December and then try to explain her master plan of turning the paper over to him so she could get back to building a life, off the island. Well, provided he survived the month. And gave her back her mug.

Ella turned back to face the four empty desks in the front part of the office. One was Pippa's, but the other three also looked like people normally sat at them. "Who's missing today?" Ella asked.

The other three women stopped talking and turned to follow Ella's gaze.

"Well, one is Marty Archer," Myrna said, pointing to the desk in the corner. "He handles advertising, classifieds, etc."

"Oh, he's doing Sid's job now?" Ella asked. She'd forgotten about Marty. He'd been the head carrier when Ella had been in high school.

Myrna nodded. "Almost two years now. Ever since Sid's double bypass."

"And Katie . . . Katie Summers sits next to me," Pippa added, nodding at the tidy desk next to hers. "She handles circulation."

"The other desk is Kurt Milligan's, but he hardly ever sits there," Maddie said.

"Kurt is the press operator and print and layout manager now," Myrna added. Ella turned to look at her. "Don't worry, he was trained by Vickie. He knows what he's doing." Ella nodded and tried to breathe. Up until that moment, the job of editor had felt more academic and hypothetical, but now . . .

"So, you start first thing tomorrow," Myrna said with a sly smile. "Enjoy your last few hours of freedom tonight."

"Hell yeah," Pippa said. Then, she paused and glanced at Myrna, her face going pale. Myrna just rolled her eyes and chuckled. Pippa grinned and looked at Ella. "You're gonna enjoy them with shot, shot, shots!"

The queasy feeling in Ella's stomach had slowly been increasing ever since she'd sat down in Clarence's office. She looked down at the assignment book she was still holding, her finger marking the page for December. Could she do this? Could she pull this off? Would she have any sanity left to speak of when it was over?

"Not tonight," Ella heard herself say. "Rain check?"

The disappointment on Pippa's face was almost comical. "But, why?"

"I need to . . . get some things taken care of," Ella said. "And I'm bushed. I just want to get to my mom's and sleep for about twelve hours. Don't let me slow the three of you down, though."

"Are you sure?" Maddie asked. Ella nodded.

"Well, I'm going to Fast Eddy's for a margarita. Any takers?" Myrna asked.

"I'm in," Maddie said.

"Me too," Pippa added. She hugged Ella. "See you in the morning," she grinned, "Boss?"

Ella rolled her eyes. "Yeah, and neither of you better be late or hungover." Maddie snapped Ella a salute and Ella sighed, moving to retrieve her suitcase.

"Come on," Pippa said. "We'll at least walk you to the gazebo. You know, so you don't get lost."

Ella rolled her eyes. "You're too kind."

While the other three women gathered up their belongings, turned off desk lamps, and put computers into sleep mode, Ella found her attention wandering back to Cal. He was facing her and from where she stood, she could see his eyes over the top of his laptop screen at an angle around the partition wall separating him from the front newsroom area. He was typing away, but as if he could feel Ella burning a hole in his forehead with her gaze, he paused and glanced up at her. When his eyes narrowed, Ella felt her "you have a problem with me, sing out, Louise" face sliding into place.

Ella wasn't big on intimidation or mind games. She usually preferred to just have it out with a person when they had beef with her. But, having a throw-down with the only other reporter on the paper before her first day even began was probably not a great way to go. She was going to have to figure out how to "kill him with kindness" as her mom would always say. Though that had never worked for her and she always imagined a big cartoon hammer with "Kindness" printed on the side whenever her mom had said it. In this case, the hammer sounded like a more plausible option for dealing with Cal Dickson. She hadn't known him long, but she already had a feeling that her first impression of him was right. And besides, Ella had more than enough doubt in her ability to pull this off without Cal Dickson giving her the stink-eye every second of the waking hours.

The sound of a phone ringing in Cal's general direction made her glance back at him before she could stop herself. He was ignoring her again, but his face broke into a smile that was genuine when he answered his phone. She felt her stomach flutter at the sight. Out of pure surprise, of course. Not any other reason, like the way he smiled with his whole face and how bright it made his eyes. No, she was just shocked. She thought she might be watching an honest-to-god Jekyll and Hyde moment.

"Billy-boy! I didn't expect to hear from you until Wednesday. What's going on?" Cal asked. He paused, smiling while he listened, and she saw his gaze turning in her direction again. She quickly turned her back to him, working to get her shoulder bag open.

"Oh, sure," Cal said to whoever was on the phone. "I can be there in about an hour? Will that work?" Pause. "Great. See you then."

Now, where did *that* Cal live when he wasn't on the phone?

She slipped Clarence's assignment book into her shoulder bag and tried to tell herself she was being dramatic when she swore it added twenty pounds to the load she was carrying. Dramatic or not, she knew that to get them through December, she didn't just need a business plan; she needed a pincer attack, a war plan, and a supply line. And there was going to be zero room for attitude-adjustment-marginal-error. *Enjoy your last cranky hours, Cal,* Ella thought. *Tomorrow, we go to war and you're not going to have the time or energy to carry around the chip on your shoulder.*

Tomorrow. Ella gripped the strap of her shoulder bag and leaned on the locked handle of her suitcase, hoping the wheels wouldn't make it go out from under her. Tomorrow was December 1st. Tomorrow was the beginning of Hope's Hellidays.

"Ready?" Pippa asked, wrapping her scarf around her neck and buttoning up her coat. Ella dragged her thoughts away from what was coming and nodded at her.

"Goodnight, Cal," Pippa called.

"Night," he called back. Ella felt a prickle on the skin at the back of her neck. Cal's voice was deep and smooth and it was . . . annoying. Quickly, she looked down at her suitcase, pretending to check the handle while she shook off the weird shiver it had sent through her. She had a feeling it was going to be a long month.

Myrna and Maddie called goodnight to him and he raised a hand to signal acknowledgment without taking his eyes off his computer screen. Ella followed the other three women out the front door and into the bustling Town Square. There was a group of high school boys helping Coach Hendricks hang the nutcracker and candy cane tinsel and light decorations from the old-style street lamps. Nearby, Ella spotted a bundled-up Mrs. Thompson standing to one side, watching them, mistletoe still clutched in her hand. Ella shook her head.

"What?" Pippa asked.

"Oh, this town," Ella said.

"No town like it," Maddie added.

"Let's hope not," Myrna said.

Ella's bag rattled across the cobblestones as they strolled toward the gazebo. Maddie and Pippa had started a conversation about Christmas plans and Myrna dropped back to talk to Ella.

"Don't worry too much about Cal," Myrna said. "I'm sure he'll get over it as soon as he sees what's coming."

Ella shrugged. "There were guys like him in my journalism classes. Moody, taciturn, and entitled."

Myrna laughed. "Oh, I wouldn't file him away with that type just yet."

"Who, Cal?" Maddie asked, turning around. Ella nodded. Maddie shook her head. "He's actually a pretty nice guy once you get to know him."

"Something to look forward to," Ella said. She didn't really want to talk about Cal. Her head was too full as it was. And she highly doubted that he was going to turn on a dime and be "nice" to the person who just waltzed in and took the job he'd been hoping to get, even though he wouldn't *want* it if he fully grasped what it meant. Ella was tired. Really tired.

"So how long are you going to stay at your mom's?" Pippa asked, interrupting Ella's thoughts.

Ella shrugged. "Well, probably for the month. If . . . if I'm still here after that, I guess I'll have to find a place of my own." That thought weighed Ella down by another ten pounds. Getting a place of her own felt like giving up and throwing in the towel. But, she didn't exactly relish the idea of staying with her mom any longer than she had to. She loved her mom, but she had a sneaking suspicion that it would only underline the "regression" Ella was already feeling in spades.

"Apartments are at a premium around here," Maddie grumbled.

Pippa nodded in agreement. "I think I heard Miss Mandie talking about the apartment over the bakery."

Ella raised her eyebrows. "It's for rent?"

Pippa frowned, trying to remember. "Maybe? Sorry. Jamie Baskin was in line in front of me and he smelled and looked like an Adonis dipped in spruce-infused flannel. I was kind of distracted."

"Understandable," Ella said.

"Mmmhmmm," Myrna and Maddie added.

Jamie Baskin had graduated with Maddie and Ella. He was not the sharpest tool in the shed, but he had a pretty face and a body that gave brain fog to everything with a pulse when he was around. He'd gone into business with his dad, and their construction company was responsible for most of the renovations and all of the new construction in Hope. Mostly because no other company wanted to make the trek out to the island.

"Well, that's almost a lead on an apartment," Ella said, more to herself than the other three. Even a month at her mom's might be too much. "I'll ask Miss Mandie about it tomorrow."

"I don't know what your hurry is," Maddie said. "With your mom's cooking and it being the holidays, their house is going to be a heck of a lot more fun than you moving into a sparsely furnished apartment over the bakery for Christmas."

Ella just smiled. If she was Maddie, she'd completely agree. But, she wasn't. She didn't have the same fondness for the island that Maddie did.

She wasn't sure why. Sometimes it pissed her off. She kind of felt like a defective unit, because she hadn't been happy to just live here her whole life. She was a little jealous of how content Maddie was. It made Ella feel like something was broken inside of her. Like every other baby on the island had been given a set of gills when they were born, but she'd been given a pair of wings. She supposed a part of her still loved the town. A small part. But a bigger part of her had spent too many years watching the sausage being made in Hope. The stress, fights, old grudges and feuds... and wounds. Ella was definitely skipped when the powers that be were handing out the rose-colored glasses for the island. Cal Dickson should thank his lucky stars for dodging that bullet. What was his story anyway? Who moves *to* the island? Everyone she knew had either been born and raised here or married in. Was he married? Who would he be married to? There were a finite number of singles in Hope. Man, she had been gone for a long time. What else had changed? There was a small pang in her chest. What else had she missed?

The street to her mom's house was ahead and she hugged the other three women again before saying her goodnights and goodbyes and turning to head toward the yellow house with the wrap-around porch. In the past four years, Ella's mom and Bill, her stepdad, had always come to the city to see her for the holidays. Being an only child, and a college student, had been a good enough excuse for them to travel to see her, so Ella had successfully resisted the island's pull for four Christmases. Now, however, she was being smacked in the face by memories with each step she took. She knew every person that lived in the houses lining both sides of Shell Street.

Luckily, because it was cold and the sun had set hours ago, most residents weren't out on their porch to strong arm her into playing an involuntary game of twenty questions. Unfortunately, that fact did nothing to stop the internal monologue and stuttering camera reel inside Ella's head as she remembered every happy, painful, and mundane memory that had happened here.

As she slowly dragged her suitcase off the road and onto the sidewalk, leaving the cobblestone pedestrians-only area, a single phrase kept repeating inside her head. *Coming home is a double-edged sword.*

8

CAL

Ella Danforth had not been what Cal expected. From the moment Myrna ended the phone call with what must have been Mrs. Danforth, and subsequently started praising Ella's name as if she was about to get her own Marvel movie, he'd been skeptical. From the way everyone was going on about her, he expected Ella to be a sophisticated Seattle woman, well-seasoned in her field with years of experience. What he hadn't expected was the Ella Danforth that had walked into the office. She had blonde, almost white hair and dark gray eyes. And she was young. Cal scowled at the cursor on his computer screen where it rested halfway through an incomplete sentence that he'd been staring at since the four women had left.

He'd been having such a good day before he had heard her name. No new voicemails on his phone from the east coast, alternating between demanding and coaxing him to come back. He'd made it downstairs to the bakery before Miss Mandie had sold out of cinnamon rolls. Then, Mrs. Ganz and Charlotte Hughes had stopped him in the street to tell him how much they liked the article he'd written about their quilting circle. That had meant a lot to him. More than he'd tried to let on. He'd worked pretty hard to slip in a couple of puns here and there in the article, just for Mrs. Ganz.

And on top of that, Christmas was in the air. Honest-to-god, eat-your-heart-out-Hallmark, Christmas. In New York, Christmas was claustrophobic. The air was heavy with expectations, guilt, and for his family, an odd sense of minimalism. No gaudy sweaters or sloppily decorated trees. Nope. His parents had a strange impressionist art sculpture made from black blown glass that was supposed to represent a tree. For the holiday, it was brought out of storage, dusted, and placed in an alcove. That was the extent of the Dickson's holiday cheer.

Cal leaned back in his chair and his gaze fell on the water cooler that Maddie and Pippa had draped in cheesy silver tinsel. On top was a motion-activated Santa in sunglasses, holding a guitar. It had lasted all of five minutes before Myrna had taken out its batteries. He could feel the familiar, and now daily smile on his face. God, he loved this town. Hope Island was the thing legends about small towns were made of. It was an island version of Mayberry. But better, because it was real. How could anyone not love Hope?

There was a prickle of heat at the back of his neck, thinking of Ella Danforth again. He scowled and tossed his pencil back onto his desk. The look of grim determination on her face when she'd talked about the upcoming events pissed Cal off. If she didn't want to be the editor and she didn't want to be in Hope for the festivities, why the hell had she come back? He understood Myrna was knee-jerk reacting to Clarence quitting, but they would have been fine.

Cal turned in his chair to look at Clarence's empty office ... which was now, he guessed Ella's office. The thought made his chest ache. He was going to miss Clarence, but the thing that hurt the most was that Clarence hadn't talked to him about being burned out or unhappy or whatever drove him to quit. Sure, they'd only worked together for the last five months, but during that time, Cal had spent more hours with Clarence than anyone else on the island. They'd been in the same building from sun-up every day to after dusk every night since Cal had taken the job. Why hadn't Clarence felt like he could talk to him? They'd had discussions about philosophy and life on the island and the future of the paper, but, Cal had to admit, Clarence wasn't exactly a chatterbox. Usually, it was just a monosyllable, a short discussion about an assignment, a funny anecdote from his early years at the paper, or something to do with someone in town that Cal was about to go interview. Still, they had a rapport. They'd had a connection. Or at least, Cal had thought they did.

He stood and took his star mug over to the water cooler. While it filled, he looked around the room. The twinge of pain in his chest over Clarence doubled. It was probably naive of him to think it, but Cal had considered Clarence a friend. He'd spent more time with him than any friend he had in New York. And Clarence had made a point of taking Cal around with him when he started and introducing him to the main figures in town. After a while, they started seeking Cal out instead of just going to Clarence when they wanted something covered. And finally, Cal had felt like he was becoming part of this zany town. Seeing how they treated Clarence had given Cal hope. Clarence wasn't a born-and-bred Islander either, but the rest of the town treated him like he was one of their own.

Cal took a drink and the annoying voice in the back of his mind cleared its throat. Killjoy Cal, as he liked to call the jerk. *Remember*, the condescending voice said, *this is temporary. You are going to have to go back eventually and face the music.*

"At least let me get through the end of the year," Cal muttered aloud to the empty office. Even three thousand miles away from his life in New York, he could feel the proverbial Brooks Brothers tie tightening around his neck like a noose. Never more than at that moment did he wish that human cloning was a reality. If it was, he could clone himself, send the clone back to New York and stay in Hope.

But you'll never really be an Islander, Killjoy Cal piped up. *I mean, look, they hired someone who is younger than you and who hasn't been on the island in a while to run the paper. You'll have to be here for years before they start treating you like Clarence.*

Cal's gaze landed on the editor's office as he walked back to his desk, feeling his emotions go full-circle back to annoyance, bordering on anger.

Ella Danforth couldn't be more than early twenties. Maybe twenty-thee at most. Guessing ages had been a game that he and Tara had always played at company dinners and fundraisers in the city. He'd gotten pretty good at it under her tutelage. "It's the eyes," Tara would say. "You can always tell how old someone is by the skin around their eyes. At least within a margin of error of six months, an alcohol bender, a face lift, a string of all-nighters, and a screaming toddler." They would check their work with Google. Everyone at those stupid functions had a public face to maintain, otherwise, they wouldn't have been there, so it was easy to find out their actual ages. More often than not, Cal was on the money.

Tara. He mentally pushed away the cauldron of acid reflux and guilt that was his feelings for her and turned his focus back to the current mental Lego in his heel.

If Ella was twenty-three, that made her at least three years younger than he was. Granted, even though he was older, Cal didn't have years of experience as an editor to improve his position in applying for Clarence's job, but hell, she couldn't either at her age. He did, however, have years of experience around the family newspaper business in New York and a journalism degree. But, she was from here. And apparently, that made her more qualified.

His phone beeped, reminding him of the four calls he'd sent to voicemail since lunch. When it rained, it poured. As if the universe had been waiting to pile on, as soon as he'd heard Ella Danforth's name, the phone calls had started up for the day. He pushed away from his desk and leaned his head back, closing his eyes. He knew he wouldn't be able to avoid them forever. Hope had been his escape. A needed one. For his sanity and if he was being honest, his soul.

New York had been suffocating him. The expectations, and engagements ...the word made his arm feel even heavier as he reached for his phone and swiped his thumb across the screen. As he'd expected, all four voicemails were from Tara. Tara Rhineholt was the heir to a magazine empire and unfortunately the victim of a two-family merger that had now been stalled for half a year. Without much enthusiasm, he brought up the latest of her voicemails and hit play before putting his phone to his ear.

"Hi Callum, it's me." He could feel himself cringing. Only Tara and his parents called him by his full name. It had been his grandfather's. And his grandfather had been one of the "hostile takeover" assholes on Wall Street whose actions had led to a lot of suicides. Just another thing he hated about his name, besides the fact that it sounded a lot like "callous".

Tara's voice droned on as the message played. "To be honest, I don't think I've ever called a guy as much as I've called you. I know you said you were going out to clear your head and get some 'perspective' or whatever, but it's almost Christmas. I've just been telling everyone that you're on some wilderness backpacking trip. Those are very 'in' right now. Anyway, I've been answering R.S.V.P.s for the two of us to the stuff we usually go to. And a couple charities your mom wants us to attend. So, when are you coming home?" There was a pause and then she gave a frustrated sigh and said, "Miss you!" The "miss you" had been perfunctory. It was as far as either of them had been able to go since both their families had shuffled them together. "Miss you" had saved them both the embarrassment of not being able to muster saying anything more. There was a lot in Cal's life that he'd faked over the years, but he'd never been able to fake love. The thought of even trying was exhausting. Tara's tone sounded exactly like it always had. He could almost hear her answering emails or painting her nails and doing her make-up while recording the message. Tara wasn't a bad person. In fact, by a long shot, she was a better daughter to the Rhineholts than he was as a son to his parents. She accepted the course her life was taking. And that, Cal knew, was the fork in the road for them. Still, she was a good person and beautifully elegant with her long, silky, black hair and dark brown eyes. He even liked the way her nose scrunched up when she was annoyed about something. Well, usually.

That had also been the face she'd made six months ago when he'd unloaded everything on her. He'd told her how much he hated the corporate life his family was shoehorning him into and how he wanted to leave the city. Then she'd looked at him with pity. Like he was a kid having a tantrum, or an old guy, yelling at a cloud for blocking the sun. Then she'd patted his hand and told him to get some sleep.

Instead, he'd gone back to his apartment and started surfing the internet.

He'd started drinking and searching "getting away from it all", "getting out of New York", "I hate my life", and finally, "need hope, feel like an island". And that's when Hope Island had popped up. The Swiss-flavored "muzak" that played on the website's homepage had broken through Cal's tipsy stupor. Before he knew it, he was staring at the tiny island, at its shops, the smiling people, the sheer distance from New York, and then he was packing a bag. He still felt like it had been a sign from the universe.

But he knew in his gut that he couldn't keep this "other life" up forever. Eventually, he'd be forced to return to his life in New York and all the bull that went along with it. Death, taxes, and his father, Richard Callum Dickson were three guarantees he couldn't outrun. Still, if he could just get to stay through the holidays and miss all the pressure of engagements and wedding planning and, god forbid, talk of kids, that happened during Christmas, he might be able to face the whole thing in the new year. He didn't really believe it, but any excuse for an extension of his time in Hope, he was willing to cling to. He'd gone so far as to tell his landlady, Miss Mandie, that he might be moving out when January arrived.

Of course, that was before Clarence had phoned in his sudden retirement on Sunday. That had been unexpected, but at the same time, Cal had to admit, there was a little hint of relief when he reasoned with himself that there was no way he could leave the Hornblower suddenly now, not when Clarence already had. There would be no one left to run it. Cal had wondered if like that Google search, this could possibly be the universe, again, telling him to be in Hope.

He knew it was a pipe dream, but Cal had come to love this strange island town and he could see himself happily living out the rest of his life at the *Hope Hornblower*, covering and being kneaded into the lives of the Islanders. Now, if only Tara and his family in New York could be suddenly hit with a spell of amnesia and forget he even existed. Then he could make that pipe dream come true; living out his life and dying happy, even if at the end he was still living over an erotic bakery.

When Cal had first come to Hope, he'd been apprehensive, not sure what people's angles were when they offered to help him get established, lended him a hand, or lended a hand to each other. They gave money, their lunch breaks, inconvenienced themselves, and on two occasions, he literally saw them give the shirt off their backs. On one of the two occasions, he had been the recipient of the shirt. It had happened after a mishap at the summer carnival when Mrs. Adams had tripped over one of the Winslow triplet's pogo sticks and thrown the bowl of fruit punch she was carrying into the air. Cal had turned just in time to see the incident and to have half a gallon of fruit punch hit him in the chest, five minutes before he had to present an award in Clarence's stead. The award was for the island's Girl Scout Troop. They'd raised enough money to build a new park shelter and become the *Hornblower's* Citizens of the Year and Cal had a very real fear that he would be immortalized in the photo with the troop, looking like a half-drowned cat. But, before he'd had to face that fate, Dale Edwards had yanked his own button-down off and traded Cal for his fruit punch-soaked shirt without saying a word. When it was over, Cal hadn't been able to find Dale to return his shirt, but the next day when he came to work, his shirt was clean and folded and sitting on his desk. He was so touched that when he'd taken Dale's clean shirt back to him, he hadn't known what to say. Dale had just smiled at the ground and shrugged, telling him it wasn't a big deal. But it had been a big deal to Cal. Something like that wouldn't have happened in New York. And it was just one of the experiences that had made Cal fall in love with the island. On any given day in Hope, you couldn't throw a rock without having five or six people retrieve it and bring it back to you before inviting you over for a barbecue, or out for a beer, or to one of the town's events. These were the real people he'd read about in nation-wide news from the time he was young. And now, finally, he was living amongst them. He just hoped that none of them were ever able to sniff out that he came from a long line of plastic people living fake lives. Everyone out here dressed, walked, and talked like they actually lived.

They had their own opinions and views and they would let you know how they felt about something, no holds barred, but more than that, they were kind. Cal had watched them for months now, trying to dissect their motivations and he'd come to the same conclusion time and time again.

Hope Islanders just wanted to live. And they wanted their neighbors to live. They never seemed to be worried about getting one over on each other or making more money than someone else. They just lived. Real people with real lives. And Cal's heart ached. That was all he ever wanted and now he was here, observing it like a naturalist in a species' natural habitat. And he didn't want to leave. His deepest desire was to join them. Why would anyone ever want to leave a place like Hope?

Behind his closed eyelids, the vision of Ella Danforth's gray eyes, defiant and challenging as she stared him down, slid into focus. Her nostrils had been flared. Which had looked ridiculous on her small button nose. Her hair had been messy. Not like she was careless with it, more like it had been a long day and she hadn't looked in a mirror since she'd left the house. And now, he worked for her.

The annoyance he'd felt when she had tried to stare him down, started to build up in his chest again. The room was warm and Cal tugged at the top closed button on his shirt until it came open. It wasn't like he'd been quiet about his interest in being Editor. He'd immediately told Myrna he wanted to interview for the job. She'd nodded, but fixed him with a look he couldn't quite put his finger on. Pity? Fear? What was Cal missing? He'd worked side-by-side with Clarence for almost half a year. How was some girl from Seattle, who hadn't been here in at least the last six months, more qualified than he was to take over the paper?

The longer Cal thought about it, the angrier he got. In the six months he'd lived in Hope, he'd never seen something so blatant and, well, unfair as what had happened at the paper today. This was the kind of backdoor-deal crap that happened in New York and one of the bonuses of leaving it.

When something like this happened in New York, the excuses were always the same, "Well, you don't know so and so, and the guy who got the job plays golf with him", or "you're just not in the same circle that the other candidate was. If you'd just make more of an effort and play golf or go to the club with so and so . . ."

But Cal refused to do it. It wasn't real. It was plastic. Plastic smiles, forming plastic words that looked one way on face-value but were cheap when you examined them closely. This reluctance of his, from an early age, had made him an outsider. An outsider there, even though it was his hometown. And now he was an outsider here, good enough to write for the paper, but not run it. The heat and anger and annoyance were now forming a hard ball in his chest. Would he ever not be an outsider? He'd probably been naive. He thought working on the paper would be a fast-track way to become a part of the community. The more stories he covered, the more people he got to know, the more . . . He blew out a sigh. He was probably kidding himself. He was a kid, hoping that by wishing, he could make summer vacation longer and delay school starting in the fall.

He smiled grimly at the peeling paint around the air vent on one wall. It had once been white but started to yellow decades before he'd arrived, probably back when it was still common for reporters to smoke indoors while they pounded on the keys of their typewriters. He could almost hear Tara's commentary on the office and his father's disgust to see the conditions he was working in. He snorted, thinking about what they'd say if they could see the little studio apartment he lived in. But Cal liked his apartment. And he liked the *Hornblower* office, exactly like it was. He chuckled, remembering the knock-down-drag-out battle he'd had with Clarence about getting high-speed internet for the office. After a month of nagging, Clarence had finally given in and after that, he'd started trusting Cal's judgment. Not just on things around the office, but also the angle Cal wanted to follow on the stories they were covering. Cal closed his eyes again. What a difference a day made. Twenty-four hours ago, he had a different boss. One that loved the island the way he'd come to love it. What would the paper look like now with an editor that seemed to hate it?

He sighed and leaned forward to study his computer screen. Hyper-focusing on Ella Danforth wasn't going to help. He needed to finish his story on the high school rowing team. Clarence had planned on running it in the Wednesday edition, so he was two days ahead of schedule. Still, it was better than going home to his apartment and spending the evening hoping Tara wouldn't call him again. At least at the office, when she called he could internally argue that he was working and he didn't have time for personal calls. He picked up his notepad and turned the page to the correct spelling for the high schoolers' names. He wondered if this would be the last non-holiday themed article he'd write for a while with what Ella had called the "Hellidays" starting.

If the holidays in Hope were anything like the hype, he wondered how long the obvious stubbornness of Ella Danforth would last. Of course, that did present Cal with a conundrum. Did he assume that she'd keep the job and follow through with his plan to head back to New York in the new year? A heavy sense of dread settled over him. Or, did he trust that the universe wanted him to wait for her to crack, quit, and then be there to take the job? That thought was much more appealing. The Clash song started playing through his head. Do I stay or do I go? Just the thought of New York had his stomach churning. If I go there could be trouble. He glanced over at Clarence's cluttered office. If I stay there could be double. For some reason, the thought of "double trouble" involving Ella Danforth as editor was strangely satisfying. He'd see how the next couple of weeks went. Then, he'd decide.

His phone beeped again, reminding him of the other unretrieved voicemails. He picked it up and erased Tara's other messages, knowing they would just be reiterations of her latest one. His phone beeped again and he groaned, glancing down at the screen. But, instead of another digital harassment from Tara, it was a text message from Bill, thanking him for being willing to come over and lend a hand. He checked the time. He had ten minutes. Then he needed to head over. He started typing. He made it another few lines before he glanced over at Clarence's empty office again. Ella. He wondered if it was short for Eleanor.

9

ELLA

The walk to the house that Ella had grown up in felt like it was at the end of a Kubrick hallway that just kept getting longer. Her feet were aching, and the day had been so long, that it was hard to believe that it had actually been a single day. It felt like the most B-Level Rocky-style montage imaginable when she looked back on it. The thought of the deep bathtub with jets in her old bathroom paired with some of her mom's cooking was the only thing pushing her on.

The muffled sound of TVs and conversation came from the houses on either side of the street creating a hypnotic hum that made Ella feel even more like a zombie as she traipsed closer to the house. She was half a block away when the banging and cursing started, interrupting the calm. She squinted at the lights on her mom's front porch. There was someone moving around, dragging something across the porch floor and muttering.

Ella felt her face split into a smile. "Bill?" She'd picked up her pace and she was close enough to see his face now. He paused and raised a hand to shield his eyes from the porch light as he squinted out at her on the street.

"El? Is that you?"

"Last time I checked," Ella said. "Though, that was this morning. At least I think it was. It could have been several years ago at this point."

Bill Benton's kind face split into a broad smile. "Your mom told me you'd had a hell of a day. Two interviews and then picking up and moving home on a whim. You must be exhausted."

Apparently, Ella's mom had given her husband the Reader's Digest version of Ella's day. "Yeah, well, there were a few more chapters in the middle of that story, but you've got the gist of it."

Bill studied her for a moment. "Well, tell me some good news."

It was a game they'd played ever since Bill had become a part of the family. Whenever Ella was moody or upset about something in high school, Bill would pretend he didn't notice and sit down in her general vicinity and ask her to tell him some good news. She'd make up something sarcastic to say and then Bill would laugh, and she'd laugh and things would be just a little bit better.

"I heard vegetables are a human construct and now there's going to be a class action suit for all of us forced to eat them as kids," she said, leaning on her suitcase.

Bill chuckled. "We both should have gone to law school."

Ella sighed. "Probably a better job market."

"Oh, I know that voice," Bill said with a nod. "And I've got good news for you. Some twelve-year-old single malt, kind of news."

"That's the best news I've heard all day," Ella said, running her hand down her face. She turned to look at her suitcase.

"I'll get that, El. You head inside. Your mom made fresh bread and beef stew for dinner. She's been waiting for you." Bill disentangled himself from the strings of Christmas lights he was doing battle with and hustled down the stairs to grab her suitcase. He was still in his deputy uniform as if he'd been "volun-told" he was hanging lights the second he got home. His service piece was still holstered on his hip.

"Why didn't you just shoot the lights?" Ella asked, looking around at the carnage strewn from one end of the porch to the other. "They clearly deserved it."

"Not worth the paperwork," Bill said, pausing to look back at the mess.

Ella was still standing next to her suitcase, taking in the sight of Bill and her old house and the Christmas carnage strewn everywhere.

"Now I'm not joking, get up those stairs before your Mom gets out here and starts in on both of us."

"Thanks, Bill," Ella said, pulling him in for a hug and pecking him on the cheek. He grinned in his bashful way that Ella found so endearing, before moving past her, carrying her suitcase up the porch steps. Ella's dad had died when she was twelve. Her mom had married Bill when Ella was fifteen. She'd told him, arms crossed and with a hostile stance, that she wouldn't call him "Dad". He'd just nodded and said that was fine. She told him she'd call him her stepdad and he said to just call him "Bill". And as Bogart would say, that was the start of a beautiful friendship.

Bill held the screen door open for Ella and with a thankful grin, she twisted the front door's knob and shoved. The door didn't budge. She paused and looked back at Bill, raising an eyebrow.

"It's the humidity," Bill said, shaking his head. "Whenever it gets wet *and* cold, the darn thing sticks something terrible. I need to work on it. It's just getting old."

Ella nodded and grinned. "I guess we'll all go the way of this door eventually."

Bill nodded. "All in need of some good sanding and refinishing."

"That's what I plan to do tonight. Does the upstairs tub still work?" Ella asked.

"Oh yeah," Bill said, shouldering the door open. "Knock yourself out."

"That's step two . . ." Ella started to say. Then, two soft and surprisingly strong arms were pulling her into a bone-crushing hug.

"El! Welcome home!" Helen Danforth Benton was not a large woman, physically. But, if size was measured by personality, she'd be the thing that ate Mothra and Godzilla. "Did Myrna treat you right? Did you get the job? When do you start? Did you meet all your coworkers? I know Maddie Burke is working there, and you already know Pippa, but . . ."

"I'm fine, mother, how are you?" Ella asked.

Her mom rolled her eyes. "So, are you going to fill your mother in on everything? Not that I'm anything less than tickled positively pink that you've moved back home . . . but is it really over with Les? I mean, is it something you could work out?"

"If you'll let me. Yes. And No," Ella said, answering her mother's questions chronologically.

She gave Ella a blank look. "What does that mean?"

"It means, I'll tell you everything if you'll hit the pause button on the questions. Yes, it's really over with Les, and no, it's not something we can work out," Ella said. She dropped her backpack and shoulder bag on the floor next to where Bill had set her suitcase down. Bill glanced from Ella to her mom and then with a knowing look, he slipped back out the front door, pulling it closed behind him.

"Honey? Are you ok?" Her mom's voice was softer now. She went to her daughter, holding her at arm's length to study her face. "What happened? On the phone, you just said it was over with him."

Ella held up a hand, trying to force down the hot knot forming in her throat. "If you want information, I will require sustenance. I've had a granola bar and three pounds of frozen yogurt today. And half a Twix."

Her mom shook her head. "Oh, honey! That's no way to eat, no wonder you look like you just came off the set of *The Living Dead*."

"Why thank you, Mom. I'm trying something new with my hair," Ella muttered.

Her mom snorted. "You know what I mean. You're just so thin. I worry that one good breeze off the Pacific will blow you all the way to Kansas." She dished up a bowl of steaming beef stew from the stove and sliced off two fresh pieces of bread, spreading them with butter from the dish on the counter. She slid the plate and bowl onto the table, in front of the chair Ella had plopped down on. Then, she seated herself at one end of the table, turning so she could watch her daughter like a pot on the stove, waiting for her to boil.

Ella ate with the same enthusiasm as someone who had just stumbled across a mixtape from high school. She couldn't eat it fast enough, savoring each bite and flavor and texture. The broth was so buttery, the meat was tender, the carrots and potatoes melted in her mouth and the seasoning was so familiar it was like hugging a friend she hadn't seen in years. Her vision began to blur as tears formed in her eyes. It was too much. After everything that had happened; the smells of her mom's kitchen, the taste of her food, the sound of her voice, and Bill's muttering on the porch outside, coupled with the plastic click of the Kit Cat Klock on the kitchen wall, was too much.

"Oh El," her mom's voice was soft as she watched her daughter.

The dam was cracking inside of Ella. No. She wasn't going to completely break down here. *Please universe. No crying,* she pleaded inside her head. The loneliness of the past few months, something that Ella hadn't really consciously acknowledged before today, was catching up with her. Despite having a boyfriend and living with him, it felt even lonelier somehow than when she'd been single. Even when Les had been around, he'd been on his phone or his computer, not that she'd been much better. Of course, *she* hadn't been sexting one of their friends. More pieces of the mental dam in her head crumbled and broke off. The day's interviews, while disheartening, were nothing compared to those months, now that she really considered it. She'd been pushing it down for so long. And today, it had all come to a head.

"What a day," Ella muttered, swiping at her eyes. Just a tear or two had escaped. That was acceptable, if not ideal. She bit down on her tongue to stop the self-pitying hill her emotions were charging up.

"We can talk about it tomorrow, dear heart," her mom said, reaching out to pat Ella on the arm. "Tonight, you should just put your PJs on and pass out."

Ella couldn't speak, so she just nodded. On the porch, there was a loud thud and then Bill let out a string of curses.

Her mom got to her feet. "Bill? What happened?" She tugged on the front door, muttering to herself when it took her two tries to get it open. She headed out onto the porch, pulling the door closed behind her. Ella stared down into her soup bowl, studying the Santa on a rocking chair pattern at the bottom. If it was after Halloween, the Christmas dishes at her mom's house were in use. The wobbling feeling in her stomach, of emotions crashing into exhaustion, was threatening to overpower her again. She was home. It felt comforting and devastating at the same time and in equal measures. She hadn't been able to "cut it" in Seattle. She'd had to come running back home. She squeezed her eyes shut. *No. No more crying. Do you hear me, brain?* Ella screamed inside her head. There was a shift change at her helm and Helga rolled up her sleeves.

Get up. Dishes in the sink. Bags upstairs. PJs. Bed. Ella slowly got to her feet. She'd taken her dishes to the sink and was about to carry her bags upstairs when Sarcastic El decided to speak up and give Ella an extra dose of motivation. *Yes, but twelve-year-old single malt, and* then *bed.*

Helga didn't object, so Ella hefted her bags upstairs with a little more spring in her step than she would have been able to manage without the promise of scotch. She did her best to turn her brain off as she mechanically dug through her bag until she found a tank top and sleep shorts. She pulled on a pair of sweatpants and her Duwamish College sweatshirt and slipped her feet into her hairy blue Cookie Monster slippers. She was about to head back downstairs when she reached up to scratch her head and immediately wished she hadn't. The hairpins from her "professional interview hairdo" were digging into her skull. She headed into the bathroom.

"I'll be seeing you later," she said, glancing at the tub and blowing it a pouty kiss. When she turned back to look at herself in the mirror, she groaned. Nothing like going all day looking like you'd lost a slap fight with a pissed-off spider monkey. She pulled all the pins out of her hair, ran a brush through it, and wrapped it into a messy ponytail to get it out of her face.

"Scotch, then bath, then bed," she told herself in the mirror. She nodded at her reflection. "A gentlewoman's agreement." She headed back downstairs in time to see her mom coming in from outside.

"Is Bill ok?" Ella asked.

Her mom smiled and nodded. "Yes, he's just locked in the eternal battle of multi-colored versus white."

"He put both kinds away in the same box last year, didn't he," Ella asked.

"Yep," she said, crossing her arms. "But, he's got help coming."

"Really?" Ella asked. "Who?"

Her mom shrugged. "He said he called one of his buddies from his bowling league."

Ella shrugged. "I can help him."

Her mom looked pained. "El, you need sleep."

Ella grinned. "I need scotch first."

Her mom rolled her eyes. "Well, he's got that out on the porch with him too. I think it's his carrot for getting the lights finished."

"I like carrots," Ella said.

"Don't you have to go to work in the morning? I heard you're starting first thing," she said, eyebrows raised.

Ella sighed. "Faster than social media; it's the Hope Island Hotline."

Her mom crossed her arms. "Well, apparently Myrna is at Fast Eddy's, celebrating. Carson Burns is a waiter there and you know he just lives on the next block. He stopped to talk to Bill and me while you were upstairs."

Ella put a hand to her face. "I guess I should be thankful that it wasn't Mrs. Thompson's rumor that made it all the way over here."

"What was Mrs. Thompson's rumor?" she asked.

Ella shook her head. "I'll tell you tomorrow. Right now, I need . . ."

Her mom sighed. "Go. But I want my Christmas lights up before you two start knocking back shots."

"You don't do shots of scotch, Mother," Ella said as she pecked her mom on the cheek before tugging the front door open and heading outside.

Bill was sitting on the porch swing, muttering under his breath as he fought to undo a knot in one of the strings of lights.

"Need some help?" Ella asked.

Bill glanced up at her. "Oh, all I can get. But aren't you supposed to be sawing logs right about now?"

Ella shrugged. "I weighed blissful sleep against manual labor in the cold and I just couldn't pass it up. I believe there was also mention of some twelve-year-old single malt."

Bill chuckled. "It's good to have you home, El."

She looked around at the chaos strewn across the porch floor. "Where should I start?"

"Eleven months ago, when I took the damn things down and didn't take the time to roll them up properly or separately before throwing them in the box," Bill muttered, going back to struggling with the knot.

"Second place to start?" Ella asked. "Do I get to use the drill?"

"Eventually," Bill sighed. "When we have something to put up."

Ella shrugged at the ball of tangled light strings. "Let's just hang it up like that. It'll be a . . . Christmas Tangle. We'll just call it art. I can probably swing getting it on the front page of the paper. Next year, it'll be all the rage."

Bill rolled his eyes. "Yeah, that would go over well with your mother."

Ella carefully stepped over the tail of the light string at her feet and started searching for its other end.

"You might want to go put on some real shoes," Bill said, noticing the Cookie Monsters on Ella's feet. "I haven't gotten around to sanding the porch in a couple of years and there may be a broken bulb or two scattered in this mess. I . . . might have tossed the strings around a little . . . and stepped on them . . ."

"I think the words you're looking for are 'thrown' and 'stomped'," Ella added with a grin. "Not that I'd blame you. This mess is what I always imagine the inside of my head looks like." It was going to take the two of them hours to get the job done. "You think we can successfully charge up this hill tonight?" She asked, staring around as Bill managed to unthread the knot he'd been working on.

"I've got some help coming. I called in a favor with one of my bowling league buddies. He's going to be over in a bit." Bill grinned. "I think you'll like him."

"He can bowl *and* hang Christmas lights?" Ella asked. "Sign me up."

"Go put your shoes on, Wisenheimer."

Ella winked at him and put her shoulder to the front door. As she headed up the stairs, a new wave of dread washed over her. As soon as everyone knew she was single again, the matchmaking would start. And if matchmaking was an Olympic sport, Hope would be the eternal holder of the gold medal. She stifled a groan and went to find her sneakers.

10

CAL

It had been an adjustment for Cal to learn that everyone in Hope walked, well, *everywhere*. There were a few delivery trucks that came over on the ferry and muscled their way around the back roads of Hope to their stops. And the police, EMS, and Bumble's Market used golf carts and ATVs. But besides that, Hope was definitely a pedestrian and bike town. The residential streets were made for cars, but for the most part, Hope's citizens left their cars in their garages to collect dust until they took them to the mainland.

    He didn't mind of course. Being from New York, he liked walking. Not that he got much of a chance to do it. His parents had lectured him about status and safety and probably another "s" or two, but he'd stopped listening by that point. He'd been distracted by the freedom he saw in people being able to walk up to food carts, in and out of bookstores, hail a cab, or go on the subway. Basically, doing whatever they wanted. His life growing up had been carefully scheduled with an endless progression of black limos, Town Cars, and the Dickson Group's company Cadillacs.

    He'd never been allowed on the subway, but it hadn't stopped him from ditching school to ride it once his sophomore year. He'd gotten mugged, a baby had puked on him, and he'd met a man with three pet parrots riding on his shoulders who wore tiny beanie hats with propellers and were named Huey, Dewey, and Louie. It had also been one of the best days of his life and the subject of his first article for the school paper.

Of course, his parents had been horrified when they'd seen the article come out, but even at fourteen, Cal had started to realize that he was different from the rest of his family. Sometimes it sucked. Why couldn't he be someone like them; interested in the same things they were, like golf, mergers, and canapes? He'd tried. He'd learned ballroom dancing for his mom. He'd studied journalism which was the only common ground between him and his father. Of course, his father just owned newspapers and was never that interested in what they put out as long as they turned a solid profit. Still, he'd always nodded when he saw Cal and told him that he would have been better off studying business. But, his dad would grudgingly say that a journalism degree would at least be some common ground between Cal and the editors at the papers when Cal took them over as Chief Executive Officer at the Dickson Group.

Cal chuckled grimly to himself. Even when he and his father had almost connected over something, they'd missed the mark. All Cal wanted to do was meet people and tell their stories. He hadn't cared about running a paper. At least, not until Clarence's job had come open. It was a good thing that Richard Callum Dickson couldn't see his son now. He could already imagine the look on his father's face when he heard Cal couldn't even get promoted to editor at a small paper in a place like Hope. That thought alone was enough to make Cal thankful to be thousands of miles away from him.

A much happier thought was the fact that while he lived in Hope, Cal could walk everywhere and make his own schedule. Walking was this strange reminder of the freedom that swelled almost embarrassingly in Cal's chest anytime he left his apartment in the morning or the newspaper office during the day. He knew most people didn't get the same giddy rush he did anytime he got to point his feet in whatever direction he chose, but six months of doing it hadn't really lessened the feeling. And he was ok with that.

He'd never been to Bill's house before, but based on the Shell Street address, he guessed it would probably take about ten minutes to walk there.

He locked up the dark newspaper office, before pausing to smile. Editor Ella Danforth wouldn't have a set of keys to get her into the office before him in the morning. Cal paused at that thought. Why was it bothering him so much? So she'd gotten the job. So what? Nothing was going to change for him. He was still a reporter for the *Hornblower*. He was still getting to do what he liked doing. She was from the island. Of course she was going to get the job. He tried to blink away the involuntary vision flashing in his head. Those stubborn gray eyes. He gave himself a mental shake just as Chill Cal, the calm, ex-stoner part of Cal's brain spoke up. *Your job hasn't changed*, Chill Cal said in his low and slow voice. *You report the news. You get involved with this community. Enjoy it while you can, man. Right now, you get to breathe on your own, live, and walk on your own.* Cal couldn't fight the involuntary smile forming on his face as the familiar giddy feeling rose in his chest. He straightened up and looked down at his watch.

"Hey, Cal." Cal turned to see Coach Hendricks waving to him. "Great article about the basketball season! I think it'll have the Selton Seafarers shaking in their Nikes."

Cal grinned. "Thanks, Coach. Glad you liked it! Can't take all the credit though. That picture of your center, Milt . . ."

"Oh, Myers," Coach laughed. "Yeah, but everyone calls him Andre, like Andre the Giant."

Cal shook his head. "Makes sense. If I was the Seafarers, I'd take one look at Andre and run up the white flag."

Coach chuckled and waved before loading the empty decoration boxes around him onto a handcart.

"You need a hand?" Cal asked, nodding at the boxes.

Five minutes later, they'd put the handcart and empty boxes into the storage shed behind Bumble's. Coach secured the padlock on the door and gave Cal a hearty slap on the back.

"Thanks, son. The team wanted to stay and help me finish, but they all have exams coming up, so I sent them home to study. Can't have them flunking out before the division championships."

Cal and Coach said their goodbyes and Cal watched Coach start a slow jog up the hill toward Aspen Circle behind the town center. Cal watched him go and then turned and started walking back toward the gazebo and Shell Street beyond it. Sometimes, Cal couldn't believe that Hope was real. Yet, here it was, a real-life Mayberry, where the high school basketball team put up holiday decorations and the local paper covered not just doom and gloom clickbait, but the lives of the people that lived there.

The cool air made him shiver and he quickly re-buttoned the top button of his shirt and tugged his sleeves back down his arms as he walked. He probably should have worn a jacket. He still wasn't used to the weather in Hope with no skyscrapers to block the wind coming off the sea.

Most of Shell Street already had their Christmas lights and decorations up. All except for a big yellow house at the end. Even from a couple of blocks away, Cal could see a figure moving around on the lit porch. When he got to the edge of the yard, he could see it was Bill and he could hear the string of curses woven through the narrative Bill was muttering under his breath.

"Problems?" Cal asked, moving to the porch steps.

Bill turned and gave him an exhausted smile. "Hey, Cal, thanks for coming. You were the only guy in the league that I knew was in town today. You have any experience with Christmas lights?"

"Not really," Cal said, looking at the tangled strings of bulbs. "But I have a little sister, so I've done some time as a professional hair-knot-untangler."

"Perfect," Bill said with a grin. "If you'll start on those white lights at that end, I think we can meet in the middle and zero in on where they're tangled due to their fraternizing with the multi-colored lights. I think if we can just separate that string out, the others will be a piece of cake."

Cal grinned and set his messenger bag down on Bill's porch swing before going to work. "We're getting holiday pay for this, right?" Cal asked, trying to untangle his left foot from a loop of lights.

"How about a scotch when we're done?".

"I can work for scotch," Cal said with a shrug. The two men worked side by side for a few minutes. Cal had carefully wound the white lights around one hand as he followed the string to the knot. He and Bill were working on getting the pronged plug end out of the mess when the front door of the house was wrenched open from the inside.

"Mary, Joseph, and a teenage pot-smoking Jesus, this door is going to kill someone," a female voice muttered. Cal felt all the hairs stand up on the back of his neck. Was that...

Ella Danforth hopped out onto the porch on one foot, trying to tie the shoelaces of the sneaker on her other foot. Cal hadn't been prepared to see this side of Ella Danforth so soon, if ever. She was wearing sweats. And her long hair was up in a messy ponytail. She was swearing as she bent over to finish tying her shoe and she had to fight the hood of her sweatshirt which had fallen forward over her eyes, impairing her vision. When she straightened up, her cheeks were pink, and even in profile, under the porch lights, he could see her gray eyes were bright. Cal almost lost his balance in his squatted position next to Bill.

"Alright," Ella said, moving over to the porch railing without glancing at him or Bill. "What does a girl have to hang in this place to get a drink?"

She snatched a drill off the railing, hit the trigger, and spun on her heel. The grin on her face was obviously meant for Bill because when she saw Cal, her eyes went wide and she quickly took her finger off the drill's trigger and lowered it.

"You."

"Uh, hi," Cal said, holding up and waving his hand wrapped in the string of Christmas lights. Too late Cal realized how incredibly dorky this was and dropped his hand.

"Oh, that's right! You two work together now, don't you," Bill said, grinning from Ella to Cal. Cal did his best to force a smile for Bill's sake.

He wasn't sure of the best way to ask how Ella Danforth was related to Bill Benton, so of course, he chose the most awkward way possible. He focused on Bill, not entirely sure of what would come out of his mouth if he addressed Ella. "Are you and Ella?"

Bill raised an eyebrow at Cal. "You think I robbed the cradle or something, son?"

"What?" Cal could feel his heart pounding in his chest. He'd interviewed Deputy Bill Benton before on new town littering policies, but he'd only started to get to know Bill as a person after he'd joined the bowling league two weeks ago. And even then, they hadn't talked about much besides sports and bowling. Frankly, he'd been surprised when Bill had called and asked for his help with his Christmas lights. If he was *with* Ella, why had she been in Seattle and...

Bill started laughing. "You should see your face, Cal." He shook his head. "Ella is my stepdaughter."

The front door was jerked open again from the inside and an older woman stuck her head out. "There's a lot more laughter than drilling and hammering out here. If you don't finish tonight, I'll..." The woman trailed off when she saw Cal.

"Oh hello!" She carefully stepped over the mess of lights near the door and extended a hand to him. "I'm Helen Benton, Bill's wife." She paused and looked over her shoulder at Ella. "And Ella's mom."

Cal reached out and shook her hand. He recognized her face from town events he'd covered, but they'd never spoken before. Too late, Cal realized that he was shaking her hand with the hand that he'd wrapped the Christmas lights around. "Cal Dickson."

Helen's eyes widened. "Oh! *You're* the Cal Dickson from the paper! I've read so many of your articles over the last few months. My goodness, do you ever get a chance to sleep? That paper seems to have you running day and night! Have you had a chance to meet Ella yet? She's going to be the new editor at the paper." The pride in Helen Benton's voice was evident. Cal slid his gaze to Ella whose face was red now. Her posture was defeated and she looked like she was contemplating suicide by Phillips-head-driver-bit.

"We've met, mom," Ella muttered.

"Oh good!" Helen said, missing the awkward tone in her daughter's voice. "Then this will be like a team-building activity! Cal, how..." She paused and glanced at her husband and then back at Cal. "How do you know Bill?"

"Oh," Cal said, barely able to suppress a snort of laughter. "We . . ."

"We're on the same bowling league team, Helen," Bill said. "Remember? I told you about him. Last week he bowled a turkey and we took the lead over Hank Melrose's team."

"Oh, Bill, I knew you had a bowling buddy coming over," Helen said, raising an eyebrow at her husband. "I guess I just didn't expect him to be so . . . young."

Cal could feel the heat rising in *his* face now.

"What? Is there a 'you must be this old and crotchety to bowl' line on the wall that I missed somewhere?" Bill muttered.

"If there was, you would be the gold standard," Helen said, pecking him on the cheek. Cal quickly turned his attention back to the string of lights in his hands. "And since Cal is so good at bowling," Helen continued, "I can see why you'd want to risk his skilled hands on stringing Christmas lights with hammers and drills." Cal glanced up to see Helen was teasing, but Bill had paused and turned to look at Cal, his face blank.

"I didn't think about that," Bill muttered.

"It'll be ok," Cal said. He glanced over his shoulder at Ella. "Besides, Ella has the drill. I'll be fine as long as she doesn't try to drill me." Cal regretted the words the second they left his mouth. He felt himself starting to sweat and he quickly looked away, now wishing that he hadn't answered his phone when Bill had called.

If he hadn't answered, he'd be at home right now, staring at his laptop screen, on his kitchen counter, while Nick Cave played on his turntable. But, instead, he was here, squatting on the Benton's front porch, wrapped in Christmas lights and embarrassing himself in front of his new bowling buddy, his new boss, and her mom. The awkward silence that followed Cal's comment was almost palpable. Desperately, Cal willed the universe to have something, anything, interrupt the tension and distract them from his words that were still hanging over them in the void. A fire, a fart, an alien landing on the lawn, literally, *anything*.

"I have been known to do some drilling in my day," Ella finally said. "And where's the hammer? Because when drilling just won't get it done, it's hammer time." Helen and Bill snorted and Cal felt relief wash over him as he felt their eyes turn to focus on Ella.

"Don't give her the hammer, Bill. And cut her off, it sounds like she's already had too much scotch."

"I'll have you know, Mother, I have yet to receive my scotch rations for this job. If Bill doesn't pony up, I'll be forced to report him to the union."

"Well, work on rationing that sass while you're out here, will you?" Helen asked, tugging on Ella's ponytail. Ella hit the trigger on the drill in protest and Helen laughed.

"Fine, while you *Home Improvement* extras work on this, I'll make some hot cocoa. Any takers?"

Ella wrinkled her nose. "Doesn't really go with scotch, Mom."

"You're right," Helen said, putting her shoulder to the door. "I'll make some coffee in a boot and then boil a tire for you all instead."

"Scotch haters gonna hate," Ella called as her mom closed the door behind her. Cal caught himself watching Ella at the same time she caught him looking at her. She quickly dropped her gaze and moved to set the drill back down. She jumped when the echoing boom of the bronze alphorn broke the stillness of the night. She let out a string of curses when the drill landed on her foot, just as Bill gave a yell of triumph. Cal tore his attention away from Ella to look at Bill.

"Got one!" Bill held up the untangled string he'd been working on. Then he paused and looked over at Ella who was doing some deep breathing. "What, did you forget about our 'beloved horn'?" Bill asked. "I remember you used to be able to sleep through that sound. On the porch, no less."

Ella shook her head. "No, that wasn't sleeping, Bill. That was hungover and passed out." She squinted out into the darkness toward the center of town. "I just forgot how loud it was. And how it happens . . . all the time."

"Kind of late for tourists, isn't it?" Cal asked, turning his gaze back to the knot he was working on.

"Oh, that's not tourists," Bill said with a sigh. "That'll be drunk high schoolers." Cal looked up in time to see Bill cut his eyes to Ella. "And it probably wasn't their lips on the horn."

Cal opened his mouth to ask him what he meant, but then it dawned on him.

Ella was rolling her eyes. "Skye Kensinger did it *one time*."

"No," Bill muttered. "His ass got *stuck* to the horn, *one time*. You jerks did it all the time. There was an outbreak of pink eye among the daily tourists and it didn't take a detective to trace it back to that godforsaken horn. They should put a plaque on the sanitation station next to the damned thing, honoring your high school graduating class."

"Well, Principal Stewart told us to go forth and leave our mark on the world," Ella said, retrieving the drill and setting it back on the railing.

"Glad I've never blown that horn," Cal muttered. He caught Ella's gaze. She was grinning at him, but then, as if they both suddenly remembered who they were grinning at, their smiles fell away.

"Alright," Bill said. "Enough jawing, let's get these up before we freeze."

Thankful for the distraction, Cal turned his attention to the rest of the tangled mess Bill had been working on, as Bill coiled a complete string of multi-colored lights. "First string is ready to hang!" Bill said proudly. Cal saw his own relief mirrored on Ella's face.

This would be easy. Just get the lights up and then go home. Cal shifted into supply and problem-solving mode. Ella kept her distance from him, preferring to stand on top of the ladder with the drill. He didn't see her look in his direction once, as she worked to secure the strings of lights, fed to her by Bill after Cal had plugged one line into the next. The whole undertaking took a little over an hour.

"Clark, you're gonna burn the whole neighborhood down," Ella said to Bill when he started fiddling with the daisy-chained extension cords leading to the newly hung lights.

"El, this is the same setup we used last year and we're all still standing. Quit being such an alarmist," Bill muttered. A few sparks flew when Bill plugged the last string of lights into the power strip connected to the extension cord and Cal took a step back. Ella caught his eye and nodded before taking a step back herself. "Ok, here we go!" Bill flipped the switch on the power strip and the lights on the house flickered and then blinked on, securing its place amongst the other houses on Shell Street.

"Awesome," Ella said. "Now we look just like everyone else."

Bill cut his eyes to her. "Your mother was never going to let us spell out, 'Suck it, Selton' on the roof."

Ella shrugged. "You don't know that. Has she ever told you about the time that Selton beat her volleyball team out as division champions?"

Bill closed his eyes. "Yes."

The front door opened and Helen poked her head out. "Well, the porch is clean. Does that mean the lights are up or did you just lose patience with them and throw them in the trash?"

"Come see for yourself," Bill called to her. Helen hurried down the front porch steps and turned to look up at the house.

"It's beautiful!" Helen breathed. She glanced up at Bill, and then over at Cal and Ella. "I guess I'll keep you all on for another season." Bill swatted her on the butt and she laughed. "Just for that, mister, you get to help me haul the light's storage boxes back up to the attic."

"Fine," Bill muttered, following Helen back to the porch. He turned back to glance at Cal and Ella. "You two hang on. I'll grab some glasses for the scotch and then we can toast our partnership and discuss a name for our lights-untangling-and-hanging service."

"Oh," Cal said quickly. "I really should be going . . ."

"Yeah, it's getting kind of late," Ella said.

"Hey," Bill said, pointing his finger at them. "Bill Benton always keeps his word. Scotch all around and then we'll call it a night."

He followed Helen inside and kicked the door closed behind him, leaving Cal and Ella standing in front of the porch. Without looking at each other, they both headed up the steps. Unfortunately, they weren't quite wide enough for two people to climb side by side. But neither of them made any move to let the other be the first up the stairs. *Why, Cal?* Chill Cal paused wrist-deep in a bag of imaginary Funions to shake his head at Cal's immaturity. *It's her house.* Just like it's her island? And her paper?

The annoyance in his chest was somewhat compromised by the soft scent invading his nose. She was so close to Cal that he could smell her perfume.

Maybe it was perfume. Maybe it was an essential oil or lotion or hell, for all he knew, that was just the way that Ella Danforth always smelled. It was earthy, like the smell of rain on a freshly-mown lawn. It was odd. He'd never known a woman his age to wear something that wasn't floral or fruity.

As soon as they got up the stairs, they each headed for different sides of the porch. Ella perched on the wide railing on one side of the stairs and Cal claimed the porch swing. A nice, heavy, awkward silence fell between them.

"So, tomorrow," Cal said before he realized the words were coming out of his mouth.

"Tomorrow," Ella repeated.

Cal forced a chuckle. "So, Myrna has been having fun with telling me how grizzly and brutal all these holiday celebrations are."

Ella shrugged. "She's probably just trying to prepare you."

Cal rolled his eyes. "Yeah, I'm sure. What? Are you in on it too?"

Ella narrowed her eyes at Cal. "Look, if you want to pretend that the next month is going to just be business as usual, you go right ahead. The rest of us know better."

Cal felt heat rising on the back of his neck. "That's right. Because you've got such a great pulse on everything that's going on here these days. When was the last time you were in Hope?"

The flash of anger that crossed Ella's face stunned Cal. Despite her messy hair and sweats, for a heartbeat, she'd looked like a wild animal, poised to attack. He was already feeling the tug to just leave the situation. Confrontations weren't his thing. Why had he said anything? He started to get to his feet just as she opened her mouth, eyes narrowed, holding him in her crosshairs. But before she could speak, the front door to the house was wrenched open and Bill came out, juggling three whiskey glasses. He snatched the scotch bottle off the low table by the door and tucked it under his arm. Ella and Cal sprang to their feet to help him.

"Here we go," Bill said, apparently missing the cloud of tension he'd just walked into. Ella and Cal each took a glass and Bill set his own down on the porch railing before proudly holding up the bottle to show them. "Glenlivet, double oak aged." He unscrewed the cap and grinned at Cal. "Normally, I'd say ladies first, but El told me years ago that she was a woman, not a lady."

"And normally that's true," Ella said, "But when scotch is involved, I'm just a damsel with the vapors."

Bill rolled his eyes. "Guests first, El. Then, you."

He poured two fingers worth of the amber liquid into Cal's glass and then turned to do the same for his stepdaughter. The three of them sipped the warming liquid and studied their handiwork as the soft glow from the lights reflected back to where they stood on the porch. Bill turned to Cal. "So, this week we're up against Manny Johnson's team. And they've got Big Jim from Baskins Construction. I heard he bowled a 270 last week against . . ."

The front door to the house was yanked open and Helen stuck her head out. "Bill, the fridge is making that revving noise again. Quick! Come listen before it stops!" Bill followed his wife back inside, shutting the door behind him.

Cal and Ella were left to their awkwardly tense silence again. Ella wasn't looking at him. She was turned so her face was profile as she looked out at the street in front of the house. Cal studied her, watching her sip and savor her drink. She closed her eyes and he saw the tip of her tongue dart out to run along her upper lip, searching for any remnants of the scotch. Cal liked scotch, but he had to say, he didn't like it as much as Ella Danforth seemed to. Cal was so transfixed with watching her that he almost missed the question that she asked, breaking the silence between them.

"Well, are you going to come out and say it or are we going to spend the whole month tiptoeing around the fact that you're pissed Myrna hired me?" Ella asked, turning her head to look at him.

The defiance was back in her eyes, either more pronounced because of the porch lighting or because of the scotch. He hadn't been expecting such a direct question. That was also something on the island he'd had to get used to. Tact was optional and often removed in the interest of time-saving in Hope, whereas the Dicksons of New York made beating-around-the-bush into an Olympic sport. Still, the annoyance and anger that had been simmering in Cal, ever since Myrna had mentioned Ella's name that morning, was now starting to boil over. It was almost a new feeling for Cal to be so angry and on the verge of showing it. He felt the heat creeping up the back of his neck again as he matched her glare for glare. His brain was telling him to just leave. Set down his glass, walk down the porch steps, and head for home. The discomfort and anxiety were starting to build inside him along with the anger and annoyance. Chill Cal was trying to talk him down. *Don't make waves. Just let it go.* For whatever reason, maybe it was the scotch, maybe it was how stubborn Ella was that made him just want to push back, or maybe it was dread and a fear of losing the Hope that he'd come to think of as his refuge, before Ella's sudden appearance. Whatever the reason, he stood his ground.

"Pissed?" Cal asked. "I don't know if that's the right word. Surprised, might be more in the ballpark. After all, I've actually *been here* for the last five months, covering stories and you know, *working* at the paper and working with Clarence. So, yeah, I guess I was a little *surprised* when this girl from Seattle waltzed in, took a ten-minute meeting with Myrna, and was announced to be the new editor, the day after Clarence quit."

Ella upended her glass into her mouth and swallowed before standing up. "What part *surprised* you more? That I'm a 'girl from Seattle' or the fact that it only took Myrna ten minutes to foist the job on me?"

Cal got to his feet too. "Well, if you don't want the job, why did you take it?"

Ella closed her eyes in frustration, her nostrils flaring as she tried to get a handle on her anger. "Because I was out of options." She opened her eyes and raised them to meet Cal's. "If I had anywhere else to be, I'd be there." She took a deep breath. "I know you don't know me, but trust me when I say you *don't* want this job. At least not at this time of year."

Cal rolled his eyes. "Oh, that's right, the big bad Hope Holidays."

Ella shook her head, the anger on her face hardening into a set-jawed expression. "I really don't have the energy to sugar-coat anything tonight.

My apologies. It's been a long day. Let's cut to the chase. You're pissed at me, Myrna, etc. But, unfortunately, we don't have time to pace circles around each other licking our wounds and jockeying for position. Tomorrow is December 1st and we will be up to our eyes in it. I know you've been here for five months, but I've lived here for eighteen years."

Cal sighed. "It's just a small-town Christmas. It's not like we're waging war."

"Look soldier," Ella said. "You think you've been covering a lot of stories in the last five months? Well, you're about to be thrust into thirty-one days of hell like you've never seen before. So, be pissed at me if you want, but if you still want to have a job and your sanity, I suggest you go home and get some sleep because, in t-minus ten hours, we hit the front lines."

Cal was too angry to speak. The desire to leave the tense situation had finally won. He upended his glass, letting the warm liquid burn his throat before setting it on the railing without looking at her. He put the strap of his messenger bag over his head and jogged down the porch steps, walking off down Shell Street faster than he normally would.

He wasn't sure if Ella was watching him leave, but he was having to fight hard against the desire to turn back to look at her one more time. He wasn't sure why. But then again, he wasn't sure why he'd even opened his mouth. On a normal day, he'd rather eat broken glass than get into a tense argument or fight with someone. It was too much like his early childhood and teenage days with his parents before he learned that just not talking to them about anything real was easier than the constant fighting. But, it hadn't been a normal day.

He kept his eyes on the road ahead of him. He tried to think of the sound of entitlement in her voice. The harsh tone she'd had the gall to use, despite the fact that she'd left this town and didn't sound happy to be back. It must be nice to have the ability to come back to Hope and be upset to be there when he would give anything to swap places with her. The anger rushing through him carried him two blocks down from the yellow house.

Ella Danforth didn't know how lucky she was. He didn't slow down until he'd turned the corner and the gazebo was in sight. The Town Square was quiet again and whoever had blown the horn had moved on to the next activity of their evening. Cal was still seething, hearing Ella's words over and over in his head, but, to his annoyance, the image of her defiant face was quickly being replaced in his mind with the profile of her drinking scotch and licking her lips as she savored it.

11

ELLA

Ella hadn't waited for Bill to come back outside. She'd watched Cal leave, and she'd had to stop herself from yelling after him to come back. The fourth thing on Ella's list of things she hated was when people walked away in the middle of a fight. They had beef to sort out and she would have liked to get it done before everything geared up in the morning. Though, she guessed she shouldn't be surprised that the day had ended with a guy doing whatever he could to get away from her. It was almost poetic. She tightened her grip on her whiskey glass as the dam carefully holding back the day's emotions began to shake. She tried to redirect her attention to something, *anything* else. She looked around the porch and the image of Cal's smiling face popped into her memory. His blue-green eyes had been lighter and almost teasing when he'd been talking to Bill. She'd even seen him chuckle once or twice. And then, when Bill had gone inside, and it had just been her and Cal on the porch, all of that had gone away.

Was that what she did to men? Her thoughts drifted to Les. The memory of his words, "I never know what you're feeling," punched her in the stomach so hard that she wanted another scotch. Unfortunately, this clear desire hadn't presented itself to her until she was inside, up the stairs, in her bathroom, naked and sitting in the tub, hugging her knees while the water rose around her. She'd stared at her empty scotch glass on the bathroom sink and something about it had been the final blow of the day for her. She'd crumbled. She was thankful for the sound of groaning pipes and running water to cover the ragged sobs that clawed their way out of her.

Ella wasn't a crier. She sucked at it. Even when she was a kid, she hated crying. It was like puking, but for your soul. And Ella hated puking almost as much as she hated crying. Anytime she was sick, she'd lay on the bathroom floor, making deals with the universe in exchange for her not having to puke. Sometimes it worked, so she'd started doing the same thing whenever she was going to cry. It didn't work this time. The universe was asleep at the wheel. Her tears were running down her thighs and no matter how much she screamed inside her head for Helga or Sarcastic El, or hell, even Numb Ella to do something about it, she couldn't stop. She squeezed her legs tighter, trying to force the air out of her and stop the open-mouthed sobs. She felt empty. Scooped out, like a Halloween pumpkin. The vision of Les, almost naked, with Wendi's arms wrapped around his chest was a vicious hand, grabbing her insides and ripping them out.

The anger that hadn't been there earlier in the day came exploding out of her with a vengeance. The water was up to Ella's chest when she finally let go of her knees, leaned forward, and plunged her face beneath its surface. She screamed her frustration into the water as the bathtub jets kicked on. She screamed for everything she hadn't been able to achieve in Seattle. She screamed for her losses. She screamed because Les had cheated. She screamed for her damn, comfy apartment that she'd given up for him. When she was screamed-out, she pulled her face out of the water and leaned back, letting the bath's warmth soothe her. She was still crying, but thankfully, it was quieter now.

Helga was tiptoeing back to the control panel in Ella's brain. *You're going to be ok,* she told Ella. *You're going to be ok now. And you don't have another second to waste on thinking about Les. Not with everything you're in charge of now. In fact, as soon as this bath water gets lukewarm, it's off to bed with you, missy.* Helga paused and then decided to throw Ella a bone. *And once you're in bed, you can spend half an hour looking at job postings back on the mainland,*

and then tomorrow night after work, we can fill out some applications. Ella drew some comfort from Helga's reasoning.

She just had to get the Hornblower through the holidays, then she could move on with her life. Maybe Cal would stop being an a-hole to her when she told him about her plan to get him ready to replace her in January. A thought occurred to her that made her shiver. Would . . . would it be enough to make him smile? Now that she'd seen it, she kind of wanted to see it again. Just as a nice change of pace to his scowl, of course. She pushed away the weird tingle that gave her and Sarcastic El decided to weigh in. *Maybe telling him about January would knock the stick out of his ass.*

An hour later, she was completely cried-out. She felt a little lighter (from dehydration she assumed) as she wrapped herself in her pj's and crawled under her covers. She plugged her phone in and started scrolling through job listings in Seattle. She copied and sent herself links to the listings and she felt the depression cloud around her starting to dissipate as the opportunities loaded on her phone screen. Helga cleared her throat after a half hour of scrolling and reluctantly, Ella put her phone down and closed her eyes. She *was* going to be ok. Maybe not right away, and that was ok too. But, eventually, she was going to be ok.

Several hours later, she lay in bed, the dim light of early morning pouring through her old bedroom window, which lacked her beloved blackout curtains. She tried to banish all thoughts of Les and Wendi. Unfortunately, those thoughts were, unhelpfully, replaced by thoughts of Cal. *This is just some kind of pendulum swing with hormones,* Helga murmured. She'd broken up with Les and her body was rebounding. First with Tony on the ferry, and now with Cal, the guy who was going to make her tenure at the Hornblower absolute hell. Not that it needed any extra help from him. She let out a soft groan as she remembered that today was December 1st.

"Are you up, El?" Her mom called to her through the door. Ella squeezed her eyes shut. She was living at home again with morning wake-up calls from her mom, just like she was back in high school. "El?" her mom called again.

"Yeah," Ella groaned. "I'm up."

"Good! You don't want to be late on your first day!" Ella cut her eyes to the closed bedroom door. She could hear her mom humming "Jingle Bells" as she moved off down the hall. Ella picked up her phone off the nightstand and checked the time.

Six a.m.

She groaned and sat up, putting her feet on the floor. Any other time of year, six a.m. would be a ludicrous start time, but for the Hope Holiday season, Ella was already running an hour late. She stumbled out of bed and pulled on a green knit shirt, black skinny jeans, and black Converses before pulling her hair up and jogging down the stairs two at a time. She grabbed her coat and shoulder bag and her hand was on the doorknob when her mom called to her.

"El? Aren't you going to have breakfast?"

"No time," Ella said.

"Well, you better make time," her mom said. "Or I'm not going to give you the envelope Myrna dropped off."

Ella turned to look at her mom. "When did Myrna drop it off?"

"This morning." She turned back to the bacon she was frying on the stove. "She came by about a half-hour ago. Poor thing. She must have really tied one on last night."

Ella had a short inner debate with herself before deciding that it was probably a good idea to at least sit down, hear her mom out, and see what Myrna had left for her before she bolted outside. "How could you tell?" Ella asked.

Her mom smiled. "Because she was wearing sunglasses, at five-thirty in the morning."

"Fair point," Ella said. "So where's the envelope?"

Her mom turned and pointed her bacon spatula at Ella. "Uh, uh. First, you eat breakfast, *then* you get the cookie."

Ella choked down a piece of toast and two pieces of bacon and held her hand out to her mom while she was still chewing. "Please. I'm going to be late."

Her mom sighed. It was the universal sigh of overburdened mothers. "Fine." She moved across the kitchen and opened the drawer next to the old wall phone and pulled out a small manila envelope, still sealed. She slapped it into Ella's hand. It was heavy and Ella could feel the outline of a key through the envelope.

"Office keys," Ella said with a sigh. "Good call, Myrna."

"Here. At least put on a scarf," Her mom wrapped a red woolen scarf around Ella's neck while Ella studied the envelope.

After finally being released by her mother, she power-walked the distance from her house to the newspaper office. Besides the De-Floured Bakery, the rest of the town appeared to be asleep. Her shoulder bag thumped with every other step as her laptop and Clarence's assignment book jostled against her leg. She tore into the envelope and tipped the keys into the palm of her hand. When she drew even with the gazebo, her footsteps began to echo off the empty square and the surrounding buildings. It was the calm before the storm. She just needed half an hour at her desk with the assignment book and she could formulate some kind of plan of attack.

Ella paused when she got to the office door and saw that the lights were on inside. She frowned. Surely Cal hadn't forgotten to turn them off before he left the night before. She tugged on the door. Locked. She fumbled with the keys from Myrna's envelope, trying each one of the three until she found the right one.

The smell of coffee greeted her when she strolled through the front door. She could hear whistling somewhere deep in the office. Was it Myrna? Somehow she doubted that hungover Myrna would be whistling what sounded like a Clash song at six-thirty in the morning, even if she had come straight to the office after stopping by Ella's house.

"Myrna?" Ella called as she moved around the dividing wall separating the office space from the small reception area. The whistling stopped. It wasn't Myrna. It was Cal. He was sitting behind his laptop, Ella's star mug in his hand. He gave her a sarcastic smile, raised the mug to his lips, and took a sip.

Well, Ella had to admit, it was about par for how she assumed the morning was going to go. "Morning, Cal," she called, moving into Clarence's office. "I see you've already brewed yourself a pot of asshole juice," she added under her breath, "to sip out of my mug."

"What was that?" Cal asked. Ella hadn't been planning to say anything about her mug, but the sarcastic smile had pushed her over the edge.

"Oh, I was just saying, that used to be *my* mug when I worked here," Ella said, nodding at the mug in his hand, pointedly.

"Was it really?" Cal asked, feigning interest. "Imagine that." He locked eyes with her as he raised it to his lips again and sipped.

Fine, Sarcastic El muttered inside Ella's head, *If that's the way he wants it, let the games begin.*

Ella gave him her own sarcastic smile until she turned her attention back to her new office and stared at the paperwork-dystopia. She felt the smile fall off her face as she stared at the mess on Clarence's desk. Yeah, the piles were going to have to go. She didn't have time to overhaul the whole office, so instead, she just knocked one of the smaller piles on the desk surface to the floor.

"Much better," she sighed. She set up her laptop, flipped on the desk lamp, and pulled out the assignment book. She set Myrna's envelope down on top of it, and a flash of yellow caught her eye. It was a piece of legal pad paper, sticking out of the envelope. Ella picked it up, studying the neatly folded square. She shook it open and scanned down the page.

Ella, thanks for taking this on. I know it probably isn't your dream job, but I'm grateful all the same. I've listed the code and instructions for retrieving voicemails from the system as well as the editor's email address and password. If you need anything, call me. I'll stop by from time to time to see how you're doing. Sometimes, life steers us off course on purpose. Not to get us lost, but to help us find what *we've lost. -Myrna*

"Helpful," Ella muttered. "And somewhat ominous." She tucked the note with the instructions and passwords under the corner of her laptop and turned her attention back to the assignment book. Time to plan. Her gaze drifted to her office window and Cal's profile, typing away on his laptop just beyond. His dark hair was tousled and he had a shadow of scruff on his cheeks. He looked as tired as she felt, but he was smiling. She shook her head. He was smiling because he didn't know what lay ahead for him.

It was close to eight when Pippa knocked on her open office door. "How's the battle plan coming?"

Ella was resting her forehead in the palm of one hand while she studied the notes she'd typed up on her computer, comparing them to Clarence's cramped writing. "Well, it's just now . . . eight . . . and we've already lost the war."

"Well, our forces held longer than I expected them to," Pippa said. She plopped down in the chair Ella had sat in the day before during her tet-a-tet with Myrna.

Ella turned her gaze on Pippa. "There are too many events happening this year."

Pippa grinned. "That's what people say every year, but everything still gets covered. Well, usually."

"Yeah, and every year, they add more events than the year before," Ella said. "But we don't have any additional reporters, making it almost certain that eventually, we were going to hit critical mass and not be able to keep up. And Pip, this is the year that the prophecy is going to be fulfilled."

Pippa's expression changed from teasing to worry in the span of a few seconds. "Are you serious?"

"As a heart attack," Ella said, getting to her feet. She leaned over her laptop and sent her notes to the printer. She glanced back at Pippa. "I've done what I can, but this is going to be a season of 'all hands on deck'. Is everyone else here?"

"I think Marty is the only one that hasn't rolled in yet," Pippa said. "But he usually turns up about now. I'll go check."

Ella nodded. "Thanks, Pip. I want to have a quick meeting with everyone to go over what we're doing today." Pippa nodded. "And," Ella added. Pippa paused to look back at her. "I think these meetings will be a daily thing this month." She nodded again and left.

Ella took a deep breath. "Ok, here we go," she said to herself. And the

Helga part of her brain nodded in approval and rolled up her sleeves. Ella marched out of the office and moved to stand in front of Maddie's desk. Maddie and Pippa joined her, and glancing at their reassuring smiles gave Ella a modicum of courage for her first meeting as Editor. At least these two were with her. The front door jingled and Myrna lumbered in, still wearing her sunglasses.

"Hi, Myrna," Ella said with a surprised grin. "I didn't expect to see you this morning."

Myrna gave a soft groan and put a finger to her lips. "A little quieter, dear."

"Have a good night?" Ella asked.

Myrna smiled and nodded before looking around the room. "Looks like the gang's all here now. Everyone, this is Ella Danforth, our new Editor-in-Chief." This was greeted by some pleasantries from Katie, Marty, and Kurt. "She may look a little green," Myrna said, grinning at Ella, "but don't let that fool you. With Clarence's departure, I didn't want to uproot any of you from your current wheelhouses to cover for him and I knew we'd need someone experienced with what was coming this month to support all of you, and that's Ella. In spades." Ella's gaze fell on Cal who was standing at the back of the gathered group, arms folded, his lips pinched into a thin line. Ella felt her blood pressure beginning to rise.

If he wants to pout, let him. We've got bigger stockings to stuff, Helga reminded her.

Really, Helga? Stockings to stuff?

Helga just shrugged and gave her the finger, so Ella turned her attention back to the other smiling faces in front of her.

"Take it away, Editor," Myrna muttered. "I'm getting coffee."

"Myrna," Maddie said. "You're holding coffee."

It was true. Myrna was holding a tall paper cup from De-Floured Erotic Bakery. She smiled and gave the cup a little shake. "Empty."

Pippa grinned. "There's a fresh pot in the break room. I'll get you a cup."

Myrna nodded gratefully and Pippa hurried off down the hall. Everyone's attention snapped back onto Ella.

"Ok, first, I know I haven't been back here in a while. I have no desire to try telling perfectly competent, experienced, and talented people how to do their jobs. If we could just go around quickly and have you tell me what you do in your own words, I can make sure I don't do anything to screw up the well-oiled machine you've already got running here."

Cal shifted his weight and Ella ignored him, keeping her attention on the rest of the group. Katie, Marty, and Kurt took turns introducing themselves to her. Katie was a mother of three elementary-aged kids. She looked slightly harassed and Ella smiled when Katie raised an arm to push a stray strand of hair out of her face, revealing what looked like dried shards of a sucker stuck to the elbow of her shirt.

"I don't take any crap from the carriers," Katie said. "And in the last quarter, we've upped our circulation by thirty percent with our ferry and mainland coverage. I'm also working on expanding our online circulation to reach more travel agencies, get copies of the paper into mainland Airbnbs, etc."

Myrna nodded. "You don't tell Katie, 'No'."

"That's excellent," Ella said. "Because we're about to put the carriers through the wringer with the holiday editions."

Katie nodded. "I remember the hell that was last year's holidays. Had to hire an extra twenty carriers for the season and with our increased circulation . . ." Katie's face was determined but the color was starting to drain from her cheeks as her eyes widened in realization.

"Don't worry," Ella said quickly. "We'll figure it out. I've got some ideas and I know you have some. Let's meet this afternoon and get it hammered out."

"Two o'clock?" Katie asked quickly.

"It's a date," Ella said. Katie started to breathe again, but Ella could tell the wheels were still turning inside her head. Ella could see Cal shifting his weight again out of the corner of her eye but she ignored him and turned her attention to Marty.

"I've had to limit how many ads the folks in town can take out during this month because we just don't have the space." Marty glanced at Kurt.

"Unless Kurt..."

Kurt sighed. "The holiday editions of the paper are already big, floppy novels. If you want to add another section, it's going to increase our run time every day by an hour or more, and that puts extra strain on the carriers..."

"Would it be possible to just put all the ads on a single insert that didn't change and was pre-printed for the month and then just insert it every day into the edition?" Ella asked. She looked at Marty. "Just tell your folks that if they want ads, it'll run for the whole month, and then we'll give them a whole month pricing for the insert space?"

Marty scratched the back of his head. "I think that would work on my end. All the stores and bazaars around here never seem to mind paying higher prices during the holidays for ad real estate. I might actually be able to cut them a better deal if it's an insert. What do you think, Kurt?"

Kurt looked doubtful. "Stuffing inserts into papers every day is going to be a chore. I'll need more help."

Ella nodded. "I think we can get it for you. Can you get me an estimate of how many extra pairs of hands you'll need?"

Kurt nodded. "We did a big insert at Easter. And we hired on a couple of extra helpers that week. I can try to model it off of that and get something to you."

"Would you have time to do it today?" Ella asked. "Today will probably be the last 'calm before the storm' day for the month."

"Probably," Kurt said. "I think I could have something roughed out by the end of the day."

"Awesome," Ella said. "I'll come and find you so you don't have to break your rhythm for a meeting." Kurt grinned and nodded.

"And I'll get on the horn with the advertisers," Marty added. "As soon as I have them on board, I should be able to use an old template, jazz it up for the holidays, and get you a draft of the insert by the end of the day, early tomorrow at the latest."

"Sounds like a plan," Ella said. "Well, the paper has been in extremely good hands." She looked from Myrna to the rest of the group. "I'm just here to help us all make it through this storm."

Katie turned to look over her shoulder at Cal. "What about you, Cal? Aren't you going to introduce yourself?"

"Cal and I met last night," Ella said. She immediately felt the heat rising to her cheeks. "I mean, when I came to the office last night, we were introduced . . ." She paused, realizing that that explanation didn't clear everything up. "By Myrna," she blurted. She couldn't look at Cal, but she could feel his eyes boring into the side of her head. She cleared her throat and glanced back at Myrna, Maddie, and Pippa for help.

Pippa smiled at Ella. "Tell us about you now."

Ella stifled a sigh. It was a change of topic, but still not one she *wanted* to talk about. But, she guessed it was better to just get it over with. She looked around at the group again. "I grew up here," she began. "I spent eighteen years doing every holiday event this town could dream up. I have been every part in the nativity play, except the sheep. I was always too tall. But I've been every human part and I was Joseph three years in a row. I've run concessions for the gazebo concerts and dance recitals. In high school, I organized the Parade of Trees and Santa's Grotto, served as an entry monitor at the Baby Jesus Bazaar, decorated, and cleaned up after the Santa Ball and Crawl, and served French toast at the Ugly Sweater Brunch, etc. So, I know firsthand how insane this place can get. But I think I've devised a plan of attack that will, hopefully, allow all of us to keep some shred of our sanity and make it through this alive." Without realizing what she was doing, Ella had clasped her hands behind her back and begun to pace like a military general addressing her troops.

"Today is December 1st, and we have no less than fifteen activities happening in town to cover. And from there, the number just goes up." She paused and looked at the crew in front of her. "Now as most of us already know," she paused for a moment to spare Cal a glance, "some of these events, installations, etc. may seem ridiculous to us, but for the ones doing them, they are the most important thing they'll do all year and it means a lot to them. And remember, they're the main customers for the paper the other eleven months of the year." She glanced at Myrna. "And we can't forget how important tourism is to Hope. Most of the businesses not to mention families in this town depend on it."

There was a low chorus of groans from the surrounding crowd. She picked up the copies of her notes that she'd printed off and handed them around. "So let's not let anyone down. Just so we're all on the same page, I would like to have daily short meetings like this one just to go over the plan for each day. We're obviously working ahead as much as possible so the tourists are hearing about the day's events with enough time to actually attend them. There's too much happening for us to do a weekly edition featuring just the events. Though, I'd like to print a complete calendar of the events for the week in the paper." She turned to Marty. "With your ads hopefully all moving to an insert, could we potentially use the usual ad space in the paper to do this? I think it'll stem a lot of complaints in case people on the mainland are planning their trip out here for a particular day of the week but might want to change which day they're coming if they know about some event or another happening."

Marty nodded without looking up at her. "Sure, we can do that." Like everyone else in the group, he was staring down at the numbered list in his hands. Katie handed Cal a copy of the notes and Ella caught the look of disbelief on Cal's face.

"This is a joke, right?" Cal asked, looking up at the rest of them. "There's no way we can fit this much in one day."

The rest of the group chuckled. It was Ella's turn for a smug smile. "Welcome to Hope."

Cal didn't say anything and Ella got back to going over the list with the rest of the group. "Now, some of this is preliminary preparation stuff, like Jim Barber's ornament topiaries in front of the library and the Girl Scouts Holiday Safety Display." Ella glanced at Maddie. "I think for these month-long installations, a nice photo with a short couple paragraphs about them will be enough. We'll have to work out a strategy to mention them multiple times throughout the month or we might be able to work out some kind of signage with the short piece to be posted at the installation to give information to the day tourists." Ella heard Cal make a weary sound, but she pressed on, focusing on Maddie. "There's so much going on, do you think you would be able to put on your reporter hat to do those short write-ups to go along with your pictures?"

Maddie nodded. "I think so."

"I'll help if you need me to," Pippa added.

The group worked their way through the list, dividing up the items. The majority of the day's events were installations and preparations for everything that was coming. "This is going to be a constant this month. We don't want to be putting out an article on an event that has already happened. We'll want a teaser piece to print at least the day before, if possible two days before, to draw in as big a crowd as we can get." She turned to look at Katie. "And live online coverage for events as they happen will be a huge draw to hopefully show folks what they're missing and what they can come be a part of, by coming out to visit Hope." Katie nodded and Ella saw Cal behind her, shaking his head.

Ella was about at the end of her rope with him. She glanced down at her notes and turned to glare at Cal. "As for full stories, the biggest thing happening today is the set-up and installation of Santa's Balloon Grotto over at Town Hall." Ella felt Maddie and Pippa suck in some air behind her, but she ignored them and continued, locking eyes with Cal. He wore his own look of defiance.

"It sounds like one of Maddie's installations to me," Cal said.

Ella slowly shook her head. "No, Santa's Balloon Grotto has been a yearly tradition since the 1920s. Paul McIntyre puts it on every year, just like his father before him, and his grandfather before him. It's a *beloved* Hope tradition and there's a very deep story there. Clarence had it earmarked as the front-page piece for tomorrow's paper. So, the clock is ticking on this one. Do you think you can handle it?"

Cal scowled at her. "Yes."

"Great," Ella said. She turned her attention back to the group. "Maddie, you're carrying most of the weight today. Let me know if you need some extra help."

Maddie shrugged. "I've got the contact information for the people putting up all the installations. I'll just schedule twenty minutes with each of them today to get pictures and tape-record a short interview with them. Eleven installations, at twenty minutes each, with transit time between them... about four hours total. Then I can be back here..."

"And I'll help transcribe the write-ups," Pippa said.

Ella nodded. "And I can handle the other three stories."

"You'll have time for that?" Myrna asked, raising an eyebrow.

Ella shrugged. "As much as anyone else has today."

"And I'm just covering some balloon grotto?" Cal asked.

"Yep," Ella said, keeping her voice short. "Paul will probably be at Town Hall when they open..." She glanced down at her watch, "in about five minutes. So you might want to head that way."

Cal spared her one last scowl before going back to his desk for his bag and coat. He caught Ella's eye as he passed by the rest of them on his way to the front door. Ella paused at the expression on his face. His scowl wasn't nearly as intense as it had been, even moments before. It was almost the playful expression he'd worn the night before as they'd helped Bill hang the Christmas lights. What was that about? She didn't have time to dwell on the enigma that was Cal Dickson, so she turned her attention back to the group in front of her.

"Alright everyone, let's get to work," Ella said. Kurt nodded and gave Ella a smile before heading down the hall to the press room.

Marty and Katie were hurrying back to their desks and Myrna smiled and waved at Ella. "I see you've got everything in hand. I'll come back this afternoon to check in with you. I think I'm going to stay in town for a few days until this hangover subsides."

"Days?" Ella asked.

Myrna shook her head. "When you're my age, hangovers can literally hang over for days." Myrna chuckled, immediately looked like she regretted it, and put a hand to her forehead before nodding at Ella and heading for the door.

Ella winked at Myrna and turned to look at Maddie and Pippa.

"Sorry you've got so much on your plate today, Maddie," Ella said.

Maddie grinned. "Honestly, I'm looking forward to having my name on more bylines than Cal's in tomorrow's paper."

"Holy crap," Pippa breathed. Ella turned to look at her. "I can't believe you sent him to the Balloon Grotto."

Ella frowned. "Well, I wasn't about to sacrifice Maddie."

"What do you mean?" Maddie asked.

Pippa grinned at Maddie. "Apparently you've never watched the Balloon Grotto as it was being built."

Maddie frowned and shook her head. "No, growing up here, I've never seen it before it was completed."

Pippa's face split in an evil grin. "The first person to see Paul when he's starting on the Grotto ends up spending the rest of their day blowing up balloons with him. It's impossible to get a word in edgewise with Paul and he's so sweet he's like everybody's grandpa so no one can bear to be mean to him."

"Oh my god, El. You just sent Cal to spend the day with him?"

Ella shrugged. "I thought it might be good for him. Get him in the right spirit for the month. Maybe knock the stick out of his ass."

Pippa snorted. "Tread lightly, Ella, and carry a big stick of your own. I don't know Cal all that well, but he looks like someone who might retaliate."

Ella's expression was deadpan. "What's he going to do? Get me fired? Do you think anyone else would want to steer this cranberry and shit-stuffed circus train?"

Both women shook their heads.

"Alright, I have calls to make," Maddie said. "Eat your heart out Cal Dickson, Maddie Burke is going to write circles around you today."

"That's the spirit," Ella said.

"I need to check some things with Kurt on supply ordering," Pippa said, heading toward the hall.

Ella nodded and after looking around the office, hard at work, she headed back to her office for her bag. She needed to jump on her own assignments for the day.

"Ella?" Katie called from behind her before Ella had made it into her office. Ella turned to find Katie standing with her phone pressed against her chest, muffling her call. "I've got a pissed-off carrier on the line that says he turned in his request for changes to his route to Clarence because I was out sick last week. He apparently has the memory of a goldfish and can't remember exactly what he wrote down. Can you see if the form is somewhere in Clarence's office? The carrier's name is Barry Hines."

Ella nodded. "I'll see if I can find it."

As she turned back to head into her office, she heard Katie return to her phone call and say, "Well, what did we learn about making a copy for ourselves before turning something in, huh?"

Ella smiled and shook her head. Katie wasn't kidding. She didn't take crap from the carriers. Ella sighed when she surveyed the stacks of paper around the office. She needed to find the carrier's form quickly. Already she could feel the day starting to slip away from her as her to-do list got longer. If the carrier had turned the form in recently, logic would dictate it would be near the top of a pile, right?

Ella moved around the desk, side-stepping and climbing over piles as she started sorting through the topmost pages of the loose papers on the floor and kicking herself for knocking them off the desk. She'd been searching for ten minutes when she came across a form that had the name Barry Hines at the top. Yes! Maybe this was a sign from the universe that she could do this. She could . . .

As she was hurrying to get around the stacks behind the desk, she caught her foot on something and stumbled, knocking over stacks of papers as she fell. Years of having an uncoordinated body that had shot up six inches almost overnight in the sixth grade had been preparing her for this exact moment. She'd fallen relaxed, so besides some soreness in her knees and elbows, she was fine. She lay for a moment, letting her forehead rest on the floor. *Thank you, Universe, for keeping me humble and not letting me get a big head about my ability to do this,* she thought. She still had the form in her hand, so she was going to call it a win, despite the mess she'd made. She rolled to her side to look back at what she'd tripped over.

The floor of the old office was made of scarred and stained oak planks. Normally these floors aged well, but even from where she was lying, she could see the rise of a loose floorboard. Ella sighed and got to her hands and knees, before crawling over to study the offending piece of wood. "Oh look, my first OSHA violation spotting. That's one for the baby book," she muttered. The floorboard was almost entirely under the desk, but the edge she'd tripped over, looked as if it had been under a stack of papers for months, possibly years. She could see the stack's outline, bordered by a darker layer of dirt and grime. What had caused the floorboard to come up now? She wasn't the most graceful person she knew, but tearing up a floor just by walking on it was definitely a first for her. She reached down and tugged at the loose board. It came up without much effort. Ella would have immediately shoved it back into place, hoping the floor coming up on her first day wasn't some terrible omen for how her tenure was going to go, but her hand brushed against something beneath the floorboard that made her pause. She held her breath as she set the piece of wood down by her side and reached into the hole. Her hands touched dusty leather, wrapped around a hard frame. A briefcase? Her fingers found a handle that was stiff but finally gave, as she lifted it out of the hole.

She set it on her lap and ran her hands across its surface, clearing away cobwebs and layers upon layers of dust. For a moment, she felt like she needed a hat, a whip, and a catchy theme song to be doing this. The leather was pale, only a shade past tan. It wasn't just dirty. There was a huge stain on the front like something had spilled on it. She turned so she was completely under the desk, but the briefcase was in the light coming from the overhead fluorescents. She stared at the stain and a cold realization slid through her stomach. She knew what that stain was. She knew because of the time she'd stepped on a nail while wearing her dad's deer skin house shoes. The permanent stain on his shoe was the same shade of brown on the briefcase.

Blood.

12

ELLA

"What the hell?" Ella muttered aloud. She hunched over the hole under the floorboard, squinting into the darkness to see if there was anything else down there.

"Any luck?" Katie's voice made Ella jump. She bashed the back of her head on the underside of her desk and let out a string of curse words. "That doesn't sound good." Katie came around the desk just as Ella shoved the blood-stained briefcase and loose floorboard behind her.

She crawled out from under the desk, rubbing the back of her head. "Yeah, sorry, just going through . . ." she glanced around the office, "paperwork."

Katie chuckled. "Better you than me. If this was my office, I'd have brought in gasoline and a match this morning." She glanced down at the paper Ella had bent down to pick up off the floor. "Is that the form?"

"Oh, yeah," Ella said, quickly handing it over to her and doing her best to block Katie's view of what was under the desk. Ella didn't know why, but her first instinct was to avoid any other staff being involved in her little mystery. At least on her first day and on the first day of the month-long battle campaign, they were about to wage.

"Thanks," Katie said with a relieved sigh. "Carriers. Can't live with them, can't kill them . . . legally" She grinned at Ella. "Never tell any of them that I said this, but I tend to think of them all like they were my kids. They just need better structure and boundaries and they'll do ok." Katie winked at Ella, took the form, and headed back out the office door.

Ella heaved a sigh and collapsed into the desk chair. She squinted at the gaping hole in the floor under the desk and then at the blood-stained briefcase. What the hell was it doing there? Did it belong to Clarence? She reached down and turned the briefcase to look at it. Instead of a combination lock, there was a rusty keyhole. It looked old. Really old. Possibly older than Clarence. If he hadn't put it there, who had? Clarence had been at the paper since 1980. Considering how little time it had taken her to find the hidey-hole in the floor, she was pretty sure Clarence had known about it, being the office's occupant for forty years.

"You're still here?" Pippa's voice called from the doorway. Ella glanced up at her. She frowned at Pippa. Pippa looked confused. "I thought you were going to cover those last three events."

Ella shot out of her chair. "Right! Yeah, I'm heading out now."

Pippa grinned. "We'll hold the fort." With a Wonder Woman-style, across her chest salute, she grinned and walked away. As soon as she was gone, Ella pulled on her coat, grabbed her phone, notebook, and pens, and then, before she could talk herself out of it, she grabbed the briefcase and replaced the floorboard.

She had to stop by De-Floured to interview Miss Mandie about her holiday season treats, interview Mrs. Thompson about her yearly door-to-door mistletoe delivery, and cover the Fire Station's annual holiday safety speech. Between the fire station and the Girl Scouts, Hope was one of the most well-informed places in the country about safety during the holiday season. She could probably recite the Fire Chief's speech in her sleep, but they'd expect the paper to cover it. And, it just so happened that Clarence's house was a block away from the fire station, according to the staff file Myrna had left on his desk. Ella wrote Clarence's address down on the palm of her hand, swung the strap of her shoulder bag over her head, and picked up the briefcase, turning the stained side toward her and hoping no one else in the office would notice or ask about it as she headed out.

Maybe it was the investigative journalist in her that was pausing and lifting her nose to sniff the wind, catching the faintest whiff of a story, or, maybe like the rest of Hope, she was just being nosy. Either way, she was going to find out the story behind the briefcase and maybe the reason for Clarence's sudden retirement if he was in a chatty mood. She didn't want to admit it with everything else that was going on, but that was a question that had presented itself to her, oh so helpfully, at 3 am that morning and made it hard for her to return to her dream about eating her way out of a ball pit filled with Skittles. What was up with Clarence? Sure, the Christmas season was hell for the Hope locals, but quitting suddenly after forty years in the same job seemed a bit extreme.

She waved to Pippa, Marty, and Katie on her way out the door. Maddie was already gone and of course, so was Cal. She smiled to herself. Depending on Cal's lung capacity, he would be somewhere between inflating his fifteenth and one-hundredth balloon at that very moment. Served him right for not giving back her mug and having the audacity to be smug about it. Maybe that was what he needed. A "smug mug". She could patent it and sell a million of them. Probably to everyone who had ever met Cal Dickson.

"Miss Mandie," Ella called when she walked through the front door of the bakery. The morning rush had died away and only a handful of customers sat quietly at the cafe-style tables, drinking tea or coffee, reading the paper, and doing the crossword. They all looked up, smiled, and nodded at Ella before returning their attention to whatever they were drinking or reading.

"Ella," Miss Mandie said, as she came through the kitchen door behind the counter, wiping her hands on her apron. "About time you made it by. Don't tell me you've been hung up at those god-awful topiaries in front of the library or talking to Eudora Thompson about her fascination with the lower half of the male physique. Though, I guess I can't really throw any rocks from my glass house on that front."

Ella grinned. "No, sorry. I was just delayed by boring office work. I haven't been to see Mrs. Thompson yet and Maddie is covering the topiaries."

"Well, tell Eudora to come find me when she zeros in on the beefcake she's going to ask to hang the mistletoe over my front door. I'll give her a free scone to let me size him up alongside her." Miss Mandie opened a drawer and pulled out a piece of paper.

Ella nodded. "Will do."

"That's a good girl," Miss Mandie said with a wink. She passed the paper to Ella. "Now, this is my holiday menu. I knew you'd be up to your ears in it today, so to save you time, I've printed out all my holiday specials for you. I'm working on my selfie skills and I want to be able to pick a flattering photo, so I'll email that over to you later. Bart said he'd show me how to do the email from my phone when he comes in this afternoon."

Ella raised an eyebrow. "Bart? You mean Bart Lofland?"

"Yeah. He works for me now. Good kid. He can frost a dozen Double D-elicious cupcakes in the time it used to take me to do one. And his fondant skills are incredible."

Ella decided against mentioning that Bart was probably so good with frosting boob-shaped cupcakes and making fondant nipple rings because he'd had years of studying the subject matter, most likely in magazines and on various computer screens.

"Hey, Miss Mandie," Ella said, struck by a sudden jolt of inspiration. "It's going to be a long month. Can I make a standing order with you to have a dozen assorted goodies, your choice as to what they are, put together for the paper every morning moving forward? I have a feeling the troops are going to need sustenance. And if they look festive and enticing, all the better."

Miss Mandie beamed. "Why of course, Ella. And I'll make sure they're things that everyone would want to put in their mouth."

"Bonus points," Ella snorted. "I can pay ahead or pay as we go," she said, reaching for her wallet.

Miss Mandie shook her head. "We can settle up at the end of the month."

With a final thanks and farewell, Ella left the shop and started looking around the town square for Mrs. Thompson. It didn't take her long to spot her. The hardest part was keeping a straight face while Mrs. Thompson talked about finding true love at Christmas and the joy in all the young people she hoped her door-to-door mistletoe would evoke. It was especially hard to take her seriously as her eyes kept wandering to the nearest man that passed them. Finally, Ella got her to stand in front of the gazebo, holding a basket of her mistletoe and she took a picture with her phone. She thanked Mrs. Thompson, and took off for the fire station, power-walking toward Evergreen Avenue. The mystery of the briefcase resurfaced in her mind as it bumped gently against her leg.

She passed Town Hall and she couldn't stop the grin on her face when she saw Paul McIntyre's truck full of the wire panels used as structure in the Balloon Grotto. *Hope you're having a good time, Cal.*

Unfortunately, it seemed that karma had heard her because when she got to the fire station, expecting to see Andy Waters, the slow-talking, doe-eyed veteran Fire Chief, she was greeted instead by Rudy "Red" Callahan.

"Ella Danforth as I live and breath," Red said, waggling his blond eyebrows at her. Red was a natural redhead and he would have been good-looking if it wasn't for the fact that he was a total ass. "I never thought I'd see you step foot back in Hope," Red continued. "Didn't you tell all of us that you'd never come back?"

"That was the plan," Ella muttered. "Now, should I be interviewing you about the holiday safety measures or . . ."

"What happened," Red asked, his smile growing wider, smug sarcasm coating every word. "Couldn't hack it in the real world so you had to come back to Hope?"

"I don't know," Ella said, finally losing her temper. "Is that why you're here?"

"I'm the Fire Chief here," Red said. "I succeeded."

Ella heaved a weary sigh. "And I'm very happy for you. Now, are you going to tell me about holiday safety or do I need to talk to someone else? I'm sure that being the Fire Chief has you very busy and that even your newest rookie recruit could give the interview without a problem."

At that suggestion, Red scowled at her before finally relenting and rattling off his safety spiel. Ella jotted down some notes and he posed in front of Hope's only fire engine, which was really a glorified pick-up truck that had been outfitted with a three hundred gallon tank, ladders, and hoses.

"So, are you . . . seeing anyone?" Red asked when the interview was over.

"Bye, Red," Ella called, heading out the front door.

She knew he hadn't asked because he was actually interested in her. It was because Hope was a town of three thousand people with a third being over the age of fifty, a third under the age of eighteen, and the last third being mostly married and parents of the under-eighteen third. Hope was a place for families. There wasn't a lot it had to offer someone living the single lifestyle. Well, except for the good-natured, but annoying rumor-mill/matchmaking industry.

Ella left the fire station and walked down the block, double-checking the address she'd written on her palm. She came to a stop in front of 340 N. Evergreen. It was a small bungalow with dark green paint and tan trim. She had a single vague memory of delivering Girl Scout cookies to Clarence here. Usually, she had delivered them to the newspaper office, but for some reason, on one occasion, she'd brought them to his house. The lawn could use mowing and there was a leaf-filled birdbath next to the paved walkway leading to the front door, but nothing that advertised that the owner of the house had recently gone around the bend. Ella tightened her grip on the briefcase and headed up the front walkway.

Before she could talk herself out of it, she rang the doorbell. She heard it echo through the house. She waited. No one came to the door. She hesitated, but the journalist in her was nagging at her to get the story behind the blood-stained briefcase, and hopefully Clarence's sudden departure. She leaned on the doorbell again. This time she heard the beginning of the ring echo inside the house, but it was silenced suddenly as if someone had cut its power.

Frowning, Ella reached up and knocked on the front door. "Clarence? It's Ella Danforth. Can you open the door?" She paused. There was silence from inside the house. "Clarence?"

The clack of the mail slot in the front door, opening from the inside, made her jump.

"Go away," a voice rasped. Before she could answer, there was a metallic click from the other side of the door.

"Clarence?" She squatted down to eye level with the mail slot and pushed on the flap of metal. It didn't budge. He'd locked it from the inside. "Wait! Clarence, I just want to ask you about something!"

But Ella's pleas were only answered with silence.

13

ELLA

Ella wasn't about to give up that easily. She reached for the doorknob, though she knew it was most likely a futile gesture. If the man had locked his mail slot, he'd certainly locked his front door. When it didn't turn, she wasn't surprised, but the frustration in Ella from the events of the last two days, the stress of worrying about where her life was headed, wondering if she was going to die alone in her childhood room at her mom's house, or if Les had made things official with Wendi and the pair of them were happy and having a laugh at her expense, combined with the weird tension and friction with Cal, and it all came bubbling to the surface. She twisted the unyielding knob and threw her shoulder against the door.

"Open up, Clarence," Ella called.

"Ella? What the hell are you doing?"

Karma, the nosy a-hole it so often was, must have been listening to her mental list of stressors and decided to conjure one right behind her. Cal was hurrying up the walkway to Clarence's front door. He wasn't wearing a jacket . . . again. Seriously, who dressed like that on a Pacific Northwest island in December? She could see his jacket, slung over his shoulder bag, mere inches away. Were jackets just *accessories* where he came from?

His dark hair was tousled and his shirt was rolled at the sleeves again. His top three buttons were undone, exposing the tan skin around his clavicle. For a second, Ella had the insane urge to reach out and run a finger along the ridge, just to see if his skin was as smooth as it looked. Immediately, she wished she could kick herself in the brain. Where did that thought come from? It had to just be the stress. She immediately yanked her gaze up to Cal's face.

He was studying the house. "Is Clarence in there?"

"I . . . I think so," Ella said. She stared at Cal. "What are you doing here?"

"Walking back to the office after my 'assignment'," Cal said, glaring at her. "There's a shortcut down Aspen Way that comes out just behind the newspaper office so you don't have to walk through the center of town to get back."

"I knew that," Ella said. Now that he said it she remembered taking Aspen on her bike when she worked at the paper in the summer, but in the years since, she'd forgotten about it.

"Thank you, by the way," Cal muttered, "for such an enlightening assignment. I think it'll be a week before I can feel my face again."

Ella rolled her eyes. "You're so dramatic." Then she frowned. "It's still early. How did you finish so fast?"

Cal raised an eyebrow at her. "So, you knew when you gave me the assignment that it would mean I'd spend most of the day blowing up balloons?"

Ella felt herself smile, so she ducked her head and shrugged. "It's a rite of passage. I had to cover the Grotto when I was in high school. The trick to getting the feeling back in your face is to do some Donald Duck impersonations and slap yourself a lot. The blood flow will come back in no time. Feel free to start now, I won't mind. I'll just see you back at the office when I'm..."

"What are you doing here, anyway?" Cal asked.

Ella sighed. "I needed to see Clarence."

Cal crossed his arms. "Well apparently he doesn't need to see you."

Ella ignored him, picked up the briefcase and stalked around the side of Clarence's house. His backyard wasn't fenced but the grass behind the house was twice as long as the grass in front.

"Clarence has a mullet lawn," Cal said, high-stepping through the tall grass.

"What are you doing?" Ella asked, watching Cal's strange gait as he searched the grass at his feet.

"I don't want to step on anything," Cal muttered.

"Anything like what?" Ella asked. "Does Clarence have a dog?"

"No," Cal said. "Not that I'm aware of."

"Are you afraid of stepping on a Washington winter rattler?" Ella asked.

Cal paused and looked back at her. "Those don't exist, do they?" Ella raised an eyebrow at him. He glared at her. "I was more worried about stepping on a rake or something."

"Don't worry," Ella muttered. "I'm sure that if there's a rake buried in this yard, I'll take it to the face before you do. Karma and I are not on speaking terms at the moment."

Cal was quiet for a minute as they moved to Clarence's small back stoop. Ella knocked on the door and waited. Silence. She knocked again.

"Clarence, it's just Ella Danforth and Cal," she called.

"Cal Dickson," Cal corrected her.

She turned to look at him. "How many Cals does he know?"

Cal gave her an incredulous look. "I don't know. How many 'Ella's does he know? Why did you say *your* last name?"

"Because I don't live here anymore," Ella said.

"I think you're in denial. Your job and the fact that you're living at your mom and stepdad's house say you do," Cal muttered.

"My mom's house," Ella snapped. "Bill moved in with her when they got married."

Cal gave her a strange look which she ignored. She headed back down the stoop and started toward one of the windows on the backside of the house.

"What . . . are you going to crawl through a window now?" Cal asked.

"Something's wrong," Ella said. "I can feel it."

Cal sighed. "Or, he just doesn't want to talk to us. I mean, we are the press after all, and if there's one thing I've learned from living in this town for the last six months, it's that anything out of the ordinary rates a story.

And everyone in town is going to want to know why Clarence quit. If I was him I wouldn't-."

Ella was only half-listening to Cal's muttering behind her. She'd come to a bald patch of muddy lawn near one of the windows on the backside of the house. She paused when she saw what was in the mud. Cal hadn't seen it yet and he was still walking toward the window.

"Stop!" She barked at him. She threw out an arm to stop him from stepping in the mud and disturbing it. Her hand slid across his smooth cotton shirt, cool from the December air, but with an underlying warmth from the hard-muscled abdomen underneath. Cal stopped his muttering mid-sentence and for a full minute, the two of them just stood there. Ella's hand was still on Cal's abs.

Get your hand off of him, Helga and El screamed at her inside her head. It took her hand longer than it should have to comply.

"Sorry," she said, wishing she could disappear on the spot when she heard her voice crack. To cover up the awkward moment and try to maintain some shred of her dignity, she pointed down at the muddy earth trying to distract Cal's attention and her own inappropriate thoughts away from the awkward moment. "Look."

"What is that? Footprints?" Cal asked, squatting down to study the impressions. He looked around. "You think Clarence made them?"

Ella glanced from the footprints to the window. "You think he was spying on himself? The footprints go up to that window."

Cal shrugged. "Maybe he locked himself out and that window's easy to get open." He closed his eyes as soon as he said it, realizing what he'd just done. But, it was too late. Ella was already moving. She side-stepped the muddy patch with the footprints and hugged the side of the house, reaching above her head to grab onto the windowsill.

"I'm too short," Ella muttered.

"That must be a new experience for you."

She glared at him over her shoulder. "You can go, you know. You don't need to stay." She turned back to the house, gripped the window sill, and moved her sneakers up the house's siding, trying to find a foothold so she could scale up enough to look in the window.

Cal heaved a weary sigh. "Hang on, let me help." She heard him move in behind her, but she still wasn't ready for the feeling of his warm hands around her waist. She almost lost her grip on the window sill at the sensation. He was quiet as he used his grip to lift her before quickly moving his hands downward. He almost dropped her, trying to skip over her lower half until he had her around the knees. When she was sitting on his shoulder, he moved her closer to the window.

"Th-thanks," she managed to grind out, gritting her teeth to prevent the escape of any other sound. She hadn't realized what a barren desert, devoid of any physical touch beyond a quick peck on the lips the last three months with Les had been. She took a deep breath and tried to steady herself. Clarence. They were here to check on Clarence. She needed to ask him about the briefcase among other things. If she had to do it in front of Cal, she guessed that couldn't be helped. "I-," her voice cracked, and she tried again. "I remember Clarence is a tall guy, but I think this window might be too high for even Clarence to crawl through on his own." Cal held her steady enough for her to cup her hands around her eyes to try to see inside. She was staring in at an empty bedroom. No Clarence. She knocked on the window. "Clarence! Clarence, are you there? We just want to talk!" She twisted, trying to see through the bedroom's open door and she felt Cal's hand move to steady her. Unfortunately, to keep her from falling, he had to put a hand on her ass. She jerked in surprise, feeling the warm heat soaking into her skin through her skinny jeans. She heard Cal let out a groan and wobble backward. She tried to grip the windowsill to keep from falling, but she missed, and they both crashed to the ground.

They lay still for a moment, trying to suck back in the air that had been knocked out of them. Ella was on top of Cal, her back partially on his chest and shoulder. She could feel his fingers curled into her side and his hip bone under her ass. She turned her head to look at Cal and make sure he wasn't dead and she realized their faces were almost nose to nose. Helga and El were once again united, screaming at her to get the hell off of him, but she was still too winded to move "Are you ok?" she gasped.

"Yeah," Cal wheezed. "Yeah, I'm fine."

Ella looked closer at Cal's face. Around his lips, the skin looked red and angry. She could see tiny blisters forming at the corners of his mouth. "Your mouth," she croaked, her voice starting to come back to her. "Did that just happen today?" A horrifying thought hit her. "The balloons," she whispered. "Are you allergic to latex?"

Color was rising in Cal's cheeks. "I said I'm fine."

Oxygen was starting to make its way through her lungs to the rest of her body and she rolled off him as quickly as she could. She staggered to her feet just as Cal pulled himself into a sitting position. She held a hand out to him and after a moment's consideration, he took it and let her help pull him up.

Ella didn't miss the unfamiliar, but not unwelcome warmth of his palm against hers. *Stop it, Ella*, Helga growled. *Get a hold of yourself. That was probably sexual harassment, falling on him like that. And you're his boss. And it's your first day.*

She glanced up to see Cal watching her. "Are *you* ok?" He asked. "You didn't hit your head or anything, did you? Because for a minute there, it looked like you were having a whole conversation inside your head."

"Yeah," Ella muttered. "I do that."

"So, I take it you didn't see Clarence?" Cal asked, glancing up at the window and wincing as he put a hand to the back of his neck.

Ella shook her head. "No."

He frowned at the house. "Maybe he just doesn't want to see anyone."

"Because that's completely normal," Ella said. "To just up and quit your job one day and then shut out everyone you know."

Cal's frown hardened as he turned to look at Ella. "We don't know what's going on with Clarence. But, I'm sure he'll tell us when he's ready. Or he won't. It's his business."

Ella scowled at him, but she decided to keep her thoughts to herself. Cal turned away from her, moving his hand to rub his lower back. His shirt had come up and she saw the muscles under tan skin flexing as he shifted his weight.

"What did I fall on? It felt like a brick." Cal stared down at the grass and Ella realized a second too late what Cal was looking at. She couldn't get to it fast enough. Cal bent down and picked up the briefcase. "What's this?"

"That's mine," Ella said quickly, reaching out to take it from him.

Cal spun away from her, holding the briefcase up to look at it more closely. "What's this stain?"

"Coffee," Ella said, blurting out the first thing that came to mind. Cal lifted it to his nose. What? Was he *smelling* it?

"It doesn't smell like coffee," Cal said.

"Well, I like unscented coffee," Ella said. "Can I have it back, please?"

Cal stared at Ella and she gave an involuntary shiver. The blue in his eyes was currently overpowering the green as his icy gaze scanned her face. Finally, he held the briefcase out to her. "I'll see you back at the office." There was no emotion in his voice. He turned away from her, heading around the side of Clarence's house without a backward glance.

It took Ella a few minutes longer to compose herself. She sat down on Clarence's back stoop and tried to untangle her thoughts. There were the "confusion and fear over why Clarence wouldn't talk to them or even open his door" thoughts. Then, there were the "bloody briefcase" thoughts, jumbled together with the questions she wanted to ask Clarence about why he'd really left the paper. To be honest, the two things were most likely not related at all, especially if Clarence had no connection to the briefcase, but some piece of innate journalist logic told her they were.

And to top it off, all of these strings of thought were being suffocated at the moment by her skin reliving the sensation of Cal's hands around her waist, her legs, her butt. The feeling of being on top of him, nose to nose. She closed her eyes and rested her forehead on her bent knees. What was she doing? This was insane. Cal *hated* her, so of course, he would be the guy that fate would have her be attracted to. Awesome. And it was her first day on the job, with a month of hell at work yet to come. *Way to start strong, Ella.* She wanted to berate Helga and El for letting it happen but the two seemed to have conveniently picked that moment to step out for a smoke break.

As she got to her feet, she did a body check for soreness from the fall. She felt pretty good. Having Cal break her fall had no doubt saved her some aches and pains. Unfortunately, there was one ache that she couldn't shake. It was the pain that had washed over her at the cold tone in his voice when he'd told her he'd see her back at the office and then walked away as if they'd just passed each other in the hall. As if nothing had happened in the twenty minutes before.

And his poor face. If he really was allergic to latex, he could have died. If he'd known he had the allergy, surely he wouldn't have agreed to help Paul blow up his balloons. It would have been a perfect excuse to get out of it. But he'd done it anyway. He must not have known.

"Well, at least I can do something about that," Ella said to the empty backyard. She checked the time on her phone. She had time to hit Willoby's Drug Store before going back to the office. Not that she was overly excited to be face to face with him again today after their . . . encounter. She squeezed her eyes shut. *Get it together, El. We've got work to do.*

14

CAL

Cal couldn't walk away from Clarence's house fast enough. He needed to clear his head. He headed for the shortcut back to the office but then veered off to walk a loop around the neighborhood. There was too much nervous energy coursing through him to sit and type. He needed to walk it off. He slowed his pace so he could think.

What the hell had just happened? His brain was tangled Christmas lights, scotch, Ella's face, and the story he needed to write.

He'd never admit it to Ella, but he'd actually enjoyed his morning with Paul. Being an island old-timer, Paul knew enough stories to outfit a historian or a journalist for a lifetime. Yeah, blowing up thousands of balloons had been a pain in the ass, but he'd done it. He'd been at it for hours when he'd realized his face was sore. But, he just figured it was from blowing up so many of the rubbery bastards. He'd been in a pretty good mood going down Evergreen when he'd heard Ella yelling and spotted her banging on Clarence's front door. If he was honest, he'd thought about going to see Clarence a half dozen times over the last day and a half, but he figured Clarence would call him if he wanted to talk. He'd be lying if he said he wasn't interested in hearing what Clarence had to say about Ella Danforth taking over for him. In retrospect though, he should have just kept walking and gone back to the office. Then, he wouldn't have . . .

An involuntary rush of heat rolled over Cal. He could still feel the soft fabric of her shirt against his palms and the warmth of her skin underneath and those legs and . . .

The echoing wheeze of the horn in the gazebo boomed through the air. He heard groans and curses muttered from islanders that passed him on their way down the street, but Cal was almost thankful for the distraction. He tried to clear his head. *She's your boss, Cal. She's the woman that just waltzed in and was handed the job as if you hadn't been the one working your ass off for the last five months.* Still, after watching her with the rest of the staff that morning, he had to admit, she wasn't half bad at the job. But, it *was* only her first day. He hadn't seen how she did under real pressure yet.

And then there was the way she'd acted about that briefcase. That nagged at Cal. What was she hiding? That briefcase was old and dirty. And the stain . . . Cal wasn't a cop or anything, but he'd bet his dad's net worth that the stain on the cracked, pale leather was blood. The question was, whose blood? And what was Ella doing with it? Where had she gotten it? He doubted it was hers. It was bulky and old. Not something he'd expect someone like Ella Danforth to own.

He gave an involuntary full-body shiver remembering the feeling of her lying on top of him. When she'd turned her head to look at him, almost nose to nose, the white-blonde hair from her ponytail trailing across the side of her neck, and her eyes so dark, like the sky over a stormy sea . . . for one maddening second, he'd had the insane urge to kiss her.

But it *was* insanity. Cal shook his head. Just the result of being alone for so long. It had been six months since he'd even been that close to a woman. He ran a hand through his hair. One of the things he liked best about Hope was the lack of single women that were looking to land themselves a husband. Something that was a welcome change from the New York social circle that he was the square peg in. There were a few single women in Hope, but there were more single guys on the island. And they were more friendly and amenable to involvement than he was. For six months, Cal had had peace. No Tara, no . . . distractions. Why did it have to start now?

He scowled at the pavement under his feet as he moved down the sidewalk. It had to be some kind of anomaly. There were only a handful of single women on the island to begin with and two of them worked at the paper. Now, three with Ella. Though, he wasn't entirely sure she *was* single. She'd moved from Seattle pretty quickly, according to what he'd overheard between Myrna, Pippa, and Maddie. But, maybe she'd left with the promise to go back and see her significant other on the weekends or something. The thought left an unexplained bad taste in his mouth. That was probably it. She'd be Editor-in-Chief and not even around half the time.

He cut across the back alley behind the paper and pulled open the man-door next to the loading dock. He waved to Kurt and his crew but didn't bother calling to him over the noise of the press. Besides the hum from the machines, the office was quiet when he came down the hallway past the break room. He subconsciously straightened his shirt and ran a hand through his hair again. Now that he was inside, the sides of his mouth were starting to sting. He stepped into the men's room, looked at himself in the mirror, and stifled a groan. God, he looked like he had herpes. The angry red blisters that had broken out on the corners of his mouth were hideous. How had Ella been able to lay so close to him? A twinge of annoyance shot through him, remembering the look of pity on her face.

Pity was something he did not need. He could feel his jaw beginning to clench remembering the look of pity Tara had given him when he'd bared his soul to her. It hadn't been the first time he'd seen that look from Tara either. The look was always covering something deeper, something calculating. If Ella was considering the same, maybe the sooner he left and went back to New York, the better. At least with Tara . . . Well, the devil you know . . .

The door to Clarence's old office was closed when he went by. He didn't pause to look in the window at Ella, but he stopped behind his chair and stared at the pink bottle and small white cardboard box sitting on the desk in front of it. Calamine lotion and a box of Benadryl. There was a neon green sticky note stuck to the box. He picked it up and stared at the chicken scratch handwriting that he guessed belonged to Ella. *"I'm so sorry about the balloons. I hope this helps. - Ella"*

Cal just stared at the items for a moment. Why? What was her game? He paused and tried to force himself to remove the cynical New Yorker filter. He'd been mostly successful in keeping it on the shelf when he interacted with the rest of the town, but Ella? There was something about her that put him on his guard. He tried to think of the gesture, just as it was. Lotion and Benadryl. Did she really just do it out of concern for his health? It wouldn't be out of character for any regular Hope Islander to do this for someone they barely knew, but coming from Ella, who as far as he could tell, despised him, he wasn't entirely convinced.

He moved the box and bottle to one side and set his laptop down in front of his chair. He slumped onto the seat and started typing up his story, pausing every five or ten minutes to look at the little bottle and the box. By the time he finished his first draft, the stinging itch around his mouth and lips was becoming unbearable. He finally broke down and took the calamine lotion into the bathroom to dab it onto the blisters. The relief was almost instantaneous. For good measure, he chased it with a dose of Benadryl and went back to work.

He glanced up when Ella and Katie came out of Clarence's (now Ella's) office. They were in deep discussion about Coach Hendricks and the high school basketball team members as potential insert stuffers and possibly some new carriers. Cal went back to work, expecting to see Ella return to her office alone. He kept typing. Still no Ella. He wasn't sure exactly why he was waiting for her to return to her office, but a slight annoyance was building inside him the longer it took her to materialize and pass by. When she didn't come back after twenty minutes, he got to his feet and looked around the front part of the office as casually as he could. Pippa was the only one at her desk.

"Did the boss step out?" Cal asked, trying to sound as if he didn't really care.

Pippa glanced up at him. "No, but I saw Katie leave. I think Ella is going to be leaving soon though."

"Knocking off early?" Cal asked, forcing a smile.

Pippa shook her head. "No, she's going over to the high school to talk to Greta Myers, the counselor. She told me she wants to start a program to help students find part-time employment for resume building before graduation."

Cal raised his eyebrows in surprise. "Oh, to be additional carriers?"

Pippa nodded. "And stuffers for the ad inserts. But maybe eventually cover some stories here and there." She paused and gave Cal a sly grin. "Why? You keeping tabs on her?"

"No," Cal said quickly. "I just figured she'd want to review this article before it went to layout."

Pippa shrugged. "Maybe. Ella's never really been a micromanager. You can send it to me if you just want a second set of eyes on it."

Cal nodded, just wanting the conversation to end. "Sure." He turned and went back to his desk. He reread his article with more diligence than he normally would as he tried to keep his thoughts away from the quickly forming enigma that was Ella Danforth.

He made sure all of his open articles were ready to go, but he didn't send them to Pippa. A plan was forming in Cal's mind. He'd send them to Ella first thing in the morning. If she took the time to read them, he'd know she was going to be reviewing his work. How much feedback she gave him would give him some more insight into the kind of person she was; how critical, open, how much she trusted those she worked with, or how much she'd try to bend the voice of the paper to her will.

It was after six when he finally packed up to head home. Pippa was sitting with Maddie, reviewing photos and the short installation pieces. Cal paused as he went past them. They both looked up.

"Yes?" Maddie finally asked.

"Do you two need any help? I've got some time, I could probably . . ."

"Thanks," Maddie said with a smile. "But we've got it."

Pippa nodded. "Enjoy that extra time. I saw tomorrow's schedule of events. Savor your freedom because you may not get another dose of it this month."

Cal gave her a tight smile and headed out. Hope was a red and green ant farm around him as he moved through the square, heading for his apartment. The air was cold, but thanks to the calamine, Benadryl, or a combination of the two, his face wasn't on fire. It was hard to be annoyed when he was surrounded by the bustle of this small town he'd come to love. But without his annoyance to distract him, it was a lot harder to keep his mind off of Ella Danforth.

***

Unfortunately, Cal's usual regime of British TV, Nick Cave on vinyl, and (as a last resort) biographies on dead politicians had all failed to put him to sleep. He'd spent the night tossing and turning because every time he closed his eyes, there was Ella's face, her nose inches from his, asking him if he was ok. He finally fell asleep just before the sun came up and when he woke a couple of hours later, he was seriously late for work. He was running down the back stairs to the street in front of his apartment ten minutes after he woke up. He held the top of his messenger bag in one hand while he sprinted across the square to the *Hornblower* office. His anxiety ratcheted up another notch when he got inside and found Pippa, Katie, and Marty working at their desks.

"Morning," Pippa said, glancing up at Cal before returning to the stack of invoices in front of her.

"Morning," Cal answered, craning his neck enough to see that the light was off in Ella's office. "No boss this morning?"

"Oh, she's been here and gone," Pippa said.

"Taking the day off?" Cal asked, hopefully.

"No," Pippa said, frowning at him. "Today's the big Christmas Cookie Bake-Off over at De-Floured. It started at seven-thirty. She'll be back after. The rest of the events are this afternoon, one on top of the other, so she thought you might need the morning to finish your other stories and clear the decks before you dive in."

"They're done," Cal muttered. "I could have covered the bake-off."

Pippa shrugged. "I told her that, but she insisted on letting you pass on this one. She took Maddie with her to get some pictures." She shook her head. "I'll bet it's a madhouse over there."

Cal nodded absent-mindedly, not really listening to what Pippa was saying. How had he missed a madhouse crowd at De-Floured? He lived right above the place. He'd taken the side exit and De-Floured was normally pretty busy in the morning . . . Still, something about Ella covering the big event for the day made Cal feel like a slacker. He headed down the hallway toward the press room, glancing back once to see if the other three were watching him. They were all working, heads down, oblivious to what he was doing. He headed out the back door past Kurt and his team who were prepping the machines for the day and cleaning up broken wraps left behind by the carriers after they'd taken their morning haul of papers. He jogged down the back alley and around the corner of the building before taking off, back across the town square toward De-Floured.

Madhouse was putting it mildly. The place was a rave, fueled by confectioner's sugar and Michael Buble's Christmas album. And possibly cooking sherry, he thought, as a woman bumped into him, blushed, and blew him a kiss before bustling over to the friends calling to her.

"One minute remaining in the speed-fondling, sorry, speed-fumbling . . . speed-fondant and decorating competition!" Miss Mandie roared over the crowd. "Put those final touches on your dangling balls and get ready to flash them!"

Cal glanced at the cookies the nearest table was rapidly frosting and throwing sprinkles at. Two cookies. A pair of round ornaments. Pink icing, red and brown, and yellow long sprinkles. Not exactly Christmas-themed, but definitely not out of place at De-Floured. He couldn't suppress the snort of laughter that fought its way out of him as he picked up snippets of conversations from the contestants.

"Now they just look wrinkly," one woman slurred as she frowned at the cookies. "They need to look more festive."

"Edna, they look like a ballsack. How are we supposed to make them more festive?" another woman asked.

"Here," a third one passed her a piece of green fondant, "put a bow on them."

"Hold this, will you?" A woman moving past Cal thrust a glass into his hand. He could smell the tequila. Whether it was on her breath or wafting out of the glass, he couldn't be sure. No, not cooking sherry; these women were fueled by Miss Mandie's Tequila Sunrises. A laugh echoed through the room, standing out over the general drunken merriment around him. It wasn't because it was unpleasant or loud. It was just . . . familiar. He glanced up to see Ella standing behind the counter being harassed by Miss Mandie. He side-stepped a woman pushing her way through the crowd, carrying a bowl of sprinkles in each hand just as another woman side-swiped him, shoving him into one of the columns by the front counter. He was half-hidden behind the column and trying to plot a course around the crush of tipsy, sprinkle-throwing women when he heard Maddie say his name. He leaned forward enough to see around the column and catch a view of Maddie standing next to Ella and Miss Mandie.

"I thought you'd have Cal covering this," Maddie said with a chuckle.

Ella shook her head. "And then deal with his passive-aggressive antics all day? No thanks."

Maddie nudged Ella. "He's not really like that."

"Could have fooled me," he heard her mutter.

Maddie sighed. "Can you really blame him for being a little ticked off? I mean, he's been waiting on Clarence hand and foot at the paper, writing all the articles, covering most of the events and then here comes this townie girl back home to the island who swoops in and gets the top job instead of him."

Ella's eyes widened and she frowned at Maddie. "But if he knew . . ."

Maddie rolled her eyes. "Yeah, if he knew everything the job entailed this month, he wouldn't want it, but it still doesn't change the fact that he didn't get it."

"So . . . what," Ella said, "it's just male pride and ego at this point? That's why he's decided to wear his ass for a hat?"

Maddie raised an eyebrow at her. "It's not as if you're being all that mature in the situation either, Cranberry Sauce."

Ella squeezed her eyes shut. "Jesus, can we just forget about the damn cranberry sauce? I still have nightmares."

"Fine," Maddie said with a grin, wrapping her arm around Ella. "Just, cut him some slack. Do the 'putting him in your shoes' thing . . . or wait . . ."

"Putting him in my shoes?" Ella asked, grinning at Maddie.

"You know what I mean. Just try to get along with him."

Ella sighed. "It won't matter. He doesn't *want* to get along."

"One of you is eventually going to have to level with the other . . . in a *non*-combative way," Maddie finished, raising her voice to cover Ella's protest.

"Well, it won't be me," Ella muttered, crossing her arms. "If he wants peace, he'll have to start by giving back my mug."

"Very mature," Maddie grumbled.

Miss Mandie had been chatting with a woman at the counter but as the woman headed back to her table, Miss Mandie turned again to face Maddie and Ella. The older woman was clutching a half-empty glass of orange juice which was also wearing half her lipstick. She put an arm around Ella and slurred, "I have to say Ella, I was surprised when you came home with no ring on your finger or even a bun in your oven. How is it that a girl that looks like you has managed to outrun the marriage lasso *and* the car seat bear traps?"

"Pure animal magnetism," Ella muttered.

"So, is there a guy?" Miss Mandie asked. "Normally I wouldn't pry but I'm all hopped up on sugar and booze at the moment and I just *gots to know*." Maddie ducked as Miss Mandie swung her glass out, sloshing some of its contents on the counter top. Cal saw Maddie and Ella exchange a look. Ella was wary and Maddie looked pained.

"Nope, no guy," Ella said. She quickly turned her attention to grabbing the glass in Miss Mandie's hand. "I'm actually in the market for an apartment and a little birdie named Pippa said you might be renting out the apartment upstairs."

Miss Mandie nodded, her head bouncing like a bobble head in her partially inebriated state. "It's not available yet, but come January . .

.″ She trailed off, studying her almost empty glass in her hand. "I swear I filled this thing up. Didn't I have a full drink a minute ago? I should get a refill."

"Hey, Miss Mandie, I think it's been a minute," Ella said, quickly, still trying to distract her enough to get the glass out of her hand. "Shouldn't you call a halt so the judges can get started?"

Miss Mandie chuckled, turning her attention back to the arguing groups of decorators. "Eh, I always say one minute at the five-minute mark. Makes them speed up. Then you can really separate the drunk from the desperate. The drunks slow down, while the desperate ones speed up."

"Like life," Maddie said. "Or . . . something."

"Are you sure *you* haven't been sneaking Tequila Sunrises?" Ella asked her.

Maddie shook her head. "No, just gobs and gobs of frosting. Here, try some."

She shoved a bowl of white frosting toward Ella. Ella shook her head. "None for me, I'm driving."

Miss Mandie chuckled. "Try it. It's my famous buttercream. You can't write about the Great Hope Cookie Bake-Off without sampling at least the frosting."

Ella rolled her eyes and looked around. "Well, I'm gonna need a spoon or something."

"No you don't," Miss Mandie said. "That's the end of the bowl, just use your finger."

"Yeah, Ella, just suck it up and use your finger," Maddie added.

Ella sighed and swiped a long finger through the frosting. She raised it to her lips and Cal felt his heart stop beating in his chest as she licked the frosting off her finger, groaned in ecstasy, and ran the tip of her tongue along her upper lip to check for any traces left behind.

"I'll take that," the woman who had thrust the drink at Cal plucked it back from his hand. The movement seemed to catch Ella's eye and she turned her head, locking eyes with him, just as her tongue made its final swipe across her lip. Cal saw color starting to rise in Ella's face as she realized what she'd just done. She raised one hand to cover her mouth and quickly dropped her wide-eyed gaze to the ground. Cal couldn't help the grin that spread across his face. Of course, when he realized it was there, the thought that followed wiped it off his lips. There was no way in hell that he could have a thing for his boss, Ella Danforth.

15

ELLA

How long had Cal been standing there? Had he heard . . . Heat rushed to Ella's face as she remembered what she and Maddie had been saying about him. Shit. And what was he doing there in the first place? Pippa would have told him that she and Maddie were covering the bake-off.

"Hey," Ella said, moving around the counter to stand in front of Cal. "Didn't Pippa tell you that Maddie and I were covering this one?"

"The Seattle Sprinklers over here are in the lead," Miss Mandie called over the chaos around them. "Better step up your game if you're going to beat them! Five minutes remaining!"

Cal raised an eyebrow at Ella. "I thought it was one minute, five minutes ago."

Ella shrugged. "Miss Mandie time defies math, science, and logic. Your only choice is to go with it."

Cal nodded. "Uh, you didn't have to cover this. I can . . . take it from here if you have other things . . ."

"Oh, no, this was *the* big time-suck today. After this is over, there's the new reindeer naming contest at the library, the Christmas Clothes Drive at the church, Ann Pettyjohn is doing the first of four special Christmas editions of her quilting circle and there's the set-up for Santa's court, so take your pick of which ones you want to tackle."

Cal blinked in surprise. "That doesn't seem like too many events. I thought you said today would have even more events than yesterday to cover."

Ella gave a mirthless laugh. "Oh, those are just the events starting at noon. And the only ones I had room in my head to memorize. I'll have to go back and check the list for the rest of what's happening today."

Cal shook his head. "This town . . ."

"Is certifiable," Ella finished, nodding. "Aren't you so glad you moved here?"

Cal grinned. "Yes, actually." That hadn't been what Ella had expected to hear coming out of Cal's mouth. She was about to ask if he really meant it, but Cal cleared his throat. "So, which reindeer gets renamed every year? Don't they already *have* names? I mean, as I recall, there's a song and everything."

Ella rolled her eyes. "Oh, the Hope reindeer is the *ninth* reindeer. Even more important than Rudolph if you believe what Abel Jakes says."

"Oh, is that so," Cal said, crossing his arms. The playful lilt in his voice was distracting her.

"Uh, yeah. So, every year, Abel Jakes brings in this ninth reindeer to name. The reindeer doesn't look like other reindeer. In fact, his legs are about four inches long and his belly almost drags on the ground, but Abel says that makes him perfect for coming through air vents in houses that don't have chimneys."

"Four inches?" Cal asked.

"Oh, yeah. The ninth reindeer is actually his Basset Hound, Louis, with a pair of felt antlers on his head and a wreath around his neck."

"Sounds like animal cruelty to me," Cal said.

Ella shrugged. "It's hard to say. Louis doesn't seem to mind, but then again, Louis never seems to mind much of anything. He likes getting pets from all the kids and they always feed him cookies. Rob, the librarian caught the kids doing it years ago and now he only serves sugar-free cookies, and gives the kids those little Milkbones for Louis so he won't end up with diabetes." Ella realized she was rambling and did her best to shut her mouth.

"Well, that's probably . . . a good thing," Cal said. "I'll cover that one."

Apparently, Ella's awkwardness was spreading. Cal absent-mindedly swiped at his mouth with the back of his hand and Ella leaped on the possibility of a new topic.

"Glad to see that yesterday didn't leave you scarred or anything," she said, nodding at Cal's face.

The playfulness in Cal's voice evaporated. "Yeah, I'm fine. I hope that's not why you thought I wouldn't be up for covering this."

Ella was back-pedaling now. "No, I just thought that after yesterday, you might need-"

Cal already had his mouth open and Ella could tell they were about to argue when Miss Mandie bustled up. "Hey you two, I'm so glad you've met." She paused and grinned from Cal to Ella. "Oh, that's right, she's your *big bad boss* now." She squeezed Cal to her side with each accentuated word. Cal forced a smile that looked more like a grimace for Miss Mandie's benefit before returning his gaze to Ella.

Fine. If he wanted to be an ass about her trying to be nice, then fine. Of course, if she went down that rabbit hole of logic, she'd have to examine the fact that none of this would have happened if she hadn't sent him into Paul McIntyre's balloon-filling arms the day before. *But* that wouldn't have happened if he'd just given her back her damn mug. She wasn't sure why exactly the mug mattered so much to her, but it did. Either way, it shouldn't have been a big enough deal to rate Cal being such an ass about it. Surely he'd been on assignments before that he'd hated. It was almost guaranteed for any reporter working in Hope. You can only "ooh" and "aww" about taxidermy fish, oddly and sometimes suggestively shaped carrots pulled from gardens, and wedding ring quilts for so long before it loses some of its "wow" factor.

"Of course," Miss Mandie had turned on Ella now. "Since you're his boss now, you can insist on all kinds of naughty after-hour . . . performance reviews."

Ella almost choked, despite the fact that she wasn't eating or drinking anything. "Uh, uh Miss Mandie, what about the contest?"

Miss Mandie snorted. "I told you, dear. This is prime time. This is when the contestants will show their true colors. Will they sabotage? Will they embellish? More sprinkles? Ruin their cookies with too many decorations? This is when you start to smell the blood in the water."

Ella and Cal gave each other a bewildered look, but Ella was inwardly thankful that the topic change had taken the squeaky toy of "naughty performance reviews" away from Miss Mandie.

"You know," Miss Mandie continued. "I'm sure glad we've got you running the paper now, Ella. Clarence, oh, he can be fun, but when it came to the paper, he was the proverbial stick in the mud that was then shoved up the ass of a church biddy." Ella was certain that Miss Mandie's blood had to be about forty percent tequila at this point. "No!" Miss Mandie slurred quickly. "Clarence's stick wasn't in mud, it was in *concrete*. You'd break him off before you could get him to budge. Of course, when he first came to town, there was a line of women that wouldn't have minded breaking a piece of him off . . ."

"Moved to town?" Ella quickly interrupted. "I thought Clarence was from here." Clarence never talked about himself and the whole time she'd been growing up, no one had ever mentioned that Clarence hadn't grown up on the island too.

Miss Mandie grinned sloppily and shook her head. "No, honey, he came in off the ferry one day. He's from somewhere east." She laughed. "I guess most people are somewhere east of us. Well, unless you're coming from Hawaii or Japan, but then again, the argument can be made that you can still go east to get to those places, so it's all semantics, isn't it?"

The alcohol breath that was coming out of Miss Mandie could have peeled paint, but now that Ella had her talking about Clarence, she didn't want to do anything to get her off course. The blood-stained briefcase and Clarence's strange behavior had been on her mind since the day before. There was a new sharp pain in her gut now. She had always thought that she knew everything there was to know about Hope, but she hadn't even known that Clarence was from somewhere else. "So Clarence came out here from somewhere east. Do you remember where?" Ella asked.

"Oh, honey, that was so long ago. We think of old Clarence as one of our own now," Miss Mandie slurred, gently shaking her head.

"But, do you remember where he said he was from?" Ella asked, trying new wording, hoping it might help dislodge the information stashed away behind erotic cake recipes and old half-remembered lines of adult film scripts in the back of Miss Mandie's head.

The older woman frowned, thinking. "Detroit? I think he said Detroit." Ella made a mental note to do some scouring of Clarence Fords, residing in Detroit forty years ago in the in-depth search engines that the newspaper subscribed to. Ella knew that there hadn't been a death in Hope that wasn't accidental or by natural causes in the last fifty years. That was a proud tradition that was touted in the town's travel brochures and every year's summer travel edition of the paper as if that fact alone would entice tourists to visit. Ella knew it was a long shot and there was definitely a possibility that her mind was turning horses into zebras, but if it *was* Clarence's bloody briefcase (which was still a big if) and if the blood on it was from an actual death rather than just an accident . . . it must have entered Clarence's life sometime prior to him coming to Hope.

Ella could feel how ridiculous all these assumptions were, but with no word from Clarence to confirm or deny them, they were the only threads she had to hold onto. Her brain was in desperate need of something to focus on that wasn't the implosion of her life in Seattle, the looming month ahead, or the annoying six feet, four inches of Cal Dickson standing in front of her. She just needed to do some extracurricular research on Clarence's pre-island life and possibly some deaths in Detroit. Then she'd have something to dangle in front of Clarence. Maybe then, he'd talk to her. A small, annoying doubt in the back of her mind told her that the stain could have been from an accident, or could even be Clarence's own blood if the briefcase was indeed his. But Helga came to Ella's rescue and told the doubt to shut up and that it wasn't very likely because why would he have felt the need to hide it? Ella tried to jerk herself back into the moment and concentrate on Miss Mandie's face, but she was distracted by the feel of Cal's eyes on her.

"Or maybe he's from Chicago," Miss Mandie said, frowning. She shrugged. "Who can remember things like that?"

Ella felt the small amount of elation leave her. Searching Clarence Fords in Detroit was going to be enough of a chore, but if Miss Mandie wasn't even sure of the city . . .

"He sure was a stud when he hit town though. Thick dark hair, those deep blue eyes . . ." Miss Mandie turned to grin at Cal. "Not unlike this one here." Ella glanced at Cal who was starting to look uncomfortable again.

"Do you remember anything else about Clarence," Ella asked, throwing caution to the wind. "I mean when he first came to town." Now she could feel both Cal and Miss Mandie's eyes on her. She tried her best to hold her ground.

"Like what?" Miss Mandie asked.

Now Ella was in a bind. With a town this small, asking something like, *"Do you remember if he was covered in blood?"* or *"Was he carrying a bloody briefcase?"* would be sure to spin out into a whole spectrum of rumors.

"Uh," Ella started, not exactly sure where she was going to go with her questions. "I mean, did he ever mention . . . a family?"

Miss Mandie frowned again. "Not that I recall. You could ask him though. Clarence used to be such a talker. At least when you got him alone."

Miss Mandie turned back to Cal. "I'll bet you're the same way. Strong and silent until the lights go out."

Ella was too distracted with the thoughts about Clarence's past that were racing through her head to immediately come up with a way to save Cal.

"Ok, Miss Mandie," Maddie said, coming to the rescue. "I think you've had enough sunrises for one day."

Miss Mandie sighed. "Getting a liquor license for this place was the best idea I ever had, you know."

"So you've told me," Maddie said, getting an arm around her and leading her away from Cal and Ella.

"Thank you," Ella mouthed at Maddie. Maddie grinned and winked at her before nodding to Cal and leading Miss Mandie over to the coffee machine.

Now, Ella was alone with Cal again. "Hey," Ella said, her mind still on Clarence. "Do you mind finishing up here? All that's left is to record the winners of the contest. We'll be doing two stories. One with the results for this year and one that we'll write and archive to be used as part of next year's article for this event as a preview."

"Where are *you* going?" Cal asked.

"Uh, I just need to take care of something," Ella said. "Maddie's already taken about fifty pictures. She'll get pictures of the winners and their cookies and then I think this is a wrap. If you can just make sure and get the correct spellings and where the winners are from. I'll cover the Clothing Drive and see you back at the office for the 12:30 meeting to divvy out the rest of today's assignments."

"What's your interest in where Clarence was forty years ago?" Cal asked, narrowing his eyes at her.

"It's nothing," Ella said. "Just curiosity." She'd known Cal for all of two and a half days and she knew he wasn't from the island either. She'd seen how he'd reacted to her caring about almost killing him with latex. She wasn't ready to share the mystery of the briefcase with him.

"Sorry about that," Maddie said, coming back to join them. "I didn't hear what was going on when Miss Mandie was talking to you, but you both turned red enough to fry an egg on your faces, so I thought it might be a good idea to step in. She can sure tie one on."

Ella turned her attention to Maddie. "Thanks, Maddie. Um, Cal is going to stay and finish getting the names of the winners. I need to run an errand. I'll see you both back at the office."

With that, Ella turned and started winding her way through the crowd.

16

CAL

Cal watched Ella leave. She bumped into a woman just before she got to the door. The woman, like Miss Mandie, must have had one too many Tequila Sunrises because she knocked into a table full of ladies putting the final touches on their cookies with pastry bags. The angry yells were followed by what Cal could only describe as "D-Day at De-Floured". Frosting was flying in every direction as the fight drew in the people sitting at nearby tables. But, it didn't turn into an all-out war until Miss Mandie came from behind the counter with a mixing bowl filled with whipped cream and a ladle.

"Now we're cooking with gas," she yelled as she started using the ladle like a hand-held trebuchet, flinging fist-sized globs of whipped cream at the contestants.

Any other time, Cal would have found this amusing, but at the moment he just wanted this assignment to end so that he could follow Ella. What was she up to? Did she have some kind of hidden history with Clarence? Was Clarence's sudden departure from the paper actually planned? Had he tapped her as his replacement because he knew he was dying or something, and this surprise return to the island was all staged? He needed to know. The journalist in him needed to know. He looked around for Maddie. She'd jumped up on the counter, her camera raised as she egged on the groups that were now laughing and squealing like fourth-graders at a sleepover.

"You gonna take that Seattle Sprinklers? The Anacortes Accessorizers are firing off warning shots at you! Retaliate with the green frosting!" she yelled, the flash of the camera was almost like a strobe light as she clicked off a dozen quick pictures. Cal tried to get behind the counter, but he wasn't fast enough. He caught a glob of pink icing on the back of his head. And just as he turned around to see who had fired it at him, he got a face full of snowflake sprinkles from another woman. Deciding to cut his losses and just try to get Maddie's attention, he put his head down and hustled around the counter, feeling another glob of god-knew-what hit him in the back.

"Maddie!' he yelled up at her.

"Use the spoon!" Maddie yelled. "The spoon! That tiny decorating brush isn't going to be able to hurl much!"

Cal gave up. The way things were going, he'd probably have enough time to slip out and come back by the time the fight ended and they were ready to declare a winner. He headed out the side door by the kitchen and started jogging down Rosario Street behind the bakery and up to the corner where he could cut over to Evergreen. She'd been at Clarence's house the day before. Maybe she was there now.

The sickly sweet smells of sugar and vanilla were assaulting his nose. He looked down at his messenger bag and groaned when he saw the smears of green, pink, and red on the flap. He could only imagine what the rest of him looked like. Tiny silver sprinkles were stuck in the mess, making it look like Christmas had used his bag as toilet paper. Spectacular. And it was only December 2nd. He was starting to think there might be something to Ella's and the rest of the staff at the paper's paranoia about how the month was going to go.

He slowed down when he got a block away from Clarence's house and crossed the street so it wouldn't be so obvious to passersby that he was checking out the house. Especially if he needed to walk by a second time. When he stepped off the sidewalk, the step down jostled some more sprinkles loose from his hair and he gritted his teeth as he felt them roll down the back of his shirt. Fantastic. When he got up on the sidewalk on the opposite side of the street, he paused to shake his shirt out in the back, hoping the sprinkles would drop to the ground instead of traveling further south and under the band of his boxers.

He scanned the street in front of him, expecting to see Ella's willowy form standing on Clarence's porch again, railing at him to open the door. He did his best to ignore the pang of disappointment in his gut when he saw the front of the house was lifeless. The street itself felt eerie. To be fair, it *was* winter and barely mid-morning on a weekday. Still, he couldn't shake the nagging feeling that something wasn't right. Of course, he had to admit that it was *possible* (however improbable) that the feeling might be coming from the fact that Ella wasn't there, yelling for Clarence to open up and talk to her. Where was she? He stared at the house, waiting for it to give him answers about where his previous and current editors were and what did they know that he didn't?

A flash of movement caught his eye. The stiff breeze was pushing around something on Clarence's cracked driveway. He squinted at the object, but couldn't make out what it was. He looked up and down the street before jogging across. The wind shifted, pushing the gray wad across the pavement and towards the side of Clarence's house. It sounded light, like leaves skittering over the cement. The breeze lifted it, and for a moment, Cal had a flash of fear that it would carry the wad past the next block, down the cliffs, and into the ocean before he got a look at it. Stupid really. What was he expecting the wad to be? He wouldn't admit it to himself, but he knew that chasing this piece of garbage had been his excuse to get close to Clarence's house. Ella had some kind of lead she was keeping close to her chest. Now, maybe he would too. He pushed away Killjoy Cal's sigh in his head along with his brain reminding him that he was chasing a wad of garbage that probably had nothing to do with Clarence. The wind abated for a moment and the wad tumbled onto the overgrown weeds at the corner of Clarence's lot. Cal dove for it, feeling a surge of triumph roll through him. Of course, the triumph quickly deflated when he held the wad up to look at it.

It was used duct tape. Just a wad of spent tape, balled up, probably out of frustration because it had stuck to itself when someone had tried to tear it. It looked like the type: far too thick to be ripped by hand and still sticky enough to pick up a spider corpse, grass clippings, and god-knew-what-else when it had been released into the wild.

Awesome, Cal. Ella has a lead, and you have a piece of garbage. He allowed himself a single growl of frustration and headed for Clarence's trash can along the side of the house. At least he could throw it away. Yea. He'd picked up a piece of litter. Community service. He didn't have leads on Clarence's story, but at least he had a bright future in litter retrieval. Cal had taken two steps around the corner of Clarence's house when his phone buzzed in his pocket.

"Are you at the library?" It was a text from Pippa.

"Crap," he muttered. He tossed the wad into the trash can and started jogging back toward the town center. He glanced back at Clarence's house as he passed by it and paused so quickly that he almost fell. The curtain in the front window was fluttering. He turned, heading for the front door. He was halfway down Clarence's walkway when his phone started ringing.

"Where are you!?" Maddie yelled in his ear. "There's a contested winner. You gotta get back here!"

Cal groaned. "On my way." He hung up and with one last look at Clarence's house, he started jogging back to De-Floured.

The rest of the day, Clarence's house was on his mind. Had Clarence been watching from the window? Was he hurt? Had Ella been in the house watching *him* from the window? He groaned at the thought of her watching him chase a stupid piece of trash across Clarence's driveway. Oh so smooth. And if she was inside, how had she gotten in? Had something Miss Mandie said made the difference with Clarence? Had it convinced him to open the door and talk to her? What was going on with her and Clarence? Clarence had never mentioned Ella to Cal. But, then again, he'd never mentioned to Cal that he was thinking about quitting.

Ella was working with Marty on the layout when Cal got back to the office after finishing up at the bake-off and the library. He hadn't had a chance to stop in front of a mirror to survey the damage to his shirt and hair from the bake-off, but he had let the Basset Hound reindeer, Louis, now renamed, "Snowfluff", lick the frosting off his bag. Seeing Ella, he felt a quick stab of annoyance with himself that he hadn't just run up the stairs at De-Floured to his apartment and changed his shirt before coming back to the office.

Ella had set up a whiteboard on an easel in the middle of the office with the daily holiday activities to cover. Cal paused next to it and scanned the list while he listened to Ella talking to Marty. He wasn't sure what exactly he was listening for, but he was wondering if he'd be able to hear something in her voice or what she was saying that would tell him if she'd been to see Clarence.

"I'd like to stick with this general layout this month if at all possible," Marty was saying. "We're going to be busy enough without having to redesign the layout every day. I heard some good feedback from the insert we put in this morning's paper. And with the high schoolers you've got coming to help stuff and deliver, I think we'll be pretty well outfitted."

Ella nodded. "Good. Then let's stick with this layout and hopefully make it possible for you to get to second base with your pillow."

Marty chuckled and Ella clapped him on the shoulder before turning back toward her office. She paused when she saw Cal. He momentarily forgot that he was supposed to be surveying the activity list on the board and not eavesdropping.

"I'd hate to see the other guy," she said, giving him the once over, her eyes pausing on his shirt. The playful smile on her face had Cal fixated on the curve of her lips. He quickly recovered, realizing he probably looked like hell at the moment and she apparently thought that was funny.

Cal glanced around the office. "Yeah, frosting fight at De-Floured. Took three pots of coffee, a case full of donuts, and about twelve purse-sized bags of Wet Ones to break it up."

Ella sighed. "Sorry I missed that."

Cal locked onto Ella's face and his mouth started moving faster than his brain. "Yeah, why is that? Where'd you have to go?"

Ella frowned at him, the hard defiance back in her gray eyes. "It's personal." Cal opened his mouth to argue, despite his brain yelling at him to shut up, but Ella cut him off before he could say anything. "Did you get the Reindeer Renaming covered?" She turned away from him and picked up the marker from the tray on the whiteboard.

"Uh, yeah."

"What was the verdict?" Ella asked without looking at him.

"The kids decided to name him 'Snowfluff'," Cal said.

Ella shrugged. "Well, that's better than four years ago, when Santa's ninth reindeer was named 'Colonoscopy' because little Johnny Higgs had just learned the word from his dad griping about having to get one." Cal didn't say anything. "Ok," Ella continued on a sigh. "For this afternoon, we have the Victorian Christmas Ornament Show at Seaside Treasures, the Confounding Carolers which are meeting at the gazebo. And in the park next to Town Hall, there's the Children's Christmas Candy Cane Obstacle Course . . . They really need to work on that name. Too many 'C's. Ok, so Maddie said she'd jump on the Victorian Christmas Ornaments grenade since you had to deal with Paul yesterday and Esther earlier this week. So, take your pick, the Confounding Carolers, or the . . ." Ella sighed. "Yeah I'm not saying that name again . . . the obstacle course." He was starting to pick up on when Ella was rambling. Was she nervous when she did that?

"I can take them both," Cal said, he could hear the annoyance in his tone and tried to mentally smooth it out. Maybe he was going about this the wrong way. Maybe by sowing some goodwill with Ella, he could get her to tell him what her connection and interest in Clarence was. It was strange that he hadn't seen Clarence even around town, at the market, the bakery . . . somewhere. At first, he just thought Clarence was hunkered down to wait out the rumor mill until he was old news so that when he did resurface in the community, he wouldn't get ambushed by everyone's questions. But now?

"I can help," Ella said, studying the list. "There's also the Ugly Sweater Decorating Party for the adults, the opening of Santa's Court tonight at Town Hall, and the first night of the Holiday Pie Sale in front of Bumble's Market. Of course, besides the sweater decorating, these are all ongoing events for the month so that makes things easier, at least from a reporting standpoint." She studied the board, nibbling on the cap of the dry erase marker and Cal was mesmerized, watching her lips on that cap. She pulled the pen away and turned to look at him, an odd pinkness in her cheeks. "Cal?"

He gave himself a shake. What was he doing? He was doing exactly what he was trying *not* to do. *Come on, Cal.*

"Cal?" Ella was asking. "How do you want to do this?"

His annoyance with himself and his frustration at the effect she was having on him came out in a harsh tone when his mouth gave his brain the middle finger and asked, "What's the story with you and Clarence?"

Ella looked confused. "What do you mean?"

Was she just that good of an actor? Cal stared at her, trying to decide.

"Look, if you've got something you want to say, just say it," Ella said.

Cal evaluated what he knew and decided he didn't have enough to show his hand. "I'll take the obstacle course and the carolers."

"Fine," Ella snapped, raising the marker and making a mark on the board. "Then I'll take the sweater decorating and the pie sale." Without looking at Cal, she walked away. She went into her office and closed the door.

Cal could feel the hot pricks of his anger climbing up the back of his neck. He didn't know whether to leave or go kick her office door open. And then what? Demand for her to tell him what's going on? Pin her to her office wall and run *his* tongue over those lips and ask her how *she* liked it? *WHAT?! No, Cal. Get it together.* He moved over to his chair and sat down. It was just exhaustion. It had to be. He wouldn't be feeling like this normally. Not about his boss and not about a woman as infuriating as Ella Danforth. Without meaning to, he turned in his chair, still thinking. He could see Ella in her office through the window where the blinds had been drawn up. She had her head down, typing on her laptop. He felt his anger simmering down into annoyance. What was she hiding?

He turned back to look at his laptop. He just needed to work, to distract himself. He started typing up his stories. Ten minutes in, he couldn't stop his knee from bouncing under the desk. He glanced over at Ella in her office again and caught her looking at him. She quickly dropped her gaze back to her laptop and started typing again. Cal sighed and pushed back from his desk. He needed to get out of there.

He grabbed his bag and headed down the hall and out the back door through the press room. Kurt and his crew were busy so no one stopped him to chat, which was lucky because Cal's thoughts were all over the place. If he could just walk off the annoyance, maybe all the other stuff running through his head about Ella would follow suit. With every step he took away from the paper, the other thoughts faded and all he could think about was Ella and Clarence. Was she actually hiding something or was she just being stubborn? If she was being stubborn, why? What did she know or think she knew?

His cell phone started to ring and he pulled it out, dreading the probability that it was Tara. His mood instantly brightened when he saw Jamie Baskin's name on the caller ID.

"Hey Jamie, what's up?" Cal asked.

"Oh, I uh, I just heard that the editor job there at the paper just opened up and I was wondering if you were gonna take it," Jamie asked, his deep voice full of the pondering optimism that Cal always associated with him.

"It's already been filled," Cal said, forcing his tone to be neutral. As annoyed as he was, Jamie didn't deserve any splash damage from it.

"Oh, already?" Jamie asked. There was a muffled sound as if Jamie was covering his phone, but doing a poor job of it, considering the fact that Cal could still clearly hear Jamie say, "Sounds like someone else already got the job."

There was a scuffling sound and then another familiar voice came on the line.

"Already? You're kidding me, right?" Cal could always count on Connor Dayton. Not only had Connor had every part Cal had needed to fix the sink in his apartment, but he'd also come over to help him fix it, and brought with him a case of beer and a pack of steaks. When Connor had nights off from his family's hardware store and Cal finished up at the paper, they would usually meet up with Jamie for a beer or two at Fast Eddy's or The

Alphorn.

"Yeah," Cal said in answer to Connor's question. "Not kidding."

"Who got the job?" Connor asked.

"You really don't know?" Cal asked. "I figured everyone in town knew by now."

"I've been on the mainland on a buying trip for the store," Connor said. "And Jamie, well . . ."

Cal nodded. "Right. Her name is Ella Danforth."

"Cranberry Sauce!?" Connor asked, his voice pitched high before he started laughing. "You're shitting me."

"Cranberry Sauce?" Cal asked, confused.

"It's a long story," Connor said. "Man, I never thought she'd come back to the island."

"Apparently that's a running theme," Cal muttered. "If someone had made book on it, they'd be raking it in now."

"Speaking of raking things in," Connor said. "It's endless fries with Jingle Burgers at Eddy's tonight. You in?"

Cal could feel his pent-up annoyance slowly being replaced by the formulation of a plan for payback. "Sure, on one condition."

"Name it," Connor said, sounding amused.

"You tell me the cranberry sauce story."

"Deal," Connor said.

Cal was smiling when he slid his phone into his back pocket and rounded the corner, heading back for the Town Square. Now, things were looking up.

The sound of Christmas carols reached him as he moved toward the gazebo. The singing halted, mid-chorus of "God Rest Ye Merry Gentlemen" and the tinny sound of a pitch pipe echoed across the square. Cal took a deep breath. These had to be the "Confounding Carolers". Cal reached into his bag and pulled out his notebook and pen.

"Hi, Cal!" The Reverend George Anderson was waving his pitch pipe at Cal. He forced a smile and waved back. George was the only preacher in town, at Hope's only non-denominational church. And he was enthusiastic about *everything*. He had the perfect career for his personality, and normally it would amuse Cal, but with everything else on Cal's mind at the moment, he wasn't as excited about it today.

"Hi George," Cal said. "Sorry, Reverend."

George made a dismissive gesture. "Please, call me George. Are you here to get the word out about the Hope Confounding Carolers?"

"I sure am," Cal said, flipping his notebook open. "So, how long have you all been caroling?"

"Oh!" George was almost bouncing with excitement as he smiled at Cal. "We've been doing this for the last twelve years."

"And what's the story behind the name?" Cal asked.

"Oh, the Confounding Carolers are not your average caroling troop! You see, we carol to raise money for various charities here and on the mainland."

"So, you collect money when you sing?" Cal asked.

"Oh, no, people hire us to surprise their loved ones with carols. Anywhere and anytime, we'll be there."

An evil thought started to form in Cal's mind. Ella threw him under the bus driven by Paul and his balloon grotto, and she was playing keep-away with what she knew about Clarence. This felt like a good option for payback, and for a good cause, nonetheless.

"George, how full is the Confounding Caroler's schedule for tomorrow?"

"Oh, wide open at the moment," George said, his eyes bright.

"I'd like to schedule your services," Cal said with a grin.

* * *

A half-hour later, Cal had gotten all the facts on the Confounding Carolers and arranged to have them scheduled for the next day. George tried to insist on having Cal stay to listen to the rehearsal, but he begged off, never so thankful to have a children's obstacle course to write a story about.

The obstacle course looked like a Christmas children's version of a *Mad Max* movie. "Oh, the children love it," Mrs. Carley Dugan cooed as the kids beat each other with PVC pipe candy canes wrapped in pool noodles and painted with stripes behind her.

"How does the obstacle course work?" Cal asked, looking past her at the chaos.

"Oh, once it's put together, there are hoops for the children to crawl through, a candy cane bridge to cross using candy cane polls, peppermint stepping stones to leap between to keep out of the fudge swamp . . ." She motioned to a muddy patch of the park that was missing grass. As Cal followed Mrs. Dugan around the park, taking notes, the fading sunlight glinted off something on the other side of the square, catching his attention. It was the front door to De-Floured. Miss Mandie was wearing dark shades and emptying a mop bucket on the strip of grass in front of the bakery. Something from that morning started nudging at him from the back of his mind. Ella had asked Miss Mandie about Clarence. She had seemed to know Clarence when he was young. When they both were. Maybe Miss Mandie would be up for talking now that she was sober. And maybe with a hangover, she'd be willing to tell him everything she knew just to get him to go away. If he could get that information out of her, he might be able to bargain with Ella so she would tell him what *she* knew.

He finished up his interview with Mrs. Dugan as quickly as he could, thankfully assisted by the screaming cries of one kid who'd taken a candy cane crook to the face. He took pictures of the progress of the obstacle course, though he wasn't sure if they should use them for the article since it wasn't completely assembled. Then, he slipped away while she went to examine the boy's injury. He hustled across the square to De-Floured, composing his argument to Miss Mandie in his head. He pulled the door open, ready to lay it all out for her, but stopped short when the sight in front of him registered. Miss Mandie wasn't alone. Sitting across from her at one of the cafe-style tables, was Ella.

17

ELLA

"Ella, my sweet summer child, not now," Miss Mandie groaned when Ella had walked into De-Floured.

The bakery was empty and it was early evening; it wasn't the most popular dinner destination in Hope. For the most part, Miss Mandie's evening crowd consisted of the "light and early supper" folks that considered 8 pm to be the middle of the night. Either the De-Floured dinner rush had just ended or it hadn't started. Ella wasn't entirely sure which, but either way, she wanted to take advantage of the bakery being empty and Miss Mandie being sober. "Miss Mandie, I just want to know about Clarence. Anything you can tell me."

Miss Mandie had a mop in one hand. It was clear she'd been scrubbing at the last of the dried frosting on the floor. She sighed and slumped into a chair at one of the cafe tables and glared at Ella over the top of her sunglasses. "Honey, have you ever had a late-afternoon hangover? It's not as nice as a regular hangover. With a regular hangover, you get to be unconscious and in your bed for the 'wearing off' process. Late-afternoon hangovers are like having an invisible vampire attached to your neck, slowly draining you until you're just a dry husk of a human."

Ella rolled her eyes. "Well, what have we learned about getting hammered on Tequila Sunrises at nine in the morning?"

"That I need to schedule Bart to cover the rest of the day when I want to do it," Miss Mandie muttered. "Thankfully, he's going to be here in a half hour so I can go home, pass out, and throw up. Though, probably not in that order."

"We can hope," Ella muttered. "I'll help you finish cleaning if you'll spare a minute to talk to me."

Miss Mandie grunted her agreement, though unenthusiastically. Ella scrubbed the tables and chairs with a rag while Miss Mandie finished the mopping. When she took the mop bucket out the front door to dump the water, Ella pitched the dirty rags into the laundry hamper in the closet behind the front counter and tried to frame the questions she wanted to ask. The rattle of the mop bucket preceded the woman back inside. She was groaning with a hand to her head as she staggered back across the bakery and flopped into her vacated chair. Ella sat down in the chair across from Miss Mandie and dove in. "Ok, how about you tell me everything you know about Clarence and then I'll leave so you can go home and get to your fun evening."

Miss Mandie groaned and put her head down on the table. The bell over the door tinkled and Ella looked over to see none other than Cal Dickson, standing in the doorway. Ella could feel her eyes narrow as she glared at him. But she was having a hard time conjuring full-blown annoyance when he was standing in the doorway, the late afternoon sun behind him, leaving not much to the imagination under his white shirt. For a second, Ella had an internal freak-out, worrying that her eyes were going to bulge out of her head and her tongue was going to unroll across the floor while she howled at him. But she was relieved when she remembered she wasn't a cartoon wolf. She gave herself a shake and tried to stir up some self-righteous irritation. What the hell was he doing here? Besides the bake-off, there wasn't anything else for him to cover at De-Floured today. Was he there to do the same thing she was trying to do? He'd probably have more luck being a young, attractive male and Miss Mandie only being human, after all.

"What are you doing here?" Ella finally managed to sputter by way of greeting.

Cal stood his ground. "Nothing. I just had some questions for Miss Mandie."

"About the bake-off?" Ella asked, raising an eyebrow.

Cal's expression hardened into the damn stubborn defiance that seemed to make his blue eyes brighter, especially surrounded by his messy dark hair and the beard scruff he seemed to be growing out. Ella had to admit that the scruff did suit him. For the span of a heartbeat, she imagined what it would feel like to run her fingers through it, trace the line of his jaw... She gave herself a mental face-slap. What the hell was she doing? Get a grip, Ella. It's Cal. Annoyed, pouty, and pissed-off Cal. And nosy. What kind of questions could he possibly have for Miss Mandie outside the story write-up?

"No," Cal said. "It's personal." He gave her a smug smile.

"I don't care if you're here to pose for the concept sketches in my new adult dessert catalog," Miss Mandie muttered, turning her head to look up at Cal. "Either of you," she added, glancing at Ella. "I'm in no mood to talk about anything right now. You two are young. How do you *not* understand the concept of hangovers?"

Ella looked back at Cal, her gaze dropping to the unbuttoned top buttons on his shirt. Green frosting was smeared around the collar and she could see a dollop of dried icing on his collarbone. The insane thought that it would be fun to lick it off of him echoed through her head, making the heat rise in her own chest and face. Hopefully, if Cal noticed, he'd just think it was an extension of her annoyance.

"Well, I was here first," Ella said, realizing how childish the excuse sounded. "And if you'll excuse us, *I* have something personal to talk to her about."

Cal opened his mouth to argue, moving closer to the table where they sat, but Miss Mandie smacked the table with the palm of her hand, silencing him before he started and drawing both of their gazes back to her. "No, I'm not talking to either one of you. Not today."

"But, Miss Mandie..." Ella quickly said.

Miss Mandie raised her head and rested her forehead in her hand. "No."

She glanced from Ella to Cal. "If you want to talk to me. Either of you, then I want something in return."

"What?" Ella asked. "Name it."

Miss Mandie nodded. "Both of you, here tomorrow morning at six am. It's going to be a long day. Tomorrow night is the Mrs. Claus bash and I have four dozen Double D-elicious cupcakes that will need to be frosted. And tomorrow is Bart's day off. You two come in and do the frosting and I'll answer your questions. Deal?"

"I'll be here," Ella said.

Miss Mandie smiled at her and shook her head. "No." She looked at Cal. "You'll both be here, or I'm not saying a peep. Got it? I'm not having two interrogations. I don't have the time for it. And it'll take both of you to get the frosting finished before the morning rush."

Ella was torn. She didn't know Cal well enough to know if she could trust him. She supposed she could frame her questions to be general so she wouldn't have to give anything away as to why she was interested in Clarence's behavior. Either way, it didn't seem like she had much of a choice.

"Fine," Ella finally said.

"Fine with me, too," Cal added.

The door jingled again and someone entered right behind Cal. They all turned to look at Bart. He had a pair of headphones around his neck and he was picking at something that had dried on the front of his David Bowie t-shirt. He looked up and an expression of confusion rolled across his face as he took in Cal's annoyed posture and frosting accents. His gaze rolled over Ella and he grinned before turning his attention to Miss Mandie who was smiling at him like someone from the graveyard shift greeting the morning crew.

"Bart, my savior," Miss Mandie muttered, groaning as she got to her feet. "The list of prep is on the fridge in the back. Please take home that last loaf of Pumpernickel with you when you leave tonight. Enjoy your day off tomorrow. I've got some frosting help for the morning." She motioned vaguely at Cal and Ella. "And I'm leaving now," Miss Mandie said, picking up her purse from the floor beside her chair and lumbering toward the front door. She patted Bart on the shoulder, nodded at Cal and Ella, and headed outside.

Bart looked from Cal to Ella. "Can . . . I get either of you something?"

"No," Ella said, crossing the room and moving past Cal. "I'm on my way out." She brushed past him, the long sleeve of her shirt sliding across his bare arm, just below his rolled cuff. She didn't allow herself time to think about the smell of his deodorant or cologne or whatever it was that she'd caught a whiff of being so close to him. She hadn't noticed it when they'd been at Clarence's house. Possibly because they were outside instead of an enclosed space or possibly because he hadn't been wearing any. Either way, she had to admit, the combination of cedar and something sharp . . . fit him. She pushed through the door and stood outside in the cold air, breathing deep, trying to get her heartbeat to return to a normal pace.

She forced herself to start walking forward, moving one foot and then the other. She'd go back to her office, close the door, sit in her chair and start banging her head against the desk until she beat all these incredibly inappropriate thoughts of Cal out of her head. Well, she would if she had time. She knew she needed to prepare for the next day. Hope's tourism was picking up speed and the events were picking up along with it. She didn't really have the time for the Clarence situation, but unfortunately, like the annoying presence of Cal Dickson, she couldn't get it off her mind. She'd tried to find a Clarence Ford in Detroit and Chicago. There were so many that it was pointless to continue down that path of research. Miss Mandie was the easiest mine of knowledge to drill into. She was a talker, she didn't mince words and she was about the same age as Clarence. And, there was something in the way she'd talked about Clarence that made Ella think that there had been something between them.

Ella adjusted her bag and when she moved the arm that had brushed against Cal, she swore she caught another whiff of his scent, but she knew it had to be her imagination. She tried to mentally shed all thoughts of him, at least for the moment. She needed to focus. She'd finalize everything for tomorrow's issue so the run could start rolling by five. Then, she'd prep for tomorrow's assignments, maybe get them assigned and then prepare her questions for Miss Mandie. A light bulb clicked on in Ella's head. Miss Mandie had asked them to be there at six. But, what if she got there early before Cal? She'd have Miss Mandie all to herself, to ask her anything she wanted *before* he got there. She couldn't suppress the smile that was starting to curl on her lips. She had a plan.

The rest of the day moved quickly with Ella and Cal doing a carefully choreographed waltz around each other, managing to both avoid *and* get in each other's way, simultaneously. They didn't speak unless it was to decide on a photo choice, agree on a layout placement with Marty's template, or approve of a story's final draft. They were the last two out, with the exception of Kurt and his crew, (now with the additional high schoolers) listening to Netflix on their phones while they stuffed inserts in the paper. Ella decided that faking Cal out was the way to go. She'd stay late at the office and not leave until after he did so he'd think she wouldn't be at Miss Mandie's until six. That way, she'd be able to almost guarantee he wouldn't show up early. There was something still bothering Ella about the whole situation. What "personal" thing was Cal going to ask Miss Mandie about? She hadn't missed the curiosity on Cal's face when he'd seen her at Clarence's house. And she hadn't missed his annoyance when she'd kept to herself why she'd been there. Then, he'd seen the briefcase. She knew he hadn't believed her lie about the stain being coffee. Was he just following her, wanting to hear what Miss Mandie told her, just to annoy Ella? Was he hoping to get dirt on her? Was he actually just worried about his former boss, Clarence? Ella rubbed her temples and closed her eyes.

"What is your game, Cal Dickson?" She whispered.

"What was that?" Cal's voice from her doorway made Ella jump. She dropped her gaze back to her computer screen.

"Nothing. You heading out?"

"Yeah. Unless you need me . . . uh, need anything else," Cal said. The phrasing sent goosebumps down Ella's arms. *What the hell, body?* Ella screamed inside her head.

"No," Ella heard her voice crack. She cleared her throat, doing her best to ignore the heat rising in her cheeks. "No, I'm good. Thanks. Uh, have a good night."

Smooth, Ella. So very smooth.

She didn't look up until she was sure Cal had left. She strained her ears to listen for the sound of him leaving through the front door. She picked up her phone and checked the time. It was just after ten. She'd wait another five minutes and then sneak out the back door. If she hustled, she could get home with enough time to pass out for seven hours before she had to be at Miss Mandie's. Bed sounded so good. It was too early in the month to feel like she'd been hit by a Mack truck. She waved to Kurt on her way out the back door and clung to the shadows until she got home.

Luckily, her mom and Bill had already gone to bed. She turned off her bedroom light and laid in the dark, thinking about Clarence and the briefcase, which she'd stashed under her bed until she could figure out what else to do with it. Then, to her annoyance, her brain took a turn, and the last thought on her mind as she drifted off to sleep, happened to be about Cal Dickson. It should not be possible to be such an ass and still smell that good.

18

CAL

"Ok, someone tell me what this 'Cranberry Sauce' nickname is all about," Cal said. He had told himself he was only going to have one beer, but as he stared at the three empty bottles on the table in front of him, he inwardly winced. It had taken three beers to finally get an opening in the conversation with Jamie and Connor. They didn't look it, especially Jamie, but they could both talk circles around Cal. It was another thing he had noticed since moving to the island. Back in New York, when he was out at a dinner or a party, there were always awkward silences where you could almost hear the whirring and clicking of everyone's minds in the room while they calibrated and calculated what topic to introduce next that would further whatever their goals were for the evening. Meanwhile, in Hope . . .

"Did you know that what sailors used to think were sea monsters were really just whale penises flopping around out of the water during mating season?" Jamie asked, eyes wide as he surveyed Connor and Cal.

"I'd believe it," Connor said, shaking his head. "Have you ever seen whales going at it? It's like a seven-car-pile-up; both mesmerizing and horrifying."

"Yeah, and the cars are their penises," Jamie added.

Cal shook his head. Normally, he wouldn't be trying to steer the conversation. For the most part, he enjoyed just being along for the ride.

But it was getting late, he was getting tipsy, and there was no way in hell he was going to miss what Miss Mandie had to say about Clarence. In fact, because he had the advantage of living just upstairs, he planned on being downstairs and chatting with Miss Mandie before Ella even got there. He probably should have just called it a night and left Jamie and Connor to their late-night National Geographic musings, but he was intrigued. "Ok, will one of you tell me what the story is behind Ella Danforth's nickname 'Cranberry Sauce'?"

Jamie and Connor both glanced over at him. Jamie's half-smile was quickly hidden behind his beer, but Connor's grin stretched ear-to-ear. "God, that was the best Town Thanksgiving we've ever had."

"I'm listening," Cal said, trying to urge him on.

"Well, if not the best, it was definitely up there," Connor added.

Cal could feel impatience mixing with his anticipation. He waved his hand in a "hurry up" gesture.

"Ok, well, it was Thanksgiving," Jamie began. Then he paused and looked at Connor. "You should tell it. After all, you were the green beans that year and you saw it happen."

"But you were one of the pies," Connor argued. "You were on the same side of the stage with her and you saw her after . . ."

"Will one of you please just tell me what happened?" Cal asked, his impatience finally getting the better of him.

"Ok, ok calm down," Connor said, raising an eyebrow at Cal. "Too much anticipation and you're going to be let down. The story isn't as funny in the retelling as it was to see in person." Cal held his tongue and just stared at Connor, waiting for him to tell the story. Connor grinned down at his beer as if he was replaying the memory in his mind. "So, you saw at Thanksgiving how the whole town comes together for a big Thanksgiving dinner, right?" Cal nodded, afraid to speak in case it slowed Connor down in spinning his yarn. "Well, you know how all the kids in the elementary school were dressed up as different foods? Yams, pie, turkey, etc.?"

"Yeah," Cal said quickly, wanting to speed him along.

"Well, when Jamie, Ella, and I were all in the fifth grade the music teacher

Mr. Grimsby decided we should make it Thanksgiving The Musical."

Cal could feel the tendrils of glee starting to curl inside of him, thinking of a fifth-grade Ella (most likely awkward and with braces in his mind) having to sing and dance dressed as a Thanksgiving side dish.

"And Ella was assigned to be the Cranberry Sauce and to do a tap dance," Connor continued.

Cal was almost euphoric. Of course she was.

"So, Ella was easily the tallest girl in the school and the can costume had been made for Marla Talbert the year before."

"Yeah," Jamie added quickly, "and Marla was like four-foot-seven."

"So," Connor said, "Ella just looked like gangly red leggings wearing tap shoes, sticking out of this giant aluminum can. Well, none of us were all that coordinated, but Ella . . ."

Jamie was chuckling. "Let's just say, I felt a whole lot better about my dancing skills after watching her."

"So what happened?" Cal asked, pushing away the tiny whiff of pity that washed over him for Ella.

"Somehow," Connor said, shaking his head, "no one has ever been able to pinpoint *how* exactly, and there has been a lot of debate about it . . ."

"A lot of debate," Jamie said. "And over the years, factions have formed, divided, and reformed over how it happened. Some think the stage floor was warped, some think her shoelaces came untied, and others think she's just the clumsiest kid to ever come out of Hope and that's saying something . . ."

"Anyway," Connor pressed on before Cal could interrupt to hurry the story along. "Somehow, Ella tripped and fell, and once her momentum was going, there was no stopping her. She fell off the stage and crashed right through the buffet table. The whole thing collapsed and then because she was stuck in a cylindrical object, she proceeded to roll back and forth over all the food, mashing it into the concrete and grass. She couldn't get up and everyone else was just . . . frozen in place, like they were trying to figure out if what they were seeing was actually happening."

"I thought people would be mad," Jamie said, shaking his head. "I mean, that was everyone's Thanksgiving dinners, like days of work and . . ."

"But they weren't," Connor said, grinning again. "Someone, I think it might have been old Hank Melrose, started yelling 'Whoa there, hoss! Hold up there, Cranberry Sauce!' and it just kind of caught on until everyone was chanting it."

Now Connor and Jamie were chuckling at the memory. Cal was torn. Yeah, the whole thing had probably been hilarious at the time, but a shiver ran down his back, remembering his sixth-grade birthday party where he and his buddies at the time had pretended to be a boy band called "Jak Mak Silver". The band name had been made up of their names, Jack and Maxwell and Silver because of Cal's braces. They'd sung a couple of Backstreet Boys songs for their families and friends at the party, but when it had come to Cal's turn to sing a solo, he'd frozen. Everyone had laughed, and then for years, whenever he'd seen Jack, Maxwell, or one of their family members or friends from the party, they'd called him Silent Silver. But they always yelled it, like the Lone Ranger saying, "Hi ho, Silent Silver!"

He couldn't torture Ella with this. Unbidden, a memory of her smug smile at him from inside Clarence's office flashed through his mind. *Well, unless she did something to really deserve it.* It did feel a little reassuring to have something on Hope's "Golden Girl" in his back pocket. Like the nuclear launch codes. He hoped he'd never have to use it, but he was glad he had it just in case.

He closed the tab for the table and in the customary Hope parting salutations, hugged Connor and Jamie and made loose plans to hang out again in the next couple of weeks.

Cal kept his head down as he moved through the town square on his way home, thinking about the strange equation that was Ella Danforth. She didn't want the job, but she'd taken it. She'd told him that she wouldn't be in Hope if she had anywhere better to be, and yet, seeing her at Miss Mandie's and with the newspaper staff . . . she just seemed to fit. And now there was this secret. Something about Clarence that she wasn't willing to share. Well, he'd know more in the morning. He was halfway up the stairs to his apartment when his phone buzzed in his pocket. He was still preoccupied with thoughts of Ella and swiped to answer before fully comprehending the name on the caller ID.

"Finally!" Tara's voice cut through Cal's thoughts like a record scratch. He paused on the stairs and closed his eyes. He'd been so careful to screen his calls and then one slip in his diligence and he was on the phone with everything he wanted to avoid. "I should have laid money on my odds of getting you to answer your phone tonight. I would have cleaned up."

Cal leaned heavily against the railing, but the damp cold forced his feet up the stairs while he internally berated himself for being so careless. As he climbed each step, he could feel his stomach sinking lower and lower.

"Hi Tara," he mustered. "How are things?"

"Things are seven shades of shit right now," Tara said. He felt himself inhaling as if he was about to dive into a pool. This was always his reaction when Tara was primed for a rant. He leaned his forehead against his door, one hand holding the phone to his ear and one hand fumbling the key into the lock as she began.

"The holidays are coming, your mother is forwarding me about twenty invitations to events a day, nudging, not very subtly I might add, about when you'll be back, confirming the dates for our engagement party and wedding, and your dad is getting snippier every time I see him, asking the same question as everyone else. When are you coming home?" Tara finished.

Cal could hear the annoyance in her voice reach a crescendo as she got to the last question.

"Never," Cal said, unable to stop himself from grinning. Consciously, he was messing with her and he knew that she'd understand that, but there was definitely a part of him that relished the thought of it being true. He didn't want to leave Hope.

"Ha ha, very funny," Tara's vocal fry-upper-Manhattan accent punched out every word.

Cal frowned as he dropped onto his bed. He'd expected Tara to laugh. How many years had they spent thrown together at parties and functions, sneaking smokes pilfered from Tara's mom's purse in the fire exits and balconies? They'd always joked about getting away and living somewhere else; cattle ranches, tiny seaside towns, the streets of Paris, anywhere but corporate New York.

"Tara?" Cal asked, quietly. "What's up?"

"I don't know, Callum, you tell me." Her voice was sharp and Cal felt a renewed sense of annoyed anger aimed at her this time.

"What is that supposed to mean?" he asked. He tried to curb the sting in his voice, but her huff of indignance on the other end of the line was making it difficult.

"I don't know what to think anymore. Have you gone crazy? Are you having a quarter-life crisis? Do you need therapy? Drugs? I've tried giving you time. I've tried giving you space."

Yeah, right, Sarcastic Cal muttered inside his head. *Daily voicemails constitute "space"*.

"But, the fact is, they all keep asking me the same questions and I still don't have any answers for them. What the hell are you doing, wherever you are, and when will you be done and come home?"

There was silence on the line between them.

"I don't know," Cal finally said. "Maybe never."

He realized as he said it that the joke-to-serious ratio had slipped from half-joking to below twenty-five percent. If he was just weighing what *he* wanted, he would never go back. But, he'd been told since birth that life was about more than just what *he* wanted.

This time, Tara did snort with derisive laughter. "Come on, Callum, be serious. Your dad and mom are starting to plan this engagement party for us. I don't know what I'm supposed to tell them."

Cal felt his spine stiffen. "Tell them to stop."

"Yeah, that'll go over big with the Dickson Group," Tara muttered. "Your dad and mom and my parents are pushing and we need you back here."

"This is bullshit," Cal finally ground out. "An engagement party? Where the hell do they get off? They didn't even consult us to see if either of us wanted this. Ever. Not on any of it," he was fuming now, pulling off his Chuck Taylors and tossing them across the room. "Not once. I mean, how can they just push us around like fucking pawns in their stupid merger game?" Tara was silent and Cal pushed on, the beer and his outrage breaking down his filters. "Tell them to go to hell for me. There. Now you have something to tell them." His gaze landed on the clock by his bed and he groaned. "Listen, I have to go. I have an early morning. I'll talk to you later." Then, he hung up before she could argue with him.

He closed his eyes, setting his phone on his chest. His heart was pounding so loudly he could hear it in his ears. He took a deep breath and savored the pine and sea salt smell of his apartment, mixed with the ever-present cinnamon smell from the bakery that seeped through the cracks in his floor. His heart rate immediately began to slow as a smile spread across his face. He had just hung up on his other life. And it had felt great. He turned his head and grabbed the battery-powered alarm clock off his bedside table, setting an alarm for five am. He set another alarm on his phone for five minutes before and got ready for bed.

He had no illusions about his phone call with Tara being the end of his east coast problems. At the moment though, he had more immediate things to worry about. *Like a blood-stained briefcase, and what the hell had happened to Clarence.* He closed his eyes and fought against the traitorous smile forming on his lips. *And of course, then there was Ella Danforth.* There was plenty for him to worry about when it came to her.

19

ELLA

The five o'clock alarm scared Ella awake. She'd been in a deep sleep, dreaming about white shirts, frosting, and that scent that rolled off of Cal. The dream had felt so real she swore she could still smell his scent when she awoke, sweaty, tired, and breathing hard. The cold morning air went a long way in waking her up and shaking off the memory and thoughts of Cal as she hustled across town to De-Floured. The streets of Hope were silent. Most people had turned their Christmas lights off sometime during the night and so the lights of the old-fashioned lamp posts around the town square were guiding her. She felt a thrill in her stomach when she saw the light on in the kitchen of De-Floured. Yes! Her plan had worked! Miss Mandie was already here and she'd have almost an hour to grill her about Clarence before Cal showed up.

She slowed her pace when she saw the shadowy outline of something in front of the bakery door. As she got closer, the thing moved. It stood up and shoved its hands into the pockets of the black leather jacket it wore.

"So, I guess I'm not the only one that was anxious to get here this morning," Cal said.

Ella was too disappointed to speak.

"Look," Cal said with a yawn. "I know you want to ask Miss Mandie about Clarence. I want to know about Clarence too. Can we just, I don't know, call a truce on this one?"

"A truce from what?" Ella growled.

"Well, *that*, to be honest," Cal said, nodding at Ella. "we've both been jerks about this whole thing . . ."

"We've *both* been jerks?" Ella sputtered.

"Yeah," Cal said. "So, why don't we just . . ."

Miss Mandie threw the bakery door open and looked out at Cal and Ella. "Well, are you two going to get in here and help or what?"

Ella glanced at Cal and she didn't miss the pink tinge on his cheeks. What had he been about to say? *No way to find out now*, Sarcastic El muttered. *Great timing as always, Miss Mandie.*

They followed her through the dark bakery, side-stepping tables, on their way to the swinging kitchen door. Cal took a step back and motioned Ella to go in front of him. If it wasn't so early, Ella might have made a comment, but she was having a hard enough time forming the questions she wanted to ask Miss Mandie and keeping her mind off of Cal's disheveled dark hair. She heard Cal enter behind her and for a moment, they just stood in the brightly lit kitchen, being partially blinded by the light reflected off of all the stainless-steel counters and appliances.

"I've already got the cupcakes mixed up and poured. I'm about to put them in the oven. You two need to mix up the frosting." She handed Ella a note card with a printed recipe and shooed her and Cal toward the tilt-stand mixer.

"Miss Mandie," Ella started to say, glancing over at Cal.

"Everything you need is on the counter. Get to it if you want to get any gossip out of me," Miss Mandie said, turning back to slide the cupcake pans into the oven. It took some maneuvering, but either Ella and Cal were too tired to be completely unpleasant to each other, or the simple act of making frosting was distracting enough that they forgot they'd each tried to dupe the other by getting to the bakery first. They were able to mix up the frosting without a single shouting match. Ella was surprised when Miss Mandie came over to add different food coloring amounts to the separated batches of frosting. "Mix those up now," she said when she was finished. Cal took two bowls to stir and Ella took the other two. The frosting was turning various skin tones as they mixed.

"Now," Miss Mandie said, wiping her hands on her apron. "What do you want to know?"

Ella glanced at Cal, but he nodded at her, telling her to go first. She couldn't decide if he was being strategic or just polite. He hadn't tried to off her with a spatula while they'd been working on the icing, so she decided to go out on a limb and pretend it was politeness.

"Miss Mandie, you said you've known Clarence since he got here?"

Miss Mandie smiled and moved to check the oven. "Yes. I'd only been here about six months when he came to town. I was looking at buying this place. I had my earnings from my previous career, so money wasn't a problem." Ella remembered learning the fact that Miss Mandie had been a pornstar before she was even old enough to know what a pornstar was. Miss Mandie told anyone who asked about her past. She never made a big deal out of it, so no one in Hope, even the church ladies, had ever made it an issue.

Ella glanced at Cal to see understanding rather than confusion cross his face. Apparently, Cal had been told about Miss Mandie's past profession as well. Probably by her. Ella's gaze fell on the blue dress shirt Cal was wearing, rolled to the sleeves again, the top two buttons undone at his throat. He looked freshly showered and the smell of his cologne that she'd been valiantly trying to ignore, now seemed to be subtly overpowering the smell of vanilla and sugar wafting around the kitchen.

"My god he was good-looking," Miss Mandie sighed. Ella jerked her gaze away from Cal, forgetting for a moment who Miss Mandie was talking about.

"Clarence?" Ella asked without thinking.

Miss Mandie nodded. "Eyes so blue. And a body that a woman could . . ."

"What else can you tell us about him?" Ella quickly interrupted. "I mean, did he know someone in Hope before he moved here?"

Miss Mandie shook her head, her eyes going soft, a sad smile settling on her face. "No. He didn't have anybody when he moved here. Just him."

"Did he ever *talk* about family, friends back home?" Ella pressed.

Miss Mandie frowned. "No. He was always tight-lipped about his past. I got the feeling that there was some pain there. Like something had happened and there'd been a falling out."

So far, dead ends. Ella paused to frame her next questions and Cal jumped in.

"Then, did he ever tell you *why* he came to Hope?" Cal asked, moving to stand next to Ella as they watched Miss Mandie.

"He said he wanted a fresh start," she said, sliding on her oven mitts. "He'd been a journalist back east and he said he'd seen an ad in the Seattle paper that there was an opening for Editor-in-Chief at the *Hornblower*. So, he came here. Myrna hired him the same day he got to town. And the rest, as they say, is history." Mandie opened the oven and pulled the first tray of mouth-watering chocolate cupcakes out.

Ella was having a hard time feeling completely disappointed at how little Miss Mandie's information was helping when she was overwhelmed with chocolate fumes.

"Have you ever known Clarence to act, well, kind of funny?" Cal asked, picking up the slack.

Miss Mandie frowned, shaking her head. "No. Usually, you can set your watch by Clarence Ford. He's at the paper in his office from six in the morning to six at night. He goes to Fast Eddy's on Thursday nights to watch the football game. He goes to The Alphorn on Saturdays for Happy Hour. He goes to the late service at church on most Sundays unless he's working, which was pretty often. He's predictable." Miss Mandie paused. "He *was* predictable anyway. I think quitting at the paper was probably the only unpredictable thing Clarence has done in all the time he's been on the island." Miss Mandie was quiet for a moment. She picked at a smear of batter on her apron and shook her head. "That's why we would have never worked."

"Did you two date?" Ella asked, finding her voice again.

Miss Mandie nodded. "Well, back then, we called it something else, but yes. For a time. But, Clarence didn't want to get serious. The man wouldn't even pose for a picture with me anytime we went to a fair or party. It bothered me at first, but he just said he didn't like having his picture taken. At the time, I thought he just didn't want to appear tied to one woman. But, as he got older, I realized that wasn't it. He really just hates pictures. I think that's why he liked being Editor. Always behind the camera, behind the story, instead of out in front."

Ella frowned. She knew Clarence wasn't big on being in pictures for the paper. But not even taking a picture with someone you were dating? That was kind of strange. As she thought over all the time she'd known Clarence, she couldn't actually remember seeing his picture anywhere. The article in the paper about his retirement hadn't even had a photo of him.

"And he never told you any *details* about his life before coming to Hope?" Cal asked before Ella could speak up again.

Miss Mandie shook her head. "No. Clarence liked to live in the now. Like I said, he never talked about the past, and rarely made plans further into the future than his next issue of the newspaper. To be honest, that was what attracted me to him in the first place." She sighed. "Most days, I wish I'd never given him a second glance. Who knows where I'd be now."

Ella frowned. "Wouldn't you be here, running your bakery?"

Miss Mandie chuckled. "Yeah. But, instead of talking to you two about what never was, I'd probably be a saber-tooth married to a hot forty-five-year-old with a firm butt."

Ella grinned. "You still could be."

Miss Mandie rolled her eyes. "Why the hell would I want that kind of headache now? No, Bart is the only man in my life and for that I'm thankful. He's not much of a talker, but he's an artist when it comes to nipples on cupcakes."

"He should put that on his resume," Ella said. "And probably his dating profile. He could just leave off the 'on cupcakes' part." She smiled at Miss Mandie, but she could only half-listen as Miss Mandie talked about what she'd told Bart to do to woo the girl he was interested in at school.

What had she been able to learn from Miss Mandie? Clarence had no family here. Possibly no family at home if he didn't want to talk about it. Or maybe he'd had a falling out with his family. He was predictable. Ella had to admit that was true. The entire eighteen years she'd lived in Hope, she could probably count on one hand all the times she'd seen Clarence outside the newspaper. Cal's voice interrupted her mental ruminations.

"So, you're not worried that Clarence quit suddenly on Sunday, breaking his predictability streak, or the fact that no one's really seen or talked to him since?"

Miss Mandie frowned. "No, not really. I mean, it wasn't expected, but considering that the many rings of Christmas hell keep increasing every year, it was bound to crack him eventually. Besides, Clarence is a grown-ass man. And he's getting up there in years. It was probably time for him to retire anyway. Once he came to that conclusion, he probably didn't want to drag it out. Quit the day of his decision or six months later, what would it matter to him? After I saw the complete list of December events at the last town meeting, I wasn't surprised he cashed in his chips when he did."

"But, do you know why he'd hide in his house after?" Cal pressed.

"Probably to hide out from all of you and the rumor mill in this town." She shrugged. "Pretty smart move if you ask me. If he waits until mid-December to start strolling around town, he'll be old news. Everyone will be talking about Gingerbread Model City Installations or the Ugly Christmas Sweater Brunch."

Cal cut his eyes to Ella. Based on his expression, Ella had the feeling that Cal had come to the same conclusion. Miss Mandie's information had scored them goose eggs as far as usefulness in the Clarence conundrum. The ding of the door into the bakery sounded like a siren overhead, making them both jump.

"Oh, sorry," Miss Mandie said. "I couldn't hear the door over the mixer so I had the Baskins boy install that." She chuckled to herself. "Mmm-mmm-mmm, Jamie Baskin." She shook her head as if to clear it and focused on Cal and Ella again. "Now, those cupcakes are for the Mrs. Claus Bash tonight so they need to not look like two reporters frosted them. So, I'll let you in on my little secret." Ella felt Cal lean in towards Miss Mandie beside her when she lowered her voice. "To have the most sensual cupcakes, you need some sensual music woven in with the frosting. So, I like to turn on some Marvin Gaye when I'm getting frosting-busy." She reached over to a small boombox on the counter and checked the CD before turning it on and adjusting the volume. "It always helps me put the sexy into the frosting," she said over the first chords of "Come Get To This". She danced around, heading for the swinging kitchen door. She glanced back at them when she reached it, winked, and with a final evil grin, disappeared. They were quiet for a moment. Ella could hear Miss Mandie talking to whatever customer had come in, but it was faint. She glanced at the boom box.

"Yeah, it was because she couldn't hear the door over the 'mixer'," Ella muttered as the loud siren overhead went off again, signaling the entrance of another customer.

She moved over to the trays of cupcakes, mostly to put some space between her and Cal, but to cover her move, she started gently removing the cupcakes from the pan. Cal came to join her after a minute, depositing the four bowls of frosting on the table in front of them.

"Here," Cal said, holding out a frosting spatula to her.

She took it from him. "Thanks." They were quiet again as they started attempting to frost the warm cupcakes.

"Yeah, I think I definitely picked the right profession," Cal muttered after a minute of silence. Ella glanced over at the cupcake that Cal was trying to smother with tan frosting.

"It's easier if you try a swirling motion from the base of the cupcake," Ella said. "Just put the frosting in the middle and then swirl around . . ." She trailed off as "Let's Get it On" started playing and she realized how her explanation had sounded.

"So," Ella said, determined to change the topic before he realized it too. "I don't know what you were hoping to learn from Miss Mandie, but she didn't seem to have anything very helpful to say about Clarence." She realized she was tipping her hand to Cal a little with this admission, but she was hoping that, in turn, he might let his guard down and do the same.

Cal shrugged, noncommittal. "That's too bad."

Ella narrowed her eyes at him. Either he'd called her bluff or he was just being an asshole. She went back to frosting her cupcake with the dark brown frosting.

"So, how do you know about frosting cupcakes," Cal asked. She looked up to see him watching her. "Are you a ringer? Have you been roped into frosting the Mrs. Claus Blast cupcakes before?"

"Mrs. Claus Bash," Ella corrected. "And no, my mom is a pretty good cook. She taught me."

"That's pretty cool," Cal admitted.

Ella glanced at him. He wasn't being sarcastic. In fact, for some reason, Cal's expression looked pained. Just as quickly as she saw it, it vanished, replaced by his typical nonchalance which seemed to be his default setting when he wasn't actively pissed off and annoyed. On someone else, the expression might make him look careless, but it seemed to fit Cal's face. "So, what is this "Mrs. Claus Bash"?

Ella grinned in spite of herself. "Well, the town's Wild Oats club, which is made up of single women like Miss Mandie and Mrs. Thompson, get together every year for a meeting about the Mrs. Claus Fundraiser which is held at the Santa Ball and Crawl on Christmas Eve. They're supposed to make all the decisions and a plan during the meeting, but they just end up getting toasted and partaking in a Christmas-themed naughty treat from Miss Mandie's. And occasionally, booking a male stripper to dress as Mr. Claus. They have to farm that job out to the mainland though. The men in Hope are too smart to get roped into doing it."

Cal raised an eyebrow at her. "You seem to know a lot about these meetings. Are *you* going to get to try these cupcakes later?"

Ella rolled her eyes. "How old do you think I am? No, my mom is a member of the Wild Oats club. Well, honorary member. She doesn't go all the time."

"And Bill doesn't mind?" Cal asked. "Wait, I thought you said it was a club of single women."

Ella nodded, feeling the familiar sharp pain in her chest. "She was single when she joined. After my dad . . ." She couldn't finish the sentence, so she cleared her throat. "She was a full member the year after. Then, two years later, she met Bill. They never really kick anyone out of the club, but they don't give her a hard time if she's not there now."

"I'm sorry," Cal said, his voice barely more than a whisper. "About your dad."

Ella nodded quickly and reached for another cupcake. "Thanks."

They were quiet for a moment and before Ella could think through the question on her mind, she blurted it out. "So why did you come to Hope?"

The easy expression on Cal's face disappeared and immediately Ella regretted asking the question.

"It's a long story," Cal finally said. She decided not to push it. After another awkwardly quiet stretch between them "Mercy, Mercy Me" started to play in the background and Cal sighed. "I guess, in a way, I'm kind of like Clarence."

"You planning to call in and quit in the morning and then hide in your house?" Ella asked, swirling the frosting around the cupcake in her hand.

"No, as much as you'd probably enjoy that," Cal muttered. Ella looked at him, trying to figure out how to tell him she'd been joking. He didn't look like he'd believe her, even if she tried to explain. She felt the urge to say *something* though. She opened her mouth to speak just as the swinging kitchen door opened and Miss Mandie stuck her head in and looked at them.

"Forgot to tell you, the fondant nipples are in the fridge. Be careful. Bart was here until ten making them. There's *exactly* enough." And then she was gone.

"On today's edition of 'Sentences I Never Thought I'd Hear and Kind of Wish I Hadn't'," Ella muttered, setting down her cupcake and spatula. She moved to the fridge and started searching for something that screamed *"We are nipples! Use us!"* She'd been searching for several minutes when she heard Cal behind her.

"Staring into the abyss?" he asked.

"I can't find them," Ella grumbled, opening drawers and moving tubs of frosting, cream filling, and fruit around.

"The nipples are M.I.A.?" She could hear the hint of laughter in his voice.

She glanced behind her and she was so surprised by the look on his face that she almost put her elbow in a Saran-wrapped bowl of egg salad. Cal Dickson was smiling. It wasn't smug or sarcastic, or even sad. It was a full-on smile that reached his eyes.

"What?" Ella asked. "What is it?"

Cal shook his head, still smiling. "I love this town."

"Really?"

He nodded. "This may be one of the only places in the world where I could work on a paper and spend the butt crack of dawn frosting boob cupcakes and searching in a fridge for fondant nipples with . . ." He looked at Ella and for a moment, he seemed on the cusp of saying something, but his smile faltered, and he cleared his throat. "With the editor of the local paper."

Ella turned back to the fridge to hide her face. She mindlessly shuffled around the Tupperware containers on the shelf in front of her. The cold air felt good on her burning cheeks. She tried to breathe slowly and get her heart to return to a normal pace. *What had he been about to say?*

"Well, there had to be other papers out there. Papers where you might only have to cover *one* story a day. And they might be about murder trials or political races instead of balloon grottos and bake-offs." She said, trying to keep her voice even as she shifted a tub of cold cuts and several blocks of cheese to look behind them.

"I like balloon grottos and bake-offs," Cal said softly. "I'd rather cover them than murder and politics, any day of the week."

Ella stopped searching, trying to understand what Cal was saying. "You actually *like* covering the little Mickey-Mouse stuff in this town?" She turned to look at him.

"I love it," Cal said.

"Why?"

He moved his eyes from her face to the shelves above her head. "Because it's real. And, I like being able to report on good things. Things that make people happy and make me happy."

Ella snorted. "No offense but based on all the glaring over the last couple of days, I didn't get the feeling that you were actually happy."

Even from her position, kneeling in front of the fridge and looking up at him, she could see a brief look of embarrassment pass across his face. "Well, I . . ."

"Oh my," Miss Mandie called from the kitchen door. "What did I just walk in on? And in front of my fridge no less. Quick, cover the meatloaf, it's too fresh to see anything so raunchy."

Cal stumbled away from the fridge and turned his back on Ella, who had stood up so fast that she bashed her head on one of the fridge shelves.

"I'm afraid they're not perfect," Cal was saying to Miss Mandie as Ella rubbed the top of her head. He was motioning to the cupcakes. "At least mine aren't. Ella's look better."

"Oh, I think they're exquisite," Miss Mandie said.

"But they don't all look the same," Cal said.

Miss Mandie cut her eyes to him. "No two boobs look the same. Don't you know that by now? Doesn't mean they aren't exquisite." Ella snorted into her hand when she saw the wide-eyed look on Cal's face. Miss Mandie moved over to look in the fridge. "Here," she said, reaching into the back of the shelf Ella had searched three times. She pulled out a Tupperware and handed it to her. She winked at Ella. "And if you two are planning on getting up to anything else scandalous back here, at least put on a hair net. This is a commercial kitchen after all." She chuckled at the look of disbelief they both gave her as she sailed back out the kitchen door.

Ella set the Tupperware down on the counter top and removed the lid. Cal drew close to her to look in at the contents.

"Those . . ." Cal paused.

"Yeah," Ella said. "I don't think I've ever seen them so..."

"So anatomically correct," Cal added.

Ella shrugged. "Alright, let's get these gals outfitted." She started placing the nipples as carefully as she could in the middle of the cupcakes.

"Careful," Cal said. "I think they're coordinated to match the frosting."

"Crap, you're right," Ella muttered, pulling off the nipple she'd just placed on the cupcake and swiping the frosting off the bottom with her finger. She moved it to a cupcake with a closer color and she stuck her frosted finger in her mouth. She heard Cal shuffle his feet next to her. With her clean hand, she held the Tupperware out to him. "Here, I'm going to wash my hands."

"So, I can't remember what today's big event is," Cal said, calling to her over the running water. She shut it off and reached for a towel. Had she imagined it . . . or had Cal's voice just cracked?

"Uh, today is the opening of Santa's Court at Town Hall," she said, moving back to stand next to him.

"Oh, that's right." He was chewing on his bottom lip as he carefully placed a nipple. Ella felt her eyes dilate as she watched his long fingers twisting the fondant until he was happy with the angle. "This one has a different kind of ring thing."

"Nipple ring?"

"Yes, but it's not a ring," Cal said, frowning at the nipple. He reached down to touch it again and Ella felt a flash of heat low in her belly.

"That's because it's a barbell," she choked out.

He raised an eyebrow at her. "You sound like someone who knows."

Ella quickly turned her attention back to put a piercing-less nipple on the nearest cupcake. "Like I said, I've lived here eighteen years. I think I was about ten when I first asked Miss Mandie about the nipple rings. She told me what the different ones were."

"When you were *ten*?" Cal asked, looking surprised.

Ella grinned. "There was a line behind me at the counter. And as I'm sure you've noticed, Miss Mandie doesn't mince words."

"And your mom was ok with her telling you all about nipple rings?"

Ella shrugged. "Yeah. Miss Mandie's been here so long, most of the adults in town grew up going into her shop for coffee and danishes in the morning. Everyone just got used to the erotic being next to the everyday. I mean, she doesn't put any of the really racy stuff in the case, at least . . . not anymore."

"Ok, let's put a pin in that," Cal said with a grin. "It sounds like there's a story there."

"If you put a pin in what I'm talking about, there would be a collective empathetic groan of pain from the entire male population of Hope," Ella said, smiling. "Let's just say, Miss Mandie had her own take on 'Ding-Dongs'. Anyway, no one makes a big deal about Miss Mandie's creations, because they're *not* a big deal. Well, at least not big enough to get upset about." Ella grinned and bit her lip. "At least, not anymore."

"Another story," Cal said, turning to look at Ella.

The memory of Maybelle Jessup's choice for her one hundredth birthday cake and the number of cake pans Miss Mandie had said it had taken to bake just the shaft made Ella chuckle.

"See?" Cal asked. "How can you not love this town? Wasn't it hard to leave?"

Ella guessed he had a point in some ways. Of course, he'd only been in Hope for six months. He didn't know what it felt like to grow up here, to feel suffocated and... haunted in some ways by the memories. Cal was standing so close to her. She could feel his body heat radiating out of his shirt. And that damn shirt was the same shade of bluish-green as his eyes. She tried to concentrate on the task in front of her. There was one cupcake still without a nipple. It was on Cal's side of the table. She wasn't sure why she did it, but she picked the last nipple out of the Tupperware and reached across him, brushing against his warm abs with her forearm. She held her breath, trying to situate it on the cupcake without betraying to Cal what she was feeling. Stupid hormones. But, even she had to admit, it had been over a year since standing this close to Les had made her feel on the verge of passing out.

"Here, let me help," Cal said, his voice softer than she'd ever heard it. He reached out and carefully situated the nipple, his hand over hers. He'd bent over slightly to check their work and when he glanced back at Ella, his face was so close to hers, she could feel his warm breath stirring the hair above her ear. Ella's heart was pounding in her chest as she locked eyes with him. There was something strange in the way he was looking at her. Warmth in the depth of those eyes. She wasn't sure if she was leaning toward him, or if he was moving toward her. To be honest, she didn't care. She subconsciously licked her lips and Cal's eyes darted down to her mouth for a moment. Ella was on the verge of closing her eyes. Her brain had stepped out for a smoke break. She didn't care at the moment about what kissing Cal Dickson would mean. Something inside her was taking a sledgehammer to the wall around her physical needs that she'd carefully been building over the past months. She *needed* this.

"What did I say about hairnets, children?" Miss Mandie's voice boomed from the front of the kitchen.

20

CAL

Oh my god, Cal thought to himself. *This is really happening. Is she leaning in? Or am I?* While one part of Cal's brain was giving him a play-by-play and urging him on, the rest of his brain had whiteboards and markers out as they calculated the possible fallout from what he was about to do. It was hard for him to concentrate on anything, let alone the list of reasons why he *shouldn't* kiss Ella Danforth. Especially when he could smell the strawberry scent of her hair mixed with the perfume she wore that smelled like rain and grass. With her eyes like the sky over the sea and her hair the color of the white-gray sand, kissing Ella Danforth would be like kissing a summer day at the shore.

Cal knew or at least he *thought* he could break the spell she held over him if he had to. He could pull away and end this, though the gate on that thought process was closing . . . fast. Then, she ran her tongue across her lips and he knew he was a goner.

"What did I say about hairnets, children?" Miss Mandie's voice was a record scratch interrupting a near-perfect moment. Ella jerked away from Cal and was halfway around the table before his brain was working again.

"I can see the two of you are hard at work," Miss Mandie teased.

"We're actually done," Ella said quickly. "All done. And, uh, I've got to get back to the office. Newspaper office. I've got a big . . . lot of . . . big things . . . to take care of." Ella squeezed her eyes shut for a moment.

"Oh honey, don't let me interrupt," Miss Mandie said. "If I hadn't gotten any in three months, I'd be all over 'old blue eyes' here."

There was red creeping up from Ella's chest and into her cheeks. She was so damn cute at that moment, Cal wanted to kick himself for not just kissing her anyway. Who cared? Miss Mandie wouldn't have. Ella kept her head down and headed out the kitchen door. She didn't even turn back to glance at Cal. He wasn't sure why, but that stung. It didn't make any sense. She'd been embarrassed, hell, so was he. Miss Mandie was looking at him like his high school buddy Danny Fisher would after walking in on Cal with a girl. He half expected Miss Mandie to lower her voice and ask for the details on what had happened.

But, Ella hadn't just been embarrassed. Had it been regret he'd seen under all that? From what he'd overheard the day before, she wasn't in a relationship. What did she have to regret? Yeah, they were boss and employee, but would anyone besides them care? In Hope of all places? The feeling like a swift kick to the stomach told Cal he'd landed on it. That had to be it. The force was strong with the Hope rumor mill and the town did like to tease . . . sometimes mercilessly he'd noticed. That had to be part of it. After all, it was Miss Mandie that had caught them almost kissing. The rumor by the end of the day would be that Miss Mandie had walked in on him, pinning Ella to the wall, her legs, wrapped around his waist. That thought sent a shock of electricity through Cal and he gave himself a shake. What the hell was wrong with him? Wasn't he, just days before, counting his blessings for the six months of quiet he'd had in Hope with no romantic entanglements? Why was he inviting some kind of involvement with one now? And with his new *boss* of all people?

Like a bucket of cold water had just hit him in the crotch, that thought sobered him up. His boss. He'd been seconds away from kissing his boss. He'd been in the process of closing his eyes so he couldn't be sure if he was the instigator or if it was Ella. Had he just harassed his boss? Was that the real reason why Ella had practically sprinted out of the kitchen? Had he misread the situation? He immediately wished he was alone in the kitchen so he could bang his head against the fridge. How stupid was he? He'd gone months without feeling this drawn to a woman. He'd assumed he was just detoxing after New York and happy to do it. And then, in waltzes this infuriating woman, who takes the top job at the paper and has the nerve to screw up his equilibrium and kick awake a part of him that had been happily hibernating. And while this was happening to him, to her, he was just an employee. He was a reporter on the paper she ran. That was it.

The longer he stood in that kitchen, the clearer it was to him that he had completely misread what was happening between him and Ella. For a second, he'd had the fleeting notion that maybe they were on the same page, and she'd wanted . . .Crap. Where did that leave him now?

"Slow down," Miss Mandie said. Cal turned to look at her, confused. "Whatever is racing through your head right now," she continued. "Take your foot off the gas pedal. I'm afraid your head is going to explode."

Cal needed air. He needed to get away from Miss Mandie and this kitchen that smelled like frosting and Ella. He couldn't close his eyes without seeing the smile she'd given him while they searched the fridge, and he was uncomfortable for so many reasons when he remembered watching her tongue lick the frosting off her finger.

"I need to go too," Cal said quickly. "Uh, we finished." He gestured at the cupcakes and then had to resist grimacing as he realized how Miss Mandie could interpret what he just said. To his relief, rather than making a comment, she just nodded and laughed.

"I suppose I'll be hearing some more Nick Cave from upstairs when you get back home tonight?" She asked, pointing a spatula up at the ceiling. "Well, unless you two can make up before then, right?"

"Miss Mandie," Cal said quickly, not sure how to hit home how serious his next statement was going to be. "Please, don't say anything about what you think you just saw."

Miss Mandie raised an eyebrow at him.

"Please," Cal said. "I'm calling in a tenant-to-landlord favor."

"Is that some kind of New York thing?" Miss Mandie asked. "Because favors call for reciprocation out here, even when they're tenant-to-landlord."

Cal nodded quickly. "I'll owe you."

Miss Mandie smiled. It was part genuine and part-teasing. "Since it's hard to collect from a fleeing favor-ower, does this mean that you've changed your mind and you *aren't* moving out after Christmas?"

In the chaos of the events of the last week and especially after his phone call with Tara, he'd been purposely ignoring the fact that he'd told Miss Mandie and himself that he would be leaving Hope at the end of the year.

"Uh, for now," Cal's mouth said before his brain could stop him. "Sorry for the . . . short notice."

Miss Mandie shook her head. "I can't blame you. I'd stay too for a pair of legs like that." She tipped her head toward the door and winked before turning away from him to start boxing up the cupcakes. Cal pulled on his coat and muttered a quick goodbye to her before heading outside.

The cold winter air was pure relief when it hit his face. The sun was up and people were slowly streaming through the town square around the gazebo. There was already a huddle of tourists from the early ferry gathered around the plaque in front of the horn. And there were kids in the group. With an inner sigh, he hoped the three EMTs for the island were on call in case of a cold metal horn-lip skin situation. As he moved around the gaggle of tourists, Cal returned waves and "hellos" to the Islanders who greeted him, but he could feel his pace slowing as he drew closer to the *Hornblower*'s office and Ella. He didn't know what he was going to say when he found her. He just knew that he eventually *needed* to find her. He needed to explain. Or, to listen. Something. He couldn't just leave it as it was . . . Unless that's what she wanted?

Killjoy Cal chose that moment to ride in and ruin any possible good outcome he could hope for. *And that is why we haven't tried to have any of these entanglements since coming here.* Cal did his best to ignore this obnoxious part of his brain, but Killjoy Cal was already doing his incredibly annoying *I told you so* dance in his head.

He'd gone six blissful months in Hope as basically a non-entity. Just doing his job and enjoying the close feel of this odd little town. Why the hell would he want to throw that away? Especially for someone like Ella

Danforth? Killjoy Cal and Sarcastic Cal paused, both raising a hand as if they were going to make a point, but then it failed them. *Great*, Cal thought. *Just fabulous. Feel free to regroup and get back to me on that, guys.*

He slowed his pace even more, the closer he got to the newspaper. He tried to hold the situation at arms' length for a moment and study it like a journalist on the outside, trying to put the story together without being *in* it. He'd been happy before Ella came. But was he happy now? No comment. Mostly because he wasn't sure how to answer that. He wasn't *unhappy*, per se. But the blissful ease was somewhat complicated now. Did he *want* to feel the way he was feeling at the moment? No. Ok. Then *why* was he chasing after something that he hadn't wanted in the first place? He's not chasing after it. At least, he didn't think he was. Was that how Ella saw it? He was chasing *her*? He still wasn't sure if he'd started what they almost . . . started . . . back there, or if Ella had. Cal let out a growl of frustration. A couple that he didn't know paused to stare at him as they passed. Judging by the copy of the *Hornblower* they carried and the number of pictures they were taking with their phones, he guessed they also belonged to the early bird tourist crew.

The realization of just how many more tourists were in the square than usual lit a fire under him, forcing him to pick up his pace. They were only a couple of days into December as it was. He had events to cover. He had a job to do. The same one he'd been doing for the last six months. And that had nothing to do with Ella Danforth. Well, except that she was his boss. But she was just another Clarence. The thought didn't quite fit, considering how he'd felt stealing glances through the window at her in Clarence's old office while she chewed on her pen cap or typed away on her laptop, chewing on her bottom lip. *Get a grip, Cal. It was a whim. An accident. It sounds like she's just having a dry spell too. Hormones. That's it*, he said to himself as he approached the front doors to the paper. *Exhaustion, coupled with stress about the job . . .* even as he said the words inside his head to try to convince himself, he could tell how pathetic they sounded. He greeted Maddie, Pippa, and Marty on his way in. Katie's desk was empty and he knew Kurt was probably in the back, cleaning the machines and restocking supplies for the next run. He let his gaze wander to Ella's office as he passed it. He paused in his tracks when he saw it was empty.

"Where's Ella?" his mouth asked aloud before his brain could weigh in on it.

"Oh, she went to interview the candidates for Mrs. Claus," Pippa said. "She forgot to put it on the list. She was already planning on being at Town Hall at the end of the day for the first night of Santa's Court."

"Geez," Maddie said, looking up from her desk. "She's going to be at Town Hall all day?"

Pippa nodded. "There are some more installations going up today too, like the building of the gingerbread model of the town, and the Mayor's holiday message for the tourists coming to Hope."

"Ho, ho, Happy Hellidays," Maddie muttered. "I'll head over there as soon as I get these shots from the bake-off sorted." She glanced up at Cal. "Is that story ready? Ella wrote the first half of it, but I think she said she emailed it to you so you could add the winners and anything she missed."

"I . . . I'll check," Cal said. He was distracted. She hadn't assigned any of today's stories to him. He paused at the whiteboard on his way by. Next to every event for the day, Ella had either put herself down or Maddie. He felt a twinge of annoyance. Had she thought he couldn't handle any of them? She'd approved his articles after she reviewed them with almost no notes. She seemed like a team player, but she hadn't assigned him much the day before, and then nothing today? What was she trying to do? Did she think if she didn't give him any assignments that maybe he'd just quit? Was that why she'd tried to kiss him at Miss Mandie's? Or if he was the one that started it, was that why she hadn't pulled away from him? Was this a mind game?

Cal just stared at the full whiteboard, anger and some kind of emotional whiplash reverberating down his spine. It had been six months since he'd had to dissect and examine someone's motives like this. He could already hear Killjoy Cal clearing his throat in his head. Cal closed his eyes and told him not to say it. Six months. Six months with no entanglements in Hope and six months without having to actually talk to anyone from New York.

Then, in came Ella Danforth, screwing up his equilibrium. And then he'd accidentally answered the phone when Tara called. Two screw-ups and his life was starting to implode. His simple summer and fall in Hope were over, or at least, complicated now. And the phone call with Tara had felt like some kind of harbinger marking the beginning of the end of his freedom. He knew he was eventually going to have to go back to New York. If he didn't... He didn't want to think about the confrontation and melt-down, blow-out that would happen. But, if he could just stick to his original plan and stay in Hope through the holidays, maybe then... He didn't know what the "maybe then" contingency plan would be.

But, at the moment, he had a more pressing annoyance. Ella Danforth. Based on the assignments for the day, either she was making a statement about how incompetent she thought Cal was, she was embarrassed by what had almost happened between them and wanted to avoid him, or it was a power play with her taking the assignments to prove she didn't need him around. In any of the three scenarios, her intent was clear. She didn't want Cal around *her*. And that was fine with him. The morning had been a close call. Too close. If Miss Mandie hadn't walked in... He gave himself a shake. Non-entity. No romantic feelings on the island. Just peace and doing what he loved to do. Right? *Right?!* he asked Sarcastic and Killjoy Cals. They were momentarily speechless. Great. He took a deep breath and turned to head back to his desk.

He sat down in his chair behind his laptop and pulled up his email. Sure enough, there was the half-finished bake-off story. Ella's email was polite and to the point:

"Here's the first half of the story. Can you add the winners and give it some polish? Thanks, Ella."

She'd asked him to polish it. If she thought he was incompetent, she wouldn't have asked that. If it was a power play, she probably wouldn't have even sent him the article. Was he wrong again? He shook his head. He was overthinking this. There was nothing to dissect in the email that might allude to how she was feeling. He closed his eyes and dropped his head back so his face was turned toward the ceiling. What if Miss Mandie let something slip? Ella was an Islander. She was the one the town was going to believe. He'd be the one run out of town on a rail if she said he'd come onto her. Had he somehow managed to screw up his job *and* living in Hope with a single miscalculation? Not even a miscalculation. An *almost* miscalculation. They hadn't even kissed. His phone started ringing. He opened his eyes and sat up, picking it up to look at the screen. Tara. Again. He felt a heavy weight in his gut. Not now. He ignored the call, sending her to voicemail, and turned his attention back to his computer screen. He just needed to work. Forget the morning with Ella had even happened. From what he could tell, Ella was already ahead of him on that front.

He opened his bag and pulled out his notebook. He'd just started typing up the end of the story when he realized that he still had no idea where Ella had gone when she'd left the bakery during the bake-off. It hadn't been to talk to Miss Mandie, and he was pretty sure she hadn't gone back to Clarence's house and somehow got him to let her in. Otherwise, why would she have been so desperate to get information from Miss Mandie? Where had she gone? Cal felt another familiar pain in his gut that he hadn't experienced in the last six months. This time, it was the feeling he got any time he knew another reporter had a lead on a story that he'd been trying to find. She was ahead of him on that front too. As much as he liked Ella. No, as much as he was attracted to . . . He tried to clear the thought. As much as he liked living and working in Hope and would like to continue doing so, he needed to find out what was going on with his new editor and how it related to his old editor. He leaned back in his chair to think. He might have to play a little dirty to find out what the connection was.

Before he could talk himself out of it, he pulled out his phone and dialed Bill.

"Hey, Cal," Bill said. "What's going on?"

"Oh, hey Bill. I was wondering if I could take you up on that offer you made to fix that loose sole on my bowling shoes."

"You bet," Bill said.

"When would be a good time?" Cal asked, already knowing what Bill's answer would be. The island had an etiquette all its own when it came to bowling equipment repair and single guys that lived alone.

"Say, why don't you come by this evening with them? You could have dinner with us and I'll get that sole fixed right up for you."

"Oh Bill, I wouldn't want to put you out," Cal said.

"You won't be. And Helen is now nodding and mouthing things like 'tell him he has to come'. So, I guess I'm telling you that you're coming to dinner."

Cal smiled. "Well, I wouldn't want to upset Helen."

"You and me both," Bill said, dropping his voice. "Is seven ok for you?"

"Should be," Cal said. "Thanks, Bill. I'll see you then."

He hung up and set his phone down on his desk next to his computer. For a long minute, he just stared at it. Stage one of his plan was officially in motion for Operation: Under Her Skin. She'd stormed into town and thrown him out of balance, now it was her turn. If he could knock her off her game, she might let something slip about where she was or be careless with her notes or not notice if he happened to ask a leading question. He cracked his knuckles. No turning back now. He went back to work on his other articles. It was just after two when he finished them up. He sent them to Marty and pulled his jacket on over his blue shirt.

"Where are you headed?" Pippa asked as Cal went by her, heading for the front door.

"Gonna grab some lunch," Cal said quickly. "I'll be back soon." Maddie was already out on her assignments and Marty was buried in perfecting the layout for the edition. Pippa was the only one to acknowledge the fact that he was leaving. That was good. Fewer witnesses to potentially notice how long he was gone.

As soon as he stepped into the square he picked up his speed, heading for Evergreen. He was going to check on Clarence's house again. He had a feeling that he might be able to get Clarence to talk to him if he was by himself. After all, they'd worked together for five months. If something was going on in Clarence's life, maybe he'd be more willing to tell Cal about it. They had similar stories as to how they got to Hope. Maybe Clarence would give him the scoop instead of Ella. Maybe Ella was working on a biographical piece about Clarence for the paper. Cal scowled in thought. It was possible, but if that was the case, why was she being so cagey about it? And what about that briefcase with the dark stain? If Clarence did open up to him, he had two options. He could keep the information to himself and scoop her on the biographical piece if that *was* what she was planning. Or, he could potentially offer the information to her as both proof that he could handle assignments that she *couldn't,* and as some kind of . . . peace offering. Right now, Cal just wanted things to go back to how they had been before Ella had come to town. At least . . . he thought he did. He did, didn't he?

This was the rational part of Cal's brain talking. The more feral part of Cal that he tried his best to keep on a tight leash, was hoping that the peace offering might get him more than just peace with Ella. *Nope. Danger, Will Robinson, Danger. Bury that thought.* She was the editor of the paper he worked for, he reminded himself. He didn't know what Ella's long-term plans were, but he knew that *he* wanted to stay in Hope and keep writing for the paper. It was a fact that had been getting clearer every day. *This* was what he wanted. The rational part of his brain didn't want to screw this up. If he could solve the Clarence mystery for her, maybe it would help clear the air between them and they could just become decent coworkers. Coworkers. The word felt hollowed-out and like a let-down and Cal didn't want to try to figure out why. It felt too much like looking over a cliff.

He turned down Evergreen. The block with Clarence's house was quiet. When he got to Clarence's overgrown yard, he headed right up the walkway to his front door without pausing. In case someone saw him, he didn't want to look suspicious. He was already in danger of being put through the rumor mill for one thing today. Better to not tempt fate with a second piece of gossip. He tried Clarence's doorbell. He didn't hear any echo of the chime inside the house, so he knocked on the door. He waited, straining his ears to listen for any sound of movement inside the house. It was silent. He looked at the window next to the door where he'd seen the curtains flutter the day before. They were still. Maybe he should break a window. After all, what if Clarence had had a stroke and was dying on the floor? He bent down and picked up a rock out of Clarence's overgrown flower bed.

Then his cell phone rang, almost causing him to jump out of his skin. He snatched it out of his pocket and answered without looking at the ID.

"Cal?" It was Reverend Anderson.

"Hi Rev, what can I do for you?" Cal asked, his gaze moving to the rock in his hand. He quickly dropped it.

"Oh, I just wanted to double-check. You said Ella would be at the newspaper for our Confounding Caroler Singing Gram, but she's not here."

Cal closed his eyes. He'd forgotten about sending the Confounding Carolers after her. That had been in retaliation for the Balloon Grotto. But, he had already gotten himself invited to dinner over at her house. And now with the Carolers on top of that . . . "Sorry Rev, but I need to cancel," Cal began.

"Oh! We just heard from the staff that she's over at Town Hall! We're heading there now! We'll make sure she knows who to thank for her Carol-Gram! Bye, Cal!"

"No, Rev . . ." But it was too late. The line was already dead. He tried redialing the Reverend, but it went to voicemail.

He took off, walking as quickly as he could without drawing suspicion, heading for Town Hall. He had to intercept the Carolers before they got to Ella. He had his head down and he almost plowed into someone walking the other way on the sidewalk.

"Sorry," Cal said quickly, glancing at the man. He was young, maybe a year or two younger than Cal, and carrying a grocery bag. Cal didn't recognize him, but that wasn't unusual since Cal had only been in town for six months. Three thousand people wasn't a large town, but it was still a lot of faces to memorize. The man didn't say anything to him. He didn't even look at Cal. He just pulled his knit cap down over his ears with his free hand and crossed the street. *How you like that? A little dose of New York "friendliness" all the way out on the island,* Sarcastic Cal muttered. Killjoy Cal cleared his throat. *Uh, Confounding Carolers?* Cal picked up his speed. He had to get to them before they got to her.

The town center was full of tourists, slowing Cal's progress as he struggled toward the Town Hall. Unfortunately, most of them seemed to be headed in that direction as well. His heart fell when he saw the crowd of Confounding Carolers ahead of him, already wearing their Santa hats and matching green and red sweaters. A pack of tourists stood between him and the Carolers and the tourists had stopped moving forward so they could have a heated debate about their next stop. Cal tried to sidestep them, but it wasn't a small group and as he moved, he heard a pitch pipe echoing around the square. He froze in his tracks and looked up in time to see the doors to Town Hall opening. Emerging, along with a crowd of gingerbread-clutching tourists, was none other than Ella Danforth.

His heart sank as he saw Reverend Anderson link arms with the ten other carolers as they formed a circle around her and began singing "Do You Hear What I Hear?" before launching into a surprisingly good rendition of The Beach Boys' "Little Saint Nick" that had a lot of hip thrusting and hat waving. The tourists all around Cal had pulled out their cameras and phones to take pictures and record the spectacle. Cal's heart had stopped beating. He was pretty sure he could hear it flat-lining in his head as he watched Ella's complete humiliation. She was trying to smile and nod and laugh, but Cal could see the bright red flush on her face. A cowardly thought occurred to Cal. Maybe she would think someone else in town arranged for the Carolers to come for her. Like her mom, or Miss Mandie . . . or Pippa . . .

"This Carol Gram," Reverend Anderson boomed out loud enough for the whole crowd to hear, "has been brought to you by Cal Dickson!"

Cal groaned. So much for that thought. The sun chose that moment to emerge from behind the clouds and shine down on him like a spotlight. He saw Ella's head swivel in his direction and then her gaze locked onto him.

"All proceeds for booking the Confounding Carolers go to the Anacortes Food Pantry!" Rev continued. "If you're interested in sending your own Carol Gram, come and see us! Thank you! We are the Confounding Carolers!" The crowd erupted in applause and Cal turned, jostling the tourists around him as he headed back toward the office. He was *not* fleeing. He wasn't. It was just . . .that look in Ella's eyes when she'd spotted him was terrifying. She'd been shooting I-will-kill-you-slowly-and-enjoy-it daggers at him with her eyes but the rest of her face had still been smiling. He needed to smooth things over, but also remove himself from the line of fire and he thought he had a way to do both. He fought his way through the remaining tourists near the newspaper office and broke into a run to get to the door. His one comforting thought was the fact that Ella would *also* have to fight her way through the crowd to get back to the office. He jogged through the reception area and skidded to a halt in front of the whiteboard.

"Where's the fire?" Pippa asked. "Which is an actual possibility with everything that's going on."

Cal checked his watch and looked down the list at the remaining assignments for the day. He picked up the dry erase marker from the tray and jerked the cap off. With his thumb, he erased Ella's name from the last four.

"Tell Ella I'll cover the Christmas Lionel Trains Display set-up over at the library, the children's Christmas Book display, the Giving Tree Community Gift Donations program launch at the elementary school, and the pre-game rally for the Powder Puff Christmas Queens Football game at the high school."

"Wow," Pippa said. "Did Ella pull out her whip and crack it all the way from Town Hall?"

Cal blocked the image that immediately came to his mind, as well as the reaction his body had to the blocked thought. "Uh, no, I just . . . she's already covering so much. And all my stories are in," Cal said quickly, heading for the hallway to the press room, one hand on his messenger bag.

"Ok . . ." Pippa said, not sounding entirely convinced. "But where are you going now? The front door puts you closer to all those assignments."

"Oh, uh, I know a shortcut!" Cal called to her before he pushed through the press room door. He didn't want to risk running into Ella when she most likely was about to put out a contract on his head. Better to slip out the back. He was halfway down the alley before his pace slowed and he remembered that he was having dinner at Ella's house that night.

Boy, Cal. When you screw up, you don't half-ass it.

Cal told Sarcastic Cal to shut up in his head and reached for his phone. Five minutes later, he was standing in front of the library, trying to get out of dinner with Bill and not having any luck.

"Helen's been cooking all day. I can't tell you how excited she is that you're coming for dinner," Bill was saying.

"Oh, Bill, I forgot I need to take care of some things at work . . . Can we . . ."

"What?" Helen's voice now. Bill must have had him on speaker phone. "I'll call Ella. She shouldn't be working *anyone* so hard that they don't have time for dinner!"

"No!" Cal almost shouted. He took a deep breath. "No, it . . . it'll be fine. I'll just finish it up tomorrow morning." He could feel the heavy weight in his stomach. "I'll . . . I'll be there at seven."

He hung up and for the second time in one day, wished he had a hard surface to bang his head against. He sighed and looked up to see Jacob O'Malley, clad in his Lionel Trains Christmas sweater and matching conductor's hat, standing in the library window, waving at him. Cal waved back, sighing inwardly. After everything today, he could at least cover these assignments for her. Some small penance. Of course, with how mad she was at him, taking her assignments might make it worse. He was counting on Pippa to soften that blow for him.

Seven o'clock came all too soon and as much as Cal wanted to drag out the Powder Puff pre-game, the girls in football pads were ready to go home by 6:45 and Cal was smart enough not to cross them. With nothing else to delay it, Cal finally started making his trek across town to Shell Street. He walked slowly, but it still felt like the shortest trip he'd ever made from one side of town to the other. The yellow house with the Christmas lights he'd helped hang only a few nights before materialized in front of him and as the Christmas lights started chasing along the edge of the roof, he felt his pulse rising to match them. What would Ella do when she saw him on her porch?

"Hi, Cal!" Bill called as he came around the side of the house.

"H-Hi, Bill," Cal called back. "I hope I'm not late." He checked his watch.

"Nope, right on time." Bill squinted past Cal to look down the street. "Which is more than I can say for Ella." He paused and looked at Cal. "Was she still at the office?"

"Uh, I don't know," Cal said. "I was over at the high school. She . . . she's not here yet?"

Bill shook his head. "No, but she'll be along any minute. If not, Helen will send out a search party."

Bill clapped Cal on the back, ushering him up the porch steps in front of him. They got to the top and Cal was starting to get his pulse under control. She wasn't home yet. Maybe by some miracle, he could come up with a good excuse to leave before she got there.

Bill turned back to face the street. "Here she comes."

Cal froze. *Thanks for that, Universe. Anything else you want to screw up while you're here? Wanna make me say out loud what Ella and I were doing in that dream last night? Bill's armed. Maybe I'll get lucky and he'll shoot me.*

"You look like you've had a long day," Bill was saying to the approaching Ella. Cal took a deep breath and turned to look. There was Ella. Her ponytail was loose and hanging down over one shoulder. She had two pens stuck in her hair and what looked like a swipe of smeared dry erase ink across her cheek. Her shirt was wrinkled as if she'd spent all day being jostled by tourists and squeezed by crowds and she looked exhausted.

"It's been a Tarantino film of a day," Ella muttered, stomping toward the porch. Her gaze was on the ground. "It started with some choice scenes reminiscent of *Pulp Fiction,* ran the gambit of *Reservoir Dogs, Four Rooms, Planet Terror, Deathproof,* and ended on *Kill Bill.* Though, if I don't get two fingers of scotch in short order, I think it may come full circle back to that scene in *Pulp Fiction* with a shot of adrenaline to the ches- . . ." She stopped when her gaze locked onto Cal. For a moment, they just stared at each other. Then Ella's gaze narrowed. "Why are you here?"

"Ella Rose Danforth!" Helen said from the doorway. "Did you leave your manners in Seattle? You may have forgotten but we do *not* talk to our guests like that on the island. Now come inside and help me get dinner on the table."

Ella side-stepped Cal and headed inside. He knew it was probably his imagination, but he swore he could feel an icy breeze emanating from her as she moved past him.

"Sorry about that," Bill muttered. "El can be a bit . . . dramatic."

Cal shook his head. "No, this is my fault. It's . . . It's been a long day. And I'm . . . I caused some of it." He turned to look at Bill. "I should just go. Let you and your family have dinner in peace."

Bill shook his head, fixing Cal with a serious look. "If you and Ella have beef, you definitely need to stay and get it sorted out. Ignoring it isn't going to fix the problem."

Cal was out of reasonable-sounding arguments, so with no other means of escape, he shot the street in front of the house a final longing look before being ushered inside by Bill.

"Here," Helen said, motioning to a chair on the long side of the rectangular dining table. It was pushed against the wall, leaving a place for one person at either end and two places, side by side on the long side. He sat where Helen had told him to, hoping either she or Bill would take the place next to him. But as soon as that happy thought crossed his mind, Cal was sure he could hear the Universe laughing at him. Bill sat down at one end and poured Cal a glass of ice water while Helen returned to the stove in the open-plan kitchen. Cal stared at the ice water in his glass, wondering if it would be the warmest thing he'd experience on his side of the table during the meal.

"El!" Helen called, moving toward the staircase. "Dinner's on. Get down here!"

Helen sat down at her place on the other end of the table and smiled at Cal. "Feel free to start filling your plate. If we wait on Ella, it'll all be cold by the time she makes it down here." She looked over at Bill. "Did she tell you why she was late or why she is in such a spectacularly foul mood?"

Bill shook his head. "Maybe it's just . . . you know . . ." Cal and Helen both looked at Bill. He was a little red in the face now. "You know . . . hormones?"

Cal caught a glimpse of Helen raising an eyebrow at her husband. "That's always your first go-to, isn't it? Never the possibility that there was something awful that happened at work or someone was being an asshole or that it was just a long day. Always hormones, huh?"

Bill started trying to back-pedal. Cal felt the nudge in his gut, telling him to fess up about the Carolers and how Ella's bad mood was most likely because of him. He was the asshole. He wavered back and forth, trying to get the courage up to say something, but the creak of wood stopped him and they all turned to see Ella stomping down the stairs in gray sweatpants, a zip-up hoodie, and Cookie Monster slippers. Her hair was twisted into a messy bun on her head again and her expression was "exhausted nun running a nightclub".

She didn't look at Cal. She paused to notice the seating arrangement and then moved to the only empty chair and purposely moved it closer to her mother and away from him. She sat down and immediately pulled a basket of rolls toward her.

Cal could hear the old cartoony black and white cat clock on the wall ticking as its eyes and tail darted from one side to the other. He was pretty sure that if he was a cat, he'd be doing the same thing at the moment. Next to him, he could feel the anger rolling off of Ella in waves as she piled three rolls on her plate and reached past Cal to push the roll basket towards Bill. Yeah, this was going to be a long dinner.

21

ELLA

Ella was going to kill Cal Dickson. *The freaking Confounding Carolers? Did the man have a death wish?* While Rev had been talking, she'd seen him disappear into the crowd of tourists. *You can run, but you can't hide.*

But she'd have to be smart about killing him. With a town as small as Hope, covering up a murder wouldn't be easy. Maybe she could make it look like a suicide. Like he hung himself by the strap of his messenger bag. Or beat his own head in with her star mug one night while working late at the paper. Or he slipped on the wet bathroom floor in his apartment. Of course, she wasn't quite sure where that was, but as Editor, she could probably access his employment file. She might have to butter Myrna up if she didn't already have access to it, but she knew Myrna's drink of choice.

"I saw the Carolers got you," Agnes Redding's voice interrupted Ella's homicidal fantasies.

"Yep," Ella said, forcing a smile and meeting Agnes' gaze. Agnes Redding and Sue Whitehorse owned Red & White Floral, Hope's only flower shop. She had her holiday cart full of poinsettias, fresh garlands, and wreaths and she was trying to muscle through the crowd without making much progress. Agnes was a small woman, barely cracking five feet. The swirl of tourists was a river, causing an eddy around her as they doubled back to look at her cart before being called to keep up with their group. When one tourist bumped into the cart and almost tipped over Agnes and her wares,

Ella stepped in.

"Here Mrs. Redding, let me give you a hand with that." Together, the two women were able to steer the cart through the crowd and back to the little shed next to her shop.

"I'm sorry you ended up being the first sacrificial victim to Rev and his Carolers this year," Agnes huffed as she began taking poinsettias off the cart and carrying them to the side door of the shop. "I was hoping it would be old Clarence. That goat's hind-end of a man deserves it."

That perked Ella up. "What do you mean, Mrs. Redding?"

She paused and grinned at Ella. "Ella, you're not a kid anymore. You can call me Agnes." She continued on into the workroom of the shop.

"Ok. Thanks . . . Agnes." Ella tussled with indecision for half a second and then grabbed a couple of plants off the cart and followed her inside. "What did you mean about Clarence?"

"Oh," Agnes said, frowning at the lack of counter space around her before settling on the large square worktable in the middle of the room and shoving the plants toward the middle. "He was supposed to run a big piece for Sue and me at the end of November, advertising our new greenery supplier and the testimonials from mainland buyers, that kind of thing." Ella nodded, hoping this would speed Agnes up in her explanation.

"And?" Ella asked.

Agnes shook her head. "And the old fart sent the kid to do it. He's alright, but he had a full plate already and Sue and I didn't get to look over the photos and pick which ones we wanted in the spread." Ella gave an inward sigh. Only in Hope would the subjects of a promotional piece get editorial control over photographs.

"I called to complain and Clarence couldn't get off the phone with me fast enough. He was so distracted; he couldn't even remember my name," Agnes muttered, heading back out to the cart.

Ella trailed after her. "What do you mean, he couldn't remember your name?"

Agnes grabbed another armload of plants and greenery and Ella followed suit. "He was babbling. Probably not expecting me to actually have the gumption to call and complain. I think his mind was starting to go anyway. Probably a good thing he quit while he was ahead. It's just too bad it had to happen while we were expecting that big boost of a piece. I think siccing the Confounding Carolers on him might be some satisfactory payback. Sue and I might even take lawn chairs over to his house and sit across the street to watch him . . ."

"Sorry . . . Agnes," Ella interrupted, hoping she wouldn't immediately piss the woman off. "What name did he call you?"

Agnes set her load down on the table and when she turned to face Ella, her annoyance was clear. Ella immediately regretted cutting her off in midstream. Mrs. Redding's lectures to misbehaving children were legendary and Ella had the feeling she was about to get her own adult-sized version. It really would be a fitting end to an exhausting day.

Instead, Agnes crossed her arms. "You know, over the last few months, Clarence has pissed off a lot of people in town. He's always been a part of the town, going to events, always stepping up to help townsfolk in need, that kind of thing. But for the last few weeks, it's almost like he's become a different person."

Ella just nodded, hoping Agnes would tell her more and she wouldn't have to risk interrupting her again. But Agnes seemed to be finished, as she started to carefully stretch the garlands out across the table before picking up a spray bottle and spritzing all the greenery. Ella took a deep breath and tried again.

"So, uh, do you remember what name he called you?"

Agnes frowned, this time in concentration. "Asen . . . Asenetta? Or something like that." She chuckled as she pumped the spray bottle and fussed over the plants. "At first I thought he was insulting me. But then I thought maybe he was just combining my name with Sue's or something." She shook her head and looked over at Ella. "I tell you, Ella, it's a good thing you came home when you did. I think the job finally got Clarence." She turned her attention back to the plants. "Still, just in case it was some kind of act, I wouldn't mind seeing the Carolers singing "Good King Wenceslas" at two a.m. on his front lawn."

Ella nodded and thanked Agnes before letting herself back out the shop's side door and heading for home. She was walking slowly, thinking about what Agnes had told her. Despite what the woman had said, she couldn't imagine Clarence's mind going.

But, she couldn't imagine the man being overwhelmed either. The Clarence Ford she'd known before leaving for school didn't *get* overwhelmed. She remembered one hectic summer weekend when Hope's marathon was happening at the same time as a weekend-long Shakespeare festival at the town gazebo, a police demonstration for the island's K-9 attack dog unit at City Park, and a Knife and Coin Show was taking place on the lawn next to Town Hall. But because Hope Island was only five miles across, the marathon had to double around and back through town several times, leading the runners between the knife demonstrations, attack dogs, and actors, some of whom were using pyrotechnics. The memory of the weekend still made Ella's pulse race, thinking of all the near misses. But she had a clear memory of looking up at Clarence, his expression never wavering from "calm amusement" as he covered every event simultaneously. Clarence Ford was a solid rock, sticking out of a sea of chaos. Unmoved and unmovable. So, that part of Agnes' story was hard to believe. But if he was messing up her name (a journalistic sin Clarence prided himself on never committing) something had to be up. Clarence would always tell Ella and the rest of the staff, "This is a community paper. Without the community, there's no paper. So, learn their names; get it right. We work for *them*."

Ella was pleasantly surprised when she found herself approaching home. Her feet had carried her through town while her mind continued to pick at the irritating puzzle that was Clarence Ford's recent behavior. Bill called to her and she was in the process of telling him about her day when she saw ... him.

Really? It wasn't enough for her day to torture her with visions of Cal Dickson all morning after their frosting fiasco? She'd just gotten the image of him, standing there, smiling down at her, bathed in the warm glow from the fridge, out of her head. Of course that was before the Carolers. Cal was standing on her front porch with Bill. Hair tousled and an almost guilty expression on his face. Instead of feeling her pulse pick up, she felt numb. Why was he on her porch? Did he come to gloat at her embarrassment? She shivered as another thought occurred to her. In high school, she'd liked a guy and he'd led her on, acting like he was into her too. Then, at the school dance, he'd laughed at her when she'd asked him to dance in front of his friends. Were the Carolers Cal's way of laughing at her for what they almost did in Miss Mandie's kitchen?

"Why are you here?" She'd asked. She knew her tone was blunt, but she didn't care anymore. Of course, her mom cared. She ignored her and Bill and headed inside. She glared at the dinner table, seeing it was set for four. So, they'd invited him for dinner. Or had Cal gotten *himself* invited to dinner? Why? To view her humiliation and discomfort up close? She went into her room and shut her door, probably harder than necessary. She tossed her shoulder bag on her bed and stared at her reflection in the mirror. She looked like she'd been road-hauled by a bookmobile. Pens stuck in her lop-sided ponytail, reading glasses still hooked onto her wrinkled button-up shirt under her jacket, a smudge of ink on her cheek, and a slight slump to one shoulder from the weight of the books, laptop, and papers in her shoulder bag. If the day had been normal and she'd found out Cal was coming to dinner, she might have tried to make herself look presentable. But now when she thought about Cal all she could see was the laughing face of a high school asshole. Echoed by the laughing crowd of tourists today in the square. And before that the laughing faces of everyone she knew at her defining moment, so many Thanksgivings ago. Laughter. The soundtrack for her humiliation. Ella glared at herself in the mirror. She started pulling pens and rubber bands from her hair. Tonight, she was going to look however the hell she wanted. Cal didn't exist. She was going to eat and then do some work and go to bed. Tonight was Ice Queen Ella's time to shine.

By the time she made her way downstairs, Bill, her mother, and "unacknowledged Asshole in chair three" were already seated, leaving only one chair for her. And unfortunately, it was right next to said asshole. Ella didn't look at him as she dragged her chair closer to her mom and sat down.

The rolls were in front of her, which from the brief consoling look her mom gave her seemed to be by design. Ella tried to not grit her teeth as she piled them on her plate. Of course, someone had probably called her mom to tell her that Ella had gotten "Caroled".

"So," Helen asked into the silence that stretched across the table. "How was everyone's day?"

Bill started talking about a couple of phone calls the station had gotten. Something about some lost tourists wandering around the residential neighborhoods after dark, but Ella wasn't really listening. It was all she could do to try to focus on her Ice Queen exterior and not stab the asshole next to her with her fork. The delicious smell of roast, potatoes, vegetables, and fresh-baked rolls was being overpowered by the deodorant or cologne or whatever it was emanating from Cal and invading Ella's nose every time he reached for plates or passed them in her direction. Ella shifted in her seat, trying to turn so the asshole wasn't even in her peripheral vision. Her mom glanced at her.

"What about you, El?" her mom asked when Bill was done.

"Oh, spectacular," Ella muttered, her mouth full of potatoes. "All other days must bow and pay homage to my day."

Helen rolled her eyes. She opened her mouth to speak and Ella braced herself for one of her mom's patented, "you pick the color of the day-whether blue or gray" speeches, but Bill spoke first.

"Well, that's a relief to hear." He had his head down, concentrating on cutting his roast. "From the way you were acting when you got home, it sounded like it must have been a doozy of a day." He glanced up and grinned at Ella. At first, she thought he'd missed the sarcasm in her voice, which would have been rare for Bill. Then she saw his gaze move to Cal before flicking back to her and the warm look he gave her told her he understood. Ella had never been able to articulate it out loud, but sometimes, she felt like her dad was looking out at her through Bill's eyes. The thought made her throat feel tight and she dropped her attention to the roll she was pulling apart as she tried to clear it.

"I'll tell you who *wasn't* having a good day," Bill said. "Gavin Blakesley."

"What's up with Gavin?" Ella heard her mom ask as she reached for her water glass.

"He's about to pull his hair out. Dirk Patterson won't let go of the idea of being a sequoia tree in the Parade of Trees. Gavin is having to arrange the dang thing this year because of Arty's triple bypass surgery."

"Dirk Patterson is five feet tall," her mom said. "If the wind blows . . ."

Bill was nodding now. "I know. I saw Gavin heading to Fast Eddy's at the end of the day. He said he needed to drink until he figured out a way to either talk Dirk out of it or reinforce his costume so the wind wouldn't throw him like a yard dart right into the ocean."

Ella chuckled in spite of herself. Dirk Patterson had always been sensitive about his height. The sequoia demand was only the latest in a series. He'd also demanded to wear stilts and be Uncle Sam at the Independence Day celebrations every year that Ella could remember as well as always demanding that he needed to stand in the back row of the Island Choir.

"And he says there are still a few businesses in town that haven't submitted their entry paperwork for the Parade," Bill said, pointing his fork at Ella. "One of them being the *Hornblower*."

Ella was about to make a comment about Gavin needing a bender weekend at Fast Eddy's if he was going to wait on her to pony up someone from the paper to *participate* in the event, but then an idea came to her, heralded by whatever the exact opposite was of the angel choir. She turned her head slowly to look at Cal who was making intense eye contact with his plate.

"Oh, did I forget to get that paperwork to Gavin? I'll do it first thing in the morning." She met Bill's gaze and smiled. "Cal is going to be the *Hornblower's* entry in the Parade."

A sound like something between a gasp and a gag came out of Cal. Ella instantly felt better. He'd effectively signed his own death warrant and then had the Carolers sing it. Cal had turned to look at her, but she'd gone back to her roll and the dish of butter her mom had passed her. She could feel his gaze attempting to burn a hole in the side of her face, but she suddenly felt too light to care.

"Oh, that's nice," Helen said, smiling reassuringly at Ella and then Cal. "What kind of tree will you be going as, Cal?"

"Uh," Cal choked out.

"Newspaper tree, of course," Ella said, grinning at her mom. "Surely you remember the costume. It's the same one the paper has been using since the Parade started in the sixties." She tried to change her tone into something that sounded mock-sympathetic. "I'm afraid it might be a little uncomfortable, but it *will* be festive."

"I'm sure," Cal muttered.

22

CAL

Well, if it was war Ella wanted, then that's what she'd get. He was at a bit of a disadvantage, having never seen whatever the hell the "Parade of Trees" was, but if it involved him being forced into a tree costume, it couldn't be anything good. He shook his head. To think he'd been on the verge of apologizing to her for the Carolers. Well, not anymore. She started it, with the damn Balloon Grotto assignment, but he was going to finish it. With what, he wasn't sure. It had to be something annoying and embarrassing. After all, he was fairly certain that both of those adjectives would describe whatever his role in the parade would entail.

A quiet voice in the back of Cal's head that didn't belong to Killjoy or Sarcastic Cal spoke up for the first time in many, many years. It was a young voice. Weak and unsure. *What about this morning at Miss Mandie's? Hadn't that meant something?* The voice sounded hopeful. Cal scowled, trying to shake off the thought. No. No, it hadn't. The only thing it meant was that it had been six months since he'd been that close to a woman he was attracted to. *No!* Now Killjoy Cal decided to make an appearance. *She's a pain in the ass and she's your boss. Fixate elsewhere.*

As he walked through the Town Square, Cal pulled the zipper up on his coat and ducked his head against the wind coming in off the sea, weaving its way between the buildings. He'd have to come up with something. Something good to use as his revenge against Ella Danforth. He'd be lying if he didn't feel a little embarrassed or . . . unsure of himself after the morning's events. The memory of her smile, her head tilted up to look at him, framed in the glow from the fridge. Something was melting at his edges and it needed to stop. He stomped up the stairs to his apartment, shouldered the door open, and threw his keys on the bed. Five minutes later, he was sitting on the counter across from his stove, watching his tea kettle heating up while Nick Cave played on the turntable. With everything that was happening in Hope, surely he could find something to volunteer Ella for that would make them even. Killjoy Cal tried to reason with him that it could just lead to even further escalation between them. Cal tamped down on this thought. He'd just have to make sure that his attack ended the war. Though, he wasn't sure what that would look like. He dragged his hands down his face, trying to banish the vision of Ella pinned against a wall, smiling that soft smile at him, her arms around his neck, legs around his waist . . . The teakettle's whistle was a welcome distraction. Still, as he dropped a tea bag into his mug and filled it with the hot water, he couldn't stop thinking about the fact that he was standing almost directly over the spot where he and Ella had almost . . .

He forced himself through his nighttime routine and then sat on his bed, staring at the comforter that had come with Miss Mandie's furnished apartment. It was patterned like a quilt, but every square had a different, realistic rendering of a fish, enclosed in a border of fishing rods. As he stared at it, all the fish gave him serious side-eye. "It's just hormones," Cal muttered to the fish. "That's it."

His phone beeped on the nightstand, and he turned to pick it up. He'd felt it buzzing in his pocket while he'd been at Ella's house for dinner, but he hadn't even looked at it.

Unsurprisingly, the call was from Tara. Again. Thinking about Tara was a double-edged sword. She was beautiful and spontaneous, but . . . but what? She was still calling him, six months after he left, asking him to come home. That was love, wasn't it? What felt like a five-pound weight seemed to be settling in his stomach. Was it love? He set his tea on his nightstand, climbed into bed, and turned off the light. Nick Cave sang through the dark, winding down on the last track on the album's B-side. Cal closed his eyes and tried to picture Tara's long black hair, saucy smile, and the way she turned every head in a room when she walked into it. He knew in his gut that she was who he was supposed to end up with. The weight in his gut grew heavier with every memory of Tara that paraded through his mind. That *was* love, wasn't it?

But, as he drifted into an uneasy sleep, the visions of Tara's dark eyes and painted lips changed to gray eyes and chocolate frosting.

The alarm sounded way too early. Cal glared at the clock and swore under his breath, realizing that he had forgotten to change his alarm time back to six. He shut it off and lay awake staring up at the dark apartment ceiling. He was replaying the events of the previous day when he remembered he had been "volun-told" that he was going to be a tree in a parade. This thought was followed by his internal edict that he would reap revenge or rain revenge . . . something with revenge (it was early) on Ella Danforth. That thought was enough to get him to put his feet on the cold floor and start his day.

He had a plan. He'd get to the office first and go through the events in the assignment book on Ella's desk. After all, it *was* Clarence's before it was hers. And he'd find something to sign her up for. Ok, he had to admit, it wasn't a great plan. Not yet, anyway. But Cal was always a last-quarter comeback when it came to retaliation. After all, he made it through high school and college and almost three years into his dad's post-graduation plan for him before he rebelled. He could play the long game with Ella Danforth. It was still early in the month.

But the universe seemed to have checked his envelope of karma money and found it to be light that morning because a warm glow was already coming from the Editor's Office when he stumbled into the otherwise dark building. He stifled an inner groan. Of course, she was already in. He really needed to master the skill of plotting revenge somewhere out of earshot of the universe. He moved past the office without looking at it and sat down behind his desk. But it was harder to ignore the pull of the inner-office light when it was constantly in his peripheral sight. He finally gave in and looked. The door was shut and he could see Ella completely absorbed in whatever she was typing on her computer. As he watched her, he couldn't shake the nagging feeling that she might be working on something other than stories for the paper. What if she was working on a story about Clarence? Maybe he should go back to Clarence's. Maybe he'd have more luck getting Clarence to talk to him early in the morning, *and* by himself. Maybe, it would be so early, Clarence would open the door to him without thinking. The thought of having another thing over on Ella, sweetening his impending revenge on her, had him out of his seat.

The bell over the office front door jingled just as he picked up his messenger bag and coat.

"Hey," Maddie said when she spotted him moving past Ella's office.

"Oh, morning," Cal said. He hesitated. If she asked him where he was going, he'd have a limited choice of reasonable responses for that early in the morning.

"El ask you to come in early too?" Maddie turned to toss her coat over her chair.

"Uh," Cal started to say.

"Oh, that's right. She probably had you come in early to try on the tree costume." Maddie's grin was far too devious for that early in the morning.

"Try on the costume?" Cal asked, dread pinning him to the spot.

Maddie nodded. "Well yeah. In case we have to do any alterations to make it fit you. Though, I'm not sure what that would be. It's not really something you can make alterations to. The *Hornblower* has been a part of the 'Walking Dread' for many years and the costume is at least half the tradition."

"Walking Dread?"

Maddie nodded, making a dismissive gesture. "It's what most Islanders call the Parade of Trees. It started as a joke about fifty years ago but then it became a town tradition and one thing you can set your watch to around here is the fact that this town will *never* abandon a tradition, whether it's been one year or a hundred. Once something is a 'tradition' in Hope, it stays. Forever. Honestly, I think that's why there's so much crap going on during the holidays."

"That sounds reasonable," Cal said.

Maddie's grin widened. "Hold onto that thought when you see the costume." She motioned for Cal to follow her down the hallway. "Marty said the last few years the staff have drawn straws to see who had to be the *Hornblower* tree. It was nice of you to volunteer."

As Cal followed her, he was pretty sure he could already feel the "Walking Dread" setting in. "Yeah, nice," he muttered.

They paused in the hallway in front of the storage closet door and Maddie fumbled with the key until she got the doorknob to turn. "Brace yourself. There's a good chance that the last time this door was opened was last year when the costume was put away."

She wasn't kidding. The closet was piled with binders and expandable files of old clippings that, based on the faded pen ink on their labels, dated back to the sixties. And those were just the ones on the shelf next to him. The room was dusty and Maddie might have been right about the last time the door was opened. In the six months he'd been at the paper, he'd never had an occasion to even pause outside the door in the hallway.

"There it is!" Maddie said with the air of a game show host revealing the grand prize to the winner.

Cal didn't feel like jumping up and down or promising to neuter his dog when he saw it. He wasn't exactly sure what he'd been expecting when he thought "newspaper tree costume", but it wasn't the three-piece bulky paper mâché monstrosity sitting in a lop-sided pile in the corner. It looked like someone with a vague notion of what a tree looked like had used three tires of different sizes as a mold for newspaper mâché that had browned and yellowed with the years.

Maddie must have misunderstood the horror on his face for confusion. "Oh, you use the suspenders to put it on."

Cal wanted to tell her that he wasn't going to wear that thing at all, suspenders or otherwise, but when his mouth opened, he was only able to articulate one word. "Suspenders?"

"Here, I'll show you." Maddie moved across the room and picked up the widest piece. It was round and so wide he wouldn't be able to get through the door while wearing it. Oh yeah, Ella Danforth was going to pay for this.

Five minutes later, he was draped in the bottom piece which fell to his knees and was held up by two "suspenders" made of thick elastic that made the piece bob up and down and almost trip him with every step he took.

"Ok, next piece," Maddie said, lifting a taller and narrower round piece which she unceremoniously dropped over his head, pinning his arms to his sides. The piece was snug around his shoulders. Maddie was frowning. "Huh, I guess the paper hasn't had anyone tall be the tree before. Looks like there's a gap."

"Oh goody, a gap," Cal muttered.

She shook her head. "Don't worry. I'll talk to El. We can cover it up with tinsel or something."

"Awesome," Cal sighed.

"Just one left." She picked up the final piece. It was pointed and frilly as if the person making the costume had started with the headpiece and hand cut bits of newspaper, glued them to thin pieces of wire, and fringed them to look like actual fir tree branches but the work was so exhausting that when it came to the rest of the costume, they just gave up. Maddie moved to stand behind him. "Can you crouch or something?"

Cal sighed again and squatted down. Almost immediately, his peripheral vision was gone and he was staring out through a hole cut for a much smaller face. His cheeks were pinched as the decades-old, hardened paper mâché cut into his skin.

"There," Maddie said, moving around to look at him, hands on her hips. Cal stood up and Maddie frowned. "Yeah, we'll have to do something about that gap too. She shook her head. "I guess people were smaller back then. Oh well, nothing some extra decorations and ornaments can't fix. You wanna show El?"

"No," Cal said quickly. Maddie raised an eyebrow at him. "It'll be more fun if it's a surprise."

Maddie grinned. "I know it's not a glamorous costume. But, I mean, you're a tree." She reached up to pull the headpiece off him. "Thanks again for doing this," she said. "I know *I* wouldn't have volunteered."

Cal saw an opening for an early strike against Ella and took it. "Why didn't Ella volunteer to do it?"

Maddie had the headpiece in her hands and her back to Cal. She froze for a moment and then shook her head slowly before setting it down in an empty space on the shelf in front of her. "I don't think El would ever do another public event if she could avoid it."

"Why?" Cal asked, leaning into the wicked smile forming on his lips. "Does it have something to do with cranberry sauce?"

Maddie turned to look at Cal and he felt himself shrink under the glare she was giving him. "So you've heard. And you think it's funny?" Maddie didn't wait for him to reply. "Imagine yourself, at your most awkward, vulnerable, embarrassing stage of life, in front of everyone you know. And all their eyes are on you. And you're nervous and scared and wearing something bulky and dangerous and expected to do something you weren't good at and didn't want to do. Then, imagine the worst possible thing that could go wrong, going wrong." Maddie crossed her arms. "And then everyone laughed at you. Not just in the moment, but for weeks. Months. Years. The whole town, reminding you of this mortifying, scarring moment for the rest of your life. After all, now it's 'tradition'. Well, that's what happened to Ella. And it wasn't just once. So, if you're going to jump on the 'cranberry sauce' wagon, you better hope you don't ever fall off and get dragged behind it. Because if you do, this town will never let you forget it."

And with that, Maddie pushed past him and left the room. Cal was stunned. The story wasn't as funny when Maddie told it. He looked down at himself. His arms were still pinned to his sides inside the costume. And in the costume, he was too wide to get through the door without help. Awesome start to the day. Eventually, his calls for help were answered by Kurt as he passed the storage room door.

"Thanks for taking that bullet for the rest of us," Kurt had told him with a wink after helping Cal out of the last two-thirds of the tree.

"Yeah, no problem," Cal said, his tone hollow as he parted company with Kurt who headed into the break room. Cal was still thinking about what Maddie had said to him, but standing in a dusty storage room wearing two-thirds of a paper mâché Christmas tree costume had shaved off a couple of layers of empathy towards Ella. She was still the reason he'd been strong-armed into the tree parade. He knew he should just tell her no, that he wasn't going to do it. But, that would mean having to actually get into a confrontation with her, and then what about his coworkers? They'd thanked him. If he backed out now . . . Killjoy Cal spoke up, *Remember, they won't be your coworkers forever.* The dread of going back to New York outweighed the dread of the tree costume at the moment. He took that as an encouraging sign and headed back to his desk. He was about to pass in front of Ella's office door when it was wrenched open from the inside and he stood face to face with her.

"Oh, morning," she said quickly.

"Yep," Cal said, before he could think of a witty and devastating greeting.

"I told her the costume fit," Maddie said, coming out of the office behind Ella.

"Oh . . . good," Cal said, his mouth moving on its own again.

Ella nodded and for a brief moment, her eyes met his. "Yeah, thanks for volunteering for that."

Ok, so she apparently wasn't telling *anyone* that she was the one that had volunteered him for it. Clever. Then, if he did back out, he would look like the ass. The annoyed anger that he'd started to associate with Ella Danforth was starting to boil up inside him again. She'd won the first battle, but he was going to win the war.

"Ok everyone, let's circle up and kick this day in the ass," Ella called to the office as she moved in front of the whiteboard.

Cal retrieved his notepad and pen from his desk, taking his time so she'd have to wait on him to start. He'd read *The Art of War*. He could get inside her head.

Half an hour later, Cal was still trying to come up with something to counter Ella's paper mâché surprise attack. He was huffing around the edge of the square to Bumble's Market, and as he moved around herds of tourists he tried to shelve his revenge line of thinking for the moment. He needed to focus on the questions he was going to ask Mrs. Bumble about the holiday discounts at the market and the bizarre and uncanny plunger and canned good holiday sculptures he was there to cover for the paper. He'd barely made it inside the door before he was hip-checked by a woman pushing a full cart of groceries topped off by three screaming toddlers. He moved down the pet food aisle to avoid the majority of the shoppers and headed for the back office. He spotted Mrs. Bumble standing next to Martha Washington, the owner of one of the women's clothing shops on Schooner Street, just off the square.

"Lisa, what are we going to do? There are only eight names on the list. We can't do it with less than ten," Martha said, wringing her hands.

Mrs. Bumble was surveying the store around her with her hawk eyes. "I know that. We'll find two more. We just . . . have to not take no for an answer."

Cal's antennae went up. Oh, Mrs. Bumble and Martha needed some volunteers, did they? Just as he thought it, Mrs. Bumble's gaze landed on Cal and he felt his blood run cold in his veins. Uh-oh. What if she tried to force him into doing it? Crap. This could backfire all over him if he wasn't quick enough.

"Oh, hi Cal," Mrs. Bumble said, waving to him.

So far, so good, Cal thought, returning her wave and moving over to join her and Martha.

"You know Martha, don't you?" Mrs. Bumble asked. "She owns Excavation over on Schooner."

"Oh, yeah," Cal said quickly. "Hi, Martha."

Martha nodded at him distractedly and then quickly returned her attention to the paper in her hand. She was chewing her bottom lip the way he'd seen Ella do so many times and for some reason, it felt like a push from the universe telling him to go for it.

"Martha, did you ask Abby White? She'd probably do it," Mrs. Bumble said.

Martha shook her head. "She's due in January, but it's her fourth and the last three have come early."

"Well that won't work," Mrs. Bumble muttered. "Still, Martha, I have yet to come up short on volunteers for a Mrs. Claus' Powder Room event."

Now, the universe seemed to be signaling to Cal.

"Oh," Cal said quickly. "Ella Danforth wanted to volunteer for that." Both women snapped their heads around to look at him.

"Ella wants to volunteer?" Mrs. Bumble asked.

"Uh, yeah," Cal said, quickly. "She thought the paper should be represented."

"Oh my goodness!" Martha practically squealed as she snatched a pen out of the front of Mrs. Bumble's apron, apparently snatching some skin with it, going by the gasp and bosom-grabbing Mrs. Bumble made in protest. "That's nine with Ella! We just need one more!"

Both women turned to beam at Cal. "You've just made our day," Mrs. Bumble said, patting him on the shoulder. "Now, did you have some questions for me?"

Half an hour later, Cal was back on the street with a story, pictures, and a spring in his step from a successful return of fire. He hoped whatever kind of event "Mrs. Claus' Powder Room" was, would be every bit as annoying as the Parade of Trees. Hopefully even more annoying. And when she found out she was signed up for it, Ella would wave the white flag.

He moved through the next three assignments on his list and headed back to the paper at lunch time for some coffee. When he came through the front door, the first thing he saw was Martha Washington talking to Pippa in the reception area. Pippa was frowning.

"I don't understand. Are you sure?" she was asking Martha.

At the jingle from the front door, Martha turned away from Pippa and her eyes locked onto Cal. "Oh yes, here he is. Our event's savior! Cal told us the good news just a few hours ago."

"He did, did he?" Pippa's gaze locked onto Cal. He tried to shake it off, but like Maddie's it gave him the horrible sensation that her laser-focused glare was actually a shrink ray. What was it with these Island girls and their glares? Maybe all the years of staring at the uncaring ocean waves beating the crap out of the rocks and eroding the ground out from under them had taught them how to parlay that into human emotion.

"Yes! He told us how Ella wanted to sign up for it and now we have nine! I just need one more."

"Martha," Pippa said, turning her attention back to the woman standing in front of her. Cal felt a wave of relief wash over him when Pippa's attention moved off him. "There's been a mistake. Ella wouldn't have volunteered for . . . "

"Lisa Bumble is right. I can't take no for an answer. Not when we're this close to the event. Her name is now on my list and I've thrown away the White-Out. I just need one more person. Pippa, would you be our tenth?"

Pippa sighed and closed her eyes. "Well, I'm not going to let El do this by herself. So, yeah. Sign me up."

Martha squealed in happiness and Cal sidestepped the women, heading back for his desk. He glanced at Ella's office and wasn't surprised to find it empty with the light off. If she'd been in, she would have been out front, talking to Martha. Ella Danforth didn't strike him as the type that would let someone else fight her battles. He sat down behind his laptop and started to type up his stories. After five more minutes of muffled conversation, there was a tinkle as the bell over the door rang out again and then he heard the sound of approaching footsteps. He looked up as Pippa stuck her head around the partition wall separating his desk from the rest of the office. Her expression was stony and the color of her face was only a shade or two lighter than her flaming red hair.

"What the absolute hell did you do, Cal Dickson?"

Cal leaned back in his chair. He had to defend himself. "Just some friendly pranking," Cal said. "Ella volunteered me to be a Christmas tree in a parade, so I volunteered her to work the Mrs. Claus event, or whatever. Turnabout is fair play."

Pippa closed her eyes and pinched the bridge of her nose. "No, turnabout *was* fair play *yesterday*, when you sicced the Confounding Carolers on her and *she* retaliated by volunteering you to be in the Parade of Trees, which by the way, is not that big of a deal. I was in it almost every year as a kid because my dad sold Christmas trees as a side-hustle. You all walk together and wave and for those that are not emotionally scarred by this town, it's a piece of cake. The only thing even slightly embarrassing is the stupid costume, but everyone is wearing one, and as a crowd, no one is making fun of a single tree." Cal just frowned at her. She shook her head slowly. "I talked to Maddie, so don't play dumb. You *know* about what happened to El. She *told* you that Ella has a trigger about being in front of people and having to perform."

Now Cal was really confused. "I don't get it. So she'll be with nine other people volunteering at this Mrs. Claus thing. She won't be . . ."

"Mainlanders," Pippa muttered under her breath. She sighed. "The Mrs. Claus' Powder Room event takes place every year at the Santa Ball and Crawl. It's the biggest event of the holiday season for the town. It's always packed and *everyone* is there."

"So?" Cal started.

Pippa redoubled her laser-focused glare on him and raised a hand, silently telling him to shut up. "So, you just signed her up to be a model in the fashion show that happens at that event every year. Every one of her fears and anxieties, all in one. Good job."

Cal suddenly felt like the bottom had fallen out of his stomach. "I . . . she can just say no. Tell them I volunteered her for it without her knowing?"

Pippa shook her head slowly. "You've never dealt with Mrs. Bumble when it comes to one of her events, have you?" She didn't wait for Cal to answer. "Lisa Bumble is the human equivalent of a Have-a-Heart critter trap when it comes to her events. You, or someone else can volunteer you to become a part of one, but once you're inside and your name is on her list," Pippa smacked her hand against the partition wall, making Cal jump, "you're trapped. And she's the only one who can let you out. But she won't. Because the only thing more important to Lisa Bumble than a balanced set of books for the market is a full docket of volunteers for her events. Thank you and goodnight." She crossed her arms. "I hope you're happy."

"I . . . I didn't know," Cal muttered, feeling his heart pounding in his chest. Shit. What was he going to do? He stared down at his hands that were now gripping the front of his desk.

"Well, now you do," Pippa said. She was gone when he looked back up.

The feeling that maybe Cal had gone too far on something was a new sensation for him. He didn't cross lines. At least, not big ones. The biggest one he'd ever crossed was leaving New York and coming to Hope and he wasn't even sure if that counted since his family and friends fully expected him to be coming back any day. But if he'd just signed her up for . . . the beginning solo for Backstreet Boys' "Shape of My Heart" started to roll through his head. The song that was his personal nemesis, remembering the taunts and laughter when he'd frozen up. If someone had forced him to sing that song now . . .

Cal was on his feet. He pulled his phone out of his pocket. He had to call Mrs. Bumble. He had to figure out a way to convince her to let Ella off the hook. If he could do that, he had a feeling Martha would go along with it. He'd set out to get some obnoxious, hopefully annoying, revenge on Ella; not to torture her. He had to fix this.

He found the number for Bumble's Market and dialed. The phone rang six times before it was picked up.

"Hello?"

Not Mrs. Bumble.

"Hi," Cal said. "I'm looking for Mrs. Bumble. Uh, Lisa Bumble."

"Oh, Mrs. B's gone for the day," the man said. "She had to go to the mainland to sign for a shipment. I can leave a message for her on her computer screen, so she'll see it first thing when she comes in in the morning."

Cal paused. He wasn't sure how to put his reason for calling into a message that could be squeezed onto a sticky note and stuck to a computer screen. Besides, if she knew why he was calling and Pippa was right about her, there was a good chance she wouldn't be calling him back.

"Uh, no, that's all right. I'll call back tomorrow. When will she be in?"

"Usually around eight."

Cal thanked the man and hung up. The uneasiness in his chest was apparently there to stay for the moment. The alarm went off on his phone and he looked down at the calendar reminder. His next assignment was about to start. No time to stew about the mess he'd made.

He grabbed his coat and bag and headed for the door. Guiltily, he thought that at least he wouldn't be in the office when Ella came back and was informed by Pippa that she'd be in a fashion show in front of the whole town. He stubbed his toe on the door on his way out and he glanced up at the sky as he moved toward the gazebo. *Ok Universe, I hear you. That was a dick move on my part.*

As if in answer, the brass alphorn squeal-honked, making Cal jump.

"Probably deserved that," Cal muttered as he zipped his coat up and told Killjoy and Sarcastic Cal to get to work on a plan to get both him and Ella Danforth out of the mess he'd made.

23

ELLA

"Oh Ella, I'm so sorry about that, here, let me help."

"Oh, it's fine Mrs. Keller," Ella said, quickly, trying to block the woman. It was a largely fruitless gesture. The woman batted Ella's hands away and started trying to brush the glitter off of Ella's chest herself.

"That damn machine. It never works right. Every year I tell George, 'Don't load the glitter cannon for the human snow globe. It always gets clogged and then blows up on some poor unsuspecting person.' But does he listen?"

"I'm guessing no," Ella muttered, watching the tourists around them pausing in their browsing to watch Mary Keller smacking the glitter off of Ella's boobs.

The sky outside the store windows was dark. Where had the day gone? She'd lost count as to how many assignments she'd covered today. She took one final picture of the human snow globe photo booth at Keller's Antiques and headed out into the cold night air. She paused to zip up her coat and looked across the street at the Excavation Lingerie Boutique. Martha Washington was in the front window putting reindeer antlers and red noses on her mannequins. It was an odd store, run by an odd merchant, but then again, this *was* Hope and the measuring stick for "odd" here was definitely more forgiving than the usual standard. As if she could hear Ella's thoughts, Martha's head snapped up from what she was doing and turned to look at her. Ella froze like a rabbit that had just been spotted by a predator. Should she just run? Something about Martha's smile was making her uneasy. Then, Martha waved at her and started mouthing something. Ella was too tired to start a mime-inspired conversation through the window glass with Martha so she decided to just wave back and mouth "Have a good night", smile, and take off. Martha stopped mouthing words at her, her smile widened, and she went back to her human reindeers in Christmas-themed teddies and thongs. Thankful that that was over, Ella hiked her bag higher on her shoulder and headed down the street. She was worn out, but she picked up her pace, still slightly worried that Martha was about to stick her head out of her store door and call her back for a chat. Ella reached the square and started back toward the office, passing other Islanders and shop owners closing up for the day.

"Hey, Ella!"

"Hey there, Cranberry Sauce!"

"Whoa there hoss! Where are you headed in such a hurry?"

With every greeting, forced smile, and pause to be polite, Ella's exhaustion ratcheted up another notch or two. By the time she got to the front door of the *Hornblower*, she was sure she could fall asleep standing up. The light was still on inside and she could see Pippa sitting behind her computer, frowning at the screen. Ella hesitated for a moment, and then made the decision to turn away from the door and head home. If Pip was mad about something, she was sure she'd hear about it in the morning and she'd want to have the energy to deal with whatever it was.

There was also the possibility that Cal Dickson was still inside at his desk and she'd have to deal with whatever passive aggressive crap she brought on herself by volunteering him for the Parade of Trees. She knew she shouldn't have done it, but Cal shouldn't have sent the Carolers after her. Now, they were even. Besides, he'd probably drop the passive-aggressive attitude when she told him that she was just there to get them through Christmas and then turn the reins over to him after the holidays.

That thought put a small spring back in Ella's step. By the time she'd turned the corner and her mom's house was in sight, Helga had formed a plan. Eat, bath, review notes, write up stories, find more Seattle job listings, and turn in more applications and resumes. Then, sleep. If time allowed.

She waved to the few neighbors on their porches that greeted her as she passed. She had to admit, it was kind of nice knowing all your neighbors. Definitely something she never did in Seattle. She paused on her porch and looked out at the row of Christmas lights on both sides of the street. She didn't just know her neighbors. She knew every person that lived on Shell Street. And every one of them knew her. And they knew every embarrassing moment that had ever happened to her. Most of them had witnessed it and would probably still be telling the story at her funeral one day.

"And that's why Hope is a nice place to visit, but you wouldn't want to live here," Ella muttered under her breath.

An hour and a half later, she was damp and wrapped in her pj's looking at job listings in Seattle. Her articles had practically written themselves. One of the benefits of having grown up in Hope meant that she never had to guess what tone to use for an article. She knew the people she was writing about. She knew what kind of energy, flattery, puns, and emphasis they'd each want regarding their holiday efforts. And she was proud of her staff. So far, they were keeping up. Myrna had even texted to tell her that sales of the paper on the mainland were almost two hundred percent higher than they'd been the year before under Clarence.

Ella's gaze drifted from her computer screen to the stained briefcase sitting in the corner of her room. She needed to see Clarence. She needed answers. Even if it was that he'd tripped over one of the stupid stacks of paper in his office, smacked himself in the nose with his briefcase, dropped it down a hidden hole in the floor, and then somehow kicked the floorboard over the hole. All before forgetting that he ever had the briefcase in the first place. She just needed to know. And she needed to know why he had suddenly quit. People didn't just quit jobs in Hope. Especially after being at them for forty years.

She leaned back against her pillows and closed her eyes. Would Cal be the next Clarence? Would he actually stay in Hope and run the paper for the next forty years? A time lapse with some pretty serious creative-license played through her head, imagining Cal aging in the job. *Huh*, Ella thought. *Looks like he's going to age fairly well.* Her eyes popped open and she frowned at the cream-colored wall across from her. Where had that come from?

"Exhaustion," Ella muttered to the empty room. "And hormones." She moved her computer off her lap and set it on her night stand. "And goodnight." She turned off the lamp beside her bed and closed her eyes. She tried to think about the job possibilities in Seattle and all her digital resumes, zooming off to inboxes all over the city. But as she drifted off to sleep, the imagined image of Cal behind Clarence's desk returned. She watched him age to silver hair with a steno pad on his knee, the phone cradled between his shoulder and ear. For some reason, the image made her genuinely smile as she drifted off to sleep.

Of course, the crack of dawn was far too impatient in breaking the next morning and Ella was only half-awake as she stumbled her way to the office. She'd poured herself a mug of coffee in her mom's kitchen and then just walked out the door, still carrying the ceramic mug. She was pretty sure she had shoes on, but she couldn't find the energy to look down at what kind. They were comfortable and she really hoped she wasn't wearing her Cookie Monster slippers for the day. She couldn't quite muster the usual morning greetings in return to the Islanders that passed her so she settled for raising her mug to them and making a grunting sound.

When Ella got to the front glass door of the paper and peered inside, her brain was confused. There were too many people standing in the lobby. She frowned and was about to check to make sure she was at the right door when the three women inside pushed the door open, forcing Ella to take a step back.

"There she is! Our savior!" The speaker was Martha Washington. Beside her was Mrs. Lisa Bumble, and trailing behind them, looking agitated and annoyed, was Pip.

"Did I found a religion I forgot about?" Ella mumbled as her brain tried to speed up and process what was happening.

"Oh you! Always with the jokes," Mrs. Bumble said, squeezing Ella's coffee mug arm.

Ella watched the hot liquid slosh inside the mug and her sluggish brain thought, *Coffee hot.*

"Now," Mrs. Bumble said quickly, pulling out a notebook and scribbling something on the top page. "Pippa's fitting is scheduled for the eighteenth, so we went ahead and just scheduled you to be right after her on that day at four." Mrs. Bumble ripped the paper off the pad and held it out to Ella.

"Four?" Ella asked, still completely lost as to what was happening.

"Yes. Pippa said it's usually a good time of day for you and with your excellent staff, I'm sure you can steal away for a half hour or so. Martha's already picking ensembles so no worries there. Well, this is excellent! Now, I really have to get back to the market." Ella still hadn't taken the piece of paper from her, so Mrs. Bumble tucked it into Ella's coat pocket. She patted her on the cheek and then moved around Ella and back out into the square. Martha wasn't far behind her.

"Oh Ella! I'm thinking dark green and silk for you! With your long legs and torso, it's going to be *gorgeous!* See you on the eighteenth!" She scurried out the front door and Ella slowly rotated on the spot to watch the women leave. She felt a hand on her back and looked behind her to see Pip giving her a look of remorse so strong, Ella felt her heart rate starting to speed up.

"Pip, what's happening? Am I . . . Am I awake?" Ella's voice was still groggy, but the look on Pip's face was activating her fight or flight instinct.

"Come on, El. I'd get you some coffee, but it looks like you literally mugged someone for theirs while they were sitting on their front porch." She nodded down at the mug in Ella's hand. Pip turned Ella toward her office in time to see the retreating foot and elbow of someone over six feet tall going down the hallway toward the break room. *Cal*, Ella's brain piped up, helpfully. *He is here.* At least he was fleeing and not casting smug, haughty, passive-aggressive shade her way.

"I have something I need to tell you," Pip said as she moved Ella by the elbows into Ella's office and closed the door. Ella moved automatically in the serpentine-pattern she'd developed for getting around the stacks of papers on the office floor. She set down her mug and pulled the strap of her shoulder bag over her head. "Good idea," Pip said, nodding. "We should sit down for this."

Ella's heart was still pounding, waking her up. Fear was stronger than caffeine. "Who died?" Ella asked. Her first thought landed on Clarence. Maybe that's why he quit . . . Maybe he was dying. She gave her head a shake. No, she had a feeling that Pippa's expression had something to do with Mrs. Bumble's and Martha's visit.

"So," Pippa started. She paused and sighed as if she didn't know where to start. Ella slumped into the chair behind her desk, and stared Pippa in the face.

"Spill," Ella said. "My brain's almost awake enough to process. Give it that last boot in the ass it needs."

Pip had on her anguished face again. "Apparently, Cal wasn't very happy with the Parade of Trees assignment you gave him." Ella opened her mouth, but Pip held up a hand. "We all figured out that you told him he was going to be the *Hornblower* tree, and he didn't actually volunteer for it. Now, none of us will tell *him* that we *know* he didn't volunteer for it. It's kind of more fun this way. But, the point is, he was pissed and he retaliated." Here, she paused again and took a deep breath. "When he went to Bumble's to cover the canned good dioramas and specials, he volunteered you for the Mrs. Claus' Powder Room event this year."

Ella felt blood rushing in her ears, the roar growing louder as realization hit her. She felt weak and her palms were sweating. She was frozen in her chair, but her heart was banging against her ribs as if it was trying to escape on its own. "He . . . what?" she croaked.

Pip nodded slowly, her anguish turning to anger. "And you know that when your name gets put on one of Mrs. Bumble's lists, it doesn't come off. You're stuck." She paused and then hurried on, trying to smile with some level of reassurance. "But, if it helps at all, I signed up too, so we'll be doing it together."

"Doing what?" Ella asked, dreading the answer. Every year, Mrs. Claus'

Powder Room event took place at the Santa Ball and Crawl on Christmas Eve to support a local business and a charity. It was always big and flashy and the whole town attended. What the absolute hell had Cal just gotten her into?

"It's . . . it's a fashion show," Pip said quietly. Ella gagged on her tongue. Pip leaned forward in her chair. "But we don't have to sing or dance or anything. We just walk down the runway and turn around and walk back. Easy-peasy, right?"

Ella was trying not to hyperventilate. The echo of laughter, people yelling and whistling, "Whoa hoss!" and "Hey Cranberry Sauce!" and the memory of the fear she'd felt as she'd fallen. And now she was going to be on a runway having to do it all over again as an adult this time. But for the people watching, they were just going to remember kid Ella, falling into their Thanksgiving dinner, collapsing tables and ruining everything. Ella rolled her chair back and put her head between her knees to keep from passing out. Pippa was at her side, kneeling on the floor between two towering stacks of paper, one hand on Ella's back and one on her knee.

"Whoa, breathe, El. Just breathe. It's going to be ok. It's not going to be like that Thanksgiving." Pippa forced a laugh. "I mean, it won't even be near the buffet table this time . . . and like I said, you won't have to dance." Ella was still having a hard time breathing, but with Pippa's coaching she finally started to regain some control. "There you go," Pippa soothed as Ella slumped back in her chair. Pippa moved back to the chair in front of the desk and for a moment they both sat in silence, thinking.

"You know, this is my fault," Ella said. Pippa glanced up at her. "I shouldn't have forced Cal into being in the Parade of Trees. I was just pissed about the Carolers."

"Well, he shouldn't have sent them after you in the first place."

"Yeah," Ella said, shaking her head. "But eventually one of us was going to have to be an adult and stop the escalation." She gave a mirthless chuckle. "I was just really hoping it would be him."

Pippa closed her eyes and leaned her head back on her chair. "If you'd shared your plan with me, I could have told you that wasn't going to work.

The two of you are actually more alike than you know. He was never *not* going to retaliate for the balloon grotto thing so, really, you just dug your own grave."

Ella glared at Pip. "He stole my mug!"

Pippa raised her head up and blinked her eyes open to stare at Ella. "That's how this whole thing started? Over a *mug*?!"

Ella's mouth was open, but nothing was coming out of it. When Pippa said it out loud like that, she had to admit it did sound kind of ridiculous.

"It was *mine!*" Ella argued.

Pippa sighed. "It was yours to use when you lived here *four years ago*. That mug was probably about to hop off the shelf, crash into the sink, and end it all from disuse. So what, Cal started using your high school boyfriend of a mug? Move on. You have a new mug in front of you. And having been to your mom's house, I can see that it's part of her matched set and she'll probably give you the third degree if it doesn't go home with you tonight."

"That's beside the point," Ella muttered, looking down at the mug in front of her.

"When the point is the escalation resulting from some ridiculous mug-based mark-your-territory power struggle between you and *an employee*, the point is bullshit and we all need to deal with the fallout and just move on." Pippa's expression had turned stony and she'd crossed her arms, glaring at Ella. Ella was about to respond when there was a knock on the door and Maddie stuck her head in.

"Am I interrupting anything?" Maddie asked, looking from Pippa to Ella.

Before Ella could answer, Pippa growled. "Just the realization that all the crap Ella and Cal have been pulling on each other originated over a *mug*."

"Really?" Maddie asked, closing the door behind her and crossing to lean on the back of Pippa's chair. She put her chin on top of Pippa's head and looked at Ella. "I thought it was because you got the job."

Ella sighed and put her face in her hands, resting her elbows on her desk. "That's how it started. I think. He was pissed. Then, I was pissed that he was pissed, and he was using my mug . . ."

"The one you used *four years ago* . . ." Maddie started.

"Yes, that one." Ella snapped. "And I know I shouldn't be holding onto something like that. But now Cal has signed me up to be a part of the godforsaken fashion show at the Santa Ball and Crawl and it's Mrs. Bumble and Martha Washington . . . and besides a grisly murder-suicide, I don't have a way to get out of it."

"Whoa," Maddie said, standing up and looking from Pippa to Ella. "I think I missed a few things. Fill me in."

Between the two of them, they got Maddie up to speed with everything that had been happening. In characteristic-Maddie fashion, she was quiet for a minute after they finished.

"Ok," she finally said in the same tone a parent would use after hearing both sides of their children's argument. "He's an asshole for volunteering you to do it . . ."

"Thank you," Ella said, vindication washing over her.

"I'm not finished," Maddie said, cutting her eyes to Ella. "But *you* are an asshole for forcing him to be the newspaper's tree in the parade and exploiting the fact that he sucks at saying 'no'."

"What?" Ella asked. "I've heard him say 'no' before." Pippa and Maddie shared a look and Ella leaned forward in her chair. "What?"

Pippa sighed and turned back to look at Ella. "It's not really saying 'no', it's just . . . we've noticed over the last couple of months that Cal has this thing about confrontation."

"Yeah," Maddie added. "You know Mr. Weller, the old guy that looks after the lighthouse and barely ever comes to town?"

Ella nodded. "I remember him. Weller the Grump."

"Exactly," Maddie said. "Well, this fall, Cal had to interview him for a story about the foliage around the lighthouse and how it was a nice day trip for tourists, etc. And Weller came into the paper, ranting and raving about how tourists were showing up outside the lighthouse and leaving trash and being noisy and-"

"It was like Cal froze," Pippa said, shaking her head. "Like he was shrinking and getting shorter the longer Mr. Weller yelled at him."

"He didn't argue with him and tell him that the newspaper can't control how the tourists act and that it's a public venue so they have a right to visit . . ." Ella started.

"Nope," Maddie said. "He just took it. And he looked so uncomfortable."

"His face was red," Pippa said. "Finally, Clarence came out and took Weller into his office to yell."

"Cal picked up his stuff and left. I thought maybe for good," Maddie said. "But he came back a couple hours later. Turned out he'd just gone on his next assignment and was back to write it up. But, I've never seen Cal so . . ."

"Embarrassed?" Pippa asked, looking at Maddie.

"Yeah, but more than that. Kind of like, mortified."

Ella knew she shouldn't be, but hearing the girls describe how uncomfortable Cal got when someone was yelling and in his face was giving her an idea. After all, the bastard had sent the Carolers after her *and* signed her up to parade on a runway and basically re-live her greatest fear and worst moments of her life in this town.

"Oh, I don't like the look on your face, El," Pip said.

"That's Plotting-Ella-Face," Maddie said. "What are you planning?"

"Nothing," Ella said quickly. She was sure that they'd do their best to dissuade her if she told them. It didn't matter. They'd known her too long. She couldn't fool them. They both fixed her with "own-up" faces, but she held her ground.

"Well, whatever it is," Pippa finally said on a sigh, "just do it quickly. I saw the pre-written list of assignments for today and there's not a lot of time to waste on diabolical plans."

Ella was about to lie through her teeth and tell her she wasn't planning anything when Maddie spoke up. "You know El, this fashion show thing might be kind of good for you." Now Pippa and Ella both looked up at her. Maddie shrugged. "You've been scared of being in front of people ever since that Thanksgiving. I mean, in high school you didn't do any of the plays, you quit the band, and the only time you didn't hyperventilate doing town activities was when you were in a crowd of other volunteers." She paused. "Hey, maybe you should trade with Cal. You be the tree in the parade and he can do the fashion show."

Ella straightened up in her chair. That didn't sound too bad.

"Only one problem with that," Pippa said quietly.

"What?" Maddie asked. "Men do fashion shows."

"It's not a *normal* fashion show."

"What do you mean?" Ella asked.

Pippa bit her lip. "Well, Martha Washington is the business owner partnering with Mrs. Bumble this year for the event, so . . ."

"Oh my god," Maddie breathed. "It's a *lingerie* fashion show?"

Ella couldn't breathe. Little black dots were clouding her vision. She was going to kill Cal Dickson. Not only had he volunteered her for a fashion show. He'd volunteered her to stand on a runway in front of her whole hometown wearing *lingerie.*

"Breathe," Maddie said softly. There were two hands on her back this time. Ella blinked her vision clear and looked up at Pippa and Maddie.

"I'm going to kill him," Ella said. The words came out as a half-gasp as she fought to suck in more air.

Maddie shook her head. "No you're not. We're more than two weeks out from Christmas and you need him. You can kill him after the new year." Ella dropped her head and she felt Maddie squeeze her shoulder and when she spoke again, her voice was right next to her ear. "El, besides, this could be an opportunity."

"To have my nickname changed to Cranberry . . . Saucy?" Ella breathed.

"No," Maddie said. "To replace that nickname with a completely uneventful performance that is completely forgotten. Maybe your outfit will be pajamas and you'll walk down the runway, smile, walk back and it'll be over. Just like that. No more running or hiding from the town and the old memory of what happened more than a decade ago."

Ella's brain was having a territory war, drawing lines and dividing itself. She heard what Maddie was saying and a part of her recognized the logic. A second part of her was still in the corner hyperventilating into a paper bag. But the third and largest part of her brain was pissed as hell at Cal Dickson for getting her into this mess in the first place. At the moment, she just needed Pippa and Maddie to return to their desks, satisfied that the crisis had passed so Ella could go big game hunting for one snotty-conflict-avoiding New York reporter.

So Ella said the first thing that came to her mind. "You're right. You're both right. It's going to be ok." Neither of the women looked convinced, but when Ella stood up, Pippa got to her feet too. "And it's time to start the day." Ella made a dramatic gesture of looking at her watch. "In fact, congratulations to us, we're already running fifteen minutes late for our morning huddle-up meeting."

That got the other two moving. "I'll round everyone in the office up," Maddie said. "I need to talk to Katie anyway."

"I'll go to the back and see if Kurt can come up for the meeting," Pippa added, following Maddie out of the office.

Ella mentally cracked her knuckles as she tried to compose the in-his-face-high-volume argument she was about to lob at Cal. He wasn't at his desk, so she headed down the hall, trailing after Pippa. Pip had just disappeared through the door at the end when she heard Cal's voice ahead and to her left. He was in the break room and from the sound of it, he was on the phone. Ella paused by the door, waiting for him to wrap up the call so she could storm in and have his full attention. She decided that after she made her big entrance, she'd stand in front of the doorway so there would be no escape for him. Then she could enjoy seeing him squirm.

"Please, Mrs. Bumble. Please," Cal was saying. No, not saying. *Pleading*. Ella frowned. She'd never heard that tone of voice from Cal. It was higher pitched than usual. "It was my fault. I didn't ask Ella. I was mad and I volunteered her. Please. I'll do anything if you'll let her out of this. I'll come help bag groceries on the weekends . . ." He was quiet. "No, I didn't know what I was volunteering her for . . . but- " Apparently, he'd been cut off mid-sentence. Ella leaned forward and she could see Cal pacing the length of the room, his free hand gripping the hair on the top of his head. When he turned toward her, she caught the expression on his face in profile. His cheeks were red and he . . . he looked on the verge of tears. "Please, Mrs. Bumble, I . . ." He stopped short and let go of his hair before pulling the phone away from his face to look at the screen. He swore under his breath and turned away from Ella. He slumped into a chair at the table and put his head in his hands.

Ella backed away from the break room and went back to her office, trying to get a handle on what she'd just seen and heard. Cal had called Mrs. Bumble and from the sounds of it, he was trying to un-volunteer her. He'd had a confrontation, just to try to save her from his screw up. But why? Why was he even bothering?

"You ready, boss?" Maddie's voice called behind her. Ella turned to see Maddie standing in the office doorway.

"Uh, yeah. Be right there," Ella said quickly. Maddie left and Ella moved to her desk to grab the notes on the day's events that she'd printed out the night before. There was a strange warmth trying to expand in her chest like the cartoon Grinch's heart growing. Maybe Cal wasn't so bad. The thought felt wrong to her somehow, but there it was. She tapped the papers on the edge of the desk and then straightened up. And maybe Maddie was right. Maybe this would cancel out that nightmare of a Thanksgiving in the minds of everyone else in town. Maybe in her own mind. She really liked pajamas. Just walk down a runway, smile, and walk back. And Cal was already uncomfortable for having caused it. Maybe they were even *now*. She tried to attribute the warmth in her chest to the satisfaction of knowing Cal had been uncomfortable for what he'd done to her, but she knew that wasn't completely true. She wasn't about to admit it to herself or anyone else, but there was a small part of her that felt for Cal. The memory of his flushed face and the glassy look of possible tears in his eyes almost shamed Ella into having caused him that, but then she remembered that he actually caused it himself and that they were even now.

She moved out of the office, doing her best to not look in Cal's direction as she headed for the circle of staff. "Morning folks, let's talk Santa's Singles and what's going on at the Spark Theatre."

She handed the stack of event rundowns to Maddie to pass around and turned to look at the whiteboard.

"That's a hell of a day," Marty said, staring down at the paper in his hand.

"Twenty-three events," Ella muttered, as she started making the list on the board.

"That's too many," Maddie muttered.

"We'll figure it out," Ella said. Her gaze drifted around her staff and finally landed on Cal. His hair was still mussed and he looked like he was standing at the edge of some kind of mental bridge, thinking about jumping. At that moment he looked so vulnerable and to Ella, game recognized game, because she knew that look. She'd been standing on the edge of that mental bridge, thinking about jumping many times before. So she smiled. Not a smug smile. A genuine smile that went from her eyes to Cal's and held. She could see him hesitate in confusion and then relax, slightly. A cautious half-smile formed in the corner of his mouth and Ella, afraid they'd be attracting attention to themselves, turned her attention back to the paper in her hand.

It took twenty minutes to dole out their daily dose of tinsel-covered madness. "Alright team, in the words of Kelsey Grammer in *Down Periscope*, let's kick this pig!" Ella said, wrapping up the meeting.

She moved back toward her office to get her bag before heading out to cover her assignments. She was halfway through the path around the desk when someone knocked on her door frame. She looked back to see Cal, standing there, one hand jammed into his jeans pocket, the other gripping the door frame awkwardly.

"Um," Cal said, without sounding like he had fully thought out what to say after "umm". He cleared his throat and tried again. "Ella, I wanted to say, I'm sorry I . . ."

Ella could feel heat rising in her own cheeks now. What was going on? She should tell him, *"Yeah, you should be sorry."* But the vision of him pleading to Mrs. Bumble stopped her in her tracks. She was actually kind of ashamed at how little thought she'd put into volunteering him for the parade.

"Hey . . . we're even now," Ella said, her mouth outrunning her brain as far as planning what to say. The tension that left Cal's posture at her words made Ella relax a little herself. She grinned and raised a hand as if swearing an oath. "I promise I will not retaliate. I'm ready to call a truce if you are."

"Truce," Cal said. "And I'll be the tree in the parade."

"Well, it's really the least you could do since I have to be in a fashion show now," Ella said. Cal looked pained. Oh god, was he going to apologize again? Already, her heart was pounding in her chest and she knew he would be able to see the color in her face. She needed a subject change. She glanced around the room for something, *anything* to change the trajectory of the conversation. Her gaze landed on the stacks of paper at her feet. "Um, so, about Clarence. You wouldn't want to help me find out what happened with him quitting, would you?" She didn't know why she said it. Desperation for a topic change was the only thing she could think of.

"Yes," Cal said, almost too quickly.

Ella raised an eyebrow at him. "Really?"

"Yes," Cal repeated. "I . . . That's why I wanted to hear what Miss Mandie had to say about him. I wasn't sure if that's why you were asking . . ."

Ella nodded slowly. "Yeah. You see . . ." She decided to take a leap of faith and just tell him. "I found this . . ."

"Hey," Pippa said, popping up beside Cal. "Mr. Gilbert is on the phone asking when one of you is going to get there for the tour of nature-made Nativity scenes."

"That's my cue," Cal said, the half-smile returning to the corner of his mouth. "To be continued . . . later?"

Ella nodded and was about to reply when Maddie squeezed into view next to Pippa. "El, it's almost nine. You're going to be late to the Kiwanis pancake feed. And I probably don't have to tell you, but you definitely want pictures *before* the dentures come out."

Ella snapped her a salute and Maddie and Pippa vanished, leaving her and Cal alone. "To be continued when the chaos dies down."

They split up and Ella was still smiling as she pushed through the newspaper office doors on her way to the big tent in City Park. There was a spring in her step that she would not have predicted, especially considering the way the morning had started. Maybe it was the fact that she and Cal had finally called a truce and it was the happiness of pure relief, knowing that she wouldn't have to constantly be waiting for the next passive-aggressive act of retaliation or be planning her own. Maybe it was the optimism of progress as she and her team tore through event after event in the holiday season to resounding success, according to Myrna. Or, and Ella did her best to force the lid down on this thought, but it was still there. Maybe it was that little half-smile on Cal's face that did strange things to Ella, like put a bounce in her step.

24

CAL

Cal hurried across the footbridge to the small patch of woods that constituted Hope State Park. Clarence had told him once that the state park was all that was left of the original face of the island. The rest had been cleared away for the five miles of town that took up the lion's share of the land. Normally, this line of thinking would spark a depressing realization and downward spiral in his mood about humans destroying nature, but today, all he could think about was the conversation he'd just had with Ella.

When Pippa had explained to him what he'd done, he'd wanted to throw up. A feeling that only increased as he paced the break room, trying to convince Lisa Bumble to let Ella off the hook. Mrs. Bumble had been polite, bordering on sociopathic, but unyielding to the point that she could probably go one-on-one with his dad and have even money on coming out on top. Cal tried to shove away the feeling of helpless desperation and panic he'd felt, trying to confront her and get her to let Ella out of it. He'd pleaded. He hated pleading. It never worked in his experience. It was just . . . embarrassing. With a deep breath of relief he was at least thankful that Ella hadn't been there to witness that scene. And then Ella had . . . just been fine with what he'd done? Cal tripped over a root in the dirt path and stumbled forward. He was able to catch himself before he hit the ground. He leaned against a trail marker on one side of the path until his balance returned. Why *had* she been ok with it? Maddie and Pippa had acted like it would be Ella's melting point. But she'd brushed it off. She'd asked for a truce . . . and she'd smiled.

Now Cal was having to regain his balance for two reasons. Cal could admit that Ella was fairly attractive, but when she smiled, he was mesmerized. Like a mouse staring at a cobra. Her eyes were soft, almost trusting when she smiled like that. He'd seen enough fake smiles on Tara, his mom, past girlfriends, and just female friends. Not to mention the fake smiles his dad and guy friends would give him whenever they were placating, or plotting, or manipulating. But when Ella smiled like that it went into her eyes, those stormy, defiant gray eyes, and opened doors to something deep inside her. That was it. She looked vulnerable when she smiled. And he felt like he was being handed a backstage pass to see what goes on behind the curtain. He didn't know why exactly, but he wanted to see that smile again. And as often as possible.

"Cal? Are you coming?" Mr. Gilbert called down the path to him. Cal looked up to see about twenty-five tourists standing with Mr. Gilbert, staring at him as if he was the slowest hiker in a team out to conquer Everest.

"Hi Mr. Gilbert! Yes, I'm coming," Cal called back. He picked up his pace as he drew toward the group, trying to shelve the mental image of Ella's smile. At least they'd called a truce. And Cal was hopeful that what she'd said about Clarence meant that she'd share with him everything she already knew. It was turning out to be a pretty good day so far. And he wouldn't have been able to predict that from the way the morning had started.

The day's assignments consisted of what was becoming the normal cup full of bizarre with a few mishaps, shenanigans, and heartwarming moments sprinkled on top. The sun had set by the time Cal made it back to the newspaper office. It was dark in the front part of the reception area but he could see the light on in the back third of the office where Ella's office and his desk were located.

"Son-of-a-bitch," he heard Ella swear as he passed her door. He glanced in and his feet paused so quickly that physics gleefully stepped in and he had to grip her door frame to keep from falling over. Legs. That was all he could see. Ella was bent over behind her desk, searching for something on the floor.

"You ok?" Cal asked, not sure what else to say and trying to tear his eyes away from the sight in front of him.

"Yeah, just . . . god!" Ella rose up and he could see her cheeks were flushed as she pushed strands of hair out of her face and glared around the office. "How the hell did Clarence ever get anything done with these *piles* everywhere?"

Cal shrugged. "Maybe he didn't and he was just really good at faking it."

Ella paused and blinked at Cal. "Had not considered that possibility." She turned to fully face him and he could have sworn he saw a flicker of something like embarrassment cross her face before she moved around the desk to lean against it and fix him with a casual, if exhausted, smile.

"So, to christen our newly established truce, do you feel like comparing notes on what we know about our dear old friend Clarence?"

Cal was surprised but did his best to hide it. "Uh, sure."

Ella nodded, looking as nervous as he felt. "Ok, let's start at the beginning. Did Clarence ever say anything to you about quitting?"

Cal shook his head. "Never. To be honest, from the way he talked, I half-expected him to die one day behind that desk."

"And no one would find the body for months because it would be decomposing under stacks of paper?" Ella asked.

Cal nodded. "I was even doubtful that we'd notice the smell. At least for a while." He looked around at the cluttered office.

"Right," Ella said. "So, he never gave you any indication that he was thinking about leaving the paper?"

"None," Cal said.

"Did you talk to him after he quit?"

"He called on Monday morning to tell me himself, but he just said he was quitting and that Myrna was going to start looking for his replacement."

"Wow, that was it?" Ella asked. Cal nodded. "Ok."

"You worked with him for years before I got here," Cal said, trying to lean against the door frame in the least awkward way possible. "From what you know about Clarence, do you have any idea about why he'd quit so suddenly?"

Ella shook her head. "Clarence never struck me as a complicated man. You got the same impression of him in five months that I had from knowing him all my life." She twisted to pick up a notepad and a pen off her desk. "Ok, so no apparent reason as to why he quit based on something he said."

Cal nodded, feeling a small dose of relief that Ella was taking notes. His fingers had been itching to go get his notepad. As he watched her scratch out notes, he felt his fingers relax and his gaze focus on Ella's face in profile as she twisted to study what she'd written under the brighter light of her desk lamp. She smiled at the notepad. A quick smile of satisfaction. A trickle of heat ran down Cal's chest as he realized that he'd seen that smile before when he'd looked at her, standing in profile on her porch, drinking scotch, all those nights ago. Scotch and information were two things that seemed to satisfy Ella Danforth. She bit down on her lower lip as she thought and Cal hadn't realized he'd been leaning forward, watching her until his shoulder slipped on the door frame and he had to quickly shift his weight to keep from face-planting.

Ella gave him a strange look and then, misreading what had happened, nodded. "It's been a long day. You've gotta be at least as tired as I am. And I didn't have a four mile stroll through the woods to look at a bunch of acorn and twig nativity scenes that Mr. Gilbert had gleefully erected. Feel like some coffee?"

Cal nodded, deciding to just go with it. He moved out of the doorway and followed Ella down the hall to the break room. They had the whole office to themselves. Kurt and his crew had finished their run and by now, most of the carriers would be on their routes to the distributors or sleeping, waiting to come in at the crack of dawn for the local routes. Then his mind circled back to his first thought. They were *alone*.

"I'll make the coffee," Cal said quickly, needing to do something to dispel some of his nervous energy.

"Thanks," Ella said. She looked a little surprised, but thankful. She curled her legs under her and sat down on the couch. "So, now the stuff both of us know. Miss Mandie told us he was from either Detroit or Chicago, and he didn't know anyone in town when he got here."

Cal nodded, keeping his back to her as he measured beans for the grinder. "So no friends or family members we can grill since he won't just open his door and talk to us."

"Right," Ella said, her enthusiasm level matching his. "And she said he'd been a journalist back east and had come to Hope for a fresh start."

Cal turned to look at her. "Wait, if he was a journalist, we could search . . ." But Ella was already shaking her head.

"I've checked. No Clarence Fords that even remotely look like him. He would have had to have a head transplant for them to be the same person."

Cal frowned. "What the hell?"

She nodded. "I know. I've had a lot of 'what the hell' moments with trying to figure out the story of Clarence Ford."

He sighed. "Ok, what else do we know about Clarence?"

"That he's usually predictable," Ella said with a shrug. "He always was when I was growing up and working for him at the paper."

Cal nodded. "He definitely had a routine every day. Even weekends, he'd usually be in his office."

"He didn't have a life outside the paper," Ella said. "So why the hell would he quit?"

Cal hit the button on the grinder and their conversation was momentarily suspended while the noise filled the room. When Cal turned the grinder off, the sudden silence was quickly broken by Ella.

"You know, Miss Mandie did say that Clarence liked to live in the now. Maybe he just got a wild hair up his ass one day and decided to quit."

"And hide in his house?" Cal asked, dumping the pulverized beans into the coffee maker and hitting the button. He turned to lean against the counter and look back at Ella. She was frowning again, but it didn't take anything away from her appearance.

"You're right," she muttered.

They were quiet for a minute and Cal raised an eyebrow at her. "Are you going to tell me about that briefcase you had with you when you were trying to break down Clarence's front door?"

Ella sighed. "Yeah. That was kind of what started the whole thing. At first, I thought that maybe Clarence had just gotten fed up, quit, and was hiding for the time being to avoid the rumor mill, but . . . here, I'll show you." She got off the couch and headed for the break room door. Cal frowned, but when she didn't come back after a moment, he decided she wanted him to follow her. He headed back for her office, but it looked empty.

"Ella?" Cal called out, listening for her to answer.

"Back here," Ella muttered from inside the office. He assumed she was either pinned under fifty pounds of un-filed obituary forms or she was behind her desk. He carefully waded through the sea of aging papers to peer down at her. She was partially under the desk, doing her best to shift a stack of slightly decaying papers out of the way to reveal a loose floorboard.

"Really? A floorboard?" Cal asked.

Ella looked up at him. "Yeah. You might say I stumbled across it. Literally." She pried it up and reached around her desk to snag something that had been sitting on the floor.

"This," she said, holding up the old, battered and stained briefcase, "was what I found *under* the floorboard."

Cal looked at the briefcase and nodded. "You had it with you at Clarence's." The light in the office wasn't great, but even with her holding it still, he couldn't identify the stain. "What stained it?"

"I think it's blood," Ella said.

Cal frowned. "Are you sure?"

"Get down here and look at it for yourself," she said, setting the briefcase down on the floor next to her and returning her attention to the crawlspace under the missing floorboard. Cal crouched down and picked up the briefcase. It looked like whatever had caused the stain had been a foot or two away from the briefcase and the leather had caught the cast-off.

"It could be blood," Cal said softly, thinking. "But why would Clarence be hiding a blood-stained briefcase under his desk, under the floorboards?"

Ella turned to look at him, still crouched down, with one arm in the hole in the floor, feeling around. "And that is why I went to see him," she said. "Maybe there's something else in the hole I missed. Something that might tell us." She sighed. "Though, I wish I'd grabbed my phone out of my bag before sticking my arm in what is probably a mouse and spider-version of Disneyland."

"Hang on," Cal said, reaching a hand back for his pants pocket. "I've got my phone." He pulled it out, turned on the flashlight and leaned forward over the hole, holding the light. He was acutely aware of how close he was to Ella in the cramped space. He could smell that rain-smelling stuff she wore and he could feel the slightest hint of her warm breath on his ear as they leaned over the hole, casting the light around. Cal was trying and failing to ignore what being so close to Ella was doing to his body.

"Knock, knock!" Cal and Ella both sat up so quickly that they knocked their heads together and then bashed them on the underside of Ella's desk. She and Cal both swore and Cal backed out of the space first, followed by Ella. They peered through red-hazy vision up at Pippa who was standing in the doorway looking surprised as her gaze shifted from Cal to Ella. "Am I . . . interrupting something?"

Ella shot Cal a look that Cal understood to mean, "I'll handle this." Fine with him.

"Filing," Ella blurted out. Cal and Pippa both looked at her, confused.

"Filing," Pippa finally said. "Is that what you crazy kids are calling it these days?"

"Cal was helping me find some papers for the files," Ella said quickly, putting a hand on Cal's arm. It was a good thing that Ella hadn't asked him to come up with an explanation because he could feel his mind starting to buzz with a busy signal as all his attention moved to focus on the warmth starting to seep through his shirt and into his arm from Ella's touch.

Pippa didn't look convinced, but she also looked tired. "Whatever. I'm too tired to give you both hell at the moment. I'll pencil something in for tomorrow and just put a pin in it for now. I just came back to the office to get an envelope of the distributor tokens for Katie. She's having to cover a route in the morning because one of her carriers just went into labor. I'm leaving now. So you two can get back to . . . filing. Night!" Pippa gave them a knowing grin and then waved as she disappeared from the doorway.

"Well, this will get them talking," Ella muttered, leaning her back against the office wall and closing her eyes. Cal wasn't sure what to say. His first instinct was to apologize. But for what? It had all been innocent, well, at least what they were doing *externally* was innocent. Cal could only be thankful that Ella Danforth couldn't read minds. To cover his discomfort, he looked down at the face of his phone.

"It's midnight," he said on a sigh.

Ella chuckled. "Of course it is." She finally opened her eyes and pushed herself up from the floor. Cal followed suit. "Maybe we save the rest of our Clarence Catch-up for tomorrow? If we stay much later, we're going to meet ourselves coming in for work."

"And punch a hole in the space-time continuum," Cal said, almost grateful to be moving away from her as she started gathering the stuff on her desk together and shoveling it into her shoulder bag. He headed for his desk to do the same before putting on his coat. Then remembered . . . "I shouldn't have made the coffee."

Ella was already bundled up for the cold night air in a dark green wool coat, her white-blonde hair spilling out of the bun on her head and over the jacket's lapels. She yawned, turning her head away from Cal while one hand worked to free the hair tie keeping her hair up. Cal felt his breath catch in his chest as it cascaded down her shoulders. She gave her head a shake and scratched her scalp as she reached for the office light switch. "It'll probably still be warm when we get back here in a few hours."

Cal followed her out the front door and turned to lock up behind them. He was surprised to see Ella standing to one side, watching him when he turned around. "Oh, you didn't have to wait."

Even in the soft, dim light from the old-fashioned lamp posts surrounding them, he could see the look of embarrassment flash across her face before she replaced it with a wry smile. "Oh, I wasn't. I was just reacquainting myself with sleep deprivation, my old friend."

"Yeah, but he can be kind of a dick," Cal said, stuffing his hands in his coat pockets. The wind was picking up around them, rushing in off the ocean and up from the port to where they stood. Ella's hair was caught in the breeze, billowing out to one side as she yawned again. In that instant, Cal wasn't sure if he'd ever seen anything more beautiful.

"Well . . ." Ella said after the yawn had subsided. "I guess I'll see you in the morning."

"Uh, do you want me to walk you home?" Cal's mouth asked before his brain could staple it shut. He thought about just walking toward the dock and then right off it into the freezing ocean. But, before he could take a step in that direction, Ella chuckled.

"Nah, I know which streets the Hope gangs hit on Tuesday nights. And I always keep some tchotchkes wrapped in dryer sheets and a picture of David Bowie as the goblin king to barter with."

He snorted. "Is that the currency of the realm?"

"On the island? Always." She shook her head. "You're a Mainlander. You wouldn't understand."

He smiled before he could stop himself. "I've got to spend more time on the street."

They stood in another awkward silence for a minute, before they both mumbled "goodnight" at the same time and split off at ninety-degree angles from each other to head home.

A cold shower. That was the first thing Cal needed. Then possibly one, probably two, dead politician documentaries. He just hoped it would be enough to keep Ella Danforth out of his dreams.

25

ELLA

The next week passed like some kind of Hallmark travesty of *Groundhog Day*. Get up, meet with Cal early at the office, prep assignments, team roll in, marching orders given out, team disperse, events covered, stories written, pictures chosen, layout completed, paper run, paper out, prep for the next day, go home in the dark, dinner, sleep, and repeat.

Now that she and Cal were on friendlier terms, they'd spend the first twenty minutes at the office in the morning swapping stories about Clarence. Then they'd talk through the different angles of what they knew about him, and anything that might have prompted him to quit. Neither of them had mentioned anything about what had happened at Miss Mandie's, but the memory had an annoying habit of slithering back into Ella's mind when she stood next to Cal, sucking down the first cup of coffee of the day in the break room. He'd since relinquished her mug and was using the one Ella had bought him at Seaside Treasures as a peace offering.

When she'd given it to him, he'd smiled that half-smile that made Ella's stomach dip. "You mean you braved Esther's talk-nado to bring me this?"

Ella had tried to nod as solemnly as she could. "It wasn't an easy mission. I had cover going in with Mrs. Gilbert bringing in a new batch of lighthouse and human face-shaped birdhouses, no I'm not joking, that she'd made to sell on commission, but when Esther saw me, shouts were fired and I was pinned down. Something about how she hadn't really seen me since I'd gotten back, blah, blah. Finally, Stanley distracted her with a price check, and I was able to make it out alive."

He'd raised the mug to her, still smiling, still making her feel like she didn't have enough air in her lungs to catch her breath. "Well, thank you kindly, soldier."

Despite the irritating and sometimes embarrassing physical effects that Cal's presence tended to have on Ella, she had to admit that she was relieved that they'd fallen into a comfortable, casual and polite working partnership that almost resembled a friendship. She was mentally ignoring the fact that she was now going to be a part of the Mrs. Claus' Powder Room fashion show because of Cal. When it did cross her mind, she reminded herself that Cal was going to have to wear the bulky tree costume, so that was something. She was sort of proud of herself when she realized her panic attacks that came in waves when she thought of being on display in front of the whole town again were getting shorter and further apart. And it hadn't escaped her notice that they'd started getting better in direct correlation to how much time she'd started spending talking to Cal. He was an outsider, but he already seemed so in tune with the town. For instance, people in town who she'd been wary of when she was a kid, because they were cranky and yelled at her when she'd chased balls or frisbees into their yards, were just ordinary people to Cal.

"Janice Rothberg stopped me on my way to lunch yesterday to tell me that she didn't like how many times the term 'candy cane' was showing up in the paper," Cal had said one morning. "She said it was 'obscene'."

Ella had been drinking coffee while he was talking and she half-choked at the mention of Mrs. Rothberg. "You talked to Mrs. Rothberg?" Ella coughed, grabbing her chest. Ella's earliest memory of the woman had been when she was seven and drawing with chalk on the sidewalk in the square to play hopscotch. Mrs. Rothberg had come screeching across the town square, yelling that she was defacing property and would burn in hell for it. She'd been wearing her traditional black dress with a web-like black shawl and her silver and black hair drawn into a tight knot at the back of her head. She'd looked like something out of a horror movie. Ella had screamed, abandoned her chalk, and run home. It had been a week before Ella's mom had been able to coax her to go back to the town square. After that, Ella had avoided Mrs. Rothberg as if she was the fifth horseman of the apocalypse. In high school, she'd sweated through a town meeting when Mrs. Rothberg had sat down two chairs away from her. Even today, the woman still scared the crap out of her.

"Of course I talked to her," Cal said, frowning as he handed Ella a napkin. "Shouldn't I?"

Ella took the napkin with a nod of thanks, still trying to clear her throat. "Of course. It's just, she's kind of scary."

Cal raised an eyebrow at her. "Scary? Mrs. Rothberg? She's barely five feet tall. And I mean, yeah, she always seems like she's dressed for a funeral, but maybe that's just her style." He drained his cup and moved away to the sink to rinse it. Ella was frozen in place, thinking.

The more she talked to Cal over the next few days, the more she heard his impressions of the people she'd known her whole life. They'd gone together to Miss Mandie's to grab the daily box of treats and some lunch to go and she'd been quiet as Cal pointed out stories the paper had done over the summer on this person or that person. From the description he gave Ella, she felt like she was seeing Hope Island in a parallel dimension. From Cal's point of view, the island didn't feel like an embarrassing underwear drawer full of bad memories. She could detect a hint of rose-colored glasses in the way he felt about the town as a whole, but he wasn't blinded by them. So Ella tried to see her assignments and the people she interviewed every day the way that Cal would see them. As if she was meeting them as an adult for the first time. After a few days, the town seemed . . . different to her. Just another benefit on top of how easily she and Cal had fallen into a routine without any pranking or passive aggressiveness to slow them down.

"Personalized ornaments at Seaside Treasures at nine," Cal said, scribbling in his assignment book. "With Esther . . ." His groan was soft and accompanied by a small head shake that made Ella smile. No rose-colored glasses when it came to Esther Jacobs. "Then, Queens Reading Christmas

Books at the library at ten, then . . ." he continued.

"Well," Ella interrupted, "if you're willing to fall on that Seaside Treasures sword for me, I'll take the library at ten. Then you'll at least have a fighting chance to extract yourself before taking the Spaghetti Feed at Town Hall."

"What does Spaghetti have to do with Christmas?" Cal asked.

Ella shook her head. "Strings and balls? When they started doing it, they tried to be clever and called it the 'Strands and Baubles Feed' but that confused everyone and no one showed up, and the mayor ended up eating spaghetti for three hundred for a month."

Cal sighed. "This town."

They had a good rhythm, covering for each other and working late into the evening to get everything done. Ella didn't see herself as Cal's boss. They were a team. And that's what she wanted, wasn't it? It definitely seemed to be what he wanted and deep down, Ella knew it was what she really *needed.*

No one had mentioned seeing Clarence out and about in the town and they hadn't spotted him when they were out on their many assignments, but Cal and Ella just assumed that like a wild animal, he'd come out when he was ready.

One evening, Ella was sitting in her office after finishing the last of her assignments for the day. She was trying to string the right words together for the article she was writing, but her mind kept wandering to Clarence. Stopping short of breaking into his house, what options did she and Cal have to get him to talk to them? He wouldn't answer his phone and he wouldn't come to the door. She frowned at her computer screen. Clarence was a loose end. Ella hated loose ends.

There were already too many in her life. She hadn't been searching for any more job listings in Seattle over the last week. She'd told herself she was too tired, she didn't have the time, and it was the holidays, anyway. But, after the holidays, she was planning to go back, wasn't she? Back to her life on the mainland? Having no job or place to live were more loose ends. And . . . she hated admitting it (even in a tiny inner voice inside her head, where hopefully Sarcastic Ella and Helga would miss it) but . . . she was a little lonely. She kind of missed having someone to fall asleep talking to, though that had stopped with Les six months ago. But she remembered how nice it had been before then. And to wake up at night and feel the warmth and weight of someone next to her, hear their breathing sounds, and of course there was sex . . . Ella's hands had dropped onto her keyboard and the screen was filling with gibberish as her fingers braced on the keys. She gave herself a shake and pulled her hands away. Those feelings were just another loose end. Eventually, she'd get the other loose ends tied up. Though the loneliness one felt like a stretch. A part of her (a sickening, annoying, whiny part of her) that she wished would just take an online enrichment course or off itself with a tub of Ben & Jerry's, still felt something for Les besides hurt and anger. And she hated it. That loose end just needed to be cut off.

With a sigh, she pushed back from her desk. More coffee. Get the blood flowing, the heart racing, the eye twitching. That's what she needed. She was picking her way around her desk when the front door jangled and she heard the now-familiar sound of Cal's long stride approaching on the threadbare office carpet. Her heart was suddenly getting a jump start on the racing, pre-coffee.

"Hey," Ella said, pausing in her office door to watch Cal unwind the scarf from around his neck and toss it onto his desk. "How was the Elf Line Up?"

Cal rolled his eyes. "They gave themselves nicknames that rhyme and all sound very similar. It'll be a miracle if I can line up the right human name, with the right elf nickname, with the right head shot."

"Paint me a word picture," Ella said, crossing her arms and leaning against her door frame.

He sighed. "Grumpy, Stumpy, Frumpy, Bumpy, and Mumpy . . ."

"Mumpy?"

"Shhh," Cal said, holding up a hand and staring into space as if he was trying to visually put the names and faces together in his head. "In that order, they are Aaron, Abby, Sharon, Karen, Lauren, and Lorraine."

"Wow, you're sure?" Ella asked.

Cal turned a little paler. "I'm not a hundred percent." He looked down at his notes and then back up at Ella. "Do you think they'll come after me with torches and pitchforks if I screw this up? I don't really know any of them that well."

Ella shrugged. "Probably lit torches and those giant PVC candy canes from Santa's court." He sighed and she grinned, glad to have switched places with him on the anxiety throne for once. "Get it as close as you can," she said, "and then I'll play the dingus card and call them, tell them I lost your notes and wanted to make sure I have the right name and nickname with the right picture. It's been a few years since I've seen them, but I think I can help on the picture front."

"They're wearing beards and sunglasses," Cal said.

"What? Why?" Ella asked.

"They said it was part of their new bad-elves persona so the kids wouldn't push them around when they come to sit on Santa's lap."

Ella blinked at him. "The maximum age limit for kids on Santa's lap is nine."

Cal nodded. "That's what I said. But, Lorraine or . . . Mumpy? God, now I'm really not sure. Anyway, she said the seven- to nine-year-olds were the worst. Apparently, they have very sharp, crotch and ass-height elbows and they're not afraid to use them."

Ella groaned. "Probably goes without saying, but don't print that part." Cal snapped her a weary salute, and she couldn't help but grin. She tried to cover it with a shake of her head. "This town. What about the follow-up interviews with the Mrs. Claus candidates?"

"Done," Cal said.

Ella didn't miss the hint of red rising in his cheeks. "You ok there, buddy? Something happen with the candidates?"

"Just . . . you didn't tell me they'd be in bathing suits."

"Oh, the Santa Swim Photo contest. A classic piece of the competition," she said with a grin.

Cal looked even more uncomfortable. "Please don't say 'classic piece' when we're talking about seventy-year-old women in swimming suits."

He closed his eyes and gave his head a shake. Then he blinked and focused on Ella. "And I know I'm going to regret asking this considering that there are only three days left before I will have to 'suit up' and I'd like to keep conveniently forgetting about it, but how'd the Parade of Trees prep meeting go?"

"Ended in a screaming match," Ella said, walking with Cal over to the assignments board. "Dirk Patterson will not give up on the idea of being a sequoia."

"Why?" Cal asked.

"Well, his argument is that sequoias *are* coniferous trees and that he shouldn't be limited to spruce, fir, or any other *traditional* Christmas trees. He said by taking away his right to be non-traditional, we're limiting his ability to get into the Christmas spirit."

Cal snorted. "Maybe I need to take Dirk out for a drink. I'll bet I could help accelerate his Christmas spirit."

"Pretty sure that the majority of the town of Hope would pony up to pay your bar tab," Ella said, as she moved past Cal. She attempted to ignore the delicious smell rolling off of him, as she headed for the white board. She made a mark next to the last three events for the day, designating them as complete. "I think Dirk just wants to be a sequoia because he's sensitive about his height. He's the only person in Hope who actually *wants* to wear the costume and be Tom Turkey. But, he's even shorter than Freddy Winston, the poor sap who ends up 'stuffing the bird', as we say, every year."

"Well, what would happen if they just *let* him be a sequoia?"

"There's a debate about that," Ella said, capping the marker and turning to look at Cal. He was standing so close to her, it took Ella a moment to breathe and think at the same time. "There's even money going around that either a strong wind will blow him and the fifteen-foot tall costume out to sea, or he'll trip, fall, and take down all the other trees with him, turning the Parade of Trees into something that resembles a lumber mill cautionary tale. Feel like laying odds on one outcome or the other?"

"No bet," Cal said with a grin.

Ella quickly replaced the marker in the tray and surveyed the board. "Ok, that's it for the day." She glanced at the clock on the wall. "And it's just six now."

"Way to go, team," Cal said.

"Speaking of," Ella said, craning her neck to look at Maddie's desk. "Do you know when Maddie will be back? All the pictures I got from the Parade meeting look like some bizarre holiday edition of Fight Club. I'm hoping Maddie has something in the archives we can use for the short write up about the Parade of Trees meeting."

"She should be back soon. She was just taking pictures for this week's round of Houses of Hope's holiday edition."

The front door banged open and Maddie stormed in. She had her phone to her ear and Ella recognized Maddie's "had it up to here" face. "Well, tell Gladys," Maddie said, doing her best to put a polite sheen on the sharp tone of her voice, "that if she doesn't *want* to be part of the Houses of Hope Holiday Edition, that's fine, but for the rest of the year, I don't want to hear her griping about not being asked." Ella felt herself smiling. There was no doubt in her mind who Maddie was talking about. Gladys Mitchell was the notorious P.I.L.L. on Hope Island. Maddie hung up and looked over at Cal and Ella.

"Good old Gladys," Ella said, grinning at Maddie.

"One of those adjectives is a stretch," she grumbled. She pulled off her knit cap and tossed it on her desk before tugging off her scarf. "Ok, what did I miss?"

Cal pointed to Ella. "Ella first. Mine can wait."

"Elves and seventy-year-olds in swimsuits, right?" Maddie asked him.

Cal nodded. "And I'd love to get all the photos off my phone and into your hands for enhancement as soon as possible, so let me know when you're ready."

Maddie nodded and then turned her attention to Ella. Ten minutes later, they'd found a suitable photo of last year's Parade of Trees and Ella was heading back to her office, already composing the article in her head.

"Hey," Cal was standing next to his desk when she turned to look at him.

"I just had a thought." His tone was low and he cut his eyes towards the front of the office. Ella instinctively took a step toward him.

"What is it?" she asked.

"Bill, your stepdad. He grew up here, right? So, he probably knew Clarence when he first got here, right?" Ella nodded. Cal's hand was on the back of his neck now as he tried to piece together something he was having a hard time spitting out. "I mean, I know he's your stepdad . . ."

Ella hated the phrase. Bill wasn't her dad and stepdad always sounded like there should be a ladder involved. He was just Bill. "What is it Cal?"

He finally sighed and she could almost hear the voice in his head telling him to just say it. "I . . . I didn't want to step on your toes, but he's a cop, so maybe you could ask him what the rules are in Hope on doing welfare checks? Maybe he could force Clarence to talk to him?"

Ella blinked at him. "I hadn't thought of that."

Cal's phone started ringing. He glanced down at it and ignored the call. He looked back up at her and she nodded.

"Yeah, I'll ask him tonight." Cal's phone started to ring again. She shrugged at him. "You should get that."

Cal shook his head. "Oh, no. No need." He punched some buttons on the phone's face and stuffed it back in his pocket. She could see the hint of color in his cheeks as he snatched up his notepad and pencil off the desk. "I better go see Maddie and offload these photos before she decides to go burn Gladys' house down." He and Ella shared a grin and she stepped back to let him pass. As he went by, she heard the faint sound of the phone vibrating in his pocket.

Ella finished her articles, checked in with Kurt in the back and couldn't come up with any other reason to stay in the office when she had Bill to question at home. A part of her (a very nosy, asshole part of her) wanted to ask Cal who kept blowing up his phone. *It doesn't matter*, Helga told her. *It's not your business.* Then, Sarcastic El decided to speak up. *Besides, he's not answering whoever it is.* While Helga told Sarcastic El to shut up, Ella smiled and said goodnight to Cal before heading out into the cool night air.

Bill was organizing his dented tackle box on the front porch when Ella arrived. The Christmas lights were blazing, and he was separating tackle and rubber worms and swearing every time a hook stabbed him.

"Thinking of doing a little ice fishing or is this some kind of Christmas protest? You know I have pull now, I could air your anti-Christmas grievances in the public forum," Ella said as she stomped up the porch stairs.

"Shhh!" Bill said, in mock excitement. "What is that I hear? The sarcastic warble of the Ella Sass bird? It's quite rare to hear on the island, but if you are going to hear it, it's usually during the holidays."

"Touche," Ella said, pecking him on top of the head before dropping onto the porch swing next to him. It took exactly five seconds for him to start handing her removable drawers from the tackle box and enlisting her help in untangling fishing line and borrowing his knife to cut it away. "So what's with the tackle box in mid-December?"

He heaved the heavy sigh of a man that had been banished to the outdoors for an activity he'd rather be inside for. "I rediscovered my tackle box in the garage this afternoon and I started thinking about going fishing this next summer. Then it hit me that with it being the holidays, I'll bet Jeb will have all the good bait and tackle marked down so people will buy it for Christmas presents and I thought it would be a good idea to stock up now, but I had to know what I needed..."

"Hitting the fast forward button," Ella muttered.

Bill nudged her shoulder in annoyance. "Anyway, long story short, I opened the tackle box on the kitchen table, your mom said it smelled like the set of a low-budget horror film and banished me out here to organize it."

Ella had already noticed the smell. "I love you Bill, but I think I have to side with mom on this one." He chuckled and Ella decided there was no time like the present to just jump in. "Bill?"

"Hmmm?"

"You know Clarence, right?"

"Clarence Ford, yeah," Bill said.

"Did you know him when he first came to the island?"

Bill paused and glanced at her. "Yeah . . ."

"What was he like?"

Bill snorted. "Exactly the same as he was the whole time you knew him, why?"

Ella decided to just level with him. She was too tired to beat her way through the bushes anymore. "No one has seen him since he quit."

Bill grinned. "Can you blame the man? He had to know that quitting the paper, but still staying on the island would be like someone coating themselves in honey and then standing in the woods, waiting for the bears. Everyone is going to start bugging him about why he quit. If I was him, I'd probably stay inside too."

"Why do *you* think he quit?" Ella asked.

Bill shrugged. "Maybe he just got tired of it." He glanced over at her. "I mean, look at you. You haven't even been at this job for a month. And some nights when you come home, you look like the living dead. No offense, but you're even scarier when you leave in the morning." Ella flicked a crusty ball of something from the plastic drawer in her lap at him and he chuckled. "All I'm saying is that I can't imagine what kept him doing it year after year for almost forty years."

"Then why didn't he just retire?" Ella asked.

Bill shook his head. "That would be a question for Clarence to answer."

"Speaking of that," Ella said. "Is there some way you and the police department could do something like a . . . welfare check on him or something? He won't come to the door to talk to me or Cal and he won't answer his phone."

Bill turned to look at Ella and she could see his cop face slide into place. "El, we can't compel him to talk to you."

"But you can check to make sure he's alive, right?" Ella asked.

"There's no need," Bill said with a shrug.

Ella frowned at him. "Why not?"

"Because, he's been calling in a grocery order to Bumble's every five or six days and one of the kids there has been delivering it to his house."

Ella felt her jaw drop. "What!?"

Bill sighed and his gaze met hers. "I was a little worried too when he just quit suddenly, so I started asking around town, casually, to see if people had seen him around. And then Tom Bumble called me at the office and told me about Clarence's orders."

A plan was starting to form in Ella's mind. "Do you know which kid was doing the grocery delivery?"

26

ELLA

"Cal!" Ella called when she jogged into the office the next morning. "I've got news."

"She yelled," Cal said, standing up from behind his desk, "as she ran through a newsroom."

"Oh, good morning Sass Fairy," Ella muttered. "I didn't see you there. I was looking for Cal."

He grinned and nodded toward the hallway. "Coffee?" She hadn't had any that morning but the excitement of possibly getting to talk to Clarence had been an effective stand in. Still, in case someone else came in while she was telling Cal her plan, talking in the break room would be better than doing it in the open. She wasn't sure why exactly, but for now, she wanted to keep the discussion about Clarence between her and Cal. As far as she could tell, only she and Cal were still bothered by his sudden departure. Everyone else was either too distracted by the holidays to worry about it or had just accepted that Clarence had been fed up.

"Ok, what's your news?" Cal asked, picking up Ella's star mug and moving over to the coffee pot.

She closed the break room door and turned in time to see Cal raise an eyebrow at her. She did her best to ignore the heat she felt in her face from the way he was studying her. She cleared her throat and tried to focus. "I have an idea about how we might be able to see Clarence." She told him about her conversation with Bill the night before.

"Whoa," Cal said, handing her mug over. "But Bill didn't know who the kid was that did the deliveries?"

Ella shook her head. "No, unfortunately. So, we'll have to ask one of the Bumbles."

"And we'll have to do it in a way that won't raise suspicion," Cal said. "Otherwise, people might start camping out on his lawn."

"And waiting for him to stick his head out and see his shadow," Ella said with a nod.

Cal took a long drink and then set his mug down on the counter. "Let me get my coat."

"Oh, you want to come with me?" Ella asked.

Cal looked at her. "Is that ok?"

She shrugged. "Sure."

"Alright," Cal said. "Let's go." He headed out of the room and Ella blinked at his retreating back.

"Oh, ok."

The town was waking up as she and Cal left the newspaper office and walked quickly towards the market. The first wave of tourists were already meandering their way into the town square from the footpath leading up from the port. Ella picked up her speed as Helga reminded her how many assignments they had to cover for the day. They needed to make this quick. Beside her, Cal seemed to notice and picked up his speed to match.

"What's up?" Cal asked.

"I was just thinking about the thirty-something stories we have to cover today," Ella said.

"Crap. Yeah, we better make this quick."

Ella nodded and led the way inside the small grocery store. There were only a few elderly shoppers, all of whom Ella knew by sight. They waved to her as she scanned the aisles, looking for Mr. Bumble, and hoping she found him before . . .

"Ella, dear!" Mrs. Bumble called from behind them. Ella turned slowly to see the woman waving at her like she was afraid Ella wouldn't see her.

"H-hi Mrs. Bumble," Ella said, attempting to plaster on a smile.

"Oh! Please, you really should call me Lisa now. You're not a little girl in pigtails selling girl scouts cookies too close to our market anymore. Especially since we'll be working together at the Mrs. Claus event."

Ella forced a smile. "Of course. Um, we were wondering if we could talk to whichever of your employees does home grocery deliveries." In the blink of an eye, Lisa Bumble's hard smile and strong-armed bubbly attitude evaporated.

"Why?" She asked with a frown. "Did something happen?"

"Oh, no," Ella said quickly, scrambling to come up with something that sounded even remotely like a good excuse.

"Um, we'd like to write spotlights on them," Cal said quickly. Mrs. Bumble's gaze narrowed on him now. Ella could hear the proverbial buzzer noise telling her that that wouldn't fly.

"A spotlight on the fact that you offer this home delivery service," Ella said, "Which can make it easier for townsfolk to get their groceries, especially during the holidays when traveling in the cold can be hard on some of them."

"Yes," Cal said quickly. "That's much better," he added under his breath.

The old woman's expression changed back to a smile as quickly as a set of shades being raised.

She beamed. "My dears! What a wonderful idea. Of course, it won't be something that the tourist types are interested in, but definitely something for our locals. As long as they *all* don't decide to go that route. We do depend on a good volume of impulse buys from our customers as part of our profits."

"Of course," Ella said.

Lisa slid her hands into the wide square pockets of her apron and looked from Cal to Ella. "Well, what do you need to know?"

"Oh, well, we know how busy you are," Ella said. "If we can just interview your employees that do the deliveries, we can let you get back to the more important store operations." Ella could feel Cal's gaze on her, but she kept her apologetic smile trained on Mrs. Bumble.

The flattery was definitely working. "Oh, I appreciate it. Well, right now we just have the one delivery boy. Tori Simmons." Mrs. Bumble paused. "You remember Tori right? He was that kid who always got things stuck in various orifices. Usually his nose and ears. Normally, I wouldn't have hired him, but well, he's in high school now, and my Thomas, well, he always had a soft spot for the boy. I mean, life is hard enough without having to find work when you have one of those little Lego men's heads permanently stuck up one nostril . . ."

"Is Tori working this morning?" Cal asked.

Mrs. Bumble nodded. "Yes, he should be around here somewhere."

"Thanks Mrs. Bumble," Ella said. She snagged the sleeve of Cal's jacket and dragged him away with her.

"Help me look for him," Ella muttered to Cal under her breath as soon as Mrs. Bumble had moved away to talk to a tourist that had just walked in.

"Lego-head-honker guy?" Cal asked.

"Yea-" Ella paused. "Are you making that his official nickname now?"

Cal shrugged. "It's already his gamer handle online. I talked to him at the post office once."

"Well, good, so you know what he looks like," Ella said, back to scanning the aisles as they paced the length of the store.

"You two aren't planning something, are you?" Mr. Bumble's gravelly voice made Ella jump. She turned on the spot to look at the old man, his bulldog jowls pulled down into a frown that was eerily similar to the one his wife had been wearing only moments earlier. "Because you both look like the shoplifting actors in the training videos we show our staff."

"Sorry Mr. Bumble," Ella said. "We're not . . ."

"We're looking for Tori," Cal said.

Mr. Bumble's face seemed to relax at that. "What did he do this time?"

"Oh, nothing," Cal said. "We're doing a little piece about the convenience of the home delivery service your store is offering to the townsfolk."

A grunt from Mr. Bumble. "My wife's idea. Tori's outside, sucking on a coffin nail, no doubt." Mr. Bumble nodded toward a side door marked Emergency Exit. Ella thanked him and they made a beeline for the door.

"He meant Tori's smoking a cigarette, right?"

"With Tori, he could literally mean sucking on a coffin nail," Ella said, distracted. "Though, I'm not sure that coffin nails are actually a thing anymore." She pushed through the side door and looked around, Cal right behind her.

Tori Simmons was easy to spot. He had a Slim Jim in his mouth and a Bic lighter in his hand. As they approached him, they saw him attempt to light the jerky stick, filling the air in the narrow alley with the smell of cooking sausage. Cal opened his mouth as if he was going to ask Tori about his current activity, but Ella cut him off, knowing it would probably not be a useful line of questioning.

"Hey Tori," Ella said. He took his thumb off the lighter trigger and swept them a bow.

"Salutations. What brings you to the Bumble Market Smoker's Area?"

"Did you deliver groceries to Clarence Ford this week?" Ella asked, deciding to get right to the point.

Tori stared off into space and for the briefest moment, Ella was afraid he'd had a stroke. "Pickles," Tori said. Ella blinked. The evidence for the stroke theory was increasing.

"And anchovies," he continued, "white bread, tomato, mayo, six bananas, Arm & Hammer Deodorant, though I told him that the off-brand was on sale this week..."

"You talked to him?" Cal asked quickly.

Tori looked at Cal and Ella like they were idiots. "I mean, we don't do telepathic orders here. I mean, like, no one can, man. Except maybe Miss Arabella on the late-night tube. That would be cool though, right? I could like take orders and smoke some beef at the same time."

"Tori," Ella said, trying to get him back on track. "So you spoke to Clarence?" Tori's nod reminded her of a bobble head. "Ok, so he ordered groceries over the phone," Ella said. "But when you dropped them off, he must have come out and paid you."

Tori shook his head. "Nope, paid for them over the phone with a credit card."

"Did you see him come out to get the groceries?" Cal asked.

Tori shook his head again. "Nope. Mrs. B was blowing up my cell phone telling me to get back to the store. So I booked."

The side door to the store opened and Mr. Bumble stuck his head out into the alley. He was frowning at Tori until he saw Cal and Ella. "Sorry, but I need Tori back at the check stand."

Tori took the Slim Jim out of his mouth, tapped it on the top of the cigarette poll and then shoved it through the narrow opening. He swept a bow to Cal and Ella. "Sorry, duty calls."

"One more thing," Ella said, digging a scrap of paper out of her pocket and snatching a pen off of the front of Tori's apron. She scribbled her cell number on the scrap of paper before handing the pen and the paper back to Tori. "Can you call me the next time Clarence calls in a grocery order? *Before* you go to deliver it to him?"

The bobble head nod again. "Certainly. You got it sister." He waved to them and meandered back through the store's side door.

"Five bucks he smokes your phone number" Cal muttered.

"No bet," Ella sighed. She turned to look at Cal and shrugged. "But I had to do something. *Maybe* he'll remember to call me. Probably better to just check in every few days or so." They headed back around the side of the store to the square.

"And what's the plan if he calls you?" Cal asked.

Ella shrugged. "I'll go with Tori and sit with Clarence's groceries on my lap until Clarence opens the door."

"And get into a slap fight with him over mayonnaise if he refuses to talk to you?" Cal asked.

"Pretty much," Ella said. "You wanna come?" As soon as she said it, she wished she hadn't. There was just a little too much eagerness in her voice and she wasn't entirely sure of its origin.

"I'm there," Cal said grinning at her. She tried to breathe.

"Sorry this little outing didn't yield that much for us," Ella said, trying to move her thoughts back to Clarence.

"Well, at least we know he's still alive and hasn't left the island," Cal said.

Ella nodded. "That's something. And he's eating what's possibly the most disgusting sandwich known to man."

"Seriously. Pickles?" Cal asked.

Ella narrowed her eyes at him. "Pickles are delicious. I meant the anchovies."

"Oh, don't be an anchovy snob. Have you ever had them on pizza?"

"Nope. And I have no desire to," Ella said as they started winding their way back through the crowds toward the office.

"Just try anchovies once," Cal said. "My treat. And if you like them, you have to do the write up on the now extra story we have to run about the home delivery service from Bumble's."

Ella groaned, remembering. She cut her eyes to Cal. "And if I hate them, you have to write it."

"Deal," Cal said, "but you have to be honest about it."

"Ella!" A voice called behind them. They stopped walking and Ella turned her head to look behind her. "You were right!" Her breath caught in her throat. It was Tony from the ferry. He was wearing a well-worn North Face jacket and a knit green beanie, pulled down to his eyebrows over his curly hair. He gave her the easy smile she remembered and with a lanky stride to match, sidled up to stand next to her.

"Hey you," she said, grinning up at him. She noticed Tony's gaze slide from her to Cal standing next to her. "Oh, this is Cal. We work together at the paper."

Tony didn't hesitate to offer his hand to Cal. Cal shook it stiffly and looked from Tony to Ella. "I'll let you old pals catch up." Ella could tell he was forcing the smile when he locked eyes with her. "I'll rain check on making you eat anchovies. I'm gonna go do that home delivery write up before the events get started for the day. We probably won't have time for it later." He didn't wait for her to reply. He looked back at Tony, and Ella saw a flicker of something like dislike flash across Cal's face before he smiled at Tony again. "Nice to meet you Tony." Both Ella and Tony watched Cal walk away. There was a knot in Ella's stomach.

"The paper, huh?" Tony asked.

Ella nodded, moving her attention back to Tony. "Yeah, the *Hornblower*." She nodded at the building ahead and to their right.

"Cool," Tony said. "So that was the job you were coming back here for?"

"Yeah," Ella said. Then she remembered what Tony had said when he'd approached. "What do you mean 'I was right'?"

He chuckled, scanning the crowd that was swarming around the Christmas decorations which today included the extremely creepy inflatable giant Frosty, Santa, and Rudolph. It was hard to say if the crowd was there for the decorations or for the argument they were causing between their "handler" Don Kring and the Swiss Daughters' Seasonal Pie stands which Rudolph's ass was now blocking. "This town is nuts."

Ella nodded, looking around. "It is. But it's never boring." Ella was a little surprised at herself. Had she really just said that? And in that tone without sarcasm? The fondness she'd just heard in her own voice was . . . unnerving.

Tony seemed to have heard it too. "Well, that's definitely a plus."

"How-how's Waldron?" She asked, not smooth at all in hiding the fact that she wanted the subject to be changed as quickly as possible.

Tony shrugged. "It's ok. Lots of fishing. It's pretty." He grinned moving his gaze from the town square back to Ella. "But not like here." Ella instantly felt heat rising in her face. Tony dropped his gaze to the ground at their feet, but he was still smiling. "To be honest, I'm just glad to be around more people than just my aunt and uncle." He jerked his head up and smiled at Ella as if something had just occurred to him. "So, what's it really like to work at a newspaper? The only point of reference I have are the newspaper rooms on TV."

Ella shrugged. "Similar, but on a much smaller scale in Hope." She paused. "Would...would you want to come look at the *Hornblower* office?"

"You'd give me a tour?" Tony asked, his dark eyes studying her face.

"Sure," Ella said, feeling the heat rising in her cheeks again. Tony was looking at her like she was the only person in the world and it was hard for her to concentrate. She did her best to make small talk with him as they walked. The tour wasn't a long one, considering how small the *Hornblower* office was. Maddie and Pippa were overly cordial to Tony, shooting Ella raised eyebrows and evil grins behind Tony's back.

"He's cute!" Pippa had mouthed at Ella, almost getting caught by a marveling Tony as he swung back around to look at her. Cal was behind his laptop and barely looked up when they stopped by his desk and the door to Ella's office. Ella studied Cal's face, creased in concentration on what he was typing while Tony gave the area a cursory glance. Was Cal mad? Ella couldn't be sure.

She and Tony spent the most time with Kurt shouting over the machines in the back. Mostly because Kurt could be a talker. Ella had to marvel at how he didn't lose his voice after yelling over the machines all day.

"Wow," Tony said, leading the way back outside to the square when the tour was over. "That place is awesome. I can see why you'd come back for a job like this."

Ella frowned. "Really?"

"Well yeah," Tony said. "You're hooked into a whole community here. And a community that by your own description, 'is never boring'. Who could ask for anything more than that?"

Ella opened her mouth to argue, not entirely sure of what argument she was going to make. But, before she could say anything, he folded his arms and met her gaze. "You haven't been totally honest with me."

Ella froze. What was he talking about?

"You're not just a reporter. I mean, you have your own office in there. And the sign next to the door said, 'Editor-in-Chief'."

Ella started to breathe again. "Yeah. Sorry, I guess it's just still new. I'm not used to saying it off hand."

"So, that day you were on the ferry with me," Tony said. "You were coming out here to start a new job as the editor for the paper?" Ella nodded. "So did the old editor get a new job somewhere else and move away?"

Ella shook her head. "No, just burned out we think. He hasn't been around town much to tell us anything about what happened."

Tony frowned. "That's kind of strange for a town as tightly-knit as this one seems to be."

Ella nodded. "It is. But, he doesn't seem to want to see anybody so, we'll just have to wait him out." Her phone buzzed in her pocket. She pulled it out and saw a text from Maddie: *Crew is assembled and ready for the day's marching orders.*

"Do you need to get back to work?" Tony asked.

Ella nodded. "Yeah." She paused and smiled up at him. "This was fun."

"Yeah," Tony said. "We should do it again some time. I guess I'll just have to plan another trip here and actually arrange to meet you with more time to . . . talk."

Ella felt a complicated twist in her chest. Tony was a cute guy that was openly interested in her and he was just visiting. Like her. Right? She'd never had a "fling" before, but maybe that's what she needed right now, just to clear the hormones out of the pipes. Before she could stop herself with a lot of unnecessary thinking, she said. "Well, next week is the Solstice Concert and Bonfire."

Tony grinned. "That sounds like fun."

Ella nodded. "It's kind of my favorite holiday event. And I mean, besides liking it, I have to be there anyway for work, so if you are . . . you know, bored or whatever on Waldron, it's . . . something to do on a Friday night?" She was babbling and Helga was hissing at her to shut up.

He nodded, still smiling. "I love having something to do. It sounds like a plan. Next Friday night. Say, seven o' clock?" She nodded. "Ok, see you then, Ella Danforth." He winked at her and tugged his ski cap down toward his ears as the wind began to pick up. She said goodbye and turned to head back into the *Hornblower* office. Realization of what she'd just done hit her when the jingle on the front door of the office jerked her out of her thoughts. Did . . . did she have a date *with Tony* for Friday night?

"Sorry about that," Ella said to Cal when she got back to her office.

"Why are you sorry?" Cal asked without looking up.

Ella just watched him for a moment; mixed feelings of Tony and Cal and her own annoyance at how Cal was reacting rolling around inside her.

"Ready boss?" Maddie called to her, snapping her out of her thoughts.

"What? Yeah," Ella said. "Just one second." She hurried into her office for her daily crew handout and got back to her door in time to see Cal stand up from his desk with his notepad and pencil. He gave her a polite smile that didn't fill her with the same warmth it usually did. It was flat and the same one that he gave to strangers. He moved past her to join the rest of the crew. She almost felt like he'd slapped her. What the hell was wrong with him? She paused. What was wrong with her? Why did she care how Cal smiled at her? She didn't, she decided. He could sort his crap out, on his own. She glanced down at the handouts she was holding. She didn't have time for it today. Not Cal's crap, and definitely not her own. It was time to go to work.

27

CAL

There was something about that guy that left a bad taste in Cal's mouth. He couldn't put his finger on exactly what it was. Maybe it was the goofy smile he gave Ella. Not because he was smiling at Ella, no, it was more of a general "have some self-respect, man" thing.

At least, this was what Cal told himself as he headed back to the office, leaving Ella alone with Tony. He wasn't listening to their conversation as he walked away. Why would he? He forced himself not to look back or hesitate when he got to the office doors. He didn't let himself pause in the reception area. He had a fluff write-up to do about Bumble's deliveries and then, if the past few days were any indicator, a dozen assignments or more to get to. No time to worry about what Ella and her curly-haired, goofy-smiled, stupid-hat-wearing friend were doing. Though he felt a pang of annoyance, he knew Ella would have her own assignments to cover. Was she going to expect him to cover them for her? On *top* of his? He pulled his laptop out of his bag, flipped it open and settled into his chair behind it. The look of pleasure and surprise on Ella's face when she'd seen the guy show up was making him scowl at his screen as he forced his fingers to type. Were they together? No, Cal didn't think so. Their greetings hadn't been those of two people who'd known each other for very long.

The jingle from the front of the office didn't interrupt the flow of Cal's thoughts.

"And this is the amazing staff that makes all the magic happen," Ella's voice was enough to make Cal pause.

"Wow, this office looks historic!"

Cal sighed, frowning at the blinking cursor on his screen again. Oh good, Tony was in the office. He heard Pippa, Maddie, Katie, and Marty introduce themselves to Tony. Cal did what he could to look busy when he heard the approaching footsteps of the pair.

"So, this printer paper purgatory is my office," Ella muttered. "And of course you've met Cal." Cal could see them in his peripheral vision, but he sped up his typing, letting his fingers pound out whatever words came to mind to increase the illusion of how busy he was. He didn't slow down until their footsteps receded and headed down the hallway. She was giving him a tour? Had she forgotten how busy they were today?

He tried to push his annoyance away and focus on what he was writing. His eyes kept darting to the small clock in the lower right corner of his screen. Ella and Tony still hadn't come back down the hallway. What were they doing? Maddie passed by the edge of his desk and headed into Ella's office with the mail.

"Hey, isn't it time for the morning circle-up meeting?" Cal asked.

Maddie raised an eyebrow at him. "Eager to get to it this morning?"

Cal shrugged, hoping his face wasn't betraying too much of his annoyance. He didn't want Maddie to get the wrong idea. "I just know that like every day, we have a bunch to cover."

"Take a chill pill. I'm sure Ella will be back in a minute, and we can go full-steam ahead." Maddie was smiling now as she studied Cal's face and it was making him nervous. He turned his attention back to his computer screen.

"Cool. Let me know when we're ready to get under way." He increased his typing speed again, tapping out whatever came to mind until Maddie walked away. When he paused, his gaze fell on the last paragraph he'd typed and he almost swallowed his tongue. He quickly highlighted and deleted it. It was early. That had to be it. He didn't really . . .

He pushed back from his desk. Coffee. That was the reason. He needed coffee. He moved down the hallway to the break room and filled the new mug that Ella had given him. The smile she'd worn when he'd opened the box and thanked her, it had been a different smile than the one she'd given Tony. He replaced the coffee pot and took the mug back to his desk. He'd just sat down again when he heard Ella and Tony coming back down the hall. Despite telling himself that he didn't care what they were talking about, he found himself pausing to listen. The tone was polite. Under the guise of needing to get something out of his bag, he stood up and picked up his bag off the back of his chair, pausing to peer around the edge of the partition wall in front of his desk. He could see Ella and Tony from the back. They weren't holding hands. In fact, there were at least four feet between them as they walked back to the reception area.

Cal leaned to his left far enough to see the front door where Tony took a step back to let Ella precede him outside. He swept her a slight bow, but Cal had to smile when he didn't hear Ella laugh. What a dork.

"Checking out the competition?" Pippa entered his field of vision, smiling in the same unsettling way Maddie had.

"What?!" Cal asked.

"Do you think Ella's going to recruit Tony to work at the paper?" Pippa asked.

Cal felt a trickle of relief, but Maddie stepped in before he could answer Pippa.

"I don't think so. I think Tony's just a friend of Ella's."

"A good friend," Pippa said.

"A *cute* friend," Maddie agreed. The jingling of the bell over the door sent them scurrying back to their desks and made Cal quickly drop into his seat again. He needed to look natural. Disinterested. Busy. So she wouldn't think . . . anything, when she walked by. When she stopped by his desk to look at him, he sucked down some more coffee that was still boiling hot. He did his best to blank-slate his face by trying to think of her as if she was someone at one of his mother's dinner parties. He didn't miss the confusion on her face, tinged with something he hadn't expected. Was that . . . hurt? He stared at the top of his desk, but he could see her walk into her office out of the corner of his eye.

"Ready boss?" Maddie asked, poking her head into Ella's office.

Cal did his best to maintain his polite expression and throw away all the questions he wanted to ask Ella about Tony. Why did he care? He drank more coffee, trying to drown out whatever line of thinking was leading him down that muddy path.

"And then at eleven, we have the Ugly Sweater Brunch to cover," Ella was saying, her back to them as she printed events on the whiteboard. "Don't worry folks, I've volunteered myself to cover it with Maddie." She paused and smiled over at her photographer. "I even took the liberty of getting us matching Ugly Sweaters. They light up *and* sing."

Maddie was chewing her bottom lip. "El, I'm supposed to be covering the children's Christmas concert in the square. Double duty since two of my baby cousins are in it and my mom will kill me if I miss it."

Ella groaned and nodded. "Sorry Maddie, we've double-booked you again. I wish I could say it was the last time, but . . ."

"Cal could probably cover it with you," Pippa interrupted. Ella turned to look at Pippa, and Cal didn't miss the flash of discomfort in her eyes. "See?" Pippa said, moving up to the board, either missing or choosing not to see Ella's eyes screaming at her to be silent. Pippa pointed at the events already assigned to Cal on the board. "He's got the Toys for Tots Drive at ten, but he could easily be done with that by eleven and then he doesn't have the Fruitcake judging contest until noon. It's perfect."

"Oh, I'm sure I can cover the event by myself," Ella said quickly. "Cal's pretty busy . . ."

"Not as busy as you're going to be," Marty muttered.

Everyone's attention turned to him and he sighed. "Do you all even *read* the ads in the paper? There's a French Toast Christmas Cottage building competition at the brunch, followed by a French toast feed. Don't worry, the French toast for the contest is not the same French toast they'll be feeding people. But, on top of that, Miss Mandie has a breakfast bar with all her seasonal drinks, the Harrys' Hope barbershop quartet is performing, there's the actual Ugly Sweater contest, and unofficially, but something that will no doubt be like a car crash to watch, Henry Watts bet Dave Buckowski that he could eat more bacon than Dave could, so that showdown is also taking place at the brunch. And all of this is happening at the same time, since they only have Town Hall for an hour before the Gingerbread Town board boots them out so the tourists can view their display." Marty scratched the back of his head. "The Gingerbread Town people are getting my pushiest event of the season vote this year." When Marty fell silent, the rest of the crew was still gaping at him.

"This is a sickness," Ella muttered. "There's too much crap going on."

Maddie snorted. "Welcome to Hope."

"So, you're going to need Cal," Pippa continued, grinning at Marty for making her point. Now everyone turned to look at Cal. "What size of Ugly Sweater are you?" Pippa asked.

"Uh, is it a standard size?" Cal asked, unsure of what else to say.

"On the island, it kind of is," Maddie said. "That and Santa suit size."

"And Thanksgiving food-size," Katie added.

"And bunny suit," Marty said.

Pippa moved around the crew and disappeared into Ella's office, returning a minute later with two bright red, knit atrocities. She was checking the tags in the collars as she approached. "Oh good, they're both size large." She thrust one at Cal and he automatically took it as she draped the other over Ella's back. Ella turned around, snatching the sweater before it hit the ground.

"There, it's all settled," Pippa said, crossing her arms. "Brunch buddies. What's next?"

The rest of the assignments were divvied up fairly quickly and everyone returned to their desks.

"Meet you at Town Hall at eleven?" Cal heard Ella ask behind him. He could hear the forced bravado in her voice mixed with something less confident.

"Yeah, see you there," he said without turning to look at her. He tucked the Christmas sweater into his bag and maybe it was how horrific it was combined with the strange note in Ella's voice, but Cal's mouth was moving before his brain had a chance to debate him about clearing the air. "Ella . . ." He turned to look behind him, but she was already gone. He was still frowning as he headed out the front door. As he crossed the square, weaving in and out of groups of tourists on his way to his first assignment, he caught himself scanning the crowd, looking for Tony. He wasn't sure why, but he didn't like Tony.

The morning rolled along quickly and he was just finishing his interview with Dotty Schwartz at the Toys for Tots drive when he heard the bells at Hope Church chiming the time. With a hint of apprehension and annoyance for something Cal couldn't completely pinpoint, he pulled the hideous red sweater out of his bag and almost dropped it when a metallic version of "We Wish You a Merry Christmas" started pouring out of it, accentuated by multi-colored lights. He couldn't stop himself from smiling. He'd never worn anything quite like this sweater. His smile widened, thinking of what his mother would say if she saw it. He paused outside the door to Town Hall and pulled the sweater down over his head. It was snug. Clearly Ella had bought the sweaters for her and Maddie and Cal was a lot broader in the shoulders than either of them. He looked down at himself and he could see the tails of his button down shirt poking out from under the ugly sweater which ended just above his belly button. An Ugly Christmas crop-top. Apparently that was a thing now. Lovely. A steady stream of townsfolk wearing similar sweaters was streaming past him on their way inside. A few of them called greetings to him as they went by, only occasionally making cracks about his too-small sweater. He bent down to get his bag and jumped when he heard Ella's voice behind him.

"Well, you ready for this?"

As Cal turned to face her, the sweater stretched tighter across his chest and "We Wish You a Merry Christmas" sounded off again. The sweater was so tight, the pressure of the fabric had triggered the metal button that he could feel an inch from his nipple. As the song thankfully ended, there was half a second of silence when he and Ella just looked at each other and then the song started over.

Ella's face split into an evil grin as she looked down at his chest. "Oh, this is going to be fun."

Cal glared at her. "Maddie is going to owe me so big for covering this for her."

"I've got your back. I'll assign her the Candy Cane Hunt and tell her we want to be able to offer every parent a personalized picture of their kiddo finding one of the candy canes."

Now Cal was grinning. "Perfect." He plucked at the fabric on his chest, setting the song off for a third time. "And make her wear this sweater."

Ella thrust her hand out to him. "We have an accord."

Cal shook her hand and he felt some of the ice that had formed between them that morning starting to thaw.

"Maybe if you slouch your shoulders, you won't set it off," Ella said.

"Do I have to keep wearing it?"

"If you want to get inside," Ella said. "It's Hope's version of a cover charge."

"Can't I just *pay* a cover charge?" Cal muttered, forcing his shoulders forward in an attempt to keep from triggering the migraine-inducing song.

"Fraid not," Ella said, leading the way inside. "Hope doesn't recognize your mainlander money when there's a chance for embarrassment involved." She was smiling, but it was a tight smile.

Cal frowned at her. "I don't think that's fair." Ella raised an eyebrow at him and he hurried on. "I mean, you kind of act like all the town is interested in is embarrassing the people that live here."

Ella nodded. "I act like it, because it's the national island pastime. I have eighteen years of proof backing me up on this."

Cal shook his head and held his hands up in a retreating gesture. "I only have six months backing up my opinion, but, if *everyone* in town takes their turns getting embarrassed and having stories told about them that they can never live down, then everyone's in the same boat, right?"

Ella frowned. "I mean, I guess when you put it that way."

"Just sounds like a close family to me," Cal said. He spotted an open table in the corner and made a beeline for it.

The sooner he could put down his bag, the less chance he had that the strap might trigger the stupid song.

"But," Ella had caught up to him and set her bag down on the table next to his, "you have to admit, if that sounds to you like a family, it's a pretty screwed up one."

Cal shrugged. "I don't know. I kind of like the idea of a family being that close." He could feel the bitterness coming out in his own voice and he quickly scanned the room looking for something to illustrate his point. "I mean, look around this place as if it was a family reunion." He pointed to the far corner where the Harry's Hope quartet was warming up while waxing and combing each other's stick-on mustaches and attaching Santa hats to the tops of their straw ones. "Your slightly embarrassing musical uncles." He saw Ella grin and he moved on, pointing at Miss Mandie behind the bar, already mixing a round of mimosas and tequila sunrises for the first thirsty sweater-wearers. "Your fun-loving, boozy aunt." His gaze roamed the room and landed on Tori Simmons who was wearing a t-shirt printed to look like a Star Wars-themed Christmas sweater.

"And that one cousin that everyone agrees is just a little different," Ella said, nodding.

"I wonder if I could buy his sweater off of him," Cal muttered.

"I wonder if he's heard from Clarence," Ella said quickly. "Come on." She grabbed Cal by the front of his sweater, setting off the song again and turning heads in their direction as they moved through the crowd toward Tori.

Cal would have been embarrassed if he could be sure Ella was the one that had set it off. At the feel of her fingers, gripping his shirt, Cal's heart had started to pound in his chest. In fact, it was pounding so hard, he couldn't be completely sure that his own chest hadn't triggered it.

"Whoa man, cool sweater," Tori said, checking out Cal as they approached. "I like the tunes and lights." He glanced at Ella. "You should tell her where you got yours. Her's is like . . . silent and lifeless."

"Tori," Ella said, her face deadpan. "We're literally wearing the same sweater."

"We are?" Tori gasped, looking down at his shirt. Cal tried to turn his laugh into a cough as Ella squeezed her eyes shut for a moment.

"Tori, have you heard from Clarence since we talked?" Ella asked.

He shook his head. "No man, it's been like, really quiet. Mrs. B said you all were going to be writing about it in the paper though so hopefully there will be more deliveries next week. I like doing deliveries. Fresh air and like walking is a freedom we don't use enough."

Ella just blinked at Tori, but Cal stepped in and patted his shoulder. "I feel you man."

"This guy gets me," Tori said, slapping Cal in the chest and setting off the tinny music again.

"Tori, are you competing in this?" Mrs. Brooks yelled. They all turned to see her pointing at the three long tables set with contestant numbers, stacks of French toast, baskets of toothpicks, marshmallows and syrup.

"Hell yeah," Tori said. "Mr. and Mrs. B sent me to represent. Plus, I gotta exercise the inside architect, you know what I mean?" He moseyed away from Cal and Ella and toward the tables.

"The what?" Ella asked, watching him go.

"Forget it Jake," Cal said, putting a hand on her shoulder dramatically, "It's Tori-town."

She snorted and then at the same time, they both seemed to notice they were touching. Ella's gaze met Cal's and he could feel his heart pounding again just as the tinny music ended. He prayed to the universe that it wouldn't set the song off again at that moment.

"Cal . . ." Ella started to say.

"Cal! Ella!" Miss Mandie was yelling at them now. They jerked apart, Cal silently cursing Miss Mandie's timing. What had Ella been about to say? "Get over here and try these. I can't tell if I made them too strong."

"But we're writing later," Ella said as they headed over to the bar. "And we don't have a designated copy editor."

"I'll write you a note," Miss Mandie muttered. "Now get over here."

Miss Mandie shoved mimosas, then the Tequila Sunrises, then a round of Bloody Mary's at them. They were successful in nursing their first drinks while they moved around the room covering the events, but the sunrises went down too quickly, and Cal barely remembered the Bloody Mary's.

"Coffee," Ella rasped, stumbling over someone's discarded coat that had fallen off a nearby table. Tori had won the French Toast Cottage contest and after Ella took his picture, he was bathing in the glory of his victory while Cal had covered the bacon eating contest and the first few people in line for the French toast feed, but like Ella, the liquor was starting to weigh him down.

"Seconded," he muttered, grabbing Ella under the elbows so she wouldn't fall.

"Over here, you two." It was Mrs. Thompson. She was running a small coffee and tea station strewn with mistletoe. "You both look like you have a snootful. Here, drink up. My Yin to Miss Mandie's Yang."

Cal and Ella both took Town Hall mugs full of the black brew she handed them and there was a second of silence while they sipped. Then as one, they both gasped as the burn traveled down their throats. It wasn't the burn of temperature heat.

"What is this?" Cal coughed.

"I call it the goblet of fire," Mrs. Thompson said, beaming at them.

"What's in it?" Cal wheezed, still struggling to clear his burning airway.

"Coffee and Tabasco," Mrs. Thompson said. "A little wasabi, and the juice from a jar of jalapenos."

"Good god, why?" Ella choked.

Mrs. Thompson shrugged. "Do you still feel loopy?"

"Not as much," Ella muttered.

The old woman smiled and nodded. "Then it did its job." She waved them away. "Now get a move on, my next soused crew is coming in for a landing."

Cal turned to see a group of five women between fifty and sixty holding each other up as they stumbled from Miss Mandie's bar toward Mrs. Thompson.

"Come on," he muttered to Ella, jerking his head back toward their table. They slumped down into chairs with their mugs of hell juice in front of them and took in the madness around them. Ella chuckled as Henry Watts, the reigning bacon-eating champion, put Dave Buckowski in a headlock and gave him a noogie. "See?" Cal asked, grinning at Ella. "How could you *not* love this place?" The smile she gave him went all the way to her gray eyes which seemed to darken the longer he held her gaze. Pulling air into his lungs was suddenly a lot harder than it usually was.

"Cal, I wish . . ." Ella started to say, her voice barely above a whisper. He could feel himself leaning forward in his chair.

Then, both of their phones started ringing. They groaned and dug them out of their pockets.

"Sorry. Alarm," Cal said, shutting it off. It was five minutes to noon. "I need to go cover the Fruitcake contest."

Ella nodded. "Maddie just sent me a text. Apparently, we missed an event scheduled for this afternoon and the person running it just called to confirm we were coming."

"What event?" Cal asked, but his heart wasn't in it. Why couldn't they have sat down five minutes earlier so Ella could have finally told him what she was about to say? She was back in Editor-mode now and they both had places to be.

"Reverend Anderson's Christmas Hot Cider bar outside the church. Open every night until Christmas Eve now. Cup for a quarter, all proceeds going to the Anacortes Shelter," Ella said, groaning as she got to her feet.

"Will you have time to cover it?" Cal asked. He stood, but he could tell he was still a little unsteady.

Ella shrugged. "I'll have to. You definitely don't have the time today. I'll squeeze it in between my next couple of assignments." She paused. "I just hope my breath doesn't smell like booze when I'm interviewing the town preacher."

Cal shook his head. "I can't believe we downed three cocktails in forty-five minutes."

"Such is the magic of Miss Mandie Cane," Ella muttered. She caught Cal's eyes and glanced down at the floor. "I actually don't drink that much anymore."

Cal shrugged. "Me either."

"Well, I think we both fell off the wagon today." She nodded at his chest "You can take that off now." Cal froze, his heart pounding until he realized she was talking about the Christmas sweater. Thankfully, Ella grinned as if she hadn't noticed Cal misinterpreting what she'd said. "Probably better to not be wearing that when the hangover sets in." Her phone pinged again and she checked the screen. "Gotta go. See you back at the office on the other side of this afternoon. Well, if we both survive."

Cal walked out with her and at the end of the ramp from Town Hall, they parted ways, both of them hurrying off to their next assignments. Maybe it was the alcohol or the cup of fire from Mrs. Thompson, or maybe it was the melted ice between him and Ella and the fact that Tony was nowhere in sight, but Cal headed off to cover the judging of fruitcakes with the same kind of giddy excitement he got from walking around the island. The air was cold, but the breeze carrying it was soft. It smelled like the sea and Christmas wreaths and the festive feel of the square was infectious. He'd blame all of this coming together as the culprit that put the image in his head of Ella Danforth, older, her hand on his chest as they left the house together in the morning, before splitting off to cover their own assignments and meet back at the office at the end of the day. Not for the first time in their acquaintance, Cal, involuntarily, he would argue, pictured kissing Ella, not as his Editor, but as . . . something more.

A group of tourists plowed into him, knocking him out of his thoughts and into one of the benches surrounding the gazebo. He gave himself a shake, trying to return his thoughts to fruitcake and expel that particularly confusing fantasy to the furthest reach of his brain. *Blame it on the booze,* he thought as he lengthened his stride, heading for Aspen Park. He could already see the red and white-striped tent that covered tables ladened down by five-to-fifty-pound fruit cakes. He pulled his notepad out and licked his thumb to turn to a clean page.

Cal was tired. And he was a little hung over as he slogged his way back to the office at the end of the day. The thought of comparing notes with Ella and maybe, finally, getting to hear whatever it was that she wanted to say drove him on. He'd just made it around the side of the gazebo when his phone rang. He gritted his teeth, hoping it wouldn't be Tara. She'd slimmed down her calls to only two a day lately, for which he was thankful. He hadn't called her again or returned her texts. The truth was, he didn't *want* to leave. That much he was sure of. He didn't know if that meant he *could* stay. That was a much more depressing question. He still had obligations in New York. Family expectations. Cal's stomach began to knot and he took a deep breath and looked at his phone. Relief crashed over him as he answered it.

"Hi, Conner, what's up?"

"Hey! You coming tonight?"

"Tonight?" Cal asked.

"Yeah, to the fruitcake fight," Conner said.

"Sorry, you say that like it's a normal thing."

"You don't know about the fight?" Conner asked, sounding confused.

"Guess not."

"Ask Ella." Cal could almost hear Conner's evil smile in his voice. "It'll be a good chance for the two of you to . . . talk."

"What are you saying?" Cal asked, frowning at his feet as he walked.

"No offense, but you're not very subtle. Rumors about the two of you are going around all over town. Apparently, you're always going places together."

"Like where?" Cal asked.

"Miss Mandie's, going to lunch, Bumble's, walking around town, and then the brunch this morning . . ." Conner said.

"All stuff for the paper," Cal interrupted.

"Maybe. But that's not what the rumors say."

"Well, I can't help that," Cal said.

"You can if you come to the fight tonight and help me and Jamie take down Ella, Maddie, and Pippa. Maddie texted me a taunt today. The three of them sneak-attacked me, Jamie, and Carl Downs senior year at the fight. This year, it's payback. And with you, we have three since Carl went off and joined the Navy. So, are you in?"

"Uh, sure," Cal said. "But I'm still not sure I know what this fight is."

"It's a fruitcake fight," Conner said again.

"But what does that . . ."

"It's a fight with fruitcake," Conner said slowly. "I'll see you at eleven in Aspen Park. Wear black." And then he hung up. Cal slid his phone back into his pocket, still frowning. Then, a light bulb blinked on in his head and he glanced back at the red and white-striped tent in the park. Oh.

28

ELLA

Ella was not going to admit to herself that the smile that would not leave her the hell alone had anything to do with a too-small, obnoxious sweater stretched across the broad chest of one Cal Dickson. So her brain needed to just forget it.

While she called upon every ounce of acting training she'd learned from her journalism classes, to appear completely enthusiastic about the community Christmas card board, proudly arranged by the Swiss Daughters, an organization of island women over seventy years old, part of her brain was still stuck on Cal. They'd laughed. And... she'd actually had *fun* at the Ugly Sweater Brunch. Something she never thought would happen. Cal Dickson was ok. The smile was back as she said goodbye to Mrs. Hurley, who waved a handful of Christmas cards at her before turning to study the giant cork board which was already full as she tried to figure out where to stick them.

As Ella hurried across the square to her next interview, there was a sharp pain in her chest remembering the last Christmas when she and Les had bought each other truly heinous sweaters and worn them all day while they watched Netflix and ate their weight in peanut brittle and toffee. Well, they'd worn them *almost* all day. A month ago, the memory would have made Ella tackle Les out of longing for what had been an excellent Christmas memory and pure horniness. Now, the longing for what she'd once had was still there, but the horniness had been replaced by the gaping hole of loneliness.

What about your Solstice date with Tony? Helga piped up. Ella *was* excited to spend some time with Tony. He was funny and nice and *not* an employee so there wasn't that whole awkward dynamic to navigate. But Tony was just visiting the island. He was impermanent. He would be a fling.

Aren't you impermanent on the island too? Helga was getting agitated now as if Ella was wasting her time. It was definitely out of deference for Helga's time and *not* the fact that Ella didn't have a good answer for the question that kept her silent.

Ella's cell phone started to ring in her pocket and she was more thankful for the distraction than she could immediately articulate. "What's up Pip?" she asked when she answered.

"The rum rides at midnight," Pip said in a low, conspiratorial voice.

"What?"

"The bourbon cherries blow sky high and fall to earth like the fires of Hades," Maddie added, matching Pippa's tone.

"Oh good, I'm on speakerphone," Ella muttered. "You two dinguses wanna fill me in?"

"Have you forgotten what tonight is?" Pippa asked, her tone returning to normal, though with a sharp edge of annoyance.

Ella sighed. "Please don't tell me that I've forgotten yet another event we have to cover today."

"I hope we're not covering it," Maddie said. "My parents would kill me."

"My gran would just be pissed I didn't bring her along," Pippa said.

"I have to go," Ella said, "The Wilkins have spotted me and are trying to wave me over like they're landing a 747."

"It's the fight," Pippa practically yelled into the phone. "Tonight's the fight!"

Ella jerked to a stop as realization hit her and the rebellious, destructive teenager that had been sleeping for four years inside her cracked open an eye. "Holy shit, I forgot."

"Now she's back," Maddie muttered. "I've already told Conner that we're coming for him and Jamie."

"Oh, I'd like to come for Jamie," Pippa said in a breathy voice.

Ella rolled her eyes. "Phrasing. Anyway, so it's going to be the three of us versus the two of them?"

"I'll bet they find a third," Maddie said. "He tried to brush off the threat I sent him, but I could hear him shaking in his Keens."

"So, we're going to meet back at the office at eleven. Wear all black," Pippa said. "And ski masks."

"Also black," Maddie added.

"I don't have a black ski mask."

"I'll bring one for you," Pippa said. "But don't tell anyone our plan. Keep it on the down-low."

"Who am I going to tell?" Ella asked. One final admonishment from Maddie and Ella was able to hang up. The smile was back and even wider now. It had been a damn good day. It started with booze, fun, and French toast and it was going to end with projectile fruitcakes, powered by a thirst to remain the reigning champions of the Fruitcake Fight, a post-Fruitcake contest Hope tradition. With less forced enthusiasm and more real excitement, she tuned into the Wilkens as they talked about the Christmas Lights Walking Tour for Hope and how it was different this year from the last.

At eight-thirty that night, she was forcing her fingers to type as her mind went a million miles an hour as the last story for her day's assignments poured out of her and onto her laptop screen. The office was quiet and whenever she paused to consider her word choice, she could hear the quiet tapping of Cal typing away on his own laptop. There was a deep winter peace that had fallen over the office. Any other night, Ella would have just leaned into it and enjoyed the quiet, but tonight was the night of The Fight. She could already imagine what the freezing temperatures were doing to the fruitcakes innocently left under the tent by the women who had carefully baked, decorated, and presented them. They'd taken their awards and their festive and fragile serving trays home, leaving the fruitcakes on paper plates to await their fate. Ella remembered there being a discussion when she was in high school amongst the women who entered the fruitcake contest every year about how if they all took their fruitcakes home that night, there wouldn't *be* a fruitcake fight and they could still enjoy them. This notion had immediately been voted down with a single statement from Mrs. Sykes, who so eloquently summed up the feelings of the rest of the ladies present. "Who the hell actually *wants* to eat all that fruitcake?"

So, it had become a Hope tradition. In the dead of night, after the fruitcake contest, all the cakes would be whipped at each other like rum-soaked, nut-studded artillery and the next morning, a group of teenagers, whoever was the first to emerge on the street, would be guilted into cleaning it up. And while they cleaned, the teenagers would be plotting out the next year's fight. And so the cycle continued. Ella had to admit, at least to herself; not everything in Hope was horrible.

"Well, that's it for me," Cal's deep voice jerked Ella out of her thoughts. She glanced up at him, standing framed in the door. He had one hand on the door frame which pulled his button-down shirt tight against his opposite side and she could see the faint definition of his hip and ribs. His hair was mussed and he was several hours past a five-o-clock shadow, but all of it just came together to really suit him.

"Crying uncle?" She asked.

Cal nodded. "I think the thousand-word argument between Harry and Micah over at the movie theater about whether *Mixed Nuts* or *The Ref* was a better Christmas movie did me in."

"Oh, yeah. They're kind of film snobs. *Miracle on 34th Street* and *It's a Wonderful Life* are plebeian choices to them."

Cal nodded and tapped the door frame awkwardly. Ella could see his awkwardness and raise him. Things had felt so easy between them that morning. She really hoped they weren't backsliding to the awkward, bordering on frigid interactions they'd had before. "Ok," Cal said, keeping his eyes on the floor. "I guess I'll see you in the morning."

"Ok," Ella said, a little too quickly. "Have a good sleep . . . bed . . . night." She wanted to crawl under her desk. *Thanks a lot, brain. And when I need you, Helga, you're nowhere.* She heard Cal chuckle and chanced a glance up at him.

"Th-Thanks. Hopefully, all of those things."

Ella was glad that she had more to do before she could head out. It offered the benefit of something to distract her from her truly awkward "goodnight" to Cal as well as give her the chance for reconnaissance as she left the newspaper. The square was completely silent and empty when she finally made it outside. The scrape of the key in the lock for the newspaper's front door seemed entirely too loud at that time of night and she swore she could hear it echoing around her off the fronts of the darkened shops. She paused as she passed Aspen Park and squinted into the darkness under the tent. No movement. So no one had gotten there earlier than was allowed to stockpile fruitcakes or take advantage of the vantage point behind the big oak tree in the middle of the park. Excellent. What the grumbling adults never realized about the Fruitcake Fight was the fact that yes, it was essentially a food fight, but there were rules and procedures and honor. And it was all observed or the perpetrator would be turned on by their own team and everyone else. At least, until the actual fight got underway. Then it kind of was a free-for-all. But what mattered was how it started.

"I made a midnight picnic basket for you and the girls," her mom told her when she breezed in through the front door. Ella had been expecting the door to stick and had hit it with more force than she'd needed to, meaning that the force had to go somewhere, so she plowed headfirst into the stairs. She just laid there for a moment, before kicking out with her foot, trying to reach the still-open front door. She heard footsteps and her mom came into view, carrying an actual picnic basket, complete with a red and white checkered cloth. "That keeps happening to me too," she said, batting Ella's feebly kicking foot away and closing the front door. "Bill had time this morning and sanded it down."

"How dare he," Ella muttered, pulling herself into a sitting position.

Her mother was giving her a doubtful, hands-on-hips, mom look. "Are you sure you want to take part in this ridiculous fight tonight? You look dead on your feet. Well, right now, dead on your butt, since you're sitting-"

"How did you know I'm going to be at The Fight tonight?"

"Oh, Pippa called," her mom said. "Asked if I could whip up some sustenance for the 'mission'."

Ella closed her eyes and chuckled. "Only Pip would ask you to make food to bring to a food fight."

"I made about thirty breakfast burritos with sausage and bacon, scrambled eggs, and home fries. Half of them are pretty spicy. I used some of that salsa Bill made last year."

"The salsa that Bill said was basically paint-stripper for taste buds?" Ella asked, blinking up at her mom.

She frowned and crossed her arms. "He was exaggerating. It's very good salsa. I marked the fifteen that have the salsa on them with an 'x' on the tinfoil wrapper. And the ones that *don't* have the salsa have *two* 'x's."

"Why didn't you just *not* mark the ones without the salsa?" Ella asked.

Her mom paused, her mouth open, and then she glared at Ella. "Because I was tired, and I didn't think of that."

"Why did you make so many, Mom? Thirty would be about ten a piece for Pippa, Maddie, and me."

"I figured you'd probably be sharing with the other kids there," her mom said with a shrug.

Ella just looked at her. "You realize this is actually a night of baked-good vandalism, right? Not an after-school picnic."

"Well excuse me for giving a rat's hairy undercarriage if you starve to death. If you don't want them, I'll just put them in the freezer." Her mom bent to pick up the basket and Ella quickly got to her feet as her stomach groaned in hunger.

"No, thanks for doing it, Mom. In fact, I'm going to have one right now." She reached into the basket and pulled out a burrito, feeling the warmth radiate through the wrapper. She looked down at the tinfoil, turning it over in her hands. "Mom, there are no markings on this one."

Her mom frowned and pulled out another burrito. "Oh crap. This one either." Her face went red and Ella raised an eyebrow at her. "I marked the tinfoil before I rolled them up. I think the X's are on the inside of the wrapper."

"So, we're playing Russian burrito roulette tonight?" Ella asked.

Her mom shrugged. "I guess. You, Maddie, and Pippa should eat somewhere where you have light enough to see which kind you're eating. Then, just give the rest to the other kids."

Ella grinned. "Sabotage assist from the home front. Keep tending that victory garden, ma'am. I like where your head is."

Her mom rolled her eyes. "If you want to sack out for an hour, I'll wake you up on my way to bed."

Ella unwrapped one end of the burrito, nodding. "That would be great. Where's Bill tonight?"

"Poker game at Eddie Clifford's."

Ella bit into the burrito and immediately felt that she was experiencing the eruption of Vesuvius in her mouth. She would have screamed but she was afraid she would choke. Her eyes darted to her mom, begging for help.

"Milk," her mom said, leading the way to the kitchen.

Ella had recovered from the intense heat of the burrito and hadn't even made it up the stairs to sleep. Instead, she'd curled up on the old, comfy couch in the living room and passed out. She felt like she had no sooner closed her eyes before her mom was shaking her awake by the shoulder. "It's ten-thirty."

Ella groaned and stumbled up to her feet. Her mom was in her bathrobe, and she snapped Ella a salute. "You're up and the picnic basket is on the table. I put a bunch of microwaveable heating pads inside it to help keep the burritos above room temperature. Now, changing of the guards. I'm going to bed. Have fun, throw cake, don't break any windows. And if you get arrested, we've never met."

"Thanks Mom," Ella muttered. "It'll be a hard case to prove, what with the burrito evidence, but if we're caught, we'll do our best to eat it before the coppers haul us in."

"See that you do," her mom muttered, kissing Ella on the cheek before breezing past her up the stairs. Ella followed her and changed into black jeans, Chuck Taylors and a thick cable-knit black sweater. She tied her hair in a high bun on the back of her head, grabbed the picnic basket, keys and her phone and headed off into the night.

"Halt," Pippa barked from the shadows around the side of the *Hornblower* office when she approached. "What's your business here."

"Burrito delivery for two dorks pretending to be 'Always Save'-brand Charlie's Angels?" Ella asked. "And I want a tip."

"Here's one," Maddie said, emerging from the shadows. "Your hair is so bright that if you went jogging right now, people would think the Olympics were about to start and the torch was passing by their house."

"Ha ha," Ella muttered. Something soft hit her in the face before landing on the cobblestone square. She set down the picnic basket and picked up the ski mask.

"There," Pippa said. "Problem solved. Now let's plan our attack."

They didn't want to attract attention to themselves by turning the lights on in the newspaper office, so they each ate a burrito by the light of one of the old-fashioned streetlamps after squinting at the inside of the wrappers to find ones with double-X markings.

"Why can't we just smell them?" Maddie asked. "You should be able to smell salsa."

"Because all of them have salsa on them," Ella said. "Mom just put the hate juice on half of them and believe me when I say, I've tried to smell the difference between the two, but I can't. It's only after you've tasted them, when it's too late."

"Great," Pip said. "We'll save those ones as a consolation prize for the boys after we cream them."

There were other dark figures starting to gather on the edges of Aspen Park when the three girls moseyed over.

"Showtime," Maddie muttered, pulling down her ski mask. Pippa and Ella followed suit, the only part of their skin now visible being their hands and the gap for their eyes.

"I wish we could wear gloves," Pippa muttered.

"Makes it too hard to dig into the over baked and partially frozen fruitcakes," Ella muttered.

"I know," Pippa whined, "doesn't make me stop wishing that I was wearing them. It's freaking cold tonight."

"Alright, everybody gather in," even in the dark, Ella could see the sharp lines of Red Callahan's face. Good. Now she had two objectives. Red and Conner and Jamie's team. "Welcome to The Fight. Now, we need to go over a few rules."

As Red droned on, repeating from the sacred text of The Fight rules which had been scribbled in black Sharpie on a brown paper grocery bag, many years before, Ella scanned the crowd. She saw Jamie standing off to one side, wearing a black beanie over his hair and a blue-plaid shirt and jeans. It was so dark under the tent that she could only make out Jamie's face and outfit because of the light coming off his phone as he scanned the screen. The two figures beside him were dressed like Pippa, Ella, and Maddie and from the angry whispering they kept hissing in Jamie's direction, she had a feeling they might be his teammates, royally pissed off that he hadn't gotten the memo about how they were supposed to dress that night and for lighting up the clandestine rules meeting with his cell phone.

"Targets acquired," Pippa whispered to Ella and Maddie. Without missing a beat, the three girls did the stupid, complicated handshake they'd come up with in high school.

"Still got it," Maddie said, nudging Ella. "It's good to have you home, El."

The warmth that spread through Ella's chest at Maddie's words, left her speechless. In that moment, arm in arm with her two best friends, and about to partake in destruction, one of her favorite pastimes, she *was* glad to be home.

"Ok, every team gets one fruitcake to start, so send one representative of your team up to pick one." Pippa hustled past Red along with half a dozen other figures and Jamie. The fruitcake Pippa returned with was the size of a late October pumpkin.

"Mrs. Gillespie's," Pippa wheezed under the weight. Ella and Maddie helped her carry it over to the nearest Aspen tree before setting it down.

"You're sure?" Ella asked. Mrs. Gillespie had won the heavyweight fruitcake class every year of Ella's childhood.

"Feel the top," Pippa said. Ella and Maddie ran their hands over it and their eyes met.

"Walnuts, pecans, *and* whole hazelnuts?" Maddie asked. "By the power of Grayskull!"

"Women, we are in possession of a true weapon of mass confection," Ella said.

"If this doesn't take them out, nothing will," Pippa said proudly. The fruitcake had to weigh more than thirty pounds. Of course, once Mrs. Gillespie had caught on to what happens to the cakes at night, Ella suspected she'd started baking for war rather than holiday festivity.

"When this is over, we need to get her a Christmas present," Ella said.

"How about two bottles of rum to replace what she poured into this monster?" Maddie choked as she started pulling the cake apart to form balls for throwing.

"Ten seconds to starting time," Red yelled. Then, everyone joined in for the count down. Ella, Maddie, and Pippa started loading up the sling bags Maddie had brought for them, made from her mom's tablecloths.

"One!" Everyone yelled. And then the air was thick with the smell of rum and cinnamon as chunks of fruitcake filled the night sky.

"I see Jamie!" Pippa yelled. "Follow me!"

Easier said than done, Pip, Ella thought. The moonlight was bright, but still not enough to be able to distinguish much beyond vague outlines. Almost as soon as Ella left her crouched position to hurry after Pip, she took a hard ball of fruitcake to the chest. She stumbled sideways just as a figure ran at her. She pulled a ball of fruitcake from the sling bag and hurled it at the figure. A male voice cried out in surprise and grabbed his head as he ducked behind one of the nearby trees. She squinted around in the dark, but she couldn't pick out Maddie or Pippa amongst the moving shadows. She did, however, know the best vantage point for the fight. The old oak tree in the middle of the park had been hit by lightning ten years before Ella had been born, but it was stubborn, like everything else in Hope and the trunk had grown back with a vengeance, though never quite capable of covering where it had been split. So now, there was a crevice, wide enough for a person to comfortably hide in on the far side of the trunk. It was the perfect place to take cover and still be able to nail any unsuspecting person that ran by. Ella stayed low, feeling the proverbial "whistle" of fruitcake sailing overhead as she hustled to the tree. She felt along the weathered bark until she got to the crevice and backed her way in.

"Uh, excuse me," a deep voice said, just as she felt the body pressed up behind her. It was Cal. She sprang away in surprise and immediately took a ball of fruitcake in her back. She turned on the spot, scooping up a ball of ammo from her sling and hurling it in the direction of the heavy breathing that was running past her. A girl yelped in surprise and dove for a nearby picnic table. Ella's face was sweating under her ski mask and she was thankful for the surrounding dark.

"Cal?"

"Ella?"

"Yeah," Ella said. "What are you doing here?"

He sighed just as another ball of fruitcake hit her in the shoulder, knocking her sideways. A warm hand reached out from the crevice in the tree and pulled her inside. "Here, just squeeze in so you're not such an easy target out in the open." The oak tree's crevice had been more than big enough for Ella and Maddie when they were kids. Once, even Pippa had squeezed in with them when they were playing hide-and-seek. But now, as an adult, crammed in, and basically sitting on the lap of another, taller, broader, and smelling good enough to distract her adult, she realized how very small the crevice was. "Sorry," Cal said. "I know it's a tight fit." There was an awkward pause and because they were so close, she could hear his barely audible "God," as he tried to shift behind her so her ass was resting against one of his lean thighs.

"So, come here often?" Ella asked, trying to keep her mind off the fact that her back was getting a full-contact view of his anatomy.

Cal chuckled and she felt his arms on either side of her, resting on the odd bark formations jutting out from the edges of the tree's trunk. "Well, it all started with me answering my phone when Conner called."

"First mistake," Ella said, feeling herself smile under her ski mask. She could feel sweat starting to run down her chin and she lifted the bottom half of the mask, rolling it up to her forehead so she could breathe.

"And he told me about this thing that happens every year in Hope, after the Fruitcake Contest."

"Did he make you sign the blood oath to never speak of it to anyone?" Ella asked.

"No, we skated over the formalities," Cal said. "So, anyway, next thing I know, I'm dressed all in black, per Conner's instructions, standing next to Jamie who definitely forgot that he was also supposed to dress in black. And then when he went and picked our fruitcake ammo, wouldn't you know it that he went for a little two-pound Bundt-style fruitcake which meant we each had exactly two, maybe three rounds of ammo before we were tapped out. So, after I ran out, I knew I had to find a place to hole up."

"And you found my tree," Ella said.

"Oh, you see, in the dark, I must have missed the sign that said it was yours."

"Well, it definitely belongs to an *islander* as a hiding place. I mean, we're the ones who know it's here."

"Oh, are you actively admitting that you're an *islander* now?" Cal asked, the teasing mixed with something more serious in his voice.

"It's not like it's a choice," Ella said. "Just like the fact that you're a New Yorker, right?"

Cal was quiet for a moment and Ella was worried she might have said something wrong, but then Cal said. "If this is Aspen Park, why is there an oak tree in it?"

Ella shrugged. "That's Hope. Have you also noticed that our Town Square is circular? It's just how we roll."

Cal snorted. "Yeah, I guess so." His hand brushed Ella's shoulder and Ella sucked in a breath. "Oh, it looks like someone nailed you with one of the over-iced fruitcakes. Do you want me to . . ? I mean, if you wanted, I could knock it off your sweater for you."

"Oh, sure," Ella said. "Thanks."

She could feel the heat from the palms of his hands seeping into her as he brushed at her shoulder and back. "Not sure if it's helping much," Cal muttered. "We're crammed in here so tight I think I'm just moving it around."

Ella felt some of the fruitcake slide down the back of her pants and she started squirming, trying to get an arm back to keep it from going down her underwear. Cal let out a faint groan behind her and she froze.

"Did I hurt you?" Ella asked.

"Nope, I'm good. I just . . . How long does this fight usually last?"

Ella listened to the running feet and yelps of pain outside. "Probably a bit longer. It still sounds like there's cake in play."

"We might need to make a run for it," Cal said. "If all the other islanders know about this tree, it's really only a matter of time before they come to poach it and find the two of us in here like sitting ducks."

"Good point," Ella said. She reached a hand into the sling at her side. "I've got some ammo I can share with you to at least get you out to find some other cover."

"How do I know you won't just nail me the second we get out of here and then claim the tree for yourself?" Cal asked.

"You don't," Ella said. "You'll just have to trust me."

Cal sighed and said very dramatically. "Alright, but if you turn on me, remember that I was the one that tried to trust first and you were the one that betrayed it."

"Duly noted," Ella muttered. Before she could even ponder the fact that she was going to miss his warmth behind her, she moved back out into the open and stuck her hand back into the tree to feel around for Cal. She grabbed his arm and quickly felt to his hand. "Here, I'll give you some ammo, but if you hit me with it, know that I was the first to trust you with ammo and you were the first to betray it." She shoved a ball of fruitcake into his hand and then another. She could feel him shifting around beside her. She gave him four of the balls she had which was half of the remaining ammo. "Alright, good luck soldier," she muttered.

"We will fight with the nuts and cherries," Cal said, "we will fight with the soaked and tortured flour, we will defend our isle, whatever the cost may . . ." A wet thump hit Cal in the chest, and he swore.

"Wasn't me," Ella called as she ran off around the tree. She wasn't lying. It had been Maddie.

"I came to find you," Maddie whispered as the pair moved back toward the stand of trees where they'd stashed the picnic basket. "I figured you'd head for the oak."

"Yeah, but someone was already in it," Ella said. "Cal."

Maddie huffed. "So, when are the two of you just going to get over yourselves and hook up?"

"What!?" Ella asked, stumbling to a halt and taking a glob of fruitcake to the boob. She scooped out a ball of fruitcake and hurled it at Jamie who was giggling as he ambled by her, his plaid shirt moving through the dark like the ghost of a childish lumberjack.

"Seriously," Maddie said. "It's been weeks and the whole town knows that you like each other. And I know there was some weirdness at the beginning, but you both seem to have figured it out since then. I just . . ."

Whack!

Maddie's turn to swear as she swiped at the fruitcake that had bounced off the side of her ski mask.

"We're going to have this conversation now? Really?" Ella asked, crouching down and pulling Maddie with her.

"Just wanted you to know what the rest of town is saying," Maddie muttered.

"Well thank you for that," Ella growled. "I'm so glad that Hope continues to live up to its reputation of making assumptions for everyone."

"What's up?" Pippa's voice now.

"Oh, I was just telling Ella that she and Cal need to-"

"Get their shit together?" Pippa asked.

"Can we just focus for a minute," Ella spat. "We're mid-battle and I don't have time to strangle both of you and take down Conner's team. That is the objective for us, isn't it?"

"Yeah, but you were just wedged in a tree with a third of that team and you didn't nail him, so I don't know if you can be trusted to complete our objective now," Maddie said. Ella could hear the teasing in her voice, but the memory of him behind her was making her sweat again. She tugged the edge of her ski cap back down.

"It wouldn't have been very sporting to pelt someone who was out of ammo and hiding."

"Whatever," Pip said. "I'm sure he's found more ammo by now. Let's just end this, I'm tired and I want to soak in a bath. I've got some kind of caramel icing leaking through my ski mask and someone has an actual frozen fruitcake and really good aim and I can almost hear the bruises forming." She stomped off across the park with Maddie and Ella hurrying to keep up.

"*Hear* the bruises?" Ella muttered to Maddie.

"So dramatic," Maddie sighed.

Most of the fruitcake fighters had tapped out from lack of ammo, the cold, or multiple bruises and head shots, leaving only a few figures still fighting. Besides Ella, Maddie and Pippa, they could see Jamie's lumbering frame moving from tree to tree and two others. One of them, was Cal. Ella was *uncomfortably* sure it was him, judging by the barely visible outline of his frame and the faint smell she caught as she moved closer. The third one let loose a battle cry, hurling ammo from the crook of his arm as he ran at the three women. Conner. Pippa leapt through the air, bringing a ball of fruitcake down on his head with both hands. She caught him in the chest with her knees and they both fell to the grass.

"I surrender," Jamie called, holding his hands up. "I don't have any more cake to throw."

"Yeah," Cal called, "I'm out too. Uh, parley?"

"What about you, Conner," Pippa asked, still on top of Conner, pinning him to the grass. "Do you surrender?"

"Never!" Conner said. "A momentary setback."

"Are you sure?" Ella asked, linking arms with Maddie. "We have breakfast burritos to share with the bravely defeated."

"Really?" Conner asked. "I'm starving." Pippa climbed off of him and pulled him to his feet.

"Me too," Jamie added. "They have bacon in them?"

"Yep," Ella said, squeezing Maddie's arm.

"Revenge served cold with hellfire hot sauce," Maddie murmured. There was a brief flare up of the fight again with the remaining ammo Conner had against the remaining ammo Ella and Maddie had when he bit into one of the hot burritos and yelled that it was sabotage. Eventually, all six of them lounged on the steps of the gazebo, one by one, breaking off to go home until just Ella and Cal were left. She wasn't sure why she hadn't headed home yet, but something in her wasn't ready to let go of the happy, light feeling in her chest.

"Tonight was great," Cal said, stretching out on the steps next to her, leaning back on his elbows, long legs crossed at the ankles as they looked up at the stars and moon overhead.

"Yeah," Ella said, hugging her knees to her chest. "It was like being back in high school where your biggest worry was getting creamed in the fruitcake fight."

"Wow, now that's a high school I wish I'd gone to," Cal murmured.

Ella turned to look at him. "What was your high school like?"

Cal shook his head and in the light from the lamp posts, she saw a shadow of anger cross his face before he shook his head and it disappeared. "Different." Ella wanted to press him. Maybe it was the investigative journalist in her, or maybe it was the nosy Hope-born islander in her, or maybe it was because she was interested in Cal Dickson and where he came from. But before she could ask him anything else, he yawned. "We probably should pack it in for the night." He pulled out his phone and grimaced at the screen. "Tomorrow is already here."

Ella groaned. "And it's going to be a mad dash to get everything in as it is." Cal sighed and got to his feet. He paused and then offered a hand to Ella. She took it and time seemed to slow down as her fingers trailed over the palm of his hand, to grip just below his wrist. He helped her to her feet and then they stood together for a moment, Ella shamelessly lapping up the feeling of human contact with the opposite sex for the second time that night.

"Ella, you ok?" Cal asked after a minute of Ella staring down at where they were still connected.

She quickly dropped his hand and straightened up. "Oh, yeah. I think I might have dozed off there for a minute. I swear, I'm so tired, I could probably sleep standing up at the moment." She could feel embarrassment and shame forming a wet knot in her throat. What was she doing? Was she that desperate and pathetic? He had just been helping her stand. And before, he had just been polite enough to share the hiding spot with her. Here she was, turning it into something else. And on top of what Hope was already saying about them? She felt the bottom of her stomach drop. What if he found out what the rumor mill was saying about them around town? She'd have to go into hiding. She could already picture the anger and annoyance on his face. After all, she'd seen that expression so many times before.

"Do you want me to walk you home?" Cal asked. The polite tone in his voice felt like a knife.

"No, I'm fine," she said quickly. "I'll see you in the morning."

She snatched up the picnic basket and started walking as quickly as she could toward home. She wouldn't allow herself to look back. How pathetic was she? She'd almost made it home when the tears finally came. What was she doing? Cal was an employee. And he was being nice and she was trying to turn it into something more. Something to replace what she'd lost.

She sat on her front porch for a few minutes, trying to lecture herself to get the stupid tears to stop. She was mildly successful, but then her mind went to Les and the easy friendship they'd had and how tender the beginning of their relationship had been. She shivered not so much from the cold as the fear that history might be trying to repeat itself. No. She just wouldn't let it. Not if she could help it. But, what was she supposed to do with all these feelings? *Let Cal make the first move*, Helga reasoned. *Then, evaluate from there.* Ella let Helga force her ass out of the porch swing and up the stairs into her room. She mechanically got ready for bed and crawled under the covers. Yes. Play it cool and let Cal act if he actually feels like there's anything he wants to act on. That thought was a lonely one, because of course, one of the worst scenarios that played itself out in her head as she drifted off to sleep, was the possibility that the whole thing was in her head and Cal felt nothing. Her brain seemed to know that she needed some happy memories to hold onto as she fell asleep and unbidden by her, flashes of time with her father as a child chased themselves through her head, hugging her mother on graduation day, and then her first dates with Les, the blanket fort they'd made in her apartment before she'd moved in with him, kissing him, making love, and just staring into his eyes. But the dream had changed and Les' dark eyes were blue, the smell of his aftershave replaced by Cal's scent.

* * *

She woke from a deep sleep and stood under the shower head for forty minutes before the pep talk she gave herself had chased away the memories of her dreams from the night before. Ok. Work to do, Ella. Tell the hormones to screw off. Cal was already in the office. He waved to her and disappeared into the break room, before returning a moment later with two mugs full of coffee.

"Thanks," Ella said, taking a mug from him. "Recovered from last night?"

"I was about to ask you the same thing," Cal said. "I think I have a bruise forming on my back and one on my . . . anyway. Brutal game you kids are into out here."

Ella shrugged. "I mean we don't like to brag, but we are responsible for a few concepts used in the Mad Max movies."

Cal grinned. "So, what's on the docket for the day?"

Ella told herself she was relieved that Cal was just acting like a friendly coworker. That was what they were *supposed* to be. She and Cal talked through the events and then joined the rest of the staff for the daily divvy up while Pippa ran across the street to get the daily box of sweets from De-Floured. While they munched on cake donut reindeer and raised donut

Santas, the meeting stretched on. The days were becoming exponentially more packed and it was making them all sweat. From the number of stories they had to cover to how they were going to cram all the content into the print and web editions without anything getting shorted.

As quickly as she could, Ella released the staff and they all threw themselves into the day's whirlwind of festive cat-herding. Ella was almost thankful for the break-neck speed of the day. She had no time to dwell on Les or her dreams or the night before with Cal and how she was projecting her own loneliness on the nearest male that was breathing and talking to her. Instead, she buzzed from one assignment to the next and when she had more than a twenty minute gap between assignments, she sprinted back to the office to pour all the information from her head onto her computer screen. She'd started taping her interviews and had found that it helped speed up her story writing exponentially.

Her afternoon assignments were a little less manic and she had enough time after her five o'clock meeting with Mr. Myers about the Food Drive trivia nights for her to type up her afternoon stories. She had one assignment left for the day and as she breezed out of the office, she almost collided with Cal on his way in.

"Like two Titanics passing in the night," Cal said, grabbing Ella around the shoulders to keep her from tumbling to the floor when she smacked into him. "And the Hellidays are our own personal iceberg."

"Sorry," Ella muttered. "My brake lights are out."

"You know, I believe that," he chuckled. "How many assignments do you have left for the day?"

"Just one. You?"

"Just finished my last one, but I'm going to have to beg for some major help on photos from Maddie."

Ella nodded. "Good luck. She should be back in a minute. She wanted to get some candid tourist shots for the website."

"Sounds good," Cal said, dropping his hands from her shoulders and giving her that half-smile that made Ella feel like something in her chest was melting.

It was so familiar, so easy. Like a memory from a previous life. Like the one Les always gave her when he was teasing her. She gave herself a shake as she and Cal said an awkward "see you later" and hurried in opposite directions. She pleaded with Helga who immediately stepped up to the plate and shelved everything except for what Mrs. Wazneicht was telling her about the town's Christmas band concert. The interview rolled along quickly, almost in 8/4 time, Ella thought. Mrs. Wazneicht was a woman about tempo with a schedule to keep. They talked for exactly thirty minutes and then with a wave of her conductor arms, cutting her off, she shooed Ella on her way and turned to face the assembling band for their rehearsal. Ella took some pictures with her phone, waved goodbye and headed back for the office. Marty had told her he wouldn't have space for the story on the Christmas concert until the issue he'd be laying out the next day, so Ella was debating going home instead of staying at the office to write the story. Either way, she needed to pick up her laptop.

Cal was standing next to Maddie's desk as they bickered over saturation and hue on the photos for one of his articles. Not wanting to interrupt their flow, Ella waved to them as she passed by on the way to her office. Besides Maddie and Cal, the office was empty and Ella decided to just get the article written while the office was quiet.

She sat down behind her laptop just as her phone started to ring. She glanced at the caller ID and her face cracked into a smile. It was Alexa Reeves, a friend of hers from Seattle. She swiped to answer and leaned back in her chair.

"Lex!" Ella said. "God, it's good to hear from you! How have you been?"

Alexa was slow with her answer. "I . . . I was about to ask you the same question."

"Oh," Ella said, frowning. "I'm good. I'm working at my old hometown's paper for now."

"Oh, so you know already?" Alexa asked. "This was a . . . something you knew about?"

"Lex," Ella said. "Is this that game where you're holding an envelope to your head and I'm supposed to guess what's in it?"

"No . . ." There was not a hint of humor in her tone.

Ella felt a jolt of fear race through her. "Lex, what happened?"

"It's . . . If you haven't seen it, I'm sorry, I shouldn't have called . . ."

"Seen what, Lex?"

"Wendi's Facebook post," Alexa's voice was so soft, Ella had to strain to hear her.

She wedged the phone between her shoulder and ear and started typing. She hadn't been on Facebook since coming to Hope. She didn't really want to be reminded of the life in Seattle she was missing. And as the days went by she'd just gotten busy and forgotten about social media. Besides the newspaper's online presence, Hope was pretty old school with everyone getting their news from their neighbors or the paper.

Wendi's page loaded and Ella scrolled down past the "Add Friend" button. She wasn't surprised that Wendi had unfriended her. When she got to Wendi's latest post, she froze.

"Ella?" Alexa's voice in her ear seemed far away. "Ella?"

But she couldn't answer her. She couldn't speak. She was staring at the professional photograph of Wendi and Les, wrapped around each other, kissing. The picture was bordered by animated bubble hearts. How thoughtful. They'd immortalized the moment as a gif. It hurt, but not as much as the caption Wendi had added.

"After five months together, Les and I are officially moving in together!"

Numb Ella put her hand on Helga's shoulder, relieving her of duty. Numb Ella sat down in the command chair as Ella stared at the caption. Five months.

"El?" Alexa's voice was soft. "Are . . . are you ok?"

"Kind of redundant, isn't it? Saying together twice in a single sentence? I mean, it's like 'we get it', right?" Ella asked. Her voice was monotone.

"I . . . I'm so sorry, El. I didn't know you and Les had been broken up for five months. I should have called sooner."

"We broke up two and a half weeks ago," Ella said.

"Oh my god," Alexa sounded pissed now. "Les is a pointless phallus. And Wendi is a douchebag."

Ella appreciated Alexa's outrage on her behalf, but Numb Ella was suddenly fighting an imminent core meltdown that she was doing her damndest to get a handle on.

"Th-thanks for calling, Lex," Ella said, hearing the pitch in her voice starting to rise. She needed to wrap up this phone call. She could feel the safeguards starting to crack inside her. She was going to cry. She pleaded to the universe to not make her cry, but the universe must have been having a "Netflix and Chill" night because the pressure was still building in Ella's throat. She was about to soul-puke.

"El?" Alexa asked again.

"Gotta go," Ella said. "Talk to you soon."

She hung up and grabbed her shoulder bag. She pulled her coat on and paused. She had two choices. She could try to sneak out down the hall and go out the back, but the machines were running and Kurt would probably spot her, not to mention his team of six, *and* the dozen or so high school ad insert stuffers. Her other choice was to power-walk past Cal and Maddie and hope they were so engrossed in what they were doing that they wouldn't look at her face. She chose door number two. She took a deep breath which almost caused the dam to break. She was almost running when she left her office.

"Hey, where are you going?" Maddie called as she rushed by her and Cal.

"Stepping out for a bit. I might be awhile," Ella called. She didn't turn to look back at them. Already, she could feel the tears stinging the corners of her eyes.

29

CAL

Cal stood, staring after Ella's quick exit. The glass front door to the office bumped closed and he turned to look at Maddie. "Was . . . was she crying?"

Maddie was frowning at the front door, deep in thought. "In all the years I've known Ella, I don't think I've ever seen her cry. At least, not in front of me." She paused and looked at Cal. "She has a thing about crying."

"What kind of thing?" Cal asked, confused.

"She won't do it in front of people," Maddie said, shaking her head. "She says it's like puking."

"Is she sure she's crying the right way?" Cal asked.

Maddie stood up from her desk so quickly, he had to take a step back. "Come on." She pushed past him and headed for Ella's office.

"What are you doing?" Cal asked. He stood in the doorway while Maddie picked her way past the piles of Clarence's papers to stand behind Ella's desk. Cal could see the light from Ella's open laptop reflected on Maddie's face. He watched her eyes scan the screen. Whatever she was reading was quickly turning her expression from curiosity to horror and disgust.

"That douchebag," she growled. She glared up at Cal. "Look at this."

Her expression was so fierce, he thought it was better to just humor her. He moved around the office to stand next to her. The screen was filled with a Facebook post. There was a picture of a tall guy in black-framed glasses wrapped around a redheaded woman, joined at the lips. Heart bubbles drifted up across the photo. Cal bent over to squint at the caption. Without context, Cal wasn't sure which person in the picture was the "douchebag". He straightened up and turned to look at Maddie.

She must have picked up on his confusion because she heaved a weary sigh and jabbed her finger at the man in the photo. "That's Ella's ex."

Cal squinted at the screen again. He frowned. He was having a hard time picturing the guy with Ella. He looked like he was too . . . something.

"So they broke up five months ago, huh?" Cal asked.

"Nope," Maddie said.

Cal frowned at her. "I don't understand."

"They broke up the day Ella came to Hope," she said, crossing her arms.

"Then why does this girl's post say they've been together five months . . ." Cal said pointing at the screen. But, by the time he'd finished his question, he knew the answer. "Oh shit."

"Yeah," Maddie said. "And apparently this girl was also her friend."

"Assholes," Cal said. Maddie nodded, her look shifting from anger to worry. "Um, should we . . ." Cal asked, pausing when he realized he wasn't completely sure about what he was planning on suggesting they do. She was apparently curious as well. She blinked at Cal, waiting. He shrugged. "I don't know, do you think she went home? Should we go see if she's ok?"

Maddie started shaking her head. "No, if I know Ella, she'll want to be alone. At least, right now." She said the words, but Cal could tell she wasn't completely convinced by them. They were both quiet for a moment. Cal glanced back at the faces of the two people on the screen, wrapped around each other, either unaware or uncaring about the carnage they had left in their wake. "Asshats," Cal muttered.

"I've got it!" Maddie said. Her sudden upbeat tone dragged Cal's eyes away from the picture and out of his thoughts that Ella was a lot prettier than the redhead.

"Got what?" Cal asked.

"A plan," Maddie said. "One that's failproof."

"I'm all ears," Cal said. "Lay it on me."

Maddie gave him a funny look. "Oh, this is kind of just a me-plan. You .

. . you don't have to do anything. Well, except help me finish the photo layout. We'll get it done and send it to Marty so Ella won't have to worry about anything else tonight."

Cal nodded quickly. "That's what I meant . . . I wasn't assuming that I could cheer her up or . . . anything." Maddie did nothing to help him end the awkward moment. She just watched him flailing like a fish on a dock. He finally stopped talking and tried to craft his expression into something that would be appropriate for a concerned coworker who'd just seen his boss leave in tears.

Maddie didn't look like she was buying it, but she pressed on. "When we're done here, I'll go over to her house with a jump drive. I'll put next week's second and third round photos on it for the remaining pieces about the month-long installations."

Cal frowned. "How is that going to help?"

Maddie shook her head. "I told you, El won't want people around her if she's crying. And she *definitely* won't want us making a big deal about it. By going over to her house, either she'll come to the door and I can see her and know she's safe, or her mom or Bill will come to the door to take the jump drive and they'll either tell me they'll take it to her or they'll give it to her when she gets home." Cal was still missing something. Maddie closed her eyes as if Cal was trying her patience. "That way I'll know if she's home safe. If they say they'll take it to her, she's home, safe and sound and I'll text her to see if she wants to talk."

"And how is that different than just going and finding her and *asking* her if she wants to talk?"

Maddie heaved a weary sigh. "I swear, you men know nothing. A text is passive. She can decide to answer it or not. It's not 'in her face' or demanding like a phone call would be. Ella may have been in Seattle for the last four years, but she's an Islander at heart and Islanders believe that not answering the phone when someone's calling is like the eighth deadly sin."

Cal chuckled. "It really is a different world out here."

Maddie grinned. "I thought you knew that by now."

"Anyway," Cal said. "What if they tell you they'll give it to her when she gets home?"

Maddie's face was worried now. "Then things get more complicated."

"Because she won't have gone home," Cal said.

Maddie nodded. "And then, I'll need to find her to make sure she's ok."

"I can help you look," Cal said, almost too quickly. He paused. No, it was ok. Coworkers would help look for their distraught boss. Right? It was just ... common human decency.

"Ok," Maddie said, raising her eyebrows in surprise. "So, you ... want me to call you after I talk to her folks?"

Cal shrugged, trying to downplay his, possibly too eager, reaction. "I mean, if she's home safe and sound, you could just text me."

"But if she's not, I'll call you," Maddie said, grinning.

"Sure," Cal said. "Now, let's finish that layout."

It was just after nine-thirty when they finished everything up. They put on their coats and bundled up against the winds that had picked up since nightfall. Maddie slipped the jump drive into her coat pocket and turned to look at Cal as she pulled her ski cap down to her ears. "Ok, I'll either call or text you."

Cal nodded. "I'll be waiting ... to hear ... I'll be on standby." His jacket and scarf were making him sweat. Maddie quickly turned away, but not before he saw the grin on her face. Cal gave himself an inward kick and, in his head, Chill Cal had been replaced by Greaser Cal, lounging in the command chair. "Smooth son, real smooth," Greaser Cal muttered.

Nothing had ever felt as good as the blast of cold air when they left the newspaper office. He waved goodnight to Maddie and headed across the square toward De-Floured. He turned his head to watch her take off down the street, heading for the Benton's house. Hopefully heading for Ella. Cal dug his hands into his pockets. He guessed he was lucky. Compared to Ella, he had the opposite problem. When he'd arrived in Hope, he thought it would only be a matter of time before Tara met someone new to take her arm and escort her to all the functions, and events. Her new guy would be someone who loved them as much as she did. But based on the volume of her calls and messages, that hadn't happened. Or at least, if it had, it hadn't been enough for her. Cal knew in his gut that Tara didn't love him, the same way he knew he didn't love her. But it was a hard battle to fight when *both* of their families were trying to shove them together.

He took a deep breath, smelling the signature Hope Island fragrance of sea air and evergreen. At least, for the moment, he was in Hope. He held onto that happy thought as he looked around the town square, now quiet and deserted for the most part. It was like living inside a holiday card. The streets were clean because of the care of Hope's citizens and the detention detail from the high school which swept up any trash left by tourists every weeknight (or longer depending on what they did to get detention). The Whorley brothers, twin hellions in the tenth grade, were apparently responsible for luring a pair of Harbor Seals into the principal's office with a five-gallon can of tuna they had pilfered from the lunchroom and from what he'd heard, would be serving clean-up detail detention until they graduated. As if his thoughts had summoned them, the pair materialized around the corner of The Hope Church. They were wearing Santa hats and carrying their push brooms over their shoulders as the harassed, matronly figure of Mrs. Cranston came huffing after them to supervise. Cal waved to the crew before heading up the stairs to his apartment.

He sat down on his bed and looked out the window, watching the Whorleys get to work, acting like a couple of curlers instead of street sweepers. He couldn't hear what Mrs. Cranston was yelling at them, but after a minute, they started to sweep and Cal smiled. If he hadn't seen Hope with his own eyes, he would never have believed that a place like it existed in the world. The people from Hope were special. His thoughts strayed to Ella Danforth. He guessed she was too. She was probably better off without her ex. He had to be a complete loser to cheat on someone like . . . he clamped down on that line of thought. Coworkers. Boss and employee. He pulled out his phone. Might as well see if Tara had called or texted. She had done both, but he didn't feel like checking them. He was waiting for Maddie's call.

He quickly got to his feet, not wanting to focus on *why* exactly he was waiting on that call. He went to his sink and filled the kettle to make some hot tea and traded out Nick Cave's *Murder Ballads* vinyl for his *The Boatman's Call*. He stood, watching the kettle on the stove, letting the music soothe him, and willing himself to not stare at his phone while he waited.

The kettle had just started to boil when Cal's phone rang.

"She's not at home," Maddie's voice was worried, and Cal was reaching for his coat before he realized what he was doing. "I had to lie to her mom. She looked worried when I asked about Ella, so I had to say I just hadn't made it back to the paper yet and I was sure she was there."

Cal frowned. "Wouldn't it be a good idea to tell her mom what's up?"

"No," Maddie said. "Not with Ella. Her phone is turned off. I need to find her." She paused and Cal moved to turn off his record player and the stove. "I'll check the bars. They're about the only thing that's open right now."

Cal pulled his phone away from his face to check the time. It was just after ten. "Ok," Cal said. "You check the bars and what do you want me to do?"

"Uh, I guess, check everywhere else?" Maddie asked.

"Right," Cal said. "It's only five miles to cover."

"It's mid-December," Maddie said. "I think I'm going to have more luck than you are."

"True," Cal said. "Ok. And whoever finds her first . . ."

"Texts the other," Maddie said.

Cal hung up, slipped his phone into his pocket, and wrapped his scarf around his neck. He hustled down the stairs as he put on his gloves. He hit the pavement and paused for a moment. Which way should he go first? There was an urgency running through him that he didn't quite understand. It was cold outside. He just didn't want her to freeze to death if she *was* outside. Though, he knew Maddie's chances of finding her were a hell of a lot better. Though, if Ella had a thing about crying in front of people, why would she go to a bar? Home was the most logical place for her to be, but she wasn't there. So, what was the next logical? He didn't know, but a need to move and search for her pushed him forward. As soon as she was found and safely headed home, he could go home and drink some tea, listen to some music and pass out. He was only worried about her because she was a coworker and a part of his daily routine. Get up, go to the paper, see Ella, get assignments, cover the assignments, go back and see Ella again, work on stories, discuss them with Ella, pick photos, captions, layout, confirm with Ella, lock up the office with Ella, and go home. He didn't like change in his daily routine and now seeing her was a *part* of his routine and he . . . didn't want that to change. That was all.

His feet had automatically taken him to the joggers' path that ran along the edge of town, flanked by city parks until it led by the old lighthouse, the Swiss Ridge cliffs and then circled back, to where it started. When he'd first moved to Hope, he'd spent a good part of most days walking on the path. It was quiet tonight as he moved down the paved trail between the pools of light from the old-style lamp posts that guided the late-night walkers and early-morning runners so they wouldn't slip on the moss-covered rocks and fall into the sea.

For the first tenth of a mile, the only sounds around him were the waves on the shore at the bottom of the cliff, thirty feet to his right, and his footsteps as they scuffed on pavement. But as he approached the boundaries of Seaside Park, he heard something ahead. It sounded like some kind of animal dying. It was groaning and growling, but it wasn't until he was within sight of Kurt and Johann's Children's Play Park that he realized the sounds were words that someone was attempting to sing. He could see one of the kids' spring riders, the one shaped like Kurt and Johann's rowboat, bouncing back and forth, almost in time with the . . . singing? He wasn't sure if that was the right word, but he stopped caring when he got close enough to see *who* was rocking back and forth in the toy boat. Ella Danforth.

"I like my town, with a little drop of poison," Ella slurred, as she sang. "Nobody knows they're linin' up to go insane." She had one hand wrapped around the neck of a bottle of Jameson, while the other flapped one of the toy wooden paddles attached to the boat, in time with her singing. For a moment, Cal just stood where he was, watching her.

"I'm all alone, I smoke my friends down to the filter . . ." She paused and raised the bottle to her lips. She took a drink and then looked at the bottle. "No I don't, do I, Jamie? No, I *drink* my friends, down to the filter . . . wait."

"Ella?" Cal asked, trying to suppress a smile.

She rolled her head on her neck to look at him. "Ahoy, matey. Permission to come aboard . . . is granted. Though, usually, I impose a three-day waiting period for hallucinations. I'll make an acceptance this time."

Cal pulled out his phone and texted Maddie that he had found Ella, and she was fine. Then he moved to stand next to the boat. It was still rocking slightly as she raised the bottle to drink again. She took a belt and then pointed at the other seat in the rowboat. "Come aboard, sailor. There's plenty of room. Old Kurt and Johann knew how to party."

"Did they now?" Cal asked as he surveyed the rider, trying to figure out how he was going to climb in it. It was much bigger than the average spring rider and the spring under it was massive. It was meant to hold two to four children, but he was skeptical about two adults. Under the heat from Ella's glare, he decided to try. He'd been around drunk women enough to know that you were best off if you just humored them. The first time he'd argued with Tara when she was drunk, he'd come back into the bedroom to find her emptying his boxers drawer off the balcony.

"You know Kurt and Johann were brothers, right?" Ella said. "Or cousins. Something. They had the same last name."

"Really," Cal said as he tried to stop the rocking boat so he could get a leg over the edge.

"Yep. Their last name was Fingelhoff, which I always thought sounded kind of dirty. And do you know what they named this fine watercraft?" She asked, slapping the metal side of the boat.

Cal had gotten one leg up, but Ella was shifting so much he was having trouble getting his other leg in. "No, what did they call it?"

"Fernweh," Ella said. At first Cal thought she was on the verge of blacking out.

"What?" Cal asked, pausing to try to look in her eyes to make sure she wasn't about to pass out and bash her head.

"Fernweh," Ella repeated. "It means, 'wanting to be somewhere else'. Like reverse homesickness. Wanting to be somewhere you're not." She paused and took another drink. "I had Fernweh once. And it led straight to an asshole." She paused. "Asshole is a funny word."

After some contortionist moves that might have gotten him an audition with Cirque du Soleil, Cal was finally sitting in the boat facing her and they were sproinging back and forth much faster with his added weight and the momentum of him "climbing aboard".

"Brace yourself, sailor, we're experiencing some . . . turbulence," Ella said.

Cal snorted. "Oh no, Captain, what do we do?"

"Drink," Ella said, thrusting the bottle at him. Cal took the opportunity to get the bottle away from her, but when he didn't take a drink, she barked the order. "Drink!" Afraid that the houses on the other side of the park would be able to hear her and they might come looking for the source of the noise, Cal took a drink. The warmth rushed down his throat and bloomed across his chest. Now he understood why Ella had been able to stand the cold winds during her stationary rowboat expedition.

"Now, the bottle please," Ella slurred, holding her hand out.

"I think you may have had enough," Cal started to say.

"Oh, a mutiny, is it?" Ella bellowed. Before Cal knew what was happening, she'd sprung from her seat and launched herself at him. Her foot caught on the metal mounting plate at the bottom of the boat, and she fell on him, chest to chest. Of course, because they were sitting in a boat, mounted to a spring, physics took over, bending the boat down toward the ground. Cal fell backward out of the boat with Ella on top of him. He'd let go of the bottle to catch her and when the boat was freed of their weight, it shot up to right itself like a slingshot and in the light from the lamp post, he saw the bottle shoot like an unlit Molotov into the park.

"Oh no! Man overboard," Ella yelled, rolling off of Cal.

"I'm fine," Cal said.

"Not you . . . you, mutininny . . . mutin-neener."

"Mutineer?" Cal asked.

"That too," she grumbled, stumbling to her feet. "We have to save Jamie. He's got no legs. He can't swim."

Cal lay on the grass for a moment, watching Ella right herself. He didn't expect her to get far, but then she took off, running into the park.

"Shit," Cal muttered, scrambling to his feet to chase after her. She was running in unintentional serpentine patterns, yelling for Jamie, who she must have forgotten couldn't answer her, what with being a whiskey bottle.

Cal tripped over the bottle before Ella could find it. "Found him," he called, bending down to pick it up.

"Oh Jamie, you gave us a scare, lad." Apparently, when Ella drank Jameson, she became a pirate. She snatched the now-empty bottle from Cal and sat down on the grass, holding it with both hands like a baby with a bottle. "You're wasting away, boy," she said to the bottle. "Barely a drop left in ye." She upended the bottle and then fell back to lay on the cold, wet grass.

Cal sighed and sat down beside her. They were quiet for a moment. Finally, Cal said, "I'm sorry about what happened."

Ella was quiet and Cal turned to look at her. In the dim light that reached them from the nearest lamppost, he could see the tears leaking out of the corners of her eyes and down the side of her face toward the grass. "Jamie's had a hard time tonight," Ella said, holding up the bottle.

Cal smiled. "I'm sorry to hear that, Jamie." He noticed Ella's eyes starting to close and her breathing starting to even out, even as more tears ran down her face. "Hey, why don't we take Jamie somewhere to warm up?"

"Mmmph," Ella said, the whiskey already dragging her towards unconsciousness.

"Come on," Cal said, standing. She didn't respond and he hesitated. He should have told Maddie to meet them. Then, he wouldn't be trying to figure out the least invasive way to pick her up. Finally, he settled on pulling her up to a sitting position by her shoulders. Once there, he took away the bottle and grabbed her hands, pulling her to her feet. She was coming around again as she swayed. He quickly moved to get an arm around her to keep her vertical.

She was looking at her hands, confused. "Where's Jamie? We can't leave a man behind."

Cal sighed, and as carefully as he could, so Ella's legs wouldn't buckle and pull her back to the ground, he bent over to grab the empty bottle. "Here," he said, handing it to her. "Don't drop him."

"Oh, I'd never drop Jamie." She dropped the bottle twice as they tried to make it back to the pavement. Luckily, both times had been on grass so he hadn't shattered. Finally, Cal dropped the bottle into a trash can as they passed, hoping Ella would forget about it. If they could walk off some of the whiskey, he might be able to caffeinate her back to enough sobriety for her to go home.

"You're a top notch first-mate, Cal Dickson," Ella said, her face was turned into Cal's side so her words were partially muffled by his coat.

He still smiled. "Means a lot, Captain."

She suddenly jerked her head up and stopped. Her face was bright as she looked up at Cal. "We should go blow the horn and let everyone know that we survived the capsizing."

Cal chuckled. "You're very 'maritime' when you're drunk."

Ella glared at him, her whiskey-addled brain apparently deciding those were "fighting words".

"I am an Islander, sir. Bap-teased by . . . by the ocean. It runs . . . through us." Then she started laughing hysterically. "If you drink it, it really *will* run through you. Happened to Alice at scout camp." She started to wobble again and Cal moved to catch her before she went down to the pavement. They were quiet for a few minutes as they made their way back to the center of town. As they passed under a pool of light, he looked at Ella. Her head was back and she was smiling with her eyes closed.

"Ella?' Cal asked.

She opened her eyes and rolled them to look at his face for a moment before looking up at the stars overhead. The storm front that the weather station had been warning them about had blown by, leaving a clear night. "I forgot the stars."

Cal glanced up and grinned. "I'm sure they won't hold it against you."

She shook her head awkwardly. "No, I forgot about them. There are so many. I couldn't see them with the big buildings. It's easy to forget how beautiful they are when they're hiding behind something."

Cal thought he knew what she meant. When he'd first come to Hope, the sight of so many stars, untarnished by light pollution or smog was almost overwhelming.

They were quiet as they made it back onto the wide, round pavement of the town center. He was afraid she was going to remember her plan to blow the horn, but instead, she just pointed at a group of manicured hedges on one side of the gazebo. "Almost lost my virginity there." Cal didn't really know what to say to that. Luckily, she didn't seem to be expecting a reply. "He was an asshole too. Ass-hole. Aaaassss hole." She chuckled. "That is a funny, funny word." She sighed. "Anyway, asshole here, asshole there. Maybe that's my brand. Have asshole, will date." She started laughing again, doubling over and pulling Cal with her. He was grinning until he heard her suck in air. Cal frowned and quickly moved the loose hair away from her face. She wasn't laughing anymore. She was sobbing. The Whorley brothers and Mrs. Cranston were gone, but there was still the possibility that someone coming from one of the bars might choose to cut through the town center and spot them. He didn't want to make tomorrow hard for Ella in case they mentioned seeing her. There were already too many rumors flying around. And her legs were starting to give out. He tried to pull her upright again, but she kept collapsing. Finally, he just scooped her up in his arms. She didn't seem to notice.

"Come on, El," Cal said, using her nickname for the first time. "Let's get some caffeine and some water in you. You'll feel better." Carrying her was so much faster. He carried her up the stairs to his apartment and turned sideways to get the door open. He set her down on the edge of his bed and waited to make sure she wasn't going to fall forward and bang her head on the floor. She lifted her hands to her face and leaned forward, bracing her elbows on her knees. He could tell by the way her body was jerking that she was trying to contain her sobs. "I'll just get the water going," Cal said awkwardly. "I've got a couple of different kinds of tea..." She didn't answer him. He turned on the stove, pulled a water bottle from the fridge, opened it, put it in her hand, and sat down in the chair next to his bed to watch her. She drank half the bottle and after a few minutes, she seemed to be getting control of herself. She swiped at her face with the sleeve of her jacket. Cal snatched a box of tissues off his nightstand and offered them to her.

"Th-thanks," she said, keeping her gaze on the floor. She wiped her face and Cal watched her giving herself some kind of mental pep talk as she squared her shoulders, still very drunk, but starting to come out of the "silly drunk" stage. "I'm a loser," Ella said. It wasn't said in self-pity. More like she was coming to a conclusion.

"No, you're not," Cal said.

She chuckled, swiping at her face again. "Yeah I am. I washed the sheets every week. They probably planned their doinking schedule around it. I just hope they did it the day *before* I washed them every week. For five months. That's like four laundry days a month, times five, like sixteen times."

Cal wasn't about to correct her. "For what it's worth," he said before he could think through what he was about to say. "That guy is definitely an asshole." Maybe it was the power of suggestion but the word made him grin.

Ella snorted. "See? It's a funny word."

The kettle started to whistle and Cal got up to shut it off. "What kind of tea would you like?"

"Surprise me," Ella said. She was starting to slur her words a little less as she began to look around her. "Where are we?"

"My apartment," Cal said.

She was still for a moment and then her eyes focused on him. "*You're* the one that lives in Miss Mandie's upstairs apartment?" Cal nodded. She frowned. "Miss Mandie said it was going to be for rent soon."

Now Cal was in a pickle. He hadn't told anyone but Miss Mandie about moving back to New York in the new year. It hadn't seemed that important, well until now, with Ella looking at him. It felt like a fork in the road that he wasn't ready to take. He was trying to figure out how to answer her when he noticed her attention had shifted off of him.

"You have a turntable?" She asked, getting unsteadily to her feet. He set the two cups of tea down on the counter and moved to be able to catch her before she fell and cracked her head open. But she put out a hand and steadied herself on the wall as she approached the record player and the small collection of vinyl he'd brought with him in his suitcase instead of clothes.

"I'll bet this one's a big hit with guests," Ella said, holding up *Murder Ballads*.

Cal grinned. "Definitely gets rid of the bad ones."

She squatted down, almost falling on her butt, but she righted herself and started pulling out some of the other records, smiling when she came across Tom Waits' *Orphans*.

"Here's the only man I need," she said, running a hand down the cover. "A rat always knows when he's in with weasels," she started to sing, "Here you lose a little, every day." She sighed and leaned her head against the window ledge next to her. "Music to 'realize your boyfriend was cheating on you for five months and you were an idiot for not figuring it out' . . . to."

Cal squatted down next to her. "Not that I don't love some Tom Waits, but if you're looking for the *best* music to 'realize your ex was a bag of dicks' to, let me suggest some Nick Cave?" He handed her the sleeve for *The Boatman's Call*.

She frowned as she read the song titles. "I don't know any of these songs."

"Allow me to make a recommendation," Cal said. He stood up and moved the needle on the record. "My personal, 'the world sucks' song."

Ella grinned. "Lay it on me."

He turned on "People Ain't No Good" and sat down on the floor beside her. She closed her eyes and started bobbing her head as the song played. Cal watched her. Somewhere between the office and her boat ride with Jamie the whiskey bottle, she'd let her hair down. It was wavy and fell in a tangled sheet over her shoulder. She leaned her head back and he caught himself watching her exposed clavicle rising and falling as she listened. The phrase "tangled sheet" took on a new meaning as his imagination took off and he struggled to stomp on that thought.

"It makes me wanna dance," Ella said. Before he could dissuade her, she was pulling herself up to stand by the window sill. She started rocking side to side, raising her arms over her head. As she turned, Cal was momentarily transfixed by the two inch strip of skin between her shirt and jeans, visible through the gap in her open jacket. He was so distracted that when she stumbled, he didn't have time to get to his feet to steady her. His hands settled on her hips as he tried to stabilize her from where he was sitting. She was still lilting to one side, eyes closed. He got to his feet, still trying to get her back to a solid stance. But, then she leaned into him. Her face rested on his chest and he was in a trance as her hands skimmed over his hips and wrapped around his back, her warmth seeping through his shirt which at the moment didn't feel like much separating them. She'd turned her face sideways and her warm breath was working its way through the gap where the shirt was buttoned, stirring his chest hair. Stirring. Also not a good thought for the moment. He tried to concentrate on Ella being a coworker that just needed a hug. Ok. Just a hug. He slowly put his arms around her small shoulders. She let out a sigh and nuzzled her face more into his chest.

She's hurting. This is a friendly hug, Cal told himself. *Just friendly. Nothing weird about that.*

"You know what the trick is," Ella said. Her voice was muffled in his chest, but she was starting to sound more sober.

"What?" Cal asked, looking down at her.

She smiled. "Your voice is loud in your chest."

"Sorry," Cal moved his arms to end the hug, but Ella tightened her hold on him.

"I like it. It sounds like thunder when you're at sea."

"I'm going to take that as a compliment?" Cal asked.

"Anyway, you know what the trick is?" Ella asked. "How you get rid of them?"

"Get rid of who?" Cal asked.

"Assholes named Les?"

"Oh, what's the trick?"

"You don't keep anything that they touched or that reminds you of them. If I hadn't gotten that call tonight, or if I just hadn't looked . . . but of course, he still would have been double dicking his dip . . .sorry double dipping his dick, for the last five months. But, when I left, I didn't take anything with me that reminds me of him. And that's the trick. Then, you just have the mental trash to take out."

"That's a good point," Cal said. She sighed and before Cal could stop himself, he rested his chin on the top of her head as they kept slowly rocking to the next track on the record. After another song, Ella paused and pulled back in Cal's arms. He told his arms to drop, let her go, end the seven-minute-hug they'd been having.

Ella looked up at him, her eyes dark, bloodshot, and puffy, but somehow not changing the way she always looked to him. "Thank you," she said. She was looking at Cal like she had that morning at Miss Mandie's. Cal felt his heart starting to pound in his chest as she leaned forward, her eyes starting to drift closed. He was leaning toward her now, closing the gap between them before he knew what he was doing.

Then someone out in the square blew the horn. The sound made them both jump. Ella groaned and closed her eyes. "If I find out who did that, I'm going to shove that horn up their ass." She was leaning in again towards Cal. God help him, he wanted to kiss her.

"El, you're drunk, we shouldn't do anything . . ." Cal was talking through his brain while the rest of him screamed at his brain to shut up. He blamed Killjoy Cal.

Ella's eyes opened and he saw a flash of hurt, quickly covered by a nervous laugh. "My god, what am I doing? I'm sorry. Uh, please, just uh," she sidestepped Cal and braced herself against the wall before straightening up and squaring her shoulders, taking careful but quick steps back across his apartment. "Thanks . . . for everything, Cal. I'll uh, see you . . . tomorrow."

"El . . . Ella, you don't have to," Cal began.

She didn't look back to see Cal poised on the edge of indecision to chase after her and kiss her or let her go. In the end, he just let her go, watching her open the door and head down the stairs. He stood in the doorway, watching until she'd safely made it to the pavement. He gave her a few minutes' head start and then followed her, keeping his distance, through the quiet streets of Hope until she climbed the porch steps of the yellow house and disappeared inside. He sighed. He wasn't sure if it was frustration over what *had* happened with Ella or what *hadn't*. As he walked home, he looked up at the stars and he heard her voice in his head. "It's easy to forget how beautiful they are when they're hiding behind something." Like a desk and a title. Tonight, he felt like, for the first time, he'd really met Ella.

30

ELLA

It took three tries for Ella to peel her eyes open. She was staring up at the ceiling of her bedroom. She frowned, thinking of the dream she'd had. There was music and . . . a boat, and . . . She shot up in bed. Cal. The pain rushing to her head wasn't just from the hangover. It hadn't been a dream. She buried her face in her hands. If all of it had actually happened, she'd tried to...with Cal . . . again. She groaned into her hands, as her memory flashed photograph after photograph behind her eyes. Cal in the kiddie park's toy boat. Laying on the grass, looking at the stars. His apartment over Miss Mandie's. A vinyl cover for a Nick Cave album. There'd been a note written next to one of the songs, "Black Hair". It was feminine handwriting which had caught her attention. It had said "Tara's song". And then . . . they'd danced. Had she forced him? Had he *wanted* to?

She leaned forward, raising her knees and burying her face in them. She'd screwed everything up. For the past two weeks, they'd fallen into a good rhythm. They were a team. Things were...comfortable. And, in the course of a single night, he'd seen her drunk, crying, and probably coming across as desperate. She groaned again. Something else from the night before surfaced in her mind, giving her a tiny moment of relief. Cal was...giving up his apartment. She assumed to go back to New York. Maybe go back *to* someone. The memory of Cal telling her they shouldn't kiss, stung. Embarrassment, she decided. That's why it stung. And the fact that the paper was about to lose their main reporter. She was drunk, she'd done something stupid, and he'd been there to see it. Lovely.

"El! Are you ok?" Her mom's voice outside her bedroom door had her wanting to crawl back under her comforter and hide. "It's kind of late for you to still be home. Are you sick?" Ella snatched her phone off her bedside table and stared at the screen.

"Shit!" It was almost eight! She stumbled out of bed.

"El?"

"I'm fine, Mom. Just overslept." Had her mom seen her come in drunk the night before? She paused and squeezed her eyes shut, trying to remember if Cal had been with her when she'd come into the house. She started breathing again when she remembered cursing out the front door for not sticking and instead launching her into the stairs when she'd pushed it open. She'd been alone. *Thank you, universe.*

She got dressed as quickly as she could and power walked her way out of the house, half out of anxiety from being late and half from anxiety about what kind of questions her mom was going to ask her. She waved and smiled back at people who called their morning greetings to her. So far, no heckling. That was a good sign. She'd taken a small handful of ibuprofen for the pounding in her head, but it almost felt satisfying like penance for what she'd done the night before. Maybe if she suffered enough physical pain, it would help repair her karma for whatever embarrassing things she'd done in front of Cal.

The office was bustling when Ella rolled in. Everyone greeted her without breaking their work flow, with the exception of Pippa who looked her over and raised an eyebrow, and Maddie who gave her a smile that was barely covering a look of pity. Great. She couldn't even bear to look at Cal's desk when she hurried past it into her office. She set her bag down and looked at her laptop. Well, that was one mystery solved. Cal knew to look for her and he knew what had happened because he'd seen what was up on her screen. And she was willing to bet dollars to donuts from the look Maddie had given her, that she knew as well and was probably responsible for filling Cal in on the Les and Wendi soap opera. Awesome. Her gaze involuntarily drifted to her window. Cal wasn't sitting at his desk. She closed her eyes. Did . . . did she do something so awful that he quit and went back to New York?

Ella could hear her pulse pounding in her ears. She was dizzy. She pulled out her chair and slumped over her desk. Shit. From a practical standpoint, if her head reporter had left, she was going to have to cover all the rest of the assignments for the month. Just her and Maddie. At least it wouldn't leave her any time to think about literally anything else. Like how she'd managed, in a single night, to screw up any kind of a relationship . . . friendship, she could have had with Cal. She tried to focus on the inconvenience of not having him at the paper, instead of letting the pain slip into her gut and point to any *other* feelings she might be having about him.

She took a deep breath, moving her hands to cover her eyes. Breathe, just breathe.

"Morning."

Ella jerked her head up and immediately wished she hadn't as the image of Cal in her doorway swam before her eyes.

"How . . ." he dropped his voice to just above a whisper. "How are you feeling?"

Ella attempted a smile, genuinely relieved to see he was still standing there, holding her blue mug with the yellow stars on it and not on his way back to New York.

"Well, you know when Janet Jackson had that wardrobe malfunction at the Super Bowl?"

"Yeah . . ." Cal said slowly.

"She should be feeling pretty good about herself compared to my bullshit last night." She forced herself to meet Cal's gaze. "I am so sorry."

Cal moved into the office and glanced behind him before he smiled at her and said, "Don't worry about it. You don't have anything to be embarrassed about."

"Cal," Ella said, "you're being kind. I *remember* some of it."

He shrugged. "It was a bad night for you. Let's just pretend nothing happened and move on." He smiled at Ella and she tried to return it, despite the stinging in her chest at his words. She quickly tried to shrug it off as residual embarrassment. If he was kind enough to move on, she wasn't going to look a gift horse in the mouth. "And don't worry about the Nativity Scene rehearsal this morning. I covered it. The rest of the events don't start until ten, so we will need you, fearless leader, to dish out the assignments after that." He grinned and dropped his gaze to the mug in his hand. In two long strides, he was at her desk, holding it out to her. "Oh, and I brought you some tea. It's peppermint. Trust me. It'll help."

Ella blinked at him. "Thanks."

He nodded. "I'll assemble the troops if you want to come do a run-down of marching orders with us." With that, he turned and headed out of the office. Ella stared at the empty doorway after he left. Cal wanted to pretend it never happened. That was good. He hadn't quit because of what happened the night before. That was also good. He wasn't on his way back to New York because he was so offended about what she did last night, and *that* was very good. If it was all so good, why did she still feel so bad?

Like Clarence's strange behavior, she needed to just shelve whatever line of thinking was causing the knot in her gut. They had work to do. She was just glad she still had her team. She got to her feet and was almost to her office door when she remembered the tea. She doubled-back, picked up the mug and took a sip. The tea was the perfect temperature, and the peppermint had an immediate effect on soothing some of the pain in her stomach. She took a deep breath and marched out to join her crew.

"Alright," Ella said on a sigh, letting the magic tea roll a wave of comfort through her. "I know you're all tired of hearing me say this, but today will be even busier than yesterday."

"Who knew," Maddie muttered.

"I'm shocked," Pippa added.

"What are our biggest fish for the day?" Cal asked.

Ella glanced over at him, a new wave of embarrassment rising in her. "Well, tonight is . . ."

Cal's face paled. "That's right. The Parade is tonight." Ella nodded.

"Dibs!" Maddie and Pippa yelled. Then they turned and looked at each other. "Jinx! Jinx! Jinx!" They yelled in unison.

Ella sighed. "Where has this enthusiasm been for the last two weeks?"

"Where has Cal, wearing a ridiculous costume, been for the last two weeks?" Pippa asked.

Ella wanted to choke Pippa, but there were too many witnesses. And, to be fair to Pip, she didn't know what Cal had done for Ella the night before. Now, the situation was even worse because tonight would be the second night in a row Cal would be embarrassed because of something Ella had done.

"But before that," Maddie said. "There's the bazaar." The dread in her voice was echoed by the groans coming from the rest of the team.

"The bazaar?" Cal asked, looking from one to the next.

The rest of the staff turned to look at him.

"The Baby Jesus Bazaar," Ella said. "I'll cover it." It was the least she could do to spare Cal from this particular flavor of absurdity. She locked eyes with him. He looked curious and a little confused. She tried to tell him with her eyes to trust her, that she was sparing him. He seemed to understand, because he let it drop. She moved down the list of events, divvying them up and then they all dispersed to try to conquer the snowstorm of events for the day.

"So, what's this bazaar about?" Cal asked, following her back to her office. She'd finished the tea he'd brought her and was feeling a lot better.

"Oh, it's just about the strangest event of the holiday season," Ella said.

Cal raised his eyebrows in surprise. "The strangest? That's a pretty high bar in Hope. Can you stick the landing?"

She grinned, leaning back on the front of her desk. "You see, it's a competition where people enter different renditions of Baby Jesus in the manger."

"Renditions?"

She nodded. "Carved, sewn, plants, animals, food, things that should never *be* food."

"Now you're just making stuff up," Cal snorted.

"Uh-uh," Ella said. "My senior year, the winner of the Baby Jesus Bazaar was Pat Templeton and his goat Marge. Marge has a white spot on her back that looks just like Baby Jesus, or at least Pat and the judges thought it did. So Pat won that year."

"What's the prize?" Cal asked.

"A fifty-dollar gift certificate to Bumble's Market and bragging rights," Ella said.

"Bragging rights," he repeated, deadpan. "For having a goat with a freak spot that looks like Baby Jesus." Ella nodded and Cal shook his head. "You Islanders pick strange things to have pride in."

She shrugged. "Everybody's gotta have something to be proud of."

Cal nodded. "I guess so. Well, if you want, I'd be *proud* to cover it with you. What time?"

"It starts at noon," Ella said. "But you really don't have to, Cal."

He shrugged. "I'm actually free at noon. Surely it would be easier with two of us covering it. How long does the event last?"

Ella studied Cal's face. She'd told him what the Bazaar was and he was *still* interested in covering it. There were Islanders that purposely avoided the spectacle. Maybe Cal was supposed to be the Islander instead of her. In that moment, the vision of Cal growing old in Hope, working at the newspaper, covering all of the town's various and sundry events came back to her. Cal would be an Islander, just like Clarence. That was, if he chose to stay. She realized he was still looking at her, waiting for an answer. She gave herself a mental shake. "They usually announce the winner at three, but they start accepting and checking in entries at nine."

"So, should I meet you there at noon?" he asked.

"Sure," Ella said. "But you don't have to . . ."

"I know I don't. But, I want to," Cal said. His voice was soft and Ella felt something strange moving through her. It wasn't the quick heat of embarrassment or even attraction. It was something slower and softer. And it terrified her.

Before she could compose what she wanted to say, her mouth was opening and Helga, Sarcastic, and even Numb Ella were screaming at her to stop. "Cal . . ."

He took a step toward her. They locked eyes and her mouth stopped moving. She was paralyzed, caught in the glow of the look he was giving her.

"Hey boss, Agatha Marley is on the phone. She sounds like she's cranked on coffee and..." Maddie had stuck her head around the doorway, but paused mid-sentence when she saw the scene in front of her. Cal dropped his gaze and scratched the back of his head and Ella tore her eyes away from him to look at Maddie.

"Right, the uh, uh..." Ella said, blinking at Maddie, trying to clear her head.

"The Tinsel Town Swingdancers," Maddie said. "They're performing tomorrow night?"

"Right," Ella said. She cleared her throat. "Tell her I'm on my way."

Maddie nodded, glanced at Cal, and then disappeared.

"And I should get moving. I've got three events to cover, but then I'll meet you back here, before noon and we can... uh, walk over to this 'Bazaar' together?"

Ella couldn't articulate words at the moment, so she just nodded. Cal gave her one of his half-smiles and then headed back to his desk.

It took a minute before Ella could feel her legs enough to move. She wasn't sure what exactly had shifted between them, but something had. Was it good? Was it bad?

The phone rang in the office again. There was a one second delay and then Maddie yelled, "El! It's Agatha again. I'm running out of plausible sounding excuses! Better get a move on!"

Cal was already gone by the time she made her way out the front door of the office and headed across the square to meet Agatha. Her assignments for the morning sped by and she wasn't sure if it was because she was dreading the Bazaar or looking forward to covering it with Cal. She was back in her office just past eleven-thirty, typing up the stories on her morning assignments when Cal hustled back in. He slowed down when he reached Ella's door and breathed an audible sigh.

"Good, I didn't miss you yet." Ella blinked at him and she saw the color in his cheeks from the cold wind outside deepen. "I mean, I've never been to this 'Bazaar' before, so I definitely wanted to go over with you."

Ella grinned. "You still sure you wanna do this? There's no guarantee that it won't scar you."

Cal shrugged, still grinning. "I think I can handle it."

The office was empty besides Cal and Ella. She tried to pull her thoughts together. Now would be a good time to try to tell him . . . something.

The front door banged open making them both jump. Cal was the first to move toward the reception area with Ella right behind him. They'd just made it through the main office when they were almost run over by Mrs. Edith Meyers.

"Thank god you two are here," she said, stopping short in front of them. She was wearing her infamous top hat that was hollowed out and housed an entire, light up nativity scene. "Everything is ruined! Ruined, ruined, ruined!"

Sarcastic Ella sat up off the fainting couch in her mind to take drama notes from Mrs. Meyers.

"What's ruined?" Ella asked.

"Everything! The whole Bazaar is ruined!"

"Why?" Cal asked.

"The flu, that's why."

"Did some of your contestants get the flu?" Ella asked.

"Contestants," she scoffed. "Lord, if it was contestants, I wouldn't have a worry. We always have too many of them anyway. And some are so . . . slap-dash. This is supposed to be a rendering of our Holy Savior in infantile form and some of them bring in a veggie dip tray in a car seat." Ella cut her eyes to Cal, which was a bad idea because he was trying so hard to hold in a laugh that he was starting to turn red. This, of course, made Ella want to laugh, but she could tell from the look Mrs. Meyers was giving them that she was not amused.

"Do you think this is *funny*?" she spat.

Ella cleared her throat. Now was not the moment for honesty. "No, sorry, it was just that entry you were describing..." She cleared her throat. "So, if it's not contestants, how is the flu ruining the Bazaar?"

"My judges, of course."

"The Hicks sisters have the flu?" Ella asked.

Mrs. Meyers closed her eyes and solemnly nodded. "This is a tragedy. I need two judges. Now. And you two fit the bill."

"Whoa," Cal said.

"Yeah, Mrs. Meyers, we can't . . ." Ella said.

Mrs. Meyers glared at them. "Don't you care that the preparation that's gone into this for the last *year* will be ruined if you don't do it?"

"But, Mrs. Meyers, we have to cover the event for the paper," Cal said, wilting somewhat when she redirected her beady laser beam eyes on him.

She threw her hands up. "You can do both! Just write the articles as the judges. It'll be a fresh new angle on the situation, and *I* won't have to go drown myself in the bay."

Ella frowned. "Mrs. Meyers, why couldn't *you* be the judge?"

She paused and for the first time since Hurricane Meyers had blown in the front door, she looked a little embarrassed. "Because I have an entry this year. As you know, it's an anonymous entry judging so the Hicks sisters never knew which entry belonged to which contestant, but of course, if *I* were the judge, I'd know."

Ella nodded. Between Mrs. Meyers' drama and near hysterics, her guilt-tripping, and the flu, she couldn't see a way out of this for her or Cal. "What do you need us to do?" Ella asked.

They followed Mrs. Meyers out to the big tent set up for the Bazaar and as they walked in her wake, Ella couldn't help but feel like she was on her way to the gallows.

"Uh," Cal's voice was soft in her ear, and she had to fight the urge to pant as she felt his warm breath on her neck. "Do you know how to judge one of these things?"

That sobered her up. She shook her head, a new kind of fear rolling over her. "No. I just know how to point and laugh at 'one of these things'. The fact that we might pick the wrong entry to win and end up pissing off a well-known and beloved town member and thereby turn ourselves into social pariahs is a very real fear and possibility."

"Awesome," Cal grumbled.

Luckily, there was a rubric that Mrs. Meyers had created for the judges. It was fairly simple with three questions on it and a sliding scale rank from zero to ten. The first question was, "Does the entry resemble Baby Jesus?" The second question was, "How creative are the materials used in the entry's construction?" And the third question was, "Would you feel comfortable giving this entry to a loved one for Christmas?" Ella and Cal shared a look when Mrs. Meyers read the third question to them. She was a little too proud of the rubric for it to be by coincidence.

"How much do you want to bet that *her* entry is something wrapped up like a gift," Cal muttered when Mrs. Meyers stepped away to answer a woman's question. The woman had a giant stick of cotton candy that looked like it was starting to lose its shape in the cold humidity.

"No bet," Ella muttered back to him with a grin.

After ten minutes of training, Mrs. Meyers sent them to stand on the other side of the one partitioning wall of the tent. "So you won't see the contestants bringing in their entries, of course," she had said when Ella asked her why.

So she and Cal stood, hands dug into coat pockets and facing into the wind as the plastic tent wall flapped behind them. They looked at everything but each other, while they waited for the event to start. She couldn't find the right words and besides, standing outside of the Baby Jesus Bazaar was not the ideal place to try to express . . . something to Cal.

"So," Ella said, casting around for something to break the tension. "What's Christmas like in New York? Does your family ever do anything quirky like a Baby Jesus Bazaar?"

Cal snorted. "Nope." He sighed. "My family's Christmas is whatever the exact opposite of the Baby Jesus Bazaar is."

Ella frowned. "So normal and sane?"

Cal shook his head. "Boring and . . . stiff."

Ella shrugged. "I mean, boring can be nice, once in a while."

"It's what comes with the boring that isn't so nice," Cal said. He looked more tired than he had even an hour earlier. He ran his hand through his hair again, gripping it, as if in frustration. Ella looked around and nodded toward the park bench that was a hundred feet in front of them and facing away from the tent.

"Let's sit."

"Do you think she'll get mad?" Cal asked, looking around in case Mrs. Meyers was perched on top of the tent like a crow, ready to swoop down on them.

Ella shrugged. "I don't see how she can. But if she does, what's she going to do, fire us?"

Cal grinned and followed her over to the bench. They sat down and Ella tried to frame a question that would just look like small talk but might reveal to her something about Cal's life in New York. But she was distracted. They were sitting close on the short bench. She could feel the warmth from his leg seeping through her leggings and it was making it hard for her to concentrate.

"So, why did you come to Hope?" Ella finally blurted out. She blamed the mix of hormones. It had to be. "I'm . . . I'm sorry . . . I shouldn't . . ."

"No, it's good," Cal said. He sighed, looking out at the square beyond the park. "I haven't really told anyone why." He turned and glanced at her. "And hey, if I'm going to tell anyone, it should be you . . . my . . . my boss." He moved his leg, knocking his knee against hers. Ella could barely breathe, let alone speak. But there must have been something encouraging in her expression because Cal continued. "I just . . . couldn't be in New York anymore. I . . . I was suffocating." He shook his head. "I guess it all boils down to the fact that I just didn't want that life anymore. I wanted something different."

"But if you just wanted something different, you could have gone abroad or to Texas, I'm pretty sure that's kind of the opposite of New York," Ella said, trying to lighten the mood.

Cal shook his head again. "Maybe. But, somehow, on a drunken bender, the universe pointed me in the direction of Hope." He shrugged. "And here I am."

"And here you are," Ella said, following his gaze as he took in the crowds of tourists milling around the square. "But once you saw what a 'bizarre' place this island is, why did you stay?"

"Why?" Cal asked. The surprise in his voice caught Ella's attention and she turned to look at him. In the mid-day, cold sunshine, his eyes were a paler blue than she'd ever seen them. He met her gaze and smiled. "I stayed because I fell in love with this place."

"You fell in love with Hope?" Ella asked, her voice coming out in a whisper.

Cal nodded. "Of course." He shook his head. "I was nervous coming into town. It was basically on a complete whim. I was so used to trying something and having it blow up in my face. So, I was just walking around, waiting for the shoe to drop. I expected it to happen immediately. Like I'd triggered some kind of alarm by leaving. Then, I'd be forced to get back on the ferry an hour after arriving and fly back to New York. And when I arrived, I would be met by a whole chorus of 'told you so's." He paused and Ella watched the slow smile spread across his face. "But, of course, when I got here, the first person I ran into was Miss Mandie."

Ella chuckled. "She was probably sizing you up as 'saber-tooth prey'."

Cal nodded. "Definitely a possibility. But, for whatever reason, she gave me coffee and donuts on the house and slipped into the conversation that she had an apartment to rent out and that if I was bored, the Summer Solstice event was looking for volunteers. Everyone involved with the event was really nice to me and made me feel like part of the team, so I worked with them for two weeks. I didn't have a day job yet, so I spent all my time working on the event. By the time the Summer Solstice happened, I was co-head of the event crew." He smiled and shook his head. "At the event, Miss Mandie pointed out Clarence to me and said he was looking for a reporter. And the rest, as they say, is history."

Ella felt like the clouds had just parted, shining down light on another piece of who Cal was. She didn't know what to say, so she just kept listening. He sighed and leaned forward, putting his elbows on his knees. "And to be honest, Ella, I can't imagine *not* being in Hope, now." He sighed. "This probably won't make sense to someone who's been born and raised around *real* people, who *is* a real person, but not everywhere is like here."

She raised an eyebrow. "Oh, it's not? Wow. Someone call Ripley's."

"Well, there are smart asses like you, but where I'm from, everyone looks at you on paper before they look at you in person. Your net worth, your name recognition, your age and 'eligibility', then, bonus points if you don't look like the dog's dinner."

"The dog's dinner?"

Cal shook his head. "Something my mom always says. She's British."

"That's cool," Ella said.

He shrugged. "She doesn't have much of an accent left. She had to take elocution lessons when she came to the U.S. My dad said people would feel more comfortable doing business with people who sounded like them rather than foreigners. So, American." He scuffed his shoe in the grass. "So she had to white-wash who she was just to keep my dad and any potential business partners happy."

"That's awful," Ella said.

"When she told me what she'd had to do to fit in, that was when I knew that I was living around toys. Programmed, perfectly painted, manufactured by the society around them. And over time . . . they break." Cal's voice cracked on the last word. He cleared his throat. "Sorry. I didn't mean to go into all this."

"It's ok," Ella said. "I know you better now, partner."

Cal's phone started to ring and he pulled it out of his pocket. Ella took the chance to move around and work off the nervous energy that had been building in her from her proximity to Cal. She stood up and walked around behind the bench. "I'll let you get that."

She moved closer to the tent's partition wall and stared at the infinite and almost blinding white in the full sunlight. Maybe if she went blind from staring at it, she wouldn't have to judge Baby Jesuses made out of chewed gum or Pixie Sticks or golf balls.

"No need," Cal said. She heard his footsteps behind her, but she didn't turn. She was thinking about what he'd told her. She had never thought

Cal was a spoiled, rich, city kid. Just a city kid. But now, from what he'd said, she was pretty sure he came from money. She felt the gap between the possibilities for her and Cal widening, even in the darkest corner of her brain where she tried to keep them hidden and starved for oxygen. They were from two different worlds. And eventually, if the fact that he was giving up his apartment was any indicator, he was going back to that world. There was sadness lingering at the edges, but she tried to push the thoughts away. She didn't want to have to examine too closely as to *why* that thought was making her sad.

Mrs. Meyers stuck her head around the partition and Ella swore she heard glass shattering. She looked confused. "What? Have you both just been standing here, staring at a blank tent wall since I left you?"

"For the most part," Ella said. "Still want us to judge?"

She narrowed her eyes at Ella. "You're not getting out of this, Ella Danforth. And I *will* call your mother."

Ella raised her hands. "We surrender."

"Good," Mrs. Meyers said. "We're ready to start." She ducked around the tent and came back with two clipboards. Ella and Cal took them and followed her around the partition wall. She paused in front of the first entry on the end of the first of twelve tables. There were ten entries per table. "You can start here. The number of the entry is on the front of the table and there should be one rubric page for each entry. Happy judging!" She practically squealed her last sentence and clapped her hands before blustering off to stand with the other contestants around a coffee carafe in a second smaller tent. Tourists were cautiously approaching the tent from the other side and Ella could only imagine how this contest would look to anyone who didn't know the entries were supposed to all look like Baby Jesus. Ella finally looked down at her clipboard and then at Cal. He was just staring at what was sitting on the table in front of them. She surveyed the tent, doing the math in her head.

After she'd figured the depressing total, she finally dragged her eyes away from the other one hundred and nineteen entries they had to judge. How do you eat an elephant? One bite at a time. Of course, the adage wasn't as appealing, considering there might actually *be* a Baby Jesus shaped like an elephant, or made from some form of elephants, hidden amongst the entries in the car wreck waiting for them under this tent. She sighed and finally looked down at the first entry.

"Is that . . ." Ella asked.

"Yep," Cal said.

"With . . ."

"Yep."

It was Baby Jesus . . . rendered in meatloaf . . . with ketchup hair and a lop-sided stick figure ketchup face.

"That's a . . ," Cal said.

"Uh huh . . ," Ella muttered.

"I think that might be . . ."

"Culinary blasphemy?"

"Yeah."

31

CAL

The Baby Jesus Bazaar was by far the strangest thing Cal had ever witnessed on the island.

"You think you would have stayed in Hope if *this* had been the first event you'd attended?" Ella asked as they stared at a Chia Pet rendering of a baby in a cardboard box.

"Uh," Cal muttered. "It definitely would have changed how I looked at the people in town." She cut her eyes to him and he shook his head. "It's probably a good thing that we don't see the names for the entry. That meatloaf..."

Ella nodded. "Yeah, I think we might have to ask them to register as a 'meat offender' and probably something religiously offensive too."

"And then immediately pitch their concept to a horror film studio," he added.

Ella shook her head. "Hollywood isn't ready for Hope's Baby Jesus Bazaar."

There was an easy lightness in the banter flowing back and forth between him and Ella. It reminded him, somewhat uncomfortably, of the way he and Tara would commentate events or things happening around them in New York. Though, he had to say, Ella was better at it. He'd missed it during the first months he'd been in Hope, but now, he felt like that gap in his life was being filled, oddly enough, by Ella Danforth.

He was shoulder-to-shoulder with her, staring at and marking scores for a bunch of Baby Jesuses, ranging from abstract, to cute, to horrifying, to nightmare fuel. But instead of feeling like they'd just been strong-armed into some kind of civic duty, Cal was enjoying himself. If he was honest, he hadn't felt this light in months. He glanced over at her, catching her expression in profile. She was staring in disbelief at the knitted baby Jesus in front of them. Her gaze was weary and her mouth was poised for another deadpan comment. *God, she was beautiful.*

Cal gave himself an internal face-slap. *She's your boss, she's pulled away twice when you've both been close to . . . something, and, according to Pippa and Maddie, she has a date for the Solstice Bonfire with that Tony guy.* Cal did his best to keep his face neutral, despite his intense desire to scowl at the reminder that someone like Tony was now in the picture.

Ella sighed and Cal looked at her again. "What do you think?" she muttered. "My brain is mush. I think they should ban succulent Baby Jesuses. It's some kind of plant cruelty to cut them down to only five-leaf things to be a head, arms, and legs. And now, we're staring at this . . ." she lowered her voice as a group of tourists passed by them on the other side of the table, "Cabbage Patch Kid-reject with holes for eyes, and I'm having a hard time remembering what Baby Jesus is supposed to look like."

Cal nodded. "It's like when you say a word too much. Like spoon. After a while, it doesn't feel like it means anything anymore, and saying it just sounds weird."

"Exactly!" Ella said, turning to look at him. "Baby Jesus is like spoon now. Not to be confused with Baby Jesus made *out of* spoons." She jerked her head toward the previous table they'd judged.

Cal nodded. "Though I have to say, the way that spoon was swaddled with a paper napkin was kind of crafty."

She turned to face him and their gazes met. At that moment, he wouldn't have been able to look away if the ground opened up under their feet. Her eyes were darker than usual but so open as if she was trying to tell Cal something. He felt his breath catch in his throat. She was blushing, but she didn't look away. There was a long strand of hair hanging in front of her ear that had slipped out of the clip thing on the back of her head. He had the sudden urge to move it and tuck it behind her ear. She bit her lip and involuntarily, Cal's gaze dropped to her mouth. No lipstick, not even gloss. Just Ella. One hundred percent. What did she taste like? Would she taste the way she smelled? Like fresh rain?

"I'm sorry about...last night," Ella said. She said it quietly. He jerked his eyes back up to meet hers. She really meant it.

"I'm not," Cal said. She looked surprised and he shook his head. "I mean, it was fine. Please, stop beating yourself up over it." He did his best to put as much feeling into the look on his face as he could. He needed her to know he meant it. Judging by the genuine smile she gave him, he knew she'd understood.

"Thank you." She looked like she wanted to say more, but either the words failed her or her courage had at that moment. She looked back down at the clipboard in her hands and picked at a curling edge of the top form clipped to it.

Cal decided it would be up to him to steer the conversation. He wanted that easy playfulness back. "And besides," he said, turning his attention back to the table of entries in front of them. "I'll expect you to carry me, dance with me, make me tea, and hold my hair back when it's *my* turn to get wasted."

"I didn't puke," Ella snapped in mock outrage.

Cal grinned at her. "Are you sure?"

Now Ella really didn't look sure. He could tell from the look on her face that she was perched on the edge of Mortification Cliff, wondering if she could keep her balance.

"Are you two almost finished?" A voice called to them. They turned to see Mrs. Meyers. She was holding what looked like orange juice, but her top hat was crooked, causing the battery-powered light inside the nativity scene to flicker when she tossed her head around.

"Just about!" Ella called to her. Cal scanned the crew around Mrs. Meyers and his eyes fell on Miss Mandie. She grinned at him and raised a pitcher of orange juice like a toast.

"Well played," Cal muttered. Ella looked at him and he nodded at Miss Mandie.

"Oh, well, that makes picking a winner easier," Ella said. "If they're all snockered, it'll be harder for them to chase us down and beat us to death with their purses, and possibly their entries."

"Just to be safe, maybe we should pick the heaviest entry as the winner so there's no chance we'll get beaten to death with it," Cal said.

"Good plan," Ella said under her breath while she smiled and waved at the glaring contestants. "I think that would make the winner either Bowling Ball Jesus or the one that's made out of old cannonballs and anchors."

They finished the rubric for the last entry on the last table and then walked back through the tables to find the heavy entries.

"I'm going with Bowling Ball Jesus," Cal said. "It's more aerodynamic and just because it's been painted so the holes are a part of Baby Jesus' face, doesn't mean someone won't stick their fingers in his eyes and mouth before throwing it at us like we're a seven-ten split."

"Deal," Ella said. "But, consider this an early 'I told you so' if we get impaled by someone throwing the one made from anchor hooks like a javelin. Or . . . the one made from an *actual* javelin."

"Agreed," Cal said. They quickly wrote down the winning entry number on a scrap of paper and shoved it into the envelope labeled "winner" that was at the back of Ella's clipboard. She licked the envelope to seal it and Cal had to look away and give his body an internal speech about baseball and Clarence hula dancing to get the image out of his head. It was almost worse now. His hands had done some innocent exploring of her curves, the heat of her skin. And she'd been so close to him, several times now. Each of those extremely memorable occasions felt like someone was throwing another log on an all-night bonfire inside him. He needed a cold shower.

"Shall we light the fuse and run?" she asked. Cal blinked at her. She waved the envelope at him. Relief flooded him when he remembered Ella couldn't read minds.

"After you," he said. They moved close enough to the group of contestants to hand over their clipboards to Mrs. Meyers along with the "winner" envelope.

"Well, this has been fun," Cal said. "But we really need to get to our next assignments. Congratulations to all of you! It was a . . ." he paused searching for a word to describe the entries.

"Pleasure," Ella said loudly. Cal looked at her in time to see her squeeze her eyes shut for a moment. Whatever embarrassment she was feeling quickly passed and she cleared her throat. "It was a pleasure being your judges and seeing all the magnificent creations you created for the Bazaar this year. You should all be very proud." She started clapping. Cal quickly joined in and eventually, the tourists around them and the contestants started clapping, eyeing each other before ultimately turning their attention to the envelope in Mrs. Meyers' hands.

"Run," Cal muttered. She nodded and they slipped out the far side of the tent, walking as quickly as they dared, not wanting to arouse suspicion, but definitely not wanting to be around when the winner was read. Just in case. They got to the office and Ella locked them inside. They hustled into the break room, which had no windows.

"Probably best to be somewhere that will be harder for them to breach with flaming Baby Jesus Molotov's," Ella said.

"We're probably making a big deal out of something that they'll be completely reasonable about," Cal started.

"Five bucks one of us wakes up with a meatloaf Baby Jesus head in our bed," Ella said.

Cal closed his eyes and shook his head. "You just aren't going to be happy until we both have nightmares about it."

She shrugged. "We're a team, partner."

They fell into an awkward silence after that. To break it, Cal turned his back to her and started making coffee for them. He felt more confident when he wasn't staring right at her. Sometimes, looking at Ella felt like he was staring into the sun; it made his skin burn and he felt stupid when he did it. "Hey," he said, trying to focus on the task at hand, and not think about how she looked, sprawled and relaxed on the couch in the corner of the break room. "I meant to thank you."

"For what?" she asked.

"For not pulling the 'boss card' on me all the time. You know, pulling rank to bend me to your will."

She chuckled. "I have no illusions about being able to bend you." Cal wasn't looking at her face, but he smiled, because he was so used to the sound she made any time she said something embarrassing that he found it endearing. "I mean," she continued with an air like she was pulling out the mop to clean up her mess. "You *are* my partner here. Really. Maddie does what she can, but with all the photographs she has to wrangle, you and I really are the ones covering the majority of the madness. And I know that there's no way in hell I could have done it without you."

He had to look at her. Her voice had sounded so sincere, he just had to know what that looked like on her face. He turned and leaned his back against the counter while the coffee pot filled. He was not disappointed. She had her hands clasped between her knees and she was looking at him. It wasn't a look that said she wanted something or expected something from him. It was earnest and for the first time in Cal's life, he felt like he was actually being seen as exactly who he was. The feeling made him nervous like she was x-raying him with her eyes. He had to tell her . . . something. She needed to know . . .

"Ella..."

She tilted her head to one side, an easy smile on her lips as if she was preparing to listen to an old friend tell her anything. Whether it was their deepest, darkest secret or the weather forecast for the next day, her face said she was here for it. Something broke inside Cal. For him, it was like observing an undiscovered species. Her expression was so honest and simple, it was giving "face-value" a new meaning. Had anyone in his life *ever* looked at him like this? He knew that to his parents and even Tara, on occasion, he was a chess piece being pushed from one square to the next, for a singular purpose. Even in Hope, though to a much lower degree, people like Clarence saw him as someone to cover the stories and give him a break, but that had been what he'd wanted anyway. But now, Ella Danforth was just looking at him, Cal Dickson, with no expectations. And that made Cal sweat. How was he supposed to react to something like that? There were no calculations for him to make. No guessing and steering what he said to meet what the other person wanted to hear.

"El, Martha Washington called!" Pippa's voice carried down the hallway. "She wanted to remind us that we're due at Excavation for our fittings in t-minus two hours . . ." Pippa stuck her head into the break room and focused her attention on Ella. "I got the feeling that if we don't show up, she's going to hunt us down."

Cal would be lying if he said he wasn't thankful for the interruption. Ella, on the other hand, was pale now. She leaned forward and put her face in her hands.

She let out a low groan and Pippa looked pained. "I'll spring for margaritas after," she said.

Ella shook her head. "I think margaritas *before* would work better, but I don't even have the time to get hammered. There's too much to do."

While Ella still had her head in her hands, Pippa glanced over at Cal. Her expression told a detailed narrative without the need for words. It said, *This is because of you. Figure out how to make this ok, or else, Tree Boy.* Pippa's "or else" wasn't something Cal ever wanted to see. He still hadn't forgotten the way she'd launched herself onto Conner and smashed a grapefruit-sized ball of half-frozen fruitcake into his face. With one final, helpless look at Ella, she backed out of the break room.

Cal wasn't sure how *he* was supposed to fix this. So, he poured coffee. Then, he brought both mugs over to the couch. "Here," his voice was softer than he'd planned. He would have liked to credit that with why Ella looked up, but he knew there was a greater chance that it was the smell of coffee that had caught her attention.

"Thanks." She took the mug and blew on it. Cal was lowering himself onto the couch next to her before he could talk himself out of it.

He held up his mug. "To our mutual day of sacrificing our self-respect to the fashion gods." Ella chuckled and clinked her mug against his.

"At least yours will be over tonight," she muttered before taking a sip.

"El," he surprised them both by using her nickname, but it had just come out. He pressed on, feeling her eyes on him. There was a mental fork in front of him. He could try to say what he'd wanted to say before Pippa had come in . . . his stomach began to knot . . . or, he could take the easier and wider path of banter. Coward Cal called dibs and he turned to look at her. "I can't fit through doorways when I'm wearing that damn tree costume. And I can't move my arms." Ella started to laugh. "I mean, if I fall, I'm cone-shaped and I'm just going to roll in a circle." She was laughing harder now. "If I bend over, and the wind catches me, I'm going to stick in the ground like a lawn dart." She was alternating between silent shakes of laughter and gasping chuckles now.

The familiar lightness in Cal's chest was back. It was happening more and more whenever he was around Ella, teasing and laughing with her. The giddy happiness in him was even stronger than the thrill he felt when he walked around Hope. The closest thing he'd ever felt to it before coming to the island, were the times he, his sister Rhone, and Tara had laughed and teased each other or their friends. That was a sobering thought. Tara. To Cal, she and Ella felt like different species on different planets, in parallel universes, but what would Ella think, if he told her about Tara? And then there was Tony.

She shifted closer to him on the couch and her rain scent filled his nose. His body was urging him on. It wanted him to just open his mouth and ask her for permission to kiss her. To hold her. To feel her laugh echoing off his chest and her hair tucked under his chin. But Killjoy Cal was there, shaking his head. *You don't deserve that, Cal. Not when you haven't leveled with her.* He tried to ignore the thought and just focus on the happiness he felt, sitting next to her.

"I'm serious," he said as her laughter died down. "Besides, the whole thing *bounces* when I try to walk in it, you know. The suspenders holding it up are *elastic.* So I'm basically a helpless, bouncing, paper-mache, windsock, just waiting for the deadly breeze with my name on it."

"Oh don't be so dramatic," Ella said when she could talk and breathe. "I'm fairly certain that no one has ever *died* from wearing that costume.

Not even of shame." She was fidgeting with her mug. "Besides," her voice was more serious now. "At least after tonight, you're done." She sighed. "I'd kill to be allowed to wear the tree costume over whatever Martha is planning for me." She took a long drink from her mug and Cal could almost hear her wish that it was bourbon instead of French roast. At first, Cal thought she was just fidgeting next to him. It was almost a minute before his brain registered that she was shaking. Shivering, like a cold puppy. She was pale again and though she kept her expression aimed at her mug, he could feel the fear and anxiety rolling off of her in waves. *Here's your chance*, Killjoy Cal yelled inside Cal's head. *Level the playing field.*

"Were you a Backstreet Boys fan when you were a kid?" Cal asked, already feeling heat rising in his chest and making him sweat as his body rebelled against him spilling his secret.

Ella glanced at him. "I mean, I guess. I wasn't big on boy bands, but of the ones out there at the time, I guess I liked Backstreet Boys the best." She looked momentarily confused. "Why?"

Cal sighed. "Because when I was a kid, two of my buddies and I made our own boy band. And we were performing for our families and friends at a birthday party. Man, there must have been about forty people there. And it was being filmed and . . ." Cal could feel his heart starting to race at the memory. He swallowed hard, trying to rein in his own anxiety. It didn't help that Ella had now sat up and turned to look at him, watching him tell the story with those huge gray eyes, boring into the side of his face as they traded places with Cal now staring into the depths of his own mug.

"Yeah?" Ella asked. "I didn't know you were a singer." There was no teasing in her voice. It was so soft and encouraging that Cal almost broke. At home, whenever even the band Backstreet Boys was mentioned, everyone would erupt with laughter and calls for "Silent Silver". It was oddly encouraging for Ella to not even crack a smile as he mentally prepared himself for her laughter when he'd finished his story.

So, he told her. His head and his body were screaming for him to stop. Laying out something so traumatizing to someone he'd known for less than a month felt a little too much like opening his shirt and pointing out the places that would be vulnerable to gunshots and knife wounds. But he pushed on, trying to focus on the fact that Ella *wasn't* laughing.

"And, I can't even hear "Shape of My Heart" without breaking out into a cold sweat now," he finished. He fell silent, waiting for the inevitable snort of laughter. It didn't come.

"Your family and friends sound like creeps," Ella said.

Cal frowned. "I mean . . . I guess. It was probably pretty funny to someone watching it, so I guess I can't . . . blame them."

"Why not?" Ella's voice was harder now. "If you can't blame them for laughing in the moment and traumatizing you, you've got to at least be able to blame them for torturing you with it for all these years."

Cal didn't know what to say to that. He finally turned to look at her, and he saw the anger flashing in her eyes. "They were assholes to you about it. It sounds like they still are."

In that moment, Cal wasn't sure if it was how beautiful she looked, like a wrathful Greek goddess ready to rain down vengeance, or if it was because she was defending him against his family and friends, but he wanted to kiss her, more than he'd ever wanted anything in his life.

Tara! Killjoy Cal yelled. Cal didn't care. Tara had laughed at him, right along with everyone else. He'd tried once to tell her how he felt about it and she told him to lighten up. But here was Ella, with a trauma of her own and empathy that he'd *never* experienced before . . .

Tony. Killjoy Cal said. *She has a date with another man. You can't kiss a woman who is seeing another man.* Cal tried to argue, but Killjoy Cal just crossed his arms. *You anxious to add* another *embarrassing memory to the pile? By asking her and being told no, because of Tony?* Unfortunately, Cal couldn't argue with that.

Ella dropped her gaze back to her mug. "People can't just treat you like a prop. Like nothing more than a funny anecdote to tell someone they just met."

"Is that what Hope does to you?" Cal asked before his brain could evaluate what he was saying.

Ella just nodded. "I know I'm probably overreacting, feeling like this, but . . ."

"No," Cal said. "You're not. I heard the story behind what happened to you from a couple of people. Maddie and Pippa are the only ones that didn't act like it was a town joke."

Ella nodded. "I guess I'm lucky. I have them. And Mom . . . she understands." She cleared her throat. "Well, what do we do about it, Cal? Do we just go the rest of our lives being haunted by a horrifying moment, frozen in time?"

Cal shrugged. "I don't know the answer to that. But, I do know that if you're going to try to get people to all stop laughing about something they've been laughing at for more than a decade, as is the case with both of us, you've got your work cut out for you."

Ella leaned forward, her elbows on her knees. He saw the grim determination on her face as she nodded. "Well, if we can't change them, I guess all we can change is how it affects us."

"Easier said than done," Cal murmured.

She nodded. "Yep." He could see from the look on her face that she was wrestling with something inside of her. He'd spent so much time with Ella over the past few weeks that he now had some of her mannerisms memorized. He could even feel the exact moment when she relaxed and nudged his knee with hers. "Of course, while I'm on the catwalk, trying to regain some stitch of dignity, you'll be forced to cover the Santa Ball and Crawl all on your own."

Cal shrugged. "No sweat, right?"

Ella nodded. "Sure, you just put on your Santa suit and try to clone yourself into five or six sets of eyes and ears. It's a huge party . . ."

"I have to wear *another* costume?" Cal asked.

Ella frowned. "Well, yeah. Everyone does. To get into the Santa Ball and Crawl, you have to be wearing a Santa suit. Complete with hat and beard, even the women." She paused. "You do have one, don't you?"

Cal shook his head. "No, but I'm sure I can probably get one here in town . . ."

Ella blinked at him. "Not this close to the ball. They usually sell out by Thanksgiving. Like I said, *everyone* in town goes to the Ball."

Cal frowned. "I guess I'll have to try to make a trip to the mainland."

Ella shook her head. "With what free time? You and I are enjoying the last," she checked her watch, "twenty minutes we'll probably get until after Christmas." She was right. His next assignment was less than a half hour away. He closed his eyes. What *was* he going to do?

"I've got it," Ella said. Cal turned to look at her. She looked nervous again. "I've got one you can borrow."

"Um, no offense," Cal said with a grin, "but if it's anything like the sweater you brought me to wear for that brunch . . ."

Ella shook her head. "No . . . no, this one should fit."

"Ok," Cal said. "Thanks." He turned his head and met her gaze. They were so close together on the couch that if he leaned toward her only a few inches, their lips would be touching. As if his body had taken that to be a dare, he was moving, despite the voices screaming in his head to stop, despite the possibility that Ella might not be thinking the same thing. He saw her eyes flutter closed and . . . was she leaning in too?

"El!" Maddie's voice this time. "I know you're going to want to kill me, and I know you have a date, but . . ."

Ella's eyes popped open at the sound of her name and she and Cal jerked backward from each other. But Cal was guessing from the look on Maddie's face that she knew what she'd walked in on.

"For which reason am I going to want to kill you?" Ella asked. Was it Cal's imagination or was there a growl in Ella's voice?

Maddie hesitated as if she wanted to comment on her editor and the paper's main reporter sitting together on a couch in an otherwise empty break room, but something in Ella's expression made Maddie decide against it. She sighed. "I know I said I'd cover the Solstice Concert and Bonfire tomorrow night, but my sister just told us she's bringing her boyfriend home for Christmas and none of us bought him presents! It's a disaster!" Cal glanced at Ella who looked like she was having to work really hard to keep the smile off her face.

"Maddie," Ella said, interrupting Maddie's rant. She paused and Ella nodded. "You're off the hook. I'll cover it."

"But what about your," she cut her eyes to Cal and then looked at Ella again. "Date?"

Ella shrugged. "I'll figure it out. It's not worth you having a heart attack over."

"I can help cover it," Cal said. Both women turned to look at him. "You know, so El doesn't have to miss her date." He almost missed the way Ella was fidgeting on the couch next to him because he was distracted by the endzone-style dance Maddie was doing. "Thank you both so much. I swear, after I hug her, I might actually strangle my sister."

"Well, just remember the island's Christmas Day rule," Ella said. "No murders until sundown. Otherwise, you'll ruin the traditional town-wide Christmas Day hangover and I'm pretty sure Hallmark will put a contract out on you."

Maddie nodded. "And you don't screw with Hallmark. Thanks again for covering it, you two. Hopefully Tony won't mind." She winked at Ella who was back to fidgeting again, and just as suddenly as she'd appeared, Maddie was gone.

"Thanks for being willing to help out with the bonfire," Ella said. "Old Island customs declare that every townsperson *must* have a gift for any visitor."

"Really?" Cal asked.

Ella nodded, getting to her feet. "Oh yeah, it's a huge faux pas to be empty-handed on Christmas Day. I honestly think that's where all the lobster nutcrackers from Seaside end up. On Christmas Day, they're wrapped and held on standby." She shrugged. "But, of course, if you're Maddie, you want your gift to be thoughtful and well-planned."

"Ah yes, the downfall of the young and caring," Cal said with a grin.

Ella turned to look at him and the playful banter that had been momentarily restored, faltered between them. He could see in her eyes what he was feeling. They'd almost . . . *again*. Was he just too chicken shit to actually make the leap? He couldn't tell if she was giving herself the same ass-chewing, but whatever she was thinking, after a moment, she gave her head a shake and her expression changed to a wry smile. "Well, since we're not covered in meatloaf and fire yet, despite *everyone else* being able to find us in here, I'd say we're probably pretty safe to carry on with the rest of today's assignments."

"Oh, yeah," Cal said, getting to his feet. They were still standing close enough that Ella had to tilt her chin up to meet Cal's gaze as he towered over her.

"I've got a break right after that stupid fitting and before my last assignment for the day," Ella began. "If you have half an hour around then, we can go get you Santa suited. I mean, the Ball is only four days away . . ." She trailed off, looking uncertain again.

Cal couldn't have that. "Sounds good. So, want me to meet you here at five-thirty? I've been told I have to be with the rest of the Parade trees by six-fifteen . . ."

Ella nodded. "Perfect. See you back here at five-thirty." She hesitated for a minute longer and Cal tried to figure out something to say, something that would reset them to the time before Maddie had interrupted. But, with one more smile from her, she turned and headed out the door.

Cal couldn't decide which was more frustrated, his body or his mind. Of course, he knew mentally that one was feeding the other. He stumbled through the rest of his assignments for the afternoon, thankfully able to hide his distraction under the guise of exhaustion. The people he interviewed were pushing through their own tiredness as the Hope Holiday season started its third lap and final run-up to Christmas. The whole town seemed to be looking forward to the Santa Ball and Crawl. From what Cal could gather, it was mostly an Islander event, like the Town Thanksgiving dinner. As Mrs. Redding put it when she mentioned it to Cal after their interview, "It's a time when the rest of the world has better things to do and the Island can let out the fart it's been holding since Thanksgiving." Cal wasn't sure if Ella would let him print that in the article, but he couldn't help smiling as he headed back to meet her at the office. Knowing her as he did now, he felt like there was a pretty good chance that her reaction to the quote would be, "Let 'er rip!"

The office was quiet when he arrived. No one was at their desks. He was about to call out when Ella emerged from her office, already bundled up for the cold, with her shoulder bag slung over one arm. "Ready?" she asked him.

He nodded and then glanced around. "Where's everyone else?"

"Well, Pip had to run some errands for her gran, Katie's youngest has an ear infection, Marty and Kurt are duking it out in the back with the machines because of some layout changes they want to make and Maddie ran home for an early dinner. She's going to be my photographer wingwoman at the Parade tonight as penance for sticking us with the bonfire."

Killjoy Cal nudged him. "Oh, and about the bonfire," Cal said. "I can cover it solo so you don't have to, you know, miss anything on your date." The words felt acidic in his mouth. Tony was probably a nice guy. He wasn't bad looking and from the one encounter with him that Cal had had, he seemed to like Ella. He needed to be a grown-up about the whole thing. If she liked Tony, he was going to have to just crate up and pack away any of his feelings that would make things harder for her.

"Oh," Ella's face turned pink. "Yeah, well, he knows what I do for a living, so he'll have to just be ok running around with me while I interview people. I'm not going to make you cover and photograph the whole thing by yourself." She cleared her throat and checked her watch. When she looked at him again, the wicked grin was back and though it usually spelled trouble for Cal, he felt himself relax. "We have barely a half hour before you turn into a newspaper tree. We better get moving."

"Where are we going?" Cal asked as Ella moved them around the square and down the road toward Shell Street.

She raised an eyebrow at him. "My house, of course."

"Oh," Cal said, feeling stupid. "That makes sense."

Helen, Ella's mom, was sitting on the porch swing, bundled in a quilt with a book and a cup of coffee when they approached. She looked surprised to see them.

"To what do I owe an early evening visit?" Helen asked, looking from

Ella's face to Cal's.

Ella pecked her on the cheek and rolled her eyes. "Honestly, mother, you act like I'm a feral cat that just shows up for food."

Helen cut her eyes to her daughter. "And what part of that is wrong?"

Ella shrugged. "I'm *at least* a feral dog. I also sleep here."

Helen sighed and Cal could see so much of Helen in Ella's mannerisms that it made him smile. "My original question still stands. Why *did* you come home in the early evening and drag Cal with you? Is the newspaper office on fire? I can't imagine anything else that would pry the pair of you away from there this close to Christmas."

"He needs a suit for the Santa Ball and Crawl," Ella said quickly. "I'm going to get dad's old one for him." Ella disappeared into the house and Helen turned her attention on Cal. He immediately had the urge to fidget under the heavy, appraising look she was giving him.

"Cal," Helen said softly. "Come sit down with me for a minute."

He was nervous, but she was only holding a book, so he probably could get away if she planned to beat him to death with it. She was also wrapped in a quilt which would slow down her mobility. She smiled at him and patted the seat on the swing next to her. So Cal went and sat down on the weathered wood.

"I like you, Cal," Helen said. "Bill likes you too." She paused and looked toward the front door to the house before meeting his gaze and nodding. "And El must like you. A lot."

Cal was confused. "Why do you say that?"

Helen's smile was honest, but there were worry lines around her eyes. "Because when Bill and I got married, El wouldn't let Bill wear her father's Santa suit. Of course, you know Bill, he didn't mind and bought one himself. When she was sad and missing her dad, I'd find her in her bed, wrapped in that Santa suit. She said it smelled like him." Helen's eyes were tearing up. She turned away from Cal and wiped them on the quilt. She was more contained when she looked back at him. "So, if she's letting *you* wear it, you must be pretty special."

The weight of Helen's words hit Cal like a punch to the chest. Did...Did

Ella trust him? As if she could read his thoughts, Helen nodded. "It's kind of a big deal. She won't act like it is, but I wanted you to know how important this is. She's been hurt, Cal. Recently."

Cal nodded. "I know." His voice had come out a lot softer than he'd intended.

Helen just nodded. "Good. So, we're kind of trusting you to not lead her on or hurt her, if you can help it."

Cal shook his head. "I never want to hurt her." The thought of Ella crying because of something he'd done made him feel sick.

Helen smiled and patted his leg. "You'll be just fine then."

He wasn't sure about that part. It was hard to predict if anything would be "just fine" when you were falling in love with someone.

32

ELLA

Ella pulled the garment bag out of her closet. The smell that still clung to it made it hard to push down the memories and emotion swirling inside her as she held the suit in her arms. Two fat tears broke through her mental defenses and rolled down her cheeks as she opened the bag and stared at the plush red and white suit. She knew her dad's smell was more in her memory now. The suit itself didn't smell like him anymore, but she could still close her eyes and run her hand over the sleeve and almost feel his strong arm under the fabric, lifting her up to twirl her around. The synthetic white beard had been soft when he'd kissed her cheek while wearing it. And she remembered him dropping the hat onto her head where it fell down over her eyes while she giggled and her father teased her. It hadn't felt right to let Bill wear this suit. She wasn't sure why. She liked Bill. But, Bill wasn't her dad.

But why did she feel ok when she thought about Cal wearing it? He was even more of a stranger than Bill was. She'd known Bill for years. She'd known Cal for less than a month. But she hadn't hesitated when he said he needed a suit. She buried her face in the fabric and talked to her dad. She hadn't done it since she was seventeen, but if there was ever a time when she needed his guidance, it was now.

"Dad," she whispered. "This is insane, but do you think I can . . . trust Cal?" The room around her was silent. She sighed. It was worth a try.

There was a crash in the closet behind her and she turned to look at what had fallen. It was the shoe box where she kept her dad's beard and hat. She bent down to pick it up and sat down on the edge of her bed, mentally preparing herself to look inside. She finally opened it and picked up the photo she always put back in the box on top of the hat and beard when Christmas was over. It was a picture of her dad holding her on his hip. She was eight. He was in his Santa suit with his beard pulled down on his chin. He was grinning at the camera, winking, and he had his free hand out in a thumbs-up. Ella smiled at the photo and touched his face. She knew *he* was where she got her sass from. Her mom could hold her own, but when she'd become a teenager, it was always her and Dad cracking jokes and driving her mom crazy. "Ok Dad, I get it," she chuckled, looking at his wink and thumbs-up. She set the photo on her nightstand, closed up the garment bag and the shoe box and headed back downstairs. She couldn't put her finger on why exactly, but she didn't feel any regret or even second-guess herself about loaning the suit to Cal. It just felt . . . right.

She opened the front door, holding the garment bag in front of her as she headed out to the porch. "Here we go," she said. Cal was sitting on the porch swing next to her mom. When he turned to look at Ella, he smiled, and she felt the consistency of her bones trying to shift from solid to liquid. Jesus, Mary, Joseph and a camel smoking Camels, Cal Dickson was gorgeous when he smiled like that. It had taken every ounce of her fear of rejection and cowardly neurosis to keep her from kissing Cal *twice* while they had been in the break room. Both times, Helga had stomped her foot, reminding her that she was Cal's *boss* and that she had a date with Tony *tomorrow night.* And then there was the "not knowing how Cal felt" at least, not being sure of how he felt. What if she leaned in to kiss him and he started laughing? But, after what he'd shared with her, his own "Cranberry Sauce"-style trauma, things had shifted between them. Just a little. Enough for her to really *see* him. And, she had to say, she'd liked what she'd seen. Realizing her mom and Cal were both still watching her, she gave herself an internal shake and moved over to the porch swing. Cal got to his feet and carefully took the garment bag and box from her.

"Thank you so much for letting me borrow your . . . spare suit," Cal said. "It . . . It means a lot to me."

Ella nodded. She couldn't look away from his blue-green eyes, but she was also acutely aware of the fact that it felt like far too intense of a moment to be having in front of her mom.

"Don't you two have to be at the Parade of Tree Taunting in a few minutes?" Her mom asked from behind her book. Ella had a feeling she'd put it up in front of her face because she'd felt the atmosphere shift around her and Cal. Her mom had pretty good instincts about things like that.

Both Cal and Ella reached for their phones. Ella, whose arms were of course now unburdened, pulled hers out first.

"Crap. Yes." She looked at Cal. "I need to catch up with Maddie and go find a lookout point before the madness gets underway. But do you need help...um, getting dressed?"

Cal quickly shook his head. "No, I'll be fine. I think I'm going to just carry it all over to the...starting line and then get someone to help me there. I think it'll be...faster."

"And less embarrassing," her mom muttered from behind her book.

"Added benefit," Cal said. He looked down at the bag and box in his arms. "I'll just stash these in the office and head over."

"Be careful," Ella said. Cal met her gaze. "Because the starting line isn't that far from the Baby Jesus Bazaar tent. In case they're lying in wait, you may have to find a taller tree to hide behind so they don't sneak up and brain you."

Her mom lowered her book to frown at Ella and then Cal. "Who's trying to brain you at the Bazaar?"

"Well, we don't *know* that they're trying to brain us. We're just taking extra precautions. We had to be the judges this morning. The Hicks sisters have the flu. But we were smart. We made the winner the heaviest entry."

"Well, almost the heaviest," Cal said.

"It was a balance between heavy and mobility."

"I think we might need to make Mrs. Meyers a new rubric for next year," Cal said with a grin.

Ella could feel her mom watching them and she had the urge to leave. "We better get back at it." Ella pecked her mom on the cheek and as she pulled away, her mom put her hand on the side of Ella's face, glanced over at Cal as he navigated the front porch stairs, and then back at Ella. She smiled and nodded. Ella felt a rush of relief she hadn't been expecting spread through her. Was she imagining things, or had her mom just given her silent approval of Cal?

They were pretty quiet as they walked back to the office, but it was a comfortable silence. Ella was grateful for it. In her head, Helga and Sarcastic El were sparring over the pros and cons of getting her hopes up where Cal was concerned. Noticeably, Numb Ella was absent from the party. Ella couldn't quit smiling.

They'd barely made it inside the office door when Maddie's voice once again interrupted her reverie. "Pip told me you drank almost her whole flask at the fitting. I'm guessing by that goofy smile you're still toasted."

Ella blinked and then frowned at Maddie. "I did *not* drink her whole flask. I barely got two sips."

"What kind of fitting *was* it?" Cal asked. "Were there blindfolds, cigarettes, and a firing squad involved?"

Ella felt her face burn. She'd gotten used to Cal's sarcastic voice, but there was a note of bewilderment there, which meant that he didn't know...

"Oh, didn't you know?" Maddie asked, wandering over and putting an arm around Ella's shoulders. "It's Excavation's fashion show that our little editor is going to be modeling in." Cal just blinked at her. "Do you know what Excavation is?"

"A clothing shop, right?" Cal asked.

"A *lingerie* clothing shop," Maddie corrected, squeezing Ella.

Ella wished she'd commandeered Pip's flask or just upended the whole thing the first time she'd gotten her hands on it. She braved a look at Cal's face and almost stopped breathing. His face was pink and he looked a little embarrassed, but there was something in his eyes that he was clearly trying to hide as he dropped his gaze to his feet. She could be imagining things, but she swore, for just a second, she'd seen heat there. Whatever it was, it chased a fleeting hot shiver down her back.

"I didn't know," Cal said, his voice lower than usual. "Well, I'm sure you'll look . . . be great."

"Yeah she will," Maddie said and then she made a cat growling noise. Ella's face burned and she turned to glare at her friend. Maddie seemed to just let the glare roll off her. "Come on, we better hustle or all the good taunting spots will be taken. And I think Miss Mandie is having an outdoors booze bar for the Parade."

God bless Miss Mandie and her penchant for cocktails. Ella felt like she needed one at the moment. Cal still hadn't looked up at her again. "And shouldn't you be carrying and or rolling your costume over to where the trees are congregating?" Maddie asked him.

"Uh, yeah," he said. Finally, he glanced up and gave them each a wry smile. "If you hear someone yelling 'timber', it's me, tripping over said costume and taking down the whole forest with me."

"Excellent," Maddie said, holding up her camera. "Just make sure you yell it loud enough for me to hear over the crowd, and at least two of Miss Mandie's cocktails, so I can capture it on film."

With that, she strong-armed Ella out the front door. "So, when were you going to tell me about you and Cal?"

"What?" Ella hissed as they waved to other Islanders, all making their pilgrimage to their preferred parade-watching spots.

"Come on, El, don't try to tell me that there's nothing going on between you two."

Ella sighed. "I don't know what you're talking about."

"Right," Maddie said. "Well, luckily, I know you. I think one hour of pushing on you and two of Miss Mandie's Christmas Crack-aritas or Stockings-Over-the-Fire," Maddie read off the sign hanging from the front of Miss Mandie's table, "and I'll get it out of you."

Ella sighed again. Sometimes having best friends could be a double-edged sword.

* * *

CAL

Cal had needed a moment after Ella and Maddie had left, to compose . . . himself. It had to be the dry spell. That, combined with the close . . . encounters he kept having with Ella. And now the fact that she was going to be on stage, like an island version of a Victoria's Secret commercial. He took a deep breath. *Walter Mondale's speech with Jimmy Carter. Grover Cleveland's cabinet members, listed in alphabetical order.* He took a deep breath. Ok. He was still holding the garment bag and box. The weight of what Ella's mom had said to him stayed with him as he set them down on his desk and wrangled the hideous tree costume out through the office's front doors. He was optimistic, but the more he thought about it, the more air was let out of the happy balloon in his chest. The fact still remained; she had a date for the bonfire. And that date was Tony. Was he kidding himself? Probably. The costume seemed to be getting heavier as he struggled toward the motley crew of people wearing stiff renderings of evergreen trees standing on the far side of Bumble's Market.

"Hey man!" Cal jerked his head up when he heard Tori's voice. The kid was coming out of the market, flapping a too-long jacket sleeve at him. "Just wanted to let you know that there's only been radio silence on the Clarence front."

Cal frowned. "He hasn't called in a grocery order yet?"

Tori shook his head. "At least, not on the phone. If he's doing the telepathic thing, I like, won't know, will I? Do you think there's, like, answering machines for telepathic orders?"

Cal just stared at Tori, marveling at the fact that he was high school age and still alive. "I.. uh..."

"Do you need, like, a helping hand with getting your tree on?" Tori asked, dropping his gaze to Cal's feet.

"What?!" Cal asked. Then he glanced down. "Oh, sure, that would be great."

Explaining how the suit went on turned out to be a largely futile effort when told to Tori. "Step aside, son," another voice barked. "I've helped with this costume for the last five years. I've got it." Tori shrugged, gave Cal the peace sign and ambled off. Cal turned to see Dirk Patterson, teetering toward him in a ten-foot-tall tube with what looked like flayed pool noodle branches sticking out of it.

"Uh, hi Dirk," Cal said. "Let me guess. You're a sequoia?"

Dirk's face lit up. "Yes! You're the first person who's actually gotten it!" Dirk cut his eyes to the rest of the chatting trees around them. "Bunch of fir tree phonies." He helped Cal step into and get situated in the bottom piece and between the two of them, they got the middle part over Cal and wedged down over his shoulders. It looked like some combination of Ella, Pippa, and Maddie had added a skirt of silver fabric and tinsel to cover the gap between the bottom two pieces. Of course, then there was the final, top piece that Cal couldn't reach for without his arms. "Hang on, I'll get it," Dirk said.

"Oh, no Dirk, we should get someone else to . . ." But it was too late. Dirk bent forward and Cal barely managed to side-step the five feet of tree trunk extending from his head. From the sounds of the people behind him, at least two, possibly three hadn't been so lucky. He turned in time to see them stumble back, knocking into the trees behind them. It was a slow-motion car-accident that Cal was unable to do anything about with his arms pinned to his sides. He thought about yelling "Timber!" for Maddie, but there was a pretty good chance she wouldn't hear them. And he couldn't see the square, so he had no idea where she and Ella were even sitting. He looked down at himself. Ella was about to see him in this ridiculous outfit. He waited for the sweating to start, the heat in his face. But it didn't come.

"Here we go," Dirk grunted, pushing himself back to stand up straight. He was holding the frilly cone head piece as he surveyed Cal. "Just lean in here and I'll get it on you."

Dirk was at least a foot and a half shorter than Cal and the "leaning in" consisted more of Cal trying to squat down enough for Dirk to shove the cone on his head.

"Whew," Dirk said, backing up and putting a hand above his head to try to steady his trunk in the breeze. He turned his attention back to Cal and looked him up and down. "They couldn't find anyone smaller to ride the *Hornblower* tree this year?"

"Nope," Cal said.

Dirk scoffed. "Well, I suppose you've all been too busy over there lately to really give the Parade much thought."

"Yeah," Cal said, only half-listening to Dirk as he looked around. "It's been a crazy month."

"Oh, I meant with the mob coming for Clarence," Dirk said.

"What!?" Cal asked, jerking his head back around to look at Dirk. He could feel the edges of the face hole cutting into his cheeks every time he moved his head, but at the moment he didn't care. "The mob?"

Dirk looked surprised. "Oh yeah, you didn't figure that out yet?"

"What are you talking about?"

"Clarence was on the outs with the mob. That's why he's gone on the run." Dirk shook his head. "I thought you were supposed to be some high-brow investigative journalist from New York."

Cal just blinked at Dirk. He'd never spent much time with the man, so legends about him were really all he had to form an opinion on. He racked his brain. What was Dirk's grip on reality like? Cal decided to skip Dirk's comments about himself and try to get him to expand on the Clarence-mob connection. "So, *why* do you think Clarence is in trouble with the mob?"

"Oh please," Dirk said, waving his hand dismissively. "Clarence comes out here, forty years ago, from back east, sweating through the only t-shirt he had with him and literally looking over his shoulder. And then he *stays* on the island? If that's not the mob, I don't know what is."

"Alright trees! Let's line up!" Mrs. Gillespie was standing on a wooden crate, clapping her hands over her head, trying to get their attention.

"Here we go," Dirk said, turning quickly on the spot to face her. Too quickly, it would seem. He let out a squeak of surprise and then waved his arms as he lost his balance, falling backward. Cal was directly behind him and his brain didn't make the connection to his legs fast enough to step out of the way. As he went down under Dirk's falling trunk, he heard the paper mache around his face crack and rip.

Instantly, the pressure on his cheeks was gone. He had time to be thankful for the relief for a single second, before the wire from one of the pool noodle branches slapped him across the face and the full weight of Dirk's trunk settled on him.

* * *

ELLA

"Are you sure you're ok?" Ella asked. She was proud of herself for barely slurring her words. She'd only had one drink with Maddie, but because it was a drink from Miss Mandie, it had packed a whole night of booze into one cup. The benefit, of course, had been the fact that the drinking had distracted Maddie from her Tony-Cal-Ella questions. They'd heard the "treefall" crash right before the parade started, but they hadn't seen the fallout until Dirk Patterson went by with the top half of his costume bent at a forty-five-degree angle, and Cal, trudging along in his wake with a swollen nose and a split head piece.

"I'm fine," Cal said, gingerly touching his nose.

"Hurry up," Maddie called back to them from where she stood, holding the newspaper office door open.

"Easy for you to say," Ella called. "You're just carrying the stupid headpiece." Ella had her arms full of the large bottom piece and Cal turned to look at her.

"I can carry that one," he nodded down at the load in her arms.

"You might have a broken nose because of this stupid thing," Ella muttered. "It's the least I can do."

Cal shrugged. "I don't think it's broken. Just pissed."

"Well, please pass on my apologies to your pissed off nose," Ella said as she paused to let Cal go through the office door first.

"I'll tell it, as soon as it's back on speaking terms with me," Cal said.

They dumped the costume back in the corner of the supply closet and

Cal and Ella stared at it.

"Kind of looks sad, doesn't it?" Ella asked.

"Yeah, I feel kind of bad about breaking it," Cal said.

"Don't," Ella said, shaking her head. "It clearly had it coming."

They said goodnight to Maddie who grabbed her stuff and headed out yelling that she'd see them in the morning.

"Hey," Cal said, dropping his voice.

Ella felt a jolt skitter through her stomach. Visions of kissing Cal, kissing his bruised nose, his eyelids, along the bottom of his jaw . . .

"Dirk Patterson told me something tonight." The visions were gone and Ella blinked up at Cal. Dirk Patterson was to Ella what baseball was to most guys.

"Did it have to do with sequoias?" she asked.

Cal shook his head. He filled her in on Dirk's mob conspiracy theory as well as the fact that Clarence hadn't ordered any more groceries.

When he was finished, Cal just shrugged. "There's a good chance that it doesn't mean anything. But, because we're . . . partners in this, I thought I'd tell you anyway."

Ella nodded. "Thanks. And I mean, the mob angle is a ridiculous stretch, but what he said about Clarence looking over his shoulder, coming to the island without much in the way of belongings. Maybe he was on the run from *something*."

"Or someone," Cal said. That happy thought hung in the air between them, doing a hell of a job of sobering Ella up the rest of the way and seeming to kill the mood of anything else between them.

When they said goodnight and split their separate directions for the evening, there was a moment of hesitation on both sides. Ella didn't have any good excuses to prolong their time together. And after the day Cal had had, he probably needed some time to himself.

"Hey," she said. Cal looked at her. There was relief on his face, as if he was thankful that she'd said something, breaking the awkward moment. She hesitated, all too aware of the pause in fighting between Sarcastic El and Helga in her head. *Play it cool*, Helga told her. She smiled at Cal. "If you feel like a drunken boat ride later, to, you know, forget about being crushed under a five-foot-tall man wearing a sequoia, give me a call. I know a place."

Cal smiled and nodded. "Will do, skipper."

He was carrying the garment bag slung over one arm with the box tucked under the other. He was carrying them so carefully, like they were precious. She met his gaze again and realized he was looking at her as if he was expecting her to keep talking.

"See you tomorrow," she said quickly, almost choking on the words along with the emotions that were swirling inside her.

"Tomorrow," he replied with a nod.

They were both smiling like idiots. *Good,* Ella thought. *At least it's not just me.*

The walk home felt a lot shorter than it usually did. She'd paused a few times to talk to neighbors who had called out to her and once to help Mrs. Armstrong grab her toddler who had just discovered running and didn't care that his mother had twin girls on her hips and not a free hand to corral him. Ella had scooped the boy up and gotten him safely back in the house. Mrs. Armstrong had thanked her and said something that broke into Ella's thoughts as she walked the last three blocks to her house.

"This really *is* the village that raised a child. And not just a child. This is the village that raises all of us, isn't it? Raises us to Hope," she'd said, chuckling at her own joke.

The sun had already set, but as Ella looked around at the merrily lit houses, cozied up next to each other and the sounds of singing, TV, and laughter coming from the houses along the road, she remembered what Cal had told her that morning and she had to agree with it.

People here are *real.* Then, a thought drifted into her mind. A thought that would have absolutely horrified her, even a week earlier.

She could stay in Hope. She could be happy in this zany little town, as long as she could see it side-by-side with Cal Dickson and see it through his eyes.

33

CAL

Despite being so exhausted that he put his tea kettle in the freezer and the sandwich he made for dinner in a kitchen drawer, Cal couldn't sleep. His insomnia, for once, wasn't caused by guilt or worry about New York. It was anxiety, but of a nervous, excited variety, rather than dread. And frankly, it was a pleasant change. He lay in bed, staring at the ceiling, waiting for the ibuprofen to kick in and reduce the swelling in his nose. What a day. Just the night before, Ella had been sitting on his bed, trying to recover from drinking what appeared to be half a bottle of Jameson by herself. She hadn't been in his apartment that long, and it could be the power of suggestion, but he swore he could still smell her in the room. He closed his eyes. When they'd first "dated", he and Tara would lay awake at night and talk until they fell asleep. It hadn't lasted that long as their shared living arrangement became more about appearance than substance. He turned his head to look at the unoccupied pillow next to him on the bed. But, if someone like Ella was sleeping next to him... Would they ever get any sleep? The last few mornings, he'd woken up with at least a dozen things he wanted to ask or tell her when he got to the office in the morning. Most of the time, he'd chicken out and keep it to himself or forget, but things were becoming so much easier between them.

His phone vibrated on the nightstand next to him. He didn't even move to pick it up. He'd moved Tara's calls to vibrate only. Little by little, he was thinking of New York less. To shut Killjoy Cal up, he promised himself that he'd figure out what to do about the whole mess on the east coast, after Christmas. He turned his head to look at the red digital numbers on his alarm clock. It was just after one in the morning. Four days until Christmas. A wave of anxious dread began to creep through his chest. Only four days left before he'd be on the downhill slope from the holidays. And waiting at the bottom of the slope were crippling expectations from everyone he knew outside of the magic bubble of Hope Island.

He put an arm behind his head and stared up at the ceiling, thinking. He still *had* four days. No need to worry about the other side of the hill until he'd reached the top. Especially when there was still plenty for him to worry about in *Hope*. Dirk Patterson's theory for one. He pushed aside the thoughts of Ella that won the majority vote in his head and body as to what to think about and tried to remember Dirk's exact prediction. Okay, the mob angle was ridiculous, but if Clarence *had* come to Hope to hide out, was it possible that he'd changed his name? Or maybe even . . . faked his own death? Cal scowled. Now *he* was starting to sound like Dirk. Still, it was something to discuss with Ella. Something he'd actually have time to do while they covered the bonfire that night. This happy thought immediately imploded on itself when he remembered the obstacle to his evening with her. Tony.

From what he'd gathered, Tony was visiting relatives on Waldron, but he wasn't from the islands. So, presumably, he'd be leaving at some point. His best guess would be after the holidays . . . just like Cal. He gritted his teeth.

Damn it. What was he going to do? On one side of the equation, there were twenty-five and a half years of one life, being raised, groomed, indoctrinated, guided, and prepared for a whole future that was as carefully detailed as a car service schedule. On the other side of the equation, he had six months of walking on his own, talking to strangers, riding the proverbial subway car with people his first life would reject in an instant, and just *living*. Bills, groceries, studio apartment, work, beer with friends that worked in construction and hardware retail rather than stocks and bonds, volunteering to do strange and beloved town events. Which road was the universe guiding him down?

He realized sleep wasn't going to come for a visit, so he sat up and turned on the lamp beside his bed. There was a small table in the corner of the room that he would occasionally use as a desk. He sat down with his laptop and a blank word document and started emptying his head onto the screen. It was a coping mechanism his shrink had taught him when he'd started having insomnia in middle school. His parents were fighting all the time, but passive-aggressively, as the Dickson family coat-of-arms decreed, rather than brawling. Still, Cal could feel the tension and every thought that whirled through his head would get caught in some kind of mental blender at night. So, he'd started emptying his head every night before going to bed and it usually helped. Since coming to Hope, he hadn't needed it. But, he needed it tonight. As words started to become sentences, then full thoughts and paragraphs on the page, what had started as just a brain dump, was shaping itself into something else entirely. There was a peace flowing through him as the words poured out of his fingers and his mind shifted to the people of Hope. Flashes of memories and faces filled his head, until the rest faded away, leaving behind a single face with deep gray eyes, framed by white-blonde hair.

* * *

ELLA

Ella hadn't slept well. Not for bad reasons, really. Though, she did feel responsible, in a way, for Cal's bruised nose. As penance, she decided to find wherever Dirk Patterson stored his sequoia costume and personally disappear it so there would be no chance of a repeat the next year. Of course, Cal wouldn't *be* in Hope the next year. Would he? That thought tied her gut in knots. She was getting too attached. A stupid crush turned into a stupid infatuation. The word "rebound" was bouncing around in her head. Followed by "boss-employee". Of course, a large part of Ella's brain, and her entire body told Helga to shut up and just for tonight, let her imagine, and dream, and enjoy. Of course, the imagining and enjoying part preceded the dreaming and left her so hot and bothered that she couldn't sleep, let alone dream. So, instead, she decided to argue with Helga. But, Helga, being the annoyingly smart jerk that she was, also pointed out the fact that she had a date with Tony in less than twenty-four hours. She hadn't forgotten. In fact, if anyone was rebound, it was Tony. He *wasn't* an employee and he would be leaving the islands . . . at some point. Like Cal, she didn't know when that would be.

A fresh cloud of anxiety settled itself on her face, prompting her to sit up. She got out of bed and moved across the room to sit down at her old desk. She turned on her desk lamp and stared at the rough wood surface where she'd doodled instead of focusing on homework, etched her initials and Maddie's, and Pippa's. There were a couple of hearts with the initials of boys she'd liked from time to time that had been scratched out when those crushes had ended. She imagined Cal's initials joining the others on the desk and the thought made her feel sick. Inevitably, whenever she'd scratched someone's initials into the desk with a heart around them, the clock would start ticking down the time until it would be scratched out, leaving a little scar on the desk to match the one on her psyche. Looking for something, anything to distract her, she started opening desk drawers. An hour later, she'd leafed through her junior and senior yearbooks and had moved onto a photo album of town events she'd been involved in over the years. The album had been put together initially when her dad died. The first thirty pages all had pictures of her and her mom with her dad at different town holidays. The pictures had been gladly donated by different town members and then, her mom had just kept adding to it. A new torrent of old emotion stung Ella's eyes as she turned the pages. Soon, she wasn't looking at herself in the pictures, just the faces of the other townsfolk that she knew so well. This was the village that had raised her.

"El!"

Her mom's morning hallway shout jerked her awake. She'd fallen asleep at her desk and there was something stuck to her face. She sat up, peeling her cheek away from a photo of Ella and Myrna dressed in Girl Scout garb. There was a knock at the door and then her mom poked her head in. "Ella? Didn't you hear me?"

"I did," Ella croaked. "But waking up from sleeping at a ninety-degree angle is kind of jarring, mother." She rubbed the back of her neck. "I couldn't remember where my mouth was."

"Well, it sounds like you've found it now. Better get a move on. It's almost eight."

That was more than enough to light a fire under Ella. She was dressed and down the stairs, rubbing her sore neck as she called goodbye to her mom and headed out into the frigid morning air. She managed to bumble a greeting to the Millers as they power-walked past her, wearing matching Christmas-themed jogging suits. She'd tried to say "Good Morning" while inwardly commenting on the dangling balls of fuzz that decorated their jogging suits, but instead, she said the quiet part out loud. "Good dangling balls this morning!" Mrs. Miller looked like she'd been about to swallow her tongue and she could still hear Mr. Miller's wheezing laugh two blocks ahead of her.

"Well, Ella," she muttered, "what did we learn about human interaction pre-coffee?" It wasn't a great omen for the day. As if in answer to this thought, the universe decided to blow a big wet raspberry at her, in the form of the godforsaken horn. There was a mixed reaction to the noise when she entered the square. The groans of the townsfolk and long-time tourists were lost under the cheers of excitement from a large group of tourists in matching sweatshirts that were huddled around the gazebo.

"Kind of handy when the obnoxious people all wear matching uniforms," Cal's voice rumbled behind her. She felt the familiar warmth rolling over her and the stubborn smile stake its territory on her face. She turned to face him and the picture of perfection was complete when she saw he was holding two huge coffees from De-Floured. "Cinnamon Hazelnut Hot Stuff," Cal said, reading off the top of the cups in his hands. He shrugged and handed one over to her.

Ella glanced down at the writing. "Pretty sure it's just Cinnamon Hazelnut and then there's a comma before Hot Stuff. I think it might be your designated Miss Mandie nickname." She grinned up at him.

"Oh, lucky me," his smile was genuine, but she could see the exhaustion under it.

"You look as tired as I feel," she said. "And I know where there is an office, full of things like calendars and voicemails, and overflowing inboxes with things like Christmas Karaoke, craft festivals, community plays, and I guarantee you, at least *one* townsperson griping about how we covered an event. Interested?"

"I'm hooked," Cal said. "Lead the way."

Besides the herds of tourists, there was a contingent of exasperated townsfolk trying to weave in and out between the crowds, carrying pieces of a mobile stage, wheeling carts of chairs, firewood, and . . .

"Oh my god, I'd forgotten," Ella breathed. She stopped to sniff the air, instantly turning herself and Cal into a rock in the river of people around them, who were then forced to alter their routes to avoid running into them.

"Forgotten what?" Cal asked.

Like a compass, her nose turned her toward the source of the smell. The sight of Mr. Bessire pushing his pretzel cart toward the bonfire set-up made her mouth water.

"Pretzels," Ella said, nodding at the cart.

"Pretzels? I thought the Solstice Bonfire was a Celtic event."

Ella cut her eyes to him. "What's your point?"

Cal was grinning. "I'm not sure if I had one."

She rolled her eyes. "I know pretzels are German, but they go perfectly with the music and the booze and the bonfire with the Yule log, which is really more like a Yule tree here. Anyway, you can scoff now, but you won't be when you try one tonight."

Without warning, Cal reached for Ella and she felt her heart starting to pound in her chest. He'd grabbed her by the shoulders and pulled her toward him. "Cal?"

"Sorry!" A voice yelled behind her. "Didn't see you!" Cal slowly let go of Ella and she turned to look at the two men behind her that were carrying heavy wooden platforms on their shoulders.

"Sorry," Cal said, his voice soft as he looked down at her. "I didn't want you to get hit."

"Thanks," she said. She twisted her sore neck, pretending to look behind her again as if she was checking to make sure there weren't more coming. Her face burned as they made it around the last of the event prepping townsfolk and tourists. Cal held the front door to the office open and she mumbled a thanks without looking up at him. She was afraid of what he might see on her face . . . For a moment, she'd thought Cal was about to kiss her and, god help her, she'd wanted him to. She was afraid that if he hadn't already seen the pitiful longing on her face in the moment, he would see it if she looked at him now.

Luckily, in some twisted way, the universe seemed to have her back on this one. The second they made it through the reception area of the office, both she and Cal were bombarded by questions and discussions from Marty and Pippa with Katie and Maddie waiting in the wings. Chaos had a lovely way of steamrolling everything else in its wake and making clocks run twice as fast. Through a wave of assignments, layout approvals, photos snapped on phones and transferred to Maddie, and stories written, Ella felt like she'd barely blinked. Then Maddie was standing in her doorway, holding one of the newspapers' Nikon cameras.

"Do you need a tutorial on this thing?" she asked, holding out the camera to Ella.

"No," Ella said. "That's the upside of the paper having a limited budget. It's the same camera I used to cover stories four years ago."

"Ah, but the lens is new," Maddie said with a grin.

Ella's look was deadpan. "I'm sure I'll be fine."

Maddie glanced behind her as if checking to see if anyone else was listening. Pointless, and most likely for dramatic effect as Cal was out on his last assignment before the bonfire and the rest of the staff had left for the day. She turned back to look at Ella, a wicked grin forming on her face. "I'm sure you'll be fine too. After all, two *very* fine and *very* tall men will be accompanying you tonight."

Ella hoped her eye roll would make the heat rising in her face appear to be from annoyance rather than . . . something else. "It's just an assignment, Mads."

"And a *date!*" Maddie practically squealed. Her expression softened. "I'm serious, El. I'm just . . . so damn happy that you're not sulking about that asshat from Seattle."

Ella nodded. "No asshat sulking for me." Maddie set the camera down on Ella's desk and bent over to peck Ella on the top of her head.

"That's my girl." Ella sighed and Maddie crouched down to eye level. "What is it?"

She couldn't hide anything from Maddie. Not really. Avoiding her had been Ella's only defense. If something was wrong with her, Maddie always found out. Ella sighed. "You ever want something to happen so badly, but you're also grateful when it doesn't because then there would be all this fallout that you'd have to sift through after it did? But at the same time, the want doesn't go away, in fact, it just gets stronger, and it drags your brain into it and . . ."

"Whoa," Maddie said gently. "Climb off the mental treadmill there and tell me what this is about."

"I can't," Ella said, staring down at the keyboard on her laptop. She loved Maddie, but she was too embarrassed to tell her everything at the moment.

"Well," Maddie said, "without specifics, I'd say go for it."

Ella turned to look at her. "Just go for it? But what about the fallout?"

Maddie shrugged. "Every decision has fallout. Very few decisions end in the destruction of life as we know it. Now, are you planning on going all Dr. Evil and, or, Bond Villain and stealing the moon or blowing up the world? Because I'm a mandatory reporter on that kind of shit."

Ella chuckled. "No, this isn't anything like that."

"Good," Maddie said. "Then do it and give me the details after. Alright? The fallout we imagine is always worse than what actually happens." She took one of Ella's hands and squeezed it.

Ella turned it over and kissed the back of her hand. "Thanks, Mads."

Maddie's cell phone beeped. "I'm being summoned," she groaned. "T-minus one hour before operation 'shopping for stupid sister's dumbass boyfriend's Christmas present' commences."

"You might want to come up with a shorter operation name. There's not going to be enough room on the mission badges for all of that," Ella said.

Maddie tweaked her nose and took off, leaving Ella alone in her office. She checked the clock on her laptop. She needed to head over to get some pictures of the bonfire as it was lit. Where was Cal? As if in answer to her question, her cell phone chirped. It was a text from him.

Esther is going long on her rant about the craft fair poaching her customers. Can't use it for the article but feels like I'm doing some form of civic duty by listening. Meet you at the bonfire?

Above the text message, there were ten others from that afternoon alone. Mostly banter about events or random thoughts. Ella smiled. Another difference between Cal and Les.

She texted back. *I'm sure I speak for all of Hope when I say, thank you for taking that bullet for us. See you at the bonfire. If you're not there in a half-hour, I'll try to come up with a way to tunnel under her shop and extract you.*

There was a pause and then the ding of a reply. *I'm holding you to that, Hogan. Better go radio silence now. Esther's changed topics to 'young people's brains turning to mush thanks to cell phones'. See you soon.*

"Cute *and* knows about *Hogan's Heroes*," Ella said to the empty office. She put on her coat and packed up her bag before slinging the camera around her neck and turning off the office lights. The light under the door to the press room was off and the absent rumble of machines told her that Kurt's crew had already finished for the day. She moved around the small office, shutting off lights and she paused when she got to the reception area to look back at the desks, now in shadow. It really wasn't a *bad* office. Working with her two best friends and a competent, small crew and . . . well, someone like Cal, definitely had its advantages. She reached for the pull cord on the lamp sitting on the side table in the reception area but paused to look down at her hand. In a moment, she'd imagined her hand looking like Myrna's, as if she'd spent the next forty years in this office. Would it be so terrible? *Yes, yes it would be.* Helga said. *Because you have dreams. And you want to do something big with your life.* Ella gave the office a final glance. Helga was right. Still, tonight, that thought made her wistful. She locked the office front door and moved through the square toward the gathering crowd where the first flickers of firelight were visible, illuminating the faces of the front row of spectators. She looked around her. No Tony yet. And no Cal. She flicked the camera on, and went in search of a front page photo.

* * *

CAL

Cal was finally able to peel himself away from Esther Jacobs, two minutes shy of Ella's timeline for extraction. He owed Esther's husband, Stanley, for the assist. He'd approached them with Esther's coat and a gentle interrupting reminder that they had a cat to feed before the bonfire and they needed to get a move on. Cal made a mental note to take Stanley out for a beer.

As he hurried across the square, he had to slow his steps as his senses were bombarded with so much Christmas festivity that his eyes began to sting.

"You know, they have all of this in New York, right?" He could almost hear Tara's voice in his ear, commentating on the elaborate displays and townspeople dressed in their festive coats, sweaters, and hats, handing out hot beverages and helping tourists find seats around the bonfire or the stage. Celtic music that teased old Christmas songs wove through the smells and sounds of the crackling bonfire and the low murmur of laughter and conversation. *No, Tara. New York doesn't have anything like this.* There was nothing he'd ever experienced in his life pre-Hope that represented the amount of love and care that this community showered on the events they birthed and raised, more than organized.

The sound of raucous giggling caught his attention as he approached the bonfire. When he spotted the source, he couldn't help but smile. Ella was holding her camera up and making funny faces at three little girls. They were wearing ski caps with pairs of pom-pom balls on top that made them look like three little bears sitting on a bench. The little girls were laughing, waving their marshmallows on sticks around while they made faces back at Ella. She snapped a few more pictures and exchanged a few words with their laughing mother who had just come back, carrying a drink carrier with four insulated cups. Cal squinted at the food cart behind them. It was Mr. Bessire's pretzel cart and he'd added a new item to his menu: hot chocolate for fifty cents a cup. His attention was drawn back to Ella who was now standing by herself, notepad in hand. She was taking notes, but she paused to rub her arms and move closer to the bonfire as if she was cold. She must have felt Cal's eyes on her because after a minute, she looked over and spotted him. There are moments in life when your mind tells you, *this is a permanent snapshot that you will carry with you forever.*

And for Cal, the picture of Ella Danforth, bundled against the cold, hair escaping the ponytail on top of her head, camera raised, and smiling at him as if he was the only person in the world, would be one he'd take with him for the rest of his life.

* * *

ELLA

"Hey Daphne, pull your finger out of your nose and make a monster face for me," Ella said to the youngest of the MacAffee sisters. The little girl growled and stuck her tongue out at Ella. She grinned and snapped a picture and soon Paige and Miranda, her two older sisters were giggling and getting in on the fun. Ella felt extra silly tonight. She wasn't sure why. It had to be the combination of Celtic music, the smell of the fire and the knowledge that as soon as she got some notes taken for the piece and a few more pictures, she could get a pretzel. That had to be it. *Not* the fact that she was covering the event with Cal and had a date with Tony.

She hadn't seen Tony yet, but while she talked to Mrs. MacAffee, she felt the familiar nudge, as if someone was watching her. She turned to see Cal, smiling and framed by the glow from the bonfire.

"My, he's a handsome one," Mrs. MacAfee said behind her. Ella turned back to look at her, but the woman had already shifted into her referee role as she moved her daughters around on the bench, separating Miranda and Paige who had started to squabble about their marshmallows. When Ella looked back across the bonfire, Cal was gone. She frowned. Had she just imagined him standing there?

"Sustenance, m'lady?" Cal's deep, soft voice sent a shiver down her spine. She turned to see him, holding out a huge soft pretzel to her.

"Why thank you, kind sir," she said. "Though, I suppose I should be buying *you* dinner, considering where you've been for the last hour."

Cal shrugged. "All in the line of duty." He nodded at her pretzel. "Now, Mr. Bessire swears that's the biggest pretzel he made for tonight, so if you see anyone walking around with a bigger one, we'll have to go back and demand a refund."

Ella just looked at him. "I've . . . never had anyone get me the biggest pretzel Mr. Bessire had before."

"Well then," Cal said, grinning and digging his phone out. "We must document this auspicious moment." Ella rolled her eyes. "No, no. You have to make me *believe* that you *want* that pretzel." She could only laugh as she watched the animation on his face as he moved her around to frame the shot. Ella could feel other townsfolk watching them, but for once, she didn't really care. It was as if at that moment, there was only her and Cal . . . and two massive soft pretzels, in the flickering fire light. "There," he finally said, his hands gently caressing her shoulders as he nudged her around so the bonfire was behind her. He hesitated, his hands still on her shoulders and Ella's breath caught in her throat as their eyes met. For the first time, instead of speeding up, her heart seemed to slow. Comfort and trust, like the feeling she got just before falling asleep was flowing through her. She'd never felt anything like it coming from another person and soothing her like this. She tried to return it through her own eyes.

A voice came over the loudspeaker, "Welcome all to the annual Solstice Bonfire and Celtic Concert, here in the beautiful city of Hope! How is everyone doing tonight?" A loud cheer erupted around them and the spell was broken. Cal grinned, took back his pretzel and raised his phone.

"Alright, Danforth," he said. "You gotta show me you want it. Attack that pretzel!"

After about ten pictures, Cal was finally satisfied with the Cookie Monster faces Ella had made at her pretzel, and they both turned to listen to the mayor, Stan Crutzfeld read the same speech he read every year at the bonfire. It wove history and jokes with fire safety and was considered a masterclass on speeches in Hope, though only the tourists still laughed at the jokes.

"What's that big open area in front of the stage?" Cal asked, keeping his voice low. He was so close to Ella, she could feel his warm breath brushing down over her ear and under a gap in her scarf to her collarbone.

"That . . . that's the dance floor," she stuttered, barely able to concentrate with the way her body was reacting to the sensory overload that was Cal Dickson.

"We should go up there," Cal said. He paused and then added quickly. "I mean, there will probably be some great photo ops."

"Sure," she said quickly. Needing, but definitely not wanting to put some distance between her and Cal.

"Unless," Cal paused. "You need to wait here for . . ." Ella turned to look at him. "Tony?" he asked.

Ella had almost forgotten Tony was coming. She scanned the crowd. No Tony. There was a tiny pang of disappointment that she would place somewhere on the scale as being worse than missing the beginning of a joke, but not as disappointing as De-Floured being out of cinnamon rolls in the morning. She shrugged. "He's not here yet. If he shows up, he can find me."

Cal blinked at her and she didn't miss the way his half-smile had turned into a full smile. She led the way to the dance floor just as the mayor finished his address. When she reached the edge of the open area, she paused to clap for him and she felt Cal's warmth stop just behind her. He hesitated and then stepped to the side and joined the applause. The mayor looked as if he was going to give an encore based on the warm reception he was getting. But the lead singer of the band met him at the microphone and amid some chuckles from his constituents, he quickly left the stage and took his wife's hand, before leading her out onto the dance floor. The band started a slow ballad and Ella started taking pictures as the floor began to fill with the couples standing around them.

"I don't want to alarm you," Cal began. Ella froze. His warmth was close behind her again. "But I'm being gently, but firmly, pushed from behind." She turned to face him. He looked slightly panicked as he reached for her shoulders, before being nudged toward her again. She could see Hank Melrose and his wife Rita turning a wide circle behind Cal. "What . . . what should we do?" he asked.

Ella tried to gulp down her nerves. Maddie's words echoed in her head. *Just do it.* "I think we should dance," Ella said. She could feel her chin jutting out in defiance. But, she knew her bravado was all show. If he started laughing at her, she'd do her best to make it off the dance floor before she crumbled.

"Oh, okay," Cal said quickly. "Um . . ." They were both still holding the remainders of their soft pretzels. He snagged hers out of her hand and opened his messenger bag to tuck them inside.

"Oh, but your bag will get all salty," Ella said.

Cal shrugged. "It'll be good for it. It's been on the island for six months. It was bound to get salty eventually." He kept his eyes on her face. She could see his nerves, and what might have been a glimpse of a nervous, young Cal, watching for guidance to make sure what he was doing was ok. She smiled and stepped into his arms, nearly forgetting to breathe. She was overwhelmed by his smell, touch, and his warmth. He folded her hand into his, and she resisted the urge to draw in a sharp breath as she felt his other hand slide across her jacket to rest on her hip. She put her free hand on his shoulder and instantly wanted to run her fingers over the ridge of bone and muscle under her palm. God, how was she going to keep her balance when she was too overwhelmed to think, let alone dance?

But, the universe took pity on the two sleep-deprived and horribly awkward journalists on the dance floor and slowly moved them through the sea of couples, more or less in time with the music. Well, moved *Ella*. Cal was actually a good dancer.

"I feel like I've just been bamboozled," Ella said, glancing down at her feet to try to keep from stepping on him. "I think you might be a ringer."

"Ballroom dancing lessons for three years," Cal muttered. Ella looked up at him, eyebrows raised. "My mom's idea," he said with a shrug.

Now that she was looking up at him, and their faces were so close, she couldn't look away. He had her. Helga was trying to flash warning lights in her head that she was in danger. *Too vulnerable. You're going to get hurt.* But, Sarcastic and Numb Ella tackled Helga and were doing a valiant job of gagging her as Cal dipped his head until his forehead was almost touching hers. The intensity of his expression, part anxiety, part hopeful, sent a shiver down her spine.

"El," he whispered. "I would really, really like to kiss you right now."

Fireworks, bells ringing, the feeling of a thousand white doves being released, John Woo-style, inside her stomach. She did her best to keep her enthusiasm under control as she tipped her face up a half-inch to look in his eyes again. "Then do it."

Cal groaned, pulling a whimper out of her as his lips crashed on hers like a wave on the shore. Despite the intensity, everything was so soft. Time stood still and with her eyes closed, nothing in the world existed except for the heat, taste, and feel of Cal. Before she could stop herself, she gently bit down on his bottom lip. He moaned into her mouth. It was a deep rumble, that made her shiver. That sound was addictive. He tasted like soft pretzels and coffee. She flicked her tongue out to run it along his upper lip and with another growl, he pulled her closer to him, pinning her to his chest. She could barely breathe, not from the pressure, but from the feeling of being held by Cal Dickson. The song ended and the loud clapping around them broke the spell of the moment. He released the intense hold he had on her, as their lips parted. She held onto the moment, trying to keep her anxiety and fear at bay as they just stared at each other.

"Wow," Cal breathed.

"Seconded," she murmured.

"If I'd have known that was what I was missing," Cal whispered, as she moved closer to him, resting her cheek on his chest. "I'd have asked to kiss you weeks ago."

"I would have let you keep my mug," Ella said, turning her face up, her lips only centimeters away from the bare skin of his neck. "In exchange for you kissing me like that."

The next song started and Cal wrapped his arms around Ella, holding her tightly against him as they slowly turned on the dance floor, watching the couples around them who were so likewise preoccupied with their dance partners that they didn't seem to have even noticed Cal and Ella's lipfest.

"Do you think," Ella started to ask, but then she froze. What if it ruined everything?

"Do I think what, El?" Cal asked, his voice gentle as his lips moved in her hair. He kissed the top of her head, and she squeezed her eyes shut, lapping up the feeling.

"Do you think there will be fallout from this? From us, you know . . ."

"I don't know," Cal said. Ella could feel his thumbs gently rubbing her back where he held her. "Do you care if there's fallout?"

She thought about it for half a second. That was all it took to evaluate the bad that could happen versus the good that *was* happening. "No."

"Me either," he whispered.

Ella's cell phone started to ring. She groaned and Cal released her so she could dig it out of her pocket. "Myrna's calling," Ella said, frowning. She glanced up at Cal.

He shrugged. "Better answer it."

She had a fleeting and irrational fear that Myrna was calling because she somehow already knew that Ella had just kissed her employee and was hoping to do more to him. If scientists could ever figure out how to channel the power of Hope's rumor mill, the world would run on clean, renewable gossip energy.

"Hi Myrna," Ella said, trying to sound nonchalant.

"Oh thank god," Myrna said. "I'm on the ferry now. The police called me because I forgot to update the first contact information from Clarence to you. And then when he didn't answer, they called me. You'd think with your stepdad being a deputy they'd know to get a hold of you . . . but anyway, I'm on my way there."

"Whoa," Ella said. "What are you talking about Myrna? The police? Clarence? Why are you on the ferry?"

"Don't tell me you don't know what happened?"

"What happened?" Ella asked. Cal slipped his hand into Ella's, and she squeezed her palm against his.

"Someone broke into the office!"

34

ELLA

Ella was speechless.

"What is it?" Cal asked. He brushed his thumb across the back of her hand and the tingling sensation cut through the fog around her brain as it tried to fully grasp Myrna's words.

"Someone broke into the office," Ella said. Cal's hand tightened around Ella's.

"Let's go."

"Myrna," Ella said into the phone, "Cal and I are on our way there now. We've been at the bonfire."

"Oh crud. That's right. I forgot it was tonight. Well, I'll meet you two at the office. The police should be there already."

Cal led the way, easily making a path through the tightly packed people dancing, drinking, and talking around the bonfire as if a crime hadn't taken place five hundred yards from where they stood.

Ella frowned when they stopped outside the office's front door. "No broken windows." She pulled on the door. "It's still locked."

"A prank call?" Cal asked. Ella squinted through the front door. There were lights on in the back of the office beyond the partition wall. Lights she *knew* she'd shut off.

"I don't think so." She pulled out her key and unlocked the door. Cal followed her in and they'd only walked a few feet before they heard voices.

The inside of the office was cold.

A stiff breeze blew loose papers around on the floor. As they drew even with Cal's desk, they found the source of the breeze. The window on the back wall had been broken. Glass shards were scattered everywhere. The voices were outside and through the broken window, Ella could see Marjorie Ellis and Mike Maxwell, two of the five patrol cops for Hope, shining flashlights around the narrow alley.

"Your laptop," Ella said, looking at Cal's desk.

"I have it with me." He sounded distracted and Ella turned to look at him. He was looking back at Maddie's desk. "What did they break in *for*? The cameras maybe? The PCs on Maddie, Marty, Katie, and Pippa's desks are all still here." Cal moved over to his desk and started checking the drawers.

"Hey! Who's that?" Mike barked, swinging back to the window and blinding Ella with his flashlight.

"Turn off your high beams, Mike," Ella called. "We come in peace."

"Mike, that's Ella Danforth. She's the new editor," Marjorie muttered, grabbing his hand to point the flashlight at the ground. "Sorry, Ella. Who's that with you?"

"Cal," Ella said. "He works here too."

"Oh, I know Cal," Mike said. "He's on our league team."

"Hang on," Marjorie said. "We're going to come around to the front to ask you both some questions."

"Can't wait," Ella muttered as the pair disappeared from the window. She knew she was probably just being paranoid, but it didn't feel like a good omen for a break in at the office to be something that happened on the same night she kissed Cal. She turned from the damage to look at her office and let out a groan.

"Oh man," Cal said, coming to join her in the open office doorway.

Most of the paper stacks around the office had been toppled. The carpet wasn't visible and Ella had the strange idea that it looked like an artist's rendition of a ball pit for accountants. The paper on the floor was at least an inch thick.

"Are...are those shoe prints?" Cal asked, pointing at a faint dirty outline on the top layer of paper.

"It looks like it," she said. She tiptoed into the office, following the shoe prints on the scattered papers.

"El, that's evidence," Cal said softly.

"I'm being careful." She followed the prints around the desk and crouched down behind it. She didn't have to push any papers out of her way to understand what she was looking at. "Son of a bitch!"

"What? What is it?" Cal asked. Ella looked up to see him picking his way around the desk to get to her.

"Whoever it was," Ella said, nodding down at the exposed hole under the floorboard, "knew exactly where to look and what they were looking for."

"The briefcase?" Cal asked.

Ella nodded and she could feel how hard her expression was when she looked at Cal. She was pissed. Not only had this bullshit interrupted a near-perfect evening, but now, some jerk had broken into her office. "Ok. This ends now," she said. "We're going to see Clarence. And if I have to break a window to get in there to see him, well turnabout is fair play."

"You think it was Clarence?"

Ella shrugged. "As far as I know, he was the only one who knew about the floorboard-hiding-spot. And I'm pretty sure Myrna gave me *his keys* judging by the 'I'd Rather Be Fishing' key chain that's still attached. So, unless he had another set made, he'd have to break in if he didn't want to see anyone when he came back for the briefcase."

Cal shook his head. "But, if he wanted it, why didn't he just take it with him when he quit?"

"I don't know," Ella said. "But I know how to find out. And if he wants any peace in his retirement, he's going to tell us what the hell is going on." With her foot, she shoved the loose floorboard back over the hole. Then she paused, looked at it, and then up at Cal. "The police will probably need to dust it for prints, won't they?"

Cal nodded. "Probably. Besides, we can't leave until we talk to them. We'll have to interrogate him after. Where's the briefcase now?"

"My house," Ella said. She crossed her arms and scowled at the mess. "What a disaster. You'd think Clarence would have been more careful with his 'filing system' when he barged in."

Cal shrugged. "Maybe he was in a hurry and just didn't think."

She sighed. "Sounds like a Clarence who would quit suddenly."

Ella and Cal left her office to stand by Maddie's desk to wait for Mike and Marjorie. They finally came in the front doors, kits in hand, crime scene camera around Mike's neck, and both with one hand on their guns. Hope didn't get a lot of criminal activity besides the odd over-intoxicated tourist causing a kerfuffle. A break-in was big news, Ella supposed. Then, she realized that she should probably be taking notes since she and Cal *wrote* the news.

Mike and Marjorie separated them for questioning.

"So what time did you lock up?" Marjorie was asking. She and Ella each had a steno pad, taking notes.

"Seven," Ella said. "Then I went over to the bonfire to cover the story."

"And you're sure you didn't see anyone hanging around outside?"

"No," Ella said. "But I wasn't really looking. How did you all find out about the break in so quickly?"

"A tourist took a wrong turn and ended up on the paper's loading dock on his way to the bonfire. He went down the alley beside the building, trying to find his way back, and when he saw the broken window, he called it in."

"But he didn't see anyone?" Ella asked.

Marjorie shook her head. "No. We held him for questioning until we could check his story out. No glass on him, cuts, or anything. And we checked his ferry pass. He'd just gotten off the eight-o-clock docking."

Ella nodded vaguely, thinking about Clarence and the briefcase. What was the connection? What was it all about? Did it have something to do with Dirk's prediction? Was someone *actually* out to get Clarence?

"Do you have any idea who could have done this?" Marjorie asked.

Ella shook her head. She didn't like lying to someone like Marjorie, but she needed to talk to Clarence before she sent the cops after him. Partly because she was worried about him, partly because she was a nosy journalist who wanted to know what was going on, and now partly because she was pissed that her office was a mess.

Marjorie finished questioning Ella a few minutes after Mike finished with Cal.

"You two will need to hang around for a bit," Mike said, with the excitement of a ten-year-old on Christmas morning. "We need to get forensics exemplars from both of you and the rest of your staff to rule you out."

"What kind of exemplars?" Ella asked.

"Shoe prints, fingerprints, hair, that sort of thing," Mike said, rubbing his hands together. Ella wondered if any cop, anywhere, had ever been more excited about a break-in.

"I'll call the staff and have them come in," Ella said. "And I better check in with Myrna."

"No need," Myrna's voice called from the front doors. "My god it's cold in here." She came to stand next to Ella and Cal and stared blankly at the broken window. "Oh, that's why."

Ella turned to look at her. "Didn't you know about the broken window?" Myrna shook her head. "I was just told 'break in'."

Ella frowned. "How did you get here so fast? Olympia is two hours from Anacortes and they only found out about the break in an hour ago."

She shook her head. "I was actually planning to come down and bring you all your Christmas presents tomorrow anyway, and I had just gotten to my sister's house in Anacortes when I got the call."

She stood with Ella and Cal while she answered the officers' questions, unable to tell them much more than Cal and Ella had. Then, Marjorie shepherded the three of them to the break room. They all sat down on the couch with Myrna in the middle and let out a collective sigh.

"I'll text the rest of the staff," Ella said. "That way I won't interrupt them with a phone call. I'll tell them to bring their work shoes to the office and then that Myrna has their Christmas presents here."

Myrna scowled. "Rephrase that when you text them, so they don't think I'm some kind of creepy old woman with a foot fetish."

Ella snapped her a half-assed salute and started typing. Myrna had a gift bag with her and she reached into it, digging around in the contents until she came up with an obscenely large summer sausage, wrapped with a big bow. She placed it on Cal's knee without explanation and started digging in her bag again until she came up with a second one which she laid across Ella's lap. Ella paused in her typing to look at it.

"Myrna, are you giving me a big sausage for Christmas?"

Myrna sighed. "Yes. They're from my brother's ranch. They're really quite good with some cheese and crackers."

"Do you want me to work this into the text message?" Ella asked, nodding down at her lap. "Bring your work shoes to the office and Myrna will surprise you with a giant sausage?"

Cal started laughing and Myrna turned on the couch to glare at Ella. "Maybe I should text them."

"No, no," Ella said, turning back to her phone. "I've got this."

They'd been waiting for an hour and only Katie had texted back saying she would come by as soon as her two-year-old conked out and relinquished the death grip he had on her shirt.

"No one else has texted back?" Myrna asked. "Check again."

Ella raised an eyebrow at her. "I can't blame them, Myrna. It's after ten."

"But what about the examples or whatever the police say they need?"

Ella shook her head. "I'm sure they'll be fine getting them in the morning."

"Myrna," Marjorie was back. Myrna shot off the couch so quickly that Ella and Cal fell toward each other into the void. Not that Ella minded.

"Yes?" Myrna asked.

"We need you to come and look over the police report for your insurance company."

"Right," Myrna said. She followed Marjorie out the door and closed it behind her.

"Should we tell Myrna about the briefcase and the hole in the floor?" Cal asked.

Ella shook her head. "Not yet. I think we do what we have to here, and then we go to my house, get the briefcase and go pay Clarence a visit. We get a confession out of him, and *then* we tell Myrna and the police. Easy-peasy."

"Why don't you want to have the police just take care of it?" Cal asked.

Ella shook her head. "I don't know. I just . . . You and I kind of started the Clarence mystery. Everyone else just acted like it was normal for him to suddenly become a hermit or at least, they acted like it was nothing to worry about. But, after what Dirk said . . . And then this? I just . . . I want to talk to him."

"Me too," Cal said, nodding.

"Ok," Ella breathed. "Now we have a plan." Without Myrna between them, they were sitting close, and their knees were touching again.

"Let me just say," Cal said, his voice deep but with a note of playfulness that made Ella smile. "I'd really like to kiss you again right now, but we're both sitting here, holding pornographic-sized sausages wearing bows on our laps, our boss and two cops are outside the door, and we're about to go interrogate Clarence."

"And as fun as that story would be," Ella said, reaching a hand up to hesitantly touch the stubble on his cheek. He leaned into her touch and smiled. She tried to gather her thoughts and continue. "There is also the possibility that Myrna could walk in on us and fire me on the spot or you or both of us for fraternizing."

Cal frowned. "Is there actually a rule about that here?"

Ella shrugged. "Not that I can recall, but tonight's been a stressful night for Myrna and she might do something rash."

"Unlike us," Cal said, smiling at her.

"Right," Ella said.

Twenty minutes later, Marjorie and Mike had taken Cal and Ella's fingerprints, shoe impressions, and hair samples. Katie had come by to give hers as well and Marjorie said she'd make house calls to get the rest. "It is getting pretty late. And at least this way they won't have to come out in the cold," she said with a professional-grade smile.

"I'll go with you," Myrna said. She was carrying the gift bag. "I have a little Christmas present for them anyway."

"Little?" Cal muttered. Ella snorted beside him and quickly turned it into a cough when Marjorie and Myrna turned to look at them.

* * *

CAL

Cal and Ella left the paper at a normal walk, not wanting to arouse any suspicion. They picked up speed as they got closer to her house. Helen was in the kitchen when they came in and for a moment, Cal was paralyzed by the intoxicating smell washing over him.

"Enchiladas," Helen said when she saw him standing still with his mouth open. "I got home from the bonfire, and just thought they sounded good. You're more than welcome to take some with you, Cal."

"Thank you," Cal said, trying to contain the emotion that was clawing at his throat. "I'll have to take a rain check on that, Mrs. Benson."

"Call me Helen, Cal, unless you want to really weird Ella out and call me 'Mom'," she said, chuckling. Cal couldn't speak.

There was a warmth in Ella's house, from her mother, from Bill, from Ella herself, that was so strong it felt like at that moment, it was manifesting as the mouth-watering smell of the enchiladas. She put a gentle hand on his arm.

"Are you doing ok?"

He pushed down what he couldn't put into words and changed directions, nodding toward the staircase. "Oh, yeah, Ella just needed something, so we ran back by to get it." Cal wasn't sure what to tell her about the break-in. "Where's Bill tonight?"

Helen sighed. "He had to go into the station. Not sure why. He was supposed to be off duty today."

Cal just nodded. He hated not telling her, but he wasn't sure what she'd do if she knew where they were headed. He was saved from having to make a decision by Ella pounding back down the stairs, briefcase in hand.

"Bye, Mom! Your midnight enchiladas smell great!" She yelled, pulling the door open and reaching back to grab Cal's hand. He had time to wave at Helen before pulling the door closed behind them.

"Did you tell her?" Ella asked, keeping her voice low as they power-walked toward Evergreen.

"No," Cal said. "I probably should have, but I thought she might want to know everything or try to stop us."

"Probably a safe bet," Ella said. She was still holding his hand, and he wasn't about to be the first to let go.

Clarence's house looked the same as it always had. They tried the front door first. They knocked, they pounded, they tried to flip the letter slot open, but it was locked.

"I thought it might be," Ella muttered. "He locked it that first time I came to visit. The post office must be holding his mail."

"Now what?" Cal asked. Ella led the way to the back of the house. She first went to the bedroom window they'd tried before.

"Help me up?" Ella asked, her voice softer as they stood close under the window. Cal nodded, feeling his pulse kick up another hundred beats per minute as he slid his arms around her legs, seating her on his shoulder so he could lift her up to the sill. She took a shaky breath and Cal looked up, trying to read her face. She gripped the window sill and tried to tug at the window.

"No luck?" Cal asked.

"No, I think it's locked. We should find a rock."

Cal was looking at the back of the house, trying to distract himself from what Ella's body was doing to his. Now that he'd kissed her, he wanted to *keep* kissing her and hopefully, go from there. But for now, he needed to focus. "Maybe not," he said, his gaze landing on another window. It was smaller, but still big enough for them to wiggle through.

He squinted at it in the dark. "Am I seeing things, or is that window open an inch?"

"Good work, Watson," Ella said, squeezing his shoulder. He set her down and they hurried over to it. Cal lifted her on his shoulder again and Ella set the briefcase on the windowsill.

"What do you see?" Cal asked, keeping his voice low in case Clarence could hear them from inside.

"It's the bathroom window," Ella whispered. "The door to the bathroom is shut. I think we can sneak in this way." She shoved the window up as high as it would go and crawled through it. Cal watched as she pulled the briefcase in with her.

She reached back through the window for Cal's hand. "It's ok, I can get up there," he said. He used the house siding to get a toe hold as he launched himself at the sill. Ella's hands were on his back and then his belt as she helped him crawl through. When they were both standing in the bathroom, he turned to look at her. She nodded at him and picked up the briefcase.

"Ok, let's go on a Clarence hunt."

They moved through the house, calling for Clarence. Now that they were inside, they *wanted* to find him or have him find them. No one answered them. They moved through the rooms on the ground floor, one by one. No Clarence.

"Did he skip town?" Ella asked.

Cal had just led the way into the kitchen when they both froze. There was a low moaning sound, accompanied by some rustling coming from a door at the back of the room. Cal led the way toward the door, and he felt Ella grip the top of his pants at the small of his back, holding on to him. He took a deep breath and threw the door open.

He heard Ella gasp beside him. He understood why. The room was a pantry and sitting in the middle of the pantry floor was an old office chair on wheels. Strapped to the chair was a gagged, beaten, and bloody Clarence Ford.

"Clarence," Cal breathed. The old man's eyes looked like they were screaming as they moved from Cal's face to Ella's. "Hang on," Cal said, moving to stand next to him. He grabbed the tape on Clarence's mouth. "Sorry about this." He tried to rip the tape off as carefully as he could. What he didn't expect was the string of cursing that came out of Clarence after the tape was off.

"What are you two doing here?!" Clarence was wild-eyed as he looked from Cal to Ella. "You have to get out of here! Now! Why couldn't you just take the hint when I didn't come to the door?"

"Who did this to you?" Cal asked.

Clarence shook his head. "It's none of your business. Either of you. We just have to get out of here before he comes ba..." He trailed off and Cal followed his line of vision to the briefcase in Ella's hand. "Why the absolute hell do *you* have *that?*"

Ella narrowed her eyes at him. "I tripped over it on my first day at the office."

Clarence sighed and hung his head. "He's going to kill me."

"Who is?" El asked.

"It doesn't matter," Clarence said, bringing his head up and looking around. "We have to get out of here."

Cal crouched down behind Clarence's chair to start working at his duct tape bonds. Clarence was shivering. He was wearing socks, pants, and an undershirt. Cal noticed angry red stripes across Clarence's exposed skin on his arms as if he'd been duct taped to the chair, freed, and then re-taped to the chair.

"El, you should call the police," Cal said.

"NO!" Clarence bellowed. "No cops."

"Why?" she asked.

Clarence looked more scared at the idea of cops than he did about the man who had tied him up and beaten him.

"You wouldn't understand," Clarence said. "It was such a freak thing..."

"Clarence, what *is* this?" Ella asked. Her voice was soft and she knelt down in front of him, holding out the briefcase.

Cal looked around the pantry. Nothing sharp to cut with.

"Hang on, I'll get a knife." Cal hustled out into the kitchen and pulled a knife out of the wooden block on the counter.

"Tell us, Clarence," Ella was saying when he got back to the pantry.

"Why were you hiding in your house? Were you being held here by the person that's been hurting you? Just tell us, who is it?"

"The nephew," Clarence groaned, looking at his lap. He was hanging, almost limply from his duct tape restraints.

"Ok, Clarence, we're gonna need a little more than that," Cal said. "Who's nephew?"

Clarence sighed and raised his head enough to glance from Cal to Ella. "It happened forty years ago, back when I lived in Chicago." He shook his head and looked at the floor, but he kept talking. "I was in Chicago at Union Station, waiting for my train to St. Louis. I'd just started working as an insurance salesman and the company I was with was sending me there for a conference. So, about twenty minutes before my train departs, I go to the men's room at the station because I have a thing about using the can on trains."

"Ok . . ." Ella said slowly.

Clarence shook his head. "I can't believe I'm telling you two this." He sighed. "So, I'm sitting in the can, minding my own business. Just me and my briefcase." He nodded at the case in Ella's hand. "It looked just like that one. When I'd gone into the stall, I'd set the case down next to me, but I'd turned it sideways and one end of it was under the stall wall, you know, like halfway into the stall next to me. Damn bathrooms back then were like chutes. Barely room for the can. And god forbid if there was more of you than the thin wasp-waisted men of the twenties when they built the thing, because then trying to fit your . . ."

"We're with you," Cal said quickly. "You can skip ahead."

Clarence nodded. "Well, while I'm in the stall, I hear footsteps, moving fast. Then, a guy sits down in the stall next to mine. Then, I hear more footsteps, heavy, and moving at a slower pace than the first guy. I didn't think anything of it, until . . ."

"Until what?" Ella breathed.

Cal had managed to free one of Clarence's arms and he raked his fingers through his cropped white hair. "Until the shooting started."

Cal froze in place, and he looked over to see Ella's eyes wide and her mouth hanging open.

"He had a silencer on his gun, but of course, I could still hear it. The guy shot right through the door of the stall next to mine. As soon as I heard the first shot, I pulled my feet up. I closed my eyes, expecting to be next. I heard the stall door next to mine open and there was some scuffling on the floor, and then those heavy footsteps left, so I grabbed my briefcase and when I saw the carnage of the man who had been shot in the stall next to me, I . . . I ran."

"Why?" Cal asked. "Why didn't you call the police?"

Clarence frowned. "Because I had a record. When I was a teenager, I used to pop cars and go joyriding around Chicago with my friends. But, that was all in my past. I had a good job that I wanted to keep. I was afraid if I missed that train to St. Louis, they would have fired me." He shook his head. "If I'd have gotten caught up in a police investigation, even as a witness, I *know* they would have fired me."

"So, what, *this* is just your briefcase?" Ella asked, looking down at the case.

"Not quite," Clarence said. "You see, when the guy got shot next to me, he kicked what I thought was my briefcase back into my stall. But, as soon as I got onto the train and it was pulling out of the station and I could breathe again and find my ass with both hands, I realized that I wasn't holding . . . *my* briefcase."

"Well, that explains the bloodstain," Ella said, looking down at the case.

"So, why didn't you call the Chicago police and drop an anonymous tip or something once you were out of town?" Cal asked.

Clarence was turning paler if that was possible, and there was a haunted look in his puffy, swollen eyes. "Because by the time I reached St. Louis and got to my hotel, there was already video footage on the news, from Union Station's security camera. It didn't show the shooter. It just showed me, running out of the men's room, clutching the briefcase." He squeezed his eyes shut. "I stole a car and drove out of St. Louis an hour after arriving. I didn't know where to go. Chicago was all I'd ever known, but I knew I couldn't go back. The news had named the victim of the shooting. He was a bagman for the Rossalini crime family. I knew that if I went back to Chicago, I'd either be arrested and immediately killed in jail, or the family would be out for my head. So, I just kept driving west. I used up most of the cash I had on me, getting to the Washington coast. I thought I'd picked up a tail, so I ditched the car in Seattle, took the rail to Anacortes and got on the first ferry."

"And ended up in Hope?" Ella asked, her voice soft despite the shock on her face.

Clarence nodded. "I changed my name, grew a beard, found a job with Myrna at the paper and did what I could to keep a low profile." Now Clarence looked angry. "Until I got sloppy."

"What do you mean?" Cal asked.

Clarence turned to look at him. "You remember that piece I wrote about my fishing team from Waldron? Well, I got lazy and didn't check with Maddie about the photo she was going to use for it. And Dale had sent her the photo of all of us together. So that's the one she used." Clarence sighed. "Well, that's how he found me. Facial-fucking-recognition software. I didn't even know it could work on newsprint lo-res pictures. But it did and he came out here and found me. He kept leaving voicemails on the machine at the paper. I didn't know for sure that it was him. It was always just... heavy breathing. And then, I got a note from him at the office saying he was coming 'for a visit'." Clarence shook his head. "So I panicked. I called Myrna and quit, called Cal here," he nodded at Cal, "and told him that I was done. Then I holed up here in my house. I thought that if I just laid low long enough and didn't show my face, maybe he'd give up on finding me. The picture in the paper hadn't had our names on the caption at least. Maddie beat herself up about it, but it bought me a little more time. However, I didn't count on him going to Waldron, finding my fishing buddies, and asking them my name."

"Who?" Ella asked. "Who is he?" Cal turned Clarence's chair, so he was facing the side of the pantry, making it easier for Cal to cut away the last of the duct tape on Clarence's leg.

"The bagman, Silvano Sanetti's, nephew," Clarence said. "Antonio

Sanetti."

There was the click of a gun hammer and all three of them froze. Cal was the first to look up at the man standing in the pantry doorway. Ella turned slowly to look behind her.

"Tony?"

35

ELLA

"Tony?" Ella could feel her voice cracking as she looked back at him over her shoulder. She wasn't sure why she asked it. It was clearly him. He wasn't wearing his ski cap now and his dark curls were frizzing from the building humidity outside. "You did this to Clarence?"

Tony looked at Ella with a cold gaze that she'd never seen before. "You mean the man who murdered my uncle?"

"But I didn't!" Clarence said, his tone desperate. "You have to believe me. Why would I kill him? I didn't even know him."

"When are you going to stop playing dumb, old man. I know you were hired by the Grizzolis. I heard about the contract. You killed him, took his briefcase, and disappeared. Sounds like a hit to me."

Ella felt pressure on the case in her arms and she realized that Cal was tugging on it gently, trying to get her to let go of it. She was still shielding it from Tony with her body. She let go and saw Cal shift it behind him so both he and Clarence's chair were blocking it from view.

"Please, Tony," Clarence cried. "I've told you. I was just using the can. That's it. I heard the footsteps of the man who killed your uncle. He took *my* briefcase. It was just a stupid mix-up."

Tony raised his arm, aiming the gun at Clarence. "You're full of lies, old man. The briefcase wasn't where you said it would be. What are you going to say now to stop me from killing you?"

Ah, Ella thought. *Tony was the one who broke into the newspaper office.*

"I didn't know it had been moved," Clarence said. Ella felt a rush of thankful relief that Clarence hadn't said *she'd* taken it.

"You're so full of shit," Tony growled. "I've run out of reasons to *not* kill you. It's not a bathroom stall, but it's still a confined space. Like a rat in a cage. Just like how you killed Silvano."

Clarence squeezed his eyes shut.

"Ok," Ella said, getting to her feet and turning to face Tony. She hadn't worked out what she was going to say before she started, but she knew she couldn't just let him kill Clarence. "I have the damn briefcase. I found it my first day on the job and took it home. I was going to bring it over here to ask Clarence about it, but . . ."

Tony narrowed his eyes at her. "Where is it?"

"My house," Ella lied. "I didn't know what else to do with it."

Tony scowled. "I knew you were going to be a problem, getting all starry-eyed over me. Once I'd seen the inside of the newspaper office and the fact that there wasn't even a security camera, I had what I needed." He shrugged, looking her over. "But, in case I need safe passage off this island asylum, it doesn't hurt to have a hostage." In a flash, his arm shot forward, and he grabbed her by the hair and started dragging her out of the pantry. "I guess you're still useful for one more thing." He paused, nudging the gun barrel under the collar of her scoop-necked shirt. "Maybe two."

"Let go of her," Cal spat. Ella was knocked sideways when he lunged past her, hitting Tony in the chest. The gun went off and a spray of blood hit the kitchen wall.

"Cal!" Ella screamed. They were rolling around on the ground and she couldn't tell who the blood was leaking out of. Cal was the first one off the floor. He got to his knees and hauled back, punching Tony in the face. She heard the crack of bone on linoleum-covered cement and Tony moaned. There was blood coming from his nose and he was feeling around on the floor. Probably for his gun. It had skidded away from him, coming to rest under the kitchen counter to Ella's right. She scrambled to grab it and held it, two-handed as she stood, shaking so much she could barely point it at him. She backed up until she could feel the wall of the pantry pressing into her back. She blinked hard, trying to keep the black-out fog and light-headed dizziness at bay.

"Cal, are you ok?" She kept the gun on Tony but turned to look at him. Cal was holding his shoulder and Ella could see the blood seeping between his fingers. "Jesus, you've been shot."

"Winged," Cal muttered. "I . . . I think that's the term. Stupid really, not like we actually *have* wings." He chuckled.

"I think you're going into shock," Ella said. "Hang on, I'm calling the police." With one hand, she kept the gun on Tony while she called 9-1-1 with the other. Both of her hands were shaking so much, she was having to use every ounce of concentration to force one set of fingers to dial and one set to be still and not squeeze the trigger. It wasn't a long call and when she hung up, she reached over and used her free hand to steady Cal as he leaned against the wall. Freed from the chair, Clarence had gotten to his feet and hobbled out of the pantry to stand over Tony's body on the floor.

"I don't think he's going to get up," Clarence said to Ella. "You mind putting down the gun? It's . . . making me nervous."

Ella set the gun down on the kitchen counter and opened drawers until she found the kitchen towels. She moved back to look Cal over and press the towel into the wound on his shoulder. Cal looked like he was working on riding out the shock he was feeling. He was breathing deep and sweating but seemed more lucid now. He took over, holding the towel to his arm and she reached up to stroke his cheek. "You sure you're ok?"

"I will be." He turned his face in her hand, rubbing his stubble against her palm and closing his eyes. When he opened them and met her gaze, the intensity of the look on his face made her feel like she was boiling and melting all at once.

"I'm an idiot," Ella muttered. Cal frowned at her. She shook her head. "If I'd just left the damn briefcase where I found it, he would have broken in, stolen it, and skipped town. And you wouldn't have been shot." She sighed. "I'm Indiana Jones in *Raiders* and I just handed the Nazis the Ark."

Cal opened his mouth to say something, but the sound of scuffling made them both turn. Clarence had been knocked to the ground by Tony. Tony was bleeding from the nose and his face was starting to swell, but he was on his feet and stumbling toward the doorway leading out of the kitchen.

"He's getting away," Clarence yelled. *No shit, Sherlock.* The gun was across the room from where she stood. Ella's never-used, high school geometry chose that moment to rear its head and tell her that the closest distance between two points was a straight line. She wasn't going to waste time by going for the gun. Helga wasn't consulted in this decision, so she stumbled after Tony and ran into him when he stopped short in the hallway. He fell forward and Ella caught herself on the kitchen doorway before she fell on top of him. She looked up, trying to figure out what had caused him to stop running. When she saw it, she was thankful to be holding onto the door frame because relief washed over her, almost taking her out at the knees.

There was Bill, in his deputy uniform. He was rubbing his broad chest and glaring down at Tony. "Jerk ran right into me."

"Bill," Ella breathed.

"You ok?" he asked.

She nodded. "Cal's been shot and Clarence is pretty banged up." She looked down at Tony on the floor. "Both sets of injuries, brought to you by this asshole."

"Looks like someone injured him too," Bill muttered.

"Oh, I think he did that to himself," Ella said. "Guilt or something."

Bill shook his head. "Guilt will do that to you, every time. I'll call for an ambulance." He looked over at Cal. "You were shot?"

"Barely," Cal said. Ella looked back to see him pulling the towel away to look at the wound on his arm. He shook his head and smiled first at Bill and then he met Ella's worried gaze. "Probably won't even need stitches." He turned his attention back to Bill. "And I'm pretty sure I'll still be able to take on Hank's team, at the next league night."

Bill chuckled. "It's a pre-Christmas miracle." He bent over to cuff Tony's hands behind his back. He pulled his radio off his belt and Ella stumbled forward, wrapping her arms around him. She closed her eyes and squeezed

Bill. She had the vaguest realization that she'd never hugged him like this before. She'd made clear to him, and clear to herself, *so many times* that Bill *wasn't* a replacement for her father, that she hadn't even noticed when he *had* become one of her two fathers. Bill must have been in shock too because it took him a minute before he hugged her back.

"You, my friend, have perfect timing," Ella said into his chest, trying not to cry.

"Only when it comes to my best girls," Bill said, patting her back. Ella finally let go of him and went to help Cal and Clarence out of the kitchen and onto Clarence's couch.

The next hour was a blur of more police questioning, first-aid care for Cal and Clarence, and Clarence retelling his story to Bill and the other officers.

"So, I . . . I guess you'll have to take me in now, right?" Clarence asked, looking down at the floor.

"For what?" Bill asked.

Clarence frowned and looked up to meet Bill's gaze. "Car theft, living under an assumed name, technically briefcase theft."

Bill shrugged. "I don't know about the assumed name part. That's something you'll have to talk to a lawyer about. But the briefcase theft was an honest mistake as far as anyone can probably prove. And if memory serves me, the statute of limitation on car theft in most states is only about seven years, so you cleared that hurdle about thirty-three years ago." Bill scratched his head. "I *will* need you to come down to the station with us to make a statement. And we'll need to call Chicago and see if they're interested in anything from you as a witness to Sanetti's murder all those years ago."

Clarence shrugged. "I don't know how I can help. I only heard the guy's footsteps."

"The security camera footage," Cal said. "If they still have it, they just need to look for a guy who came out of the men's room before you did, also carrying a briefcase which would have been yours."

"A big man," Clarence said, "going from the sound of his footsteps."

"So, what's in the briefcase you ended up with?" Ella asked Clarence.

He shook his head. "I don't know. The key to my briefcase wouldn't open it. I probably could have forced it, but I barely wanted to touch it, let alone pry it open. I slept better when it was under the floorboards."

Bill frowned. "Where is this briefcase?"

Ella went back into the pantry and carried it out, setting it on the kitchen island in front of Bill. He studied the key lock by the handle. "I have a feeling that Chicago might be interested to see what's inside. And we should probably give them the first crack at it." Bill carried the briefcase over to Marjorie who had shown up with Mike to take Tony away.

Missy Tolliver, one of Hope's two paramedics, was talking to Cal where he sat on the couch and Ella moved over to sit down beside him. "Well, you're not clammy anymore. I think the shock is passing. And you were lucky. The wound is really just a graze. I don't think you'll even need stitches. But," she reached into her bag and pulled out a stack of sterile bandages in paper wrappers and put her finger on the top of the stack. "You will need to change that dressing later tonight and probably in the morning." Missy moved her gaze from Cal to Ella. "You'll have to help him. Because of where the wound is, it's not something that a person can do easily by themselves and if he tries to, he could end up tearing any scabbing the wound is trying to do to heal."

Ella hesitated. He'd need the bandages changed *during* the night? She swallowed hard and just nodded at Missy. The woman smiled at them both and got to her feet before picking up her bag and moving off to talk to Bill in the kitchen, leaving Ella and Cal alone in the room.

He turned to grin at Ella. "Wanna see my battle wound?"

Ella rolled her eyes and heaved a dramatic sigh. "You mean your *graze?*"

Cal dropped his jaw in feigned outrage. "I was *shot!*"

Ella felt the soft vulnerability that Cal brought out of her, rising to the surface of her face. "You were. And I'm so sorry. You were . . . trying to save me."

Cal dropped his eyes from hers. "I was afraid. I thought he might . . ."

"Cal . . ." Ella breathed.

He raised his eyes back up to meet hers. "I saw him. Walking on

Clarence's street. It was days before you introduced me to him. He was wearing a hat the first time I saw him, just like he was that day he came to tour the office. But, I didn't put it together before tonight. I'm sorry."

"You're sorry?" Ella asked. "You just took a bullet and punched an a-hole in the face because said a-hole was threatening me."

Cal shook his head. "I just didn't want him to hurt you. I didn't . . ."

Whatever Cal was going to say after that was lost when Ella leaned forward and pressed her lips against his. She traced his lips with her tongue and he let out a low groan. Ella felt his warm fingers trailing through her hair, gently pulling her closer to him. She felt his tongue dart out to trace her bottom lip and a burning heat shot through her to the pit of her stomach and then moved lower.

"Alright," Bill's voice growing louder was a mental cold shower. Ella jerked away from Cal and they managed to look only mildly guilty when Bill, Missy, and Marjorie emerged from the kitchen. "I think we've got what we need and Mike will be back at the station with Clarence and our suspect." Bill paused in front of the couch and looked from Ella to Cal. "You two need a ride? We brought both golf carts over."

Ella shook her head. "No, I think we'll be fine. I . . ," she hesitated, trying to arrange her words in a way that would sound plausible to Bill. "I'll probably sit up at Cal's and make sure he gets to sleep ok. Missy says he'll need to change his bandages and he can't do it himself."

Bill's face stayed neutral except for the faintest hint of teasing in his eyes as he nodded at Ella. "I'll tell your mom so she won't worry." Ella thought she was in the clear and was about to breathe a sigh of relief. But then, Bill winked. She felt her face starting to burn and did her best to hide it by turning to look at Cal.

"We should go. They probably need to lock up Clarence's house." Something occurred to her and she frowned, turning back to look at Bill. "How did Tony get in here in the first place? We had to crawl in through a bathroom window."

Bill chuckled. "Clarence said that he went out his front door to get his groceries off his porch the last time they were delivered, and Tony showed up before he could get back inside and held his gun on him. So, he had to let him in."

Cal and Ella followed the others out and Bill locked the front door behind them.

"You know," Cal said as he and Ella waved and watched the dim lights of the two golf carts, trundling off toward the police station, "I normally love how much Islander is in you."

Ella turned to frown at him. Love?

"But," he said, turning to look at her, "maybe there's a *little* too much sometimes. Especially when there's a gun in play." He pulled Ella to him with his uninjured arm, wrapping it around her waist as he hugged her to his chest. Though unexpected, Ella definitely didn't mind. "When he had that gun on Clarence," Cal said softly, "and then you stood up . . . I was afraid he'd . . ." He shook his head and closed his eyes.

Ella hugged him gently, trying to be careful of his arm. "But he didn't shoot me, because of you." They were still for a moment, just holding each other. Ella closed her eyes, thinking of how hard she would have laughed if three weeks ago someone had told her that she would be here, in Cal's arms at this moment. She decided she didn't need anything for Christmas. Her arms were already full.

"What do you mean, 'how much Islander I have in me'," she muttered without opening her eyes.

"Oh El," Cal chuckled, moving his lips to brush against the bare skin on her neck. "You're an Islander, through and through. Just accept it."

She sighed, tipping her head to give him more access. The fire was burning in her belly again, moving lower and making her squeeze her thighs together. The cold breeze had become a wind, carrying the smell of the sea and evergreen across a clear and star-studded night. She smiled. And then the quiet night was broken by the warbling sound of the whale-fart horn. She and Cal both groaned as they separated.

"We should get you somewhere warm," Ella said, looking at Cal.

He searched her face. "Will you come with me? I mean, you heard the professionals. I can't be trusted to bandage myself."

Ella sighed. "I guess I'd feel kind of guilty if you somehow managed to hang yourself with an ace bandage." She threaded her arm around Cal's waist, and they started the walk back toward the square and Cal's apartment.

36

CAL

Cal could barely feel the stinging in his shoulder as he walked with Ella snuggled into his side. He was fairly certain an anvil could fall on his head in the next five minutes and he wouldn't notice as long as he could still feel Ella's warmth next to him. What a night. It felt like days packed into only a few hours. He'd finally kissed her. And it had been even more incredible than he'd imagined it would be. It had been sensory overload, for his body, but also for his mind. As they walked in comfortable silence back toward his apartment, not for the first time that night, his mind was flooded with the vision of Ella, growing older with him as they worked at the paper and watched the seasons change together on Hope. He subconsciously squeezed her shoulder where his hand was resting and she responded by tightening her hold around his waist.

"Well, that's one mystery solved," Ella said, as they reached the square. Cal looked down at her, momentarily confused. She nodded behind them. "Now we know the story on Clarence."

Cal nodded. "Yeah. I . . . didn't expect *that* story."

Ella shook her head. "Me either."

Cal groaned. "I can't believe I'm actually going to have to buy Dirk a beer."

"Do the whole town a favor," Ella said. "Don't tell him he was right. It'll have dire ramifications for the Dirk-ecosystem."

"Oh, come on," Cal said. "It wouldn't be that bad."

Ella paused and looked up at him. "You want to play newspaper tree to his sequoia *again* next year?"

Cal paused. "I do not." He felt Ella stiffen next to him. "What is it?"

"I guess . . . that's not something you'll have to worry about, is it?" Her voice was hollow.

Cal frowned. "Are you saying you're not going to strong arm me into being in the Parade of Trees next year?"

She turned to look at him. "You're not going to *be* here next year, are you?" It was a question, but it didn't sound like one. Either way, it cut Cal like a knife.

"What if I stayed?" Cal asked. He could hear the vulnerability he felt, coming out in his voice. "What if I didn't leave?"

Ella pulled away from him. He froze but started to relax when he saw the look on her face, illuminated by the lights from the old-fashioned lamp posts.

"You'd really stay?"

Cal had a hard time forming words as he took in the nervous, hopeful expression on her face. "Would you want me to?" he finally asked, his voice coming out as a whisper.

"Yes," she said softly.

Cal felt his heart picking up speed in his chest. "I already loved it here," he said. "Even before I met you. But now, with you here, I don't want to be anywhere else." He watched her face and he saw a reflection of everything that was battling inside of him; vulnerability, fear, desire, and something strong that he couldn't quite put a name to. But it didn't matter. Ella's lips were on his again and fire was traveling down his chest and further south. He groaned at the soft feel of her lips moving from his mouth to his chin and he stopped breathing when he felt her tongue tentatively lick his neck.

"We should get upstairs," he panted, barely recognizing his own voice. "I don't know about you, but I don't think what I'm feeling should be happening just feet away from the Girl Scouts' holiday safety display." He felt his eyes roll back in his head as the sensation of Ella's lips on his collarbone reached him in his haze of desire.

"That display is also only feet away from Miss Mandie's. I doubt we'll be the crushing blow to its innocence," she mumbled. But, with a final flick of her tongue, she stepped back and held her hand out to Cal. They couldn't get up the stairs fast enough. In the security light outside the door to his apartment, he paused to look at her. Not for the first time, he stood in awe of the woman in front of him. Over the previous weeks, he'd seen; disheveled Ella, sweatpants and relaxed Ella, stressed and professional Ella, scotch-drinking Ella, vulnerable and drunk Ella, and brave Ella. Now, he was being treated to yet another facet of her and he felt the privilege, wondering how many people had ever gotten the chance to see the aroused and incredibly beautiful side of Ella Danforth that he was now staring at.

She raised an eyebrow at him and smiled. "Are there keys? Or is there a secret knock?"

"A secret knock? So what, the taxidermy trout bouncer can let us in?" Cal asked.

She shrugged. "I don't know. I don't remember how you magicked your apartment door open last time." Cal dug his keys out of his pocket and fumbled with the knob. Ella followed him inside and he flicked the lights on. The fact that at least a third of his apartment was taken up with the queen-sized bed immediately made the energy in the room shift. Ella took a step away from him and turned to look at the stuffed trout mounted on the wall next to the door. Cal tried to tamp down the arousal that had been threatening to overpower him seconds before. They'd *just* kissed, only hours before and already he was thinking . . .

"Do you want some tea?" Cal asked, realizing how pathetic it sounded after the words had already left him.

"I'm good," Ella said. He could feel the same nervous energy in her voice that was slowly replacing the overwhelming desire in him.

"El," Cal said, fear almost choking him before he could say her name. She turned to look at him, her emotions raw on her face. She was nervous and hesitant, but her eyes were still dark and he could see her tongue worrying the inside of her cheek. "I know we just kissed tonight, and this is all happening, really, *really* fast, but . . ."

She slowly shook her head. "It doesn't feel fast." She closed her eyes and he recognized the body language of someone steeling themselves to say something that would leave them vulnerable. "I've wanted to kiss you and . . . you know, I've thought about . . . you, for a while now."

Cal felt relief rush through him, bringing an easy smile. "Me too."

That seemed to put her more at ease. She crossed the room and stood in front of him. "May I?" she asked, running a finger under the edge of his jacket. Cal could only nod. He wasn't sure what it said about his past relationships, but, no one had ever looked at him with as much heat as Ella was at that moment. She eased the coat off his shoulders and bit her lip when she looked at the blood-stained fabric of his shirt where it was stretched across his shoulder, bulging over the bandages. "Your shoulder. I'm sorry. I should just . . ."

"Shhh," Cal said softly. "I'm fine."

She frowned, keeping her eyes on the wound. "We might need to change the bandages. I can see some blood coming through." Cal had to focus on his breathing as her long, slender and slightly cold fingers teased the skin on his chest as she unbuttoned his shirt and helped it off his shoulders. He wasn't shy about his body, but the thought of Ella seeing him without his shirt, made him hold his breath until he saw her pupils dilate and the pleased, but embarrassed smile on her face. His heart was already beating so fast that when he felt her fingers on his bare skin, he had to bite down on his tongue to keep from moaning again. She was so gentle as she changed the bandage on his arm. He glanced over at the wound. There was a dark bruise starting to form around the nickel-sized section of torn flesh. It was throbbing in time with his pounding heart, but the pain was registering as minor in his brain, especially compared to the other sensations gently assaulting him.

"There," Ella said with a sigh, as she finished with his bandages. She pushed a loose piece of hair behind her ear and smiled at Cal. Her cheeks were pink. "Whew, it's hot in here." She slid off her jacket, leaving her standing before him in her black scoop-necked t-shirt, dark jeans, and Chuck Taylors. Cal's eyes traveled from her smiling face and the wicked half-grin on her lips to her long neck, downward, feeling his body reigniting. "What?" Ella asked after a moment of silence.

"You're beautiful," Cal said before he could think about the words pouring out of him. Inside his head, Chill Cal had knocked out Killjoy Cal, at least for the moment. He heard her breath deep before taking a step closer to him. He could feel goosebumps forming on his exposed skin and he tried to keep his breathing steady, even as she drew so close that he could feel her warm breath stirring the hairs on his chest.

"Funny," she whispered. "I was thinking the same thing about you."

"I really want to kiss you again," Cal breathed.

"I thought you'd never ask." Ella's voice went up an octave on her last word as Cal lowered his lips to the curve of her neck. God, she was addictive. And the more he kissed her, the more he wanted to. She was the sea and he was a shipwrecked sailor, drinking from her desperately, but instead of being sated, he only wanted more. Ella's hands were exploring his chest and when their lips broke apart, her lips followed her hands. He couldn't control the noises he was making. It had been so long since he'd felt so connected to someone and *wanted* someone so badly. But, something important, something from Killjoy Cal's corner of his brain was fighting its way to the surface. When it hit him, he pulled back, holding Ella by her shoulders to put enough space between them for his brain to work. Her eyes were wide and the scared, stung expression on her face at the interruption almost broke his resolve.

"El," he breathed, trying to get his heart rate to slow down enough to stop pumping all his blood south. "We just kissed tonight, for the first time." She bit her lip and looked down. He had to make her understand what he was feeling. "Don't get me wrong. *I'm* completely here for this." He squeezed her shoulders. "I've . . . for weeks been thinking about you . . . like this." She raised her head to meet his gaze again and her expression was starting to shift to playful. "But," he forced himself to continue, "I completely understand if you aren't . . ."

"Ready?" she asked.

"Right," Cal said.

Ella shook her head slowly, the wicked smile on her face widening. "No, I'm asking if you're ready."

And then, she reached down and slowly pulled her shirt over her head. Cal swore he heard his heart flatline, as his gaze fell to Ella's breasts, encased in black silk.

"Now," Ella's voice wavered and he jerked his gaze up to meet hers. She was still smiling, but there was an edge of nerves, pinching the corners of her eyes. "Full disclosure, it's been... awhile for me."

"Me too," Cal said. Then, the real ramifications of that fact hit him and it was his turn to feel nervous. "It's been a pretty long time for me."

She bit her lip and took another deep breath. "And Cal, also in full disclosure . . . I don't do one-night stands."

Cal wasn't sure if he'd ever heard more reassuring or comforting words. "Neither do I." He reached for her and his senses became too overwhelmed for thinking or analyzing. It was sensory overload before they'd even shed all their clothes.

"Protection?" he whispered.

"We're covered," she moaned as his lips returned to her throat and began moving south. He'd never made love with so much emotion coursing through him before. He was in awe of Ella Danforth. Not because she was physical perfection or some kind of goddess to be worshiped. It was because she was supremely *real* and he could feel the emotions rolling through her to meet his with every sound and whisper that got louder and louder as the sweat rolled down his chest as he tried to suppress the inevitable.

"El, I'm not going to last . . ."

"Filing," she moaned.

"What?" he panted.

"Filing, just think of filing, that's the only way I'm holding on."

"Filing," Cal growled.

"All those stupid papers strewn all over my office that I'm going to have to pick up. It's the only thing that's . . ." she moaned. "But you're not making it easy to concentrate on filing."

Cal grinned. "I'd be disappointed if I was." He leaned forward and kissed her, their tongues caressing the inside of each other's mouths. He tried to think of filing. But, Clarence's hoarding tendencies couldn't drag his attention away from the amazing creature moving under him. She wrapped her legs around him and he knew he wouldn't be able to keep holding on.

"Cum with me, Ella," he breathed. As if she'd been waiting for him to say it, she moaned and he felt her clench around him. Bliss exploded from inside him and he clung to her, smoothing her loose hair away to plant kisses on her cheeks, nose and forehead.

"Wow," Ella panted.

"Wow," Cal agreed. He moved to lay beside her and she arranged the pillows so his shoulder was protected and they drifted to sleep, Cal holding her against him. A funny thought occurred to him just before he slipped into blackness. It was odd and brought with it a ragged realization that almost made him gasp in joy. His eyes stung and he felt a tear roll down his cheek as he turned his face, burying his nose in Ella's hair. For the first time in his life, Cal felt like he was home.

He drifted off, vaguely aware of a rhythmic buzzing somewhere in his apartment.

* * *

ELLA

Ella was awakened by an air raid. Once she'd blinked herself awake and remembered she wasn't living through World War II, she turned her attention to the obnoxious digital alarm clock on Cal's bedside table. She was about to reach out to unplug it when a long, lean arm, reached past her and smacked the top of it. She shivered and drew a shaky breath, feeling warm skin against her back.

"Morning," Cal mumbled.

Ella turned to look at him, smiling. She vaguely remembered worrying as she fell asleep in his arms that she hoped her brain wouldn't be a jerk and make her regret this in the morning. Well, it was morning. And she didn't regret it. She could see tension in Cal's face and she frowned. "Does your arm hurt?"

Cal glanced at his shoulder and then back at her, shaking his head. "No, I mean, it's a little sore, but . . ." The flash of vulnerability on his face melted Ella's heart. "I just . . . I hope you don't . . . Last night was . . ."

"Last night was amazing," Ella said, leaning forward and kissing the end of his nose. "And I would request an encore right now if I could." She sighed and turned her head to look at the alarm clock for the time, rather than how many ways she could destroy it. "Unfortunately, we're due at the office and I'm pretty sure we'll each have more than a dozen stories to cover today. Let alone the bonfire write-up from last night." She put a hand to her forehead and turned to look at Cal. "And then there's what to do about the story of Clarence and Tony Sanetti."

Cal rested a hand on the side of her face, running his thumb over her cheek. "I say we sit on it until after Christmas day."

Ella nodded, a naughty thrill running through her at the realization that she was talking journalism and paper business with Cal while they were both naked with their legs entwined under his comforter. "I agree," she said. "It's not like it will do much for the holiday tourism."

Cal blinked at her. "Oh, yeah. I was mostly thinking of the fact that there wouldn't be room in the layout with everything we already have to cover."

"Also true," Ella said. She sighed and looked around the room. "Why can't time stop when you're comfy in bed?"

"I don't know," Cal said, his voice muffled as he started kissing his way down her neck, "but it's ridiculously inconvenient that it doesn't."

They finally made their way out of bed, and Ella pulled on her clothes from the night before. "I need to run home and shower. But I still need to print out the notes for today."

Cal nodded. "Well, I'm going to take a shower and if you'll email it to me, I'll head over and print out the notes so we'll be ready for the team huddle-up when you get there."

"Really?" she asked.

"Of course," Cal said.

Too fast, they were dressed, and he was walking Ella to the door. She paused, chewing on her lip as she thought.

"What should we say about . . . us? I mean, to . . . people?"

Cal smiled. "You mean to Maddie and Pippa?"

Ella sighed. "I'm terrible at hiding things. They always, *always* figure it out. I just . . . I don't want to say anything that would make you uncomfortable."

"Ella," Cal said. "Nothing about this is uncomfortable to me. It's actually uncomfortably comfortable." He paused and frowned. "If that's a thing."

She kissed him, hard. And he wrapped his arms around her. It was another minute or two before Helga, yelling in her ear about being late, forced them apart. She took the stairs two at a time and started power-walking across the square toward home. She was surprised to realize that it wasn't because she was embarrassed or worried that someone would see her leaving Cal's apartment. It was because she wanted to shower and get back to the office to see him again. To write articles with him and discuss assignments, tease Maddie and Pippa with him . . . To do it all with him.

Her mom was in the kitchen, but she didn't grill Ella when she bounced in and headed up the stairs, after yelling a hurried "good morning" to her. She showered, doing her best to try to keep the fog and thoughts of showering with *Cal* at bay. She dressed and met her mom as she came back down the stairs.

"You feel like breakfast?" her mom asked, smiling. Ella studied her. Her mom wasn't smiling like she was gearing up for an interrogation. It was just a happy smile.

"Actually," Ella said, an idea coming to her. "I think I'll grab something at Miss Mandie's. I need to pick up the paper's daily box of donuts anyway."

Helen nodded. "Very good. Only a few more days until Christmas!" She wrapped Ella's red scarf around her neck and kissed her forehead. Ella pecked her on the cheek and headed back out. She felt giddy, like a kid on the first day of summer, walking on clouds as she navigated the quickly filling square with the first ferry-load of tourists for the day. She rolled through the door of De-Floured and joined the line for the bakery counter.

"Morning, Madam Editor," Miss Mandie smiled when she saw Ella. "Here for the paper's box?"

"And . . . two of those cinnamon hazelnut coffees," Ella said, thinking of Cal. She thought about getting more for the whole crew, but she wasn't sure how they'd feel about cinnamon hazelnut. She *knew* Cal liked it. She was still on the fence, wondering if she should cancel the coffees, considering what the other staff members might say. She looked at the line behind her which was now twice as long as it had been when she'd joined it. The woman waiting to be served right after her looked like Seattle upper-crust. She was wearing a tailored white suit, gold jewelry and sunglasses on her head that were probably worth two years of Ella's salary at the *Hornblower*.

"Here you go, sweet thing," Miss Mandie said, setting the donut box and coffee carrier on the counter. Ella swiped her card quickly and scooted down the counter so Miss Mandie could serve the woman while she tried to maneuver the coffee carrier and box into her arms.

"What can I get you?" Miss Mandie asked her.

"Oh, I don't . . . want anything," the woman's voice was polite, but more formal than the usual tourist on Hope. "I'm looking for someone and I'm wondering if you can help me."

"I'll help you if I can," Miss Mandie said. Ella didn't miss the subtle sarcasm in the older woman's tone.

Ella got the box of donuts settled into the crook of one arm and was working on inching the drink carrier off the counter and into her other, when the woman said, "I'm looking for Callum Dickson."

Ella paused and looked over at the woman. Miss Mandie was frowning. "Do you mean Cal?"

The woman in white looked annoyed and tossed her long black hair over one shoulder. "I suppose. His full name is Callum."

Miss Mandie frowned, looking less and less impressed with the woman. "And just who is looking for him?"

The woman crossed her arms. "His fiancé."

37

ELLA

The coffee carrier slipped off Ella's arm and crashed to the floor. When they hit the ground, the lids popped off of the cups and the hot liquid sprayed her legs, soaking through her jeans and burning her skin. But the burning pain in her legs was nothing compared to what was happening in her chest.

"Whoa there, Cranberry Sauce," Bart's voice echoed in Ella's head. "Did you burn yourself? I've been telling Miss Mandie we need to get the carriers with the handle instead of these flat ones. They're just not sturdy enough."

Ella needed to get out of there. There were too many thoughts, too many emotions, too many people. She set the donuts down on the tray table next to the trash can and bent down to scoop up the coffee cups and carrier. She dumped them into the can as Bart wheeled the mop bucket over. "Don't worry, I've got this," he said. He kept talking but Ella's heart had started beating again and it was now pounding in her ears as she tried to force herself to not look at the woman in white who had been watching Ella's coffee-redecorating demonstration.

"You ok, El?" Miss Mandie had left the woman and come down the bakery counter to stand in front of her. Ella nodded quickly. Now her fear was that Miss Mandie would mention that Cal worked with Ella and she'd have to talk to this woman. She just needed to get out of there.

She scooped up the donuts. "Sorry about the mess, Bart," she muttered before nodding at Miss Mandie. She put her head down and used the donut box to help clear a path for her through the waiting line. The cold breeze on her face helped, but she was still surrounded by people as they hurried around the square from shop to shop, from event to event. The Helga part of her brain was frozen in place, mid-to-do-list. Numb Ella was waiting in the wings with Sarcastic Ella, but for the moment, they were speechless. What was going on? His fiancé? Was she lying? Or had *Cal* lied to *Ella?* What if he *was* engaged? She thought of Clarence. He'd come to Hope, running from something . . . a sick, cold feeling slid into her stomach. What if Cal had done the same thing? But, if he *was* engaged, why hadn't he told her? A vision of Les and Wendi, framed in her apartment door, her arms around him. Ella froze, ignoring the annoyed mutters of the tourists that bumped into her. As they streamed around her, Ella tried to get a handle on the horror and anger swirling inside her. Was *she* Cal's Wendi?

She needed to see him. She needed to see his face and have him tell her the woman was wrong. She needed to hear that she *wasn't* his Wendi.

* * *

CAL

Cal couldn't get the stupid smile off his face. He couldn't remember a time when showering in the tiny box shower had ever felt so good. The worn out thrift-store sweater he'd picked up that fall had never felt softer and the walk across the square had an extra layer of freeing ecstasy than it usually did. He was looking around it, imagining being able to look at it every day for the next forty years of his life. He imagined being old and walking around the square, hand in hand with Ella. The thought was a little unnerving. The future had always depressed Cal while he was growing up. As soon as he learned that the "you can grow up to be anything you want" speech was for all the other kids, he hadn't had a lot of enthusiasm for getting older. But now . . . It almost knocked the air out of him when he stopped to really think about the last twenty-four hours. Twenty-four hours ago, it had been a normal day. He'd of course, done the same friendly dance around Ella that he'd been doing for the last week and a half. Then, Tony had stood her up at the bonfire, they'd kissed, and everything had changed. He paused in his thoughts, waiting for Killjoy Cal to pipe in his two cents and let him have it about the fact that he was moving too fast. *I'll wait.* No Killjoy Cal. He couldn't be entirely sure, but he guessed it was possible that Killjoy Cal was currently too distracted by the infrequent cloud of euphoria coursing through him to rain on his parade.

He strolled into the office, smiling.

"What are you so happy about?" Pippa muttered. Cal paused and looked from one employee face to the next. Everyone was wearing their coats and as the stiff breeze rolled over him, he understood why. Oh. He moved around the partition to look at the window that was shattered the night before. The police had screwed a sheet of plywood over the hole, but it was an inch too narrow, allowing for cold air to roll into the room under it.

"Oh good," Cal said, looking at his chair. "Right at neck level."

"So spill," Maddie said. "What really happened last night?"

Cal turned to look at her, feeling his heart pounding in his chest. What did she know? Maddie gestured at the window, looking at him like he was an idiot. "Myrna said you were here after the break in."

"Oh, yeah," Cal said.

"So?" Pippa asked. "What did they take?"

Cal shrugged. "We don't know. We looked around and it didn't seem like anything important was taken . . ."

"Wait," Maddie said. "Where's El?"

Cal could feel the heat rising in his face. He tried to shrug and glance at her office as if he was just a polite coworker, mildly interested in where the boss might be. Of course, even from where he stood, he could see the papers scattered across her office floor and the phrase "filing" floated through his mind bringing with it the memory from the night before. The room was suddenly too warm, despite the cold breeze that was making the others hunker down in their coats.

"I don't know," Cal said, hoping his tone wouldn't draw any attention, especially from Maddie or Pippa. "I'm sure she's probably on her way in."

Maddie's cell phone started to ring, and she looked at the screen and rolled her eyes. "Oh good, Gladys. Can this morning get any better?"

"Pippa?" Kurt's voice called from the hallway. "I found the shipping form, but the part listed on it isn't the part we got. You have a second to come look at it?"

"Coming," Pippa said. She slid her gaze to Cal for a moment, a tiny frown forming on her face. Cal started to sweat. But, she didn't say anything. Instead, she turned and headed for the hallway.

"Well, until Ella gets here, I've got a couple of advertisers to call," Marty said.

"And I have a carrier to ream out," Katie muttered, scrolling on her phone. "Apparently, he forgot the newspapers when he went out to deliver them."

The office was suddenly filled with overlapping conversations, accentuated by puffs of fog as the employees wrapped more layers around themselves and clutched their phones to their ears.

The landline phone for the office started to ring.

Cal set his messenger bag down on his desk, thankful for the cold breeze that would do a lot in helping him keep a lid on his body's reaction around Ella. Even if he couldn't control the thoughts in his head.

"Cal, can you get that?" Maddie called from the front part of the office. "The rest of us are either chewing ass or having our asses chewed at the moment. We're kind of busy."

"Uh, sure," Cal said. He moved over to the cordless phone extension in the middle of the office. *"Hope Hornblower,"* he said, momentarily panicking and trying to remember what Pippa and Maddie always said when they answered the landline phone.

"Oh good! I tell you, you lose one resume and it's like letting go of a balloon in the park and watching your perfect employee float away!" a woman's flustered voice chittered in his ear.

"Uh, what can I do for you?" Cal asked. Of course, the first time he answered the phone, it would be someone like this.

"Oh, sorry, yeah, my boss is just really peeved because I misplaced her resume and she wants to hire her. Well, have her come for an interview, but mostly, so she can meet her, and hire her on the spot. Because, oh man, after seeing everything you all do out there on the island, she will be *perfect* for our publication."

"Who?" Cal asked, frowning.

"Oh, didn't I say?" The woman's laugh was manic. "I'm so sorry. Too much coffee. Or not enough. I'm not sure. Sorry, this is Maisie Little from *Seattle Center Community Weekly*. I'm calling because Ella Danforth applied to be our lead community reporter. And we've just got to have her. Like, now. I mean, as soon as we can. Her cover letter sounded like her bags were already packed, so I'm hoping we can snap her up before anyone else gets her. But, because I lost her resume, the only thing I could remember was that she was currently the editor at this *Hope Hornblower*. It's such an odd name. I mean, how did the paper get that name anyway? Oh well, doesn't matter. Can I talk to her?"

Cal felt numb. Ella had applied for jobs in Seattle? She really was leaving. Had she lied to him last night? Why? The image of growing old, working at the paper with her, and going to all the holiday events together, began to implode.

"So is she available?" the woman chirped in his ear.

"Uh, she's not in yet," Cal said.

"Oh, well I'll give you my number, and please have her call me as soon as she arrives!"

Cal scratched down the number and hung up. He stared down at the green sticky note in his hand and he felt his heart sinking into his gut.

What had he done? If the night before hadn't happened, he wouldn't be feeling like he'd just been punched in the gut, would he? He tried to imagine how he would feel if he'd taken that phone call three weeks ago. Would he be excited? Yes. Because he would have been excited for the paper to go back to the way it was before Ella had arrived. But, over the last three weeks, he'd started to understand that as much as he loved the paper and the people in this small town, he was never going to be better at the job than Ella. It needed her. And, in a quieter internal voice, hoping that Killjoy

Cal wouldn't hear it and then punish him for it, he knew that *he* needed her. Ella Danforth *was* the Island, no matter how much she would disagree if he tried to tell her that. She was independent and nosy, ruled by her heart, loving but not naive. And the way he'd clung to the island, he'd clung to her. But now, in the harsh light of day and with the beginnings of tinnitus giving him a headache, caused by the voice of Maisie Little, still ringing in his ears, he felt like a fool. His father had always told him growing up that he was too much of an idealist and that it would bite him one day.

He slumped down in his chair and stared at her empty office, papered with the years of hoarded layouts and articles and clippings and general paperwork. His face felt numb. He'd thought Hope was an oasis, perfect, and genuine. But, how could it be now if the woman who personified the island to him, wasn't what she appeared to be. Anger and defeat swirled inside him as he waited for the sound of the bell jingling over the front door and to hear the familiar steps of Ella Danforth.

38

ELLA

The jingle over the office's front door was a little too upbeat for Ella at the moment. As she trekked across the square, her anger had slowly boiled away, leaving her hollow. She kept hoping that Numb Ella would step up to the plate and wrap her in the same defensive shield that she put around Ella when she found Les and Wendi, but Numb Ella was nowhere to be found. As hollow as she felt, she was holding on moment to moment, fighting down the knot in her throat and willing the stinging in her eyes to stop. The office was busy when she walked in. Maddie, Katie, and Marty were on their phones and Pippa wasn't at her desk. She had a brief moment of relief, thinking maybe Cal had run into his fiancé and just left, disappeared with her. Then, maybe Ella could just pretend that he'd never been there.

The moment ended when she got to her office door and came eye-to-eye with Cal. He just looked at her, stone-faced. "I need to talk to you." There was no warmth in his voice and she didn't expect any. Was he going to try to explain? Had someone already called to tell him that his fiancé was in town? That was stupid. She was his fiancé. Of course he already knew she was in town.

"Yeah," Ella said. She could hear the ice in her own voice. "Me too." The overlapping, muffled conversations of the others reminded her that they were not in a good physical location to have their argument out. She looked around, unable to fully look at him. He was showered and his hair was disheveled, and he smelled like he always did. The pain in her chest for what had been lost before it had really been something in the first place, almost took her breath away as she said, "Break room?" She forced herself to look at him in time to see his nod before she turned and headed down the hallway, not bothering to look behind her to see if he was following.

Ella marched across the room to stand by the far wall, facing away from him. *Please universe, if you get me through this without crying, I'll . . . stop cussing so much. Just please, don't let me cry in front of him.*

She heard him close the break room door behind them, but she didn't turn around. For a moment, they were both quiet, listening to each other breathe.

"So," Cal finally said, his voice cracking on the word. "Is there something you want to tell me?"

Ella frowned at the wall. Was he going to try to act like this was *her* fault? Like Les had?

"I don't know what you're talking about," Ella said. Maybe if she played dumb, he'd be forced to start the fight.

"I just got off the phone with Maisie Little," Cal said.

Ella frowned. "Who?" She turned to look at him.

He was leaning against the counter next to the coffee machine and she could see he was gripping the edge with both hands. It could have been in anger, but the look on his face was puzzling her. He was angry, but there was something else there. Anxiety? Fear?

"Apparently, she works for the *Seattle Center Community Weekly*," Cal said. Ella could feel his eyes on her as she looked down at his knees, thinking. Was that . . ? And then she remembered. One of the last resumes and applications she'd sent off, over three weeks ago.

"Why did she call here?" Ella asked, frowning. Usually, they emailed to tell her they weren't interested.

"Apparently she lost your resume," Cal's voice was growing quieter, but she could see his anger rising in his face. "But she remembered you worked for the *Hornblower*. They want to hire you. Congratulations." Ella didn't know what to say. As she'd fallen asleep in his arms the night before, she'd been relieved to think that she wouldn't need to send out any more resumes or applications or receive any more rejections. It was a small perk, compared to being able to work with Cal during the day, and spend her nights *not* working, but with him. It had been a dream built on a lie, and this was the harsh light of day, kicking her in the ass. The universe must have seen it coming and decided to give her a way out.

"Uh, did she leave a number for me to call her?" Ella asked, before her brain could vet the question.

Cal shook his head. "I'm such an idiot."

Ella frowned at him. "What? Why?"

"To think you were serious about wanting to stay here with the paper . . . with me."

Ella felt like he'd slapped her. "I *was* serious."

His eyes shot up to meet hers. "And yet, you were planning to leave all along. I'm curious, if you'd answered the phone, how long would it have taken for you to tell me you were leaving? Would you have strung me along through the holidays? New Years? Or would you have just disappeared one day and left a note?" He shook his head. "I can't believe how much I was trusting you."

The anger was back, raging through Ella as she listened to him, but there was a full minute of flared-nostril, heavy-breathing, silence before she could find the words.

"You want to talk about trust?" Ella was having a hard time controlling the volume of her voice, but she really didn't want an audience for this humiliating conversation, so she paused to take a breath and try to lower her voice. Cal looked livid. He crossed his arms and glared at her, looking like there was nothing she could say that would change his belief that *she* was the one that couldn't be trusted. "I just bumped into your fiancé at the bakery."

That did it. Cal blinked at her and then she watched as his face ran a full gamut of emotion; confusion, followed by disbelief and then horror. "What?! Tara's *here!?*"

Ella felt the dam starting to break inside her. "Apparently," she ground out, internally demanding that Numb Ella get her ass in the command chair and under no circumstances, let her cry in front of Cal. "Though, I didn't know her name."

Cal's face was back to disbelief. "And why do you think she's my fiancé?"

Ella bit down on her tongue, hoping the pain would throw some extra fuel on the fire and force the tears back behind her eyes. "Because she said so." She paused, remembering what the woman had said was Cal's full name. Ella hadn't even known that about Cal and she'd kissed him, jumped into bed with him. *Way to go, El. You're batting five thousand in the 'good decision-making' area.* "Callum," Ella said.

Cal's face clouded over, anger turning his eyes dark and his cheeks red. He glared at the floor and shook his head. Ella silently counted to ten, trying to breathe and hold everything in. When he didn't say anything else, Ella heard the warning bell in her head moments before the anger erupted out of her like lava, like soul vomit.

"Nothing else to say?" She paused. He just kept glaring at the floor. "You know, I'm curious, how long were *you* planning on yanking me along when the entire time, you were *engaged* to someone else? You made me be your side-play. You made me an accomplice in the same thing I had to go through less than a month ago." She squeezed her eyes shut and shook her head. "And *I'm* the idiot for falling . . ." she paused, as all the voices in her head screamed, *"No!! Don't say it!"* She took a breath. She wouldn't. She didn't want him to see her that vulnerable ever again and she didn't want to hear out loud how pathetic the truth was.

"It's not what you think," Cal muttered.

Ella looked at him, but she was having a hard time processing what he'd said. "What do you mean, 'it's not what you think'? Is she your fiancé?"

He groaned and put his head in his hands. "Technically."

"Then honey, it *is* what I think," Ella moved around the room toward the door.

"Ella, wait," Cal's voice was pleading as she reached for the doorknob. Her bravado was the only thing holding her together at the moment. He paused beside her, reaching out with his hands, but stopping before they touched her. "Please. Please look at me." His voice cracked and the desperation in his tone made her think of the day she'd eavesdropped on him begging Mrs. Bumble to let Ella off the hook. She forced herself to look at him and was momentarily distracted when she looked in his eyes. She could see the shine of tears, threatening to spill out any second. He was practically shaking, his hands still held out as if he'd been reaching out to draw her to him, but lost the courage halfway and just stayed in that pose.

"It's... it's like an arranged marriage. My family and hers have *wanted* us to get married for years. It's all a part of this plan that they have for us, to merge the companies and then run this big media empire." Cal shook his head. "I ran away from all of it six months ago." Ella didn't say anything. She couldn't decide if she believed him or if this was the punchline of the joke being on her; something he and his fiancé and his New York friends would laugh at, over pizza and beer. "So, when I ran, I came here. I've been..."

"Hiding?" Ella asked, her voice hollow.

"I guess that's the word," Cal said, dropping his arms to his sides and his gaze to the ground. "I was just hoping it would go away. And I could live the life I wanted instead of the one I was destined for."

There was a knock on the break room door and Maddie stuck her head in. She was still bundled in her jacket and her look of annoyed confusion turned to apprehension when she looked from Ella to Cal. "S-sorry to interrupt... but, there's someone here for Cal. Though, I'm not entirely *sure* she's here for you. She says she's looking for Callum Dickson."

Ella watched Cal's face as he closed his eyes, looking like a man on his way to the gallows. She wanted to say something to him. To tell him to ditch his fiancé, stay in Hope, stay with her. But she couldn't form the words. She was having a hard enough time wrapping her head around everything she hadn't known about Cal Dickson before she slept with him, and everything she knew now. Maddie backed out of the room, leaving the door open.

"Ella, I..." Cal started to say.

"There you are!" The woman in the white suit strolled into view. "For a tiny, kitschy town, that took way too long to find you." The woman wrapped her arms around Cal's neck and pulled him down toward her chest. "Oh, I missed you. You know, I actually think you've gotten taller since I last saw you. Must be all the trees and . . . mountain-people out here. I wonder if it's confusing for them when they remember they're on an island."

Ella felt Sarcastic El lining up the woman in her sights. "Oh, all the time," Ella said. "But the city people that come for a visit get confused when they have to do something like *walking*, so somehow, we all just muddle through."

The woman gave Ella an appraising look and then her face twisted into a smile that was all lips and blindingly white teeth, with no warmth behind it. "Oh, didn't I see you in the bakery? Dropping coffees? I didn't know this town was big enough to have a coffee delivery service. I mean, that must be why you're here."

"Ella is the editor of the paper," Cal said.

The woman's eyebrows almost disappeared under her hairline. "Really? She's the editor?"

"Ella, this is Tara Rhineholt."

"Callum's fiancé," the woman said, holding out her hand to Ella. She couldn't decide if the woman was waiting for Ella to shake it or kiss it. Ella just nodded at the woman.

"Nice to meet you." Sarcastic El was doing all she could to join forces with Numb Ella to keep her together while Helga reviewed maps and charts and drew formulas on a grease board. She needed to leave the room. Tara's arms were still around Cal and though he looked unhappy, he wasn't doing anything to dissuade her. "If you'll both excuse me, I've got a meeting to run." She forced herself not to look at Cal as she put one foot in front of the other and moved out of the break room and down the hall.

The room was cold, thanks to the poorly patched broken window. She made a mental note to call Myrna about when the window would be replaced. *That's good.* Numb Ella said. *Just think about paper business. Not* about Cal or what happened last night or how he's in the next room with his fiancé. Ella's eyes burned. *No. You're not going to cry. Not right now.* She had a fleeting vision of herself being able to scream into her bathwater and she held onto that thought. She still had work to do and, as a silver lining, she wouldn't have to tell Maddie or Pippa about what had happened the night before and why she couldn't stop smiling. *No! Abort! Don't start thinking about that!* At the moment, Ella wasn't convinced that she'd ever smile again.

"El? Everything ok?" Maddie called to her. Ella turned to look at Maddie and Pippa standing together by Maddie's desk.

"Yeah," Ella said, forcing the bravado armor to close around her before cinching it tight. No vulnerabilities showing. "Give me a minute to print out the notes for the day and we can get into our huddle up."

"What about Cal?" Pippa asked, nodding toward the hallway.

Ella took a shaky breath. "I don't know that he'll be joining us at the meeting." Without waiting for a reply from them, she turned on her heel and waded into her office, kicking aside paperwork until she could get the door closed. She wanted to break then. She wanted to cry and scream and throw things and then curl into a ball and just become another piece of paper in Clarence's mess.

But you're not going to, Helga said, pushing the other two out of her way and sitting down in the command chair. *You're going to march over to your desk, print off seven . . . no six copies of the notes for the day and then you're going to go out there and run the meeting. And then, with all your assignments, you won't have any time left to think about . . . him.*

She put a hand on the edge of Clarence's desk to steady herself, and then she set down her bag and pulled out her laptop. Helga did a good job of keeping her mechanically moving forward, despite every fiber of her being wanting to go back to yesterday, when everything was good, and nothing hurt.

39

CAL

Cal was in hell. Not "waxing poetic hell", absolute hell. It was the circle of hell where consequences came home to roost. So, probably the lobby. He'd thought he could out bluff them, for just a few more weeks, but as Tara talked on and on about how she'd just had this psychic connection to him the night before and knew he needed her, he realized that the universe was punishing him early. He knew he should have never kept the facts from Ella. He'd just thought he'd have more time to figure things out before he told her about all the baggage he carried with him.

"And you mom has arranged for our engagement party to be on Christmas Eve. Technically, it'll be in the afternoon, but still, I think it'll be a nice pre-Christmas opportunity to do the glad-handing and the pictures for the media, and . . ."

"I don't want to get married," Cal said. He wanted to add, "to you", but the thought of having the huge screaming match that he knew would follow, here in the break room of the paper that he loved, kept it quiet.

"It's not like I'm a hundred percent sold on the idea either, but Callum, our parents, our families and friends, are all *expecting* it. And we can't just blow that up. You have responsibilities, I have responsibilities. We just have to adult-up and do it." Cal didn't say anything. At that moment, he wished the night before had been his last on earth. He could have died happy, content, with everything he wanted. "Now, I have us on a one o'clock flight back to LaGuardia Airport and then . . ."

"I don't want to go," Cal said.

Tara closed her eyes and pinched her lips together as if she was trying to force herself to be patient. "Callum, it's not about what you want anymore. You ran out here for half a year, leaving me to bear the entire weight of everything in New York. I was patient and I let you do . . ." She looked around at the break room warily, "whatever it was you needed to do out here. But now, it's time to go home and get on with our lives. We're taking the one o'clock flight. Your dad is sending a car for us when we land. And then there's a dinner tonight that we'll probably be late to. And tomorrow is final preparations for this last-minute party, thanks to you being out here, and then it's Christmas Eve."

"I'm not going," Cal said, his voice stronger, though Killjoy Cal and Chill Cal were holding each other and shaking, waiting for Tara to go full-Banshee.

"You're going," Tara said. She opened her arms and glared at him. "You don't belong here. You know that. I can see it in your eyes. You're not one of these island-people. You're a New Yorker and a member of one of the most influential families on the east coast. My god, you're the heir to that family. If you want to play cub reporter- His Girl Friday after we get married, then fine. We'll figure that out. But *this* isn't your home. Your home is with me and your family and our friends. Now let's go. The floating barge thing leaves in twenty minutes. I've already talked to that erotic cake woman about having your stuff shipped to New York." Tara shook her head. "And if the apartment you rented from her is anything like *her*, you might as well call her on the way to the airport and just have her burn whatever you left behind."

Cal felt hollow. He wanted to tell her no, to stay, to beg Ella to forgive him, but the thought of all the fallout from doing that stopped him. The thought of a shouting match with Tara in front of the rest of the *Hornblower* staff whom he'd come to think of as friends. To have his last memory of this place be one with screaming, as they all looked on, wasn't how he wanted to think about his time in Hope. A tiny part of him knew there was always a very, very slim chance that he'd get to stay on the island, but he hadn't been prepared for the raw pain that ripped through him as he followed Tara down the hallway and through the office. Everyone was at their desks and he didn't see Ella. He wanted to say goodbye to all of them, but he didn't have the words, or, if he was being truthful, the courage. He was being led away from his paradise like a kid getting picked up from school by his mother.

As much as he wanted to, he knew that if he said *anything* to them, they'd ask questions and then he'd have to explain . . . everything to them. He'd have to tell them who Tara was and she'd be awful to them and it would all lead to the screaming he was so desperate to avoid. So, instead, he was leaving without saying goodbye, the same way he left New York. There one moment, gone another. He dragged his feet, holding onto the strap of his messenger bag with both hands as he looked around the town square, poised to pounce on Christmas. The wind was picking up, making the tourists hold onto their hats and burrow deeper into their coats and scarves. They turned away from Tara and Cal as they moved through the square. He knew they were turning away from the wind which was blowing him toward the footpath to the ferry, but it felt symbolic and he couldn't blame them. By leaving, he was turning his back on the island. Why shouldn't they do the same? He forced himself to *not* think of Ella, but the vision of her turning on her heel, and leaving the break room without even looking back at him was tearing him up inside. His eyes stung and he knew it was from more than the wind. Tara was still talking to him, but he wasn't listening. He tried to counter the feeling of loss tied to Ella with anger for the fact that she hadn't told him she was looking for jobs off the island, but it didn't hold up. Of course she was. She'd made no secret of the fact that she didn't really want Clarence's job. Maybe in a few days, she'd be leaving too and what they had, what they *almost* had, what they *could* have had, would be lost in time. A single point of possibilities missed.

For the first time, in six months, he stepped onto the ferry. Tara was standing too close to him as she talked, as if she was afraid he'd leap off the ferry and swim back to the island if she didn't keep an eye on him. And, to be honest, Cal had considered it. But, he'd die in the December water, and what would he be swimming back to? Maybe Tara was right. He'd had six months of what he wanted. Maybe that was all he was ever going to get.

They moved from the ferry, to a waiting hired car, to the SEA-TAC airport, through security and then, they were in the air, and the heavy, crushing sensation was pushing down on Cal's chest, even worse than it had on his way from New York. There was snow on the ground when they deplaned at LaGuardia and moved through the gates to the street exit. Cal frowned at the purse on Tara's shoulder.

"You didn't bring any luggage?" Cal asked.

Tara turned to look at him, eyebrows raised. "Oh good, you can speak. I was starting to worry you'd left your vocal cords on that island." She shook her head. "No, Callum, you forget, I know you. I knew I wouldn't need to pack anything, not when I was flying out and returning on the same day."

Cal felt a new anger scalding his insides. What did she mean by that? She knew him and that's why she didn't need to worry about staying overnight when she came to Hope?

"Why hello wandering traveler," a familiar voice called out. Cal jerked his head up to look ahead of them. His sister Rhone was smiling and waving at them from in front of one of the family's black limos.

"Rho," Cal breathed. "When did you get home from Switzerland?" She pushed past Tara and yanked Cal down in a bear hug.

"Grrrr," she said. "Bear hug!" Her hug felt like it had dislodged some of the weight on his chest as he wrapped his arms around her, picking her up and swinging her around. She laughed. "Stop! Put me down! The nuns will see and Mom will send me back to Eidenhorn."

Cal finally set her back down, laughing. He glanced at Tara who had her cell phone out, texting away and ignoring the siblings' reunion. Cal turned his attention back to his sister. "So?"

Rhone shrugged. "I finished up a month ago, the nuns gave me a piece of paper saying they'd had enough of me, put me in a funny gown and booted me out the door."

Cal's heart fell. "You graduated? And I missed it?"

Rhone rolled her eyes. "You know I would have hated it if you'd been there. I didn't even tell Mom and Dad until it was too late for them to get the jet there in time." Her smile faded a little as she studied Cal's face.

"Do you two mind if we continue the reunion in the car?" Tara asked. "I'm freezing my ass off out here."

"And we can't have that," Rhone muttered under her breath. They piled into the limo and Cal smiled at Harry in the rear view mirror. He'd been hired as the family driver at the beginning of the year and Cal had immediately liked him.

"Good to see you, Cal," he said with a wink.

"Right back at you, Harry," Cal said.

"My apartment, please, Harry," Tara said, sliding in last and closing the door. She glanced at Cal. "I mean, *our* apartment."

Harry nodded and pulled into traffic. Cal was having a hard time just looking out the window when he could feel his sister's eyes boring a hole in the side of his head. He looked back at her and he could almost see the wheels turning behind her eyes. After a minute, she gave him a short nod and turned to talk to Tara on her other side.

"So Tar," Cal had to fight the instant smile he got whenever Rho called Tara, Tar. It was a nickname Rho had given her when they were all really young, but once Rho figured out how much Tara hated it, she'd decided to keep up the tradition. "You look *exhausted*. I mean, you must have had to keep the claims stubs for those bags under your eyes. Why don't we drop you off so you can rest and then Cal and I will go get something to eat and check on you later?" Rho knew where all the pressure points were for Tara and at the first mention of bags, Tara was digging through her purse and pulling out a folding mirror.

"Fine," Tara said, snapping the mirror closed and tossing it back in her purse on a yawn. "I do feel Mr. Jetlag trying to be my best friend." She turned her gaze on Cal. "Just don't let *him* out of your sight."

Rho snapped Tara a smartass salute that was so reminiscent of Ella, Cal felt sick. They dropped Tara off outside their old building on the upper east side of Manhattan and after the door was closed behind her, Harry turned his head to look back at the Dickson children for their next destination.

"Harry, my good man," Rho said. "Take us to the finest dive bar in the area, that is conveniently located near a parking garage so that you can join us."

"You got it," Harry pulled into traffic again.

"Ok," Rho said. "Do you want to spill your guts here, or wait until there's a beer in front of you?" Cal just looked at her. She sighed and rolled her eyes. "Cal, I just got back from eleven months with Swiss nuns. Guilt, shame, regret, and pain are now things I can spot at fifty paces."

"Money well spent," Cal said, forcing a grin.

Rho gave him a sad smile. "Cal, I always knew that despite me being a girl and the baby, *you* were the black sheep of our family." She sighed. "Do you know how happy I was when you sent me that email, telling me you were just *going* west? Just picking up and leaving?"

Cal frowned at her. "You were happy?"

"Yes!" she said, slapping her hands against her thighs. "Because for once, *you* weren't just going with the flow and letting Tar, and Mom and Dad make your decisions for you."

"Hey," Cal said. "They don't make all my decisions for me."

Rho sighed. "No, they don't. But you'd just been 'the good son' for so long that, frankly, it was refreshing when you gave the rest of us the middle finger and flew off into the sunset."

Cal shook his head. "I've missed you."

"Of course you have," she sniffed. "Everyone always does. Isn't that right, Harry?"

"Oh I always miss you, Miss Rho," Harry said with a grin.

"Christmas is coming," she said. "And I'm going to make sure your bonus reflects how often you help me make a point."

They parked in a lot down a side street that had seen better times and Rho tipped the lot attendant a hundred dollar bill to watch the car. "So Harry can relax and tie one on. If we have too much, we'll all just hail a cab and come back for the car later."

The dive bar was half-full of what looked like folks from the neighborhood. A few people looked up when they entered, but no one stared. That was the benefit of being well-off, but unknown in New York. Harry volunteered to retrieve the first round and Rho pecked him on the cheek in thanks. She sighed as he disappeared into the throng crowded around the bar and the single TV showing a hockey game. "One day, I'm going to marry that man."

Cal chuckled. "Good luck getting Mom and Dad on board with that." The sick feeling in his gut was growing as he pulled his phone out of his pocket and set it on the table. He hadn't missed the fact that there were no missed calls or texts. Not even from Maddie or Pippa asking what happened. He could only imagine what the rumor mill in Hope was saying about him now.

Harry came back with three beers and after Rho patted the seat next to her, he slid in on her side of the booth. They all took a long drink from their bottles and then Rho and Harry fixed their gazes on Cal.

"Now, spill," Rho said.

Cal shook his head. "There's nothing to . . ."

Rho pointed to her eyes. "Nuns, Cal." She pointed at his face. "I can see it. Now tell me what I'm looking at."

40

ELLA

It had been an exhausting day, and Ella, for the first time in living memory, was thankful for it. She'd been covering almost twice the amount of daily events that she usually did without Cal there. Maddie, and even Pippa, had stepped up and taken some of the events when they were happening at the same time. It was after ten and she'd just finished hammering out the last of her articles for the day. Unfortunately, that meant that reality was starting to creep up on her in the quiet office. Her gaze fell on the empty desk on the other side of her office window and she felt the dam inside her rumble.

No. Helga boomed in her head. *Bathtub water tonight.* That's *when you can break.* She just needed something to tide her over until then. Mostly for something to do, she started pulling open the desk drawers, searching for something she knew she couldn't find in a desk drawer, namely her dignity, a time travel device, and a naked Cal under a fishing quilt. *No. He's someone's fiance. You are* not *Wendi.* Helga was very loud tonight. *Maybe bring it down a notch*, she told Helga. Helga was not amused. Finally, in the bottom drawer of the desk, she found not what she was looking for, but something that might help anyway. She ran her hand over the bottle's label. "Twelve-year-old Dewar's. Not bad, Clarence," she said to the empty office.

There was a knock on the open office door and she looked up at Maddie and Pippa. "We were about to head out," Maddie said, looking around at the paper scattered all over the floor. "But...we saw...the light on." She shook her head. "What are you going to do with all this paper?"

Ella shrugged. "Katie had a good idea about gasoline and matches."

"Now you're talking," Pippa said. The pair just stood in the doorway for a moment, squeezed in side by side.

Ella sighed. "You two look like two-thirds of the three stooges, standing there like that. Just go ahead and ask what you wanted to ask." She'd been rehearsing in her head all day what to tell people when they asked her why Cal had left. She'd decided on "He had a family emergency." It wasn't true, but it was the only way she could think of that would stem the tide of follow-up questions. It was even possible that she could feign ignorance. But no one at the paper had asked and she guessed everyone else in town hadn't noticed yet. It was incredibly busy on the island right now.

"El, are you ok?" Maddie asked.

Ella felt the hand holding the scotch start to shake and she lowered it to rest the bottle in her lap. She hadn't been expecting that question. She opened her mouth to speak, trying to figure out what to say. The dam shook inside her and she could hear the mental crack of cement and the groan of metal as it threatened to rupture.

"No, you're not," Pippa said, nodding. She turned to look at Maddie. "Call Dante's Pizza and tell them we need a Ninth Circle, Extra-Hedon-size, delivered here in twenty minutes." She pulled her phone out of her pocket. "I'm going to call in our loser-beer favor to Conner, since he owes us a free, delivered six-pack for beating their team at the fruitcake fight." Maddie nodded and disappeared from the doorway.

"Guys," Ella croaked. "I don't need . . ."

Pippa put the phone to her ear and held her hand up to silence Ella. "Shhh, honey, adults are calling in favors. We'll get to you in just a minute." Ella chuckled and hugged the bottle of scotch to her chest. As much as she wanted to get to her scream-cry session in her bathtub, she had to admit she was glad she wasn't alone at the moment.

Conner brought the beer and Maddie and Ella pushed the mountains of paper towards the walls enough to clear a spot to sit and sprawl on the office floor. They didn't push her at first. They talked about the insanity of the day and articles, town gossip that *didn't* involve Cal, but then they finally rounded the corner on topics and ended up back at the obvious.

"So, who was that woman that Cal left with this morning?" Pippa asked, taking a second slice of pizza out of the giant box.

"His fiancé," Ella muttered. She was going back and forth between her coffee cup that held two fingers of scotch, and the cold beer in front of her.

"Eat more pizza," Maddie said, pushing the box at her. "You need something to soak up all the booze."

"But I like the booze," Ella muttered, staring into the depths of her mug. "The booze are warm and they make me happy."

Pippa rolled her eyes. "No, whatever was going on *yesterday* was making you happy. The booze just makes you drunk."

"But a happy drunk," Ella argued. Maddie reached over and snagged the bottle of Dewar's from beside Ella before she could stop her. "Hey, give that back."

"I will, once you eat another piece of pizza," Maddie said, nodding down at the box.

"And," Pippa added. "Once you tell us why Cal really left."

Ella did her best to ignore this second request and focused on the piece of pizza in her hand. "What are all these toppings?"

Pippa shrugged. "The Ninth Circle has everything on it. Just eat it this time instead of dissecting it."

She sighed and took a bite. There was something savory and salty on this piece that she'd missed on the last. She pulled the piece away from her face and stared at the long dark object she'd bitten into, partially hidden under melted cheese. "What's this?" She turned her slice to show Pippa.

Pippa stopped eating and squinted at the pizza. "Anchovy." She went back to chewing.

Ella stared at the pizza, a forgotten conversation echoing in her head. Anchovies. With a final groan that echoed out through Ella, the dam broke.

"Oh El!" Maddie dropped her pizza and she and Pippa moved around to hug Ella between them on the floor. She couldn't talk. She just sobbed. She didn't know how long it lasted. It could have been several minutes or several years. She gasped for air and held onto their arms like they were a human life raft. For a few minutes, or maybe it was a few hours, the three of them just held each other and sat in the middle of forty years' worth of life stories and accounts of events that they'd each been wrapped in from birth, leading them to that exact moment.

"I was worried you were going to get hurt," Maddie murmured, tightening her grip on Ella.

"I wasn't," Pippa said. Maddie and Ella just looked at her. She shrugged. "I've never seen you so happy." She squeezed Ella's arm and looked at Maddie. "I don't know if the two of you know this or not, but being younger, I kind of watched the two of you all the time, and El, I never saw you as happy with any guy you dated through high school, as you've looked these last two weeks." She shook her head. "And I mean, I know I haven't really seen you in four years, and I never met Wes, or Les or whatever his name was, but something about the way you acted around Cal was . . . different."

Ella felt heat stinging her face that was now wet from her tears. Had the whole office guessed about what had been happening between them?

"And he seemed . . . different," Maddie said, frowning. "Different than he'd been acting since he got here. I never saw him show any interest in any of the other women on the island, until you came."

Ella hung her head. "Probably because he has a fiancé." The collective gasp from the other two was almost comical.

"No! You were actually serious!?"

"What?! I thought you were joking!"

Ella nodded. "Yep. The woman in the white suit."

"That rat bastard," Maddie muttered. "He was jerking you around, and the whole time he had a *fiancé*?"

Ella nodded again. "Apparently."

"I don't buy it," Pippa said. Ella cut her eyes to her in time to see Pippa shaking her head. "No, I'm sorry, but no guy is *that* good of an actor. If you were just his side-hustle, there would have been signs. Like lots of personal phone calls he'd step out to take..."

Ella remembered something. "He wouldn't answer his phone one day when we were talking, even though I told him it was fine if he wanted to. Then, he changed his phone to vibrate."

"That could have been her," Maddie said.

Pippa frowned. "But if it *was* his fiancé, why would he be able to blow her off?"

Ella filled them in on what Cal had told her in the break room that morning before he left, about his family and the merger. "And he said it was like an arranged marriage."

They were quiet for a moment and then Pippa sighed. "Poor guy." With the heat of a thousand fiery suns blazing daggers from their eyes, both Ella and Maddie turned to look at her. "Oh please," she said, rolling her eyes. "The 'daggers of a thousand burning suns' look doesn't work on me. Hello, Redhead here. I patented that shit." She shook her head. "No, I mean, it doesn't sound like Cal has had much say in his life. And, considering how much he avoids anything to rock the boat..."

"That's bullshit," Ella said, anger replacing, at least for the moment, the pain in her chest. "He's a grown-ass man. He can tell everyone where to get off if he wants to. But instead, he just followed her out like a puppy and went back, I'm guessing, to New York."

"Very good point," Maddie said. Ella recognized Maddie's tone and she couldn't meet her gaze, knowing what she was about to do. "But, it's not easy to face the thing we fear the most. Is it?"

Ella shook her head, needing to not think about this anymore. The two of them didn't even know the extent to which she and Cal had... The recently repaired dam that was holding back a second wave of emotion shook. She could even see the tiny dam builders pausing in their efforts to shake their fists at her.

She wiped her eyes on the sleeve of her shirt and sniffed hard. "It doesn't matter now." She cleared her throat. "He's gone and there are two more full days of events until Christmas to cover."

"And after Christmas?" Pippa asked, her voice sounding smaller than it usually did. Ella looked at her. "What about after Christmas?"

"Yeah," Maddie said. "Are you going to . . . will you stay, or go back to Seattle?"

Something Cal had said floated back to the top of her memory. "Actually, I need to make a call in the morning. There's a community events paper in Seattle that wanted me to come in for an interview."

"Oh . . . good," Maddie tried to smile, but Ella wasn't fooled. Maddie and Pippa looked at each other and Ella felt something hacking away at the seedling of excitement that had sprouted up in her head. It was the chance she'd wanted before coming to Hope. She'd be covering something big in a big city. Something important.

"But El," Pippa said, "Cal . . ."

Ella shook her head, thankful that Helga was strapping into the captain's chair. "I don't want to hear anything else about Cal, ok? I just . . . want to forget about him and finish out this season." They both looked like they wanted to argue, but Ella got to her feet and picked up her beer from the floor before knocking back the dregs and letting out a warrior-cry of a burp. "Now, tomorrow's coverage starts in . . ." she checked her watch, "eight hours. So, I suggest we all go whisper sweet nothings to our pillows and meet back here at eight."

They didn't look convinced, and Ella had to keep her eyes on the mess of used napkins and beer cans she was picking up so her bravado wouldn't crack. She took out the trash and without her jacket, the freezing wind had a lovely "cold shower" effect on her that helped her exchange the depression of loss for the joy of swearing about various parts of her anatomy freezing off.

"Yeah," Maddie said, watching Ella stomp back toward her office, trying to get the feeling back into her arms and feet. "They're predicting snow on the island on Christmas Eve." Maddie's phone beeped and she pulled it out to check it, as she turned to get her coat.

"Man," Pippa said, tugging a pink knit hat down to her eyes. "I think the last time it snowed here, we were in middle school."

Maddie nodded, still clicking around with her thumb on her phone. "And we tried to go sledding and almost flew off the cliffs and into the ocean."

Ella chuckled. "And Mrs. Bukowski's chicken coop saved us."

"Which is more than I can say we did for the coop," Maddie muttered.

Ella hugged them both a little longer than she normally would have. "I'll lock up and head out the back," she told them. Then she watched Maddie and Pippa leave, arm in arm, their breath rising in a fog around them as they chatted and power-walked across the square, lit by the light of Maddie's phone.

Ella slid the bolt home on the front door, still searching for more distractions to occupy her mind. She turned back toward her office and paused to look at the newly installed window, replacing the temporary plywood. Clarence and Tony. Bill might have some updates on what was happening with them and the briefcase. She should get something written up for that story before she left the island. As a journalist, she had an obligation. She kept her gaze on the spot as she went back to her office, purposely avoiding the empty desk in front of it. Obligation. Cal's words echoed in her head, and she did her best to silence them. Everyone had obligations. But they also had a choice as to whether they wanted to follow the obligations or the voice in their own heads and hearts.

The last thought made her stomach cramp. She turned her back to the room and stared into the paperwork abyss that was her office. She told herself she needed to file, but even saying the word inside her head made her think of Cal's husky moan as he said it and they were... A wave of heat crashed into the cold stillness of despair inside her, raising the pressure against the dam's wall. She sagged against the door frame and looked around the room. Near where they'd been sitting, eating pizza, a splotch of red caught her eye. Pizza sauce. She pictured herself stepping on it's congealed surface in the morning and then traipsing around the office and town with the paper stuck to her shoe like journalism toilet paper. She sighed and, somewhat grateful for the momentary distraction, retrieved the paper and cleaned it off with a paper napkin. Her eyes drifted over the print on the page; *The Curious Case of Hans Horn and the People Who Hate It by Clarence Ford*. She smiled, reading down the article as Clarence's familiar tone told the old story with tongue firmly in cheek.

But, the article continued, *as obnoxious, and bizarre, and often startling as the old horn is, even I, a transplanted Islander of more than three decades, have to admit, that nothing suits this town better. Hope is a town of human alphorns. We can be beautiful and melodic and picturesque, staunchly rooted in our traditions and using our loud voices to tell the world that "we are here" and "all are welcome to be here too". And just because we're small, doesn't mean we aren't proud. Of course, some of us have talents outside the musical realm, so when we blow the horn, something entirely different emerges, convincing me that we will one day, unintentionally summon Cthulhu with some little-known mating call. But that is the reality of Hope. It's not always pretty. Sometimes it's hilarious, or obnoxious, or painful. But it's steady. Like the people of Hope. Always enduring. And as a proud editor, of a proud paper, in a borderline haughty about how proud we are town, I felt it only right that I took the time today, on the anniversary of Hope's incorporation, to "blow our own horn".*

Ella leaned back against the front of her desk and held the paper to her chest.

Hope endures.

41

CAL

"Wow," Rhone said, setting down her empty beer bottle. "You done screwed up."

Cal nodded and then buried his face in his hands. "How did this happen?"

"Your 'never fighting, go with the flow' mantra sailed you up the river," she said, leaning her head against Harry's shoulder as she surveyed her brother.

Cal was drunk. And not just a little drunk. Cal would be looking for a rowboat on a spring and a bottle of Jameson if he was still on the island. That thought alone was so painful, it cut like a knife through his beer goggle fog and made a painful knot in his throat.

"I had it Rhone," he muttered, one elbow slipping off the table. He jerked his head up before it hit the battered and sticky surface.

"Had what?" Rhone asked, trying to keep her tone serious, though, from her smile, Cal could tell how much she was enjoying seeing her older brother snockered.

"Everything," Cal croaked, trying to force the knot down in his throat. "Life. Happiness. Purpose. It was in my hands," he paused and looked down at his palms, feeling the twinge in his shoulder from the healing bullet graze. "But I couldn't keep it."

He reached up and felt around on the bandage wrapped around his shoulder. Ella had been the last person to change it. And thankfully, Tara hadn't seen it. That was a fight that he was going to avoid for as long as possible.

"Why?" Rhone asked.

Cal dragged his gaze up to her face, frowning. Was she in his head? "Because I hate fighting."

"That's why you couldn't keep your life, happiness, purpose?" she asked, raising an eyebrow at him. "Because you hate fighting?"

Cal felt realization trickling through him like a strong cup of coffee, pushing back the haze and shock of the day.

Rhone chuckled. "By George, I think he's got it."

Cal frowned at her, blinking to try to keep her in focus. "What are you talking about?"

"Exactly what you just said. You lost everything because you hate the act of fighting for it." He opened his mouth to argue and she shook her head. "Cal, I'm not saying that you won't go after something you want, but when it comes to others telling you what they want *you* to do for *them* with *your* life, you become Surfer Cal, just deciding to ride the wave, instead of dropping trough, telling the wave to suck it, and walking out of the ocean." She sighed. "That's what I thought you were doing when you left for the west coast. If that stupid finishing school had had internet or even let us use the telephone without a nun warden breathing down our necks, I would have called or emailed to tell you how *proud* of you I was."

Cal shook his head. "But me going out there didn't change anything. It was pointless. All it did was delay the inevitable."

"I can't speak to the rest of it," Rhone said. "But it changed you. Even after," she paused and counted the empty bottles on the table in front of her, "six beers, I know that in the twenty years I've known you, I've never seen you buck the system like you did when you left." She reached across the table and squeezed his hand. "And to be honest, I never thought that was possible. I know what tide brought you back. Mainly because I can still smell the stink of Chanel No. 5 on both of us . . ." she paused and sniffed Harry's coat. "Jesus, even on *my* boyfriend." She sighed. "I know that Dad has always planned for you to run the family business, and I'd be lying if I said I hadn't spent several years hating you for being the one that was being groomed for it, even after I aced my business classes in high school and spent every summer working there, *but . . .*" she paused and Cal felt himself grinning at her. Rhone was definitely the one that should have been born first. She smiled at him and squeezed his hand again. "That's what *Dad* wants. And frankly, that's *his* problem. You're a great journalist, Cal. You're a writer and you love talking to people the way that I love projections and spreadsheets. And we should both be able to do what . . ," she paused and cut her eyes to Harry, "and *who* we love." He chuckled at her and she kissed his cheek.

"Rho," Cal mumbled, "Even after," he stared at the bottles on the table in front of him and felt his eyes slide out of focus, "many, many beers, I still know that it's easy to say that, but the explosion that would happen if I told Dad . . ."

"When you imagine that explosion, is it better or worse than the explosion of your head when you spend the next forty years married to Tar and all the corporate matched luggage that comes along with her and Dad's hand-me-down career?"

Cal tried to imagine both scenarios, but his stomach started churning and the room started spinning. He put his head down and felt his forehead glue itself to the sticky tabletop.

"You just had the one beer," he heard Rhone say to Harry, "but are you ok to drive?"

"Of course." Harry's voice was smooth. "There was no way I was going to let my best girl take a cab."

Then Cal was moving. He wasn't sure if he was moving of his own volition or if he was being carried. At one point, he pried his eyes open enough to look down at his feet which were scuffing along the pavement, but he couldn't feel them. It was like they were someone else's legs. He wished he was that person. With legs walking, going wherever he wanted. Going back to Hope, back to Ella . . .

"Hey, hey," Rho's voice was soft. "It's ok, Cal." He could feel her head next to his ribs as they walked, and she kept a short arm around him. He could hear Harry huffing on his other side, most likely baring the lion's share of Cal's weight, while someone nearby sobbed. His eyes blurred and his face was wet. Was it raining? It wasn't until they were back in the limo when Rho dug a Kleenex box out from under the seat and started wiping at his face, that he realized *he* was the one that was sobbing.

"I love her, Rho," he choked. He hadn't thought about the words before they'd come out, but even in his drunken stupor, Killjoy Cal wasn't stepping up to object. He'd never really loved a woman before Ella. He'd liked, been fond of, and "missed" them. But Ella Danforth was . . . she *was* hope. Hope for possibilities, freedom, and a life well-lived. An even quieter, innocent and more naive voice that Cal was usually able to silence when he was sober, took a tentative step forward and cleared his throat. *Hope for a real family.* He thought of Bill and Helen and the feeling he got when he walked into their house. The feel of Ella's hand in his. All the corniness and simple bliss of being able to always say what he meant and mean what he said. All without worrying about an angle, or how shiny his plastic sheen was and what the other plastic people would think if it didn't meet their standards.

"I know," Rho said. "I knew that was what I was looking at in your eyes the second I saw you come out of the airport. I just needed to hear you say it." She coaxed Cal into laying down with his head on her knee and he closed his eyes. "I don't want him to have to see Tar tonight. Let's go to my apartment."

"Yes ma'am," Harry said.

"Smartass," she chuckled. "You'll pay for that later when I get you alone."

"Yes ma'am!"

Cal didn't remember the lobby of Rho's building or the elevator ride or even when Rho accidentally knocked his head against the door frame of her guest room as she and Harry half-carried him in. When he woke up, he was still drunk, and from the lack of non-artificial light coming in through the bedroom windows, he knew it was still night. He sat up in bed and looked around. His messenger bag was on the floor beside him. At the moment, it felt like the only link to Hope he still had. He had to talk to her.

The thought of calling her made him sweat. What would he say to her? What *could* he say? Words on the page. That was his strength. He'd send her an email. He'd pour everything out to her. He'd let her know . . . he'd tell her . . . what? *I love you, but I'm going to marry someone else and go through with the life I've been expected to live?*

He opened the laptop and woke it up. The bright white light from the screen was blinding, and Cal immediately second-guessed his plan. Maybe he should wait until he was sober.

"Can't sleep?" Rho's voice from the hallway made him jump. The bedroom door was open, and he could see her, wrapped in a fluffy pink robe and holding two-pint glasses of ice water. She moved into the room. "I made one of these for Harry, but he kept all the brains for himself and didn't try to drink his body weight in beer like you and I did, so he can wait." She handed one of the glasses to Cal and clinked hers against his. They both groaned at the sound. She sat down next to him on the bed and they both upended their glasses.

"So," she said into the silence that followed. "Are you going to email her?"

Cal sighed. "I was thinking about it."

She shrugged. "I mean, it is the chicken shit way to say you're sorry."

He glared at her. "It's not . . ." She raised her eyebrows, and he dropped his gaze to the bright screen. "Ok. It's chicken shit."

"Well, Chicken McShit, let's see what you've penned thus far." She jerked the laptop out of his hands and Cal's inebriated reflexes were too slow to stop her.

"Rho, that's personal." He knew what document he'd left up on his screen. He knew, because after Ella had left his apartment, after a night he knew he'd never forget, he'd opened up the brain-dump from the night before and added to it and then he'd just left it up when he put his computer to sleep.

"You're telling me." She turned so she was out of Cal's reach as he tried to reclaim the laptop. Cal's head started to spin again and he sagged back onto the bed, closing his eyes. So Rho was going to read everything he'd written. She'd torture him with it for a while, but he could deal with Rho's teasing torture. She wouldn't show it to Tar or his parents so the chances of there being a screaming match because of it were low. He was losing his grip on consciousness again, slipping back into the dark, vaguely aware of the soft clicking near him as Rho started to type.

* * *

RHO

"Wow, Cal. This is . . ." Rho started to say when she'd finished reading. She looked over at her brother. He was passed out again. His forever-disheveled hair had fallen over his eyes and his mouth was half-open as he drooled on the pillow. She glanced back down at the screen. *Ella Danforth, you have ensnared a hell of a guy.* As she read about the island town and the woman that her brother was internally self-destructing and fighting his own nature over, an idea started to form in her mind.

"Uh oh," Harry's deep voice murmured from the hallway. "I know that face." She jerked her head up to squint out at him. He was scratching the back of his head as he moved across the room to sit down on the bed next to her. The extra weight on the mattress shifted Cal, turning his face into the pillow. They both paused as they listened to the new sound of him trying to inhale the pillowcase.

"Will you fix that," Rho nodded at Cal, before turning her attention back to the email program she was scrolling through.

Harry re-positioned Cal's face and then sat back down beside her. "Rho-Rho-Rho-your-bout to get a spanking if you don't spill what you're doing to Cal."

She cut her eyes to him. "Promises, promises." She looked back at the screen and sighed. "I'm just trying to undo twenty-six years of damage."

"That's a pretty tall order for three am," Harry said with a yawn.

"I know. And I know what I'm doing won't be anywhere near enough. But maybe, it'll be a nudge."

For the last half hour, she'd been editing Cal's document. She wasn't sure what it was supposed to be. It didn't have a title. It was just thoughts about Hope Island and his editor, and apparently the woman that had captured his heart, Ella Danforth. She scrolled back to the top of the edited document and passed the computer to Harry.

"Here, read this. I just need a title to go with it."

She watched his eyes move line to line as a frown grew on his face. "Rho, you can't submit this as if Cal had written it. That's not going to . . ."

"I didn't write it." She nodded at her brother's unconscious body. "He did." Harry raised an eyebrow at her. "Before," she said. "When he was conscious. And I think before Tar got a wild hair up her butt and went out there to drag him back."

Harry sighed. "I like your brother, but I doubt Tara had to do much dragging. My guess is that she said 'heel' and he fell in line."

Rho nodded and picked at her nails in her lap. "When we were kids, Cal would always cry and hide when Mom and Dad yelled. It didn't matter if they were yelling at each other or at him. He couldn't handle it. But Cal wouldn't run and hide when the parents started in on me. And I was a screw up kid. I colored on walls, left my shoes on the sidewalk outside our building, left my toys in the elevator. And every time they were about to start in on me, Cal would stand beside me and hold my hand. I remember being mad at them, but I could feel Cal's hand shaking in mine and I wouldn't argue because I wanted it to end too, so Cal would stop being so scared."

Harry put an arm around her shoulders. "I'm sorry."

She turned to look at Cal, putting a hand on his knee. "Well, it's time for me to stand beside him." She shook her head and took the computer back from Harry. "I don't know if it'll do any good, but something this strong shouldn't be left unsaid." She changed tabs back to the email program and hunted through the list of contacts, cross-checking them with previous emails.

"Madison Burke," she muttered. "*Hornblower* Photographer and Layout Assistant. Ok." She started typing up an email, trying to imagine herself as Cal and get the professional journalist tone right. When she was done, she turned to look at Harry. "Still waiting on that title."

"You act like titles are easy," he huffed. They were quiet as she pulled up the document again and passed the computer back to him. "How about 'The Thing About Hope'?"

Rhone smiled. "Perfect." She leaned in and kissed Harry. "And since you're so good with titles, as soon as we're done with this, you can give a title to whatever we're doing for the rest of the night." She giggled as he ran his tongue down the side of her neck. She titled, saved, and attached the document to the email. Cal stirred in his sleep, groaning before turning onto his back. "Cal, if you want to stop me, you better wake up right now and smack this computer out of my hands," she called softly to him. In the ghostly glow of the artificial light, she saw Cal smile in his sleep. She grinned back at the computer and clicked. "Sent." She closed the laptop and slid it under the bed. She and Harry both got to their feet and she pulled the blankets up and over Cal.

"Now," Harry said, wrapping his arms around her from behind. "I believe there is a spanking and some titling to be done?"

"Lead the way," she whispered.

42

ELLA

The day had been so long, and full of so much that she hadn't expected to happen when she'd woken up, that she didn't think she could be surprised by anything else. But, the universe shattered this belief as she dragged her feet down Shell Street towards the one house that still had its porch *and* Christmas lights on. There was someone sitting on the porch swing and for a single, shining moment, she thought it was . . .

But it was Bill. He was rocking slowly, staring down at his lap, a frown on his face that over the years Ella had learned either meant that the football team he was rooting for had lost, her mom was making something he didn't like for dinner, or he was disappointed about something he couldn't change. Since there hadn't been a major football game that day and it was the middle of the night, she was going to go with door number three.

"Hi Bill. What's wrong?" She had to admit that it felt like a nice change up to be the one asking the question instead of the one expected to answer it.

He looked up at her and the frown turned to confusion. "El? I thought you were in bed by now."

She shook her head. "Late night at the paper." She paused next to the swing before sitting down. "Your butt isn't frozen to the swing, is it? If it is, you've got to tell me before I sit down. If we both freeze to the swing, we'll die of exposure because the ear plugs I got mom for Mother's Day are military-grade."

Bill chuckled. "I can always count on you to put things into perspective."

"How so," she asked, slumping down beside him.

"Well, our bowling team may have lost our best player, but at least my ass isn't frozen to a porch swing." She didn't say anything. Of course. She'd been naive to think in some selfish way that Cal leaving Hope would only affect her. "So," he said, turning to look at her. "Tell me some good news."

"Uh," Ella said. "Well, it's going to be hard to top the fact that we're both still in possession of the skin on our buttocks and free to move around, but . . ." she racked her brain and remembered the job in Seattle. "A paper in Seattle called to ask me to come interview for a job."

"Are you going to do it?" Bill asked.

Ella forced herself to nod. "Yeah."

"Well, alright then." He sighed. "If you can put it off, don't tell your mother until after Christmas." He winked at her. "Consider it an early Christmas present to me."

She grinned. "Too late. Mom and I already got you your presents." She shrugged. "But even if I interview before Christmas, there's a good chance I won't know if I got the job until after the holidays anyway."

"Good," he nodded.

"Your turn," Ella said. "Tell me what's happening with Clarence."

"Oh," Bill's face brightened and he smiled, turning to look at Ella. "It's been fairly straight-forward. Apparently old Clarence's real name is William Clarence. When he got to Anacortes, he had to sign his name when he bought his ticket and he hadn't figured out what name he was going to use and there was a line behind him, so he said he just panicked, wrote his last name as his first name and the car he'd stolen was a Ford, so he just wrote that as his last name, hoping no one would look at C. Ford and think William Clarence."

Ella chuckled. "So is he in trouble?"

Bill shook his head. "There's some legal kerfuffle about him living under an alias that Lawrence Elton is helping him navigate through, but other than that, it sounds like he's going to be in the clear. He didn't open that briefcase, so he's not even in a pickle with the Feds or Chicago P.D."

"Did *you* get to see what was in the case?" she asked.

Bill nodded. "Money and some hand-written notes pointing back to the protection scheme the Rossilinis were running."

She shook her head. "I still can't figure out why Tony would want to avenge an uncle that died before he was even been born."

"Initiation, apparently," Bill wasn't smiling now. His expression had settled back into his hard-jawed police face. "Tony was coming up in the family and in order to earn his wings, they told him he had to go track down and kill the man who killed Silvano and retrieve the loot."

"So glad we could all be a part of his special day," Ella muttered. She still felt a pang of shame for falling for his face and easy demeanor. It had all been an act. Tony *and* Cal. She closed her eyes and laid her head against the back of the swing, letting the gentle rocking lull some of the anxiety out of her. Numb Ella high-fived and switched places with Helga, giving Ella some comfortable, emotional distance from the events of the day.

"Clarence did have a message for you," Bill said softly.

Ella opened her eyes and turned her head to look at him. "Really?"

Bill nodded, shifting on the swing to search his pockets. "He told me to tell you that the editor job is all yours. And . . ," he fished a scrap of folded yellow legal paper out of his shirt pocket, "he gave me this to give to you." He handed it to her.

She unfolded the note and read, *Ella, I always knew you were going to grow up to do great things. Enjoy your time at the paper. I know you'll steer her right. – Clarence*

She smiled. "He still signed his name 'Clarence'."

Bill shrugged. "Change is hard. Maybe the comfort of holding onto something familiar will be what makes it possible for him to keep going."

Ella pecked Bill on the cheek and said goodnight. She decided she was too dehydrated and too tired to sit up and cry. She laid in bed, waiting for exhaustion and the quiet, dark of the house to carry her off to sleep, and she thought about Cal. Wondering if he was holding Tara tonight the way he'd held her the night before. It wasn't a helpful line of thinking and she could feel the muscles in her stomach starting to clench, so she tried to force her mind down another path. She thought about Bill's words and Clarence's note and the article he'd written, and life and her last thought as she finally slipped out of consciousness was the fact that she *did* have something familiar to hold on to so she could keep going. She had Pippa and Maddie, her mom and Bill, Miss Mandie, this kooky town . . . and the most unexpected thing to happen to her of the day, turned out to be the smile on her face as she drifted off to sleep.

Unfortunately, the happy feeling didn't stick around to greet her when she woke up. She stared at the empty place in the bed next to her and thought of Cal. The mental force she had to use to try to turn the thoughts of despair into anger, had her so distracted that she almost broke her toe off when she stubbed it on the doorway into the bathroom. Lovely start to the day. She looked in the mirror and immediately wished she hadn't. She did what she could with her hair, pulled on some clean clothes and headed down the stairs. Her mom and Bill weren't up yet and Ella was only a little late for the sunrise. The town was in that state of opening its mouth wide to yawn out all its delightful morning breath before the tourists started arriving. Mr. Vernon was on his porch in his robe, drinking his coffee and meditating. Ella was supremely thankful that it was winter, because she knew firsthand that in the spring and summer, Mr. Vernon didn't wear a robe in the morning. She greeted the morning joggers and early shoppers on their way to Bumble's and paused in her tracks when she opened the newspaper door and interrupted a conversation between Maddie and Pippa. They both looked exhausted, but smiled and jumped to their feet when she came in.

"Morning?" Ella asked. If the pair of them had been replaced by body snatchers, it would be good to know before she put her bag down.

"Morning," Pippa almost squealed. Ella frowned and Pippa cleared her throat. "Sorry. I mean, good morning," she said, pitching her voice lower.

"Coffee?" Maddie asked, cutting her eyes to Pippa.

"Right, coffee," Pippa said. "Can I get you a cup?" she asked Ella.

"Sure," Ella said. "But I'll have mine with the cocaine on the side. Seriously, what is with you two this morning? And why are you here so early?"

"Oh, just . . . lots to do," Maddie said. She dropped back into her chair, typing something at lightning speed as Ella approached. She moved her mouse and clicked, as Ella drew even with her computer monitors, and when Ella looked at the screens, it was to see the *Hornblower's* standard desktop background.

"Uh huh," Ella said.

"Oh," Maddie peeled a sticky note off the edge of her desk. "A Maisie Little called again for you. Well, she said she was calling again. She said she called yesterday, but . . ." She handed over the note. Under the name and number, she'd scrawled "Seattle Center Community Weekly".

"Thanks," Ella said. She jerked her head up to look at Maddie, just as Pippa returned with her star mug. "Let's have the huddle-up meeting as soon as everyone is here today. It's going to be another big one."

"But tomorrow's not too bad," Pippa said. "I checked the calendar. Just the Santa Ball and Crawl and the typical installations."

Ella nodded. "Yeah. I'm hoping that if we can knock everything out today, I can give you all tomorrow off. We just need to make sure everything is ready for the issue coming out on the 26th by the end of the day."

Pippa and Maddie both snapped her a salute. "You know," Ella said to the coffee in her hand, "I think I'm a bad influence on them."

She prepped for the huddle-up and then stared back down at the sticky note she'd set on her desk. *Just do it.* Helga said. Yes. It was a good opportunity and a way to hold onto something familiar. She'd be covering community events while moving on to make changes and doing something big. She held her breath as she dialed and waited for Maisie Little to pick up.

"Oh my gods, Ella! You had me terrified that you were never going to call back. I kid you not, my boss fell in *love* with the resume you sent us. Of course, then it was misplaced and there was some drama, but it turns out, that accidentally deleted emails from trash cans *can* be retrieved by the IT

Squad. So, we would love, love, love to have you come in and interview as soon as possible."

"Oh," Ella said, slightly reeling from the woman's enthusiasm. Maybe she was on whatever Maddie and Pippa were taking. *See Ella,* Sarcastic El spoke up. *The early woman gets the crack donut.* "I could come as early as the day after Christmas?"

Maisie Little tittered on the line. "How about tomorrow morning?"

"T-tomorrow? Christmas Eve?"

"Like I said, my boss is in *love* with your resume. She wants you here like, yesterday. So, can I pencil you in for ten?"

"Uh, I guess. Sure." Probably not good to argue with someone as geared up as Maisie. Even though they were on the phone, Ella couldn't rule out the possibility that she might still somehow lose a finger.

"Coolio! We'll see you then! And score, now I have your cell number!" Then Maisie hung up.

"Ok, then," Ella said to the empty office. She had a moment of joy, thinking about retelling the story to . . . but then her gaze fell on his empty desk and the joy was gone as if it had never been there.

To keep functioning for the day, Ella hung onto everything familiar around her, namely writing too many stories, covering too many assignments, and dealing with too many townsfolk coming in to sing a carol in exchange for using the paper's bathroom, even though Ella assured them they could just use it *without* having to sing for it.

"I'll finish up the layout," Maddie said at seven o'clock. "You look beat. And you already finalized the layout for the day after Christmas edition."

Ella frowned. "Are you sure? I thought we needed to do some article Tetris to fit in Dirk Patterson's editorial."

"Already done," Maddie said, her voice loud enough for Ella to take a step back. The two women just stared at each other. "Sorry," Maddie said, quieter. "I'm just . . ."

"Tired?" Ella asked. "Exhausted? Strung-out?"

"Yes, yes, and yes," Pippa said with a yawn as she emerged from the hallway.

Ella bit her lip. "But we're all good for the next couple of days, right? So everyone can take tomorrow off?"

Pippa nodded. "Well, everyone else. You and I of course have a date with destiny on the catwalk."

Ella groaned. She'd purposely been avoiding any thoughts straying toward the stupid lingerie fashion show almost as much as she'd been avoiding any thoughts of Cal. Her stomach quickly got to work, tying itself in knots. Oh well. If the interview went well the next morning, it would be her final embarrassing performance in front of the town.

"Oh, just in case either of you needs me tomorrow morning," Ella said quickly. "I'm going to be on the mainland for that job interview in Seattle." She chewed her lip as she looked from one to the other. She saw the disappointment, but they both nodded.

Her mom had a similar reaction to the news. She didn't argue with Ella, but that was almost worse. The look of pity she kept giving her throughout dinner and the way that the roll basket kept parking itself next to her plate, made Ella wonder what her mom knew. She remembered the way Cal had sat with her mom on their porch the day she came to get him the Santa suit. A new blow to the gut. She'd *trusted* him with her dad's suit. Something she'd never thought she'd even trust *Bill* with. And he was still there, still steady after almost eight years. Cal, on the other hand, had been in her life for three weeks and then disappeared, like a bad cough. She could feel the dam rumbling inside her again and she said goodnight to Bill and her mom.

She did go through with her bath and the screaming, crying depression that went with it. She felt like she needed to get it out of her system. Needed to get *him* out of her system. But, the universe and her subconscious must have been in cahoots, because as soon as she closed her eyes and tried to will herself to sleep, she was back, on that trout quilt with him, warm and steady, and . . . loving him. She opened her swollen eyes and stared at the ceiling. She'd thought that she'd been in love with Les. She'd even felt sure of it at times. And she'd felt so sure because it had taken *time*. Love took time, didn't it? It wasn't something that could spring into existence in three weeks. Infatuation happened that fast, but... As she lay there, staring out her bedroom window at the stars above Shell Street, she couldn't keep her thoughts off of Cal, as painful as they were, and hoping that wherever he was sleeping, he was actually happy and content. *Change is hard.* Bill's words came back to her. She had to agree. She'd changed since coming back to Hope. Change wasn't pretty or smooth. It was embarrassing and painful. She smiled. After all, before coming back to Hope, the thought of being in a fashion show in front of the town would have had her projectile vomiting in fear. But now, she just had a mild to moderate stomach ache. See? Progress. Progress towards change. And that was the happy thought in her head as she drifted off to sleep. She decided not to look too hard at the fact that the voice she kept hearing it in was Cal's.

* * *

For the first time since coming to the island, Ella put on her interview suit and actually did her hair and make-up. Her mom had gotten up early to make breakfast for her and she ate while her mom sipped coffee and they both stared out into the dark pre-dawn morning.

"Do you know how much this other job will pay?" her mom asked, her voice soft.

Ella shook her head. "The job description said it would depend on experience."

"Well, what if it's not as much as you make at the paper here?"

She met her mom's gaze. "Mom?"

Her mom squeezed her eyes shut. "It's selfish. I know I'm being selfish." She opened them and looked at Ella. "But, I've really liked having you home."

"Mom, I hate to burst your bubble, but I was never going to move back in forever."

Her mom shook her head. "I know that. I didn't mean having you here in the house. I meant here in town. In Hope. It's just . . . I don't know what it is, but for me, El," she reached out and squeezed Ella's hand, "even though I've lived here my whole life, it feels more like home when you're around."

Ella didn't know what to say. She tried to imagine spending the holidays on a friend's couch in Seattle, alone and with no job. Alone in that big city and she thought she understood, at least a little. She kissed her mom goodbye and went to board the seven a.m. ferry. She'd just taken a seat in the ferry's lounge when her phone pinged in her pocket.

It was a text message from Maddie. *Check out today's edition of the paper.*

Ella squeezed her eyes shut. *Great.* What was wrong? She knew she should have stayed to help Maddie triple-check the layout. Kurt had already started the presses after Maddie had done the initial and double-check, but they could have stopped it to fix whatever was wrong. She left her seat and went in search of the roving newspaper kiosk. She found the squat man pushing the cart on the upper deck and bought a copy of the paper. She scanned the first few pages. So far, so good. Then, she got to the page with what Maddie said was an editorial from Dirk Patterson. Ella had been so busy she'd just told Maddie to proof it before she printed it as long as Dirk wasn't just ranting about sequoias.

But it wasn't an editorial from Dirk. It was a letter entitled *The Thing About Hope* and under the title, *by Cal Dickson.*

Ella's legs wobbled and she stumbled over to sit on a bench. The cold morning wind off the ocean whipped at her hair, but she didn't care.

The most important thing to know about Hope is its humility. I guess it's understandable, only being a five-mile-wide spit of land, shaped like a human heart and, as a well-informed Islander once told me, originally called Hoffnung by the Swiss settlers who reached the uninhabited island in 1816. The island was nothing but forests and cliffs with no indigenous wild game or natural resources, at least, until the people moved in.

Like its namesake, the people of Hope can be fragile, naive, and idealistic. But they are also steady, humble, and persevering. They are humble about the pride they hold in their town and more important than that, they are giving with everything they have. As an outsider looking in, I knew in my head that I would never be a true Islander, but that wasn't the story that the island and its people were telling my heart. And my heart is forever changed by the unabashed and steady hope I've been given by this tiny, unassuming place. I've had the honor and privilege to write for this newspaper for nearly the past six months, and I cannot express in words, how my days here have impacted me as a human being.

This is a village, this is a family, this is home. And as all three, it is not immune to change, because it is inhabited by and made of people, uniquely real, who change. We move away, come back, are introduced in, age, retire, and we die. Nowhere in the world is the true meaning of life more evident than on Hope Island. And that is because life has meaning because we give it meaning. Being mortal. It means something to us because it ends. So we have to seize the day, climb every mountain, ford every stream. And that, more than anything, is what Hope Island is. There has not been a day in my six months of residence here where the town has not seized every moment, holding charity events, entertainment, quirky bazaars, and just good old-fashioned excuses to get together and live. Truly live.

Hope is humble because Hope knows the secret to having lives well-lived. I never thought I'd meet a person that combined everything that Hope is into a single human spirit. But that person is the new Editor of the Hornblower, Ella Danforth. She's stubborn, and bossy, nosy, giving, sarcastic, fragile, but steady and strong. I have been luckier than I can say to stumble across Hope Island and even luckier still to meet and work with someone like Ella Danforth. After forty years, Clarence, our previous editor, has retired and passed the torch. And I cannot think of anyone better to keep the lighthouse lit, shining Hope to all who seek it, than Ella. Every issue of this paper is a love letter to this island. A love letter to its people. And no one pours more love into composing that letter, than Ella. You're lucky to have her Hope. And I'm lucky to know her.

43

ELLA

The tears had started without her noticing. It wasn't until she reached the end of the letter and the words blurred together, forcing her to blink her eyes to clear them, that she noticed the damp spots on the newsprint. The waves gently rocked the ferry as Ella tried to force the dam to hold, repaired again while she slept and through the morning as she thought about the job interview and tried to outline all the happy possibilities. The builders in her head were wary, tired of the repair work, and demoralized at the probability that it wouldn't hold a third time, leaving the dam weak and not strong enough to hold against Cal's letter.

She felt exposed, vulnerable, and raw. This was in print, rushing as she sat, all over Hope, and onto the mainland, where everyone could read his words. The heat of embarrassment that immediately rushed over her made her face burn, but just as suddenly, it was beaten back, by a second realization. His words were out where everyone could read them. He was exposing himself, every bit as much, more even, than she was. She reread his letter. It wasn't a love letter to her, but it *felt* like a love letter. Not just to her, but the island. She turned in her seat to look behind the ferry and the shrinking speck on the horizon that was Hope Island. Her island. Her home. Faces passed before her eyes, and stories told, stories written, and the thrill of being there when those stories were made. That was what living was, wasn't it? People and the things they do for one another, the dreams they do for themselves, and the funny, and yes, embarrassing lessons they learn along the way. That *was* what the Hokey Pokey, Monty Python, Tree of Life, Hitchhiker's Guide, all of it, were about. A giddy thrill that she hadn't felt since childhood was filling her up. It was a freedom, a realization, a joy and relief that comes only with unraveling a difficult and complex problem. She had to tell someone. She pulled her phone out and scrolled through her contacts, selecting a name before she processed who. She was about to punch the call button, when her brain caught up with her heart. Cal's contact information stared back at her on the screen.

She squeezed her eyes shut. She couldn't call him. He was engaged. That door was closed. For a moment, she let herself grieve for what she missed and could never experience. She let the images pass by behind her eyes; Cal, growing old behind the editor's desk, seeing him every day as they covered stories and flirted and drank coffee, spending their nights talking about life and about the paper, naked and entwined, before falling asleep. She let the memories that would never be, fill her up, and then, slowly and painfully, she let them go, one by one. She was still crying when she opened her eyes, but Numb Ella was nowhere to be found and Helga was one-cheeking it on the command chair with a new guest at the party. Ella recognized the scrawny eighteen-year-old version of herself, but where the constant anxiety and embarrassment that had followed her through high school had always been apparent on her face, there was now a look of peace and what had to be a healthy dose of Sarcastic El. *Let's kick this pig,* the new Hope Ella said. It took Ella a few minutes to be composed enough to carefully fold the paper and slide it into her bag. She went to the washroom to fix her makeup and hair, but she was one of the first off the ferry when it docked. She got onto the shuttle bus and started making a game plan in her mind with Helga sketching the whole thing out. She had to put her phone away to keep the temptation of texting Cal out of reach. Move on. He was getting married. She'd have to let go of those feelings . . . now . . . soon . . . as soon as she could. But, for now, there was another love that had been slowly creeping up on her over the past weeks. And she couldn't turn her back on that.

When she got off the shuttle, the Uber she'd ordered was waiting across the street. Twenty minutes later, it dropped her off outside an unremarkable office building downtown. Ella followed the directions Maisie had given her to get to their office on the tenth floor. She paused by a window to look out at the cityscape, remembering the thrill she'd had coming to Seattle as a teenager and vowing that this would be where she'd make her mark, where she'd live her life. But even though she'd lived there for four years, it was impossible to tell that she'd been there at all. There was no phone tree the day she left, wondering where this member of the community had gone after suddenly disappearing from their midst. There was no one on the mainland waiting to welcome her as she walked through the streets or hug her and tell her how much they missed her. And yet, she'd had *all* of those things when she'd gone home. How stupid she'd been, thinking all the town wanted to do was embarrass her. All they'd been trying to do was reconnect to a part of their community that had been removed. And they were only human, doing it in the only way they knew how.

"Ella Danforth?" Ella turned to see a short woman with a wide smile and a cloud of curly black hair. "Oh awesome! I'm Maisie. Thank you sooooo much for coming in today. Tomorrow is going to be a shitstorm, so the sooner we can get through the paperwork, the better." Ella followed Maisie through a reception area, and a large cubicle area where at least two dozen people worked, bent over computers in their individual cubes. Beyond them, Maisie led her into an artistically furnished office. "Ella, this is our Editor Lauren Lynch."

She was a middle-aged woman with brown hair shot through with silver. She shook Ella's hand with both of hers and gestured for her to sit in one of the leather chairs in front of her desk. "Ella, I'm so glad you could make it." She set both hands on her desk, palms down and leaned forward to look Ella in the eye. "Let me tell you, as soon as I read that you were the new editor of that charming little paper on the island, I knew I wanted you. My husband and I have been going out there once a year for the past fifteen years. And there's *always* something going on! A festival, a fair, some obscure holiday, and all of it treated by your paper as if it was the most important thing to happen all year. *That* is the kind of energy and care that we need here at the *Seattle Center Community Weekly*."

Ella had set her bag on her lap when she'd taken her seat and as she thought of the folded newspaper, tucked inside, resting under her folded hands, her voice chose that moment to find her. "I'm so sorry Ms. Lynch. I'm very flattered by the invitation for the interview. And as of this morning, I was really excited to interview for this job, but . . ."

Lauren Lynch straightened in her chair, eyes wide. "Is it the pay? Because I will double your salary at the *Hornblower*. And we've got a block of apartments for new hires. My husband owns the building. He's a great landlord and doesn't expect anything down from employees. And we pride ourselves on having the best rent in the city for our reporters."

Ella smiled and slowly shook her head. "No, it's not that. Three weeks ago, I would have leapt at this chance. I would have camped out outside your office, waiting for the chance to interview with you and hopefully get the job. But, halfway here this morning, I realized that I already have a job. An important job. A job that, despite everything that it entails, I love." As calmly as she could, and with her heart pounding in her ears, she got to her feet, sliding the strap of her shoulder bag over her head. She reached out and shook Lauren Lynch's hand and then Maisie's. "And I should be getting back to it. Merry Christmas to you both. And I hope we'll have the pleasure of seeing you out on the island one day soon. When you do come for a visit, please stop by the *Hornblower* office and let me treat you to lunch."

Then, with fear making her legs shake as every step hammered home the realization of what she was voluntarily giving up, she left the office. She wound her way back through the cubicles of reporters and employees, and out the door of the reception area. She didn't start breathing until she was back in the elevator, but by the time she'd reached the bottom floor, she couldn't stop smiling. She was terrified that she'd just spit in the eye of the possibility of any kind of glamorous, famed future, but as she waited for the Uber she'd ordered to arrive, she wasn't afraid that she'd destroyed her hope of having an *important* future.

She waited until she boarded the ferry back to the Island before she called Maddie. "First of all," Ella said, "now that I know what you were doing with not letting me check the layout for today's paper, I want you to know that you have made me forever paranoid, and you'll never get the chance to pull something like this again."

"So you read it?" Maddie asked.

"I did," Ella said, her voice cracking.

"And?"

"And I'm not taking the job in Seattle." She yanked the phone away from her ear as Maddie screamed in celebration.

"Oh my god, El, so does that mean . . . are you going to stay in Hope?"

"For now," she said. She smiled. Just saying the words felt like a weight had been lifted off her shoulders. "Do you mind telling Pip?"

"Already texting her as we talk!"

"Of course you are." Ella chewed on her bottom lip. "Mads, when did you get that editorial from Cal?"

Maddie was quiet for a moment. "I got the email from him the night after he left."

"He sent it to you *after* he left?"

"Yeah."

She hadn't expected that. Why had he sent it *after* he'd left with his fiancé? She hung up with Maddie and stared at her phone. Her thumb found Cal's contact info, but she couldn't bring herself to dial. She wanted to know *why*. Why, after he'd already left with his *fiancé*, had he sent a letter like that to the paper? To her?

She greeted Mrs. Thompson and Mr. Welks and let the stream of midday tourists carry her into the town square. She paused by the gazebo, not sure of where to go. The newspaper was closed for the day, with no big events to cover besides the ball that night. She turned her feet towards home and went wide to avoid a group of tourists wearing Santa hats and posing on one side of the square.

"Hey, Madam Editor," Miss Mandie called to her. The older woman was out on a smoke break, wearing a red sweater with a sequined bra outlined on it with "Jolly my Holidays" printed underneath.

"Hey, Miss Mandie. How are things coming for tonight?" Miss Mandie was always in charge of the giant candy cane-shaped spice cake for the party at large and the erotic eclairs and Double D-elicious cupcakes that were smothered with booze and smuggled into the pockets of party-goers.

"Done. And I'm airing out the old Santa Slay-wear." She winked at Ella, but the smile didn't last long, giving way to worry. "Are you . . . Is Cal . . ." She sighed. "I've never been good with a bat and shrubbery, so I'm going to just come out and ask. Did something happen between you two?"

Ella sighed. So far, she was doing ok, at least a C-plus grade, at keeping thoughts of Cal from overwhelming her. She took a shaky breath. "He had to go back to New York."

"With his fiancé, apparently, right?" Miss Mandie asked. Ella nodded. "I thought so. But no, what I was thinking had more to do with what I about walked into in my kitchen the morning you two were frosting cupcakes and then what I kept catching hints of after. I was about to blame the Marvin Gaye for getting your engines running. Were you two seeing each other?"

Ella gave her a mirthless smile. "How could we be seeing each other when he had a fiancé?"

Miss Mandie crossed her arms. "One thing has nothing to do with the other. I know this, because Cal was one way for the first five months he was here and then after you got back, things changed. Unless he met that girl on the internets and did that virtual sex shit, I think she was baggage from his previous life which begs the question as to why he moved thousands of miles away from her if they were engaged."

Ella didn't know what to say to that. The whole thing was too raw for her to try to make logic out of. It was an exposed nerve that Miss Mandie was prodding. "I don't know," Ella finally said.

"Well, in any case, my upstairs apartment is now for rent. Come on, I'll give you the tour."

"Oh, no, Miss Mandie, it's ok."

"What? Have you already seen it?" The wicked grin she gave Ella was enough to get her to follow Miss Mandie and feign ignorance. Miss Mandie got to the top of the stairs and unlocked the door.

"Miss Mandie!" Bart's panicked voice made them both turn.

"On the back stairs, Bart!" Miss Mandie called.

Bart was sweating through his hair net as he skidded to a stop at the foot of the stairs. "Something's going wrong with the eclairs. They're in the oven and the . . . uh, the . . . shafts are uh . . . engorging."

Miss Mandie chuckled. "If I had a nickel." She looked at Ella. "You go ahead and look around. I'll be right back in case you have anything you want to ask me."

"Miss Mandie, I really," Ella started to say.

"I'll be right back." She headed down the stairs and on a sigh, Ella turned back to face the door.

Ok, this was going to suck. But when you're going through hell, keep going. One step in front of the other. She nudged the door open and was smacked in the face by the smell of Cal. The bed was made and it looked as if he had just left it. Had he even come back to his apartment after he'd left with Tara? Were his clothes still here? She moved through the tiny studio, stopping next to his turntable and the handful of vinyl. There were fuzzy moments of the night he'd brought her to his apartment after she'd found out how long Les had been with Wendi. She crouched down and pulled out the Nick Cave album he'd played. *The Boatman's Call.* The record was still on the turntable. She started the album and "Into My Arms" started playing. She held the album jacket to her chest and closed her eyes as she leaned back against his kitchen counter. Holding something that had belonged to Cal, standing in his apartment, surrounded by his smell, she could almost trick herself into believing that he was there, somewhere just beyond her eyelids.

When the song ended, she opened her eyes and took some deep breaths. Ok. So far, so good. She was sad, but she wasn't bawling. As the next song started, she turned the album jacket over to look at the song list. That was when she saw the note written next to the song "Black Hair". It said, *Tara's Song.* She bit her lip, willing herself to keep the lid firmly clamped down on the sob that was threatening to escape her. She blinked her eyes and set the album jacket down on the counter. Another deep breath and she tried to look around the apartment and imagine her belongings on the walls and counter top. It wasn't easy. She kind of liked the apartment as it was. *Do you really like it? Or do you like it because it reminds you of him?* Damn you, Helga.

There was a sliding closet door opposite the turntable. It was cracked open and Ella took a step toward it. *Danger! Danger!* Helga tried to warn her. Seeing Cal's clothes wasn't going to help. But she couldn't stop herself. Her hands were moving on their own, pushing the door open. Her fingers reached out and ran the soft fabric of his sweaters and t-shirts over her palms. Then, she saw the garment bag and shoe box she'd given him. Her dad's Santa suit. The song changed and "People Ain't No Good" started to play and Ella broke. She was crying so hard that she could barely see to pull the bag off the railing. She hugged the garment bag to her chest. She'd been wrong. So wrong to trust him.

"I'm sorry, Dad," she whispered to the suit. She was trying to control the gasping sobs, but she was having a hard enough time standing. She set the box down on the bed and collapsed, more than sat, down next to it. She hugged the suit to her chest and let herself cry.

44

CAL

"You did *what!?*" Cal had a hangover and he couldn't tell if that was the reason his head felt three times its size, or if it was due to what Rhone had just told him.

"I just gave you a little nudge," she said, waving her cereal spoon at him. "You can thank me later."

"Thank you!? You took some half-baked ramblings that I just vomited onto the page and sent them to the paper to be printed!" Cal's heart was pounding in time with his head. "Ok, well maybe no one will read it . . ."

"Wouldn't count on that," Rho said around a mouth full of cereal. Cal turned to look at her. At the moment, she looked just like the mischievous thirteen-year-old she'd been, planning ways to torture him his senior year of high school.

"What do you mean?"

She swallowed and grinned at him. "Because Madison Burns said she'd make *sure* she saw it."

Cal slumped down onto a kitchen chair and held his head in his hands. "Oh no."

"Why are you so upset about this?" She brought her cereal bowl over to the table and sat down across from him. "It was a *beautiful* letter. And I took out the really personal stuff about how she smelled like fresh rain at sea, and the stuff about wanting to . . . feel her long hair and lips trailing down your . . . and you wanting to . . ."

"Rho!" Cal moaned. "Just please, stop talking. I can't even look at you right now. You read my private, personal . . ."

She sighed. "Ok, that probably crossed some line. But in my defense, you had the document *already opened*. And you were about to pass out, so really, you should be glad that I saved your laptop from falling on the floor. Huh?" Cal groaned in reply. "Sorry. I thought I was helping. Look, Cal, you get *one life*. One. Is avoiding a temporarily uncomfortable situation *worth* having to miss out on what you want, and instead living the life that someone *else* wants you to live?"

"It's not that simple . . ."

"Just answer me this," she snapped, tapping the table in front of her. Cal could feel the reverberation in his head and it felt like a battering ram. With another groan, he raised his head to look at her. "I'm going to ask you one more question, and then I'm going to leave it alone. I promise. Unless you ask me to *not* leave it alone."

"Fine," Cal said, his stomach churning for a different reason now.

"Ok. Now, let's look at this like a business projection. A . . . life projection. If you stay the course, Mom and Dad will be happy. They'll pay for this big wedding with Tar's parents, they've already bought you your apartment, and you've got a job with a starting pay of $1.2 million a year, moving up to, let's just say infinity when you take over the firm, because, Slugger, the sky's the limit. Now, those are the pros. The cons of staying the course are being married to Tar, which only you can decide how you feel about. And you'll have to stay in New York unless you're going on vacation to one of the pre-determined *appropriate* destinations, also per Mom and Dad. You will have a schedule you'll have to keep and that you don't get to set, at least until Dad is toes up. And you'll spend most of your time in the office, staring at merger paperwork, projections, and tax accountants named Hugh and Larry." Cal rested his forehead back down on the table. "Or," Rho continued, "you can stand up to Dad, tell him for once that you don't want the life he planned for you, weather the storm of his rage, Mom's theatrics and possible dramatic fainting, Tar's screeching, and the very real possibility of being disinherited. All the cons, but then you'd get to have the pros of doing what you want, where you want, for as long as you want . . . and with *whoever* you want."

The apartment doorbell rang. Rhone sighed and went to answer it. The second he heard Tara's voice, he felt his stomach clench.

"You two really tied one on last night, didn't you?"

Cal turned his head to look at Tara. She looked like she'd just walked off a promotional shoot for Saks.

"Thanks for keeping an eye on him," she said, lightly tugging on a loose piece of Rho's hair. Cal saw Rho make a face. "Come on, Callum. Dad wants us to come over to look at the linen for our party tomorrow. And then you'll need to get your tux fitted. I think you've lost a few pounds since going on your 'wilderness excursion'. And then, there might be enough time for us to have an . . . early night in." She ran her fingers through Cal's hair, scratching his scalp and sending a shiver down his spine. Though, it wasn't the same shiver it once gave him. "Thanks again, Rhone."

"No problem, Tar."

Cal saw Tara's back tense as she headed for the front door. He struggled to get to his feet and pick up his messenger bag.

Rho came around the table to stand in front of him. The apartment door opened and they heard Tara's heels leave the hardwood floor as she crossed onto the carpeted hallway. "Remember what I said," Rho hissed. "Temporary," she gave his face a quick slap and he reeled back, blinking at her. "But permanent is that slap, every second of every day, for the rest of your life. Just think about it."

Cal hugged her.

"Callum! Come on!!!" Tara's voice was already one level below screeching. He groaned and followed her out of the apartment and down to the car. His body was present while they visited Tara's parents and pointed at table cloths and god-knew-what-else, but Cal's mind was thousands of miles away, wondering how Ella had reacted when she'd read the editorial. It had been printed in the online edition and when Rho had shown him, he'd wanted to go down to her building's basement and start digging a fifty foot hole to hide in. While Tara and her parents were talking about having a string quartet play the party, Cal pulled out his phone and scrolled through his contacts. His finger hovered above Ella's number. He wished he could just hear her voice. Even if she wasn't talking to him. He doubted that she'd answer the phone if he called. He'd hidden Tara from her. He'd hidden his whole New York life from her. But it hadn't felt like hiding. Not really. Because after he'd spent nearly six months actually *living*, everything before that, felt like it was a vague memory of a story from someone else's life. He needed to know that everything he'd had wasn't a dream, wasn't gone forever. He stewed through the evening, thinking. His anxiety ratcheted up another couple of notches when they went to his parents for dinner. His Dad was silent and brooding, glaring at Cal and only speaking in harsh certainties about the upcoming wedding and Cal's first day back at the office which was going to be the day after Christmas. Not asking. Telling. Cal's mother made small talk with Tara about the wedding, but she smiled and hugged Cal before they left, telling him she was glad he'd come to his senses and come back.

They went back to Cal's old apartment which Tara had completely moved into. He sat down on the new, uncomfortable modernist couch and pulled out his phone.

"I'm going to take a bath and a quick nap," Tara called to him. "Would you . . . like to join me?"

Cal looked up at her. Her hair and make-up were perfect. She was elegantly casual in her "loungewear". But, nothing about the woman he was looking at made him feel the way he felt when he thought of sweats, messy ponytails, and blue, furry Cookie Monster slippers.

"Uh, no. I've . . . got some stuff to take care of."

She nodded, but he didn't miss the hurt expression on her face. She closed the door to their bedroom and a moment later he heard the bathtub running in the en suite. He closed his eyes and leaned his head back against the hard couch cushion. Was he an idiot? Any guy would have to be to *not* want to be with someone like Tara. He got to his feet and moved across the room to the Park Avenue view. He stared down at all the people moving around on the streets below him. He could see Christmas decorations and lights on the store fronts and people bundled against the cold. As he watched, a light snow began to fall. There had been no Christmas decorations at Tara's parents' house, his Mom and Dad's, or even Rho's. Though, she had a good excuse, having just got back into town as well. He closed his eyes and rested his forehead against the cold glass, thinking of sitting on the gazebo steps in the cold sea-smelling air, next to Ella after the fruitcake fight, with the whole town square lit up with tinsel decorations. Hanging up Christmas lights with her and Bill, the guitar-playing singing Santa at the office, the Baby Jesus Bazaar... He opened his eyes and blinked out at the city. But that life was thousands of miles away now, and New York, looked as if he'd never left it, or as if he'd never been there in the first place. Just like Hope. He moved over to the wet bar, and poured himself two fingers of scotch.

The next morning found him sprawled across the uncomfortable couch. He'd only had the one drink, but his head was throbbing from the moment Tara started talking. With her pushing and shoving, he was in the limo with Harry, on his way to get his tux fitted. Then, he was being chauffeured over to his parents house, where the engagement party was being held. The apartment was packed and Cal's first thought was to marvel at the fact that all of the people in attendance didn't have something better to do on Christmas Eve. A feeling of desperation had been growing in Cal's chest all morning, making it harder to breathe. Now, at three o'clock he was pacing around the party, barely managing to be civil with the people who wished him well and then asked where the bar was located. He had his phone in his hand and he'd almost called Ella a dozen times. If he just *knew* where she was in this whole mess, it might give him the courage to...

"You know, they used to weigh the brides down to make it harder for them to run away." Cal turned to look at Rho who was dressed in business formal, arms folded, watching him pace. She must have seen the mental anguish on his face because her haughty expression evaporated and she put an arm around him, guiding him out onto the snowy balcony where they could be alone. "You look like you're currently being haunted by an

Edgar Allen Poe character. What's going on?"

Cal shook his head. "I don't want to do this, Rho. I don't want to. But, I know I'm supposed to, so I feel like I have to. And I don't even know how she feels. She was looking for jobs in Seattle and I know she hates me now because I didn't tell her about Tara and what I was *destined* to do here and if I just *knew* if she was still there and if I had even the tiniest . . ."

"So, your whole decision about whether to stay on course or do what you want is based on whether or not a girl hates you?"

Cal stopped pacing and sighed. "Not entirely. First of all, she's not just any girl. Second, it's just . . . if I knew how she was feeling, or what her plans were, it would give me the courage to . . ." Rho snatched the phone out of his hand. "What are you doing?"

"Calling her."

Cal dove for the phone. "No! You can't."

Rho spun away from him. "Watch me. And remember to thank me later." She huddled over the phone so Cal couldn't get it away from her and put it on speaker phone. With every ring, he stopped breathing, only to start again when she didn't pick up. Finally, someone answered on the last ring.

"Ella's phone." Cal recognized Maddie's voice.

"Maddie?" Cal asked.

"Yeah. Wow. I can't believe you're calling her. Does your fiancé know? Did she see your letter?"

Cal squeezed his eyes shut. "There's a lot to explain."

"Tell me about it."

"Why are you answering her phone?" Cal asked, frowning. Had something happened to Ella?

"I've got her bag. She and Pippa are in the bathroom. Miss Mandie found her, curled up in your bed in your apartment, hugging a Santa suit."

"Oh my god," Cal said, running his fingers through his hair. "I forgot about her dad's suit."

"You stole her dad's Santa suit?"

"What? No. She was lending it to me to wear to the Santa ball."

"She lent you her *dad's* suit? You know she wouldn't even let Bill use it?"

"I know. Just . . . I need to know, Maddie. You're her best friend. Is there . . . hope for me with Ella?"

The silence on the line was the longest Cal had ever experienced in his life.

"I don't know," Maddie finally said. "I've never seen her as crushed as she is right now. She's doing ok, until she's not. But when she's not, she's barely holding together. Pippa is pissed as hell at you right now. And I am too, but I'm reserving judgment for the moment. Right now though, the odds aren't in your favor."

"Fair enough," Cal said. "Should . . . should I talk to her? Can I talk to her?"

"I have a feeling she wouldn't want to talk to you. Besides, she and Pip have the rehearsal for that fashion show in a couple of hours and the last thing in the free world that Ella needs is to be crying her eyes out while modeling lingerie and creating a new favorite story for the town to torture her with. Lovingly torture, but still."

"What should I do?" Cal breathed. "How can I win her back?"

"It's not about winning her back," Maddie snapped. "It's about apologizing, embarrassing yourself enough to actually face someone you've hurt and telling her the truth."

"Ok, how do I do that if she won't talk to me?"

"I don't know, but you better think of something. I have to go." And Maddie hung up.

Rho turned to look at him. "I like her."

Cal was sweating, despite the snow that was settling on his shoulders. Now was the moment he'd been dreading and pretending would never happen his whole life. He had to make a choice. And it would likely close one door to him forever. He turned to look back into the apartment and took a slow, deep breath.

"What are you going to do?" Rho asked.

Cal reached out and took his sister's hand. "The right thing."

They walked back into the party, side by side.

45

ELLA

"I swear it was bigger when I tried it on," Ella said, before upending the flask.

"Hey, hey! Save some for me!" Pippa muttered, snatching it out of her hand. "And it wasn't bigger. I was here. You were just tipsy. Lots of things probably seem bigger when you're drunk."

"That's the spirit," Miss Mandie muttered.

All ten women in the fashion show had been practicing walking the catwalk in their sweaters, jeans, and boots. None of them were fashion models and all ten of them looked nervous. So, in sisterly solidarity, Maddie had called Miss Mandie in as reinforcements.

"It's the least I could do since I can't be in the show with you," Maddie said, giving them a fake pouty frown.

"Next year, on the catwalk," Ella said, pointing at Maddie. "I'm going to let Mrs. Bumble know that you're already raring to go for next year."

Maddie narrowed her eyes at Ella. "Then *I'll* tell her that *you* want to do it again too!"

Pippa sighed. "To save us all time and Mrs. Bumble from having three conversations, I'll just sign all three of us up for it again. Problem solved."

"I'm never doing this again if I can help it," Ella muttered. She cut her eyes to look at the dark green scraps of silk hanging on the rack next to Pippa's Santa red teddy. "How come you get to wear a teddy and I have to wear . . . *that?*"

Pippa sighed. "Because you were blessed with long legs, and I was blessed with a boo-tay."

"Yeah, that must be it," she muttered, glaring at Pippa.

"Alright, Ella, you're next!" Martha Washington's voice was cheerful but to Ella, at that moment, she sounded like the harbinger of doom. She grimaced at Pippa and Maddie and trudged down the narrow walkway behind the partition wall that had been set up to separate the backstage from the catwalk and the audience. "Ready, Ella?"

"Ready," she called. She just needed a blindfold and a cigarette and her feeling of being minutes away from a firing squad would be complete.

"Now this is going to be your music, when you hear it start, come out. And *sashay*! These looks need to sell the sexy side of the holidays."

"Yes, I think the Pope said it first," Ella muttered. The song started and Ella felt her palms starting to sweat. "Really?" she muttered to herself. It was a bouncy pop version of "All I Want For Christmas is You".

"Ella? Hello?" Martha called over the music.

Ella sighed and squeezed her eyes shut. Unbidden, Cal's face floated into her mind, squeezed into the headpiece for the newspaper's tree, bruised nose, still smiling and waving as he walked in the parade. Before she could stop herself, she was smiling. She stepped out onto the catwalk and stared at all the empty chairs and the standing room around the stage. Her legs began to shake under her jeans and she was infinitely thankful that she wasn't wearing the ridiculous clear plastic heels they would have to model in.

"Work it, Ella!" Maddie called, running out from the backstage area to stand by Martha at the end of the catwalk. She held onto the memory of Cal, smiling and calm as people commented about his nose and the shabby costume that he was too tall for, as she moved stiffly down the catwalk.

"Smile, Ella! And don't forget to pause and pose! We're selling lingerie for charity! We need to make that money, so let's see those money-makers!"

Ella looked over at Maddie who was looking at Martha with her mouth hanging slightly open. The Town Hall was currently deserted except for the women involved in the fashion show. Maybe it was because she was standing in the same room where she and Cal had fallen into comfortable banter at the Ugly Sweater Brunch, or maybe it was the way Martha and Maddie were dancing, but for whatever reason, Ella decided to have some fun. The more she screwed around on the catwalk, the more excited Martha got.

"Yes!!! Yes! Ella yes!!! Just do that tonight!!!"

By the time Ella made it backstage again, she was laughing. Pippa was waiting for her, mouth hanging open. "What's gotten into you? I've never seen you have that much fun doing something you were dreading."

Ella shook her head. "I just . . . I keep picturing something funny in my head."

"Well, whatever you're doing, just do it tonight and you'll be fine!"

Ella swiped Pippa's flask off the makeup counter and shook it. "I think it might also have a lot to do with what's in your magic flask. Or what *was* in it. You need a refill."

"I'm on it," Miss Mandie said, muscling her way through the other girls and taking the flask from her. She unscrewed the top and stuck her nose over the opening. She sniffed and nodded. "I've got just the thing." Miss Mandie turned to leave and Pippa and Ella watched her go.

"Five bucks she comes back with tequila in that thing," Pippa muttered.

Ella frowned. "Wasn't it whiskey?"

Pippa nodded. "Won't stop her. Tequila is Miss Mandie's meaning of life."

A life well-lived. Ella felt a stab of pain in her chest, remembering Cal's letter. She tried to force her face into a smile when Pippa turned to look at her.

"So, you're really going to stay?"

Ella nodded. "Now, I don't know if it'll be forty years or not. Frankly, if next Christmas is as bad as this one, I give myself *maybe* another five years if I cut out sugar, carbs, and swearing."

Pippa chuckled. "But that's not living." She grinned at Ella. "So, what are you going to do with all the free time you're going to have at work, now that the holidays are winding down and there's less going on? I suppose you'll finally have some time to get some filing done."

A new twinge ran through Ella, not entirely unpleasant, especially considering the voice and tone she now heard that word spoken in inside her head every time she thought about it.

"Uh, yeah..."

"Ok," Maddie came bursting through the side door to the backstage. "I don't know what got into you, El, but *that!* Just do *that* tonight and you'll be perfect!"

"Well, most of Pip's flask got into me."

"It was empty, but Miss Mandie's on it," Pippa added.

"You know it's going to come back, filled with tequila, right?"

"Pippa! You're next!" Martha called. Ella went to join Maddie out front to cheer Pippa on. Of course, as her teddy was red with a black Santa style belt, she was saddled with "Santa Baby" as her song. As she and Maddie cat-called Pippa, who responded with twirls and middle-fingers raised, Ella looked at her two best friends and she felt more sure about her decision to stay than ever. There was pain in staying, especially considering the empty desk she stared at through her office window and the sense of loss for all that could have been, but wasn't. But with Pippa and Maddie, she could laugh. And if she could laugh, she could live. And that was what mattered.

"Alright girls," Martha called. "Everyone out on the catwalk." When they were assembled, squeezed together like a Land's End commercial, Martha clapped her hands together once. "Now, tonight, we're not smart Island women in sensible shoes and warm underwear. Tonight, we're sexy Christmas fairies, selling clothes for a good cause! And, as tradition goes, everyone will wear their Santa hats and beards with their outfits." There was a collective groan from the girls. "I know, I tried to argue that it would ruin the ensembles, but they said that the models have worn them every year in the fashion show and there's never been a problem raising money, so just wear them. You'll all look beautiful anyway." Martha put a hand to her forehead as if she had a headache and Miss Mandie was at her side in an instant with a glass of orange juice.

"Here Martha, your blood sugar must be low." Martha happily accepted the drink and Miss Mandie glanced over at Ella and winked.

"God bless us, everyone," Ella muttered. "But especially the steadiness of Miss Mandie's pouring hand."

Martha chugged the drink and with a satisfied smile handed the empty glass back to Miss Mandie. "Thank you. That was . . . delicious." Martha turned her attention back to the women in front of her. "Now, all of you need to have Santa suits for before and after the fashion show of course. And be back here by eight to get ready. Heels are not optional, just as your Santa beards and hats are not optional. They *will* be worn with your ensembles. The show starts at nine sharp. So, unless anyone has questions, you're all free to go!"

"Freedom being a relative term," Ella muttered, looking at her watch. "Two hours until we have to be back here." She looked from Maddie to Pippa. "Anyone else up for running away and joining the circus?"

"I mean, beards on the runway, beards at the circus," Pippa said, weighing her hands, "either way is sixes."

Ella was quietly thankful for the tradition of all fashion show volunteers wearing their outfits with their beards and hats. Maybe, there was a chance, no one would recognize her.

46

ELLA

"Ten minutes, ladies!" Martha's voice was as welcome as Hans' stupid horn in the middle of a porch nap.

Ella tried to breathe. Pippa couldn't carry her down the catwalk. She was going to have to get her legs back under her. All around them, the other eight girls were stripping down and hustling back and forth through a cloud of hairspray, back lit by the bulbs around the makeup stations.

"Just breathe," Pippa was saying as she pulled off her beard and hat, still watching Ella.

Ella breathed. Slowly, she started taking off her Santa suit while Helga gave her a mental pep talk. The catwalk was only about twenty five feet long. That's fifty feet total that she'd have to walk. It would only take her about a minute, minute and a half to walk that. She could do this. She could do this. She dropped her Santa pants and stepped out of them. The cold air hit her ass and legs and she started to shake again. She knew it was not because of the cold, but because of sheer terror. She could hear the loud mumbling of conversation from the crowd over the Christmas music.

"Ok, ladies, let's line up!" Mrs. Bumble was marching through the dressing room, waving her hands to usher girls into line. Pippa was last and Ella was right before her.

"Can we sit until it's closer to our time?" Pippa asked Mrs. Bumble when the old woman turned her beady eyes on them.

"Fine. But don't miss your entrance!"

When she'd moved off, Pippa squeezed Ella's hand. "You can do this, El. I know you can."

Ella nodded, unable to string together everything that was running through her mind. A part of her *wanted* to do this. She *wanted* to face this fear and come out the other side. She didn't want Cranberry Sauce to be written on her headstone. If she could pull this off, it might be enough . . .

"Good Evening Hope!" Conner's voice boomed out across the crowd. This was greeted by a roar of applause and cheers. "Tonight, we've got an Excavation exclusive fashion show for you, with fifty percent of all proceeds from sales of tonight's ensembles going to the Hope Pantry and the other half going to help our very own local business, Excavation." More cheering. "But before that, we have a very special, last minute treat for you." Pippa and Ella frowned at each other. "Our very own, Cal Dickson is here tonight and he's going to sing something he would like to dedicate to a very special lady."

"What the..." Ella breathed.

Pippa pulled her up out of her chair and began pushing her way through the other girls. "Sorry. Emergency. Ex-Coworker about to embarrass himself. We have to see this." The girls seemed to understand and when they were at the edge of the curtains leading out to the stage, Pippa crouched down so they could both peek around the edge.

It was him. Cal. He was back. Conner handed him a cordless microphone and Cal looked up and down the stage. There were no stairs, making it easier to get up, so with a shrug, he set the mic down and climbed up the side. It wasn't graceful and a couple people in the audience chuckled.

"He came back," Pippa breathed. Ella couldn't speak. Her mind was having trouble believing what she was seeing.

"Hi everyone." There was an obvious waver in Cal's voice. She saw him wipe his free hand on his pant leg as he started to shift his weight. He was wearing a Santa suit . . . a very *familiar* Santa suit.

"Is that my dad's . . ," she started to say.

"Before you get mad," Pip said. "He called and asked, and Maddie is just as guilty as I am, so you'll have to kill both of us in your revenge sequel."

Ella couldn't put description to her emotions at the moment, but she knew anger wasn't one of them.

"So, I screwed up pretty bad, with an amazing woman." Cal was saying, his voice growing stronger. The crowd was silent. "And it was because I was scared." He took a deep breath and Ella could feel her own anxiety reverberating off of him. "Scared of my past. Scared of facing my fears. And, when I was a kid, I had an embarrassing, scarring experience that has haunted me my whole life. I tried to sing this song, but when I opened my mouth, nothing came out. And everyone that was there, wouldn't let me ever forget that moment." The crowd was tittering now.

"Nail them, Cal," Pippa muttered.

"And it made things worse," Cal said. "But, ultimately, I think I've always known that the only way I was going to get over that experience, was to face it. And, thankfully, I can face it tonight, because, for the first time in my life, I have someone to sing this sappy, terrible, pop song to, and mean every word. Merry Christmas, Hope. And Ella," he turned on the stage and Ella froze as his gaze sought hers behind the shadows thrown by the curtains. He smiled. "This is for you."

He turned around to face Conner and nodded. The familiar notes of the corny Backstreet Boys' "Shape of My Heart" started playing and Ella felt something breaking inside of her. But, it wasn't painful. Tears were springing to her eyes, but she couldn't stop smiling as she listened to Cal sing. He wasn't a singer, but it was still the most beautiful thing she thought she'd ever heard.

As he sang, the audience cheered and laughed and Ella peeked out again to see Cal doing some truly goofy dance steps.

She laughed and she felt Pippa squeeze her hand. "You know that if you take him back, he's going to have to top this next Christmas Eve. And the one after that."

When the song wound down, the crowd went wild. Cal bowed to the crowd and then he turned and looked right at Ella. She knew that for as long as she lived, she'd never forget that look of complete vulnerability on his face. He put his right hand over his chest and bowed his head. When he looked back up at her. He winked and mouthed, "You've got this."

He climbed back off the stage and handed the mic back to Conner.

"Girls! Back in line! Quickly now! We're already running behind." Martha was smiling, but Ella could hear the annoyance in her voice.

In a daze, she followed Pippa back to the end of the line.

"Wow," Ella said. "I can't believe it."

"Yeah." She could hear the awe in Pip's voice. "I didn't think he'd do *that*."

Ella felt lighter. Cal was back. That was a whole realization on its own. But, beside that, he'd just gotten on stage, in front of the whole town, and sang the song that had haunted him since his childhood. She looked down at herself. Well, it wasn't a cranberry sauce can, but at that moment, it felt like a toss-up as to which was more embarrassing. She stepped into the clear plastic heels under her chair and squared her shoulders.

Pippa grinned at her. "Uh oh. Is this going to become a new escalation thing between you two?"

Ella frowned at her. "What are you talking about?"

Pippa sighed. "Are you two now going to try to out-self-humiliate each other for the rest of your lives? He sings, you model and dance and then next year, you'll both be trying to top the other again, so he'll model dad shorts and you'll rap or something?"

"Good god, no," Ella said, shaking her head. "This is my one-night-only performance." She took a deep breath, trying to shove down the jitters which were trying again to get a toehold for an anxiety attack. "I'm going out there, to do the same thing he just did: Wipe the slate clean. No more Silent Silver for him. No more Cranberry Sauce for me."

Pip looked a little doubtful. "That's great and everything, but I don't know if you'll be able to *completely* get other people to stop with the nicknames."

Ella shrugged, a smile spreading across her face. "That's their problem. *This* is for me. I don't want to think of myself as Cranberry Sauce: the girl that wrecked Thanksgiving for the town. If they call me that, I want to be able to laugh it off, because I know that I stood in front of them tonight and gave a damn good performance."

"Hell yeah!" Pippa squealed, pumping a fist in the air. She paused. "So, I guess you don't need a sip from my flask."

Ella held her hand out to her. "Nope, I'm still going to chug the whole thing. Hand it over."

"Pippa, Ella, get in line!" Martha squawked. They complied, Ella hiding the flask behind her back until Martha had moved out onto the stage to give her welcoming speech.

"Do you think Santa would be a twerker? Ella asked, feeling the heat from the whiskey mixing with the tequila in her stomach. There were butterflies there and she could feel the slightest sheen of cold sweat on her palms, but Helga had put on her stubborn girl scouts uniform and was rolling up the sleeves.

"I say yes," Pippa said, giving Ella a wicked smile.

* * *

CAL

"Hey Cal! The 90s called and said they wanted their pop music back!" Cal turned to see Rudy "Red" Callahan, the Fire Chief smirking at him.

"That's funny," Cal said, smiling. He'd dealt with Red before. The guy was Ella's age and a jerk from what he'd seen. Cal held the man's gaze but didn't say anything else. This was his town now, too, and Red was going to have to work a lot harder than that to get a rise out of him. After a minute, Red moved away.

Conner took the microphone from him and slapped him on the back. "That was cool, man. Dorky song, but hey, what love song isn't?"

Cal chuckled at his friend. "Just wait until the right person comes along for you. Then, you'll be willing to do any number of dorky things for them."

Conner laughed and shook his head. "No man, I'm a player for life. I . . ." he trailed off as Martha Washington bustled onto the stage in a light pink Santa suit. "Show time."

Cal started to back away, but paused when he felt a hand on his back. He turned on the spot to see Miss Mandie grinning up at him. "A little humiliation for love is good for the complexion. Here." She handed him a Bloody Mary.

"Oh, Miss Mandie, I . . ."

"Don't drink it," she warned. "That one's mine. I just want you to hold it so my hands are free for this."

Cal decided not to ask. The music started and Martha hurried back behind the curtains. Cal took a deep breath.

Ok universe, this ask isn't for me. But, please, cash out any good karma I have and shift that over into Ella's balance. Please, make this good for her.

He gripped the cold drink in his hand and held his breath, trying to will the universe to come through for him.

* * *

ELLA

The fashion show was moving too fast. The line of girls in front of Ella was getting shorter by the minute and she was back to deep breathing exercises as she got closer to the front. The lyrics of the song Cal had sung were circling through her head, and as she breathed, and watched, and waited, she started thinking about what would happen *after* the show. Would they fight? Could she just forgive him and move on? Would he have anything else to tell her?

The girl in front of her disappeared through the curtains as "Jingle Bell Rock" started. Ella's outfit wasn't the one with the most exposure, but it was up there. She twisted the short lace hem of her see-through nightie.

"Pretend you're just modeling for him," Pippa whispered.

Ella turned to stare at her, eyes wide. Pippa sighed and rolled her eyes. "Don't act so surprised. Maddie and I knew you two were going to hook up before either one of you did. The only surprising part about it was how long it took. Talk about waiting for the fourth quarter." Ella mouthed at her, trying to figure out what to say. "But don't worry about that right now," she continued. "Just find him in the crowd and dance just for him."

The girl in front of her returned through the curtains, smiling and waving behind her as the crowd applauded and the music faded out. "All I Want for Christmas is You" started playing and Pippa gave her a shove. "Go!"

* * *

CAL

Cal was having fun watching the crowd as they watched the fashion show. He'd pulled out his cell phone to take pictures of the crowd cheering and especially Miss Mandie, who was whistling and hollering as the girls flounced down the runway. Even . . . spanking herself at one point . . . which Cal was infinitely glad he *hadn't* caught on camera. Cal was thankful for his beard because he was having a hard time containing his laughter when he recognized some of the other women in the crowd like Mrs. Bumble, and Mrs. Meyers, who was wearing her nativity hat instead of a Santa hat. "Jingle Bell Rock" faded out and a pop version of "All I Want for Christmas is You" started.

When she walked out onto the stage, he was doubly thankful for his beard. He felt his jaw fall open. He couldn't take his eyes off her. Ella was all long legs and torso and twitching hips as she shimmied down the runway, barely clothed in green silk. He had to force himself to think about the ass-kicking he was still due from her, to keep his mind off the last time he saw her wearing so little.

She paused on the runway, crouched down and went to hands and knees, crawling to the end of the stage, shaking her hips from side to side. The crowd went wild. They only got louder when she rolled over on her back and kicked her legs in the air, twirling her finger around her beard. Cal was laughing and whistling now too. His face hurt from smiling. God help him, he was in love with that girl. She was doing it. And in lingerie, on a stage, wearing a Santa hat and beard.

She wasn't just *doing* it. She was *owning* it. Like his stupid, uncoordinated dance moves, she wasn't taking herself seriously. And not a single person in the crowd was yelling "Cranberry Sauce" at her. There were so many sides to Ella, and he knew he hadn't seen them all. She was real, god, she was so real that he felt like he'd been asleep for twenty-six years and was just learning what life could be like. She skipped back up the runway, pausing to shimmy and shake, before blowing a kiss at the crowd through her beard, giving a little finger wave, and disappearing.

He whistled and whooped and clapped as the music died down, replaced by Eartha Kitt's "Santa Baby", followed by the entrance of Pippa. She was wearing what looked like a Santa suit turned into a teddy. He could tell it was her by the red curls bouncing as she walked. She got to the end of the runway, turned away from the audience and started twerking. The crowd lost it. He was laughing so hard, Miss Mandie turned and took her drink back from him. When Pippa had disappeared behind the curtain and the lights were brought back up, the older woman turned to look at him.

"I don't know if it was your 90s pop display or my liquor, but between the two of us, she made it through."

"Here, here," Cal said with a grin.

"I need to get back to my specialty bar," she said. She patted him on the arm. "I haven't rented out your apartment yet, but I think you might have to wrestle Ella for it. She'd been asking about it before and I'm going to leave it to the two of you to work that out." She winked and without another word, disappeared into the crowd.

Cal managed to skirt the group of a cappella Santas, warming up, now that the official festivities had kicked off. Beside them, there was a group of keg standing Santas taking their places around a couple of fifty-five gallon drums, dressed up to look like chimneys. He was almost run over by a gang of walker-toting and Rascal-riding Santas, and then there was a group of dancing Santas forming as the runway was quickly deconstructed. It *was* a ball, after all. He pulled out his phone and started taking pictures. He wasn't sure that he'd be able to talk Myrna and Ella into giving him his old job back, but he was hopeful. And maybe a good way to start clawing his way back into their good graces would be to cover the event. Of course, he knew that was just superficial reasoning. The lightness in his chest as he took in the spectacle that was Hope Island in its natural state, told him that this was just him, loving his new town. Bar none, he couldn't remember ever feeling as happy as he did at that moment. He'd said it before, but this time, he meant it with every fiber of his being. He *was* home.

"Hey," Ella's voice broke into his thoughts, and he turned to face her, back in her Santa suit, Pippa beside her, fighting with her beard.

"I..." Where to start?

"Need a drink," Pippa finished for him. "It's unanimous."

Cal felt himself relax. "I think Miss Mandie is back at her specialty bar, if that sounds good." Ella moved toward him, and he held his breath. She paused and then reached for his hand.

47

ELLA

Ella grinned, feeling her heart pounding in her chest as the warmth from his palm seeped through her skin, traveling up her arm and right into her heart. "Good. Let's get in there before the crew around her start doing belly shots off each other."

Cal shuddered. "Yeah, with the beards and fake fur suits, that could get ugly."

Pippa led the way and Ella fell in step beside Cal. She could feel the eyes of the people they passed following them, but she didn't care. She wasn't sure if it was the rush of adrenaline she was still riding after the over-the-top performance she'd done on the runway, or if it was because of the semi-anonymity she felt, wearing her Santa suit. Either way, she was just taking in the thrill of holding Cal's hand. She didn't know what to say to him. There was so much. She needed time to put her thoughts in order. The area beyond the stage, bottle-necked into the large meeting room where the bars were set up and they had to pause when they reached the doorway to look around.

"Wow. It is just . . . wall to wall Santas in here," Cal said. "Like the backrooms of all the Macy's in the U.S. had a magic portal for Santa to go through and this is where it dumped all of them."

"I think that's what the decoration crew was going for," Ella said. There was a crowd around Miss Mandie now, so Ella motioned toward one of the bars on the side of the room. They took three beers from the bartender Santa and Cal raised his up.

"To making it through the Hellidays," he said. He paused, and even behind his Santa beard, Ella could see the intensity in his gaze as he locked eyes with her. "To standing up to people trying to control us and telling them where to get off, and then facing our pasts."

Ella was speechless. New York? Tara? Was he saying . . .

"Not just facing them," Pippa interrupted. "You two sang and . . . crawled all over them." She hip-checked Ella who stumbled sideways but quickly caught herself, before cutting her eyes to Pippa.

Pippa seemed immune from her glare. She waggled her eyebrows at Cal and then Ella. "You both know you're going to be tapped by everyone in town to do something like this next year. When there's even *more* to do for the Hellidays." Pippa sighed. "And don't forget, we're not through them yet."

"Almost through," Ella said, rubbing the back of her neck. She saw Cal shift his weight next to her. "We just have some post-Christmas stuff and New Year's. And then it quiets down until Martin Luther King, Jr. Day, and Valentine's Day, and President's Day . . ." She had to stop talking because Cal's lips were on hers. She had artificial beard hair in her mouth, her Santa hat was trying to slip off the back of her head and she was still wearing lingerie under a Santa suit, but she did not care. Ella threw her arms around his neck, nearly spilling her beer down his back, and pulled Cal closer.

"Santa on Santa action!" Someone in the crowd shouted.

Ella groaned. Reluctantly, she loosened her grip on Cal. He laughed, but he didn't let her go. He held her in front of him, his eyes finding hers. Then he started making some spitting sounds and reached up to tug at his beard.

"Sorry. Beard hair, "Cal said.

"Yeah, I feel for Mrs. Claus." She smiled at him, trying to force all the feelings rolling through her into the mold of words she could say to tell him . . .

"Ella! Pippa!"

"Oh good," Ella groaned. "It's the melodic warble of the Martha Washington bird." The three of them turned to see Martha waving them over.

"We need to get a picture! I want to blow it up and frame it for the wall in my store. Come on! Come on!"

"To be continued," he whispered. He had phrased it like a question and there was hope but also vulnerability in his eyes.

"To be continued, definitely," Ella whispered back. She moved off with Pippa to pose against a wall with the other eight girls. Thankfully, they were allowed to keep their Santa suits on. She could feel Cal's eyes on her the whole time, and she was starting to feel self-conscious when she made her way back over to him.

"You were phenomenal," Cal whispered, reaching for her. For a split-second, Ella had a dilemma. She knew they needed to talk everything out. But, it was Christmas Eve, and he was there. The look in his eyes was telling her that he wasn't going anywhere. And, she'd just faced down the biggest monster in her past. No, tonight, she just wanted to live. So, as Cal pulled her close to him, it was Ella's turn to make the first move. She leaned in, her hands on the side of his face, separating his fake mustache to find his lips, still managing to push some of it into his mouth, but he acted like he couldn't care less. She flicked her tongue playfully against his and she felt him wrap his fist in the jacket of her Santa suit.

* * *

CAL

"Am I playing with fire?" she whispered, breaking the kiss to move her lips closer to his ear.

"Ella Danforth, you are playing with lava," Cal said, trying to make his voice as deep and husky as he could. But he couldn't hold it together. He snorted and she started to laugh too. "Do you want to dance?" he asked.

Ella nodded. Even under her beard, he could see her smile. "Can I bring my beer?"

"Well, I'm bringing mine," Cal said. "And it would be a shame to break them up." A pop cover of "White Christmas" came on and they danced. He kept one hand on her waist, the other on his beer while she kept one on his shoulder, innocently stroking his collar bone through his suit while she held her beer with her free hand.

"Lava, Ella," Cal growled, when she traced a forefinger under the collar of his jacket.

She paused and Cal could hear doubt creeping into her voice. "Cal, about New York."

"There is no New York anymore," he said, softly. "No more Tara, no more family expectations, no more career in the Big Apple waiting for me. As of today, I'm a disinherited, college educated, possibly unemployed reporter for the *Hope Hornblower*. Oh, and Miss Mandie says I might be homeless, too."

Ella leaned forward, her gray eyes wide. The raw emotion there was making Cal feel weak. "I think I might be able to help you with the job area, but that apartment is just so cute . . ." She leaned in and he met her half-way, their kiss deepening.

When she pulled back, he saw worry in her eyes. "Is . . . Is this too fast?" She sounded like she wasn't sure if she was asking herself or Cal. She dropped her gaze to his chest, and he watched her face. "I mean. Let's be honest, we've only known each other for a little over three weeks, but . . ." Her expression told him that she was standing on some mental precipice, considering jumping. He rubbed his thumb over the small of her back. If she jumped, he would be there to catch her. Her voice was soft. "I think I'm falling in love with you."

He slowed down in his dancing steps. "Ella." He waited for her to look up and meet his gaze. He kept his voice low, but he tried to put a lot of reassurance in it. "I *am* in love with you. But I won't push for anything you don't want." If Ella Danforth wanted to wait for a year, or two or five or ten to do more than kiss him now, after what he'd put her through, he would wait and write articles and spend every day just *living* with her and breathing the same air. She was giving him margins of grace, much wider than he deserved. He would do whatever she wanted.

"No," Ella whispered in his ear. "It doesn't feel fast. And that's what's scaring me."

"I'm in the passenger seat on this El, you get to control the gas."

She sighed. "But you'll tell me if I'm taking a curve too fast or something?"

"Oh, say that again, but slower," Cal said. She laughed and he pulled her closer to him.

"God, what a day," she said, resting her head against his shoulder.

"What a month," Cal said with a smile.

"At least the mystery of Clarence and the blood-stained briefcase is finally solved," she said doing a pretty good impression of Velma from Scooby-Doo. "And the Hellidays are almost over."

Cal smiled. "And we all made it through in one piece."

Ella lifted her head and speared him with her gray eyes. "And you're home."

"I'm home," Cal said. There was a happy, painful knot in his throat as he looked at her. He *was* home.

She raised a hand to his cheek. "Are you sure you're ok? I mean, after everything?"

"Perfectly fine," Cal said. "In fact," he took a deep breath to steady himself, in case this was the wrong thing to say at the moment, but he wanted her to know, "I'm feeling so good, and I *do* owe you, so I'd even be up to do all the filing in your office."

There was mischief and something naughty in Ella's gaze, and if she hadn't been wearing that ridiculous Santa beard, Cal was willing to bet he'd currently be treated to the sight of her biting her lip in that way that drove him crazy. There was something about Ella's lips. Her whole face was expressive, but there was something so . . . bewitching . . . about her mouth, whether she was telling him off or licking scotch or eating frosting. Her eyes moved off his face and he turned to see what she was looking at. She was staring out the dark windows that faced the town square.

"Come on," she said quickly, grabbing his hand and leading him off the dance floor.

"Is . . . Is that snow?" Cal asked when they got to the doors. "I didn't think it snowed on the island."

"It's rare," Ella said. She turned to look at Cal. "You wouldn't want to stand out in it with me for a minute, would you?"

"No," Cal said, shaking his head. He could feel her hand wilt a little in his. He squeezed it. "I want to stand out in the snow with you forever. Or five minutes. Or until frostbite sets in, whichever occurs first." She rolled her eyes and they headed outside. They heard some yelling and looked over to see a crew of drunk Santas rolling around in the few flakes on the ground, trying to make snow angels. As one, Cal and Ella pulled out their phones to take pictures.

"What do you think? Cover photo to lead the story?" Cal asked.

"Definitely," Ella said. She sighed and Cal looked over at her.

"Since we're technically outside the Ball, do you think we could get away with taking down our beards?" he asked.

Ella looked around. "Maybe to our chins. You don't want to get caught flaunting the rules by the mayor's wife or she'll make us work the event next year."

Cal raised an eyebrow at her. "Really?"

"Where do you think the Santa bartenders come from?" Ella asked. "That's mayoral detention in this town. If you get in trouble one year, you have to serve drunk Santas the next year, *and* you can't drink."

"Wow," Cal said. "Hope does have a purgatory."

"Yep," Ella said. "And it's exactly as awful as you'd expect."

They pulled down their beards, and Cal suddenly felt more exposed with nothing to hide behind, but it was definitely worth it to see Ella's flushed face. She was smiling and he could tell she was forcing herself to breathe and keep her eyes on his face.

"I actually wanted to ask you about something," Ella said.

"Sounds serious."

"It kind of is. I should have asked you weeks ago, when I thought of it, but with everything that was happening and . . ." She shook her head. "Sorry, I'm babbling." She took a deep breath. "You're staying, right?"

Cal grinned and nodded. "Yes."

Ella's face broke into a relieved smile. "Ok. In that case, how would you feel about coming back as the head reporter?"

"Really?" Cal asked. "But I left."

She took their beers and set them down on the railing before taking both of his hands in hers. "But you came back. And if you hadn't been here this month, I wouldn't have survived." She shook her head. "And, because if it hadn't been for you, Callum "Cal" Dickson, lost Backstreet Boy, and loon that gave up a shit ton of money and a whole life in New York to move to the island . . ." Cal laughed and Ella squeezed his hands, her face earnest as she held his gaze, "I would never have faced my fears in this town." She paused.

"And I would have never seen the truth. That letter you wrote . . ." Cal thought about interrupting her and telling her about Rho and Maddie, but she continued, and he decided it could wait. "You were right. Working with and being a part of this community *is* doing something big. It's big enough and it makes a difference all on its own. I would never have seen it if someone like you hadn't shown me what to look for. Living here my whole life, it's easy to miss the forest for the trees." She leaned forward and stretched up to kiss him on the cheek. Cal's face was warm long before and after her soft lips trailed over his skin. "Thank you," she whispered.

Cal ran his thumbs over her fingertips. "El, I should be thanking you." He felt the heat in his face changing from longing to embarrassment. "For so much of my life, I just went with the flow. Never wanting to rock the boat and say what *I* wanted, what *I* needed, or do anything about it. And then, I met you. You never back down from a fight. You made me want to be stronger." He shook his head. "You make everyone around you feel stronger, just by encouraging them. *You* deserve to be the Editor. You know what you're doing, you know this town, and you have the heart to make it real. It's not just a fluff paper when you run it. It breathes and lives and connects people. You want to know why tourism has been off the charts this last month?"

"Because Miss Mandie started selling alcoholic eggnog at ten in the morning?" Ella asked.

"Well, that might be a contributing factor, but do you want to know the real reason?" Ella nodded. "It's because people fall in love with Hope. The *Hornblower* really is a love letter, every day, to this town. And people are searching for a romance like that. They need it. *I* needed it. That's why I had to come back. Well . . . one of the reasons." He squeezed her hands.

"Couldn't kick the eggnog habit?" Ella laughed.

"It's the whipped cream and booze combination," Cal growled. "Miss Mandie's got my number. She sprinkles some cinnamon on top and I'm a full-blown eggnog abuser."

Ella laughed and pulled him to her. This kiss, sans Santa beards, standing in the snow, looking out at the town center was one of the moments that Cal knew would be a perfect moment that he would use to measure all other moments for the rest of his life. Normally, when he added moments to his list of great moments, it was depressing, knowing it could be the last moment to make the list and it would make every moment after it seem insignificant. Somehow, as he pulled Ella closer to him and knocked her Santa hat off her head while he ran his fingers through her hair, he didn't feel the old depression. Only pure, *real* joy. Because he knew that every second with Ella had the potential to top this moment.

When he finally loosened his hold on her and she pulled her head back, he saw the devilish glint in her eye, despite the snow that was starting to accumulate on her shoulders. "Well, Mr. Head Reporter, I believe you are obligated by your job description to do 'other duties as assigned'. So as penance for leaving us in a lurch, I would like you to help me *file* all the papers in my office. Tonight, preferably."

"Oh *now* you're talking about filing, huh," Cal sighed, trying to frown as if he was considering it to be a deal breaker, as well as pretend that they were actually talking about filing.

"You know," Ella said, wrapping her hands around the collar of his Santa suit. "I think Miss Mandie is onto something with the chocolate frosting and Marvin Gaye. When you're doing something like frosting cupcakes, or filing, you just need the right music and atmosphere, and it can be . . . fun." She leaned forward and Cal felt every nerve in his body stand at attention when she started kissing her way up his neck.

"Ella Danforth, I would file papers with you all night long," he growled, pulling her close and kissing her under her ear.

She chuckled. "Well, maybe we should practice. You know, besides that single night of . . . filing, it had been months since I'd . . . filed."

"For me too," Cal said. Ella met his gaze and the softest smile formed on her lips.

"Really?"

He nodded. "Besides that night, I haven't filed for at least the last six months, probably more. I could definitely use the practice. And besides, there may be some filing we need to do in my apartment. I hear I might be getting a roommate?"

"Oh, so now it's *your* apartment again and *I'm* going to be the roommate?" Ella asked. Cal grinned and kissed her. When she pulled back, she said. "Ok, but if we're going to file all night long, I'm sorry, but we'll need better filing music than Nick Cave."

Cal grinned. "Don't worry, I have a plan."

48

Epilogue

MISS MANDIE

The snow was a two-inch thick blanket covering Hope. Any other day, she would have thought it was pretty, but Miss Mandie was nursing a hangover and the glint of the snow under the light from the lamp posts would have caused snow blindness if she'd forgotten to wear her sunglasses. She felt her way through the dark bakery and groaned when she flipped on the bright kitchen lights.

"Never again, Mandie," she muttered, putting a hand to her head. "Tequila is the devil." She poured herself a tall glass of water from the pitcher in the fridge and pulled out a bowl of chocolate frosting. She just needed to get into her routine. It was Christmas morning, traditionally a pretty busy time in Hope. Unlike most places, the townsfolk in Hope didn't keep their celebrations to themselves. They'd wander through town, snow or no snow, just for the chance to wish everyone they came across a merry Christmas. *Crazy town*, she thought with a smile. She started mixing up the day's cupcakes and donuts. Something was missing.

"I need my Marvin," Miss Mandie mumbled to the empty kitchen. Without looking away from her mixer, she reached for the little boombox.

Her hand hit the empty counter top. She moved it around, searching. Nothing.

EPILOGUE

Finally, she dragged her tired gaze from her humming mixer and looked at the spot where the boombox usually sat. It wasn't there. She frowned and turned to look around the kitchen. The boombox was gone.

"What the . . ."

Then she paused. There were muffled sounds coming from overhead. She reached over and turned her mixer off. The smooth sounds of "Sexual Healing" filtered down to her through the ceiling. She shook her head and chuckled. "Well, it's about time." She sighed. "Blame it on the Marvin Gaye."

Would you like to leave a review for Deck The Headlines? Click the links below to tell other readers how much you enjoyed it!

Amazon
https://tinyurl.com/DeckTheHeadlinesAReview
GoodReads
https://tinyurl.com/DeckTheHeadlinesGR
BookBub
https://tinyurl.com/DeckTheHeadlinesBB

For access to a bonus epilogue in which we catch up with Cal and Ella two years later, head to the link below and join Teagan's Hopeful Romantics mailing list: https://tinyurl.com/DeckBonusEpilogue

Teagan Hart

Spicy. Snarky. Small Town Shenanigans.

49

Sleigh Ride Or Die Preview

ABBY

"No. I'm not going to join your ritual torture cult," Abby muttered as she stuffed the papers from her ninth-grade biology class into the drawer of her desk.

"You didn't even let me finish the whole sales pitch," Dana said. "Wait until you hear about what we wear when we make our nightly sacrifices."

"Well if this gets graphic, feel free to keep it to yourself," Abby sighed, dropping down onto the stool she used in lieu of a desk chair.

Dana snorted. "I don't know about you, Locke, but I could use some 'graphic' these days." Abby looked up at her friend in time to see Dana glance toward the classroom door. "Of course, not *all* of us can live next door to a stack of tall, bookish pancakes."

Abby blinked and shook her head. "Ok, now I can't tell if you're horny or hungry."

"Yeah, I missed lunch. Still, when are you going to, you know . . . jump on it?" Dana jerked her head towards the hallway.

"Dana, what did we say about your House of Pain consumption during work hours?"

"I couldn't help it. I was working on the Poe display. I needed my jams."

"Well . . . I *guess* that makes sense."

"Yeah. What *doesn't* make sense is how someone can live next door to a person who speaks the same weird nerd language they do, is single, would drop anything they're doing to help with whatever hair-brained project comes up, *and* looks like everyone's college professor they had a crush on, *and* yet this someone *still* doesn't check that book out."

Abby stared at her, deadpan. "I'm sorry. I got lost in that run-on sentence. Send help, a compass, and some sled dogs. Is that *someone* supposed to be me?"

"Yes you, you Vulture."

"You mean Vulcan?" Abby asked with a sigh.

"Yes, pointy ears, emotionally clueless, yet lovable," Dana said. "And don't play coy with me, Abs. I'm in the middle of a serious dry spell. I need to live vicariously through someone."

"Not that it's any business of yours," Abby said, dropping her voice, "but I'll see your dry spell and raise you a 'dystopian-level drought'." It was a truth Abby had been feeling more strongly lately. She wasn't sure if it was because of her looming thirty-third birthday on the other side of Christmas, a random spike in her hormones, or some kind of feral pull brought on by the excitement and expectations of the holidays. Probably a combination of all three.

"An entirely self-imposed dystopian drought," Dana muttered. "Literally cross your porch and there's paradise, wrapped in tweed, one door down . . ."

Abby felt her skin flushing in annoyance. "Dana . . . he's my best friend. Just. . .let it go," Abby muttered, rubbing her temples.

She heard Dana sigh. "If you don't, someone else is going to, but fine. I'll let it go if that's what you *really* want."

Abby glanced up and squinted at her friend. "That was too easy."

"You didn't let me finish," she said, crossing her arms. "*Fine.* So you have no reason to *not* sign up for Santa's Singles this year."

"Ah yes, circling back to your ritual torture cult," Abby said again. "What would Hope's holiday season be without it? Nothing like awkward blind dates periodically accentuated by the giant whale-fart alphorn in the town square. I think I'd rather stay in my dry desert like the Road Warrior." The thought of volunteering for forced, paired dating as some kind of hellish carpool lane out of her dry desert was enough to have her thinking fond thoughts about the impending Christmas break and the vibrator under her bed.

"Hey, I'm willing to cross the desert in search of a thunderstorm," Dana said. She bit her lip and ran a hand through her hair, striking a pose.

Abby raised an eyebrow. "Is that your time-traveling audition for the cover of Penthouse or something?"

"More like 'Pent-up'. Abs, I'm serious," Dana sighed and Abby rolled her eyes. Dana had at least *had* relationships during the current presidency. It had been three years since Abby's last romantic endeavor had blown up in her face like a Whorley brothers' chemistry experiment.

"Hey, you two," a low voice called. The color drained from Dana's face, her eyes grew three sizes behind her glasses, and Abby had to stifle a snort of laughter as her old friend, the demure school librarian resurfaced.

Abby turned to look at Fred Goss, the gym teacher, poking his head into her classroom. He was a good-looking guy with deep tan skin and kind eyes.

"Did either of you happen to see a couple of miscreants smuggling dodgeballs?"

"The Whorley brothers again?" Abby asked.

Fred cut his eyes back to the hallway. "I suspect." He cleared his throat and gave Dana a half-smile. "Hey there, Dana. I-I meant to tell you how much I liked the new Poe display in the library."

"Oh, well, you know, it's his birthday next month . . . and, I didn't want to disappoint . . . him," Dana trailed off.

Abby stared at the space between Fred and Dana, and for a moment, she swore she could actually *see* the awkwardness, break-dancing on the floor, as well as feel it in the air.

"Well," Abby clapped her hands together and got to her feet. Either the sound or her movement jerked Dana and Fred out of their game of social freeze tag. "I've got Jake Whorley in my nine o'clock chemistry class in the morning, and Aaron has Turk in his sophomore English class at the same time across the hall. So, we could divide and conquer. If either of them is suddenly found to be 'with dodgeball', say under their Metallica shirts, we'll be sure to let you know."

"Uh," Fred cleared his throat. "Good . . . Th-thanks, Abby."

She swept him a bow.

"Oh, I know that bow," a deep voice rumbled behind Fred. "Whenever Abs breaks out a bow, I know that there has just been some mid-grade sass bandied about."

Abby shrugged. "Eh, low-grade at best." She grinned at Aaron where he towered over Fred in the door frame.

He raised one dark eyebrow behind his black-rimmed glasses and she saw his hazel eyes glance from Fred, back to her. "Let me guess, the Whorley brothers?"

Fred turned to look up at Aaron. "How did you . . . ?"

Aaron nodded back across the hall to his classroom. "I saw them out the window, throwing dodgeballs at each other. I assumed it was 'unsanctioned play'."

"You assumed right," Fred muttered. "See you all tomorrow. I've got two Whorleys to skin alive."

"Jake has a paper due," Abby called after him, "So don't just skin him. You better finish him off."

When Fred was gone, Aaron grinned at her. "You about ready?"

Abby nodded. "Yeah. I think I've done enough damage for today. Let me get my coat."

Aaron nodded. "Always good to stop when you're ahead."

He disappeared from the doorway and Dana grinned at her. Now that they were alone, her old confidence seemed to be back, performing an encore.

"What?" Abby asked, blinking at her.

Dana shook her head slowly and Abby felt a stab of annoyance at the wicked smile her friend was now giving her.

"Drought," Dana nodded at Abby. Then she jerked her head back toward the hallway. "Meet thunderstorm."

"Seriously Dana, not having this conversation with you again. He's my neighbor and right now, he's looking like he's unseated you as my best friend. You were neck and neck, but I'm pretty sure he just came out ahead." Dana's eyes widened, her mouth opening, ready to twist Abby's words into some kind of tantric double-entendre. "And if you rearrange what I said into something about necking, coming, or . . . head, I'm dis-inviting you from my 'Teachers Gone Wild' start of break party." Abby narrowed her eyes at Dana while she weighed the satisfaction of saying something saucy versus missing out on the annual teachers' cutting loose party.

Finally, Dana blew out a sigh. "Fine. But, you should at least *think* about joining Santa's Singles this year. Since you and your new 'ride or die bestie' across the porch won't climb into that sleigh together, you should be out there looking for someone to jingle your bells."

Abby closed her eyes and pinched the bridge of her nose. "Really?"

Dana sighed. "Cut me some slack. I'm high on Christmas cookies. The staff break room looks like some kind of mis-decorated cookie Valhalla. Bob got them cheap from Miss Mandie. Apparently they're the rejects from the Bake-Off over at De-Floured."

"Whatever happened to 'just say no'," Abby muttered.

"Sugar overdose or not, I'm being serious, Abs." Abby opened her eyes and looked at Dana. She was taller than Abby, not that that was unusual. She was often dwarfed by her own freshmen. Dana pulled Abby into a hug and Abby went with it because she knew resistance was futile because Dana was an octopus when she wanted to hug someone. "You're not getting any younger," Dana murmured. "And I'm not either. You don't want to die alone, do you?"

Before Abby could respond, Aaron was back, his beanie pulled down all the way to his eyebrows, squashing his dark hair flat against his forehead. She and Dana broke apart and Abby couldn't help the smile that spread across her face. Aaron looked like a gangly teenager. Like a six-foot-five version of their students, despite the fact that they'd celebrated his thirty-fifth birthday over the summer.

"What?" Aaron asked, narrowing his eyes at her.

Abby shook her head. "Nothing."

"Uh huh, Nessie. Let's go. See you tomorrow, Dana."

"Nessie?" Dana whispered, glancing at Aaron's retreating back. "That new?"

Abby rolled her eyes and sighed. "Scotland documentary. Loch Ness."

"And your last name is Locke," Dana chuckled. "It's cute."

"It's annoying."

"Thunderstorm," Dana stage whispered, flashing jazz hands at her.

"I can do that too," Abby muttered, giving Dana her own, single-fingered, version of jazz hands.

"Santa's Singles," Dana said. "Think about it."

So Abby thought about it. She only thought about it for the twelve seconds it took for her to put on her coat, sling her backpack over her shoulder and cross her classroom. But hey, it still counted. By the time she reached for the light switch, she'd already stopped thinking about it. She joined Aaron in the hall and they started their daily exodus from Hope High.

"So, what's Dana gotten herself into? Something about a . . . cult?" he asked.

"Damn your Vulcan hearing," Abby muttered as they pushed through Hope High's front doors. She felt a momentary shiver of panic that he'd heard *everything* Dana had said.

"You know, Vulcans having better hearing than other races is a myth," Aaron said.

"I know," Abby muttered. "Voyager, season two."

"Just checking, since you're haphazardly throwing around *Star Trek* race misnomers," Aaron said.

"Thanks, Spock," Abby muttered. Relief was creeping in. She knew that if he *had* heard what Dana had said about him being a thunderstorm and Abby's dry spell, he'd be torturing her relentlessly about it at that moment. Neither of them were very patient when the opportunity to goad each other presented itself.

"So, I heard there were reject Christmas cookies in the break room,"

Abby said.

"Yep." Aaron pulled a napkin out of his coat pocket and handed it to her.

"Aw man, you're the best . . ." she kept her gaze on the napkin, feeling the stupid heat rise in her cheeks. *It's just cookies, Abby. It's what besties do. You'd have gotten him cookies if you'd been the one to make a pit stop in the break room.* She unwrapped the napkin and stared at the two round cookies. They were frosted pink and decorated by long brown sprinkles. "I . . . I don't know what to say," her voice was deadpan as she tried not to laugh. "A pair of balls, all my very own."

Aaron sighed. "Believe it or not, but those were the *tamest* of the cookies. I don't think Bob inspected them before he set the box out for staff."

"Didn't want to look a gift ball cookie in the mouth, huh?" Abby asked, picking up one of the cookies to study it. The smell of the buttercream made her think that maybe she could just close her eyes and eat it.

Aaron snorted. "Something like that . . . I think."

"So, if these are my cookies and they're the *tamest,* what, pray tell, did your cookies resemble?"

Aaron sighed. "I'm not telling."

"What?!" She clutched her invisible pearls in mock outrage, "That is most ungentlemanly of you, sir. To have me show you mine without even *describing* yours." She waited for the inevitable pink rise in his cheeks and she wasn't disappointed. She tried to hold onto the playful annoyance she was putting up as a front as they continued on, but she couldn't. She was too distracted. They'd just stepped outside the school and her vision was cluttered with the sight of the whole town of Hope in the throes of a full-body holiday dry-heave. The high school basketball team was already assembled, helping with the town decorations in front of the school and wearing their new Hope High Goats-themed sweat suits. The orange and red material was turned all the way up to "eye assault".

"I knew it," Aaron muttered as they waved and moved down the sidewalk toward them.

"Knew what?"

"That Michaels was yanking my crank about his elbow. He said he wasn't taking notes in class because he'd hurt it in practice and he needed to save his arm for this weekend's game."

Abby glanced up at the team's center, Adam Michaels, who was currently standing on a ladder, both arms over his head, securing a tinsel Santa to the light pole. The ladder was short and Adam's face was buried between Santa's black tinsel legs.

"Well, his arm seems fine now. But, he might need therapy after he climbs out from under Santa."

"Yeah, well, he'll deserve it. I can't believe I fell for that."

Abby shrugged. "You're kind. You take your students at their word."

Aaron shook his head. "I'm a pushover."

Abby smiled. "But the good kind. Like those breakfast things."

He raised an eyebrow at her. "Ok, either you mean turnover, or you mean popover. A pushover isn't a breakfast item."

"Both. Or neither. Whatever," Abby said, her attention drawn to the festive window displays they were passing as they headed down Main Street. "I don't know why people bother naming anything that's for breakfast. Everyone's half-asleep when they eat it anyway. Just shove it in your mouth and chew."

Aaron chuckled. "You know, this sounds like a rant worthy of Miss Mandie. Wanna stop off for something before we make the long slog home?"

"Sure," she shrugged. "I think I'll need something to wash down these balls. I wouldn't want to choke." For a moment, Aaron sounded like *he* was choking. She grinned, unable to help herself. "But if there's a line, I'll have to catch you later. I have to soak Mr. Burns in some warm water tonight and scoop up some of his poop."

A man passing them paused and looked at Abby, his eyes growing wide.

"She's talking about her lizard," Aaron said quickly to the man. The man still looked confused, but he gave them a quick nod and hurried on his way.

"He's not a lizard," Abby said, cutting her eyes to Aaron. "Mr. Burns is a dragon."

"He lives in an aquarium, under a heat lamp and you make him outfits out of tube socks. Name another dragon that lives like that," Aaron said, hooking his thumbs into his backpack straps and grinning at her.

Abby shrugged. "You don't know what Smaug's home life was like! Maybe he liked tube socks and heat lamps."

"At least *that* was what that guy heard instead of the choking on balls thing."

She shrugged. "Who knows, maybe it's an important safety tip he needed to hear. After all, it is the holiday season, the most wonderful time of the year *for accidents.*"

Aaron just shook his head. "Oh look, no line," he muttered, as they reached Miss Mandie's window.

He was right. Abby could see the larger-than-life proprietor behind the counter, leaning on the display case and sipping coffee. Abby was so used to Miss Mandie and her erotic bakery, De-Floured, that the sight of the Double D-elicious boob cupcakes and the Well-Endowed eclairs didn't make her bat an eye. She glanced at Aaron and she had to drop her gaze to the sidewalk to hide her smile. When Aaron Burns had been hired at Hope High as the new English teacher and took the classroom across the hall from her, she'd immediately decided to make it her mission to get him accustomed to all the . . . unique aspects of Hope Island. Well, she hadn't decided to make it her mission *immediately.* To be honest, when she first met Aaron, she could hardly speak around him. He was tall and good-looking, and he read Middle English, which Abby thought he'd been joking about until he started reciting Chaucer's jokes from *The Canterbury Tales* in the mercifully dead, vaguely-discernible language. Not unlike said dead language, after a while, she'd gotten the hang of Aaron's rhythm, and she'd started to see what he was really like. They'd been best friends ever since. He was a nerd. And he was alone. He'd gone to school in Seattle, but the only family he had left was his dad and they weren't close. The first holiday season he was in town, when she'd found out he would be spending it alone, the training-from-birth of every Hope Island-born person had kicked in. No one was allowed to be alone in Hope. On a five-mile island

and a town of just over three thousand, (not counting all the day-tripping and weekend-warrior tourists), it wasn't physically possible.

"Look what the school children spit out," Miss Mandie called to them when they pushed through the bakery's front door. "What's the going rate for paying off high schoolers to leave you with enough sanity to feed and dress yourselves?"

"I've got them on a lay-a-way program," Abby said.

"I told them I'd bring them a treat tomorrow," Aaron muttered, reaching for his wallet.

"Oh yeah?" Miss Mandie asked, arching her perfectly-penciled eyebrow at him. "What kind of treat?"

"I'm thinking maybe a pop quiz and some surprise homework. That's what the kids are into these days, right?"

Miss Mandie snorted. "Maybe when you were a kid. You look the type."

Abby dropped her backpack off her shoulders so she could dig out her wallet. "It sounds like Miss Mandie has you pegged, Burney."

Aaron sighed. "Two large coffees please, Miss Mandie. If I'm going to have to defend myself against *both* of you, I'm going to need caffeine."

"You're going to need more than caffeine if you're planning on drinking both of these," Miss Mandie said, filling the cups. "This is my special Christmas Chaos blend. Triple the usual amount of caffeine." She winked at them over her shoulder. "I like to serve it for December and then the day after New Year's, I switch everyone over to decaf. Makes January more interesting."

Abby shook her head slowly. "Miss Mandie, when they come for you with torches and pitchforks, I'm not saying that I'll join them, but defending you might be a hard case."

"Oh honey, I can handle myself."

"Of that, I have no doubt," Abby said, moving up to the counter. Aaron lifted one of the cups to his lips and Abby noticed the familiar glint in Miss Mandie's eyes. It took a lot to flap Aaron, but in Miss Mandie's hands, he was underwear on the clothesline, helplessly caught in her breeze.

"Hmmm, he's a good coffee drinker. Gentle. Full-lips. You ever wish you were a cup lid?" Miss Mandie asked, glancing from Aaron to Abby. "Because I'm kind of thinking it wouldn't be so bad right now." Aaron choked, spewing coffee across the counter and making Miss Mandie take a step back. "Well, his dismount could use some work."

Abby felt like her cheeks were on fire. She was torn between embarrassment for Aaron and a desire to weigh in on the cup lid argument and escalate that embarrassment. It was a game she and Aaron had been playing for the last three years. They called it Chicken-Too-Far, with each of them always seeing how far they could push something before it moved out of the comfort zone of the other person, who would finally admit it was "too far" for them. They'd always played it jokingly, and always knowing that revenge would be coming for the person who started it. Lately, Chicken-Too-Far had started to become a real challenge. Their friendship had just gotten so . . . comfortable. Abby felt herself smile. There was something indescribably nice about having Aaron Burns as her best friend.

At the moment though, Aaron was still coughing. His face was bright red, so Abby decided to take a rain check on the Chicken-Too-Far. It wouldn't really be fair anyway. Not with Miss Mandie piling on.

"Just *one* of your chaotic coffees for me please, Miss Mandie," Abby said, pulling out her card. "Still have another week before Christmas break and I have to keep a leash on my sanity while the students are around."

Still choking, Aaron shook his head and pushed the second to-go cup toward her.

"Oh, this is for me?" Abby asked, frowning at Aaron. "I thought you were planning to go for some kind of record by drinking both of them."

With a final gasping throat-clear, Aaron had control of his voice again. "What? You actually thought I was going to drink *two* of Miss Mandie's aneurysm-inducing, barely-legal-caffeine-level coffees? No. I don't feel like spending the rest of the day slowly vibrating into a million pieces while *smelling* the colors on YouTube videos."

Abby shrugged. "I don't know. Sounds like a pretty good evening to me."

"I especially like the 'vibrating into a million pieces part'," Miss Mandie added, reaching into her apron for a pack of cigarettes. "Bart, I'm going on break," she called over her shoulder. She turned back to Abby and Aaron, stuck a cigarette between her lips, and made a shooing gesture at them as if they were feral possums. "It's my night to clean the floors in this place, so if you're going to have an aneurysm or vibrate or whatever, kindly take it outside. I'll send you Bart's floor-cleaning schedule if you want to come back in for a repeat."

They turned and headed back outside in front of Miss Mandie. The cold air was crisp, and Abby heard all three of them draw in a collective, deep breath. It was thick with the smell from Miss Mandie's coffee roaster, wood-burning fireplaces, the salty sea air, and fresh greenery from the piles of garlands that were being wound around anything in the town square that stood still long enough.

"I love this place," Abby said softly. She hadn't meant to say it out loud, but at that moment, with her senses on overload from the sight in front of her, the smell around her, and the warmth of her bestie beside her, she hadn't been able to stop herself. Aaron caught her eye and she saw the corner of his mouth twitch up in a half-smile.

They said their goodbyes to Miss Mandie and cut through the town square.

"Thanks for the coffee," Abby said, tapping her to-go cup against Aaron's. "Next one is on me."

"I'll hold you to that," Aaron said. "Of course, if this coffee is as strong as I suspect, the next one might be at my funeral."

Abby shrugged. "I'll pour one out for my homey."

"Yeah, just put it in my hand while I'm in the casket," Aaron said. "I'll bet it'll make a good cup holder when I go into full rigor."

"That doesn't last," Abby said. "Bodies come out of full rigor after a while." She shivered. The thought of Aaron in a casket, even jokingly, stabbed at something deep in her chest. If it happened, she'd have to just ride into the afterlife and drag him back out. That was the kind of machine she'd need to invent.

"So," Aaron's deep rumble interrupted her stroll down Morbid Lane,

"*Mystery Science Theater 3000* marathon tonight? I've got some grading to do, but I'd love to have a dangling carrot at the end of it to motivate me."

Abby nodded. "Sounds good. I just have to take care of Mr. Burns first. I don't know if you want to be present for . . . that."

"Dragon poop-scooping?" Aaron asked. "What's going on with him anyway?"

Abby shook her head. "I don't know. Doc Winters said she needed a stool sample to analyze. She thinks he might just be getting . . . old." Abby gritted her teeth against the hard lump forming in her throat. The thought of losing Mr. Burns was a second quick stab of pain in her chest. Why couldn't bearded dragons just be immortal? Sometimes she hated biology and the inevitable entropy of life and the universe.

She liked her little apartment world with Mr. Burns in his aquarium and Aaron right next door. The thought of losing either of them knocked the breath out of her. *Stop it, Abby. Geez. The anxiety is strong with this one today.* Abby didn't usually focus on depressing shit. What was with her? After a moment of racking her brain, the light bulb blinked on. Damn it, Dana. She could still hear her words, *"you don't want to die alone, do you?"* It wasn't something Abby had really dwelled on in the last three years. But in comes Dana, Captain of the U.S.S. Depression, and it was instantly invading her post-classroom thoughts. She was going to have to think of an appropriate retaliation for Dana. Post-Classroom time and brain space were sacred. Maybe editing her Spotify playlist. Swap her House of Pain out for Mariah Carey. That would show her.

"Home at last," Aaron sighed. She glanced up at the green and white A-frame house in front of them. It had been divided right down the middle by the owner, Todd Miller. In doing so, he'd turned the three-bedroom, two-bathroom house into two, two-bedroom, one-bathroom halves with a wall dividing the master bedroom right down the middle. Aaron lived in the right half and Abby in the left. It was quirky and strange, like everything else that Abby really liked about her life. The porch creaked under Aaron's heavy boots as he headed up the stairs in front of her.

"Should we name the hammer and make it a stocking for Christmas?"

Aaron asked, pausing next to Todd's abandoned hammer, still lying under the railing.

"We could," Abby sighed, "but then we'd have to figure out visitation schedules with the hammer and whose apartment it would spend Christmas at, Easter, etc. It's just easier to call Todd again and tell him to come get it."

"I called the last time," Aaron said. "It's your turn."

"I'll get right on that," Abby muttered. "Just as soon as I have three to five hours to spend on the phone with him, while he retells me the story of every Hope Goats baseball game he's ever watched. Watching baseball is boring enough, *hearing* about someone *else* watching baseball is something I'm sure Dante wrote about. You're the English scholar. Was it in his description of the eighth or the ninth ring of hell?"

"It was in the seventh-inning-stretch ring." He grinned and Abby rolled her eyes.

"Walked right into that one. Not unlike my future trip to hell."

"I call shotgun," Aaron chuckled. "After all, we both know you can't navigate for crap."

She sighed. "I get us lost *one time* and I never hear the end of it."

He blinked at her. "We were in Bumble's."

She glared at him. "Right after their remodel. The *pet food* was in the *front.* The *greeting cards* were in the *back.* It was 'Apocalypse Now', baby!"

"At least we survived," Aaron muttered.

"And I made sure the troops had sustenance," Abby said, stomping up the porch stairs.

"Shoving a still-wrapped Twix in my mouth to get me to stop narrating our harrowing journey does *not* count as supplying sustenance."

She shook her head slowly. "I should have left you to die on the field of the appliances and dish towels aisle."

He chuckled. "Well, hindsight. Since you have Mr. Burns to tend to, I think I'll get started on that grading."

"Meet you on the other side?" Abby asked, glancing over at him as she dug her keys out of her coat pocket.

"Meet you on the other side of Hamlet essays and lizard poop," Aaron said, nodding.

"Dragon poop," Abby corrected.

"Right," Aaron said. "Dragon. Hopefully, Mr. Burns doesn't consider it to be a part of his horde."

"From your lips to Smaug's ass," Abby called to him. He flashed her the half-smile again and for a strange second, Abby forgot how to breathe. She'd seen that smile a thousand times, her gaze always drawn to his mouth, his slightly crooked canine tooth and the single dimple in his right cheek. This time, she'd been looking at his eyes. And . . . the smile had looked . . . different.

The comforting sound of the *Star Trek* "whooshing" doors sound effect greeted her when she passed the novelty motion sensor and slipped inside. She shut her door and leaned against it. *Great. Now you're not only catastrophizing about everyone dying, you're also imagining things. It's not even Friday yet.* She listened to the comforting quiet of the apartment around her and felt another irrational stab of fear in her chest. What would she do if things changed? If she lost a piece of this world? Aaron or Mr. Burns or her cozy apartment? As the floating thoughts landed in her brain she frowned. *What the hell!?* It wasn't like her to jump off the deep end like this. Abby prided herself on her logic and practical thinking. What was causing all these bullshit thoughts? She felt her forehead. *Nope, not a fever.* She did an internal check. She didn't feel like it was low blood sugar. She systematically named off and dismissed possibilities and hypotheses, letting the comforting hand of cold data guide her. Nothing biological that she could think of. She wasn't even PMSing. There was only one other possibility. She'd suspected it all along, but she was hoping she'd been wrong. But as Sir Arthur Conan Doyle wrote, *"Once you eliminate the impossible, whatever remains, however improbable, must be the truth."*

"Dammit Dana," Abby muttered. "I hate you." All her talk of dry spells and thunderstorms and dying alone. She groaned and pushed off the door. She just needed to forget it and distract herself. And what better way than dealing with dragon poop? "Well, Mr. Burns, your Smithers-stand-in is home. And the time has come." She stopped in front of Mr. Burns' aquarium in time to see the bearded dragon roll his eyes at her.

* * *

She was partially soaked and chasing the wet dragon around the bathtub when her phone rang.

"You win this round, Monty," Abby muttered.

He hissed at her and bobbed his head in triumph as she dug her phone out of her pocket and sat down on the bath mat.

"Hey mom," Abby muttered, rubbing the back of her neck.

"Abby! Your father and I just heard from your sister! She's engaged! She and Ken are planning an island wedding this summer."

Abby felt her heart pause in her chest. Her *little sister*, Barb, was getting married. Wow. "That's great," Abby said quickly before the shock really set in. She could feel Mr. Burns crawl up the side of the bathtub and onto her shoulder. He wasn't hissing now and as he nudged her under the chin, she had the feeling that he was trying to make up with her for soaking her shirt. Or maybe he could sense that she was stunned and he was standing by to administer CPR. After a few seconds, she finally found her voice. "I thought Barb and Ken had only been dating for a few months."

"Six weeks," her mom said. "But, sometimes when you know, you know right away. She's bringing Ken home for Christmas in a few weeks. We're having a lunch to celebrate on Saturday. Ken has to work but Barb is coming in on the ferry that morning. Can you make it? I'll be making everyone's favorite Seven-Layer-Sin chocolate cake."

"Can I bring Aaron?" Abby asked automatically.

Her mom sighed. "I suppose if you want to bring your *neighbor friend* with you, you can."

"He's my *best* friend, Mom," Abby said automatically. "And he's *family*." There was a pause, and Abby held her breath, counting down to the inevitable in her head.

"I know he's alone. But you two are *friends*. Not boyfriend and girlfriend, not in a relationship beyond pulling pranks on each other, everyone else, and taking part in your *hobbies*." Abby sighed, but her mother wasn't done. "Friends are great, honey, but they're not who you marry. When are *you* going to have someone to introduce us to at Christmas?"

"I'm thinking maybe my mid-fifties, mid-sixties," Abby said, running a crooked finger under Mr. Burns' chin. This argument with her mom was so old, she had a *Thunderdome*-style wheel in her head that she'd just nod at the raggedy man to spin and feed her any response it landed on.

"Abby," her mom said with a sigh. "You're not getting any younger, dear heart. Mr. Burns can't dial the telephone if you have a heart attack and die."

"You don't know that. We've been working on his dexterity," Abby said.

"It's all those toys in your apartment," her mother added, not missing a beat and completely ignoring Abby's sarcasm. She was immune. "Any person who steps in the door is immediately confused, not sure if they just walked into a grown woman's apartment or some teenage geek's dream house."

"They're not toys, Mother," Abby said. "They're action figures and replicas."

Her mom's sigh was put-upon. "Whatever they are, they'll scare away anyone who even has a fleeting thought about having a serious relationship with you. I mean, just look what happened with Sam." That mental kick landed in Abby's gut. In the final round of the final boss fight she'd had with Sam, he'd been talking about moving in and helping her sell her collectibles on Ebay so she could "grow up". That was when Abby had shown him the door. Perfunctory sex and her parents' approval hadn't been enough for her to forgive and forget what he'd said.

"And has there been anyone since? Any man willing to brave your 'fortitude of solitaire'?"

Abby pinched the bridge of her nose. "Fortress of solitude?"

"That's what I said," her mom continued, the frustrated edge in her voice becoming more pronounced. "It's been *three years* since you two broke up. What about the family you always wanted? You *love kids.*"

Abby did her best to push aside the old ache. "Yeah, well, the shine comes off that apple when you teach science to teenagers all day, every day."

"I'm being serious, Abs. You don't want to die alone."

"I don't know, Mom. It could have its advantages. It means I wasn't murdered." Abby felt Mr. Burns leap off her shoulder and touch down in the tub, sending a splash of warm water in a wave down her back.

"And having a friend that's a *man* and that you're close to is not going to help you find someone to get serious with either. It would probably be better for you both if you didn't spend so much time together," her mom continued.

Mr. Burns was splashing in the tub and Abby wasn't in the mood to discuss distancing herself from Aaron, or what her odds were at finding a relationship beyond friendship. She didn't know how to tell her mom that she didn't think that was in the cards for her anymore. It was too painful to say out loud, even though it was a realization she'd been coming to over the past few years. "I need to go, Mom. I'll call Barb this week to congratulate her. Love you."

Twenty minutes later, Mr. Burns was back under his heat lamp, wearing his trademark *"Excellent"* t-shirt, and enjoying a treat of meal worms while Abby double-bagged his dookie and put it on the porch. She'd have to figure out how to get it to the vet's in the morning. She'd forgotten about her early morning detentions.

"A problem for Morning Abby. Though, that bitch be crazy and tomorrow's Afternoon Abby will probably pay for it. Oh well. Now that the dirty work is done," Abby said, cutting her eyes to Mr. Burns while she washed her hands at the sink, "it's time to have some fun." She opened YouTube on her TV and hunted for the classic *MST3K* episode, *The Undead*. An ad started and she turned her attention back to the few dishes in her sink from breakfast.

"Do you live alone?" the ad began, *"Are you worried about what would happen if you fell? Who would find you?"*

Abby paused, soapy sponge in hand. She cut her eyes to the TV.

"With LifeCall Alert, you can have peace of mind while you live alone. With

the push of a button, help can be on the way. You are never truly alone with LifeCall Alert."

Abby squeezed her eyes shut and sighed. Three times in one day? Really? Were Dana, her mom, *and* YouTube conspiring against her?

Abby glanced up at the ceiling. "Et tu, universe?"

Continue with Abby, Aaron, Mr. Burns (my favorite!) and all of the wonderful denizens of Hope Island with Sleigh Ride Or Die on Kindle Unlimited!

SLEIGH RIDE OR DIE

A HOPE ISLAND ROMANTIC COMEDY

TEAGAN HART

About the Author

Spicy, snarky, small town shenanigans. "Like a spicy Hallmark movie."

Teagan Hart is a Kansas farm kid, transplanted to Oregon. She is irreverent, incorrigible, and loves a good steamy scene. Hart writes small town romantic comedy with a side of snark, building fun and outlandish places for her characters to fall in love. Her work has been described as "spicy Hallmark movies in book form" and that not only is very accurate, but made her smile.

You can connect with me on:
- https://linktr.ee/teaganhart

Subscribe to my newsletter:
- https://tinyurl.com/teaganhartb

Also by Teagan Hart

The Hope Island Holiday Romances are your passport to small town holiday romantic comedy hijinks spanning six spicy, snarky, hilarious love stories.

Sleigh Ride Or Die

Two ride-or-die besties are living their best life in nerdy, platonic bliss. But a dare gone wrong lands them in a holiday dating game that lights a fire where only friendship had been before.

Will they stay in the friend zone or end up unwrapping each other on Christmas morning?

A Christmas For Carol

She was sure she'd missed the boat. He's the sole survivor of a shipwrecked relationship.

Will working together to save a beloved theater be enough to keep their heads above water?

Auld Lang Mine

You never forget your first love. Especially when your first is a wounded warrior. When some good-natured meddling from their hometown ropes them into a support group that more closely resembles an obstacle course, they're forced together to confront their past and try to build a future.

Will the new year give them both a second chance at love?

Cupid Can Suck It

Love sucks. Or so two coworkers think when they look out at all the sickening hearts and naked baby cupids stuck to everything that stands still on Hope Island. So, they decide to burn it down. The whole holiday.

But when their pranks start to backfire on them, will the growing heat between them leave them both burned?

Reel Love

All Cara's ever wanted is to be accepted into Julliard and fulfill her dream of becoming a professional ballerina. There are only two things Ian wants since leaving Ireland; the sea and music. Well, until he meets Cara.

Can they work out a rhythm that will keep them moving to the beat? Or will the beats that move them around and towards each other end up being the beats of their hearts?

Printed in Great Britain
by Amazon